WARD NUMBER SIX
AND OTHER STORIES

ANTON CHEKHOV was born in 1860 in south Russia, the son of a poor grocer. At the age of nineteen he followed his family to Moscow, where he studied medicine and helped to support the household by writing comic sketches for popular magazines. By 1888 he was publishing in the prestigious literary monthlies of Moscow and St. Petersburg: a sign that he had already attained maturity as a writer of serious fiction. During the next 15 years he wrote the short stories—50 or more of them—which form his chief claim to world pre-eminence in the genre and are his main achievement as a writer. His plays are almost equally important, especially during his last years. He was closely associated with the Moscow Art Theatre and married its leading lady, Olga Knipper. In 1898 he was forced to move to Yalta, where he wrote his two greatest plays, *Three Sisters* and *The Cherry Orchard*. The première of the latter took place on his forty-fourth birthday. Chekhov died six months later, on 2 July 1904.

RONALD HINGLEY, University Lecturer in Russian at Oxford, has edited and translated The Oxford Chekhov (9 volumes), and is the author of *A New Life of Anton Chekhov* (also published by Oxford University Press).

THE WORLD'S CLASSICS

ANTON CHEKHOV

Ward Number Six
and Other Stories

Translated with an introduction
and notes by
RONALD HINGLEY

Oxford   New York
OXFORD UNIVERSITY PRESS

Oxford University Press, Walton Street, Oxford OX2 6DP

Oxford New York
Athens Auckland Bangkok Bombay
Calcutta Cape Town Dar es Salaam Delhi
Florence Hong Kong Istanbul Karachi
Kuala Lumpur Madras Madrid Melbourne
Mexico City Nairobi Paris Singapore
Taipei Tokyo Toronto

and associated companies in
Berlin Ibadan

Oxford is a trade mark of Oxford University Press

Translations and editorial material © Ronald Hingley 1965, 1970, 1971, 1974
This selection first issued in Oxford Paperbacks 1974
First issued as a World's Classics paperback 1988

British Library Cataloguing in Publication Data
Chekhov, A. P.
1. [Seven stories], Ward numbr six and other stories.
I. [Seven stories]   II. Title
III. Hingley, Ronald
981.73'.3[F]   PG3456.P3
ISBN 0-19-282174-1

Library of Congress Cataloging in Publication Data
Chekhov, Anton Pavlovich, 1860-1904.
Ward number six and other stories. (World's classics)
Rev. ed. of: Seven stories. 1974
Bibliography:—
Contents: Ward number six—The butterfly—
Ariadne—A dreary story—Neighbours—An anonymous
story—Doctor Startsev.
I. Hingley, Ronald.   II. Title.   III. Title: Ward
number 6 and other stories.
IV. Series.
PG3456.A15H56   1988   891.73'3   87-21959
ISBN 0-19-282174-1
The text of the seven stories in this volume is taken from volumes 5, 6, 8, and
9 of the Oxford Chekhov, translated and edited by Ronald Hingley.

5 7 9 10 8 6

Printed in Great Britain by BPC Paperbacks Ltd, Aylesbury, Bucks

CONTENTS

CONTENTS

INTRODUCTION

Chekhov and the Short Story

CHEKHOV came of humbler social origins than the leading Russian fiction-writers of earlier generations: he was the third son, born in 1860, of a struggling grocer in the southern Russian port of Taganrog.

He was a lively boy: a gifted mimic, a keen attender of the gallery at his home-town theatre, a great practical joker. He read widely, and was fortunate in attending the local grammar school, where the study of Latin and Greek loomed large in the curriculum. Though these studies bored the boy—whose school marks tended to be average— his school provided him with a stimulating social framework within which to develop. It also helped to qualify him for entering Moscow University.

In 1879 the nineteen-year-old Chekhov moved more than six hundred miles north from Taganrog to settle in Moscow, after which that city and its environs remained his base for two decades. He qualified as a doctor in 1884, but was to practise only sporadically, having already become an established writer of short humorous sketches and tales. From the proceeds of these the undergraduate Chekhov had already been helping to support his family—including his once strict father (now often unemployed) and mother as well as a sister and two younger brothers.

Chekhov's first writings were published under a variety of comic pseudonyms in a variety of scurrilous comic magazines, and seem to have little in common with his mature work. Though he turned them out by the hundred, he had all along been unobtrusively experimenting with a more serious—at times tragic—approach. Meanwhile he was being awarded a sequence of literary promotions as his work found its way into increasingly respectable periodicals or newspapers published in the capital city, St. Petersburg: *Fragments* (1882), *The St. Petersburg Gazette* (1885), *New Time* (1886). Finally, in 1888, Chekhov breaks into one of the 'fat journals': literary monthlies in which nearly all the major works of Russian literature have first appeared in print.

With this event—the publication of the story *Steppe* in the *Northern Herald* in 1888—Chekhov has been accepted, in effect, as an author who might hope to claim a permanent place in Russian literature.

Henceforward most of his longer stories are first issued in one or other of the 'fat journals' as a prelude to publication in book form. He is now concentrating on quality rather than quantity. He has also transformed his humorous approach, for though humour always remains a basic ingredient in his technique it is no longer cultivated for its own sake.

In 1890 Chekhov suddenly astounds his friends by undertaking a one-man expedition across Siberia to the convict settlement on the island of Sakhalin. He conducts a painstaking sociological survey and publishes the results in *Sakhalin Island*: a treatise as well as a travelogue, and a landmark in Russian penological literature.

In 1892 Chekhov buys a country estate at Melikhovo, about fifty miles south of Moscow, and embarks on the most fruitful period of his work as a short-story writer—all but two of the items in this volume belong to his Melikhovo period. But he is increasingly incapacitated by tuberculosis. Compelled to winter in the south on doctors' orders, he builds a villa near the Crimean resort of Yalta in 1899 and abandons Melikhovo while continuing to return to Moscow as his health permits. His output of short stories declines, but he is now first making his mark as a dramatist with the successful production of his four-act plays *The Seagull* and *Uncle Vanya* by the newly founded Moscow Art Theatre. In 1901 Chekhov marries the actress Olga Knipper, a member of the Art Theatre Company. Between his marriage and his death in 1904 he writes two plays specially for the Art Theatre: *Three Sisters* and—his last work—*The Cherry Orchard*.

Chekhov did not belong to the heroic epoch of Russian fiction: that of Pushkin, Gogol, Turgenev, Dostoyevsky and Tolstoy. With the grand age of the Russian novel—the reign of the Emperor Alexander II (1855–81)—he was involved only in the sense of witnessing it from afar as a provincial schoolboy.

Alexander II's reign had begun with general optimism and sweeping social reforms sponsored by the Emperor himself, among which the Emancipation of the Serfs had been the most important—it was enacted in 1861, when Chekhov (whose paternal grandfather had actually been a serf) was a mere babe in arms. As a schoolboy Chekhov was made aware, without becoming keenly interested, of political opposition to the Russian autocracy such as was now first finding serious organized expression. It was now that oppositionists of a more modern type than had hitherto surfaced in Russia—whether termed liberals, radicals or revolutionaries—first made themselves felt as a collective force, albeit on a small scale. Resistance to the Reforming Tsar (and for not reforming fast enough) culminated in his assassination on 1 March 1881 by a group of extremists. This momentous event coincided fairly closely with the deaths of Dostoyevsky and Turgenev, as also with the end of Tolstoy's major period as a novelist. The assassination was, accordingly, a literary as well as a political landmark, simultaneously signalling the end of the old heroic era and the beginning of a new and less flamboyant period.

Chekhov's début as a writer came at just this time: it was in the Reforming Tsar's last year of life, to be precise, that he first began to publish his work.

With Alexander II's sudden death the age of reform and generous hopes—already in sad decline—seemed to have ended for the foreseeable future, and the political police moved in to crush the small but virulent revolutionary movement. Meanwhile the assassinated Emperor's successor, Alexander III, was embarking on 'counter-reforms' designed to put the clock back and protect the autocracy against the activities of political terrorists such as those who had blown his father to pieces. Despite all curbs on political and social reform, however, Russia under the new Tsar never developed into the police state which the world still seems to insist on conceiving it. Admittedly the peasants' condition remained unenviable, and they were exposed to terrible famines and epidemics. Equally unenviable was the plight of the urban proletariat, which still remained comparatively small in numbers. Of such sufferings Chekhov's own works provide eloquent illustration. But, as they also show, at least the professional section of society, to which he himself belonged as a doctor and author, suffered from few indeed of the disadvantages associated with a police state. Despite the existence of a literary censorship (a continual nuisance) and despite many another handicap, the Russian intellectual of the last two decades of the nineteenth century enjoyed—provided always that he did not belong to the rump of active revolutionary conspirators insignificant until the mid-1890s—a degree of real freedom for which later generations and societies may well envy him.

Himself no admirer of the autocratic system and on occasion its outspoken critic, Chekhov was even less sympathetic to revolutionary conspiracy. Not that this issue loomed prominently in his consciousness. As is abundantly clear from his voluminous surviving letters (over four thousand), and also from the many memoirs of his contemporaries, the emphasis was on quite other matters. Here was a lively, vigorous society—not least in Moscow: Chekhov's spiritual home at times, and an exhilarating milieu in which to write, paint, carouse, make love, gossip and argue about the meaning of existence over a combination of oysters, champagne, sturgeon, vodka, beer or tea in one of the many *traktiry* (taverns) in which Muscovite intellectuals seemed to spend half their time. Nor did the continued espousal of reactionary policies by Nicholas II, who came to the throne in 1894, succeed in suppressing the general feeling of excitement.

In enjoying these amenities fairly extensively, until frustrated by ill health, Chekhov was a man of his age. Yet he was conscious all the time of those less fortunate than himself, and more effectively conscious than many a contemporary who posed as champion of the poor and downtrodden. Eloquent in words—as witness those numerous artistic works in which he depicts the plight of the unprivileged—Chekhov was also a man of action, working as doctor, health officer, builder of schools, patron of libraries and so on.

Though chosen (as noted in the Preface) for their excellence as short stories, the items in the present selection well typify Chekhov and his period by covering a wide spread of contemporary Russian settings. The Russian countryside provides the background for *Neighbours* and *Ariadne*, while provincial towns—characteristically anonymous— supply the stage for *Ward Number Six* and *Doctor Startsev*. In *A Dreary Story* and *The Butterfly* Moscow (loved and hated by Chekhov) appears to be the scene, though unavowedly so, while the capital, St. Petersburg, figures memorably as the setting of *An Anonymous Story*. Less typically, Chekhov permits himself an excursion outside Russian national territory in the last-named story, and also in *Ariadne*. In each case his description of foreign parts seems to accord with a formula evolved in another context: that 'abroad is a bloody place'. Such was, incidentally, Chekhov's own frequent but by no means invariable reaction to his travels outside the Russian Empire.

So much for the geographical background. As for the social setting, we have provided a less characteristic spread, since—as stated above— stories focused on the life of the peasants have been omitted, as have studies of merchants, the urban lower middle class and the industrial worker. The main emphasis in this volume is on the gentry and on the professional class which Chekhov himself entered as a young man by becoming a doctor and self-supporting writer. Within that category the range is fairly wide. In *Ariadne* and *Neighbours* the dramatis personae belong to the landowning milieu, while high officialdom is unforgettably described in *An Anonymous Story*. The academic world dominates *A Dreary Story*, as do artistic circles *The Butterfly* and—on a pathetic provincial level—*Doctor Startsev*.

As these stories richly illustrate, Chekhov particularly liked to draw his heroes from the profession of medicine in which he himself had qualified but which he practised only occasionally (very rarely, incidentally, does he make a writer his hero). How little the mature Chekhov dealt in stereotypes, how rarely—if ever—he essentially repeated himself when creating new characters, the various doctors in the present volume richly illustrate. The saintly Dr. Dymov of *The Butterfly* becomes a victim of his own inability to assert himself and of his devotion to his profession. By contrast, Dr. Ragin of *Ward Number Six* is—ideologically speaking—a villain, or at least a non-approved figure. He is shown unavowedly espousing Tolstoy's doctrine of non-resistance to evil—a doctrine which Chekhov had briefly shared before rejecting it and embodying his changed attitude in this and other stories as well as in his correspondence. Between these two types falls Doctor Startsev, hero of the story of the same name, for he changes from hero to villain in the course of the narrative. But the fullest portrait of all—and the most remarkable of all Chekhov's innumerable fictional doctors—is the professor-hero whose litany of uninterrupted laments constitutes *A Dreary Story*. This is one of the most astonishing works ever penned by a Russian writer: on one level a hymn to the futility of existence, and yet a work which produces anything but the 'dreary' effect advertised in its title.

How, we may now ask, does Chekhov fit into the general pattern of nineteenth-century Russian literature? His is the last big name among the great Russian masters. He was the last great representative of the 'realist' school which has origins in the work of Pushkin and Lermontov, but which really began—according to a commonly accepted view—with Gogol, continuing with Turgenev, Goncharov, Dostoyevsky, Tolstoy and others.

Realist authors were concerned—some more, some less—to describe Russia contemporary to themselves, evoking a feeling of authenticity by a plain, factual, functional descriptive technique, emphasizing character rather than plot and showing sympathy with all manner of men: even with such unfashionable targets for compassion as the rich and virtuous as well as with those more conventionally patronized: the poor, the downtrodden and the criminal. Determined to be more than mere story-tellers, all cultivating in some degree the role of prophets, teachers or guides, they surveyed the Russian and general human condition with high seriousness and deep concern. Some of them (notably Gogol, Dostoyevsky, Tolstoy and Saltykov-Shchedrin) were at times actively engaged in propagating specific philosophical, social, political or religious doctrines. Others—such as Turgenev, Leskov and Goncharov—considered the doctrines and social problems of their time from a less committed angle, yet often seemed to feel bound by an obligation at least to include these weighty issues in their thematic material.

Chekhov shared with these formidable predecessors a preference for subject-matter taken from contemporary Russian life experienced at first hand. He too tended to emphasize character rather than plot. He showed comparably wide human sympathies, he was similarly concerned with the Russian and general human predicament. He was, however, far less committed than his great predecessors to the propagation, illustration or exposition of specific social, political, philosophical and religious panaceas. He differed from them also in adopting a less heavy and detailed descriptive technique. Hardly, indeed, did he need such a technique since he possessed an uncanny flair for conjuring up a human personality, a social setting or an entire complex situation with one or two deft strokes—as when (in *Ariadne*) he sums up the boredom of jaded tourists with the magnificent phrase 'like gorged boa-constrictors, we only noticed things that glittered'.

Adept at knowing what to leave unsaid, Chekhov is laconic, terse, pointed. He proceeds by hints, suggestions and telling silences. Where his great predecessors had orchestrated major climaxes in multi-decker novels, Chekhov did not even find it necessary to write novels at all, for he could say more in twenty pages than many another could convey in eight hundred. Where they dealt in climaxes, he cultivated anti-climaxes. He was above all the master of the miscued effect, the mis-directed pistol shot, the bungled seduction, the whimper which replaces the expected bang. Murder, lunacy, prostitution, felony . . . Chekhov by no means avoided such themes, as he himself liked to claim. On the contrary, he handled them expertly, with a deadly touch, while yet preserving his usual economy of means. His rare scenes of violence—such as Dr. Ragin's death in *Ward Number Six* and the slaughter of a religious maniac in *Murder*—are depicted with a lightness of touch spectacularly un-Tolstoyan, un-Dostoyevskian and un-Gogolesque; but are no less horrific for that.

Himself well aware of the gulf separating him from the literary dinosaurs of Russia's past, Chekhov takes issue with them in occasional ironical passages of fiction, as is well illustrated by his story *The Duel*. From Pushkin's and Lermontov's time onwards almost all major Russian writers had gone out of their way to portray splendid duelling scenes, these armed clashes between individuals being superbly qualified to provide fictional conflicts of the most dramatic kind. How differently though, does the anti-dramatic Chekhov handle this same bloody theme! When, at the climax of his narrative, pistols have been duly produced at dawn, it turns out that neither the contestants nor their seconds have the faintest idea what to do next.

> A hitch occurred. . . . It transpired that none of those present had ever attended a duel in his life, and no one knew exactly how they should stand, or what the seconds should say and do. . . . 'Any of you remember Lermontov's description?' Von Koren asked with a laugh. 'Turgenev's Bazarov also exchanged shots with someone or other——'

That Chekhov's duel ends in fiasco—with one contestant firing into the air and the other put off his aim by a comic intruding cleric—need hardly be said.

In the present volume we find Chekhov once again pointing to the generation gap in Russian fiction. Zinaida, the heroine of *An Anonymous Story*, in effect gives up everything to follow her lover to the ends of the earth, and is thus a parody of the idealistic self-sacrificing girls whom Turgenev created in such large numbers. Unfortunately for her she does not find herself matched with one of Turgenev's no less numerous wishy-washy young men, but has a more modern lover to reckon with: the urbane and cynical Orlov, who explicitly states that he is not a Turgenev hero. He also goes out of his way to dissociate himself from Turgenev's Insarov; the heroic Bulgarian freedom-fighter in *On the Eve*, whose Russian lady-friend—the heroically self-sacrificing Helen—joins him in the battle to free his country from Turkish oppression. Orlov's is, as he points out, a different nature. 'Should I ever require to liberate Bulgaria I could dispense with any female escort.'

Such was the irony with which Cheknov occasionally referred to his great precursors, and he could go beyond mere ironic flashes. In a private letter he once called Dostoyevsky's work long, immodest and pretentious. He seems to have held a fairly low opinion of Goncharov. And though an unstinting admirer of Tolstoy's art, he came to reject Tolstoy's teachings and didacticism. But Chekhov came nowhere near to any blanket condemnation of earlier Russian writers and their work. Nothing could have been further from the temperament of a man who was always generous in his praise of fellow-authors and quite incapable of disparaging others in order to boost himself. Throughout his life he showed a modesty astounding in anyone and especially remarkable in a creative artist. Certainly he did not regard himself as the superior of his chief precursors as writers of Russian fiction. Equally certainly, though, he knew that he was a different man using different techniques and operating in a different age.

What of Chekhov's outlook on life as expressed in his stories?

To this question no neat, all-embracing answer will ever be given. Chekhov was no builder of watertight philosophical systems, but even less was he a pure aesthete indifferent to the ethical or other non-artistic implications of his work. A few of his stories are explicitly didactic—especially those reflecting his brief and fictionally disastrous flirtation with Tolstoyism in the late 1880s. Others, by contrast, are mere 'slices of life' devoid of any homiletic element. More typical are items, of which all those in the present volume are samples, which fall between these two extremes. Here the author is doing more than just describing people and situations: he also seems to be saying something about how they ought—or at least about how they ought not—to behave.

Of the works in the present volume *Doctor Startsev* comes nearest to conveying such an author's message. It is typical of Chekhov in pillorying the futility of existence in the Russian provinces: a favourite theme. The town of S——, in which the story is set, is yet another of those anonymous Chekhovian provincial backwaters where the inhabitants do nothing but eat, drink, sleep, play cards, gossip, ill-treat their servants, indulge in frivolous litigation . . . and engender children who will continue the eating, drinking, sleeping, card-playing, ill-treating and litigating processes. Their futility is only further emphasized by such pathetic cultural activities as they can contrive: Mrs. Turkin's novels, her daughter's piano-playing, her husband's 'wit' and the posturings of their servant Peacock. What, indeed, 'could be said of a town in which the most brilliant people were so dim'?

Doctor Startsev is much more than a mere denunciation of provincial Russia. It is one of those many stories in which Chekhov shows worth-while human values succumbing to trivial vulgarity and petty everyday material cares—to what the Russians call *poshlost*. These perils can surface just as easily in the Russian countryside or St Petersburg as in the town of S——. They can also appear in Moscow, as *The Butterfly* shows. On Chekhov's characteristic use of symbolic consumables to stress his approval and non-approval of his characters this particular story provides an eloquent commentary, especially in the use made of food: the approved Dymov never seems to get anything to eat or drink, while his non-approved wife, her lover and their artistic friends are tainted by numerous food associations from caviare and grouse to wine and cabbage stew. Similarly, in *Ward Number Six*, the discredited Doctor Ragin is for ever nibbling gherkins and swilling vodka and beer.

It is, incidentally, often Chekhov's women who drag down the more idealistic men to the level of *poshlost* and vulgar domesticity—especially by the non-approved activity of making jam. The Professor's wife in *A Dreary Story* with her tendency to fuss about food and money; Ariadne, who has to be served with roast beef and boiled eggs in the middle of the night; Zinaida in *An Anonymous Story*, with her frills and fusses and copper saucepans . . . all these are typically female intruders on a male world comparatively unmaterialistic.

And yet Chekhov himself enjoyed his food, his drink, and even his female company—at least until his later years, when illness made inroads on his appetites. Nor, despite the high-minded implications of many of his stories, was he any philosophical idealist. He was, rather, a materialist with a straightforward, typically Victorian belief in human progress: to which we must hasten to add that this belief tended to sag and recede at times—and that it was in any case no 'burning faith', as some memoirists and critics have maintained. By training a scientist, Chekhov on the whole contented himself with observed fact, and if he showed any passion in his thinking it was in rejecting metaphysical and religious speculations. Similarly, he avoided the extravagances of artistic experimentation and 'modernism' which (one would hardly suspect from his own work) were coming into fashion during his mature years as a writer. Nor did he hold fanatical political views such as have been so tediously and catastrophically fashionable among Russian intellectuals of his own and other periods. Still less, though, would it be fair to repeat the criticism often levelled at Chekhov during his lifetime: that he was a-political, a-philosophical, and lacked principles of any kind. The accusation infuriated him, and he rightly thought it ill-founded. Chekhov held a variety of convictions, they fluctuated as his life developed, they were often mutually inconsistent—in other words, they resembled the views or convictions of many another educated and intelligent man who has never sought to work out an all-embracing system of belief. To claim that his views on life are all-important to his writings is as misleading as to maintain that they have no bearing on his work at all. In discussing such matters critics would do well to cultivate the restraint and common sense of the man whom they often misrepresent.

Chekhov's stories are by no means as shapeless as is commonly suggested. In the present volume *The Butterfly*, *Ward Number Six* and *Doctor Startsev* all have a well-defined plot, constructed with considerable balance and symmetry, and culminating with the death—actual or spiritual—of a main character. By contrast, other stories do indeed fizzle out in accordance with the formula so often applied to Chekhov: 'life goes on. . . .' One such tale is *Neighbours*, where the very pointlessness of the action or non-action *is* the main point of a saga which also hinges on a characteristic ironical twist: the man who so eloquently denounces his sister's ineffectual lover is his spiritual twin, being just as futile as the object of his tirades.

As the superb harangues in this story so richly illustrate, Chekhov by no means always depends on mere hints and pregnant silences. The eloquent over-statement of a case is often as important to the characterization of his figures as is the frequent use of deadly understatement. *A Dreary Story* is all harangue—and nowhere is its submerged irony more telling than in the passages where the Professor so violently carps at a university colleague . . . for continually carping at *his* university colleagues.

Arrivals, departures and journeys seem to have had a particular significance for Chekhov, almost every one of whose mature stories offers such a change of scene. One function of these episodes, without which no story or play of Chekhov's seems complete, is to extend a work's frame of reference by taking it temporarily out of its immediate spatial context. The same function is also performed in a different way by the frequent evocation of distant noises such as bands playing, church bells or drunken shouting. Similarly, Chekhov will extend his temporal frame of reference by constant harkings back to the past: often to the period when one or other of the characters was a child. ('Long ago, when he had been a small boy, his mother had. . . .') The same function is also performed by the many occasions on which characters look forward—hopefully, but often so pathetically—to the future when everything is somehow going to be wonderful, and when those of them who have never yet done a stroke of work will—they unconvincingly predict—devote their days to honest toil. ('Life in X years will be wonderful. . . .')

Illusions about the future, regrets for the past, high hopes collapsing among jam jars, fried onions and copper saucepans, the incongruities and inconsistencies of human beings, their mannerisms, their selfishness and their unselfishness, their tendency to say far too much or far too little, their inability—whether silent or garrulous—to communicate effectively with each other . . . these are some of the elements which make up Chekhov's thematic arsenal. His artistic aim—as he himself kept repeating—was simply to reflect the world as he saw it. And though life could never, in his portrayal, be fitted to a single all embracing pattern, it was not altogether lacking in patterns and parts of patterns either. An observer rather than an inventor, dependent on watchful personal experience rather than on a fertile creative imagination, he had the knack of noticing ordinary aspects of human behaviour such as had existed—but existed unrecorded—ever since civilization began. Chekhov observed and registered, often embedding in his record some strong implicit bias of his own, while yet leaving the reader unharassed by overt homilies and exhortations.

Rarely did he operate this technique more movingly and effectively than in the seven samples of his work which now follow.

SELECT BIBLIOGRAPHY

W. H. Bruford, *Chekhov and his Russia: A Sociological Study* (London, 1948).

The Oxford Chekhov. Tr. and ed. Ronald Hingley. Nine vols (London, 1964–80).

Letters of Anton Chekhov. Tr. Michael Henry Heim in collaboration with Simon Karlinsky. Selection, Commentary and Introduction by Simon Karlinsky (New York, 1973).

Letters of Anton Chekhov. Selected and edited by Avrahm Yarmolinsky (New York, 1973).

T. Eekman, ed., *Anton Chekhov, 1860–1960* (Leiden, 1960).

Ronald Hingley, *Chekhov: a Biographical and Critical Study* (London, 1950).

—— *A New Life of Anton Chekhov* (London, 1976).

Robert Louis Jackson, ed., *Chekhov: a Collection of Critical Essays* (Englewood Cliffs, N. J., 1967).

Karl D. Kramer, *The Chameleon and the Dream: the Image of Reality in Čexov's Stories* (The Hague, 1970).

Virginia Llewellyn Smith, *Anton Chekhov and the Lady with the Dog.* Foreword by Ronald Hingley (London, 1973).

A CHRONOLOGY OF ANTON CHEKHOV

All dates are given old style.

1860   16 or 17 January. Born in Taganrog, a port on the Sea of Azov in south Russia.

1876   His father goes bankrupt. The family moves to Moscow, leaving Anton to finish his schooling.

1879   Joins family and enrols in the Medical Faculty of Moscow University.

1880   Begins to contribute to *Strekoza* ('Dragonfly'), a St. Petersburg comic weekly.

1882   Starts to write short stories and a gossip column for *Oskolki* ('Splinters') and to depend on writing for an income.

1884   Graduates in medicine. Shows early symptoms of tuberculosis.

1885–6 Contributes to *Peterburgskaya gazeta* ('St. Petersburg Gazette') and *Novoye vremya* ('New Time').

1886   March. Letter from D. V. Grigorovich encourages him to take writing seriously.
        First collection of stories: *Motley Stories*.

1887   Literary reputation grows fast. Second collection of stories: *In the Twilight*.
        19 November. First Moscow performance of *Ivanov*: mixed reception.

1888   First publication (*The Steppe*) in a serious literary journal, *Severny vestnik* ('The Northern Herald').

1889   31 January. First St. Petersburg performance of *Ivanov*: widely and favourably reviewed.
        June. Death of brother Nicholas from tuberculosis.

1890   April–December. Crosses Siberia to visit the penal settlement on Sakhalin Island. Returns via Hong Kong, Singapore and Ceylon.

1891   First trip to western Europe: Italy and France.

1892   March. Moves with family to small country estate at Melikhovo, fifty miles south of Moscow.

1895   First meeting with Tolstoy.

1896   17 October. First—disastrous—performance of *The Seagull* in St. Petersburg.

1897   Suffers severe haemorrhage.

1897–8   Winters in France. Champions Zola's defence of Dreyfus.

1898   Beginning of collaboration with the newly founded Moscow Art Theatre. Meets Olga Knipper. Spends the winter in Yalta, where he meets Gorky.

         17 December. First Moscow Art Theatre performance of *The Seagull*: successful.

1899   Completes the building of a house in Yalta, where he settles with mother and sister.

         26 October. First performance by Moscow Art Theatre of *Uncle Vanya* (written ?1896).

1899–1901 First collected edition of his works (10 volumes).

1901   31 January. *Three Sisters* first performed.
         25 May. Marries Olga Knipper.

1904   17 January. First performance of *The Cherry Orchard*.
         2 July. Dies in Badenweiler, Germany.

THE BUTTERFLY

I

ALL Olga's friends, everyone she knew well, came to her wedding. 'Just look at him,' she told her friends. 'There's something about him; isn't there?'

And she nodded towards her husband as if trying to explain just why she was marrying so simple, so very ordinary, so utterly undistinguished a man.

The bridegroom, Osip Dymov, was a rather junior doctor on the staff of two hospitals: a temporary registrar in one, and an assistant pathologist in the other. He saw his patients and worked in his ward from nine till noon every day, then took the horse-tram to his other hospital in the afternoon and performed autopsies on deceased patients. His private practice was negligible, worth about five hundred roubles a year. That's all. What else can one say about him? Whereas Olga, her friends and her cronies were not quite ordinary people. Each one of them was somehow distinguished and somewhat famous, was already something of a name and was reckoned a celebrity. Or even if he wasn't quite a celebrity yet, he at least showed brilliant promise. There was an established and extremely gifted actor from the 'straight' theatre: an elegant, intelligent, modest man with a superb delivery who had taught Olga elocution. There was an opera singer, a jolly fat man who sighed that Olga was ruining herself. If she hadn't been lazy, he told her, if she had taken herself in hand, she might have become a distinguished singer. Then there were several artists, headed by the genre-painter, animal-painter and landscapist Ryabovsky, a very handsome, fair young man of about twenty-five who had exhibited successfully and had sold his last picture for five hundred roubles. He touched up Olga's sketches and used to say that she might possibly come to something. Then there was a 'cellist whose instrument sobbed and who openly declared that Olga was the only woman he knew who could play an accompaniment. And there was also an author, young but already famous, who wrote short novels, plays and stories. Who else was there? Well, there was a Vasily Vasilyevich: squire, landowner, amateur illustrator and vignettist with a great feel for the old Russian style, for the folk ballad and for epic. On paper, china and smoked plates he could work absolute miracles. In this spoilt, free-and-easy, Bohemian milieu—admittedly sensitive and modest, but conscious of such as doctors only at times of illness—the name Dymov cut no ice whatever. In this ambience he seemed an alien, superfluous, shrunken figure, tall and broad-shouldered though he was. He looked as if he had borrowed someone else's coat, and his beard seemed like a shop-assistant's. Had he been a writer or artist, though, they would have called his beard Zolaesque.

With Olga's flaxen hair, the actor said, and in her wedding dress, she much resembled a shapely young cherry-tree festooned with delicate white blossom in spring.

'Now, just listen to me,' Olga told him, clutching his hand. 'How did all this happen so suddenly? Well, listen, won't you? The thing is, my father worked at the same hospital as Dymov. When poor Father fell ill Dymov watched at his bed-side day and night. Such self-sacrifice! Now, listen, Ryabovsky. And you'd better listen too, Mr. Author, this is most interesting. Come closer. What self-sacrifice, what true sympathy! I stayed up every night too and sat with Father, when suddenly—what do you know?—the handsome prince is at my feet! Brother Dymov's in love, head over heels! Funny things do happen, I must say. Well, he took to calling after Father's death, or we would meet in the street. Then, one fine evening, suddenly—hey presto! He's proposing! You could have knocked me down with a feather! I cried all night and fell fiendishly in love myself. And now I'm Mrs. Dymov, as you see. There's something tough and rugged about him, isn't there, a sort of bear-like quality? You see him in three-quarter face now and badly lit, but when he turns just you look at that forehead. Ryabovsky, what say you to that forehead?

'We're discussing you, Dymov,' she shouted to her husband. 'Come here. Hold out your honest hand to Ryabovsky. That's the spirit. Now, be friends.'

With a good-natured, unsophisticated smile Dymov held out his hand to Ryabovsky.

'How do you do?' he said. 'There was a Ryabovsky in my year at college. I don't suppose he's a relative of yours?'

II

Olga was twenty-two years old, Dymov thirty-one. They settled down splendidly after their wedding. Olga plastered all the drawing-room walls with sketches—her own and other people's, framed and unframed—while assembling around grand piano and furniture a picturesque clutter of Chinese parasols, easels, gaudy rags, daggers, busts and photographs. She stuck folksy wood-cuts on the dining-room walls, she hung up bast sandals and sickles, and she stood a scythe and rake in the corner, thus creating a dining-room *à la russe*. The bedroom walls and ceiling she draped with dark cloth to create a cavernous effect, also hanging a Venetian lantern over the beds and placing a figure with a halberd by the door. A very cosy little nook the young people had, or so everyone thought.

Olga rose at eleven o'clock each day and played the piano. Or, if the sun was shining, she painted in oils. Then, at about half past twelve, she drove to her dressmaker's. She and Dymov were very hard up, so she and her dressmaker were put to ingenious shifts to enable her to appear frequently in new dresses and make a bit of a splash. Out of an old, dyed frock, very often—or from scraps of tulle, lace, plush and silk costing nothing—some miracle of seductiveness, some dream of a dress would emerge. From her dressmaker's Olga usually drove to an actress friend to cull the theatre news and incidentally to wangle a ticket for a first night or benefit performance. From the actress she would drive to some artist's studio or picture exhibition, and then to one of her celebrities to ask him home, pay a visit or just gossip. She found a joyous welcome everywhere, being splendid, charming, very special, people told her.

Her celebrities and 'great men', as she called them, accepted her as a friend and equal, predicting with one accord that her gifts, taste and intellect would take her a very long way indeed if she didn't try to do too much at once. She sang, played the piano, painted, modelled, took part in amateur dramatics: and all this with great style, not just any old how. Whether she made lanterns for the illuminations, put on fancy dress or tied someone's cravat, the effect was always highly artistic, graceful and charming. But the brightest of her talents was a knack of striking up acquaintance with celebrities and hitting it off with them. Someone only had to make a bit of a name and get himself talked about for her to meet him and make friends with him that very day and invite him home. Every new contact was a red letter day to her. She adored notabilities, exulted in them and dreamt about them each night. She craved for them with a thirst which nothing could slake. The old ones disappeared and were forgotten, and new ones took their place, but soon growing used to them too, or disappointed, she began eagerly seeking new and ever newer great men . . . and, finding them, began the search afresh. One wonders why.

She would have a meal with her husband at about half past four. His good nature, common sense and kindness had her in transports of joy. She kept jumping up, impulsively hugging his head, bestrewing him with kisses.

'You're so clever, Dymov, you're such a fine man,' she would say. 'But you do have one great defect. You take no interest whatever in art. Music, painting . . . you reject them both.'

'I don't understand them,' was his gentle reply. 'I have worked at science and medicine all my life, and I've had no time to be interested in the arts.'

'But I say, that's absolutely awful, Dymov.'

'Why so? Your friends know nothing of science and medicine, but you don't hold that against them. Everyone has his own line. I don't understand landscapes and operas, but if highly intelligent people give their whole lives to them and other intelligent people pay vast sums for them, then they must be important, as I see it. I don't understand, but not understanding doesn't mean rejecting.'

'Let me shake your honest hand!'

After their meal Olga would visit friends, then go to a theatre or concert and come home after midnight. So it went on every day.

On Wednesdays she was 'at home'. Hostess and guests did not play cards or dance on these occasions, but diverted themselves with various artistic activities. The actor recited, the singer sang, the artists sketched in albums (of which Olga had many), the 'cellist played and the hostess herself also sketched, modelled, sang and played accompaniments. In the gaps between recitals, music and singing there was talk and argument about literature, theatre and painting. Ladies were not present since Olga considered all women dreary and vulgar, actresses and her dressmaker excepted. Not one party passed without the hostess trembling at every ring.

'It is *he*,' she would say triumphantly, understanding by 'he' some new invited celebrity.

Dymov would not be in the drawing-room, nor would anyone remember his existence. But at exactly half past eleven the dining-room door would open and he would appear, smiling his good-natured, gentle smile.

'Supper is served, gentlemen,' he would say, rubbing his hands.

Then all would go into the dining-room, where they always saw the same array on the table: a dish of oysters, a joint of ham or veal, sardines, cheese, caviare, mushrooms, vodka and two carafes of wine.

'My dear *maître d'hôtel*,' said Olga, throwing up her hands in ecstasy. 'You're too, too adorable! Look at that forehead, gentlemen. Turn your profile, Dymov. See, gentlemen: the face of a Bengal tiger, but a kindly, charming expression like a fawn. Now, isn't he perfectly sweet?'

The visitors ate and looked at Dymov.

'He really is a splendid chap,' they thought, but soon forgot him and went on talking about theatre, music and painting.

The young couple were happy and everything went swimmingly. The third week of their married life was not altogether serene, though —it was rather the opposite. Dymov caught erysipelas in hospital, spent six days in bed and had to have his magnificent black hair shaved to the scalp. Olga sat by him weeping bitterly, but when he felt better she put a white kerchief round his cropped head and began to paint him as a Bedouin. That was great fun, they both found. Then, a day or two after he had recovered and gone back to his hospital work, a new misfortune befell him.

'I'm out of luck, my dear', he said at dinner one day. 'I did four post-mortems today and I went and scratched two fingers. I only noticed when I got home.'

Olga was scared, but he smiled and said it was nothing, and that he often cut his hands when dissecting.

'I get carried away, my dear, and don't concentrate.'

Olga was worried. She feared blood poisoning and prayed about it every night, but all was well and their quiet, happy life resumed its course free from worry and alarm. The present was wonderful and spring was at hand, already smiling from afar and promising a thousand delights. They would live happily ever after! For April, May and June there was a holiday cottage some distance from town. There would be walking, sketching, fishing and nightingales, and then, from July right through till autumn, a painting party on the Volga, in which trip Olga would take part as an indispensable member of their society. She had already had two linen travelling dresses made, and she had bought paints, brushes, canvases and a new palette for the journey. Ryabovsky visited her almost daily to see how her painting progressed. When she showed him her work he would thrust his hands deep into his pockets, purse his lips and sniff.

'Quite so,' he would say. 'That cloud of yours is a bit off, the light's wrong for evening. The foreground's rather chewed up and there's something, you know, not quite. . . . And your cottage has choked on something, it's more than a bit squeaky. And you should dim out that corner a shade. But altogether it's not so dusty. Nice work.'

And the more obscurely he spoke the more easily Olga understood him.

III

On Whit Monday afternoon Dymov bought some food and sweets, and set off to visit his wife at their cottage. Not having seen her for a fortnight, he missed her terribly. While in the train and then while searching a huge wood for the cottage, he felt famished and exhausted, looking forward to an informal supper with his wife, after which he would flop into bed and sleep. It cheered him up to look at the bundle in which he had wrapped caviare, cheese and white salmon.

By the time that he had found and identified his cottage the sun was setting. An ancient maid said that the mistress was out, but would be home directly for sure. The cottage was extremely unprepossessing, its low ceilings papered with writing-paper and its floors uneven and cracked. It had only three rooms. In one stood a bed, in another chairs and window-sills were bestrewn with canvases, brushes, greasy paper, and with men's overcoats and hats, while in the third Dymov found three strange men. Two were dark with little beards, while the third was clean-shaven and fat: an actor, apparently. A samovar hissed on the table.

'Can I help you?' boomed the actor, surveying Dymov frigidly. 'Looking for Olga, are you? Then wait, she'll be here any moment.'

Dymov sat and waited. One of the dark men gave him a few sleepy, languid glances and poured himself some tea.

'Perhaps you'd like a glass?' he asked.

Dymov was thirsty, and hungry too, but refused tea, not wanting to spoil his supper. Soon he heard footsteps and a familiar laugh, the door slammed and Olga swept into the room in a wide-brimmed hat with a box in her hand, followed by jolly, rosy-cheeked Ryabovsky carrying a huge parasol and camp-stool.

'Dymov!' shrieked Olga, flushing with joy.

'Dymov!' she repeated, laying head and both hands on his chest. 'Can it be you? Why have you been so long? Why, why, why?'

'But I never have time, my dear. I'm always busy, and when I am free the railway timetable never fits.'

'Now, I'm so glad to see you! I dreamt of you all night long, I was afraid you might be ill. Oh, if you did but know how sweet you are, you've come just in the nick of time, you'll be my salvation: only you can do it!

'We're having a quite fantastic wedding here tomorrow,' she went on, laughing and tying her husband's tie. 'A young telegraph clerk at the station's getting married, one Chikeldeyev. He's a good-looking boy, er, by no means unintelligent, and there's something rugged about his face, you know, a sort of bear-like quality. He could model a young Viking. We holiday visitors are all taking an interest in him and we have promised to be at his wedding. He's not well off, he has no relatives, he's a bit bashful and to let him down would be unforgivable, of course. Just think, the wedding will be after the service and then everyone will troop off from church to the bride's house. We'll have the copse, see? We'll have bird-song, sunlit patches on grass and all of us as variegated blobs against a bright green background: quite fantastic, in French impressionist style.

'But what can I wear in church, Dymov?' Olga asked with a tearful simper. 'I have nothing here, literally nothing: no dress, no flowers, no gloves. You must save me. The very fates bid you rescue me, your arrival shows it. Take your keys, dear man, go home and get my pink dress from the wardrobe. You remember it, it's hanging in front. Now, on the right of the closet, on the floor, you'll see two cardboard boxes. When you open the top one you'll find tulle all over the place and various bits and pieces, and underneath those some flowers. Take all the flowers out carefully, try not to crush them, darling, and I'll choose the ones I want later. And buy me some gloves.'

'All right,' said Dymov. 'I'll go back tomorrow and send them.'

'*Tomorrow?*' Olga stared at him in amazement. 'But you won't have time tomorrow: the first train leaves here at nine in the morning and the wedding's at eleven. No, darling, you must go tonight, tonight without fail, and if you can't come yourself tomorrow you must send the stuff by messenger. Come on, now, hurry up! There's a passenger train due in directly. Don't miss it, darling.'

'Very well.'

'Oh, how I hate letting you go,' said Olga, and tears came to her eyes. 'Oh, silly me, why ever did I promise that telegraph clerk?'

Dymov gulped a glass of tea, seized a roll, smiled gently and made for the station. His caviare, cheese and white salmon were consumed by the two dark men and the fat actor.

IV

One quiet, moonlit July night Olga stood on the deck of a Volga steamer, gazing alternately at the water and the picturesque banks. Ryabovsky stood by her side. The black shadows on the water were not shadows, he told her, but phantoms. This enchanted water with its eerie glitter, this unplumbed sky, these sad, pensive banks eloquent of our life's vanity and of some higher world of everlasting bliss . . . they were sights to make one swoon, die, become a memory. The past was vulgar and dreary, the future was meaningless, and this superb, unique night would soon end and melt into eternity. So why live?

Lending an ear, now to Ryabovsky's voice, now to the night's stillness, Olga thought that she was immortal and could never die. Turquoise-hued water such as she had never seen before, sky, banks, black shadows, mysterious joy flooding her inmost being . . . these things said that she would be a great artist and that out there, beyond that far horizon, beyond this moonlit night, in the vastness of space, she was heading for success, fame and a place in people's hearts.

She gazed unwinking into distance for some time, her fancy picturing crowds, lights, solemn music, triumphant shouts, herself in a white dress, flowers strewn on her from all around. She also reflected that by her side, leaning his elbows on the ship's rail, stood a truly great man, a genius, one of God's elect.

His present achievements were superb, fresh, extraordinary, but what he would achieve in time, with the mature development of his peculiar gifts . . . that would be something spectacular, something ineffably sublime, as could be seen by his face, his way of expressing things, his attitude to nature. He had his own special language for describing shadows, evening tints and moonlight, so that his power over nature cast an irresistible spell. He was a very handsome man, very much of an individual. Independent, free, a stranger to everything pedestrian, he seemed to live the life of a bird.

'It's a bit chilly,' said Olga with a shiver.

Ryabovsky wrapped his cloak round her.

'I feel I'm in your power,' he said mournfully. 'I'm your slave. Why are you so bewitching tonight?'

He gazed at her, he could not take his eyes off her and those eyes so scared her that she feared to look at him.

'I love you madly,' he whispered, breathing on her cheek. 'Say the word and I'll end my life.

'I'll abandon art,' he muttered with violent emotion. 'Love me, love me——'

'Don't say such things.' Olga closed her eyes. 'That's terrible. What about Dymov?'

'And what about Dymov? Why Dymov? What do I care for Dymov? There's Volga, moon, beauty, there's my love, my ecstasy, but there's no such thing as Dymov. Oh, I don't know anything, I don't care about the past. Just give me one second, one fleeting moment.'

Olga's heart was thumping. She tried to think about her husband, but all her past life—her wedding, Dymov, her At Homes . . . it all seemed so small, worthless, dull, superfluous and far, far away.

What *did* Dymov matter, actually? Why Dymov? What did she care about Dymov? Did such a phenomenon really exist? Or had she just imagined him?

'For so simple, so very ordinary a man the happiness which he has already received is quite adequate,' she thought, covering her face with her hands. 'Let them condemn me, let them curse me back there, but I'll ruin myself just to annoy them, I'll just jolly well wreck my life. One must experience everything in this world. God, how frightening, and how marvellous!'

'Well, what do you say?' muttered the artist, embracing her and hungrily kissing the hands with which she feebly tried to push him away. 'Do you love me? You do, don't you? Oh, what a night, what a fantastic night!'

'Yes, what a night!' she whispered, gazing into his eyes now bright with tears. Then she looked quickly round, embraced him and kissed him firmly on the lips.

'We're approaching Kineshma,' said someone on the far side of the deck.

Heavy footsteps were heard as the waiter came past them from the bar.

'Waiter!' said Olga, laughing and crying for joy. 'Would you bring us some wine?'

Pale with emotion, the artist sat on a bench and gazed at Olga in grateful adoration, then closed his eyes.

'I'm tired,' he said, smiling languidly.

He leant his head against the rail.

V

The second of September was a warm, calm, but overcast day. A thin early-morning mist drifted over the Volga, and at nine o'clock it began to drizzle. There was no chance of the sky clearing. Over morning tea Ryabovsky told Olga that painting was the most ungrateful and boring of the arts, that he was not an artist and that only idiots thought he was any good. Then suddenly, with absolutely no warning, he snatched up a knife and made scratches on his best sketch. After his tea he sat gloomily by a window, gazing at the Volga. No longer did the river glisten. It was dim and lustreless, it had a cold look to it. Everything around seemed to presage a melancholy, gloomy autumn. Sumptuous, green-carpeted banks, brilliantly reflected sunbeams, translucent blue distance . . . nature seemed to have taken everything showy and flamboyant from the Volga and packed it away until the coming spring, while crows flew above the river taunting its nakedness with their raucous caws. Hearing their noise, Ryabovsky reflected that he had gone to seed, that he was no good any more, that everything in this world is conditional, relative, idiotic—and that he should never have become involved with this woman.

He was in a bad mood, in other words, and felt depressed.

Olga sat on the bed behind a screen, running her fingers through her lovely flaxen hair and imagining herself first in her drawing-room, then in her bedroom, then in her husband's study. Her fancy bore her to the theatre, to her dressmaker's, to her famous friends. What were they up to now? Did they remember her? The season had started and it would have been time to think about her soirées. And what of Dymov? Dear old Dymov! How tenderly, in what childlike, pathetic terms his letters begged her to hurry home! He sent her seventy-five roubles each month, and when she wrote that she had borrowed a hundred roubles from the others he sent her the hundred too. How kind, how generous a man! Olga was weary of travelling, she was bored, she wanted to get away as fast as she could: away from these peasants, away from that damp river smell. She wanted to shed the sensation of physical impurity which she always felt while living in peasant huts and wandering from village to village. If Ryabovsky hadn't promised the others to stay till the twentieth of the month she could have left today, which would have been wonderful.

'Ye gods, will the sun *never* shine?' groaned Ryabovsky. 'How can I get on with my sunny landscape if it's not sunny?'

'But there is that cloud scene you're doing,' said Olga, coming out from behind the screen. 'With the wood in the right foreground, remember, and a herd of cows and some geese on the left. Now would be the time to finish that.'

'Oh, really!' Ryabovsky frowned. 'Finish it! Do you really think I'm such an ass that I don't know my own mind?'

'How you have changed towards me,' sighed Olga.

'And a very good thing too.'

Olga's face trembled, she moved away to the stove and burst into tears.

'Crying! Oh, this really is the limit. Stop it. I have umpteen reasons for tears, but you don't find me crying.'

'Reasons?' sobbed Olga. 'The chief one is that you're fed up with me.

'Yes,' she said, bursting into sobs. 'You are ashamed of our affair, truth to tell. You keep trying to hide it from the others, though it can't be concealed and they've known all about it for ages.'

'I ask only one thing of you, Olga,' begged the artist, laying his hand on his heart. 'Just this: stop tormenting me, that's all I want from you.'

'But swear you still love me.'

'Oh, this is sheer hell,' Ryabovsky muttered through clenched teeth and jumped to his feet. 'I'll end up throwing myself in the Volga or going mad. Leave me alone.'

'Then why don't you kill me?' shouted Olga. 'Kill me!'

She sobbed again and went behind the screen. Rain swished on the thatch, Ryabovsky clutched his head and paced the room. Then, with the resolute air of one bent on proving a point, he put on his cap, slung his gun over his shoulder and left the hut.

For some time after he had gone Olga lay on the bed crying. Her first thought was to take poison so that Ryabovsky should find her dead when he came back, but then her fancies swept her into her drawing-room, into her husband's study. She saw herself sitting quite still by Dymov's side, enjoying physical calm and cleanliness, she imagined hearing Masini in the theatre one evening. And a pang of longing for civilization, for the bustle of the city, for famous people, plucked at her heart. A local woman came into the hut and began slowly lighting the stove so that she could cook dinner. There was a fumy smell, and the air filled with blue smoke. The artists arrived in muddy top-boots, their faces wet with rain. They looked over their sketches and consoled themselves by saying that the Volga had a charm of its own, even in bad weather. The cheap clock on the wall ticked monotonously. Cold flies crowded and buzzed in the corner by the icons, and cockroaches were heard scuttling in the thick portfolios under the benches.

Ryabovsky came home at sunset and flung his cap on the table. Pale, exhausted, in muddy boots, he sank on to a bench and closed his eyes.

'I'm tired,' he said, and twitched his brows, trying to lift his eyelids.

Olga wanted to be nice to him and show that she wasn't angry, so she went up, silently kissed him and ran a comb through his fair hair. She wanted to do his hair properly.

'What's this?' he asked, starting as if from a cold touch.

He opened his eyes. 'What's going on? Oh, leave me alone, for heaven's sake.'

Pushing her away, he moved off—looking disgusted and dismayed, she felt. Then the peasant woman brought him a bowl of cabbage stew, carrying it with great care in both hands, and Olga saw the stew wetting her thumbs. The dirty woman with her tightly belted stomach, the stew so greedily gulped by Ryabovsky, the hut, this whole way of life so adored at first for its simplicity and Bohemian disorder . . . it all struck her as perfectly odious now. She suddenly felt insulted.

'We must separate for a bit,' she said coldly, 'or else we may quarrel seriously out of sheer boredom. I'm fed up with this, I shall leave today.'

'How, pray? By broom-stick?'

'It's Thursday today so there's a boat at half past nine.'

'Eh? Yes, quite so. All right then, you go,' said Ryabovsky gently, wiping his mouth on a towel instead of a napkin. 'You're bored here, you're at a loose end and it would be most selfish of me to keep you. So go, and we'll meet after the twentieth.'

Olga cheerfully packed her things, her cheeks positively glowing with pleasure. Could it really be true, she wondered, that she would soon be painting in a drawing-room, sleeping in a bedroom, dining with a cloth on the table? She felt relieved and was no longer angry with the artist.

'I am leaving you my paints and brushes, Ryabovsky dear,' said she. 'You can bring me anything I leave behind. Now, mind you aren't lazy when I'm gone, and don't mope. You do some work. You're a good chap, Ryabovsky old sport.'

Ryabovsky kissed her good-bye at ten o'clock—this was so that he needn't kiss her on the boat in front of the others, she thought—and took her to the landing-stage. The steamer soon came and bore her off.

Two and a half days later she arrived home. Breathless with excitement, she went into her drawing-room without removing hat or raincoat and thence into her dining-room. Dymov was sitting at the table in his shirt-sleeves with his waistcoat unbuttoned and was sharpening a knife on a fork. There was a grouse on the plate in front of him. At the time of entering her apartment Olga had been quite sure that she must keep her husband in ignorance and that she possessed the requisite wit and strength to do so, but now that she saw his broad, gentle, happy smile and his eyes alight with pleasure, she felt that deceiving the man would be mean, odious, out of the question—and as far beyond her as bearing false witness, robbing or murdering. So she made a sudden decision to tell him all. She let him kiss and embrace her, then knelt before him and covered her face.

'Now, what is it, my dear?' he asked gently. 'Did you miss me?'

She lifted her face, red with shame, and looked at him guiltily and beseechingly, but fear and embarrassment stopped her telling the truth.

'It's all right', she said. 'It's nothing——'

'Let's sit down,' he said, lifting her up and seating her at the table. 'There you are. Have some grouse. My poor darling, you're famished.'

She eagerly breathed in the air of home and ate the grouse, while he watched her tenderly and smiled happily.

VI

Half-way through winter Dymov evidently began to suspect that he was a deceived husband. It was as if *he* was the guilty party, for he could no longer look his wife in the face, nor did he smile happily when they met. So as to be alone with her less he often asked his colleague Korostelyov in for a meal. This was a small, close-cropped person with a wrinkled face who kept buttoning and unbuttoning his jacket in embarrassment when talking to Olga, and would then start tweaking the left side of his moustache with his right hand. Over their meal both doctors would talk about how an upward displacement of the diaphragm is sometimes accompanied by pulse irregularities, about how widespread compound neuritis is nowadays, and about how Dymov had found cancer of the pancreas when performing yesterday's autopsy on a cadaver bearing a diagnosis of pernicious anaemia. Both apparently discussed medicine only to give Olga the chance to remain silent, and hence to avoid lying. After the meal Korostelyov would sit at the piano.

'Ah me, old chap,' Dymov would sigh. 'Ah, well. Play something melancholy.'

Hunching his shoulders and splaying his fingers, Korostelyov would strike a few chords and start singing in his tenor voice:

> 'Do you know any place in all Russia
> Where no suffering peasantry groans?'

Dymov would sigh again, prop his head on his fist and sink into thought.

Olga had been behaving most indiscreetly of late. Each morning she woke up in an appalling temper, with the notion that she no longer loved Ryabovsky and that the affair was over, thank God. By the time that she had finished her coffee she was fancying that Ryabovsky had taken her husband from her, that she was now bereft of both husband and Ryabovsky. Then she would recall her friends' talk about how Ryabovsky was working on something outstanding for exhibition, a mixture of landscape and genre *à la* Polenov—visitors to his studio were in ecstasies about it. But that work had been done under *her* influence, had it not? It was her influence, by and large, that had changed him so much for the better. So beneficent, so vital was this influence that he might well come to grief should she abandon him. She also recalled that he had worn a kind of grey, flecked frock-coat and a new tie on his last visit.

'Am I handsome?' he had asked languorously.

Elegant he indeed was with his long curls and blue eyes, and very handsome too—unless that was just an illusion—and he had been nice to her.

After many rememberings and imaginings, Olga would dress and drive to Ryabovsky's studio in a great pother. She would find him cheerful and delighted with his picture, which really was marvellous. He would skip about and fool around, returning joke answers to serious questions. Olga was jealous of that picture, she hated it, but she would stand in front of it without speaking for five minutes out of politeness, then sigh like one contemplating a holy relic.

'No, you've never done anything like this before,' she would say quietly. 'It's positively awesome, actually.'

Then she would implore him to love her, not to desert her, and she begged him to pity poor, unhappy her. She would weep and kiss his hands as she insisted on him swearing that he loved her, arguing that he would go astray and come to grief without her good offices. Then, having spoilt his mood, feeling degraded, she would drive off to her dressmaker's or to an actress friend to wangle a theatre ticket.

Should she miss him in his studio she would leave a note swearing to poison herself without fail if he did not come and see her that day. He would panic, go along and stay to a meal. Ignoring her husband, he spoke to her rudely and she repaid him in kind. Each found the other a drag, a tyrant, an enemy. Growing angry, they failed to notice in their rage that both were being indiscreet, that even crop-headed Korostelyov knew what was going on. After the meal Ryabovsky was quick to say good-bye and leave.

'Where are you off to?' Olga would ask him in the hall, looking at him with hatred.

Scowling, screwing up his eyes, he would name some woman known to them both, obviously mocking her jealousy and trying to annoy her. She would go to her bedroom and lie on the bed, biting the pillow and sobbing aloud in her jealousy, vexation, humiliation and shame. Dymov would leave Korostelyov in the drawing-room and come into the bedroom, embarrassed and frantic.

'Don't cry so loudly, my dear,' he would say gently. 'Why should you? You must say nothing about it. You mustn't let on. What's done can't be undone, you know.'

Not knowing how to tame this bothersome jealousy, which even gave her a headache, and thinking that matters might still be mended, she would wash, powder her tear-stained face and rush off to see the woman friend in question. Not finding Ryabovsky, she went to a second, then a third.

She was ashamed of going about like this at first, but then it became a habit and there were times when she toured all her female acquaintance-ship in a single evening—looking for Ryabovsky, as everyone very well knew.

She once told Ryabovsky that 'that man' (meaning her husband) 'overwhelms me with his magnanimity.'

Such a liking did she take to this sentence that she always used it on meeting artists who knew of her affair with Ryabovsky.

'That man overwhelms me with his magnanimity,' she would say with a sweeping gesture.

Her routine remained that of the year before. There were the Wednesday soirées. The actor recited, the artists sketched, the 'cellist played, the singer sang and at half past eleven without fail the dining-room door opened.

'Supper is served, gentlemen,' Dymov would smile.

As of old, Olga sought great men and found them—but then found them wanting and sought more. As of old, she came home late each night. Dymov would no longer be asleep as in the previous year, though, but sat in his study doing some work. He went to bed at about three o'clock and rose at eight.

One evening, when she was standing in front of her pier-glass before going to the theatre, Dymov came into the bedroom in his tails and white tie. He smiled gently and looked his wife in the eye as delightedly as of old. He was beaming.

'I've just been defending my thesis,' he said, sitting down and stroking his knees.

'And did you succeed?' Olga asked.

He chuckled and craned his neck to see his wife's face in the mirror, for she was still standing with her back to him, doing her hair.

He chuckled again. 'I shall very likely be offered a lectureship in general pathology, you know. It's in the air.'

His beatific, beaming expression showed that if Olga were to share his joy and triumph he would forgive her everything, both present and future, and would dismiss it from his mind. But she didn't know what a lectureship was or what general pathology was. And besides, she was afraid of being late for the theatre, so she said nothing.

He sat there for two minutes, then went out with a guilty smile.

VII

It was a very disturbed day.

Dymov had a bad headache. He took no breakfast, stayed away from hospital and just lay there on his study sofa. Olga set off for Ryabovsky's at about half past twelve as usual to show him her still-life sketch and ask why he hadn't visited her on the previous day. She didn't think the sketch was very good and she had only done it to give herself an excuse for visiting the artist.

Entering his apartment without ringing, and removing her galoshes in the hall, she heard the sound of someone running quietly through the studio and the rustle of a woman's dress. She quickly peeped inside and just glimpsed a flash of brown petticoat whisking past to vanish behind the large picture draped down to the floor with black calico, easel and all. That a woman was hiding there was beyond doubt —Olga herself had taken refuge behind that picture often enough! Obviously much embarrassed, Ryabovsky held out both hands as if surprised at her arrival.

'Aha, delighted to see you,' he said with a forced smile. 'And what news do we bring?'

Olga's eyes brimmed with tears and she felt bitterly ashamed. Not for a million roubles would she have consented to speak before that strange woman, her rival: the false creature who now stood behind the picture, probably giggling at her discomfiture.

'I have brought you a sketch,' she said timidly in a thin little voice, her lips trembling. 'A still life.'

'Aha, a sketch?'

The artist picked up the sketch. As he examined it he went into the next room, affecting a disinterested air.

Olga followed him submissively.

'A *nature morte*, the finest sort,' he muttered, seeking a rhyme. 'Resort, port——'

From the studio came the sound of hurried steps and the rustle of a skirt. So the creature had left. Olga felt like shouting aloud, hitting the artist with a blunt instrument and leaving, but she could see nothing for tears and she was overwhelmed with shame, feeling as if she were no longer Olga, no longer an artist, but a small insect.

'I'm tired,' said Ryabovsky languidly, looking at the sketch and shaking his head to conquer his drowsiness. 'It's all very charming, of course, but a sketch today, a sketch last year and another sketch in a month's time . . . I wonder you don't get bored with it. I'd give up painting if I were you and take up music really seriously, or something. You're no artist, after all, you're a musician. I say, I am tired, you know. I'll have tea served, shall I?'

He left the room and Olga heard him giving orders to his servant. To avoid farewells and explanations, and above all to avoid bursting into tears, she darted into the hall before Ryabovsky came back, put on her galoshes and went into the street. There she breathed more easily and felt free once and for all: free from Ryabovsky, from painting, from the load of shame which had so overwhelmed her in the studio. It was all over.

She drove to her dressmaker's and then to see the actor Barnay, who had only arrived the day before. From Barnay she went to a music shop, brooding the while on how she would write Ryabovsky a cold, harsh letter full of her own dignity. That spring or summer she and Dymov would go to the Crimea, where she would shake off the past once and for all and start a new life.

Reaching home late that night, she sat down in the drawing-room without changing her clothes in order to write her letter. Ryabovsky

had said that she was no good at painting, so she would revenge
herself by telling him that he painted the same picture year in year out
and said the same thing day in day out, that he was stagnating, and that
he would achieve nothing beyond what he had already achieved. She
also felt like telling him how much he owed to her good offices, whereas
if he behaved badly it was only because her influence was paralysed by
sundry dubious personages such as the one who had hidden behind the
picture today.

'My dear,' Dymov called from the study, not opening the door.
'My dear!'

'What is it?'

'Don't come into my room, dear, just come to the door. Look, I
must have caught diphtheria at the hospital the day before yesterday,
and now I'm feeling awful. Send for Korostelyov as quick as you can.'

Olga always called her husband by his surname, as she did all the
other men she knew. She disliked the name Osip because it reminded her
of Gogol's Osip. And wasn't there that jingle about the old fellow called
Osip, who 'grew hoarse from a surfeit of gossip', or something vaguely
like that? Now, however, Olga shouted: 'That's not possible, Osip!'

'Send for him, I'm in a bad way,' Dymov said behind the door, and
was heard going back to the sofa and lying down.

'Send for him.' His voice had a hollow ring.

Cold with fear, Olga wondered whatever the matter could be.
'Why, this is dangerous!' she thought.

For no special reason she took a candle and went into her bedroom,
where, as she tried to work out what to do, she chanced to glimpse
herself in the pier-glass. Her pale, frightened face, her jacket with its
high sleeves, the yellow flounces at her breast, her skirt with the stripes
running in unorthodox directions . . . these things made her seem
horrible and disgusting in her own eyes. She felt a sudden stab of pity:
for Dymov, for his boundless love of her, for his young life and even
for this orphaned bed in which he had not slept for so long, and she
remembered his usual smile, so gentle and so meek. She wept bitterly
and wrote a note imploring Korostelyov to come. It was two o'clock
in the morning.

VIII

When Olga came out of her bedroom at about half past seven, her
head heavy from lack of sleep, her hair unbrushed, ugly, and guilty-
looking, some gentleman with a black beard—a doctor, apparently—

went past her into the hall. There was a smell of medicine. Near the study door Korostelyov stood twisting the left side of his moustache with his right hand.

'I can't let you go in, I'm sorry,' he told Olga grimly. 'It's catching. And actually there's no point, he's delirious anyway.'

'Is it really diphtheria?' Olga whispered.

'It should be a criminal offence, actually, asking for trouble like that,' muttered Korostelyov without answering Olga's question. 'You know how he caught it? He sucked some diphtherial membrane from a boy's throat on Tuesday, through a tube. Whatever for? It was so stupid, sheer folly——'

'Is it dangerous? Very?' asked Olga.

'Yes, it's the malignant kind, they say We should really send for Schreck.'

There arrived a red-haired little man with a long nose and a Jewish accent, then a tall, stooping, shaggy individual who looked like an archdeacon, then a very stout, bespectacled young man with a red face. These were doctors coming to take their turns at their colleague's bedside. Korostelyov had done his stint, but stayed on instead of going home, positively haunting the flat. The maid served tea to the doctors on watch and was constantly running to the chemist's. There was no one to tidy the rooms. It was quiet and gloomy.

Olga sat in her bedroom and thought how God was punishing her for deceiving her husband. A silent, uncomplaining, mysterious creature, robbed of individuality by its very gentleness, characterless, weak from superfluity of kindness, was dumbly suffering without complaint somewhere in there on the sofa. And were it to complain, even in delirium, the doctors at the bedside would know that the fault was more than just diphtheria alone. They could ask Korostelyov: he knew all about it, and it was not for nothing that he looked at his friend's wife as if she were the true, the chief culprit, the diphtheria being merely her accomplice. Oblivious now of that moonlit evening on the Volga, of declarations of love, of their romantic life in the peasant's hut, she remembered only that an idle whim, sheer self-indulgence, had made her smear herself all over, hand and foot, with sticky filth that would never wash off.

'Oh, how horribly false I have been,' she thought, remembering her turbulent affair with Ryabovsky. 'Damn, damn, damn all that!'

At four o'clock she joined Korostelyov for a meal. He ate nothing, just drank red wine and frowned. She too ate nothing. At times she prayed silently, vowing to God that, should Dymov recover, she would love him again and be a faithful wife. At times she lost track of things and gazed at Korostelyov.

'How boring,' thought she, 'to be an ordinary, utterly obscure nonentity, besides having a wrinkled face and no social graces.'

At other times she felt that God would strike her dead that very instant because she had never once been in her husband's room, fearing infection. There was also a general sensation of hopelessness, a certainty that her life already lay in ruins beyond all hope of recovery.

After the meal it grew dark. Olga went into the drawing-room and Korostelyov slept on a couch with a gold-embroidered silk cushion under his head. He snored raucously and rhythmically.

The doctors came to do their stint and went away again without noticing this disarray. A snoring stranger asleep in the drawing-room, the sketches on the walls, the quaint furnishings, the mistress of the house with her dishevelled hair and slovenly dress . . . none of that aroused the faintest interest now. One of the doctors chanced to laugh at something, and his laugh had a ring strange, timid and positively unnerving.

When Olga returned to the drawing-room Korostelyov had woken up and sat smoking.

'He has diphtheria of the nasal cavity,' he said in a low voice. 'His heart's not too good either. Things are pretty bad, really.'

'Then send for Schreck,' said Olga.

'He's been. It was he who noticed that the infection had passed to the nose. What is Schreck, anyway? He's nothing, really, Schreck isn't. He's Schreck, I'm Korostelyov—and that's that.'

Time dragged on terribly slowly. Olga lay fully-clothed on her unmade bed and dozed. She fancied that the whole apartment was jammed from floor to ceiling with a huge chunk of iron, that if only one could remove this iron everyone would be happy and cheerful. Then she woke and realized that it was not iron that weighed her down, it was Dymov's illness.

'*Nature morte*, port,' she thought, lapsing into forgetfulness again. 'Sport, resort—. And what of Schreck? Schreck, greck, Greek, shriek—. But where are my friends now? Do they know we're in trouble? Lord, help us, save us! Schreck, greck——'

And again the iron appeared. Time dragged terribly, a clock on the ground floor kept striking. The door-bell was continually ringing as doctors arrived. The housemaid came in with an empty glass on a tray.

'Shall I make the bed, ma'am?' she asked, and went out after receiving no answer.

The clock struck downstairs, Olga dreamt of rain on the Volga and once again someone came into the bedroom: a stranger, it seemed. Olga jumped up and saw that it was Korostelyov.

'What's the time?' she asked.

'About three.'

'Well, what is it?'

'What indeed? I've come to tell you that he's sinking.'

He gulped, sat by her on the bed and wiped his tears with his sleeve. Unable to grasp it all at once, she turned cold all over and began slowly crossing herself.

'He's sinking,' he repeated in a shrill voice and sobbed again. 'He's dying because he martyred himself.

'What a loss to science!' he said bitterly. 'Compared with the rest of us he was a great man, he was quite outstanding. What gifts!

'What hopes we all had for him,' Korostelyov continued, wringing his hands. 'Lord above us, he was a real scientist—you don't find his sort any more. Osip, Osip Dymov, how could you? Oh, oh, my God!'

Frantic, Korostelyov covered his face with both hands and shook his head.

'And what moral strength!' he went on, his anger mounting. 'That kind, pure, loving heart as clear as crystal. He served science, he died for science. He slaved away day in day out, nobody spared him—and a young scholar, a budding professor, had to tout for private patients and spend his nights translating to pay for these . . . disgusting rags!'

Korostelyov glared at Olga with hatred, snatched the sheet in both hands and tore it angrily as if he blamed the sheet.

'He didn't spare himself and no one spared him. Oh, what's the use of talking?'

'Yes, he was quite outstanding,' said a deep voice in the drawing-room.

Olga remembered their life together from beginning to end in all its details and she suddenly saw that he really had been an outstanding, rare person: a great man compared with everyone else she had known. Recalling what her dead father and all his doctor-colleagues had thought of Dymov, she realized that they had all seen him as a future notability. Walls, ceiling, lamp, the carpet on the floor . . . all seemed to wink at her sardonically.

'You're too late now,' they seemed to say. 'You've lost your chance.'

She rushed wailing out of the bedroom, darted past some stranger in the dining-room and ran to her husband's study. He lay quite still on the sofa, covered to the waist with a quilt. His face was terribly thin and sunken, with a greyish-yellow hue never seen on living man. Only the forehead, black brows and familiar smile showed that this was Dymov. Olga quickly felt his chest, forehead, hands. His chest was still warm, but his forehead and hands were disagreeably cold. And his half open eyes gazed at the quilt, not at Olga.

'Dymov!' she called aloud. 'Dymov!'

She wanted to tell him that there had been a mistake, that all was not yet lost, that life could still be wonderfully happy, that he was a rare, an outstanding, a great man—and that she would worship him all her life, adore him, revere him and do him homage.

'Dymov!' she called, feeling his shoulder, unable to believe that he would never wake again. 'Dymov! Answer me, Dymov!'

In the drawing-room Korostelyov was speaking to the maid.

'It's perfectly simple. Go to the church lodge and ask for the alms-house women. They'll wash the body, they'll lay it out and do whatever needs doing.'

WARD NUMBER SIX

I

In the hospital courtyard stands a small building surrounded by a jungle of burdock, nettle and wild hemp. The roof is rusty, the chimney half collapsed. The porch steps have rotted and are overgrown with grass, and only a few traces of plaster are left. The front faces the hospital and the rear looks into open country, cut off from it by a grey hospital fence with nails on top. Those nails with spikes uppermost, the fence, the hut itself . . . all have the melancholy, doomed air peculiar to hospital and prison buildings.

Unless you are afraid of nettle stings, let us take the narrow path to this shack and see what goes on inside. Opening the first door we enter the lobby, where great stacks of hospital rubbish are piled by walls and stove. Mattresses, tattered old smocks, trousers, blue-striped shirts and useless, dilapidated footwear . . . all this junk is dumped around any old how, mouldering and giving off an acrid stench.

On the rubbish, a pipe always clenched between his teeth, lies the warder Nikita, an old soldier with faded chevrons. He has a red nose and a stern, haggard visage to which pendulous eyebrows give the look of a prairie sheepdog. Short of stature, he appears gaunt and sinewy, but has an air of authority and knows how to use his fists. He is one of those dull, self-assured, punctilious simpletons who believe in discipline above all things and who are therefore convinced that people need hitting. He hits them on face, chest, back or anywhere handy, being firmly convinced that this is the only way to keep order in the place.

Next you enter a large, capacious room which is all the hut consists of, apart from the lobby. Its walls are daubed with dirty blue paint, the ceiling is caked with soot as in a chimneyless peasant hut, and you can tell that these stoves smoke and fill the place with fumes in winter. The windows are disfigured by iron bars on the inside, the floor is grey and splintery, and there is such a stink of sour cabbage, burnt wicks, bed-bugs and ammonia that your first impression is of entering a zoo.

The room contains beds which are screwed to the floor. Sitting or lying on them are people in navy-blue hospital smocks and old-fashioned nightcaps: the lunatics.

There are five in all. Only one has genteel status, the rest being of the lower orders. The nearest to the door is a tall, lean working-class fellow with a glistening ginger moustache, tear-filled eyes and a fixed stare, who sits resting his head in his hands. He grieves all day and night, shaking his head, sighing, smiling a bitter smile. He seldom joins in any conversation and does not usually answer questions. At feeding time he eats and drinks like an automaton. His excruciatingly racking cough, emaciation and cheeks with red spots seem to be symptoms of incipient tuberculosis.

Next comes a small, lively, very nimble old man with a pointed little beard and black curly hair like a Negro's. He ambles about the ward from one window to another in daytime, or squats on his bed Turkish-fashion, whistling irrepressibly like a bullfinch, humming and giggling. At night-time too he evinces the same infantile gaiety and liveliness, getting up to pray: to beat his breast with his fists and pluck at the door with his finger, in other words. This is Moses the Jew, a loon who lost his reason twenty years ago when his hatter's workshop burnt down.

Alone among the denizens of Ward Number Six he is permitted to leave the hut and even to go out of the hospital yard into the street. He has long enjoyed this privilege, probably because he is a veteran inmate: a quiet, harmless idiot and the town buffoon, long a familiar sight in the streets with his entourage of urchins and dogs. In his great smock, comic night-cap and slippers, sometimes barefoot and even untrousered, he walks the streets, stopping at gates and shops to beg. He gets kvass here, bread there, a copeck elsewhere—and so he usually returns to the hut well-fed and in funds, but Nikita confiscates all the takings for his own use. This the old soldier does roughly and angrily, turning out Moses's pockets, calling God to witness that he will never let the Jew out in the street again and saying that if there is one thing he can't stand it's disorder.

Moses likes to be helpful. He brings his ward-mates water, tucks them up when they are asleep, promising to bring them all a copeck from the street and make them each a new hat. He also spoon-feeds his left-hand neighbour, who is paralysed. This is not done through pity or from humanitarian considerations, but in imitation of—and in automatic deference to—his right-hand neighbour Gromov.

Thirty-three years of age, a gentleman, a former court usher and official of the twelfth grade, Ivan Gromov has persecution mania. He either lies curled up on his bed or paces from corner to corner as if taking a constitutional. He very seldom sits. He is always excited, agitated and tense with some dim, vague premonition. The merest rustle in the lobby, a shout outside, is enough to make him lift his head and cock an ear. Someone has come for him, haven't they? It is him they're after, isn't it? At these times his face expresses extreme alarm and disgust.

I like his broad face with its high cheek-bones, always pale and unhappy, mirroring a soul racked by struggle and ever-present terror. His grimaces are weird and neurotic, but there is reason and intelligence in the subtle traits carved on his face by deeply felt suffering, and his eyes have a warm, healthy glint. I like him as a person polite, helpful and outstandingly delicate in his manner towards all except Nikita. If someone drops a button or spoon he leaps from his bed to pick it up. Every morning he wishes his fellow-inmates good day, and he bids them good night when he goes to bed.

Besides grimaces and unrelieved tension, his insanity also finds the following outlet. Some evenings he wraps himself in his smock, and starts pacing rapidly from corner to corner and between the beds, trembling all over, his teeth chattering. He acts as if he had a high temperature. His way of suddenly stopping to look at the others shows that he has something extremely important to say, but then he shakes his head impatiently and resumes his pacing, evidently considering that no one will heed or understand him. But soon an urge to speak swamps all other considerations and he unleashes an eager, passionate harangue. His speech is jumbled, feverish, delirious, jerky, not always comprehensible, but there is a fine ring about it, about his words and his voice. As he speaks you recognize both the lunatic and the man in him. It is hard to convey his insane babble on paper. He talks of human viciousness, of brutality trampling on justice, of the heaven on earth which will come to pass in time, of the bars on the windows which constantly remind him of the obtuseness and cruelty of his oppressors. The result is like a chaotic, untidy, miscellany of old songs: old, but not yet stale.

II

Twelve or fifteen years ago a civil servant called Gromov, a man of weight and substance, was living in a house which he owned on the town's main street. He had two sons, Sergey and Ivan. Sergey contracted galloping consumption in his fourth year at college. He died, and this death seemed to herald a whole series of disasters which suddenly befell the Gromov family. A week after Sergey's funeral the old father was prosecuted for forgery and embezzlement, and died soon afterwards of typhus in the prison hospital. His house and all his effects were sold up at auction, Ivan and his mother being left utterly destitute.

While living in St. Petersburg and attending the university during his father's lifetime, Ivan had received sixty or seventy roubles a month and had not known what hardship was, but now he had to change his way of life abruptly. All day long he had to do coaching for a pittance and he had to take on copying work—yet still go hungry since he sent all his earnings to keep his mother. Ivan couldn't stand the life. He lost heart, fell ill and gave up the university to come home. Through his connections he obtained a job as teacher in the county school here in the little town, but he didn't get on with his colleagues, his pupils disliked him and he soon dropped it. Then his mother died. He was out of work for six months, living on bread and water, after which he became a court usher: a post which he held until dismissed through illness.

Even as a young man at college he had never looked healthy. He was always pale, thin and subject to colds, he ate little, he slept badly. One glass of wine went to his head and made him hysterical. He had always needed company, but his petulance and touchiness prevented him from making close contacts and friends. He always spoke with contempt of the townsfolk, whose crass ignorance and torpid, brutish lives were, he felt, loathsome and nauseating. He spoke in a loud, urgent, high-pitched voice, always furiously indignant or admiringly ecstatic, always sincere. Whatever you spoke about he always reduced it to a single theme: the town was a stuffy, boring place to live, society lacked higher interests, leading a dim, meaningless existence and varying it with brutality, crude licentiousness and hypocrisy. Scoundrels were well fed and well dressed, honest men ate crumbs. They needed schools, a local newspaper with an honest view-point, a theatre, public recitals, intellectual solidarity. Society must recognize its own nature and recoil from it with horror. In his judgements about people he laid things on with a trowel—seeing everything in black and white, acknowledging no intermediate shades. He divided humanity into honest men and scoundrels with nothing in between. Of women and love he always spoke with fervid enthusiasm, but he had never been in love.

Extreme though his views were, touchy as he was, he was popular in town, where he was fondly known as 'good old Ivan' behind his back. His innate delicacy, helpfulness, decency and moral integrity inspired kindness, sympathy and sorrow, as also did his shabby old frock-coat, ailing appearance and family misfortunes. Besides, he was well educated and well read. He knew everything, according to the locals, and the town reckoned him a sort of walking encyclopaedia.

He read a great deal. He would sit in the club sometimes, nervously plucking at his beard and leafing through magazines and books, and showing by his expression that he was not so much reading as gulping the stuff down with barely time to chew it. Reading must have been one of his morbid symptoms since he pounced with equal zeal on whatever came his way, even last year's newspapers and calendars. At home he always lay down to read.

III

His coat collar turned up, Ivan Gromov was splashing his way through the mud of alleys and back lanes one autumn morning to collect a fine from some tradesman or other. He was in a black mood, as he always was in the mornings. In a certain alley he came across two convicts wearing foot-irons and escorted by four guards with rifles. Gromov had met convicts often enough before—they had always made him feel sympathetic and uncomfortable—but now this latest encounter had a peculiarly weird effect on him. Somehow it suddenly dawned on him that he himself might be clapped in irons and similarly hauled off to prison through the mud. He was passing the post office on his way home after paying this call when he met a police inspector of his acquaintance who gave him good day and walked a few steps down the street with him. This somehow struck Gromov as suspicious. At home he was obsessed by convicts and armed guards all day, and a mysterious psychic unease prevented him from reading and concentrating. That evening he did not light his lamp and he lay awake all night, brooding on the prospect of being arrested, clapped in irons and flung into jail. He had done nothing wrong so far as he knew and could vouch that he would never commit murder, arson or burglary in the future. But was it so difficult to commit a crime accidentally and against one's will? Can false accusations—can judicial miscarriages, for that matter— really be ruled out? And hasn't immemorial folk wisdom taught that going to jail is like being poor: there isn't much you can do to escape from either? Now, a judicial miscarriage was only too possible with present-day court procedures, and no wonder. People with a bureaucratic, official relationship to others' woes—judges, policemen and doctors, for instance—eventually grow so callous through force of habit that they can react to their clients only on a formal level, much as they would like to do otherwise. In this respect they are just like the peasant who slaughters sheep and cattle in his backyard without noticing the blood. Having this formal, heartless attitude to the individual, a judge needs only one thing to deprive an innocent man of all his citizen's rights and sentence him to hard labour: enough time. Only give the judge time to carry out certain formalities, for which he is paid a salary, and that is the end of the matter. A fat hope, then, of finding justice and protection in this filthy little town a hundred and twenty miles from the railway! And how absurd to think of justice, anyway, in a society which welcomes every kind of brutality as a rational and functional necessity, while every merciful act—the acquittal of an accused person, for instance—provokes a great howl of indignation and vindictiveness!

Next morning Ivan Gromov rose from his bed aghast, his brow cold with sweat, now fully convinced that he was liable to be arrested any minute. If yesterday's irksome thoughts had remained with him so long, he reflected, there must be a grain of truth in them, they really couldn't have occurred to him for no reason whatever.

A police constable strolled past his windows: no accident, that. And over there two people had stopped near the house. They were not speaking. Now, why not?

Days and nights of agony began for Gromov. When anyone passed his windows or entered his courtyard he took them for spies and detectives. At noon a police inspector usually drove down the street in his carriage and pair. He was on his way to police headquarters from his near-by country estate, but Gromov always felt that he drove too fast, with a special air, and was evidently hastening to report that a most important criminal was in town. Gromov trembled at every ring and knock on the gate, and he suffered when he met any stranger visiting his landlady. On encountering policemen and gendarmes he would smile and whistle to convey an air of nonchalance. For nights on end he lay awake expecting to be arrested, but snoring aloud and sighing as if in slumber so that his landlady should think him asleep. If he couldn't sleep he must be suffering the pangs of conscience, mustn't he? Rather a give-away, that! Facts and common sense argued that all these phobias were neurotic nonsense, and that there was really nothing so terrible about arrest and prison, if you took the broad view and had a clear conscience. But the more intelligent and logical his reasoning, the stronger and more harrowing became his mental anguish. He was like a certain hermit who wanted to hew himself a home in virgin forest, but the more forcefully he plied his axe the more densely and vigorously did the trees burgeon around him. In the end Gromov saw how useless it all was, gave up reasoning altogether and yielded to utter despair and terror.

He began seeking seclusion and avoiding people. His job had always been uncongenial, but now it became downright unbearable. He was afraid of trickery: of having a bribe slipped surreptitiously into his pocket and then being caught, of making a chance error tantamount to forgery with official papers, or of losing someone else's money. Never, oddly enough, had his imagination been as supple and ingenious as it now was when he daily concocted thousands of miscellaneous pretexts for serious apprehension about his freedom and honour. But with this went a considerable weakening of interest in the external world, especially in books, and his memory began to fail notably.

When the snow melted in spring two semi-decomposed corpses were found in a gulley near the cemetery: an old woman and a young boy bearing signs of death by violence. These corpses and the unknown murderers became the talk of the town. To show that he was not the killer Gromov would walk the streets smiling, and on meeting anyone he knew he would blench, blush and assert that there was no fouler crime than the murder of the weak and defenceless. But soon wearying of this lie, he decided on reflection that the best thing for someone in his position was to hide in the landlady's cellar. He sat in that cellar for a day, a night and another day, frozen to the marrow, then waited for darkness and crept stealthily up to his room like a burglar. He stood in the middle of that room until dawn, perfectly still, his ears cocked. In the early morning before sunrise some stove-makers called on his landlady. They had come to rebuild the kitchen stove, as Gromov was well aware, but his fears told him that they were policemen in stove-makers' clothing. Stealing out of the flat, he dashed panic-stricken down the street without hat or coat. Barking dogs chased him, a man shouted somewhere behind him, the wind whistled in his ears, and Gromov thought that all the violence on earth had coiled itself together behind his back and was pursuing him.

He was caught and taken home, his landlady was sent for a doctor. Dr. Andrew Ragin (of whom more later) prescribed cold compresses for his head and laurel-water drops, then shook his head sadly and went away, telling the landlady that he did not propose to call again because one shouldn't do anything to stop a man taking leave of his senses. Unable to afford living and being treated at home, Gromov was soon sent to hospital and put in the ward for venereal diseases. He could not sleep at night, he behaved childishly, he disturbed other patients and soon Dr. Ragin arranged for his transfer to Ward Number Six.

A year later the town had quite forgotten Gromov, and his landlady dumped his books in a sledge in an out-building where they were pilfered by urchins.

IV

As I said before, Gromov's left-hand neighbour is the little Jew Moses, while his right-hand neighbour is a bloated, nearly globular peasant with an obtuse, utterly witless expression. This is an inert, gluttonous animal with dirty habits. Long bereft of all capacity to think and feel, it constantly exudes a sharp, acrid stench.

Cleaning up the mess, Nikita beats the creature cruelly, takes a real swing, doesn't pull his punches. The odd thing, though, is not the beating, because you can get used to that, but the failure of that stupefied animal to respond to blows with any sound, movement or expression of the eyes: it only rocks gently, like a heavy barrel.

The fifth and last denizen of Ward Number Six is a townsman of the lower sort, a former post-office sorter: a small, thin, fair man with a kindly but somewhat sly expression. To judge from his clever, quiet eyes with their serenely cheerful look, he has his wits about him and knows some momentous and delightful secret. He keeps under his pillow or mattress an object which he never shows to anyone: not from fear of its being removed or stolen, but from modesty. Sometimes he goes to the window, turns his back on his fellows, puts something on his chest and crooks his head to look at it. Should one approach him at these times he will grow flustered and snatch something off his chest. But his secret is not difficult to guess.

'You must congratulate me,' he often tells Gromov. 'I have been put in for the Order of St. Stanislaus, second class with star. The second class with star is only given to foreigners, but for some reason they want to make an exception in my case.'

He smiles, shrugging his shoulders in bewilderment. 'I must say I never expected this.'

'I know nothing about these things,' Gromov grimly avers.

'But do you know what I'm going to get sooner or later?' continues the ex-sorter, slyly screwing up his eyes. 'I mean to have the Swedish "Pole Star". That's a decoration worth angling for: a white cross with black ribbon. Most handsome.'

This hut is probably the most boring place on earth. Each morning the patients (the paralytic and the fat peasant excepted) wash from a big tub in the lobby and dry themselves on the tails of their smocks. Then they drink tea in tin mugs brought from the main building by Nikita. Each rates one mugful. At noon they eat sour cabbage stew and gruel, in the evenings they sup on gruel left over from lunch. In between times they lie, sleep, look out of the windows, pace the ward. And so it goes on every day. Even the ex-sorter always talks about the same old medals.

Fresh faces are rarely seen in Ward Number Six. The doctor stopped admitting new lunatics long ago and there are few people in this world with a taste for visiting asylums. Simon the barber attends the ward once every two months. How he shears the maniacs, how Nikita helps him, how the appearance of this drunken, grinning barber always strikes panic into the patients . . . over all that we shall draw a veil.

No one ever looks into the ward besides the barber, the patients are doomed to see no one but Nikita day in day out.

Recently, though, a rather odd rumour has swept the hospital.

The rumour is this: Ward Number Six has, allegedly, begun to receive visits from the doctor!

V

An odd rumour indeed!

Dr. Andrew Yefimovich Ragin was a remarkable man in his way. In early youth he was extremely pious, it is said, and he was preparing for a church career, proposing to enter theological college after leaving school in 1863, but his father, a Doctor of Medicine and surgeon, supposedly uttered a scathing laugh and announced categorically that he would disown the boy if he became a cleric. How true that is I have no idea, but Ragin himself has often confessed that he never had any vocation for medicine or for science in general.

Be that as it may, he did not take holy orders after graduating in medicine. He evinced no piety, bearing as little resemblance to a man of God at the beginning of his medical career as he does now.

He has a heavy, rough, uncouth look, his face, beard, flat hair and powerful, clumsy build reminding one of some paunchy, high-handed, cantankerous highway inn-keeper. His face is stern and covered with blue veins, the eyes are small, the nose is red, he is tall and broad-shouldered, he has enormous hands and feet, and he looks as if he could kill a man with a single blow. But he treads softly, walking cautiously and stealthily. Meeting someone in a narrow corridor, he is always first to stop and give way, apologizing in a gentle, reedy little voice: not in the bass tones which one might have expected. He has a small growth on his neck which prevents his wearing hard, starched collars, so he always goes about in a soft linen or cotton shirt. Altogether he doesn't dress like a medical man. He wears the same suit for ten years on end, while his new clothes, which he usually buys in a Jewish shop, look just as worn and dishevelled on him as the old. He sees his patients, eats his meals and goes visiting, all in the same old frock-coat: and this not out of meanness but because he just doesn't care about his appearance.

When Ragin came to town to take up his post in the hospital, that so-called charitable institution was in a parlous plight. In wards, corridors and hospital courtyard you could barely draw breath for the stink. The ambulance men, the nurses and their children slept in the wards with the patients, complaining that the cockroaches, bed-bugs and mice made their lives a misery. There was endemic erysipelas in the surgical department, the entire hospital boasted only two scalpels and not a single thermometer, and potatoes were kept in the baths. The manager, the matron and the assistant doctor robbed the patients, and the old doctor (Ragin's predecessor) was reputed to have sold surgical spirit on the sly, having also set up a regular harem among his nurses and women patients. These irregularities were common knowledge in town and were even exaggerated, but people took them calmly. Some defended them by saying that only lower-class townsfolk and peasants went to hospital, and such people couldn't complain because they were far worse off at home. They could hardly expect to be fed on the fat of the land! Others pleaded that the town lacked the resources to maintain a good hospital on its own, unaided by the Rural District. People should be grateful to have any hospital at all. But the newly established Rural District Council opened no clinic either in the town or its environs on the grounds that the town already had its hospital.

Having looked the hospital over, Ragin concluded that it was an immoral institution, detrimental to its inmates' health in the ultimate degree. The wisest course would be to discharge the patients and close the place down, he felt; but he decided that he lacked the will-power to accomplish this on his own, and that it would be useless anyway. Expel physical and moral filth from one place and it will only crop up elsewhere, so one should wait for it to evaporate spontaneously. Besides, if people have opened a hospital and tolerate it they must have a need for it. Now, these superstitions and all these sickeningly foul living conditions *are* needed since they become transformed into something useful in due course, as dung produces fertile soil. There is nothing on earth so fine that some element of pollution was not present at its birth.

Having taken on the job, Ragin adopted an attitude of apparent indifference to the irregularities. He only asked the orderlies and nurses not to sleep in the wards, and installed two cupboards of instruments. The manager, the matron, the chief medical assistant and the surgical erysipelas all stayed put.

Andrew Ragin much admires intellect and integrity, but lacks the character and confidence to create a decent, intelligent environment. As for issuing orders and prohibitions or insisting on anything, he is positively impotent, as if he had taken a vow never to raise his voice or use the imperative mood. He finds it hard to say 'give me this' or 'bring me that'. When he feels hungry he will cough indecisively.

'I wouldn't mind a bit of tea,' he will tell his cook. Or: 'How about a spot of lunch?'

But to tell his manager to stop pilfering, to sack him, to do away with his parasitical sinecure entirely . . . such things are absolutely beyond him. When people try to hoodwink Dr. Ragin, when they flatter him or bring him some blatantly falsified account to sign, he turns red as a beetroot and feels guilty—but signs it all the same. He squirms when his patients complain of hunger or rude nurses.

'All right, all right,' he mutters guiltily. 'I'll go into it later, it's probably a misunderstanding.'

At first Dr. Ragin worked very hard, seeing his patients daily from early morning until lunch, performing operations—attending confinements, even. The ladies used to say how considerate he was, and what a first-class diagnostician, especially of children's and women's ailments. But in due course he has become obviously bored with the monotony and palpable futility of his job. He will see thirty patients today, and tomorrow, like as not, thirty-five will roll up, then forty on the next day—and so on, day in day out, year in year out. But the town's mortality rate does not decline, the patients don't stop coming. To give serious help to forty out-patients between breakfast and lunch is a physical impossibility, and the upshot can only be total fraudulence. In the current year twelve thousand out-patients have been seen, and so twelve thousand people have been cheated, not to put too fine a point on it. But it was also out of the question to install seriously ill patients in the wards and treat them on scientific principles since such principles as they possessed had nothing scientific about them. Moreover, if one left theory out of it and stuck blindly to the rules like other doctors, then the crying need was for hygiene and ventilation instead of dirt, for healthy food instead of stinking sour cabbage stew, and for decent subordinates instead of crooks.

And then, why stop people dying if death is every man's normal, regular end? Who cares if some huckster or bureaucrat survives an extra five or ten years? And then again, if one sees medicine's function as relieving pain with drugs the question naturally arises why pain *should* be relieved. Firstly, suffering is said to bring man nearer to perfection. And, secondly, if mankind should really learn to relieve its sufferings with pills and drops it would completely turn its back on religion and philosophy which have hitherto furnished a bulwark against all manner of ills, and have even brought happiness too. Pushkin suffered terribly before he died, and poor Heine lay paralysed for several years. So why should an Andrew Yefimovich or Matryona Savishna be spared pain when they lead such blank lives: lives that would be utterly void and amoeba-like but for these sufferings?

Depressed by such considerations, Dr. Ragin let things slide and ceased to attend hospital every day.

VI

His routine is as follows. He usually rises at about eight a.m., dresses and has breakfast. Then he sits in his study reading or attends hospital. Here in the narrow, dark, little hospital corridor sit out-patients waiting to see him. Orderlies and nurses dash past them clattering their boots on the brick floor, scrawny in-patients go through in smocks, corpses and slop-pails are hauled past, children cry, there is a piercing draught. Dr. Ragin knows what sufferings such an ambience causes to those stricken with fever and tuberculosis, as also to impressionable patients in general, but it can't be helped. He is met in the surgery by his assistant Sergey Sergeyevich. This little fat man with his clean-shaven, freshly washed, plump face and soft, fluid manners resembles a senator more than a doctor's *aide* in his ample new suit. He has a vast practice in town, wears a white tie and thinks himself better qualified than the doctor, who has no practice at all. In a corner of the surgery stands a large icon in a case with a heavy icon-lamp and near that a big candle-holder with a white cover. On the walls are archbishops' portraits, a view of Svyatogorsk Monastery and wreaths of dry corn-flowers. Sergey Sergeyevich is religious, he likes pomp and ceremony. That icon was put here at his expense. On Sundays a patient reads the hymns of praise aloud in the surgery on his orders and after the reading Sergey Sergeyevich tours the wards in person, wafting incense from a censer.

The patients are many and time is short, so transactions are confined to brief questions and the issue of some nostrum such as ammoniated liniment or castor oil. Dr. Ragin sits plunged in thought, his cheek propped on his fist, and asks his questions like an automaton. Sergey Sergeyevich also sits there, rubbing his hands and occasionally inter-vening.

'The reason why we fall ill and suffer privation,' says he, 'is that we pray badly to All-Merciful God. Yes, indeed.'

Dr. Ragin does not perform operations during surgery hours. He has been out of practice for so long and the sight of blood upsets him. When he has to open a child's mouth to look in its throat, his head spins from the din in his ears and tears appear in his eyes if the child shouts and tries to ward him off with its little hands. Hurriedly pre-scribing something, he gestures for the mother to remove her child quickly.

At surgery he soon wearies of his patients' timidity, of their muddled talk, of the proximity of the grandiose Sergey Sergeyevich, of the portraits on the wall and of his own questions which he has been asking for over twenty years without variation. So he leaves after seeing half a dozen people and his assistant receives the rest after he has gone.

With the pleasant thought that he has not practised privately for ages, thank God, and that he won't be interrupted, Dr. Ragin sits down at the desk in his study and starts reading the moment he arrives home. He reads a lot and always much enjoys it. He spends half his salary on books, and three of the six rooms in his apartment are crammed with books and old magazines. His preference is for historical and philo-sophical works, and in the medical field he subscribes only to *The*

Physician, which he invariably starts reading from the back. He always reads non-stop for several hours on end, without tiring. He does not read rapidly and jerkily, as Ivan Gromov once did, but slowly, penetratingly, often pausing at passages which he likes or cannot understand. Near his book he always keeps a carafe of vodka, while a salted gherkin or pickled apple lies directly on the tablecloth, not on a plate. Every half hour he pours himself a glass of vodka and drinks it without taking his eyes off his book, then gropes for the gherkin and takes a small bite.

At three o'clock he cautiously approaches the kitchen door and coughs. 'Daryushka, how about a spot to eat?'

After a rather poor and messy meal Dr. Ragin paces his quarters, his arms folded on his chest. He is thinking. Four o'clock strikes, then five, and still he paces about, deep in thought. From time to time the kitchen door creaks and Daryushka's red, sleepy face appears.

'Isn't it time for your beer, Doctor?' she asks anxiously.

'No, not yet,' he answers. 'I'll just, er, wait a little——'

Towards evening Michael Averyanovich, the postmaster, usually arrives: the one person in town whose company does not depress Dr. Ragin. Once a very wealthy landowner and cavalry officer, he lost all his possessions and was driven to take a job with the post office in late middle age. He has a sound, healthy look, prolific grey side-whiskers, cultivated manners and a loud, agreeable voice. He is kind and sensitive, but irascible. When a post-office customer protests, expresses disagreement or simply starts an argument, Michael Averyanovich turns crimson and trembles from head to foot.

'Silence!' he thunders.

His post office has, accordingly, long rated as an institution terrifying to its visitors. Michael Averyanovich respects and likes Dr. Ragin for his erudition and high-mindedness, but he looks down on the other townsfolk, regarding them as subordinates.

'Well, here I am,' says he, entering Ragin's quarters. 'Hello there, my good fellow. You must be tired of me by now, what?'

'Far from it, I'm delighted to see you,' answers the doctor. 'You're always welcome.'

The friends sit on the study sofa, smoking in silence for a while.

'How about a spot of beer, Daryushka?' says Dr. Ragin.

They drink their first bottle in silence, the doctor rapt in thought, Michael Averyanovich with the jolly, vivacious air of one with something fascinating on his mind. It is always the doctor who opens their discussion.

'What a pity . . .' says he slowly and quietly, shaking his head, avoiding his companion's eyes (he never looks people in the eye). 'What a great pity, my dear Michael, that our town so totally lacks people who either can or will conduct an intelligent, interesting conversation. We're under such an enormous handicap. Even our professional men don't rise above vulgarity—they're no better than the lower classes in their level of maturity, you take it from me.'

'Perfectly true. Agreed.'

'As you well know, sir,' the doctor continues with quiet emphasis, 'everything in this world is trivial and boring, higher spiritual manifestations of the human intellect excepted. The intellect marks a clear boundary line between animal and man, it intimates man's divine nature and even compensates him to some extent for not being immortal. It follows that our intellect is our only possible source of pleasure. Neither seeing nor hearing anything intellectual around us, we are, accordingly, deprived of pleasure. We do have books, granted, but that's nothing like living conversation and interchange. If you will permit a rather dubious comparison, books are sheet music, while conversation is song itself.'

'Perfectly true.'

Silence ensues. Daryushka comes out of the kitchen and pauses in the doorway to listen with an expression of dazed grief, propping her face on her fist.

'Ah me,' sighs Michael Averyanovich. 'You get no sense out of people these days.'

How healthy, happy and interesting life was in the old days, he says, and what a brilliant intelligentsia Russia once had: how highly they had prized the concepts of honour and friendship. They lent money with no security, and withholding help from a friend in need was thought disgraceful. And what crusades, adventures and skirmishes there were, what comrades, what women! And the Caucasus . . . there was a wonderful land. A certain battalion commander's wife, an eccentric, would don officer's uniform and ride up into the mountains of an evening, alone and unescorted. She was said to be having an affair with a local princeling in some tribal village.

'Holy Mother, help us,' sighs Daryushka.

'How we drank and ate, what frantic liberals we were!'

Dr. Ragin listens without hearing as he muses and sips his beer.

'I often dream of talking to clever people,' he says unexpectedly, interrupting Michael Averyanovich. 'My father gave me an excellent education, but then forced me to be a doctor, swayed by the ideas of the sixties. If I had disobeyed him then I think I should be at the very heart of the intellectual movement now, I'd probably belong to some faculty. Not that intellect lasts for ever, either—it is transitory, of course—but you already know why I have such a weakness for it. Life is a deplorable trap. When a thinking man attains adulthood and mature awareness he can't help feeling hopelessly ensnared. And it *is* against his will, actually, that he has been called into being from nothingness by certain chance factors.

'What for? What's the meaning and purpose of his existence? He wants to learn, but he isn't told—or he is fobbed off with absurdities. He knocks, but no one opens. Death approaches, and he hasn't asked for that either. You know how prisoners linked by common misfortune feel better when they're all together? In the same way the life-trap can be ignored when men with a flair for analysis and deduction forgather and pass the time exchanging proud, free ideas. In that sense intellectual activity is a unique pleasure.'

'Perfectly true.'

Avoiding his companion's eye, quietly, between pauses, Dr. Ragin continues to talk about conversing with intelligent people while Michael Averyanovich listens attentively and agrees.

'Perfectly true.'

'But don't you believe in immortality?' the postmaster asks suddenly.

'No, my dear Michael, I do not, nor have I any grounds for so believing.'

'I admit I have my doubts too. Actually, though, I do sort of feel I shall never die. Dear me, thinks I to myself, it's time you were dead, you silly old buffer, but there's a little voice inside me saying don't you believe it, you aren't going to die.'

Michael Averyanovich leaves just after nine o'clock.

'Dear me, fate *has* landed us in a dump!' he sighs as he dons his fur coat in the hall. 'The most maddening thing is, we have even got to die here. Ah, me.'

VII

After showing his friend out Dr. Ragin sits at his desk and resumes his reading. The quiet of evening, and of the night which follows, is unbroken by any sound. Time appears to be standing still, sharing the doctor's immobility as he pores over his book, and nothing seems to exist beside that book and the green-globed lamp. The doctor's coarse, rough face gradually lights up with a smile of joyful delight at the stirrings of human intellect.

'Oh, why can't man be immortal?' he wonders. 'Why does the brain have its centres and crannies? Wherefore vision, speech, self-awareness, genius, if all these things are doomed to go into the soil and finally to cool along with the earth's crust—and then to rotate with the earth round the sun for millions of years, all for no reason? Cooling, rotating . . . these were no reasons for calling forth man, with his lofty, almost divine intellect, out of nothingness and then turning him into clay as if to mock him.

'The transmutation of matter? But what cowardice to console one-self with such makeshift immortality! The blind workings of the natural process are even more primitive than human folly since folly does at least imply awareness and deliberate intent, of which natural processes are entirely devoid. Only a coward, one whose fear of death exceeds his self-respect, can find comfort in the thought of his body being reborn in due course as grass, as a stone, as a toad. To see one's immortality in the transmutation of matter is as strange as to forecast a brilliant future for the violin-case after a valuable fiddle has been smashed and rendered useless.'

When the clock strikes Dr. Ragin lolls back in his arm-chair, closing his eyes for a spot of meditation. Then suddenly, swayed by the fine ideas culled from his book, he casts a glance at his past and present. His past is odious and better forgotten, and the same is true of his present. He knows that, at the very time when he is mentally rotating round the sun along with the cooled earth, people are suffering from illness and unhygienic conditions in the large hospital block adjoining his own quarters. There may be someone who can't sleep and is fighting off insects while someone else is contracting erysipelas or groaning because his bandage is too tight. Patients may be playing cards with the nurses and drinking vodka. Twelve thousand persons will have been swindled in the current year and the hospital's whole activities are still based on pilfering, squabbles, tittle-tattle, jobbery and rank charlatan-ism, just as they were twenty years ago. The place is still an immoral institution, detrimental to its inmates' health in the ultimate degree. Ragin knows that Nikita thrashes the patients behind the bars of Ward Number Six and that little Moses runs round town begging every day.

On the other hand, Ragin is also well aware of the fantastic changes which have taken place in medicine in the last quarter of a century.

In his college days he used to feel that medicine would go the way of alchemy and metaphysics, but now, when he reads at nights, medicine moves him, arousing his admiration—his enthusiasm, even. And, in very truth, what a dazzling break-through! What a revolution! Thanks to antiseptics, operations are performed such as the great Pirogov never even dreamt of. Ordinary general practitioners venture on resections of the knee-joint, abdominal surgery produces only one fatality per hundred operations and stone matters so little that no one even bothers to write about it. There is a radical treatment for syphilis. And then there is the theory of heredity, isn't there, and hypnotism? There are Pasteur's and Koch's discoveries, there are hygiene statistics, there's our Russian rural medical welfare service. Psychiatry with its modern methods of classifying disorders, its techniques of diagnosis and treatment . . . a gigantic stride forward, all that! The insane no longer have cold water poured over their heads, they are not put in strait-jackets, they are treated decently, they even have theatrical performances and dances arranged for them—or so the newspapers say. Modern views and tastes being what they are, Dr. Ragin knows that an abomination like Ward Number Six can only exist a hundred and twenty miles from the railway in a small town where the Mayor and Council are all semi-literate yahoos who regard a doctor as a sort of high-priest to be trusted blindly even when he's pouring molten lead down your throat. Anywhere else the public and the newspapers would have made mincemeat of this puny Bastille ages ago.

'But what does it matter?' Ragin wonders, opening his eyes. 'What does it all matter? There are antiseptics, there is Koch, there's Pasteur—yet the essence of things has not changed a bit, sickness and mortality still remain. People arrange dances and shows for the lunatics, but they still don't let them loose. So it's all a snare and delusion, and between the best Viennese clinic and my hospital there is no real difference at all.'

Yet grief and a feeling akin to envy prevent him from feeling detached: through fatigue, presumably. His heavy head slumps towards his book and he cushions his face in his hand.

'I am serving a bad cause,' thinks he, 'and I get a salary from those whom I swindle, so I'm dishonest. But I am nothing in myself, am I? I'm only part of an inevitable social evil. All the provincial officials are up to no good, they all get paid for doing nothing. So it's not my fault I'm dishonest, it's the fault of the age. If I had been born two hundred years later I'd have been different.'

When three o'clock strikes he puts out his lamp and goes to his bedroom. He doesn't feel sleepy.

VIII

In a fit of generosity Rural District had decided two years previously to make a yearly grant of three hundred roubles towards reinforcing the town hospital's medical staff until a country hospital should be opened. The town invited a local doctor, a Eugene Khobotov, to help Dr. Ragin. This Khobotov is very young, still in his twenties. He is tall and dark with broad cheek-bones and small eyes: his ancestors must have been Asiatics. He arrived in town penniless with a small suitcase and an ugly young woman whom he calls his cook, and who has a young baby. Dr. Khobotov wears a peaked cap, jack-boots, and a short fur coat in winter. He is very friendly with Dr. Ragin's assistant Sergey Sergeyevich and with the local treasurer, but calls the other officials aristocrats for some reason and shuns them. In his whole flat there is only one book: *The Latest Prescriptions of the Vienna Clinic for 1881*. He always takes this book with him when visiting a patient. He plays billiards in the club of an evening, but dislikes cards. He is very much given to such expressions as 'rigmarole', 'mumbo-jumbo with trimmings', 'don't cloud the issue' and so on.

He attends hospital twice a week, does his ward rounds, sees his patients. Though dismayed by the cupping-glasses and total lack of antiseptics, he does not introduce improvements lest he offend Dr. Ragin. He considers his colleague Dr. Ragin an old rogue, suspects him of being pretty well off and secretly envies him. He would like Ragin's job.

IX

One spring evening at the end of March, when the snow had all melted and starlings sang in the hospital garden, the doctor came out to see his friend the postmaster to the gate. At that very moment the little Jew Moses was entering the yard on his way back from a foraging expedition. He wore no hat, he had thin galoshes on bare feet and he carried a small bag which contained his takings.

'Give us a copeck,' he asked the doctor, shivering with cold and smiling.

Dr. Ragin, who could never say no, gave him a ten-copeck piece.

'This is quite wrong,' he thought, looking at the bare feet and thin red ankles. 'And in this damp weather too!'

Moved by mingled pity and distaste, he followed the Jew into the hut, glancing now at the bald pate, now at the ankles. As the doctor entered Nikita sprang from his pile of junk and stood to attention.

'Good day, Nikita,' said Dr. Ragin softly. 'You might perhaps give this Jew some boots or something, or else he'll catch cold.'

'Very good, sir. I'll notify the manager, sir.'

'Please do. Ask him in my name, will you? Tell him I said so.'

The door leading from lobby to ward was open. Ivan Gromov was lying on his bed, leaning on one elbow and listening anxiously to the strange voice, when he suddenly recognized the doctor. Vibrating with fury, he leapt up and ran into the centre of the ward, his face crimson with rage, his eyes bulging.

'The doctor's here!' he shouted with a bellow of laughter. 'And about time too! Congratulations, gentlemen! The doctor honours us with his presence!

'You bloody rat!' he shrieked, stamping his foot in a frenzy never witnessed in the ward before. 'Kill the vermin! No, killing's too good for him—drown him in the latrine!'

Hearing this, Dr. Ragin peeped into the ward from the lobby.

'What for?' he asked softly.

'What *for*?' shouted Gromov, approaching with a minatory air and frantically wrapping his smock around him. 'Well may you ask!

'Thief!' he brought out with abhorrence, his lips working as if he wanted to spit. 'Charlatan! Butcher!'

'Calm yourself,' said Dr. Ragin with a guilty smile. 'I have never stolen anything, I do assure you. As for the other things, you are probably much exaggerating. I see you are angry with me. Calm yourself, please, if you can, and tell me quietly what you're so angry about.'

'Well, why do you hold me here?'

'Because you are ill.'

'Yes, I am. But aren't there dozens—hundreds—of other madmen at large because you're too ignorant to distinguish them from the sane? So why should I—why should these other wretches—be cooped up here as scapegoats for everyone else? You, your assistant, the manager and all the other hospital riff-raff are immeasurably lower on the moral scale than any one of us. So why are we shut up? Why not you? Where's the logic of it?'

'Morality and logic are neither here nor there. It's all due to chance. Whoever has been put in here stays put, and whoever hasn't runs about outside, that's all. There is no morality or logic about my being a doctor and your being a mental patient, it's sheer blind chance.'

'That gibberish means nothing to me,' said Gromov in a hollow voice, and sat on his bed.

Little Moses, whom Nikita hesitated to search in the doctor's presence, had deployed some hunks of bread, pieces of paper and little bones on his bed. Still shivering with cold, he intoned something quickly in Yiddish. He probably imagined that he had opened a shop.

'Let me out of here,' said Gromov in quavering tones.

'I can't.'

'Why not? Why ever not?'

'It's not in my power, that's why. And just think: what would you gain if I did release you? If you went off the townspeople or police would only pick you up and bring you back.'

'Yes, yes, quite true,' said Gromov, and wiped his forehead. 'It's awful. But what am I to do? You tell me that.'

Dr. Ragin liked Gromov's voice and intelligent, grimacing young face. Wanting to comfort the young man and soothe him, he sat down on the bed beside him.

'You ask me what to do,' Ragin said after a little thought. 'The best thing in your position would be to run away, but that's no use unfortunately as you'd only be picked up. Society's all-powerful when it protects itself from criminals, mental patients and other awkward customers. There's only one thing you *can* do: accept the idea that you're a fixture here.'

'But what use is it to anyone?'

'Since there are such things as prisons and lunatic asylums someone must be shut up in them, mustn't they? If not you, then I, if not I, then someone else. Just wait until prisons and asylums cease to exist in the distant future, then there won't be any bars on the windows or hospital smocks. Sooner or later, of course, that time will come.'

Gromov smiled derisively.

'You're joking,' he said, screwing up his eyes. 'You and your minion Nikita . . . you have no concern with the future, your sort of gentry haven't. But better times *are* on the way, my dear sir, you can take that from me. I may sound banal, you may laugh at me, but a new life *will* dawn. Justice shall triumph, our day will come. I shan't see it, I shall be dead, but someone's great-grandchildren will live to see it. I greet them with all my heart and I'm glad for their sake: glad, I tell you! March forward, my friends, and may God be with you.'

Eyes shining, Gromov arose and stretched his arms towards the window.

'From behind these bars I bless you,' he continued in throbbing tones. 'Long live justice! I rejoice!'

'I see no special cause for rejoicing,' said Dr. Ragin, who found Gromov's gesture theatrical, yet most pleasing. 'There will be no prisons or asylums, and justice shall indeed prevail: as you say, sir. But the real essence of things won't change, will it? The laws of nature will stay as they are. People are going to fall ill, grow old and die, just as they do now. And gloriously as your dawn may irradiate your life, you'll still end up nailed in your coffin and thrown in a pit.'

'But what about immortality?'

'Oh, really!'

'You may not believe in it, but I do. Someone in Dostoyevsky or Voltaire says that if God hadn't existed man would have invented him. And I profoundly believe that if there's no such thing as immortality human genius will sooner or later invent it.'

'Well said,' remarked Ragin, smiling delightedly. 'I'm glad you're a believer. With such faith a man can live a merry life, even immured inside a wall. Did you receive any education, sir?'

'Yes, I went to university, but didn't take my degree.'

'You're a thinking man and a thoughtful one. You can find consolation inside yourself in any surroundings. Free, profound speculation on the meaning of life, utter contempt for the world's foolish vanities . . . those are two blessings higher than any other known to man. And you can possess them though you live behind triple rows of bars. Diogenes lived in a barrel, but was happier than all the emperors of this world.'

'Your Diogenes was an ass,' Gromov pronounced morosely. 'But why all this stuff about Diogenes and the meaning of something or other?'

He jumped up in sudden rage.

'I love life, love it passionately! I have a persecution complex, I suffer constant, agonizing fears, but there are moments when such a lust for life comes over me that I fear my brain will burst. I have such a tremendous appetite for life, tremendous!'

He paced the ward excitedly.

'In my day-dreams I see visions,' he said in hushed tones. 'People sort of haunt me, I hear voices and music, I seem to be walking through a forest or along a beach, and I do so long for the hum and bustle of life.

'Tell me now, what's the news?' Gromov asked. 'What's going on?'

'In town, you mean, or in general?'

'Oh, tell me about the town first and then about things generally.'

'All right. The town is an abysmal bore, what with no one to talk to, no one to listen to and no new faces. Actually, though, a young doctor did turn up recently: Khobotov.'

'He came while I was still in circulation. What's he like then, pretty crude?'

'Well, he's not exactly cultured. It's odd, you know, there's no mental stagnation in St. Petersburg and Moscow, so far as one can see. Things are humming there, so they must have some pretty impressive people around. But why do they always send us people of whom the less said the better? Unfortunate town!'

'Yes, unfortunate indeed,' sighed Gromov, and laughed. 'But how are things in general? What do the newspapers and magazines say?'

The ward was already in darkness. The doctor stood up to describe what was being written, abroad and in Russia, and spoke of current intellectual trends. Gromov listened carefully and asked questions, but then suddenly clutched his head as if gripped by some hideous memory and lay on the bed, his back to the doctor.

'What's the matter?' the doctor asked.

'Not one more word will you hear from me,' said Gromov roughly. 'Leave me alone.'

'Why, what's the matter?'

'Leave me alone, I tell you. To blazes——'

Dr. Ragin shrugged his shoulders, sighed and went out.

'You might clean up a bit, Nikita,' he said as he passed through the lobby. 'The smell's absolutely frightful.'

'Oh, yes sir. Oh certainly, sir.'

'Now, what a nice young man,' thought Ragin as he went to his quarters. 'I think he's the first person I've been able to talk to since I've been here. He can use his brain and he is interested in just the right things.'

While reading, and then as he went to bed, he kept thinking of Gromov, and on waking up next morning he remembered meeting so intelligent and entertaining a person on the previous day, and decided to call on him again at the first opportunity.

X

Gromov lay in the same posture as yesterday, his head clutched in his hands, his legs tucked beneath him. His face was hidden.

'Hello there, my dear friend,' said Ragin. 'Not asleep, are you?'

'Firstly, I'm not your dear friend,' said Gromov into his pillow. 'And secondly, you are wasting your time. Not one word will you get out of me.'

'Odd,' muttered Ragin, flustered. 'We were having such a friendly chat yesterday, but you suddenly took offence and broke off abruptly. I put something clumsily, very likely, or I may have expressed an idea contrary to your convictions.'

'Catch me trusting you? Not likely!' said Gromov, raising himself slightly, and looking at the doctor with contempt and misgiving. His eyes were bloodshot. 'Do your spying and snooping somewhere else, there's nothing for you here. I spotted your little game yesterday.'

'What a strange delusion,' the doctor laughed. 'So you take me for a spy?'

'I do. A spy or a doctor I'm to be examined by . . . what's the difference?'

'Oh, really, I must say! I'm sorry, but you *are* a funny chap.'

The doctor sat on a stool near the bed and shook his head reproachfully.

'But let's suppose you are right,' he said. 'Let's suppose I am a deceiver trying to catch you out and give you away to the police. You'll be arrested and tried, but will you be any worse off in court and prison than you are here? And if you're sent to Siberia as an exile—or as a convict, even—would that really be worse than sitting cooped up in this hut? I don't think so. So what have you to fear?'

These words obviously had their effect on Gromov. He quietly sat up.

It was about half past four in the afternoon: the time when Ragin usually paced his rooms and Daryushka asked if it was time for his beer. The weather was calm and clear.

'I came out for an afternoon stroll,' the doctor said, 'and I'm calling on you, as you see. Spring is here.'

'What month is it now, March?' asked Gromov.

'Yes, it's the end of March.'

'Is it muddy outside?'

'No, not very. The garden paths are walkable.'

'I'd like to go for a carriage drive now, somewhere out of town,' said Gromov, rubbing bloodshot eyes as if half asleep. 'Then I'd like to come home to a warm, comfortable study where some proper doctor would cure my headache. It's ages since I lived like a human being. This place is so foul, it's unbearably disgusting.'

He was tired after the previous day's excitement: inert and reluctant to speak. His fingers shook and he looked as if he had an acute headache.

'There's no difference whatsoever between a warm, comfortable study and this ward,' Ragin said. 'Man finds peace and contentment within him, not in the world outside.'

'Meaning what?'

'The man in the street seeks good or evil in externals—in carriages and studies, that is—but a thinking individual looks to the world within him.'

'Go and preach that philosophy in Greece where it's warm and smells of oranges. It doesn't fit our climate. Now, who was I discussing Diogenes with—not you, was it?'

'Yes it was—yesterday.'

'Diogenes needed no study or warm building. It was warm there anyway, and he could just lie around in his barrel munching oranges and olives. Now, if he had to live in Russia he'd be begging to be allowed indoors in May, let alone December. He'd be doubled up with cold, you mark my words.'

'No. One can ignore cold, just like any other pain. "Pain is the vivid impression of feeling pain," Marcus Aurelius said. "Will yourself to change that impression, jettison it, stop complaining—and the pain will vanish." That's quite right. Your sage, or your ordinary thinking, thoughtful individual . . . it's this very contempt for suffering which distinguishes them. They are always content and nothing ever surprises them.'

'I must be an idiot then, since I suffer, since I'm discontented and since I am surprised at human depravity.'

'Don't say that. If you meditate more you will appreciate the insignificance of all those externals that so excite us. One must seek the meaning of life, for therein lies true happiness.'

'Meaning of life. . . .' Gromov frowned. 'Externals, internals. . . . This makes no sense to me, sorry.

'I know only one thing,' he said, standing up and looking angrily at the doctor. 'I know God made me of warm blood and nerves, that I do know, sir. Now, organic tissue with any spark of vitality must react to every stimulus. So react I do! To pain I respond with shouts and tears, meanness makes me indignant, revolting behaviour sickens me. This is what life means, actually, or so I think. The lower the organism the less sensitive it is and the weaker its response to stimuli, whereas the higher it is the more receptively and forcefully does it react to reality. Why, it's so obvious! The man's a doctor and doesn't even know a little thing like that! Contempt for suffering, permanent contentment, never being surprised . . . it just means sinking to *that* condition.'

Gromov pointed to the obese, bloated peasant.

'Or else it means so hardening oneself through suffering that one loses all sensitivity—gives up living, in other words.

'I'm no sage or philosopher, sorry,' Gromov went on irritably. 'These things are beyond me and I'm in no state to argue.'

'Far from it, you argue very well.'

'The Stoics whom you caricature . . . they were remarkable men, but their doctrine ground to a halt two thousand years ago, it hasn't budged an inch since. Nor will it, impractical and moribund as it is. It has only succeeded with the minority which spends its time studying and sampling various creeds. The masses haven't grasped it. A doctrine of indifference to wealth and comfort, of contempt for suffering and death . . . it's quite beyond the great majority of people since both wealth and comfort have passed them by. If such people despised suffering they would be despising life itself. Hunger, cold, injury, loss, fear of death à *la* Hamlet . . . why, these feelings are the very essence of being a man! They're the whole of life, these sensations are. Life may irk you, you may loathe it, but despise it you mustn't. And so, I repeat, Stoicism can never have a future, whereas sensitivity to pain, the capacity for response to stimuli . . . these things have been moving forward from the beginning of time to our own day, as you can see for yourself.'

Gromov suddenly lost track of his thoughts, paused and rubbed his forehead with annoyance.

'I had something vital to say, but I've lost the thread,' he remarked. 'Now, where was I? Oh, yes. Now, this is my point. A Stoic once sold himself into slavery to ransom a neighbour. So even a Stoic reacted to a stimulus, you see, since so generous a deed as self-denial for one's neighbour's sake presupposes feelings of outraged sympathy. In this prison I have forgotten everything I ever studied, or else I should remember a few other things too. Well, take Christ. He reacted to the external world with tears, smiles, grief, wrath—with anguish, even.

He didn't greet suffering with a smile or despise death, but prayed in the Garden of Gethsemane that this cup should pass Him by.'

Gromov laughed and sat down.

'Let's admit that man's peace and contentment are within him, not outside him,' said he. 'And let's admit that one should despise suffering and never feel surprise. But you, now—what grounds have *you* for preaching this doctrine? Are you a sage? A philosopher?'

'No, I'm no philosopher, but everyone should preach this doctrine, because it's rational.'

'Now, why do you think yourself competent in the search for meanings, contempt for suffering and the rest of it? That's what I'd like to know. Have you ever suffered? Have you any idea what suffering is? Tell me, were you beaten as a child?'

'No, my parents abhorred corporal punishment.'

'Well, my father beat me cruelly. My father was a cantankerous government official with a long nose, a yellow neck and piles. But let's go on about you. No one ever laid a finger on you in your life, no one ever frightened you, no one hit you. You're as strong as an ox. You grew up under your father's wing, you studied at his expense, you picked up a soft job straight away. For twenty years and more you've had rent-free accommodation with heating, lighting and service, besides which you have been entitled to work how you liked, as much as you liked: even to do nothing at all. Being lazy and spineless by nature, you tried to arrange things so that nothing bothered you or budged you from the spot. You delegated your job to your assistant and those other swine while you sat in the warmth and quiet, saving money, reading a book or two, indulging yourself with speculations in the sphere of higher nonsense, and also'—Gromov looked at the doctor's red nose—'by hitting the bottle. You've never seen life, in other words, you know nothing about it. You're conversant with reality only in theory. And why *is* it you despise suffering, *why* don't you ever feel surprise? There's a very simple reason. The vanity of vanities, externals, internals, despising life, suffering and death, the meaning of existence, true happiness . . . it's the philosophy best suited to a typical lackadaisical Russian. Say you see a peasant beating his wife. Why meddle? Let him beat away, they're both going to die anyway sooner or later. Besides, that peasant is degrading himself with his blows, not the person he's hitting. Getting drunk is stupid, it's not respectable, but you die if you drink and you die if you don't. A peasant woman comes along with toothache. So what? Pain is just the impression of feeling pain, besides which no one can get through life without sickness and we are all going to die. So let that woman clear out and leave me to my meditations and vodka. A young man wants advice on what to do, how to live. Anyone else might reflect before answering, but you have your ready-made reply: seek the meaning of life or true bliss. But just what *is* this fantastic "true bliss"? That, of course, we're never told. We are kept behind these bars, we're left to rot, we're given hell, but that is all splendidly rational because there's no difference between this ward and a warm, comfortable study. Oh, it's a convenient philosophy, this is! You don't have to do anything, your conscience is clear and you think yourself a sage.

'No, sir, there is no philosophy, no thought, no breadth of vision in that, there's only laziness, mumbo-jumbo and a sort of drugged trance.

'Yes, indeed,' said Gromov, angry again. 'You may despise suffering, but you catch your finger in the door and I bet you'll scream your head off!'

'Or perhaps not,' Ragin said with a gentle smile.

'You damn well would! And suppose you suddenly became para-lysed. Or say some crass upstart used his rank and position to insult you in public, and you knew he was bound to get away with it—that would teach you to refer people to the meaning of existence and true bliss.'

'This is highly original,' said Dr. Ragin, smiling with pleasure and rubbing his hands. 'Your bent for generalizations impresses me most agreeably, while your character-sketch of me . . . quite brilliant, sir! I enjoy talking to you hugely, I do confess. Well, sir, I've heard you out. Now will you be so good as to listen to me?'

XI

The conversation lasted another hour or so and obviously made a great impression on Ragin. He took to visiting the ward daily. He went there in the mornings and afternoons, and the evening darkness often overtook him deep in discussion with Gromov. Gromov was wary of him at first, suspecting him of evil intent and expressing open hostility, but then grew used to him, changing his harsh attitude for ironical condescension.

Soon rumours of Dr. Ragin's visits to Ward Number Six spread through the hospital. Why did he go there? Why did he stay for hours on end, what did he talk about, why didn't he write any prescriptions? His assistant, Nikita, the nurses . . . none of them could make sense of it.

His conduct seemed peculiar. He was often out when Michael Averya-novich called, which had never happened before, and Daryushka was extremely put out because the doctor no longer had his beer at a definite hour and was even late for his meals sometimes.

Once, at the end of June, Dr. Khobotov called to see Ragin about something. Not finding him at home, he sought him in the yard, where he learnt that the old doctor was visiting the mental patients. Khobotov went into the hut and paused in the lobby, where he heard the following conversation.

'We shall never see eye to eye and you'll never convert me,' said Gromov irritably. 'You are totally ignorant of life, you have never suffered, you've only battened, leech-like, on others' woes, whereas I've never stopped suffering from my day of birth until now. So I frankly tell you I think myself your superior, more competent in every way. I have nothing to learn from you.'

'I have absolutely no idea of converting you,' Ragin brought out quietly, regretting the other's unwillingness to understand him. 'Anyway, that's not the point, my friend. The point is not that you have suffered and I haven't. Suffering and joy are transitory, so let's ignore the wretched things. The point is that you and I are thinking beings. We see each other as people capable of meditation and dis-cussion, and that makes for our solidarity, different as our views may be. My friend, if you did but know how bored I am with general idiocy, mediocrity, obtuseness—and how glad I always am to talk to you. You are an intelligent man and I revel in your company.'

Khobotov opened the door an inch or two and peeped into the ward. The nightcapped Gromov and Dr. Ragin sat side by side on the bed. The madman grimaced and shuddered, frenziedly wrapping his smock about him, while the doctor sat perfectly still, his head lowered, his face red, helpless and sad-looking. Khobotov shrugged his shoulders, grinned and exchanged glances with Nikita. Nikita too shrugged.

Next day Khobotov came into the hut with Dr. Ragin's assistant. Both stood and eavesdropped in the lobby.

'The old man seems to have a screw loose,' said Khobotov, coming out of the hut.

'Lord, have mercy on our souls,' sighed the grandiose Sergey Sergeyevich, carefully avoiding the puddles so as not to dirty his brightly polished boots. 'Quite frankly, I've been expecting this for some time, my dear Eugene.'

XII

From now onwards Dr. Ragin began to notice an aura of mystery around him. Orderlies, nurses and patients would shoot him quizzical glances when they met him and then whisper to each other. Little Masha, the manager's daughter, whom he used to enjoy meeting in the hospital garden . . . when he smiled and went to stroke her head she now ran away for some reason. The postmaster Michael Averyanovich no longer said 'Perfectly true!' when listening to Ragin, but became mysteriously embarrassed, looked thoughtful and sad, and muttered 'Yes, quite so.' For some reason he was advising his friend to give up vodka and beer, but he didn't come straight out with this, he hinted at it, as a man of tact, and spoke of some battalion commanding officer ('grand chap') or else of a regimental chaplain ('first-rate bloke') who had taken to drink and fallen ill, but completely recovered after going on the wagon. Dr. Ragin's colleague Khobotov visited him a couple of times, also advising him to give up spirits, and recommending him to take potassium bromide for no obvious reason.

In August Dr. Ragin received a letter from the Mayor asking him to call on most urgent business. Reaching the town hall at the appointed time, Ragin found the district military commander, the county school superintendent, a town councillor, Khobotov, and also a stout, fair individual who was introduced as a doctor. This doctor had an unpronounceable Polish surname, lived on a stud farm about twenty miles away and happened to be passing through town.

'There's a memorandum here that's up your street, like,' the councillor told Ragin after they had exchanged greetings and sat down at the table. 'Dr. Khobotov here says there ain't enough space for the dispensary in the main block. It ought to be moved to one of the huts, he reckons. Now, moving it ain't no problem, of course—but the thing is, that hut's in need of repair, like.'

'Yes, there will have to be repairs,' said Ragin after some thought. 'Say we take the corner hut as our dispensary, then I suppose it will require five hundred roubles at least. It's an unproductive expense.'

There was a short pause.

'Ten years ago,' Ragin continued quietly, 'I had the honour to report that this hospital as it stood was a luxury which the town couldn't afford. It was built in the forties, but things were different then, weren't they? The town spends too much on unneeded buildings and unnecessary posts. If we changed the system we could maintain two model hospitals on the same money, I reckon.'

'Oh, so it's the system we want to change now, is it?' the councillor asked forcefully.

'I have already had the honour of reporting that our health depart- ment should be transferred to the Rural District.'

'You give the R.D.C. money and they'll only steal it,' the fair-haired doctor laughed.

'That's the way of it,' agreed the councillor, also with a laugh.

Dr. Ragin gazed with dull, lack-lustre eyes at the fair-haired doctor.

'One should be fair,' he said.

Another pause followed. Tea was served. Very embarrassed for some reason, the military commander reached across the table to touch Ragin on the arm.

'You've quite forgotten us, Doctor,' he said. 'But then you are a bit of a monk—don't play cards, don't like women. You're bored with the likes of us.'

Living in this town . . . oh, what a bore for any self-respecting man, they all started saying. There was no theatre, no music. At the last club dance there had been about twenty ladies and only two gentlemen. Young people didn't dance, but they were always swarming round the bar or playing cards. Without looking at anyone, Dr. Ragin spoke slowly and quietly about what a great, great pity it was that the towns- folk squandered their vital energies, their hearts and their minds on cards and gossip, that they neither could nor would find time for interest- ing conversation and reading, that they had no use for intellectual pleasures. Intellect was the one fascinating and remarkable thing, all the rest was vulgar triviality.

Khobotov listened carefully to his colleague. Then he suddenly asked a question.

'What is today's date, Dr. Ragin.'

After receiving an answer, Khobotov and the fair-haired doctor began questioning Ragin in the manner of examiners aware of their own incompetence. What day of the week was it? How many days were there in the year? And was it true that Ward Number Six housed a remarkable prophet?

Ragin blushed at this last question.

'Yes, it's a patient, but an interesting young fellow,' he said.

They asked no more questions.

As Ragin was putting his coat on in the hall the military commander laid a hand on his shoulder.

'It's time we old fellows were put out to grass,' he sighed.

As he left the town hall, Ragin realized that this had been a commission appointed to assess his sanity. He blushed as he remembered their questions and for the first time in his life he somehow found himself terribly upset about the state of medicine.

'My God,' thought he, remembering the doctors who had just investigated him. 'Why, these people took a course in psychiatry only recently, they sat an examination. So why such crass ignorance? They have no conception of psychiatry.'

And for the first time in his life he felt insulted and enraged.

Michael Averyanovich called that evening. He came up to Ragin without greeting him and took him by both hands.

'My dear, good friend,' said the postmaster in a voice vibrant with emotion, 'prove that you believe in my sincere good will and consider me your friend. My friend . . .

'I like you because you're so well-educated and generous-hearted,' he went on excitedly, not letting Ragin speak. 'Now, listen to me, my dear fellow. Medical etiquette obliges those doctors to keep the truth from you, but I'm going to give it you straight from the shoulder, soldier-fashion. You're not well. I'm sorry, my dear fellow, but it is so—everyone round here noticed it some time ago. As Dr. Eugene Khobotov was saying just now, you need rest and a change for your health's sake. Perfectly true, that—a capital idea! Now I'm taking my leave in a day or two and I'm going away for a whiff of fresh air. So prove you're my friend—come with me. It will be quite like old times.'

'I feel completely well,' said Ragin after a little thought, 'and I can't go with you. Permit me to prove my friendship in some other way.'

Going off on some trip without rhyme or reason, without books, without Daryushka, without beer, while so brusquely shattering a routine of twenty years' standing . . . at first the idea struck him as wildly grotesque. But remembering the interview at the town hall and his depressed state on the way home, he suddenly warmed to the prospect of a short break from this abode of morons who thought him insane.

'Now, where are you thinking of going?' he asked.

'Moscow, St. Petersburg, Warsaw. I spent the five happiest years of my life in Warsaw. A staggering city, that! Let's go, my dear fellow!'

XIII

A week later Dr. Ragin was invited to 'take a holiday': to resign, in other words. He didn't mind and a week later he and Michael Averyanovich were bowling along in a post-chaise on their way to the nearest railway station. The days were cool and bright, the sky was blue, the distant view was clear. They did the hundred and twenty miles to the station in forty-eight hours, with two overnight stops. Whenever they were served tea in dirty glasses at the coaching inns, whenever harnessing their horses took too much time, Michael Averyanovich turned crimson and shook all over.

'Shut up!' he would shout. 'Don't you bandy words with me!'

In the carriage he kept up a non-stop account of his trips in the Caucasus and Poland—so many adventures he had had, such meetings! He spoke so loudly and he looked so amazed about it all that he might have been supposed to be lying, besides which he breathed into Ragin's face while describing all this and guffawed into his ear. This irked the doctor—prevented him from thinking and concentrating.

On the train they went by third-class non-smoker to save money. Half the passengers were of the respectable sort. Michael Averyanovich quickly got to know them all, moving from one seat to another and loudly averring that one shouldn't use these disgusting railways: the whole thing was such a racket! Now, horseback riding was a different matter! You could knock up your sixty miles a day, and you felt healthy and hearty afterwards. Now, the reason why we had bad harvests was the draining of the Pripet Marshes. By and large things were in a pretty pickle! He grew heated, spoke loudly and no one else could get a word in edgeways. This endless natter interspersed with loud guffaws and eloquent gestures . . . , it wearied Ragin.

'Which of us two is the lunatic?' he wondered indignantly. 'Is it I, who try not to annoy the other passengers? Or this megalomaniac who thinks he is cleverer and more interesting than everyone else, and so won't leave anyone alone?'

In Moscow Michael Averyanovich donned a military tunic without epaulettes and trousers with red piping. He wore an officer's peaked cap and cloak in the streets, and the soldiers saluted him. The man had squandered all the good patrician qualities which he had once possessed, Ragin now felt, and had kept only the bad ones. He liked being waited on, even when it was completely pointless. There might be matches on the table in front of his eyes, but that wouldn't stop him shouting for a waiter to bring him a light. When the chambermaid was in his room he walked around in his underwear and made no bones about it. He was very off-hand with all the servants, even the old ones, and called them oafs and blockheads when he lost his temper. These were the manners of the squirearchy, Ragin thought, but they were odious.

Michael Averyanovich first took his friend to see the Iverian Madonna. He prayed fervently, bowing to the ground and weeping, and sighed deeply when he had finished.

'Even if you aren't a believer you'll feel easier somehow after a spot of prayer. Kiss the icon, old man.'

Embarrassed, Ragin did so. Michael Averyanovich mouthed a whispered prayer, while his head swayed and his eyes once more brimmed with tears. Then they went to the Kremlin, where they saw the 'Tsar Cannon' and the 'Tsar Bell', even touching them with their fingers. They enjoyed the view across the river, they visited St. Saviour's Temple and the Rumyantsev Museum.

They dined at Testov's. Michael Averyanovich scrutinized the menu for some time, stroking his side-whiskers and adopting the tone of a lusty trencherman completely at home in restaurants.

'Now, my good man,' he would say. 'What treat have you in store today?'

XIV

The doctor went about, saw the sights, ate and drank, but his sole sensation was of annoyance with Michael Averyanovich. He wanted a holiday from his friend, he wanted to go away and hide, but his friend felt in duty bound not to let Ragin out of his sight and to furnish him with as much entertainment as possible. When there were no sights to see he entertained Ragin with talk. Ragin stood it for two days, but on the third he told his friend that he was ill and wanted to stay in all day. In that case, said his friend, *he* would stay in too. They did need a rest, actually, if their feet were going to stay the course. Ragin lay facing the back of the sofa and listened, teeth clenched, to the friend who fervently assured him that France would certainly smash Germany sooner or later, that Moscow was teeming with crooks and that one should never judge a horse's qualities by its looks. The doctor's ears buzzed and his heart pounded, but he was too tactful to ask the friend to go away or be quiet. Luckily Michael Averyanovich tired of being cooped up in a hotel room and went for a stroll in the afternoon.

Left on his own, Ragin relaxed completely. How pleasant to lie perfectly still on a sofa and know you are alone in the room! True happiness is impossible without privacy. The fallen angel probably betrayed God because he wanted the privacy denied to an angel. Ragin wanted to think about what he had seen and heard during the last few days, but he was obsessed with thoughts of Michael Averyanovich.

'He took his holiday and made this trip with me out of friendship and generosity, didn't he?' the doctor brooded in dismay. 'There's nothing worse than such paternalism. Oh, he seems kind and generous all right, he is cheerful enough, but he's such a bore, such a shattering bore! He is like those people who can't speak without uttering witticisms and *bons mots*, yet leave you feeling how very dull they are.'

On the following days Ragin said he was ill and did not leave his hotel room. He lay facing the back of the sofa, suffering while his friend entertained him with conversation or resting during his friend's absence. He was angry with himself for making the trip, and angry with his friend who became more garrulous and hail-fellow-well-met every day. Ragin simply could not pitch his thoughts in a serious and elevated key.

'I am suffering from the very environment that Ivan Gromov spoke of,' he thought, incensed at his own pettiness. 'Anyway, that's all nonsense. When I'm back home everything will be the same as ever.'

St. Petersburg was no different. He stayed in his hotel room for days on end, lying on the sofa, and only got up for a glass of beer.

Michael Averyanovich kept urging him on to Warsaw.

'What do I want there, old man?' pleaded Ragin. 'You go by yourself and let me go home, I beg you.'

'Most certainly not!' Michael Averyanovich protested. 'It's a staggering city. It was there that I spent the five happiest years of my life.'

Lacking the strength of character to get his own way, Ragin went to Warsaw much against his will. There he stayed in his hotel room and lay on the sofa, furious with himself, with his friend and with the servants who stubbornly refused to understand Russian, while Michael Averyanovich—hale, hearty and jolly as ever—scoured the city from morning till evening looking up his old pals. Sometimes he didn't come home at all. After one such night, spent heaven knows where, he returned in the early morning, greatly agitated, red-faced, with hair awry. He spent some time pacing the room muttering to himself, then stood still and said:

'Honour above everything!'

After a little more pacing he clutched his head.

'Yes, honour above everything!' he pronounced tragically. 'I curse the moment when I first thought of coming to this hell-hole.

'Despise me, dear friend,' he told the doctor. 'I have lost all my money gambling. You must lend me five hundred roubles!'

Counting out five hundred roubles, Ragin silently handed them to his friend, who, still crimson with shame and rage, mumbled some superfluous oath, put his cap on and went out. Returning two hours later, he flopped in an arm-chair and gave a loud sigh.

'Honour is saved,' said he. 'So let us be on our way, my friend. I won't stay one minute longer in this bloody city. Swindlers! Austrian spies!'

It was November when the friends returned to their town and snow lay deep in the streets. Dr. Khobotov was doing Ragin's job, but was still living in his old lodgings, waiting for Ragin to come back and move out of his hospital rooms. The ugly woman whom he called his cook was already established in one of the out-buildings.

In town new rumours were circulating about the hospital. The ugly woman was said to have quarrelled with the manager, and he was alleged to have gone down on his knees and asked her forgiveness.

Ragin had to find himself new lodgings on the day after his arrival.

'Excuse an indiscreet question, my friend,' said the postmaster timidly, 'but what are your means?'

Ragin silently counted his money.

'Eighty-six roubles,' he replied.

'I didn't mean that.' Michael Averyanovich was embarrassed, not grasping the doctor's purport. I meant how much money do you have altogether.'

'I've just told you, eighty-six roubles. I have no more.'

Michael Averyanovich had thought the doctor a man of honour and integrity, but he still suspected him of having tucked away at least twenty thousand. Now that he knew Ragin for a pauper with nothing to live on, he suddenly burst into tears for some reason and embraced his friend.

XV

Dr. Ragin was now living in a three-windowed cottage belonging to a Mrs. Belov, a townswoman of the lower sort. This cottage had only three rooms apart from the kitchen. Two of them, with windows on the street, were occupied by the doctor while Daryushka,

Mrs. Belov and her three children lived in the third and the kitchen. The landlady's lover, a rowdy, drunken yokel who terrified the children and Daryushka, sometimes stayed the night. When he turned up and installed himself in the kitchen, clamouring for vodka, everyone felt uncomfortable. Taking pity on the crying children, the doctor took them into his room and laid them to rest on the floor, which gave him great pleasure.

He still rose at eight in the morning, had tea and then sat down to read his old books and magazines—he couldn't afford new ones. Whether because the books were old, or perhaps because of his changed circumstances, reading no longer held his attention, but tired him. For the sake of something to do, he was making a detailed catalogue of his books, gluing labels to the spines and finding this meticulous, mechanical work more interesting than reading. In some mysterious way the monotonous fiddling relieved his brain, his mind would go blank and time passed quickly. Peeling potatoes in the kitchen with Daryushka or picking dirt out of the buckwheat . . . even that he found interesting. On Saturdays and Sundays he went to church. Standing by the wall and screwing up his eyes, he listened to the choir and thought about his father, his mother, his university and about different religions. He felt relaxed and sad. Leaving the church later, he would find himself regretting that the service had ended so soon.

He twice went to the hospital to talk to Gromov, but on each occasion Gromov was unusually agitated and angry. He asked to be left in peace, saying that he was utterly sick of trivial tittle-tattle and required of these damn blackguards only one recompense for his sufferings: solitary confinement. Would they deny him even that? As Ragin was taking farewell and wishing him good night each time, Gromov snarled and told him to go to hell.

Now Ragin didn't know whether to go and see Gromov a third time. He wanted to, though.

Ragin had been accustomed to patrolling his rooms in the afternoons and thinking, but now he would lie facing the back of his sofa between lunch and afternoon tea, indulging in niggling reflections which he was quite unable to repress. He was hurt at receiving neither a pension nor a lump sum in return for more than twenty years' service. He hadn't done an honest job, admittedly, but all functionaries receive pensions without distinction, don't they, honest or dishonest? It's just the way things are done nowadays, to be fair to every one—it isn't your moral qualities or competence, it's just doing your job, however you do it, that earns you your rank, medals and pension. So why should Ragin be the one exception? He had absolutely no money. He was ashamed to pass the local shop and see the woman who kept it. There were thirty-two roubles owing for beer already and Mrs. Belov was owed money too. Daryushka was selling old clothes and books on the side, and she lied to the landlady: said the doctor was expecting a large sum of money shortly.

He was angry with himself for spending a thousand roubles' savings on his holiday. How useful that sum would be now! He was also annoyed at not being left in peace. Khobotov thought himself in duty bound to visit his sick colleague from time to time. Everything about the man disgusted Ragin: his smug face, his bad manners, his patronizing air, his use of the word 'colleague', his jack-boots. Most odious of all, Khobotov felt obliged to give Ragin medical treatment and believed that he was actually doing so. He brought a phial of potassium bromide on each visit, and some rhubarb pills.

Michael Averyanovich also felt obliged to visit his friend and amuse him. He always entered Ragin's room with an air of bogus nonchalance, uttering an affected guffaw, and assuring his friend that he looked splendid today and that matters were on the mend, thank God—from which it might be deduced that he thought his friend's situation desperate. He still hadn't paid back the money borrowed in Warsaw and was weighed down by a burden of guilt. Being on edge, he tried to guffaw the more uproariously and to tell funnier stories. Now apparently never-ending, his anecdotes and tales were excruciating both to Ragin and himself.

Ragin usually lay on the sofa during these visits, listening with his face to the wall and his teeth clenched. Layers of scum seemed to be forming inside him, and after each of his friend's visits he felt as if these deposits were mounting higher and higher until they seemed to be clutching at his throat.

Trying to suppress trivial worries, he quickly thought about himself, Khobotov and Michael Averyanovich all being bound to die and vanish without trace sooner or later. If one imagined a ghost flashing through space past the earth in a million years' time, it would see nothing but clay and naked crags. Culture, moral laws . . . it will all disappear, it won't even have burdocks growing on it. So what if you *are* ashamed to face a shopkeeper? What *of* the wretched Khobotov? Or Michael Averyanovich's irksome friendship? These things were mere insubstantial trifles.

Such arguments no longer helped, though. Barely had he pictured the earth's globe in a million years' time before jack-booted Khobotov popped up behind a naked crag—or Michael Averyanovich, forced guffaw and all. One could even hear his mortified whisper about that Warsaw loan.

'I'll pay you back in a day or two, old man. You rely on me.'

XVI

One afternoon Michael Averyanovich arrived when Ragin was lying on the sofa and Khobotov chanced to turn up with his potassium bromide at the same time. Ragin rose ponderously to a sitting position and braced both hands on the sofa.

'Well, old man, you're a far better colour than you were yesterday,' began Michael Averyanovich. 'You look no end of a lad—by golly, so you do!'

'It's high time you were on the mend, dear colleague,' yawned Khobotov. 'You must be sick of all this rigmarole.'

'Oh, we're on the mend all right,' said jolly Michael Averyanovich. 'We shall live another hundred years, shan't we now?'

'I won't say a hundred, but we'll hold out for another twenty,' Khobotov consoled him. 'Don't worry, dear colleague, don't despair. And don't cloud the issue, now.'

'We'll show what stuff we're made of,' guffawed Michael Averyanovich, slapping his friend on the knee. 'We'll show them a thing or two. We'll be off to the Caucasus next summer with a bit of luck, and we'll ride all over it on horseback—clip-clop, clip-clop, clip-clop! And when we get back from the Caucasus it'll be wedding bells for us, I shouldn't wonder.'

Michael Averyanovich gave a crafty wink.

'We'll marry you, my dear old pal, we'll marry you off.'

Ragin suddenly felt the deposit of scum reach the level of his throat. His heart pounded violently.

'That's pretty cheap,' he said, quickly rising to his feet and going over to the window. 'Can't you see you're talking vulgar nonsense?'

He wanted to continue gently and politely, but suddenly clenched his fists in spite of himself, lifting them above his head.

'Leave me alone!' he shouted in a strange voice, turning crimson and trembling all over. 'Clear out of here! Both of you, clear out!'

Michael Averyanovich and Khobotov stood up and stared at him: first with amazement, then in fear.

'Get out, both of you!' Ragin kept shouting. 'Imbeciles! Half-wits! I don't need your friendship, you oaf, or your medicines. Oh, what a rotten, dirty business!'

Exchanging frantic glances, Khobotov and Michael Averyanovich backed towards the door and debouched into the lobby. Ragin seized the bottle of potassium bromide. He hurled it after them and it crashed, ringing, on the threshold.

'You go to hell!' Ragin bellowed tearfully, rushing into the lobby. 'To blazes with you!'

After his visitors had left Ragin lay on the sofa, trembling as if with a fever.

'Imbeciles! Half-wits!' he kept repeating for some time.

His first thought on calming down was how terribly embarrassed and depressed poor Michael Averyanovich must feel, and how horrible all this was. Nothing like it had ever happened before. Where were his intellect and tact? What of his search for the meaning of things, his philosophical detachment?

Ashamed and annoyed with himself, the doctor lay awake all night and went to the post office at ten o'clock next morning to apologize to Michael Averyanovich.

The postmaster was deeply moved.

'We'll forget the whole thing,' sighed he, firmly shaking Ragin's hand. 'Let bygones be bygones.

'Bring a chair, Lyubavkin!' he suddenly yelled, so loudly that the postal staff and customers all started.

'And *you* can wait!' he yelled at a peasant woman who was thrusting a registered letter towards him through the grille. 'Can't you see I'm busy?

'We'll forget all about it,' he continued, addressing Ragin affectionately. 'Now, sit down, my dear chap, I do implore you.'

He stroked his knees in silence for a minute.

'I never even dreamt of taking offence,' he said. 'One must make allowances for illness, I know that. Yesterday's attack alarmed the doctor and myself, and we had a long talk about you afterwards. Why won't you take your health seriously, old man? You can't go on like this.

'Excuse an old friend's bluntness,' Michael Averyanovich whispered, 'but you do live under most unsuitable conditions: cramped and dirty, with no one to nurse you and no money for treatment. My dear friend, the doctor and I do beg you most earnestly to heed our advice and go into hospital. You will be properly fed there, you'll be nursed and you'll receive treatment. Eugene Khobotov may be a bit uncouth, between ourselves. Still, he does know his stuff and he is completely reliable. He has promised to attend to you.'

Ragin was moved by the postmaster's sincere sympathy and by the tears which suddenly glistened on his cheeks.

'Don't believe a word of it, my good sir,' he whispered, laying his hand on his heart. 'Don't believe them, it's all a trick. There's only one thing wrong with me: it has taken me twenty years to find a single intelligent man in the whole town, and he is insane. I'm not ill at all, I'm just trapped in a vicious circle from which there is no way out. But I don't mind, I'm ready for anything.'

'Then go into hospital, my dear fellow.'

'It can be a hole in the ground for all I care.'

'Promise me you'll do everything Dr. Khobotov says, old man.'

'All right, I promise. But I repeat, sir, I am caught up in a vicious circle. Everything, even my friends' sincere sympathy, tends the same way now: to my ruin. I'm finished and I'm man enough to recognize it.'

'You'll get better, old chap.'

'Why talk like that?' asked Ragin irritably. 'What I am now experiencing . . . most people go through it at the end of their lives. When you are told you have something like bad kidneys or an enlarged heart and you take treatment, when you're called a lunatic or a criminal— when people suddenly take notice of you, in other words—then you can be sure you are trapped in a vicious circle from which you will never escape. The more you try to get away the more you are enmeshed in the toils. You may as well give in because no human effort will save you now, or that's what I think.'

Meanwhile a crowd was gathering by the grille. Not wanting to be a nuisance, Ragin stood up and began saying good-bye. Michael Averyanovich made him repeat his promise and saw him to the outside door.

Late that afternoon Khobotov unexpectedly presented himself to Dr. Ragin in his short fur coat and jack-boots.

'I have some business with you, dear colleague,' he said in a tone which seemed to dismiss the previous day's happenings. 'Now, how about coming along to a little consultation, eh?'

Believing that Khobotov wanted to take him for a stroll or really would help him to earn some money, Ragin put his hat and coat on, and they went into the street together. Ragin was glad of the chance to redress the wrong which he had done on the previous day and to make peace, so he felt grateful to Khobotov for not breathing a hint about the matter: evidently, to spare his feelings. Such delicacy was hardly to be expected from a being so uncivilized.

'And where is your patient?' asked Ragin.

'In the hospital. I've been wanting to show you this for some time: a most fascinating case.'

Entering the hospital yard, they skirted the main block on their way to the hut where the lunatics were housed: all this in silence for some reason. When they entered the hut Nikita jumped up as usual and stood to attention.

'One of these people has a lung complication,' said Khobotov in an undertone, entering the ward with Ragin.

'Now, you wait here, I'll be back in a moment. I'll just fetch my stethoscope.'

He left.

XVII

Darkness was already falling and Ivan Gromov lay on his bed with his face buried in his pillow. The paralysed patient sat immobile, quietly weeping and moving his lips. The fat peasant and the former post-office sorter were asleep. It was quiet.

Ragin sat on Gromov's bed and waited. But half an hour passed, and instead of Khobotov it was Nikita who came into the ward with a hospital smock, underclothes and slippers clasped in his arms.

'Kindly put these on, sir,' he said quietly.

'Now, here's your bed, you come this way,' he added, pointing to an empty bed which had obviously been brought in recently. 'It's all right, you'll get better, God willing.'

Now Ragin understood. He went wordlessly to the bed indicated by Nikita and sat down. Seeing Nikita standing there waiting, he took off all his clothes and felt embarrassed. Then he put on the hospital clothes. The pants were too short, the shirt was too long, the smock stank of smoked fish.

'You'll get better, God willing,' repeated Nikita.

He collected Ragin's clothing in his arms, went out and closed the door behind him.

'Oh, who cares?' thought Ragin, bashfully wrapping his smock around him and feeling like a convict in his new garb. 'Nothing matters. Tail-coat, uniform or smock ... whatever you wear, it's all the same.'

What about his watch, though? And the notebook in his side pocket? What of his cigarettes? And where had Nikita taken his clothes? Now perhaps he would never have occasion to put on his trousers, waistcoat and boots for the rest of his life. All this was a bit weird at first—mysterious, even. Ragin was still convinced that there was no difference at all between Mrs. Belov's house and Ward Number Six, that everything on this earth is folly and vanity—yet his hands trembled, his legs grew cold, and he was afraid of Gromov suddenly standing up and seeing him in this smock. He got up, paced about, then sat down again.

He sat for a further half hour, then another hour, and was bored to tears. Could one really spend a day or a week here—years, even, like these people? Here he was having sat down, walked about, then sat down again. One could go and look out of the window and cross the room again. But what next? Was one to sit like this all the time like a stuffed dummy, just thinking? No, one could hardly do that.

Ragin lay down, but at once stood up again, wiped the cold sweat from his brow with his sleeve and smelt his whole face stinking of smoked fish. He paced about again.

'This is some misunderstanding,' he said, spreading his arms in perplexity. 'It must be cleared up, it's a misunderstanding——'

Then Ivan Gromov awoke, sat up, propped his cheeks on his fists. He spat. He gave the doctor a lazy glance, obviously not understanding for a minute, but then a malevolent leer suddenly came over his sleepy face.

'Oho, so they've shoved you in here too, have they, old man,' he said in a voice hoarse with sleep, closing one eye. 'Welcome, indeed. So far you've been the vampire, now it's your turn to be thrown to the bloodsuckers! An excellent idea!'

'This is some misunderstanding,' Ragin said, fearing Gromov's words. He shrugged his shoulders.

'It's a misunderstanding,' he repeated.

Gromov spat again and lay down.

'Oh, blast this life!' he grumbled. 'And the really galling, wounding thing is that it won't end with any recompense for sufferings or operatic apotheosis, will it? It will end in death. Some peasants will come and drag one's corpse into a cellar by its hands and feet. Ugh! Oh well, never mind, we'll have our fun in the next world. I shall come back from the other world and haunt these rats. I'll scare them, I'll turn their hair white.'

Little Moses came in, saw the doctor and held out his hand.
'Give us a copeck,' he said.

XVIII

Ragin went over to the window and looked out into open country.
Darkness was already falling and a cold, crimson moon was rising above
the horizon on the right. Not far from the hospital fence, no more than
a couple of hundred yards away, stood a tall white building with a
stone wall round it: the prison.

'So this is reality,' thought Ragin, terrified.

Moon, prison, the nails on the fence, a distant flame in the glue
factory . . . it all terrified him. Hearing a sigh behind him, Ragin
turned and saw a man with shining stars and medals on his chest who
smiled and artfully winked an eye. That too struck Ragin as terrifying.

Ragin told himself that there was nothing peculiar about a moon and
a prison, that even sane persons wear medals, and that everything
would rot and turn to clay in time, but despair suddenly overwhelmed
him and he clutched the window-bars with both hands, shaking them
with all his strength. The iron grille did not yield.

Then, to lull his fears, he went to Gromov's bed and sat down.

'I don't feel too grand, old chap,' he muttered, trembling and wiping
off the cold sweat. 'I'm feeling a little low.'

'Then how about a spot of philosophy?' jeered Gromov.

'Oh, God, my God! Yes, er, quite so. You, sir, once remarked that
there's no Russian philosophy, but that all Russians, nonentities included, are philosophers.

'But the philosophic theorizings of nonentities don't do any harm,
do they?' Ragin asked, his tone suggesting that he wanted to weep and
arouse sympathy. 'So why laugh at my misfortunes, dear friend? And
why shouldn't nonentities talk philosophy if they're dissatisfied? An
intelligent, well-educated, proud, freedom-loving man made in God's
image . . . and his only outlet is to be a doctor in a dirty, stupid little
town surrounded by cupping-glasses, leeches and mustard plasters all
his life! How bogus, how parochial, ye Gods, how cheap!'

'Stuff and nonsense. If you hated doctoring you should have been
a Minister of the Crown.'

'There's nothing one _can_ be, I tell you. And we're so feeble, my
friend. I used to be detached, I used to argue confidently and sensibly,
but it only took a bit of rough handling to make me lose heart and cave

in. We're a rotten, feeble lot. You are the same, my dear chap. You're intelligent, you have integrity, you imbibed high principles at your mother's breast, but barely were you launched on life before you tired and sickened. You're feeble, I tell you.'

Besides fear and resentment, some other depressing sensation had been nagging at Ragin ever since nightfall. In the end he realized that he wanted his beer and a smoke.

'I'm just going out, my dear chap,' he said. 'I'll tell them to bring us a light. I can't manage like this, can't cope——'

Ragin went and opened the door, but Nikita jumped up in a flash and blocked his path.

'And just where do you think you're off to?' he asked. 'None of that, now! It's bed-time.'

Ragin was flabbergasted. 'But I only want a turn in the yard for a minute.'

'None of that, now. It ain't allowed, you know that.'

Slamming the door behind him, Nikita leant his back against it.

Ragin shrugged his shoulders. 'But what does it matter if I go out for a bit?' he asked.

'I don't understand, Nikita, I *must* go out,' he said in quavering tones. 'I've got to.'

'Don't you give me no trouble, we can't have that,' Nikita cautioned him.

'Oh, what the blazes *is* going on?' Gromov suddenly shouted and jumped up. 'What right has he to stop you? How dare they keep us here? The law, I think, states clearly enough that no one may be deprived of his liberty without a court order. It's an outrage, it's sheer tyranny!'

'Of course it is,' said Ragin, encouraged by Gromov's shout. 'I *must* go out, I've got to! He has no right to do this. Let me out of here, I tell you!'

'Do you hear me, you stupid bastard?' shouted Gromov, banging his fist on the door. 'Open up or I'll break down the door, you bloody savage!'

'Open up!' shouted Ragin, shaking all over. 'I insist!'

'You just say one word more!' Nikita answered from behind the door. 'Just you try it, that's all!'

'At least go and fetch Dr. Khobotov. Tell him I asked him to come over, er, for a minute.'

'The doctor will be along tomorrow anyway.'

'They'll never let us out,' Gromov was saying. 'They'll let us rot here. Oh Lord, can there really be no hell in the next world, will these blackguards really get away with it? It's so unfair!

'Open up, scum, I'm choking!' he shouted hoarsely, charging the door. 'I'll beat my brains out! Murdering bastards!'

Nikita swiftly opened the door, roughly shoved Ragin back with both hands and a knee, then swung and punched him in the face. Ragin felt as if a vast wave of salt water had broken over his head and swept him to his bed. And his mouth did indeed taste salty—because blood was coming from his teeth, probably. As if trying to swim away, he struck out and gripped someone's bed. As he did so he felt Nikita hit him twice in the back.

Gromov gave a loud shriek. He must have been hit too.

Then all was quiet. Moonlight filtered through the bars, a network of shadows lay on the floor. It was horrible. Ragin lay down and held his breath—terrified, awaiting another blow. He felt as if someone had stuck a sickle in him and twisted it a few times inside his chest and guts. He bit the pillow in his pain and clenched his teeth. Then suddenly a fearful thought past all bearing flashed through the chaos of his mind: that just such a pain must be the daily lot, year in year out, of these men who loomed before him like black shadows in the moonlight. How could it be that for twenty years and more he had ignored that—and ignored it wilfully? He had not known pain, he had had no conception of it, so this wasn't his fault. And yet his conscience proved as tough and obdurate as Nikita, flooding him from head to heels with an icy chill. He leapt up, wanting to shout at the top of his voice, wanting to rush off and kill Nikita, then Khobotov, then the manager, then Khobotov's assistant and finally himself. But no noise came from his chest, his legs would not obey him. Panting, he ripped the smock and shirt on his chest, and flopped unconscious on his bed.

XIX

On the next morning he had a headache, his ears buzzed, his whole body felt exhausted. He was not ashamed to recall his feebleness of the previous day. He had been cowardly yesterday, he had even been scared of the moon, he had frankly expressed feelings and thoughts which he had never suspected himself of harbouring: those ideas on the discontents of theorizing nonentities, for instance. But now he cared nothing for all that.

He neither ate nor drank, but lay still and silent.

'I don't care,' he thought as they asked him their questions. 'I'm not answering, I just don't care.'

Michael Averyanovich arrived that afternoon with a quarter of a pound of tea and a pound of jam. Daryushka came too and stood near the bed for a whole hour, her face expressing dazed grief. Dr. Khobotov also visited. He brought a bottle of potassium bromide and told Nikita to fumigate the ward.

Late that afternoon Ragin died of a stroke. His first sensation was of a devastating feverish chill and nausea. Something quite sickening seemed to permeate his whole body, even his fingers, sweeping from his stomach to his head, swamping his eyes and ears. A green light flashed in his eyes. Knowing that his end was near, Ragin remembered that Gromov, Michael Averyanovich and millions of others believed in immortality. Now, what if there really were such a thing? But he didn't want any immortality, he only thought about it for a moment. A herd of deer, extraordinarily handsome and graceful, of which he had been reading on the previous day, darted past him. A peasant woman held out a registered letter, Michael Averyanovich said something.

Then it all vanished. Dr. Andrew Yefimovich Ragin plunged into eternal oblivion.

The peasant orderlies came, seized his hands and feet, and hauled him off to the chapel. There he lay on the table, open-eyed and bathed in moonlight at night. On the next morning Sergey Sergeyevich came, prayed devoutly before the crucifix and closed his ex-boss's eyes.

A day later Ragin was buried. Only Michael Averyanovich and Daryushka went to the funeral.

ARIADNE

On the deck of the Odessa–Sevastopol steamer a rather good-looking man with a full beard came up and asked me for a light.

'Notice those Germans sitting by the deck-house?' he asked. 'When Germans or Englishmen meet, they talk about crops, the price of wool or personal affairs, yet somehow when we Russians meet, we always talk about women and abstract ideas. Mainly women, though.'

I knew him by sight because we had both come in on the train from abroad the day before and I had seen him at the customs at Volochisk, standing with his lady companion before a mountain of suitcases and hampers full of feminine attire. He was annoyed and much disheartened at having to pay duty on some odd bit of silk, and his companion protested and threatened to complain. Then on the way to Odessa I saw him taking cakes and oranges along to the ladies' compartment.

It was rather damp and the sea was a little rough, so the women had gone to their cabins. The bearded man sat down beside me.

'Yes,' he went on. 'When Russians meet they only discuss abstract subjects and women. We're pompous intellectuals forever laying down the law and we can't tackle a problem at all unless it's on a very lofty plane. A Russian actor can't act the fool—even in a farce he feels he has to be profound—and the rest of us are just the same. Even our small talk must be on the most exalted level. We're not bold, sincere or natural enough, that's why. And why do we keep on about women so? Because we aren't satisfied, I think. We idealize women too much and make demands out of all proportion to what we're actually likely to get. We don't get what we want or anything like it. Hence our dissatisfaction, shattered hopes and wounded spirits, and you can't have a sore point without wanting to talk about it. Would it bore you if I went on?'

'Not at all.'

'Then may I introduce myself?' he asked, rising slightly from his seat. 'I'm Ivan Shamokhin, a landowner from the Moscow district, you might say. As for you—I know you well.

He sat down again and went on, looking into my eyes in a frank, friendly sort of way.

'This endless talk about women—a second-rate philosopher like Max Nordau would put it down to sex mania, the serf-owning mentality or something, but that's not my view. We're dissatisfied because we're idealists, I tell you. We want the creatures who bear us and our children to be superior to us and everything else on God's earth. As young men we feel romantic adoration for our beloved. To us love and happiness are one and the same. We Russians look down on anyone who doesn't marry for love, we find lust ridiculous and disgusting, and our most successful novels and stories are those in which the women are beautiful, romantic and exalted. Russians have raved over Raphael's Madonna and worried about women's rights for years, but that isn't a pose, believe me. The trouble is this, though. No sooner do we marry or have a love affair than in a couple of years we feel disappointed and let down. Then we have more affairs and more dreadful disappointments. In the end we decide that women are mean, restless, lying, unfair, primitive, cruel creatures. Indeed, far from thinking them man's superiors, we completely look down on them. Dissatisfied and deceived as we are, we can only grouse and talk in and out of season about being let down so badly.'

While Shamokhin spoke I noticed how much he relished his native language and environment. He must have been terribly homesick abroad. He praised Russians and called them great idealists, but without disparaging foreigners, and that was rather in his favour. Clearly, too, he was feeling a little upset and it was himself rather than women that he wanted to talk about. I was in for a long story, a confession of some kind.

Sure enough, after we had ordered a bottle of wine and drunk a glass each, he began.

'I remember someone in a tale of Weltmann's remarking, "I say, what a story!" But someone else answers, "That's no story, it's only the beginning of one." Well, what I've told you so far is only the beginning. What I'd really like is to tell you my latest romantic adventure. Excuse my asking again, but would it bore you to hear it?'

I said no and he went on as follows.

The action takes place in the north of Moscow Province. The country round there is just wonderful, indeed it is. Our estate is on the high bank of a swift-flowing stream by some rapids, with water thundering past day and night. Picture a large, old garden, pleasant flower-beds, beehives, a vegetable-plot and the river down below with feathery willows that seem to lose their gloss and turn grey in heavy dew. Across the river there is a meadow and beyond it on a hill is a grim, dark pinewood with masses and masses of orange mushrooms. Elks live in the heart of it.

Those early mornings, you know, with the sun actually hurting your eyes—when I am dead and in my grave I think I shall still dream of them. Then there are the wonderful spring evenings with nightingales and corncrakes calling in the garden and beyond, the strains of an accordion floating over from the village, someone playing the piano in the house and the river roaring past—such music, indeed, that you want to cry and sing out loud. We haven't much ploughland, but the pasture helps us out, bringing in about two thousand a year with what we get from the woods. I'm the only son. My father and I live modestly and with Father's pension this was quite enough for us to live on.

For three years after taking my degree I stayed in the country, running the farm and expecting all the time that some job would turn up. But the point is, I was very much in love with an extremely beautiful and charming girl. She was the sister of our neighbour Kotlovich, a bankrupt squire whose estate sported pineapples, superb peaches, lightning-conductors and a fountain in the courtyard, though he had not a copeck to his name. He was idle, incompetent and somehow mushy like a boiled turnip. He treated the peasants by homœopathy and went in for spiritualism. He was a mild, tactful sort of person, actually, and no fool, but I have no use for anyone who talks to spirits and treats village women by magnetism. To start with, this kind of limited outlook always goes with muddled thinking, and such people are very hard to talk to. And then they aren't fond of anyone usually and they don't live with women, which gives them an air of mystery that puts sensitive people off. I didn't like his looks either. He was tall, fat and white, and had a tiny head, tiny glittering eyes and plump white fingers. He didn't shake your hand, he massaged it. He was always saying how sorry he was—if he asked for something it was 'so sorry', and if he gave you something, it was 'so sorry' again.

But his sister was quite a different story. By the way, I hadn't known the Kotloviches when I was younger, for my father was a professor at N. and we lived in the provinces for years. The girl was twenty-two by the time I met them, had left school long ago, and had lived in Moscow for a year or two with a rich aunt who brought her out. The first time I met her I was greatly struck by her unusual and beautiful christian name—Ariadne. It suited her so well. She was a brunette, very slim, very dainty, svelte, elegant and amazingly graceful, with exquisite and really handsome features. Her eyes were bright, like her brother's, but whereas his had a cold, sickly glint like boiled sweets, it was youthful beauty and self-confidence that shone in hers. I fell in love with her at first sight, and no wonder. First impressions were so strong that I have still not lost my illusions and would like to think that nature created this girl as part of some splendid grand design.

Ariadne's voice, her footsteps, her hat—even her footprints on the sandy bank where she fished for gudgeon—thrilled me, delighted me and put new life into me. To me her lovely face and figure were pledges of her inner self. Ariadne's every word and smile bewitched me, charmed me, made me feel that hers was indeed a noble nature. She was affectionate, talkative, gay and natural. Her belief in God seemed infused with poetry, as did her reflections on death. So rich and subtle was her inner nature that it lent even her faults delightful qualities all her own.

Perhaps she wanted a new horse, but couldn't afford one. Well, why worry? There was always something to sell or pawn. And if the estate-manager swore that there was not, then why not strip the metal roofs off the lodges and dispose of them to the local factory? Or take the cart-horses to market and let them go dirt cheap just when the farm work was at its height? These wild urges sometimes drove everyone on the estate quite frantic, but she expressed them with such style that she was always forgiven in the end and allowed to do as she pleased, like a goddess or Caesar's wife.

There was something rather moving about my love and soon everyone—Father, neighbours, village people—noticed it. They were all on my side and if I happened to stand the men a round of vodka, they would bow and say, 'Here's hoping you may wed Miss Kotlovich, sir.'

Ariadne herself knew that I loved her. She often rode over to see us, or drove over by cabriolet, and sometimes spent whole days with me and Father. She made friends with the old man and he even taught her to ride a bicycle—his great hobby. I remember helping her onto her bicycle one evening when they were just going for a ride. She was so beautiful. I felt that touching her was like scorching my hands. I was trembling, I was in ecstasy. And when she and the old man, both so handsome and graceful, bowled off down the road together, a black horse—coming the other way and ridden by our manager—lurched to one side because it too was dazzled by her beauty, or so I thought. My love and adoration greatly moved Ariadne and she longed to feel the same magic and love me in return. That would be so romantic, you see.

But unlike me she couldn't love truly, for she was cold and already rather corrupted. Day and night a devil inside her whispered that she was so charming, so divine. What was she doing in this world? What had she been born for? She had no clear idea and saw her own future purely in terms of fame and fortune. She dreamt of dances, race-meetings, liveries, a sumptuous drawing-room, her own *salon* with a swarm of counts, princes, ambassadors, famous painters and enter-tainers—the whole lot at her feet, raving about her beauty and fine clothes.

This lust for power, this ambition and unswerving concentration on a single goal—it makes people insensitive. And insensitive Ariadne was, about me, about nature and about music.

Meanwhile time was passing and so far there were no ambassadors in evidence. Ariadne continued to live with her spiritualist brother and things went from bad to worse until she could not afford to buy dresses and hats and was put to all sorts of shifts and dodges to hide how badly off she was.

Typically enough, a Prince Maktuyev—rich, but an utter worm—had paid his addresses to her when she was living at her aunt's in Moscow. She had refused him out of hand, but now there was some-times that little nagging doubt. Had she been right to turn him down? Just as your peasant blows disgustedly on a glass of kvass with beetles in it, but still drinks it, so she frowned and turned up her nose when she remembered the prince—yet remarked to me, 'Say what you like, but there's something mysterious and delightful about a title.'

She dreamt of titles and gracious living, yet she did not want to let me go either. Dream of ambassadors as you will, you are not made of stone after all, and it's hard to forget that you are only young once. Ariadne tried to fall in love, pretended to be in love, and even swore that she loved me.

Now I am a highly strung, sensitive person. I can tell when someone loves me, even at a distance, and I need no assurances or vows. But this was like a breath of cold air. When she spoke of love I seemed to hear the singing of a mechanical nightingale. Ariadne herself felt that there was something missing. That distressed her and I often saw her in tears. Then once, believe it or not, she suddenly flung her arms round me impetuously and kissed me—it happened on the river bank one evening. I could tell by her eyes that she did not love me, but had embraced me purely out of curiosity, as a sort of exercise. She wanted to see what would happen. But it horrified me. I took her hands.

'It makes me so unhappy when you kiss me without loving me,' I brought out in desperation.

'Oh, you are a—funny boy!' she said irritably and went away.

I should probably have married her after a year or two, which would have been the end of my story, but fate decided to give our romance a different twist. A new personality happened to swim into our ken when Michael Lubkov, a university friend of Ariadne's brother, came to stay with him. He was a charming fellow and even the coachmen and servants called him 'the amusing gentleman'. He was of medium height, a bit scraggy and bald. His face was that of a good bourgeois—unattractive, but presentable, pale, with a bristly, carefully tended moustache. He had goose-flesh and pimples on his neck and a large Adam's apple. He wore pince-nez on a broad black ribbon and couldn't pronounce *r* or *l* properly. He was always in high spirits and found everything great fun. He had made a peculiarly stupid marriage at the age of twenty, and receiving two houses in Moscow near Devichy as part of his wife's dowry, had had them repaired, built a bath-house and then lost every penny. Now his wife and four children were living in terrible poverty at the Oriental Apartments and he had to support them. All this was great fun. He was thirty-six and his wife was forty-two and that was fun too. His mother, a stuck-up, pompous person—a frightful snob—looked down on his wife and lived alone with a horde of dogs and cats and he had to pay her seventy-five roubles a month, quite apart from what his wife got.

Lubkov himself was a man of taste and liked lunching at the Slav Fair Hotel or dining at the Hermitage Restaurant. He needed a lot of money, but his uncle only let him have two thousand a year, which was not enough, and for days on end he ran round Moscow with his tongue practically hanging out, trying to cadge a loan. That was funny too. He said that he had come to stay with Kotlovich to recover from family life in the heart of the country. At lunch, at supper and on walks he talked about his wife and mother, about creditors and bailiffs, and laughed at them. He laughed at himself too and claimed to have met a lot of very nice people through his knack of borrowing.

He laughed all the time and we joined in. And during his stay we passed the time differently. I was given to quiet and 'idyllic' pleasures, being fond of fishing, evening walks and mushroom-picking. But

Lubkov preferred picnics, fireworks and hunting. Two or three times a week he arranged a picnic and Ariadne, looking solemn and dedicated, would list oysters, champagne and chocolates, and dispatch me to Moscow—not asking, naturally, if I had any money. Toasts were drunk at the picnics, there were lots of laughs, and more gleeful stories about how old his wife was, how fat his mother's dogs were, and what nice people creditors were.

Lubkov was fond of nature, but took it very much for granted, thinking it thoroughly beneath his notice and created only for his amusement.

'Not a bad place to have tea,' he would say, pausing in front of some magnificent view.

Once, seeing Ariadne walking some way off with a parasol, he nodded towards her.

'What I like about her is, she's thin,' he said. 'I don't like fat women.'

I was shocked and asked him not to speak of women like that in my presence. He looked surprised.

'What's wrong about me liking thin ones and not fat ones?' he asked.

I made no answer. Then there was another occasion, when he was in a good mood and had had a drop to drink.

'I've noticed that Ariadne likes you,' he said. 'But I can't make out why you're so slow off the mark.'

This embarrassed me and I rather shyly gave him my views on love and women.

'I don't know,' he sighed. 'Women are women, the way I see it, and men are men. Ariadne may be the poetical, exalted creature you make her out, but that doesn't put her outside the laws of nature. She's at an age when she needs a husband or lover, you can see that for yourself. I respect women every bit as much as you do, but I don't think certain relationships are incompatible with poetry. Poetry is one thing. A lover's another. It's just like agriculture—natural beauty's one thing and the income from forests and fields is something else again.'

When Ariadne and I fished for gudgeon, Lubkov lay near us on the sand and poked fun at me or instructed me in the art of living.

'How do you manage without a mistress?' he asked. 'It baffles me, man. You're young, handsome, attractive—in fact, you're one hell of a fellow. But you live like a monk. I've no use for these old men of twenty-eight! I'm nearly ten years older than you, but which of us is the younger? You tell us, Ariadne.'

'You of course,' Ariadne answered.

When he tired of us saying nothing and keeping our eyes on the floats, he would go indoors.

'It's a fact,' she would say, looking furiously at me. 'You're not a man. You're such a ninny, God forgive us! A man should be swept off his feet, do crazy things, make mistakes and suffer! A woman will forgive you if you're rude and impudent, but she'll never forgive you for being so stuffy.'

She was genuinely angry.

'You must be bold and dashing if you want to get anywhere,' she went on. 'Lubkov isn't as good-looking as you, but he's more attractive and he'll always be a success with women because he's not like you, he's a real man.'

She sounded really vexed. One evening at supper she started off without looking at me about how she wouldn't vegetate in the country if she was a man. She would travel and spend the winter abroad somewhere—in Italy, say. Oh, Italy! Now my father inadvertently added fuel to the flames by making a long speech about Italy—how splendid it was with its wonderful weather and museums. Ariadne suddenly yearned to go there. She actually banged the table with her fist and her eyes flashed as if to say, 'Let's be off!'

This started a lot of talk about how nice it would be in Italy. 'Oh, Italy, lovely Italy!' We had this every day. When Ariadne looked at me over her shoulder, her cold, stubborn look told me that in her day-dreams she already had Italy at her feet—salons, famous foreigners, tourists and all. There was no holding her back now. I advised her to wait—put the trip off for a year or two—but she frowned disdainfully.

'You're so stuffy!' she said. 'You're like an old woman.'

But Lubkov was in favour of the trip. He said that it would be very cheap and he would be glad to go along himself and recover from family life in Italy. I'm afraid I behaved as innocently as a schoolboy. I tried to leave them alone together as little as possible, not from jealousy, but because I thought that something outrageous might happen. They pulled my leg—pretended to have been kissing, say, when I came in the room and that kind of thing.

Then one fine morning her plump, white, spiritualist brother arrived and evinced a desire to speak to me in private.

He was a man with no will-power. If he saw other people's letters on a table, he simply couldn't stop himself reading them, for all his education and tact. Now, as we spoke, he admitted that he had happened to read a letter from Lubkov to Ariadne.

'This letter shows she's going abroad soon. I'm terribly upset, old boy. For goodness' sake tell me what it's all about. It makes no sense to me.'

He panted straight into my face as he spoke and his breath smelt of boiled beef.

'Excuse my revealing the secrets of this letter,' he went on. 'But you're a friend of Ariadne's and she thinks highly of you. You might know something. She wants to go away, but do you know who with? Mr. Lubkov proposes to go with her. I must say, Lubkov's behaviour is decidedly odd. He's a married man with children, but he tells Ariadne he loves her and calls her "darling". All most peculiar, I must say!'

A chill came over me. My arms and legs grew numb and I felt a sharp pain in my chest. Kotlovich flopped helplessly in an easy chair with his arms hanging limply down.

'But what can I do?' I asked.

'Influence her. Make her see sense. She and Lubkov—well, judge for yourself. They're not in the same street. Oh God, it's so awful!' he went on, clutching his head. 'Awful! She has such wonderful prospects—Prince Maktuyev and . . . and the rest of them. The prince adores her and only last Wednesday his deceased grandfather Ilarion definitely confirmed in so many words that Ariadne would be his wife—no doubt about it! Grandfather Ilarion may be dead, but he's amazingly clever. We call up his spirit every day.'

I lay awake all night after this conversation and felt like shooting myself. Next morning I wrote five letters and tore them all in little pieces. Then I wept in the barn. Then I borrowed money from Father and left for the Caucasus without saying good-bye.

Women are women, of course, and men are men, but is all that really as straightforward these days as it was before the flood? Must I, an educated man with a complex spiritual nature, really put down my yearning for a woman to the fact that her body is a different shape from my own? What a ghastly thought! I should like to think that man's genius has taken up the cudgels against carnal love as part of his battle with nature, and that if he hasn't beaten it, he has at least managed to enmesh it in illusions of comradeship and affection. For me at any rate these things were not just a function of my biological organism as if I were a dog or frog, but true love—every embrace inspired by a pure impulse of the heart, by respect for womankind.

Actually a revulsion against animal instincts has been built up over the centuries in hundreds of generations. I've inherited it—it is part of my blood, part of the very fibre of my being. And if I now romanticize love, isn't that just as natural and inevitable these days as the fact that I can't waggle my ears and am not covered with fur? I think this is what most educated people feel, since love without anything moral and poetical about it is treated as an atavistic phenomenon these days, and is said to be a symptom of degeneracy and many forms of derangement. Granted, when we romanticize love we do endow the loved one with virtues that are often just non-existent, and that's why we're always doing the wrong thing and suffering for it. But it's better that way in my opinion. I mean it's better to suffer than to console oneself with women being women and men men.

In Tiflis I had a letter from my father. He wrote that Ariadne had gone abroad on such-and-such a date and intended to be away all winter.

A month later I went home. It was autumn. Every week Ariadne sent my father letters on scented paper, most interesting letters too, written in an excellent literary style—I think any woman could be an author. Ariadne described in great detail how hard she had found it to placate her aunt and obtain a thousand roubles from her for the trip, and how long she had spent in Moscow hunting up an old lady, a distant relative, to persuade her to go with them. There was a highly contrived air about this excess of detail and I realized of course that she was travelling without a chaperon.

Soon afterwards I too had a letter from her—also scented and well-written. She wrote how much she missed me and my beautiful, clever, love-lorn eyes, reproached me in a friendly way for wasting my youth and stagnating in the country when, like her, I might live in paradise under palm-trees and breathe the fragrance of orange groves. She signed herself, 'Ariadne, whom you have deserted'. A day or two later there was a second letter in the same style signed 'whom you have forgotten'. I was in a complete daze. I loved her passionately and dreamt of her every night, and here was all this 'deserted' and 'forgotten' stuff. Why? What was I to make of it? Besides, there was the tedium of country life to put up with, and the long evenings and nagging thoughts about Lubkov.

I was tortured by uncertainty that poisoned my days and nights until I could stand it no more. I gave in and left.

Ariadne wanted me to go to Abbazia. I arrived on a fine, warm day

after a shower had left drops hanging on the trees, and took a room
in the huge, barrack-like hotel annexe where Ariadne and Lubkov
were staying. They were out. I went into the local park, strolled along
the paths for a while and then sat down. An Austrian general passed
by with his hands behind his back. He had red stripes down his trousers
just like one of our own generals. A baby was pushed past in a pram,
with a squeaking of wheels on the wet sand. A doddery old man with
jaundice passed by, followed by a group of Englishwomen and a
Polish priest, then the Austrian general came round again. Military
bandsmen, just in from Fiume, plodded off to the bandstand, carrying
their glittering trumpets, and struck up a tune.

Were you ever in Abbazia? It is a filthy little Slav town. Its only
street stinks, and when it has been raining you can't get along it without
galoshes. I had been so carried away by all the things I had read about
this earthly paradise that I was annoyed and embarrassed to find myself
hitching up my trousers as I gingerly crossed the narrow street and
bought some hard pears from an old countrywoman out of sheer
boredom. Seeing that I was a Russian, she made a pathetic attempt to
talk our language. I was puzzled where on earth to go and what to do
in the place, and was forever running across other Russians who felt
as cheated as I did.

There is a quiet bay crossed by steamers and boats with coloured
sails. You can see Fiume and distant islands shrouded in mauvish mist.
It would be all very picturesque if the view of the bay wasn't blocked
by hotels and their annexes in the inane suburban architectural style
favoured by greedy speculators who have built up the whole of that green
coast, so that you hardly see anything of paradise but windows, terraces
and odd spaces with little white tables and waiters' black tail-coats. There
is the sort of park that you find in any foreign resort nowadays. The
dark, still, silent foliage of palms, the bright yellow sand on the paths,
the bright green benches, the flash of soldiers' blaring trumpets and
the red stripes on generals' trousers—it takes just ten minutes for all that
stuff to bore you stiff. Meanwhile you are somehow forced to spend
ten days or ten weeks in the place!

Drifting from one resort to another, I have noticed more and more
what mean, uncomfortable lives the rich and overfed lead. Their
imaginations are so feeble and stunted, their tastes and desires so
unadventurous. How much happier are travellers, young or old, who
cannot afford hotels, but live where they can, admire the sea while
lying on green grass high in the hills, go about on foot, see forests

and villages at close quarters, study a country's customs, listen to its
songs and love its women.

It was growing dark as I sat in the park. Spruce and elegant as any
princess, Ariadne appeared in the twilight, followed by Lubkov in
a new, loosely fitting suit that he must have bought in Vienna.

'Why do you look so cross?' he asked. 'What have I done wrong?'

She saw me and gave a joyful shout, and would certainly have
thrown her arms round my neck if we had not been in a park. She
squeezed my hands, laughing, and I joined in, moved almost to tears.
Then the questions began. How were things in the village? How was
Father? Had I seen her brother? And so on. She insisted on me looking
her in the eyes and asked if I remembered the gudgeon, our little
quarrels and the picnics.

'It was so marvellous, wasn't it?' she sighed. 'Not that it's dull here
either. Darling, we've lots of friends! Tomorrow I'll introduce you
to a Russian family here. Only for goodness' sake buy another hat.'
She looked me up and down and frowned. 'Abbazia isn't a village,'
she said. 'It's the thing here to be *comme il faut*.'

We went to a restaurant. Ariadne kept laughing, behaving skittishly
and calling me a 'dear', a 'darling' and 'such a clever boy', as if she
could scarcely believe I was with her. We sat around till about eleven
and departed very pleased with our supper and each other. Next day
Ariadne presented me to the Russian family as 'the son of a distinguished professor whose estate is next to ours'. She talked of nothing
but estates and harvests to these people, continually referring to me.
She wanted to pass as a member of a rich 'county' family, and I must
say she succeeded, having the superb manner of a true aristocrat—
which indeed she was.

'Isn't Aunt funny!' she suddenly said, smiling at me. 'We had a
bit of a tiff and she's gone off to Merano. What do you think of
that?'

'Who's this aunt you were talking about?' I asked her later when
we were walking in the park. 'What's all this about an aunt?'

'Oh, just a little white lie,' laughed Ariadne. 'They mustn't know
I'm unchaperoned.' After a moment's silence she snuggled up to me.
'Please, darling, do be nice to Lubkov,' she said. 'He's so miserable.
His mother and wife are simply dreadful.'

With Lubkov she seemed to keep her distance, and when she went
to bed she wished him good night with a 'till tomorrow', just as she
did me. And they lived on different floors, which made me hope there

was nothing in the idea that they were lovers. So I felt at ease with him and when he asked for a loan of three hundred roubles, I was glad to let him have it.

We spent the whole of each day amusing ourselves, strolling about the park, eating and drinking. And every day we had these conversations with the Russian family. One thing I gradually got used to was that if I went in the park I was sure to meet the old man with jaundice, the Polish priest and the Austrian general, who always had a small pack of cards with him and whenever possible sat down and played patience, nervously twitching his shoulders. And the band kept playing the same tune.

At home in the country I was always ashamed to face our peasants when I went fishing on a working day or drove out for a picnic. And I had the same feeling of shame with the servants, coachmen and workers that I met here. I felt they were looking at me and wondering why I never did anything. I felt this sense of shame every day from morning to night.

It was a strange, unpleasant, monotonous time, varied only by Lubkov borrowing money from me—now a hundred florins, now fifty. Money was to him what morphine is to an addict. It soon cheered him up and he would roar with laughter at his wife, at himself or at his creditors.

Then the rains and cold weather set in. We left for Italy and I telegraphed Father, asking him for God's sake to send me an eight hundred rouble money-order in Rome. We stopped in Venice, Bologna and Florence, and in each city invariably found ourselves at expensive hotels where we were charged extra for lighting, service, heating, bread with our lunch, and the right to dine in a private room. We ate an enormous amount. We had a large breakfast and lunched at one o'clock on meat, fish, some kind of omelette, cheese, fruit and wine. At six o'clock we had an eight-course dinner with long intervals when we drank beer and wine. About half-past eight tea was served. Towards midnight Ariadne would declare herself hungry and demand ham and boiled eggs and we would have some too to keep her company.

Between meals we dashed round museums and exhibitions, haunted by the fear of being late for lunch or dinner. I was bored with pictures and longed to go home and lie down.

'Marvellous! What a feeling of space,' I would repeat hypocritically after the others, looking exhaustedly for a chair.

Like gorged boa-constrictors, we only noticed things that glittered. Shop windows mesmerized us, we were fascinated by cheap brooches and bought a lot of useless junk.

It was the same story in Rome where there was rain and a cold wind and we went to inspect St. Peter's after a greasy lunch. Because we had been stuffing ourselves, or perhaps because the weather was so bad, it did not impress us, and having caught each other out not caring about art we almost quarrelled.

The money arrived from Father. It was morning, I remember, when I went to fetch it and Lubkov went with me.

'So long as one has a past,' he said, 'one can't lead a full, happy life here and now. My past is a great handicap to me. True, if I had money it wouldn't be too bad, but I'm broke. Do you know I've only eight francs left?' he went on, lowering his voice. 'Yet I must send my wife a hundred and my mother another hundred. Then there's living here. Ariadne's such a child. She just won't understand, and she squanders money like a duchess. Why did she have to buy that watch yesterday? And why should we still pretend to be as innocent as new-born babes? You tell me that! Why, it costs us an extra ten to fifteen francs a day to conceal our relationship from servants and friends by taking a separate room for me. What's the point?'

I felt a sharp stab of pain in my chest. Now I knew what was going on—no more uncertainty. I felt cold all over and at once found myself deciding to see no more of these two, but to escape and go home at once.

'Starting an affair with a woman's easy enough,' Lubkov went on. 'It's just a matter of undressing her. It's what comes later that's such a bore—oh, what a lot of nonsense!'

I counted my remittance.

'Lend me a thousand francs or I'm done for,' he said. 'Your money's my last hope.'

I gave him it and he cheered up at once and started laughing at his uncle—the silly fool hadn't managed to keep Lubkov's address from his wife. I went back to the hotel, packed and paid the bill. It remained to say good-bye to Ariadne.

I knocked on her door.

'*Entrez!*'

Her room was in a typical morning mess—tea things on the table, a half-eaten roll and eggshells. There was a strong, stifling reek of scent. The bed had not been made and it was obvious that two people had slept in it. Ariadne herself had only just got up and was wearing a flannel bed-jacket. She had not done her hair.

I said good morning and sat for a moment in silence while she tried to tidy her hair.

'Why, oh why did you send for me?' I asked her, trembling in every limb. 'Why drag me abroad?'

She evidently guessed what was in my mind and took me by the hand.

'I want you here,' she said. 'You're such a decent person.'

I was ashamed of being so shaken and distressed—I should be bursting into tears next thing! I went out without another word, and an hour later I was in the train. All the way home I somehow pictured Ariadne as pregnant and she seemed repulsive. And somehow all the women I saw in trains and stations appeared pregnant and, like her, repulsive and pathetic. I felt like a fanatical miser who suddenly finds that his gold coins are all counterfeit. Those pure, graceful visions which my imagination, inspired by love, had so long cherished, my plans, my hopes, my memories, my views of love and woman—all that seemed to be mocking me and jeering at me.

'Could this be Ariadne,' I asked in horror, '—this young, strikingly beautiful, educated girl, the daughter of a senator—conducting an intrigue with that vulgar, humdrum mediocrity?'

'But why shouldn't she love Lubkov?' I answered. 'Is he any worse than me? Oh, let her love who she likes. But why lie? And then again, why on earth should she be honest with me?' And so on and so forth until I felt I was going out of my mind.

The train was cold. I was travelling first class, but there were three people to a side and no double windows. There was no corridor either and I felt like a man in the stocks—cramped, abandoned, pitiable. My feet were dreadfully cold. Meanwhile I kept thinking how seductive she had looked that morning in her jacket with her hair down. I felt such pangs of jealousy and I jumped to my feet in such agony of mind that my neighbours looked surprised and even scared.

At home I found snow-drifts and nearly forty degrees of frost. I like winter because my home has always been so warm and snug even in the hardest frosts. I like putting on my fur jacket and felt boots on a fine, frosty day and doing a job in the garden or yard, reading in my well-heated room, sitting in Father's study by the fire, or taking a country-style steam-bath. But when one has no mother, sister or children about the place, winter evenings are somehow eerie and fearfully long and silent. The warmer and cosier the home, the more you feel that something is missing. After my return from abroad that winter the evenings seemed interminable. I was so dreadfully depressed that I could not even read. It wasn't so bad in the daytime when you could clear snow in the garden or feed the hens and calves, but the evenings were more than flesh and blood could stand.

I used to hate visitors, but I was glad to see them now, knowing that they were bound to talk about Ariadne. Kotlovich, our spiritualist, often drove over for a chat about his sister, and sometimes brought along his friend Prince Maktuyev who loved her as much as I did. To sit in Ariadne's room, strumming on her piano and looking at her music—this was a necessity for the prince. He could not live without it. And the spirit of Grandpa Ilarion was still predicting that she would be his wife one day. The prince usually stayed for a long time, from lunch to midnight perhaps, and hardly spoke. He would drink two or three bottles of beer without a word and now and then he would give a staccato, sad, silly laugh just to show that he was still with us. Before going home he always took me on one side.

'When did you last see Miss Kotlovich?' he would ask in a low voice. 'Is she well? She's not bored there, is she?'

Spring came round with the woodcock-shooting and the corn and clover to be sown. There was a sad feeling, but this was springtime melancholy and one felt like making the best of things. Listening to the larks as I worked in the fields, I wondered if I should not settle this business of personal happiness once and for all by simply marrying an ordinary village girl. Then suddenly, when the work was in full swing, I had a letter with an Italian stamp.

Clover, beehives, calves and village girls . . . all that vanished in a flash. Ariadne now wrote that she was profoundly, unutterably miserable. She blamed me for not coming to her rescue, for looking down on her from the pedestal of my own virtue, and deserting her in her hour of danger—all this in large, shaky writing with smears and blots, evidently dashed off in great distress. At the end she begged me to come and save her.

Once more I slipped my moorings and was swept away. Ariadne was living in Rome. I reached her late one evening and she burst into tears when she saw me and flung her arms round my neck. She had not changed at all during the winter and looked as young and lovely as ever. We had supper and drove round Rome till dawn while she told me about her doings. I asked where Lubkov was.

'Don't mention that man to me!' she shouted. 'Disgusting, loath-some creature!'

'But you did love him, I think.'

'Never! He seemed a bit unusual to start with and made me feel sorry for him, but nothing more. He's shameless and takes a woman by storm, which is attractive. But don't let's talk about him—that's a dreary chapter of my life. He's gone to Russia to fetch some money and jolly good riddance to him! I told him not to dare come back.'

She was not staying in a hotel now, but in a two-room private apartment which she had decorated to her own taste, with chilly luxury. She had borrowed about five thousand francs from friends since Lubkov's departure, and my arrival really was her last hope. I was counting on taking her back to the country, but I did not succeed—though she was homesick for Russia, memories of past hardships and shortcomings, and of the rusty roof on her brother's house, made her shudder with disgust. When I suggested going home she clutched my hands convulsively.

'No, no!' she said. 'I'd be bored to death.'

It was now that my love entered its last, waning phase.

'Be a darling again and love me a little,' said Ariadne, leaning to-wards me. 'You're so solemn and stuffy. You're afraid to let yourself go and you keep worrying about what might happen, which is a bore. Please, please be nice, I beg you! My good, kind, precious darling, I love you so.'

I became her lover. For at least a month I was crazy with sheer undiluted happiness. To hold her beautiful young body in my arms, to enjoy it, and feel her warmth every time one woke up and remember that she, she, my Ariadne, was here—well, it took a bit of getting used to! Still, I did get used to it and gradually found my bearings in my new position. The main thing was, I could see that Ariadne loved me no more now than she had before. Yet she longed for true love, fearing loneliness. And the point is, I was young, healthy and strong, while she, like all unemotional people, was sensual, so we both acted as if our affair was a grand passion. That, and a few other things, became clearer as time went on.

We stayed in Rome, Naples and Florence. We went to Paris for a while, but found it cold there and returned to Italy. We passed every-where as man and wife, rich landowners. People were glad to meet us and Ariadne was a great success. She took painting lessons, so they called her an artist, and do you know, that really suited her, though she had not a scrap of talent. She always slept till two or three in the afternoon and had coffee and lunch in bed. For dinner she took soup, scampi, fish, meat, asparagus and game, and then when she went to bed I used to bring her something else—roast beef, say—which she ate with a sad, preoccupied look. And if she woke up in the night she ate apples and oranges.

The woman's main and more or less basic characteristic was her fabulous cunning. She was up to some trick every minute of the day. There was no obvious motive for it, it was just instinctive—the sort of urge that makes a sparrow chirp or a beetle waggle its antennae. She played these tricks on me, on servants, porters, shop-assistants and friends. She could not talk to anyone or meet anyone without all sorts of posturing and antics. Just let a man come into our room—waiter or baron, it made no difference—and the look in her eyes, her expression, her voice changed. Even the contours of her figure altered. If you had seen her then, you would have called us the smartest and richest people in all Italy. Not one artist or musician did she meet without telling him a string of fatuous lies about his remarkable genius.

'You're so brilliant!' she would say in a sickly drawl. 'You frighten me, really. I'm sure you see right through people.'

The point of all this was to be attractive, successful and charming. Every morning she woke with but a single thought—to attract! That was the aim and object of her life. If I had told her that in such-and-such a house in such-and-such a street there lived someone who did not find her attractive, it would really have spoilt her day. Every day she must bewitch, captivate, drive people out of their minds. To have me in her power, converted into an utter worm by her charms, gave her the pleasure that victors once felt at tournaments.

My humiliation was not enough, though, and at nights she lounged about like a tigress—with no clothes on, for she always felt too hot—reading letters from Lubkov. He begged her to come back to Russia, or else he swore he would rob or murder somebody to get money and come and see her. She hated him, but his ardent, abject letters excited her.

Having an extremely high opinion of her charms, she thought that if a great assembly of people could see what her figure and complexion were like, she would vanquish all Italy and indeed the entire globe. This talk about her 'figure' and 'complexion' shocked me. She noticed this, and when angry she tried to annoy me with all sorts of vulgar taunts. It reached the point where, losing her temper once at some woman's villa, she told me, 'If you don't stop boring me with your sermons, I'll take off all my clothes this instant and lie down naked on those flowers!'

When I watched her sleeping, eating or trying to look innocent, I often wondered why God had given her such outstanding beauty, grace and intelligence. Could it really be just for lolling in bed, eating and telling lies, lies, lies? Indeed, was she really intelligent? She thought the number thirteen unlucky—three candles too. She was terrified of the evil eye and nightmares. She spoke of free love—and freedom in general—like some pious old granny, and maintained that Boleslav Markevich was a better writer than Turgenev! But she was diabolically sharp and cunning, and in company she had the knack of passing as educated and progressive.

Even when she was in a good mood she thought nothing of insulting a servant or killing an insect. She liked bullfights and reading about murders, and was angry when accused people were acquitted in court.

For the kind of life that we were leading, Ariadne and I needed plenty of money. Poor Father sent me his pension and all his odds and ends of income, and borrowed for me where he could. Once when he answered that he had no money left, I sent a frantic telegram begging him to mortgage the estate. A little later I asked him to raise funds on a second mortgage. He did both without a murmur and sent me the money down to the last copeck. Ariadne despised the practical side of life and took no interest in any of this. While I squandered thousands of francs to gratify her mad whims and groaned like an old tree in the wind, she just gaily hummed, '*Addio, bella Napoli*'.

I gradually cooled towards her and grew ashamed of our liaison. I dislike pregnancy and childbirth, but now I sometimes longed for a child, if only as some formal justification of our way of life. To retain some shreds of self-respect, I began visiting museums and galleries and reading books, ate little, and gave up drinking. If you keep yourself on the go like that from morning to night it does seem to help a little.

Ariadne tired of me too. It was only mediocrities, by the way, who were so taken with her, and her ambassadors and *salon* were still as far away as ever. Money was short and that upset her and made her cry. In the end she announced that perhaps after all she wouldn't mind going back to Russia. So here we are on our way back. In the last few months before our departure she has been very busy corresponding with her brother. She is obviously up to something, but what, God only knows. I'm tired of puzzling over her tricks. But we aren't going to the country—it's to be Yalta and then the Caucasus.

She can only live in holiday resorts these days. If you did but know how I loathe all such places—they make me feel I'm choking, they embarrass me so. I want to go to the country! I want to work and earn my bread by the sweat of my brow and make good my mistakes. I'm so full of energy just now. And I feel that if I really put my back into it I could clear the estate of debt in five years. But there's a snag, you see. We're not abroad now, this is dear old mother Russia and there's the question of holy wedlock. Of course my infatuation's over, my love has gone beyond recall, but be that as it may, I'm in honour bound to marry her.

Shamokhin was excited by telling his story and we went below, still talking about women. It was late. We were sharing a cabin as it turned out.

'Nowadays it's only in the villages that women keep up with men,' said Shamokhin. 'There women think and feel like men. They grapple with nature, they fight for civilization just as hard as men. But the urban, bourgeois, educated woman long ago dropped out. She's reverting to her primeval condition, she's already half animal and, thanks to her, many triumphs of the human spirit have just been thrown away. Woman is gradually disappearing and her place is being taken by an archetypal female. This backwardness of the educated woman is a real menace to civilization. Retreating, she tries to drag man back with her and arrest his progress, no doubt about it.'

'Why generalize?' I asked. 'Why judge all women by Ariadne? Women's urge towards education and the equality of the sexes, which I take to be an urge for justice, simply can't be reconciled with any idea of retreat.'

But Shamokhin was hardly listening. He smiled suspiciously. By now he was a fanatical misogynist and was not going to change.

'Oh, get away with you!' he interrupted. 'Once a woman sees me, not as a man and her equal, but as a male animal, and is bent solely on attracting me—possessing me, that is—her whole life through, the question of equal rights doesn't arise. Don't you believe them, they're very, very cunning! We men make a great fuss about their freedom, but they don't want to be free at all, they're only pretending. They're up to all sorts of dirty tricks.'

Tired of arguing and wanting to sleep, I turned my face to the wall.

'Yes indeed,' I heard as sleep came over me. 'Indeed yes. It's all the fault of our upbringing, man. What does the upbringing and training of an urban woman boil down to? To turning her into a human animal so she can attract a male and conquer him. Yes indeed.'

Shamokhin sighed. 'Our girls and boys should be brought up together and never be separated. A woman should be trained to know when she's wrong, like a man. As it is she always thinks she knows best. Impress on a little girl from the cradle that a man is not first and foremost her escort and suitor, but her comrade and equal. Teach her to think logically and to generalize, and don't keep telling her that her brain weighs less than a man's and so she needn't bother with learning, the arts or cultural matters. A boy—a cobbler's or house-painter's apprentice—also has a smaller brain than a grown man's, but he takes part in the general struggle for existence, he works and suffers. We must also give up this trick of putting it all down to physiology, pregnancy and childbirth. And why? Firstly, a woman doesn't give birth every month. Secondly, not all women have children anyway. And thirdly, a normal village woman works in the fields the day before she has her baby and is none the worse for that. Then there should be complete equality in everyday life. If a man gives up his seat to a lady or picks up her handkerchief, let her do as much for him. I don't mind a girl of good family helping me on with my coat or giving me a glass of water——'

I fell asleep, so that was the last I heard.

As we approached Sevastopol next morning the weather was wet and unpleasant and the sea was a little rough. Shamokhin sat with me in the deck-house, thoughtful and silent. When the bell rang for tea, men with turned-up coat collars and pale, sleepy-looking ladies began going below. A young, very pretty woman—the one who had been angry with the customs officers at Volochisk—stopped in front of Shamokhin and spoke to him, looking like a naughty, spoilt child.

'Ivan dear, poor little Ariadne's been sick!'

Later on, while staying in Yalta, I saw this lovely creature dashing about on horseback followed by two officers who could hardly keep up with her. Then I saw her one morning wearing a Phrygian cap and a small apron, sitting on the sea-front and sketching while a large crowd stood a little way off admiring her. I was introduced to her. She shook me heartily by the hand, gave me an enraptured look and thanked me in a sickly drawl for the enjoyment that my writings gave her.

'Don't you believe it,' Shamokhin whispered. 'She hasn't read a word of yours.'

Strolling on the front late one afternoon, I met Shamokhin who was carrying some large parcels of delicatessen and fruit.

'Prince Maktuyev's here!' he said delightedly. 'He arrived yesterday with her spiritualist brother. Now I see what she was writing to him about. My God!' he went on, looking at the sky and pressing the parcels to his chest. 'If she and the prince hit it off, I'm free, don't you see! I can go back to the country, to Father.'

He ran off.

'I'm beginning to believe in spirits,' he shouted, looking back. 'Grandfather Ilarion's prophecy seems to have come true. God, I hope so!'

The day after this meeting I left Yalta and how Shamokhin's story ended I do not know.

A DREARY STORY

FROM AN OLD MAN'S MEMOIRS

I

THERE is in Russia an eminent professor, a Nicholas Stepanovich Such-and-such—a man of great seniority and distinction. So many medals, Russian and foreign, does he possess that when he wears them his students refer to him as an icon-stand. He knows all the best people, having been on terms of intimacy with every celebrated Russian scholar of the last twenty-five or thirty years at least. His present life offers no scope for friendship. But if we speak of the past the long list of his famous friends ends with names like Pirogov, Kavelin and the poet Nekrasov, who all bestowed on him an affection sincere and warm in the extreme. He is a member of all Russian and three foreign universities, and so on and so forth. All this, and a lot more that might be said, makes up my so-called name.

It is a popular name. It is known to every Russian who can read and write, and is invoked in foreign lecture-rooms with 'famous and distinguished' appended. It's one of those few lucky names—to abuse it, to take it in vain in public or in print, would be a sign of bad taste. And this is as it should be. My name is, after all, closely linked to the image of an illustrious, brilliant and unquestionably useful man. I work hard. I have the stamina of an ox, which is important, and I have flair, which is a great deal more important. I'm also a well-behaved, modest, decent sort of chap, incidentally. Never have I poked my nose into literature and politics, or curried favour by bandying words with nitwits—nor have I ever made after-dinner speeches or orated at my colleagues' funerals.

My name as scholar is free from blemish, by and large. It has nothing to grumble about. It is a fortunate name.

What of the bearer of this name—of myself, in other words? I present the spectacle of a sixty-two-year-old man with bald head, false teeth and an incurable nervous *tic*. I'm every bit as dim and ugly as my name is brilliant and imposing. My head and hands tremble with weakness. Like one of Turgenev's heroines, I have a throat resembling the stringy neck of a double bass, my chest is hollow, my shoulders are narrow. When I speak or lecture, my mouth twists to one side. When

I smile, senile wrinkles cover my whole face, and I look like death. There is nothing impressive about my wretched figure, except perhaps that, when I suffer from my nervous *tic*, a special look comes over me— one bound to provoke in those who observe me the grim, arresting thought that 'the man will soon be dead, obviously'.

I still lecture quite well, I can still hold my audience for two hours. My enthusiasm, the skill with which I deploy my theme, and my humour almost hide the defects of my voice, which is dry, harsh and sing-song, like that of some snivelling preacher. But I write badly. The bit of my brain which controls the writing faculty has ceased to function. My memory is going, my ideas lack consistency, and when I put them down on paper I always feel I've lost all feel for their organic links. My construction is monotonous, my language is poverty-stricken and feeble. I often write things I don't mean, and by the time I reach the end of what I'm writing, I've forgotten the beginning. I often forget ordinary words, and I always have to waste a lot of energy avoiding unnecessary sentences and superfluous parentheses in my writing. These things are clear evidence of declining intellectual activity. The simpler the subject the more agonizing the effort, oddly enough. I feel more at ease and more intelligent writing a learned article than when composing a congratulatory letter or memorandum. Another thing—I find it easier to write German or English than Russian.

As to my present mode of life, I must first mention the sleeplessness from which I've been suffering lately. If anyone should ask me what constitutes the essential core of my life at the moment, I should answer insomnia. From force of habit I still undress and go to bed at midnight exactly. I fall asleep quickly, but I wake up between one and two o'clock feeling as if I hadn't slept at all. I have to get up and light the lamp. I walk up and down the room for an hour or two, and look at long-familiar pictures and photographs. When I tire of walking I sit at my table—sit motionless, thinking no thoughts, experiencing no desires. If there's a book in front of me I pull it towards me mechanic-ally and read listlessly. Not long ago I read an entire novel in one night in this mechanical way—it had an odd title: *The Song the Swallow Sang*. Or I make myself count a thousand to occupy my mind. Or else I imagine a colleague's face and start recalling when and how he took up academic work. I like to listen for sounds. My daughter Liza sometimes mutters rapidly in her sleep two rooms away. Or my wife walks through the drawing-room with a candle—and never fails to drop the

match-box. A warping cupboard squeaks, or the lamp burner gives a
sudden buzz. All these sounds excite me, somehow.

To miss one's sleep of a night is to feel abnormal every minute,
which is why I yearn for dawn and the daytime when I have the right
not to sleep. Much exhausting time passes before the cock crows
outside—my first herald of good news. At cock-crow I know that the
house-porter downstairs will awake within an hour and come up on
some errand, angrily coughing. Then the air beyond the windows will
gradually grow pale and voices will be borne in from the street.

The day begins for me when my wife comes in. She arrives in her
petticoat with her hair in disarray—but washed, smelling of flower-
scented eau-de-Cologne, and looking as if she has dropped in by
accident. She always says the same thing.

'Sorry, I'll only be a minute. Had another bad night?'

Then she turns out the lamp, sits by the table and starts talking. I'm
no prophet, but I can predict her theme, which is the same every morning. After anxious inquiries about my health, she'll suddenly mention
our son—an officer stationed in Warsaw. We always send him fifty
roubles after the twentieth of the month, and this is our chief topic of
conversation.

'We can't afford it, of course,' my wife sighs. 'But we're bound to
help the boy till he finds his feet. He's abroad, and his pay's not much.
Anyway, we'll send him forty roubles next month instead of fifty if
you like. How about that?'

Daily experience might have taught my wife that constant talk about
our expenses does nothing to reduce them, but having no faith in
experience, she regularly discusses our officer son every morning, and
tells me that the price of bread is down, thank God, but sugar has gone
up two copecks—all this with the air of one communicating matters of
moment.

I listen and grunt encouragement mechanically, while strange,
unsuitable thoughts obsess me, probably because I had such a bad
night. I look at my wife and feel a childlike wonder. This elderly
woman, very stout and clumsy, with her stupid look of petty anxiety,
her fear of falling on evil days, her eyes clouded by brooding on debts
and poverty, her capacity for harping on the price of things, and for
smiling only when it comes down—can this woman, I wonder in
amazement, really be the slim Varya with whom I once fell so deeply
in love because of her good, clear brain, her pure heart, her beauty,
and because she felt the same 'sympathy' for my profession which

Desdemona felt for Othello's? Can this really be my wife Varya who once bore me a son?

I stare intensely at this fat, clumsy old woman's face, seeking my Varya, but of her old self nothing remains except her anxiety over my health, together with her habit of calling my salary 'our salary', and my cap 'our cap'. She's a painful sight to me, so I let her say what she likes to give her what comfort I can, and I don't even answer when she criticizes others unfairly, or nags me for not taking up private practice and publishing textbooks.

Our conversation always ends in the same way—my wife suddenly remembers that I haven't had my tea, and panics.

'But what am I doing here?' she asks, standing up. 'The samovar's been on the table ever so long, and here I am chattering. Dear me, how forgetful I'm becoming.'

She moves off quickly, but stops by the door.

'You know we owe Yegor five months' wages?' she asks. 'We shouldn't let the servants' wages run up, I've told you that again and again. It's far easier to pay them ten roubles a month than fifty every five months.'

She goes through the doorway and stops again.

'Poor Liza's the one I'm sorry for,' she says. 'The child studies at the Conservatory and moves in good society, but her clothes aren't fit to be seen. Her fur coat is—well, she's ashamed to go out in it. If she was just anyone's daughter it wouldn't matter, but of course everyone knows her father's a distinguished professor, one of the heads of his profession.'

Having reproached me with my rank and reputation, she goes out at last. This is the start of my day. Nor does it improve as it proceeds.

While I'm drinking tea, my daughter Liza enters in her fur coat and little cap—carrying some music, and all ready to go off to the Conservatory. She's twenty-two years old, but seems younger. She's pretty, and looks a bit like my wife when young. She kisses me affectionately on temple and hand.

'Good morning, Father,' she says. 'Are you well?'

She was very fond of ice-cream as a child, and I often used to take her to a café. Ice-cream was her yard-stick of excellence. 'You're ice-creamy, Daddy,' she would say if she wanted to praise me. We used to call one of her fingers 'pistachio', another 'cream', a third 'raspberry', and so on. When she came in to say good morning I would usually put her on my knee and kiss her fingers.

'Cream, pistachio, lemon,' I would say.

I still kiss Liza's fingers for old time's sake. 'Pistachio, cream, lemon,' I mutter—but it doesn't come off at all, somehow. I feel as cold as ice myself, I'm embarrassed. When my daughter comes in and touches my temple with her lips, I start as if stung by a bee, give a forced smile and turn my face away. Ever since I first contracted insomnia, a single question has been nagging at me. My daughter often sees me, a distinguished elderly man, blushing painfully because I owe my servant money, she sees how often worry over petty debts stops me working and has me walking up and down the room for hours on end brooding. Then why has she never come to me without telling her mother and whispered: 'Here are my watch, bracelet, ear-rings and dresses, Father. Pawn them all, you need the money'? When she sees her mother and me trying to keep up appearances by concealing our poverty—why doesn't she give up the expensive pleasure of music study? I wouldn't accept her watch, her bracelet or any other sacrifices. God forbid, that's not what I need.

I also happen to remember my son, the officer stationed in Warsaw. He's an intelligent, honest, sober fellow, but that's not good enough for me. If I had an old father, and if I knew that he had moments when he felt ashamed of his poverty, I think I'd give someone else my officer's commission, and take a job as an ordinary labourer. Such thoughts about my children poison me. What good are they? To harbour ill-will against ordinary mortals for not being heroes—only a narrow-minded or embittered man can do that. But enough!

At a quarter to ten I have to go and lecture to my dear boys. I dress and walk along the road which I've known for thirty years, and which has a history of its own for me. There is the large grey house containing the chemist's shop. Here was once a small house with an ale bar where I thought out my thesis and wrote Varya my first love letter—in pencil, on a page headed *Historia Morbi*. Next comes the grocery once kept by a little Jew who sold me cigarettes on credit, and then by a fat countrywoman who loved students because 'each of them has a mother'. Its present occupant is a red-headed shopkeeper, a very stolid man who drinks his tea out of a copper teapot. Now come the gloomy university gates so long in need of repair, the bored janitor in his sheepskin coat, the broom, the piles of snow.

On a bright boy fresh from the provinces with the idea that a temple of learning really is a temple, such gates cannot produce a salutary impression. By and large the university's dilapidated buildings, its gloomy corridors and grimy walls, the dearth of light, the melancholy vista of steps, coathooks and benches, have played an outstanding part as a conditioning factor in the history of Russian pessimism.

Here is our garden—it seems neither better nor worse than it was in my student days. I don't like it. Instead of these wizened limes, that yellow acacia and the skimpy pollarded lilac, it would be far more sensible to have some tall pines and fine oaks growing here. Most students' moods depend on their environment, and their place of learning should confront them exclusively with loftiness, strength and elegance at every hand.

God preserve them from scraggy trees, broken windows, grey walls and doors upholstered in tattered oilcloth.

When I reach my own entrance, the door is flung open and I'm greeted by my old colleague, contemporary and namesake—the porter Nicholas. He lets me in and clears his throat.

'Freezing weather, Professor,' says he.

Or, if my fur coat is wet he says: 'A bit on the rainy side, Professor.'

Then he runs ahead, opening all the doors on my way. In my study he solicitously removes my fur coat whilst contriving to purvey some item of university news. Such is the close fellowship between all university porters and caretakers that he knows all about what goes on in the four faculties, the registry, the vice-chancellor's study and the library. He knows pretty well everything. For instance, when the vice-chancellor's retirement is in the air, or a dean's, I hear him talking to the young door-keepers—listing the candidates for the vacancy, and immediately explaining that So-and-so won't be accepted by the Minister, and Such-and-such will turn it down. Then he goes into fantastic details about certain mysterious papers which have turned up in the registry and concern an alleged secret discussion of the Minister's with the County Education Officer, and so forth. These details apart, he's practically always right. His sketches of each candidate's character have their peculiarities, but they're dependable too. Should you need to know the year when So-and-so was vivaed for his thesis, took up academic work, retired or died—then enlist this old soldier's portentous memory, and he'll not only tell you year, month and date, he'll also furnish the details attending this or that circumstance. No one can have a memory like this unless he loves his subject.

He's a custodian of academic tradition. From his predecessors as porter he has inherited many university legends, to which treasures he has added stocks of his own amassed in the course of his career. Many are the tales, long and short, which he'll tell you should you wish. He can speak of fantastic pundits who knew *everything*, about tremendous workers who went without sleep for weeks on end, about scholarship's many victims and martyrs. In his stories good triumphs over evil, while the weak, the wise, the modest and the young always vanquish the strong, the stupid, the proud and the old.

There's no need to take all these legends and fantasies at face value, but sift them carefully and you'll be left with something vital—our fine traditions and the names of real paragons who are generally recognized.

Society at large knows nothing of the academic world beyond anecdotes about the grotesque absentmindedness of elderly professors, and two or three witticisms variously ascribed to Gruber, me or Babukhin. For an educated community this is rather poor. If society loved learning, scholars and students as Nicholas loves them, its literature would long ago have included whole epics, legends and chronicles such as it now unhappily lacks.

After telling me the news, Nicholas adopts a stern expression, and we proceed to discuss practical matters. If an outsider could observe the freedom with which Nicholas handles technical terminology at such times, he might take him for a scholar masquerading as an old soldier. Those stories of college porters' erudition are grossly exaggerated, by the way. True, Nicholas knows over a hundred Latin terms. True, he can put a skeleton together, he can prepare the occasional specimen, and he can amuse the students with some long, learned quotation. But a theory as straightforward as that of the circulation of the blood, say—it's as deep a mystery to him today as it was twenty years ago.

Hunched over a book or preparation, my demonstrator Peter Ignatyevich sits at a desk in my study. This industrious, modest, not very bright person is about thirty-five years of age, but already bald and potbellied. He slogs away morning noon and night, reads a great deal, and has a good memory for what he has read, in which respect he's a real treasure. But in all other respects he's an old hack—a dull pedant, in other words. The old hack's characteristic features—those which distinguish him from a really able man—are as follows. His horizon's restricted and narrowly confined to his subject—outside his own special field he's like a baby, he's so naïve. I remember going into the study one morning.

'What terrible news!' say I. 'I'm told Skobelev's died!'

Nicholas crosses himself, but Peter Ignatyevich turns to me and asks who this Skobelev is!

Another time—this was somewhat earlier—I announce that Professor Perov has died, and dear old Peter Ignatyevich asks what he used to lecture on!

If Patti sang in his very ear, if Chinese hordes invaded Russia, or if an earthquake struck, I don't think he'd move a muscle—he'd just go on squinting down his microscope, imperturbable as ever. 'What was Hecuba to him?' in other words. I'd have given a lot to see this fossilized specimen in bed with his wife.

Another feature is his fanatical faith in the infallibility of science, and above all in anything written by a German. He has confidence in himself and his preparations, he knows the purpose of life, and is a total stranger to the doubts and disillusionments which turn more able heads grey. Then there's his grovelling deference to authority, his lack of any urge to original thought. It's hard to change his views on any subject, and there's no arguing with him. How can you argue with a man so deeply convinced that medicine is the queen of the sciences, that doctors are an élite, that medical traditions are the finest of all? Only one tradition has survived from medicine's bad old days—the white tie still worn by doctors. For a scholar—for any educated man, indeed—the only possible traditions are those of the academic world as a whole, without any distinction between medicine, law and so on. But it's hard for Peter Ignatyevich to accept this, and he's prepared to argue about it till doomsday.

I can picture his future clearly. In the course of his life he'll have made several hundred preparations of exceptional purity, he'll write a number of dull but highly respectable articles, and he'll do a dozen conscientious translations. But he'll never make a real splash. For that you need imagination, inventiveness, flair—and Peter Ignatyevich has nothing of the kind. He's no master of science, in brief, he's its lackey.

Peter Ignatyevich, Nicholas and I speak in low voices. We feel a certain unease. It's a peculiar sensation, this, to hear your audience booming away like the sea on the other side of a door. Thirty years haven't hardened me to this sensation, I still feel it each morning. I nervously button up my frock-coat, ask Nicholas unnecessary questions, betray irritation.

Panic-stricken though I may look, this is no panic, but something else that I can neither name nor describe.

I look at my watch quite unnecessarily.

'How about it?' I say. 'Time to go.'

We parade in sequence. Nicholas walks in front with the preparations or charts, and I follow—while after me, his head modestly lowered, trudges the old hack. Or, if necessary, a corpse is carried in first on a stretcher, followed by Nicholas, and so on. At my appearance the students stand up, then they sit down and the sea's boom is suddenly hushed. We are becalmed.

I know what I shall lecture about, but just how I shall lecture, what I shall start with, where I shall end—that I don't know. I haven't a single sentence on the tip of my tongue. But I only have to glance round my lecture hall, built in the form of an amphitheatre, and utter the timeworn phrase 'last week we were discussing—', for sentences to surge out of my inner self in a long parade—and the fat is in the fire! I speak with overwhelming speed and enthusiasm, feeling as if no power on earth could check the flow of words. To lecture well—interestingly, that is, and with some profit to the audience—you need other qualities besides ability of a high order: experience, a special knack, and the clearest possible conception of your own powers, of your audience, and of the subject of your lecture. Furthermore, you need to have your head screwed on, keep your wits about you, and never for one moment lose sight of your object.

When a good conductor interprets his composer, he does twenty things at once—reads the score, waves his baton, watches the singer, motions sideways towards drum or French horn, and so on. My lecturing is the same. I have before me a hundred and fifty faces, all different from each other, and three hundred eyes boring into my own. My aim is to vanquish this many-headed hydra. If I can keep its level of attention and comprehension clearly in view throughout every minute of my lecture, then I have it in my power. My other adversary is within myself. This is an infinite variety of forms, phenomena and laws, and the welter of ideas—my own and other people's—thereby conditioned. I must maintain a constant facility for seizing out of this vast material the most significant and vital element, keeping time with the general flow of my lecture as I clothe my idea in a form suited to the hydra's understanding and calculated to stimulate its attention, remaining on the alert to convey my thoughts—not as they accumulate, but in a certain order essential to the proper grouping of the picture which I wish to paint. Furthermore, I try to make my language as elegant, my definitions as brief and precise, and my wording as simple and graceful as I can. Every moment I must check myself and remember that I have a mere hour and forty minutes at my disposal. I have my work cut out, in other words. I have to play the scholar, the pedagogue and the orator at one and the same time, and it's a poor lookout if the orator in one preponderates over the pedagogue and scholar, or vice versa.

After a quarter or half an hour of lecturing, you notice the students looking up at the ceiling or at Peter Ignatyevich. One feels for his handkerchief, another shifts in his seat, a third smiles at his thoughts.

Their attention is flagging, in other words, and something must be done about it—so I seize the first chance to make some joke. The one hundred and fifty faces grin broadly, the eyes glitter merrily and the sea briefly booms.

I laugh too. Their attention has been revived, and I can go on.

No argument, no entertainment, no sport has ever given me such enjoyment as lecturing. Only when lecturing have I really been able to let myself go, appreciating that inspiration isn't an invention of the poets, but really does exist. And I don't think that even the most exotic of Hercules' labours ever left him so voluptuously exhausted as I've always felt after lecturing.

So it was once, but now lecturing is sheer agony. Not half an hour has passed before I feel intolerable weakness in legs and shoulders. I sit in an arm-chair—but I'm not accustomed to lecture sitting down. I stand up a minute later, and carry on standing—but then sit down again. My mouth feels dry, my voice grows husky, my head reels.

To conceal my condition from the audience, I keep drinking water, I cough, I frequently blow my nose as if I had a cold, I make random jokes, and I end up announcing the break before time. But my main feeling is one of shame.

Conscience and reason tell me that my best course would now be to deliver the boys a farewell lecture, say my last words to them, give them my blessing, and yield my post to a younger and stronger man. But, as God is my judge, I lack the courage to obey my conscience.

Unluckily I'm neither philosopher nor theologian. I'm perfectly well aware that I have less than six months to live. My main concern should now be with the shades beyond the grave, one might suppose—with the ghosts which will haunt my entombed slumbers. But somehow my heart rejects these issues, though my mind recognizes their full import. On the brink of death my interests are just the same now as they were twenty or thirty years ago—purely scientific and scholarly.

Even at my last gasp I shall still believe that learning is the most important, splendid and vital thing in man's life, that it always has been and always will be the highest manifestation of love, and that it alone can enable man to conquer nature and himself. Though the belief may be naïve and based on incorrect premises, it's not my fault if I hold this faith and no other. Nor can I shake this conviction within me.

But this is beside the point. I only want people to indulge my weakness, and realize that if a man's more interested in the fate of the bone medulla than in the ultimate goal of creation, then to deprive him of his professorial chair and pupils would be like taking him and nailing him in his coffin without waiting for his death.

My insomnia, and the strain of fighting my increasing weakness, have caused a strange thing to happen to me. In the middle of a lecture tears suddenly choke me, my eyes begin smarting, and I feel a furious, hysterical urge to stretch forth my arms and complain aloud. I want to cry aloud that fate has sentenced me, a famous man, to capital punishment, that within six months someone else will be officiating in this lecture theatre. I want to shout that I've been poisoned. New thoughts, hitherto unfamiliar, have been blighting the last days of my life, and they continue to sting my brain like mosquitoes. Meanwhile my situation seems so appalling that I want all members of my audience to leap from their seats in terror and rush panic-stricken to the exit with screams of despair.

Such moments are not easily endured.

II

After the lecture I stay at home working. I read journals and academic theses, or prepare my next lecture. Sometimes I write. I work in fits and starts because I have to receive visitors.

My bell rings. A colleague has come to discuss some professional matter. Entering my room with his hat and stick, he thrusts both at me.

'I'll only be a minute, only a minute,' says he. 'Don't get up, dear colleague, I only want a couple of words.'

Our first concern is to demonstrate how extremely courteous we both are, and how delighted to see each other. I sit him in an arm-chair, he asks me to sit too. Meanwhile we're cautiously stroking each others' waists, touching each others' buttons, and seem to be feeling each other over as if afraid of burning our fingers. We both laugh, though our remarks are devoid of humour. Once seated, we incline our heads towards each other, and speak in subdued tones. However affectionately disposed we may be towards each other, we can't help embellishing our speech with all manner of mumbo-jumbo like 'as you so justly deigned to observe', or 'I have already had the honour to inform you'. And we can't help laughing aloud if one of us makes a joke, however poor. His business completed, my colleague stands up jerkily, and begins saying good-bye with a wave of his hat in the direction of my work. Again we finger each other, again we laugh. I see him out into the hall. Here I help him on with his coat, while he makes every effort to evade so high an honour. Then, when Yegor opens the door, my colleague assures me that I shall catch cold, while I pretend that I'm ready to escort him into the street, even. And when I get back to my study at last, my face still smiles—through inertia, no doubt.

A little later the bell rings again. Someone comes into the hall and spends some time removing his coat and coughing. Yegor announces a student.

'Ask him in,' say I.

A little later a well-favoured young man comes in. Our relations have been strained for the last twelve months. He makes a frightful hash of his examinations, so I give him the lowest mark. Each year I always have half a dozen of these young hopefuls whom I fail—or 'plough', in student parlance. Most of those who fail an examination through incompetence or illness bear their cross patiently, they don't bargain with me. The only ones to bargain and visit my home are gay, uninhibited spirits who find that the examination grind spoils their appetite and prevents them visiting the opera regularly. The first sort I spare, the second I go on 'ploughing' throughout the year.

'Sit down,' I tell my visitor. 'Now, what can I do for you?'

'Sorry to disturb you, Professor,' he begins haltingly, not looking me in the eye. 'I wouldn't venture to bother you if I, er——. I've taken your examination five times now and, er, have ploughed. I beg you, please pass me because, er——'

All idlers defend themselves with the same argument. They have passed with distinction in all other subjects, they have only failed mine —which is all the more amazing because they've always studied my subject so industriously, and know it inside out. Their failure is due to some mysterious misunderstanding.

'I'm sorry, friend,' I tell my visitor, 'but I can't pass you. Go and read your lecture notes again, then come back—and we'll see about it.'

There is a pause. I feel the urge to torment the student a little for loving beer and opera more than learning.

'Your best course,' I sigh, 'is to give up medicine altogether, I think. If you, with your ability, can't get through your examination, you obviously don't want to be a doctor, and you've no vocation for it either.'

The young hopeful's face lengthens.

'I'm sorry, Professor,' he smiles. 'But that would be a bit odd, to put it mildly—study five years, and then suddenly throw it all up!'

'Oh, I don't know—better lose five years than spend the rest of your life doing a job you dislike.'

But then I immediately feel sorry for him.

'All right, suit yourself,' I hasten to add. 'Do a bit more reading, then, and come along again.'

'When?' asks the idler in a hollow voice.

'When you like—tomorrow would do.'

'Come I may,' his good-natured eyes seem to tell me, 'but you'll only plough me again, you swine!'

'If I examine you fifteen times over,' I tell him, 'it still won't make you any more learned, that's obvious. But it will train your character, and that's at least something.'

Silence ensues while I get up and wait for my visitor to leave, but he stands looking at the window, plucking at his beard and thinking. This grows tedious.

Our young hopeful's voice is pleasantly fruity, his eyes are alert and sardonic, his face is complacent and somewhat the worse for wear from too much beer-drinking and lolling on his sofa. He would obviously have a lot to say about the opera, his love affairs and his student friends. But it's not done to discuss such things, unfortunately, much as I'd like to hear about them.

'On my word of honour, Professor, if you pass me I'll, er——'

When we arrive at that 'word of honour', I make gestures of despair and sit down at my desk, while the student spends another minute in thought.

'In that case good-bye,' he says despondently. 'I'm sorry.'

'Good-bye, dear boy. Look after yourself.'

He walks hesitantly into the hall, slowly dons his coat and goes into the street, where he probably ponders the matter further, but without hitting on anything new beyond the term 'old devil' with reference to myself. He goes into a cheap restaurant for some beer and a meal, then returns home to bed. May your bones rest in peace, honest toiler!

The bell rings for the third time, and a young doctor comes in—

wearing a new black suit, gold-rimmed spectacles, the inevitable white tie. He introduces himself, I sit him down and ask what I can do for him. Somewhat nervous, this youthful devotee of scholarship tells me that he has this year passed the examination qualifying him to go on to a doctorate, and all he has to do now is to write his thesis. He would like me to be his supervisor, and I should oblige him greatly by giving him a research subject.

'Delighted to be of assistance, dear colleague,' say I. 'But can we first agree about what a research thesis is? The term normally implies a dissertation based on original work—or am I wrong?—while a composition written on someone else's subject, under someone else's supervision, is given a rather different name——'

The doctorate-seeker remains silent.

'Why do you all come to me? That's what I don't see!' I blaze out angrily, leaping from my chair. 'Think I'm running a shop? I'm not hawking research theses! Why won't you all leave me in peace, for the umpteenth time! I'm sorry to be so blunt, but I'm absolutely sick and tired of it!'

The doctorate-seeker makes no reply beyond a slight flush in the region of the cheek-bones. Though his face expresses deep respect for my distinguished reputation and erudition, I can read in his eyes how he despises my voice, miserable figure and nervous gestures. Angry, I seem a kind of freak to him.

'I'm not keeping a shop!' I say wrathfully. 'But why won't any of you be original, that's what baffles me? Why do you hate freedom so?'

I talk a great deal, he says nothing. In the end I gradually calm down —and give in, of course. He'll receive a subject from me not worth a brass farthing, write an utterly pointless thesis under my supervision, hold his own in a tedious disputation, and obtain an academic degree of no possible use to him.

Sometimes the bell never seems to stop ringing, but I shall confine myself here to four visits only. With the fourth ring I hear familiar footsteps, the rustle of a dress and a well-loved voice.

Eighteen years ago an oculist colleague of mine died, leaving his seven-year-old daughter Katya and about sixty thousand roubles. He appointed me guardian in his will, and Katya lived with us as one of the family till she was ten, after which she went to boarding-school and spent only the summer holidays in my home. Having no time to attend to her upbringing, I only observed her sporadically, which is why I can't say much about her childhood.

My first memory of her—and one that I'm very fond of—is the amazing trustfulness with which she entered my house, which showed in her manner towards the doctors who treated her, and which always glowed in her little face. She would sit somewhere out of the way with cheek bandaged, and she was always examining something attentively. I might be writing or leafing through some books while my wife busied herself about the house, the cook peeled potatoes in the kitchen, or the dog played—seeing which things, her eyes always retained the same unchanging expression.

'All things in this world are beautiful and rational,' they seemed to say.

She was inquisitive and much enjoyed talking to me, sitting on the other side of my desk, watching my movements and asking questions—curious to know what I was reading, what my job was at the university, whether I was afraid of corpses, and what I did with my salary.

'Do the students have fights at the university?' she asks.

'Yes, dear.'

'And do you make them go down on their knees?'

'I do.'

She was tickled by the idea of student fights—and of me making them kneel—and she laughed. She was an affectionate, patient, good child. I often chanced to see something taken off her—or saw her punished for something that she hadn't done, or with her curiosity left unsatisfied. Her unfailing expression of trustfulness took on a tinge of sadness at such times, but that was all.

I was incapable of standing up for her and only when I saw her sadness did I long to draw her to myself and console her in the voice of an old nanny, calling her my 'poor darling orphan'.

I remember too how fond she was of dressing up and using scent, in which she resembled me, for I too like fine clothes and good scent.

I regret that I lacked the time and inclination to observe the origin and development of the great passion which engulfed Katya when she was fourteen or fifteen. I mean her passion for the stage. When she came home from school for the summer holidays, she spoke of nothing with such delight and eagerness as plays and actors, wearying us with her incessant talk of the theatre. My wife and children wouldn't listen, and only I was too cowardly to deny her an audience. When she felt an urge to share her enthusiasm, she would come into my study.

'Nicholas Stepanovich, let me talk to you about the theatre,' she would plead.

I would point to the clock.

'You can have half an hour,' I'd say. 'Commence.'

Later she began bringing home dozens of portraits of actors and actresses whom she adored. Then she tried to take part in amateur theatricals several times, until finally, when her schooldays were over, she informed me that she was born to become an actress.

I never shared Katya's enthusiasm for the theatre. If a play's any good, one can gain a true impression without troubling actors, I think—one only needs to read it. And if the play's bad, no acting will make it good.

As a young man I often went to the theatre, and now my family takes a box twice a year and 'gives me an airing'. That's not enough to entitle me to judge the theatre, of course, but I shan't say much about it. I don't think the theatre's any better now than it was thirty or forty years ago. I still can't find a glass of clean water in corridors or foyer. Attendants still fine me twenty copecks for my coat, though there's nothing discreditable about wearing warm clothes in winter. The orchestra still plays in the intervals without the slightest need, adding to the impression already conveyed by the play a further new and quite uncalled for impression. The men still go to the bar in the intervals and drink spirits. Where there's no progress in small things it would be idle to seek it in matters of substance. When an actor, swathed from head to foot in theatrical traditions and preconceptions, tries to declaim a simple, straightforward soliloquy like 'To be or not to be' in a manner anything but simple, and somehow inevitably attended with hissings and convulsions of his entire frame, when he tries to convince me at all costs that Chatsky—who spends so much time talking to fools and falls in love with a foolish girl—is a highly intelligent man, and that *Woe from Wit* isn't a boring play, then the stage seems to exhale that same ritual tedium which used to bore me forty years ago when they regaled me with bellowings and breast-beatings in the classical manner. And I always come out of the theatre more conservative than I went in.

You may convince the sentimental, gullible rabble that the theatre as at present constituted is a school, but that lure won't work on anyone who knows what a school really is. What may happen in fifty or a hundred years, I can't say, but the theatre can only be a form of entertainment under present conditions. Yet this entertainment costs too much for us to continue enjoying it. It deprives the country of thousands of healthy, able young men and women who might have become good doctors, husbandmen, schoolmistresses and officers, had they not devoted themselves to the stage. It deprives the public of the evening hours, which are best for intellectual work and friendly converse—not to mention the waste of money, and the moral damage to the theatre-goer who sees murder, adultery or slander improperly handled on the stage.

Katya held quite different views, however, assuring me that the theatre—even in its present form—was superior to lecture-rooms, books, and anything else on earth. The stage was a power uniting all the arts, the actors were missionaries. No art, no science on its own could make an impact on the human psyche as powerful and sincere as the stage—no wonder, then, if a second-rate actor enjoyed more popularity in the state than the greatest scholar or artist. Nor could any form of public service give such enjoyment and satisfaction as the stage.

So one fine day Katya joined a theatrical troupe and went away—to Ufa, I think—taking with her a lot of cash, a host of rainbow-coloured hopes and the most lordly views of the matter.

Her first letters written on the road were wonderful. I read them, simply astounded that these small sheets of paper could contain so much youth, spiritual integrity and heavenly innocence—yet also subtle, practical judgements such as would have done credit to a good male mind. The Volga, the scenery, the towns which she visited, her colleagues, her successes and failures—she did not describe them so much as rhapsodize them. Every line breathed that trusting quality which I was used to seeing in her face—and with all this went masses of grammatical mistakes and an almost total lack of punctuation marks.

Within six months I received an extremely romantic, ecstatic letter. 'I'm in love,' it began, and with it was enclosed the photograph of a clean-shaven young man in a broad-brimmed hat with a rug thrown over his shoulder. The ensuing letters were still as magnificent as ever, but punctuation marks had now appeared, grammatical mistakes had vanished, and there was a strong masculine flavour about them. It would be a good idea to build a large theatre somewhere on the Volga, Katya wrote. It must be a joint-stock company, and rich businessmen and steamship owners must be brought into the project. There would be lots of money in it, terrific takings, and the actors would play on a partnership basis.

Perhaps it really was a good idea, but such schemes can originate only in a man's brain, I feel.

Be this as it may, all seemed to go well for eighteen months or two years. Katya was in love, she had faith in her work, she was happy. But later I began to notice in her letters the obvious signs of a decline. It started with complaints about her associates—the first symptom, and a most sinister one. If a young scholar or literary man begins his career by complaining bitterly about other scholars and literary men, it's a sure sign of premature fatigue and unfitness for his work. Katya wrote that her colleagues missed rehearsals, and never knew their lines. By the fatuous plays which they put on, by their bearing on stage, they each revealed utter disrespect for the public. For the sake of box-office receipts, their sole topic of conversation, serious actresses sank to singing popular songs, while tragic actors performed musical skits on deceived husbands, the pregnancy of unfaithful wives and so forth. The wonder was, what with one thing and another, that the provincial stage hadn't yet collapsed entirely—that it could still hang on by a thread so flimsy and rotten.

I wrote Katya a long answer—a very boring one, admittedly.

'I've had many occasions,' I wrote, amongst other things, 'to talk to elderly actors, extremely decent folk sympathetically disposed towards myself. From our conversations I could see that their activities were governed less by their own intelligence and free choice than by fashion and society's moods. The best of them had had to play tragedy, operetta, Parisian farce and pantomime in their time, and whichever it was, they always felt they were on the right lines, and were doing good. So, you see, one mustn't seek the root of this evil in actors, but more deeply—in the art itself, in society's attitude to it as a whole.'

This letter only irritated Katya.

'We're completely at cross purposes,' she replied. 'I was not referring to these extremely decent folk sympathetically disposed towards yourself, but to a gang of crooks without the faintest shred of decency—a pack of yahoos who only went on the stage because no one would take them anywhere else, and who only call themselves artists out of sheer impudence. There's not one talent among them, but there are plenty of mediocrities, drunkards, schemers and scandal-mongers. My adored art has fallen into the clutches of people odious to me, and I can't tell you how bitterly I feel about it. And I'm bitter because even the best of men will only look on evil from a distance, won't go any nearer, and won't stick up for me—but only write me pompous, platitudinous, futile sermons instead.'

And so on. It was all in that vein.

A little later I received the following letter.

'I've been cruelly deceived, I can't go on living. Do what you think fit with my money. I've loved you as my father, my only friend. Farewell.'

Her young man, it turned out, also belonged to that pack of yahoos. I later gathered from certain hints that there had been an attempt at suicide. I think she tried to poison herself. That she fell seriously ill afterwards seems likely because her next letter reached me from Yalta, where her doctors had presumably sent her. Her last letter contained a request to send her a thousand roubles in Yalta quickly.

'I'm sorry my letter's so gloomy,' she ended. 'Yesterday I buried my baby.'

She spent about a year in the Crimea, and then came home.

She had been on the road about four years, during the whole of which time I had played a pretty invidious and curious role in our relations, I can't deny it. When she originally told me that she was going on the stage, and then wrote about her love, when she was periodically seized by fits of extravagance and I had to keep sending her a thousand or two roubles at her demand, when she wrote of her intention to die and then of her baby's death—I always felt disconcerted, and could express my sympathy for her lot only by much meditation, and by composing long, boring letters which might just as well never have been written. And all this time I was supposed to be a father to her, don't you see? I loved her as a daughter!

Katya lives a few hundred yards from me now, having taken a five-room flat and fixed herself up rather comfortably, and in her own peculiar taste. Were one to portray her surroundings, the picture's dominant mood would be laziness—with soft couches and soft stools for lazy bodies, rugs for lazy feet and faded, dim or pastel colours for lazy eyes. A profusion of cheap fans on the walls caters for the lazy psyche, as also do the wretched little pictures wherein eccentricity of technique predominates over content, the welter of little tables and shelves stocked with utterly superfluous and worthless objects, and the shapeless rags in place of curtains.

Add to all this a dread of bright colours, symmetry and space, and you have evidence of perverted natural taste in addition to temperamental indolence. Katya lies on the couch reading books day in day out—chiefly novels and stories. She only goes out of doors once a day, to visit me in the afternoon.

While I work, Katya sits near me on the sofa in silence, wrapped in a shawl as if she felt cold. Either because she's so congenial, or because

I was so used to her visits as a little girl, her presence doesn't affect my concentration. I automatically ask her a question from time to time, and she replies very briefly. Or, for the sake of a minute's relaxation, I turn towards her and watch as she pensively scans some medical journal or newspaper. At such times her face no longer carries its former trustful look, I observe, her present expression being cold, listless and abstracted—as with passengers who have a long wait for a train. She still dresses beautifully and simply, but carelessly. Her dress and *coiffure* have clearly taken no little punishment from the sofas and rocking-chairs on which she sprawls for days on end. Nor is she inquisitive as of old, having given up asking me questions, as if she'd already seen what there is to see in life and didn't expect to learn anything new.

Towards four o'clock movement begins in hall and drawing-room—Liza is back from the Conservatory, and has brought some girl friends with her. They are heard playing the piano, exercising their voices and laughing. In the dining-room Yegor lays the table with a clatter of crockery.

'Good-bye,' Katya says. 'I shan't call on your family today. I hope they'll excuse me, I haven't time. Do come and see me again.'

As I escort her to the hall she looks me up and down severely.

'You keep getting thinner,' she says regretfully. 'Why don't you see a doctor? I'll call on Sergey Fyodorovich and ask him to look you over.'

'Don't do that, Katya.'

'What's your family playing at? That's what I don't see! A fine lot they are, I must say.'

She puts her coat on abruptly, and inevitably a couple of pins fall from her carelessly dressed hair to the floor. She's too lazy to do her hair, hasn't the time. She awkwardly hides the straying locks under her hat and leaves.

I enter the dining-room.

'Wasn't that Katya with you just now?' my wife asks. 'Why didn't she come and see us? It's rather peculiar——'

'Mother,' says Liza reproachfully, 'if she doesn't want to, never mind. We can't very well go down on bended knee.'

'Say what you like, but it is rather off-hand. To spend three hours in the study without one thought for us. Oh, anyway, let her suit herself.'

Varya and Liza both hate Katya. This hatred is quite beyond me, one must probably be a woman to appreciate it. Among the hundred and fifty young men whom I see almost daily in my lecture-theatre, and among the hundred or so older men whom I run across every week, there's barely one, I'd stake my life, capable of understanding this hatred and disgust for Katya's past—her pregnancy and the illegitimate child, in other words. And yet I can't recall one woman or girl of my acquaintance who wouldn't harbour such sentiments, consciously or unconsciously. Nor is this because woman is purer and more virtuous than man, for virtue and purity differ precious little from vice unless they're free from malice. I attribute it simply to women's backwardness. The despondency, the sympathy, the conscience-pangs which the spectacle of misery evokes in your modern male—they say a lot more for his cultural and moral level than would hatred and disgust. Now, your female is as tearful and insensitive today as she was in the Middle Ages, and those who advocate educating her like a man are being perfectly sensible, or so I believe.

My wife also dislikes Katya for having been an actress, for being ungrateful, proud and eccentric, and for all those many other vices which one woman can always find in another.

Besides myself and my family, two or three of my daughter's girl friends lunch with us, as also does Alexander Adolfovich Gnekker—Liza's admirer and a suitor for her hand. He is a fair-haired young man under thirty, of medium height, very stout and broad-shouldered, with ginger dundreary whiskers near his ears and a tinted little moustache which makes his plump, smooth face look like a toy. He wears a very short jacket, a gaudy waistcoat, trousers very broad on top, very narrow down below and patterned in large checks, and yellow heelless boots. He has bulging eyes like a crayfish, his tie resembles a crayfish's neck. The young man's whole person gives off a smell of crayfish soup, or so it seems to me. He visits us daily, but no one in the family knows where he comes from, where he went to school, or what his means are. He doesn't play or sing, but he's somehow implicated in singing and music as a salesman for someone or other's pianos who's always in and out of the Conservatory, knowing all the celebrities and officiating at concerts. He criticizes music with a great air of authority, and I've noticed that people are quick to agree with him.

As rich men are always surrounded by toadies, so are science and the arts. There seems to be no art, no branch of learning free from 'foreign bodies' of friend Gnekker's ilk. Not being a musician, I may be wrong about Gnekker—not that I know him very well, anyway. But his authority seems to me rather suspect, as does his air of profundity when he stands by a piano listening to someone sing or play.

You may be a gentleman and a leading member of your profession a hundred times over, but once you have a daughter there's nothing to protect you from the lower-class vulgarity so frequently obtruded upon your home and mood by courtship, marriage negotiations and wedding. For instance, I simply can't abide the triumphant look on my wife's face when Gnekker's in the house, and I can't put up with bottles of Château Lafite, port and sherry served solely to provide him with ocular evidence of our generous and lavish way of life. Neither can I stomach Liza's laugh which she has picked up at the Conservatory, or her trick of screwing up her eyes when we have men in the house. Least of all can I comprehend why I should be visited daily by —and lunch daily with—a creature so totally alien to my habits, my studies and the whole tenor of my life, who is also so utterly different from anyone dear to me. My wife and the servants mysteriously whisper about him being 'Liza's young man', but I still can't see what he's doing here, and I feel as nonplussed as if they'd sat a Zulu down beside me at table. What also seems odd is that my daughter, whom I'm used to regarding as a child, should love this tie, these eyes, these soft cheeks.

In the old days I used to enjoy my lunch, or was indifferent to it. But now it only bores and irritates me. Since I became a professor, since I've been a Dean of Faculty, my family has found it necessary to make a complete change in our menu and lunching procedures for some reason.

Instead of the simple dishes familiar to me as student and ordinary doctor, I'm now given 'purée'—or soup with things like white icicles floating in it—and kidneys in Madeira. Professorial rank and fame have for ever cut me off from cabbage stew, tasty pies, goose and apple, bream and kasha. They have also robbed me of our maid Agasha, a chatty old woman who liked a bit of a laugh, and in whose stead a dim, haughty creature called Yegor, with a white glove on his right hand, now serves meals. The intervals between courses are short, but seem excessively long because there's nothing to occupy them. Our former gaiety, the carefree talk, the jokes, the laughs, the expressions of fondness for each other, the delight which used to stir the children, my wife and myself whenever we met in our dining-room—these are all things of the past. To a busy man like myself lunch was a time for relaxation and sociability, while for my wife and children it was a holiday—brief indeed, but bright and gay—when, for one half hour, they knew that I belonged not to science, not to my students . . . but to them, and them alone. Now I've lost the knack of growing merry on one glass of wine, and there's no more Agasha, no more bream and *kasha*, no more uproar such as once greeted minor meal-time scandals like the cat and dog fighting under the table, or Katya's bandage falling off her cheek into a bowl of soup.

To describe my present style of lunch is as unappetizing as the eating of it. Solemn in its pompous affectation, my wife's face wears its usual careworn expression.

'I see you don't like the joint,' says she with an anxious glance at our plates. 'Now, you don't like it, do you? Tell me.'

'Don't worry, dear,' I have to answer, 'the joint's very nice.'

'You always agree with me, Nicholas,' says she. 'You never tell the truth. But why is Mr. Gnekker eating so little?'

So it goes on right through the meal, with Liza laughing her staccato laugh and screwing up her eyes. I watch them both, and only now at lunch does it dawn on me that their inner life has long since vanished from my field of vision. Once I lived at home with a real family, I feel, but now I'm just the lunch-guest of a spurious wife, looking at a spurious Liza. A great change has taken place in them both, but I have missed the long process by which it occurred, so no wonder I can't make sense of anything. What caused that change I don't know. The trouble is, perhaps, that God gave my wife and daughter less strength than he granted me. I've been used to holding out against external pressures since boyhood, I've steeled myself pretty well. Such disasters in life as fame, reaching the top of one's profession, abandoning modest comfort for living above one's means, acquaintance with celebrities and all that—these things have barely touched me, I've kept a whole skin. But on my weak, untempered wife and Liza the whole business has collapsed like an avalanche of snow, crushing them.

Gnekker and the young ladies talk fugues, counterpoint, singers, pianists, Bach and Brahms, while my wife smiles sympathetically, fearing to be suspected of musical ignorance.

'How splendid,' she mutters. 'Really? You don't say!'

Gnekker eats solidly away, making his solid jokes and lending a patronizing ear to the young ladies' observations. Evincing an occasional desire to speak bad French, he finds it necessary for some reason to dub me *Votre Excellence* at such times.

But I'm morose. They're as uneasy with me, obviously, as I am with them. I had never come up against class hatred before, but that's what plagues me now, or something like it. I seek only the bad in Gnekker, I find it soon enough, and suffer agonies at the thought of someone outside my own circle as suitor for my daughter's hand. His presence affects me badly in another way too. When I'm on my own or with people I like, I don't brood on my own virtues as a rule—or, if I do, I find them as trifling as if I'd only spent one day in academic life. But when I'm with someone like Gnekker, my merits loom before me like some great mountain with its summit lost in cloud, while down on the foothills squirm Gnekkers scarce visible to the naked eye.

After lunch I go into my study and light my only pipe of the day, a relic of my bad old habit of puffing away morning noon and night. While I smoke my wife comes in and sits down for a talk. As in the mornings, I know what we're going to talk about in advance.

'You and I must have a serious talk, Nicholas,' she begins. 'About Liza, I mean—. Why won't you put your mind to it?'

'To what?'

'You pretend you don't see anything, but that's wrong, one mustn't be so off-hand. Gnekker has intentions towards Liza—what do you say about it?'

'That he's a bad man I can't say because I don't know him. That I don't like him I've told you a thousand times already.'

'Oh, this is impossible, really——'

She stands up and walks about in agitation.

'You can't adopt that attitude to a serious step,' says she. 'With a daughter's happiness at stake, one must put all personal considerations aside. All right, I know you don't like him—but if we turn him down now and break it off, what guarantee have you that Liza won't hold it against us for the rest of her life? There aren't too many young men about these days, heaven knows, and another one may not come along. He's very much in love with Liza, and she obviously likes him. He hasn't got a proper job, of course, but that can't be helped. He'll get fixed up somewhere in time, God willing. He's of good family and he's well off.'

'How do you know?'

'He said so himself. His father has a large house in Kharkov and an estate near by. What it comes to, Nicholas, is that you must definitely visit Kharkov.'

'What for?'

'You can go into things there—you know some of the local professors, and they'll help you. I'd go myself, but I'm a woman and I can't——'

'I shan't go to Kharkov,' I say gloomily.

My wife takes fright, and an anguished expression appears on her face.

'For God's sake, Nicholas,' she begs between sobs. 'For God's sake, take this burden from me—I'm in agony.'

The sight of her causes me suffering.

'All right then, Varya,' I say tenderly. 'All right, I'll run down to Kharkov if you like and do what you want.'

She presses her handkerchief to her eyes and goes off to cry in her room while I'm left on my own.

Somewhat later a lamp is brought in. Arm-chairs and lampshade throw on walls and floor the familiar shadows of which I have long since tired. Watching them, I feel as if night had fallen and my damned insomnia had started already. I lie on the bed, I get up and pace the room, then lie down again.

As a rule my nervous excitement reaches its highest pitch in the late afternoon. I begin crying for no good reason, and bury my head in the pillow—afraid of someone coming in, afraid of dying suddenly, ashamed of my tears, and altogether in the most unbearable state of mind. No longer, I feel, can I bear the sight of my lamp, of my books, of the shadows on the floor, nor can I endure the voices ringing in the drawing-room. Some force, unseen and inscrutable, is thrusting me roughly out of my home, and I leap up, quickly dress and slip into the street, heedful to elude the attention of my family. Where shall I go?

The answer to that question has been in my mind for some time—to Katya's.

III

As a rule she's lying on a Turkish divan or sofa, reading. Seeing me, she idly lifts her head, sits up and stretches out her hand.

'You're always lying down,' I say after pausing for breath. 'That's bad for you, you should be doing something.'

'Eh?'

'You should be doing something, I say.'

'Doing what? A woman can only do menial work or go on the stage.'

'Well then, go on the stage if you can't do the other kind of work.'
She says nothing.

'You ought to get married,' I say, half joking.

'There's no one to marry—no point in it either.'

'You can't go on like this.'

'Without a husband? A lot that matters—I could have as many men as I liked if I wanted.'

'That's not very nice, Katya.'

'What isn't?'

'What you just said.'

'Come on,' says Katya, noting my distress and wishing to remove the bad impression. 'Now, come with me—there you are.'

She takes me into a small, extremely comfortable room.

'There you are,' she says, pointing to the desk. 'I arranged this for you, you can work here. Come here every day and bring your work—they only interrupt you at home. You will work here, won't you?'

To avoid the offence of a refusal, I reply that I will indeed, and that I like the room very much. Then we both sit down in that comfortable room and start talking.

Warmth, comfort, a congenial presence—instead of pleasure, as of old, these things now evoke in me only a strong urge to complain and grouse. I'll somehow feel better, it seems, if I fuss and grumble.

'Things are in a bad way, my dear,' I begin with a sigh. 'Very bad——'

'What is?'

'Well, it's like this, my dear. The greatest, the most sacred right of kings is the right of pardon, and I've always felt like a king because I've availed myself of this right up to the limit. I've never judged, I've been indulgent, I've gladly forgiven all and sundry. Where others protested or waxed indignant, I merely advised or persuaded. Throughout my life my sole concern has been to make my company tolerable to my family, students, colleagues and servants. This attitude to others has had a formative influence on those around me, I know. But now I'm a king no longer. Something is going on inside me—some process fit only for slaves. Day and night evil thoughts haunt me, feelings hitherto unfamiliar have settled in my heart—hatred, scorn, indignation, outrage, fear. I've grown excessively severe, exacting, irritable, disagreeable, suspicious. What once provoked me to an extra joke and a jolly laugh, no more—even those things depress my spirits now. And my sense of logic has changed too. Where once I despised only money,

I now harbour malice against rich people, as if they were at fault—not against their money. Where once I hated violence and tyranny, I now hate those who employ violence, as if they alone were to blame—and not the rest of us for our inability to educate each other. What's the meaning of this? If these new thoughts and new feelings proceed from changed convictions, then where did this change come from? Has the world grown worse? And I better? Or was I blind before, and apathetic? Now, if the change derives from a general decline in my physical and intellectual powers—and I am ill, after all, I do lose weight every day—then my situation's pathetic, for my new thoughts must be abnormal and morbid. I should be ashamed of them, make little of them——'

'Illness is neither here nor there,' Katya breaks in. 'Your eyes have been opened, that's all, and you've seen what, for some reason, you once preferred to ignore. The main thing is, you must make a clean break with your family and get away—that's what I think.'

'Nonsense.'

'You don't love them, so why pretend? Call that a family! Nonentities! If they dropped dead today, not a soul would miss them tomorrow.'

Katya despises my wife and daughter as much as they hate her. Nowadays one can hardly talk about the right to despise other people. But put yourself in Katya's place, and admit such a right—then she's clearly as entitled to scorn my wife and Liza as they are to hate her.

'Nonentities!' she repeats. 'Did you get any lunch today? Don't tell me they remembered to tell you it was ready! Or that they haven't forgotten your existence!'

'Please be quiet, Katya,' I say sternly.

'Think I enjoy talking about them? I wish I'd never set eyes on them! Now, listen, my dear. Throw everything up and leave—go abroad, and the sooner the better.'

'Oh, rubbish! What about the university?'

'Leave the university as well—what do you want with it? It makes no sense, anyway. You've been lecturing for thirty years, and where are your pupils? Are there many distinguished scholars among them? Just try counting them! As for breeding the sort of doctor who exploits ignorance and earns his hundred thousand roubles—it doesn't need a good man or a brilliant intellect for that! You're not needed.'

I am aghast. 'My God, you're so harsh, so very harsh! Now, be quiet, or I'll leave—I don't know how to answer such rudeness.'

The maid comes in to announce tea, and over the samovar we

change the subject, thank God. Having had my grouse, I now wish to indulge another senile weakness—reminiscences. I tell Katya about my past—informing her, to my own amazement, of details that have survived all unsuspected in my memory, while she listens with bated breath, delighted and proud. I particularly like telling her how I was once at a school for clergy's sons, and dreamt of going on to the university.

'I used to walk in our school garden,' I tell her. 'A song or an accordion's grinding floats on the breeze from some faraway tavern, or a troika with bells careers past the school fence—and that's quite enough to fill my heart, and even my stomach, legs and arms, with a sudden happy glow.

'Listening to an accordion, or a dying peal of bells, I'd imagine myself a doctor, and paint pictures of the scene—each better than the last. Now my dreams have come true, as you see. I've received more than I dared to hope. For thirty years I've been a well-loved professor, I've had excellent colleagues, I've enjoyed honours and distinction. I've loved, I've married for love, I've had children. When I look back, in fact, my whole life seems a beautiful and accomplished composition. Now it only remains not to spoil the finale, for which purpose I have to die like a man. If death really is a menace, I have to meet it as befits a teacher, a scholar and the citizen of a Christian country—confidently and with equanimity. But I'm spoiling the finale. I feel I'm drowning, I run off to you, I ask for help, and—"Drown away," say you, "that's just what you should be doing".'

Then a bell sounds in the hall. Katya and I recognize the ring.

'It must be Michael Fyodorovich,' we say.

A minute later my colleague, the literary specialist Michael Fyodorovich, comes in—a tall, well-built, clean-shaven man of fifty with thick grey hair and black eyebrows. He's a good-natured man, an excellent colleague, and comes of an old, rather successful and accomplished family of gentry which has played a prominent part in our literary and educational history. He himself is intelligent, accomplished, highly educated—but he has his foibles. We're all peculiar, we're all freaks in some degree, but his quirks are somewhat extreme, and they're rather a menace to his friends. I know quite a few of them whom his eccentricities have blinded to his many virtues.

He enters and slowly peels off his gloves.

'Hallo,' says he in a deep, velvety voice. 'Having tea? How convenient. It's hellishly cold.'

Then he sits down at table, takes a glass and starts speaking immediately. Nothing is more typical of his delivery than his unfailing jocularity—a sort of cross between philosophy and buffoonery reminiscent of Shakespeare's grave-diggers. He always treats of serious topics—but never treats them seriously. Though his judgements are always harsh and acrimonious, the soft, level, jocular tone somehow prevents the harshness and acrimony from jarring, and one soon grows used to them. Each evening he brings along five or six items of university gossip with which he leads off when he sits down at table.

'Oh Lord,' he sighs with a sardonic twitch of his black eyebrows. 'There are some clowns in this world, I must say!'

'Meaning what?' asks Katya.

'I'm leaving a lecture this morning when I meet friend So-and-so on the stairs, the old fool. He walks along with that horsy chin jutting out as usual, looking for someone to hear him moan about his migraine, his wife and the students who won't go to his lectures. Well, think I, he's spotted me, and I'm lost, the game's up——'

And so it goes on, all in that style. Or else he leads off like this.

'I went to dear old Such-and-such's public lecture yesterday. The less said about this, the better—but I'm astonished that the dear old *alma mater* dares put such numskulls as this creature, such certified boobies, on public display. Why, the man's an imbecile in the international class—oh yes he is, European champion! He lectures, believe it or not, as if he was sucking a boiled sweet—champ, champ, champ! He panics, he can't keep track of his notes, while his wretched thoughts crawl along about as fast as an abbot on a bicycle, and above all you can't make head or tail of what he's driving at. It's so fiendishly dull, the very flies drop dead. The only comparable bore is the annual ceremony in the university hall, the day of our traditional oration, damnation take it!'

Then he makes an abrupt transition.

'About three years ago, as Nicholas here will remember, I had to give that oration. It was hot and stuffy, my uniform was too tight under the arms—sheer hell it was! I lecture for half an hour, one hour, an hour and a half, two hours. "Well," think I, "I've only ten pages left, praise the Lord!" And there are four pages at the end that I needn't bring in at all—I'd reckoned on leaving them out. So I reckon I've only six pages left. But then I glance in front of me, see? And I notice some general with a medal ribbon, and a bishop—sitting together in the front row. The poor creatures are bored rigid, their eyes are popping

out of their heads in their efforts to stay awake, yet they try to look as
if they're attending, they make out that they understand and appreciate my lecture. "Very well," think I, "if you like it so much you can
damn well have it, and serve you right!" So I go ahead and give them
the last four pages too.'

As is the way of these sardonic people, only his eyes and eyebrows
smile when he speaks. His eyes then express neither hatred nor malice,
but a great deal of wit, and the peculiar foxy cunning only seen in
very observant people. And talking of eyes, I've spotted another
peculiarity in his. When he takes a glass from Katya, listens to her
speak or glances after her as she leaves the room on some brief errand,
I notice something tender, supplicatory and innocent in his look.

The maid takes the samovar away, and serves a large piece of cheese,
some fruit and a bottle of Crimean champagne—a poorish vintage of
which Katya had been fond in the Crimea. Picking up two packs of
cards from the shelves, Michael Fyodorovich plays patience. But
though he claims that certain forms of patience require much imagination and attention, he doesn't pause from his conversational diversions
as he plays. Katya follows his cards keenly, helping him more by mime
than words. She drinks no more than two glasses of wine in an evening,
and I drink a quarter of a glass.

The rest of the bottle devolves upon Michael Fyodorovich, who can
put away a great deal without ever getting drunk.

We discuss various problems, mainly on the loftiest level, during
the game of patience, and our great love—science—comes in for
rougher treatment than anything else.

'Science has had its day, thank God,' enunciates Michael Fyodorovich. 'It's day is done, indeed it is, and mankind already feels the need
for some substitute. Science grew out of superstition, it was fed on
superstition, and it now represents superstition's quintessence, like its
outmoded granddams—alchemy, metaphysics and philosophy. And
what have people got out of it, anyway? Between learned Europeans
and the entirely unscientific Chinese, there's precious little difference,
isn't there—and that purely external? The Chinese have done without
science, and what have they missed?'

'Flies don't have science either,' I say. 'What of it?'

'Don't be angry, Nicholas, I only say this here, you know, it's
between us three. I'm more discreet than you think, I wouldn't talk
this way in public—God forbid! The masses hold the superstitious
view that science and the arts are a cut above agriculture, trade and

handicraft. Our section of society lives on this superstition, and God forbid that you and I should destroy it.'

As the game of patience proceeds, the younger generation also finds itself in hot water.

'Our people have gone to seed,' sighs Michael Fyodorovich. 'I say nothing of ideals and all that, but if they could only work and think sensibly! It's Lermontov's "How sadly I regard the present generation" all over again.'

'Yes, they've degenerated terribly,' Katya agrees. 'Tell me, have you had one outstanding student in the last five or six years?'

'I can't speak for other professors, but I don't remember any, somehow.'

'I've seen many students in my day, many of your young scholars, many actors. And what do you think? Not once have I been privileged to meet an ordinary interesting person among them, let alone any star performers or high flyers. They're all so dim, so mediocre, so puffed up with pretensions——'

All this talk about things going to the bad—it always affects me as if I'd accidentally overheard unpleasant gossip about my daughter. I'm insulted by the sweeping nature of indictments built on such hackneyed truisms and bugbears as degeneracy, lack of idealism and harking back to the good old days. Every criticism—even one expressed in ladies' company—should be formulated with maximum precision, or else it isn't criticism, it's just baseless calumny unworthy of a decent man.

I'm an old man, I've been in university work for thirty years, but I see no degeneration or lack of idealism, I don't think things are worse now than they used to be. My porter Nicholas, whose experience has some bearing on the matter, calls today's students no better and no worse than those who went before.

If asked what I dislike about my present students, I shouldn't answer at once or say much, but I should be adequately specific. Knowing their defects, I don't need to resort to a fog of platitude. I dislike their smoking, spirit-drinking, marrying late in life, and being so happy-go-lucky—and often so callous—that they condone starvation among their fellows by not paying their dues to the students' aid society. They don't know modern languages, nor do they express themselves in correct Russian. Only yesterday a colleague—a specialist in hygiene—was complaining to me that he has to give twice as many lectures because their physics is weak and they're wholly ignorant of meteorology.

They gladly fall under the influence of the latest writers, and not the best ones at that, but they're quite indifferent to such classics as Shakespeare, Marcus Aurelius, Epictetus or Pascal, say, and this inability to distinguish great from small reveals their lack of practical experience more than anything else. All difficult problems of a more or less social nature—for instance, that of colonizing unpopulated areas of the country—they decide by getting up a public subscription, not by scientific investigation and experiment, though this last procedure is well within their grasp and has a close bearing on their mission in life. They gladly become assistant surgeons, registrars, demonstrators and housemen, and they're ready to do these jobs up to the age of forty, though independence, a feeling of freedom and personal initiative are just as much needed in science as in art or commerce. I have pupils and audiences, but no helpers and successors. So I like them, I'm enthusiastic about them—but without being proud of them. And so on and so forth.

However numerous such defects may be, they can breed a pessimistic or abusive mood only in a poor-spirited, feeble individual. They're all adventitious and temporary, they derive exclusively from living conditions. A few decades will see them vanish or yield to other, new defects such as cannot be avoided, and will also alarm the craven-hearted in their turn. Students' misdemeanours often annoy me, but such vexation is nothing to the thirty years of enjoyment which I've had through talking and lecturing to my pupils, keeping an eye on their attitudes and comparing them with people in different walks of life.

Michael Fyodorovich casts his aspersions, and Katya listens, neither noticing the bottomless pit into which they are gradually sucked by the patently innocent diversion of condemning their neighbour. They don't sense how ordinary talk gradually turns into sneering and scoffing, or how they both start employing the techniques of downright muck-raking.

'You meet some really killing characters!' says Michael Fyodorovich. 'I dropped in on friend Yegor Petrovich yesterday, where I run across a student type, one of your medicals—in his third year, I think. He has a face in—well, in the Dobrolyubov style, with that stamp of profundity on his brow. We get talking.

'"Oh yes, young man," say I, "I was reading that some German, whose name I forget, has extracted a new alkaloid from the human brain—idiotin."

'Know what? He falls for it! And even adopts a respectful expression, as if to say "Good for us!" Then I went to the theatre the other day. I take my seat. Just in front, in the next row, sit a couple of them—one a member of the Chosen Race and evidently a law student, and the other shaggy creature a medico. The medical boy's as tight as a coot, pays no attention to the stage at all, and just snoozes away, nodding his head. But as soon as some actor launches into a noisy soliloquy, or simply raises his voice, my medico starts and pokes his neighbour in the ribs.

'"What's that?" he asks. "Noble sentiments, eh?"

'"Yes indeed," answers the Chosen One.

'"Hurray!" bellows our medico. "Elevating stuff, this! Bravo!"

'This drunken clot hasn't come to the theatre for art, you see, but for noble sentiments. He wants to be edified!'

Katya listens and laughs. She has a strange kind of guffaw, breathing in and out in rapid, even rhythm, as if playing a concertina, while her nostrils are the only part of her face to express amusement. But I feel downcast, and don't know what to say. I lose my temper, I flare up, I leap from my seat.

'Why don't you just shut up?' I shout. 'Why sit here poisoning the air with your breath like a couple of toads? Stop it!'

Without waiting for an end to their calumnies, I prepare to go home. It's high time anyway, gone ten o'clock.

'Well, I'll stay a bit longer,' says Michael Fyodorovich. 'Have I your permission, Miss Katya?'

'You have,' Katya answers.

'*Bene*. Then have them bring on another little bottle.'

They both see me into the hall with candles.

'You've grown very thin of late, and you've aged,' says Michael Fyodorovich as I put on my fur coat. 'What's up? Ill, are you?'

'Yes, a bit.'

'And he won't see a doctor,' Katya puts in gloomily.

'But why ever not? This won't do! God helps those who help themselves, dear man. My regards to your family, and my excuses for not calling on them. I'll come round and say good-bye in a day or two before I go abroad—I'll make a point of it. I leave next week.'

As I come away from Katya's I'm irritable, alarmed by the talk about my illness and annoyed with myself. I wonder whether I really should consult a colleague about my health. Then I immediately picture him sounding my chest, after which he goes towards the window without speaking, thinks a little, and then turns to me, trying to prevent me from reading the truth in his face.

'I see nothing to worry about at the moment,' says he in a neutral voice. 'Still, I'd advise you to give up work, dear colleague.'

And that would rob me of my last hope.

What man lives without hope? Now that I am diagnosing my own condition and treating myself, I have times when I hope that I'm deceived by my own ignorance, that I'm wrong about the albumen and sugar that I find—wrong about my heart, too, and about the oedemas which I've twice noticed in the mornings. Perusing textbooks of therapy with true hypochondriac fervour, and changing my nostrums every day, I still fancy I may stumble on some consolation. But this is all so trivial.

Whether the sky's cloudy or aglow with moon and stars, I always gaze at it on my way back, thinking how death will shortly overtake me. One might suppose that my thoughts must be as profound as that sky on these occasions, and as bright and vivid.

Far from it! I think about myself, my wife, Liza, Gnekker, students, people in general. My thoughts are wretched and trivial, I'm not honest with myself, and all the time my outlook is that expressed by the famous Arakcheyev in a private letter: 'Nothing good can exist without evil in this world, and there's always more evil than good.' All is vile, in other words, there's nothing to live for, and the sixty-two years of my life must be written off. Catching myself thinking like this, I cultivate the conviction that such ideas are accidental, temporary, superficial.

'But if that's so,' I immediately think, 'why am I drawn to see those two toads every evening?'

I swear I'll never go to Katya's any more—yet I shall visit her again the very next evening, I know.

Tugging my door-bell and walking upstairs, I feel I've lost my family and don't want it back. These new, Arakcheyev-like ideas of mine obviously aren't accidental or temporary at all, they dominate my entire being. Sick in conscience, despondent, indolent, scarce moving my limbs, and feeling about fifty tons heavier, I go to bed and soon fall asleep.

Follows another sleepless night.

IV

Summer comes, life changes.

One fine morning Liza enters my room.

'Come, sir,' says she in jocular tone. 'All is ready.'

Sir is taken into the street, put in a cab and driven off. For want of anything better to do, I read the shop signs backwards as I pass. *Traktir*, the word for 'tavern', comes out as *Ritkart*, which would do as a baronial surname—the Baroness Ritkart. Then I drive through fields past a graveyard, which makes no impression on me at all, though I'll soon be lying there. Then I go through a wood, then through fields again. This is boring. After travelling for two hours, Sir is taken into the ground floor of a summer cottage and placed in a small, very jolly room with light blue wall-paper.

At night I sleep as little as before, but instead of waking and listening to my wife in the morning, I lie in bed—not asleep, but a prey to drowsiness, that semi-conscious state when you know you're not asleep, yet dream. I rise at noon and sit at my desk through force of habit, but instead of working I amuse myself with French books in yellow wrappers, which Katya sends me. To read Russian authors would be more patriotic, of course, but I'm not particularly disposed in their favour, I must confess. Two or three veterans apart, all modern literature seems to me less literature than a variety of cottage industry which exists solely to enjoy the patronage of persons reluctant to avail themselves of its products. Even the best of these homely artefacts can't be called noteworthy, nor can one praise them sincerely without qualification. The same applies to all those literary novelties that I've read during the last ten or fifteen years and which include nothing noteworthy, nothing which can be praised without a 'but'. Such a product may be witty and uplifting—but lacks talent. Or else it's talented and uplifting, but lacks wit. Or, finally, it may be talented and witty, but lacks uplift.

I wouldn't call these French books talented, witty or uplifting. They don't satisfy me either. But they're less boring than the Russian, and it's not unusual to find in them that element vital to originality—a feeling of personal freedom such as Russian authors lack. I can't remember one new work where the author wasn't at pains to hobble himself with all sorts of conditions and contracts with his conscience from the first page onwards. One fears to speak of the naked body, another has tied himself hand and foot with psychological analysis, a third requires a 'warm attitude to man', while a fourth deliberately pads the thing out with whole pages of nature description so as not to be suspected of tendentiousness.

One insists on his work showing him as a townsman of the lower orders, another must be a gentleman and so on. They have premeditation, caution, an eye to the main chance, but they lack the freedom and courage to write what they like, and hence they lack the creative spirit.

All this relates to so-called belles-lettres.

As for learned Russian articles—on sociology, say, on art and all that —the reason I don't read them is sheer nervousness. As a boy and youth I was terrified of hall-porters and theatre ushers for some reason, and that terror is with me to this day. I still fear them. One fears only what one doesn't understand, it's said. And hard indeed it is to see quite why hall-porters and ushers should be so pompous, overweening and sublimely unmannerly. Reading learned articles fills me with just the same vague dread. That fantastic pomposity, this air of magisterial banter, those familiar allusions to foreign authors, the ability to preserve one's dignity while on a wild-goose chase—it's all rather beyond me, it terrifies me, and it's most unlike the modesty, the calm, gentlemanly tone to which I've grown accustomed when reading our natural scientists and medical authors. Articles apart, I find it hard to read even translations made or edited by your serious Russian. The presumptuously condescending tone of the introductions, the profusion of translator's notes which stop me concentrating, the question marks and the word *sic* in brackets with which the liberal translator has bespattered the whole article—these things encroach on the author's personality and on my independence as a reader, or so I feel. I was once called in to give expert evidence in a county court. During the adjournment a fellow-expert pointed out how rude the prosecutor had been to the accused, who included two ladies of good social standing. I don't think I was exaggerating in the least when I told my colleague that the prosecutor's manner was no ruder than that obtaining between the authors of learned articles. So offensive is this manner, in fact, that one can't speak of it without distaste. They either handle each other, or the writers whom they criticize, with such egregious obsequiousness that it lowers their own dignity—or, conversely, treat them with far scanter ceremony than I have my future son-in-law Gnekker in these jottings and musings. Allegations of irresponsibility, of impure motives—of all kinds of criminal activity, even—are the staple embellishment of learned articles. And that is, as young doctors like to say in their papers, the *ultima ratio*! Such attitudes are inevitably reflected in the morals of the younger generation of writers, which is why I'm not one bit surprised that the new items accruing to our literature in the last ten or fifteen years contain heroes who drink too much vodka and heroines whose chastity leaves something to be desired.

I read French books and look out of the open window. I see the sharp points of my garden fence, two or three wizened little trees, and then—beyond the fence—a road, the fields, a broad belt of pine-wood. I often enjoy watching a little boy and girl, both with fair hair and torn clothes, as they climb the fence and laugh at my hairless pate. In their gleaming little eyes I read the words: 'Go up, thou bald head.' They must be pretty well the only people who care nothing for my fame and rank.

Out here I don't have callers every day, and I'll mention only the visits of Nicholas and Peter Ignatyevich. Nicholas usually comes on a Sunday or saint's day—supposedly on business, but really to see me. He arrives quite tipsy—which he never is in winter.

'What news?' I ask, going to meet him in the hall.

'Sir!' says he, pressing a hand to his heart and looking at me with the fervour of a lover. 'Sir! May God punish me, may lightning strike me where I stand! *Gaudeamus igitur juvenes* tra-la-la!'

He kisses me eagerly on shoulders, sleeves and buttons.

'Is all well?' I ask.

'Sir, I swear by Almighty——'

He keeps on swearing to no purpose and soon grows tedious, so I send him to the kitchen where they give him a meal.

Peter Ignatyevich also comes out on holidays, especially to look me up and share his thoughts. He usually sits at my table. Modest, dapper, judicious, not venturing to cross his legs or lean his elbows on the table, he recounts in a soft, level, smooth, pedantic little voice sundry supposedly fascinating and spicy novelties culled from journals and pamphlets. All these items are alike, all add up to something like this. A Frenchman has made a discovery. Someone else, a German, has caught him out by proving that this discovery was made back in 1870 by some American. Now someone else again, another German, has outmanœuvred both—proving that they slipped up by taking air bubbles for dark pigment under the microscope. Even when trying to amuse me, Peter Ignatyevich discourses in long-winded, circumstantial fashion like one defending his dissertation—giving a detailed catalogue of his bibliographical sources, endeavouring not to misquote his names or the dates and issues of his journals, and never calling someone plain 'Petit', but always 'Jean-Jacques Petit'. Sometimes he stays for a meal, and spends the whole time telling these same pithy anecdotes which depress the whole table. Should Gnekker and Liza mention fugue and counterpoint, or Brahms and Bach, in his presence, he modestly drops his eyes and betrays embarrassment, ashamed for such trivialities to be invoked before two serious people like him and me.

In my present mood five minutes of him is enough to bore me as if I'd been seeing and hearing him from time immemorial. I loathe the poor fellow. His quiet, level voice and pedantic speech shrivel me up, his stories numb my brain.

He has the greatest good will for me, he only talks to me to give me pleasure, and I repay him by goggling back as if trying to hypnotize him.

'Go!' I think. 'Go, go, go!'

But not being susceptible to telepathy he just stays on and on and on.

When he's with me, I'm obsessed by the thought that he'll very likely be appointed to succeed me when I die, and my poor lecture-room seems to me like an oasis with a dried-up spring. I'm surly with Peter Ignatyevich—taciturn and gloomy, as if these thoughts were his fault, not mine. When he praises German scholars in his usual fashion, I no longer make fun of him good-humouredly, as once I did.

'Your Germans are asses,' I mutter gloomily.

It reminds me of when Professor Nikita Krylov was alive. He was once bathing with Pirogov in Revel, and lost his temper because the water was so cold. 'These Germans are scoundrels!' he cursed. I treat Peter Ignatyevich badly. Only when he's leaving—when I look through the window and glimpse his grey hat flickering behind the garden fence—do I want to call him back and say: 'Forgive me, dear fellow!'

Lunch is more boring than in winter. That same Gnekker, whom I now loathe and despise, eats with me almost daily. Where once I endured his presence in silence, I now make cutting remarks at his expense, causing my wife and Liza to blush. Yielding to malice, I often utter complete imbecilities without knowing why. For instance, I once gave Gnekker a long, contemptuous stare. Then I suddenly barked out, apropos of nothing:

'An eagle on occasion may swoop lower than a hen,
But the clouds the eagle soars through are beyond that chicken's
   ken.'

Most aggravating of all, Hen Gnekker turns out far cleverer than the professorial eagle. Knowing that he has my wife and daughter on his side, he pursues the tactic of answering my cutting remarks with condescending silence.

'The old boy has a screw loose,' he implies. 'So why talk to him?'

Or else he teases me good-humouredly. It's astonishing how petty one can be—I can spend the whole meal brooding on the day when Gnekker will turn out an impostor, Liza and my wife will realize their mistake, and I shall make fun of them. But fancy conceiving such inane ideas with one foot in the grave!

Nowadays we also have disagreements such as I could once conceive only through hearsay. Shameful as it is, I'll describe one which occurred the other afternoon.

I'm sitting in my room smoking a pipe. In comes my wife as usual, sits down and says what a good idea it would be to pop over to Kharkov now that the weather's warm and we're free, and find out what sort of man this Gnekker really is.

'All right, I'll go,' I agree.

Pleased with me, my wife gets up and goes to the door, but comes back at once.

'By the way, I've another request,' says she. 'I know you'll be angry, but it's my duty to warn you—. I'm sorry, Nicholas, but there's talk among our friends and neighbours about your visiting Katya so much. She's a clever, educated girl, I'm not denying that, and she's good company. But for someone at your time of life, and in your social position, to enjoy her society—well, it is rather odd, you know—. What's more, her reputation is hardly——'

I have a rush of blood to the head. My eyes flash, I jump up, I clutch my head, I stamp my feet.

'Leave me alone!' I shout in a voice unlike my own. 'Leave me alone! Leave me!'

My face must look terrible, and my voice must be strange indeed, for my wife suddenly blenches and shrieks, also in a desperate voice unlike her own. At our shouts Liza and Gnekker run in, followed by Yegor.

'Leave me alone!' I shout. 'Get out! Leave me!'

My legs are numb and bereft of sensation, I feel myself fall into someone's arms. Then I briefly hear the sound of weeping, and plunge into a swoon which lasts for two or three hours.

As for Katya, she visits me daily in the late afternoon, and neither our neighbours nor our friends can fail to notice that, of course. She comes in for a minute, then takes me out for a drive. She keeps her own horse, and a new chaise bought this summer. By and large she lives pretty lavishly—having taken an expensive detached villa with a big garden, she has moved all her belongings there from town, and keeps two maids and a coachman.

'Katya,' I often ask her, 'what will you live on when you've spent all your father's money?'

'We'll see about that,' answers she.

'That money deserves to be taken more seriously, my dear. It was earned by a good man's honest labour.'

'So I'm aware, you've told me that before.'

First we drive through open country, then through the pine-wood which can be seen from my window. Nature seems as lovely as ever, though the devil whispers that when I'm dead in three or four months' time, none of these pines and firs, these birds and white clouds in the sky, will miss me. Katya likes driving, and is pleased that the day is fine, and I'm sitting beside her. She's in a good mood, and doesn't speak harshly.

'You're a very fine man, Nicholas Stepanovich,' she says. 'You're a rare specimen—no actor could play you. Now, take me, say, or Michael Fyodorovich—even a poor actor could play us. But no one could act you. I envy you too, I envy you terribly. What do I add up to, after all? What indeed?'

She thinks for a minute.

'I'm a negative phenomenon, aren't I?' she asks. 'Well, Nicholas Stepanovich?'

'Yes,' I reply.

'H'm. Then what am I to do?'

What can I tell her? 'Work', 'Give all you have to the poor', 'Know yourself'—these things are easily said, so easily that I don't know how to answer.

When teaching the art of healing, my colleagues on the therapy side advise one to 'individualize each separate case'. Following this advice, one comes to see that the techniques recommended in the manuals as best—and as fully applicable to a textbook case—turn out quite unsuitable in specific instances. Moral ailments are the same.

But I have to give some answer.

'You have too much spare time, my dear,' I say. 'You should find an occupation. Now, why shouldn't you go on the stage again if that's your real line?'

'I can't.'

'Your tone and manner are those of a victim. I don't like that, my dear. It's your own fault. Remember, you began by getting angry with people and the way things were done? But you did nothing to improve the things or the people. You didn't resist evil, you just caved in—so you're a victim of your own weakness, not a battle casualty. Well, you were young and inexperienced then, of course, but now everything may be different. So go ahead, honestly! You'll be working, serving the sacred cause of art——'

'Don't be so devious, Nicholas Stepanovich,' Katya breaks in. 'Let's agree once and for all that we can talk about actors, actresses and writers—but we'll leave art out of it. You're a marvellous, rare person, but you don't know enough about art to be sincere in calling it sacred. You have no feel for art, no ear. You've been so busy all your life, you've had no time to cultivate this feel. And anyway—I don't like this talk about art!' she goes on nervously. 'I dislike it! The thing's been vulgarized enough already, thank you very much!'

'Who vulgarized it?'

'Some by drunkenness, the newspapers by their patronizing attitude, and clever men by their theories.'

'Theories are neither here nor there.'

'Oh yes they are. When someone theorizes, it shows he doesn't understand.'

To prevent unpleasantness, I hurriedly change the subject, and then remain silent for a while. Only when we emerge from the wood and make for Katya's villa do I take up the topic again.

'You still haven't answered me,' I say. 'Why don't you want to go back to the stage?'

'Nicholas Stepanovich, this is really cruel!' she shrieks, suddenly flushing crimson. 'Do you want it spelt out for you? All right then, if that's what you want. I'm no good at it. I have no talent, and—and I have a lot of vanity. So there!'

After making this confession, she turns her face away and gives a powerful tug at the reins to hide the trembling of her hands.

Driving up to her villa, we see Michael Fyodorovich from afar strolling near the gate and impatiently awaiting us.

'There's that Michael Fyodorovich again,' says Katya, annoyed. 'Can't you get rid of him—please! I'm sick of him—he's half dead, confound him!'

Michael Fyodorovich should have gone abroad long ago, but puts off his departure every week. One or two changes have occurred in him of late. He looks pinched, somehow. Wine makes him tipsy, which it never used to, and his black eyebrows are going grey. When our chaise pulls up by the gate, he can't hide his delight and impatience. He fussily helps the two of us down, firing rapid questions, laughing, rubbing his hands. That tender, supplicatory, innocent look which I'd previously noticed only in his eyes—his whole face is now suffused with it. He rejoices—yet feels ashamed of his joy, ashamed of this habit of calling on Katya every evening, and he finds it necessary to motivate his appearance with some obvious absurdity such as: 'I was just passing on an errand and thought I'd look in for a minute.'

We all three go indoors. First we drink tea, after which objects long familiar appear on the table—the two packs of cards, the large piece of cheese, the fruit, the bottle of Crimean champagne. Our topics of conversation are not new, they haven't changed since winter. The university comes in for abuse, as do students, literature and the theatre. Calumny clogs the stifling air, and it is no longer two toads, as in winter, which exhale their poisonous breath, but a whole trio of them. Besides the velvet baritone laugh and the loud guffaw like the sound of a concertina, the serving maid can also hear an unpleasant rattling snigger resembling the chuckle of a stage general in a farce.

V

There are terrible nights with thunder, lightning, rain and wind—'sparrow nights', country people call them. There was once such a sparrow night in my personal life.

I wake up after midnight, and suddenly jump out of bed. I'm on the point of dying quite suddenly, I somehow feel. Why this feeling? There's no physical sensation pointing to a sudden end, yet terror clutches at my heart, as if I'd just seen the huge glow of some sinister conflagration.

I quickly strike a light, drink water straight from the carafe, rush to the open window. The night is superb, with a smell of hay and some other very sweet scent. I see the sharp points of my garden fence, the sleepy, wizened little trees by the window, the road, the dark strip of wood. There's a very bright, peaceful moon in the sky, and not a single cloud. It's quiet, not a leaf moves. I feel as if all these things were looking at me, and listening for me to start dying.

It's an eerie feeling. I close the window and run to my bed. I feel for my pulse. Not finding it in my wrist, I feel for it in my temple, then in my chin, then again in my wrist—and all these places are cold, clammy with sweat. I breathe faster and faster, my body trembles, all my inside is moving, my face and bald pate feel covered with a spiders' web.

What shall I do? Call my family? No, there's no point—I've no idea what my wife and Liza could do if they came in.

I hide my head under the pillow, close my eyes and wait—just wait. My back's cold, and feels as if it was being sucked inside me, and I sense that death is sure to sneak up quietly from behind.

'Kee-vee, kee-vee!' something suddenly shrieks in the night's stillness, and I don't know where it comes from—my chest or the street.

'Kee-vee, kee-vee!'

God, how appalling! I'd have another drink of water, but I'm scared to open my eyes, afraid to lift my head. This is an unreasoning, animal fear. Why I'm so scared, I haven't the faintest idea—whether because of an urge to live, or because new, as yet unknown, pain is in store for me.

In the room above me someone is groaning or laughing. I listen. Soon afterwards footsteps are heard on the stairs. Someone goes quickly down, then back up again. A minute later steps are again heard downstairs. Someone stops near my door and listens.

'Who's there?' I shout.

The door opens, I boldly open my eyes and see my wife—her face pale, her eyes tear-stained.

'Can't you sleep, Nicholas?' she asks.

'What is it?'

'Come and have a look at Liza, for God's sake. There's something wrong with her.'

'All right—I'll be glad to,' I mutter, delighted not to be alone. 'Very well—straight away.'

I follow my wife and hear her speaking, but am too upset to take in any of it. Her candle throws jumping patches of light on the steps, our long shadows quiver, my legs trip in the skirts of my dressing-gown, I gasp for breath, I feel as if someone's chasing me and trying to seize my back.

'I shall die here and now on these stairs,' I think. 'Now——'

But then we pass up the staircase and along the dark corridor with the Italian window, and enter Liza's room. She sits on the bed in her night-gown with her bare feet dangling. She is groaning.

'God, God!' she mutters, frowning in the light of our candle. 'I can't stand it, I can't——'

'Liza, my child,' I say. 'What's the matter?'

Seeing me, she shrieks and throws herself on my neck.

'My kind father,' she sobs. 'My good, kind father, my darling, my dearest! I don't know what's the matter, I feel so awful.'

She puts her arms round me, kisses me and babbles endearments such as I used to hear from her when she was a little girl.

'Be calm, child—really!' I say. 'You mustn't cry. I feel awful myself.'

I try to tuck her in, my wife gives her some water, and we both potter about haphazardly at her bedside. I jog my wife's shoulder with my own, reminded of the days when we used to bath our children together.

'Help her, can't you?' begs my wife. 'Do something!'

But what can I do? Nothing. Something's depressing the child, but I understand nothing, know nothing.

'Never mind,' is all I can mutter. 'It'll pass—. Sleep, sleep——'

To make things worse, dogs suddenly howl in our yard—quietly and hesitantly at first, but then in a rowdy duet. I never used to bother about omens like dogs howling or owls hooting, but now my heart sinks in anguish, and I hasten to find an explanation for the howling.

'It means nothing,' I think. 'It's just the way one organism affects another. My extreme nervous tension infected my wife, then Liza and the dog, and that's all. Such infection is behind all forebodings and premonitions.'

Returning to my room soon afterwards to write Liza a prescription, I no longer brood on my impending death, but just feel so downcast and forlorn that I actually regret not having died suddenly. I stand motionless in the centre of the room for a while, wondering what to prescribe for Liza, but the groans above my ceiling fade away, and I decide not to prescribe anything. But I still stand there——.

There's a deathly hush, a quiet so intense that it makes your ears tingle, as some writer once put it. Time passes slowly, and the strips of moonlight look as if they had congealed on the window-sill, for they don't budge.

Dawn is still a long way off.

But then the garden gate squeaks. Someone creeps in, breaks a twig off one of the scraggy saplings, and cautiously taps the window.

'Nicholas,' I hear a whisper. 'Nicholas Stepanovich!'

I open the window and feel as if I'm dreaming. Beneath the window, huddled against the wall and bathed in moonlight stands a black-garbed woman whose huge eyes stare at me. Her face is pale and stern —and weird, like marble, in the moonlight. Her chin quivers.

'It's me,' she says. 'Me—Katya.'

By moonlight all women's eyes look large and black, and people seem taller and paler, which is probably why I had failed to recognize her at first.

'What do you want?'

'I'm sorry,' she says, 'but I suddenly felt unutterably depressed, some-how. I couldn't bear it, so I came here, there was a light in your window and—and I decided to knock. I'm sorry—. Oh, I was so depressed, did you but know. What are you doing now?'

'Nothing—I can't sleep.'

'I had some premonition—it doesn't matter, anyway.'

She raises her eyebrows, tears shine in her eyes, and her whole face glows with that familiar, trustful look which I have not seen for so long.

'Nicholas Stepanovich,' she beseeches, stretching out both arms to me. 'My dear friend, I beg you—I implore you—. If you don't despise my affection and respect, do grant me this request.'

'What request?'

'Take my money.'

'Oh, really, don't be silly! What do I want with your money?'

'You can go somewhere for your health—you need treatment. You will take it, won't you, my dear?'

She stares avidly into my face.

'You will,' she repeats, 'won't you?'

'No, my dear, I won't,' I say. 'No thank you.'

She turns her back on me and bows her head. I must have refused her in a tone which brooked no discussion of money.

'Go home and sleep,' say I. 'We'll meet tomorrow.'

'So you don't consider me your friend?' she asks dejectedly.

'That's not what I'm saying, but your money's no good to me now.'

'I'm sorry,' she says, dropping her voice an octave. 'I see what you mean. To borrow money from someone like me—a retired actress—. Good-bye, anyway.'

And she leaves in such haste that I don't even have time to say good-bye.

VI

I'm in Kharkov.

It would be pointless, and beyond my powers, to fight against my present mood. So I've decided that the last days of my life shall at least be above reproach in the formal sense. If I'm in the wrong where my family's concerned—as I fully realize I am—I'll try to do what they want. If I'm to go to Kharkov, then to Kharkov I will go. Besides, I've grown so indifferent to everything lately that I really don't in the least care where I go—Kharkov, Paris or Berdichev.

I arrived at noon, and took a room in a hotel near the cathedral. The train's jolting upset me, I had draughts blowing right through me, and now I'm sitting on my bed, clutching my head and waiting for my nervous *tic* to start. I ought to visit some professors of my acquaintance today, but I have neither strength nor inclination.

The old corridor servant comes in and asks if I have bed linen. I keep him for five minutes, putting several questions about Gnekker, the object of my errand. The servant turns out to be a Kharkov man who knows the city inside out, but he doesn't remember any house belonging to a Gnekker. I ask about the country estates and the answer is the same.

The corridor clock strikes one, then two, then three.

These last months of my life, this waiting for death, seem to last far longer than the rest of my life put together. Never before could I resign myself to the slow passage of time as I can now. Waiting for a train at the station, or sitting through an examination once used to make a quarter of an hour seem an eternity, but now I can sit motionless all night on my bed, reflecting with total unconcern that tomorrow night will be just as long and colourless, and so will the night after.

Five o'clock strikes in the corridor, then six, then seven.

It grows dark.

There is a dull ache in my cheek—the onset of the *tic*. To occupy my mind, I revert to a point of view which I held before I became so apathetic.

'Why', I ask, 'should a distinguished man like myself, one of the heads of his profession, sit in this small hotel room, on this bed with the unfamiliar grey blanket. Why do I look at this cheap tin wash-stand? Why listen to that wretched clock rattling in the corridor? Is this in keeping with my fame and high social position?' I answer these questions with an ironical smile, tickled by my own youthful credulity in once exaggerating the importance of fame and of the exclusive position supposedly enjoyed by notabilities. I'm well known, my name is invoked with awe, I've had my picture in *The Meadow* and *World Illustrated*—I've even read my biography in a German magazine. And the upshot? I sit all on my own in a strange town, on a strange bed, rubbing my aching cheek with my hand.

Family squabbles, hard-hearted creditors, rude railway officials, the nuisance of the internal passport system, expensive and unwholesome food in the buffets, general loutishness and rough manners—all these, and many other things too time-consuming to mention, affect me no less than any humble citizen unknown outside his own back alley. So what is there so special about my situation? Granted, I'm a celebrity a thousand times over, a great man, the pride of Russia. Granted, bulletins about my illness appear in all the papers, and my mail includes addresses of sympathy from colleagues, pupils and the general public. Yet these things won't save me from dying a miserable death on a strange bed in utter loneliness.

No one's to blame, of course, but I dislike being a celebrity, I'm sorry—I feel cheated, somehow.

At about ten o'clock I fall asleep, despite my *tic*. I sleep soundly, and would have gone on sleeping for a long time, had not someone woken me—soon after one o'clock comes a sudden knock on the door.

'Who's there?'

'A telegram.'

'You might have left it till the morning,' I say angrily, taking the telegram from the servant. 'Now I shan't get to sleep again.'

'Sorry, sir, but your light was on, so I thought you were awake.'

Tearing open the telegram, I first glance at the signature—my wife's. What can she want?

YESTERDAY GNEKKER SECRETLY MARRIED LIZA COME HOME

Reading the telegram, I feel momentary panic—not at what Liza and Gnekker have done, but at my own indifference to the news of their marriage. Philosophers and true sages are said to be aloof, but that's false, for such dispassionateness is spiritual atrophy and premature death.

I go to bed again, wondering how to occupy my mind. What shall I think about? I seem to have thought everything over already, and have nothing left capable of stimulating my ideas.

When dawn breaks, I sit up in bed, arms round my knees—and for

want of anything better to do I try to know myself. 'Know thyself'—
excellent practical advice, that, and the only pity is, it didn't occur to the
ancients to tell us the technique of following it.

When I wished to understand some other person or myself, it was
not their actions—so dependent on other factors, all of them—that I
used to consider, but their desires. Tell me what you want, and I'll tell
you who you are.

Now I scrutinize myself. What do I want?

I want our wives, children, friends and pupils to love us as ordinary
people—not for our reputation, not for how we're branded and labelled.
What then? I'd like to have had helpers and successors. And then?
I'd like to wake up a hundred years from now and cast at least a cursory
glance at what's happening in science. I'd like to have lived another ten
years or so.

And then?

The rest is nothing. I go on thinking—for a long time—but can't
hit on anything. And rack my brains as I will, broadcast my thoughts
where I may, I clearly see that there's something missing in my wishes
—something vital, something really basic. My passion for science, my
urge to live, my sitting on this strange bed, my urge to know myself,
together with all my thoughts and feelings, and the conceptions which
I form about everything—these things lack any common link capable
of bonding them into a single entity. Each sensation, each idea of mine
has its own separate being. Neither in my judgements about science,
the stage, literature and my pupils, nor in the pictures painted by my
imagination could even the most skilful analyst detect any 'general
conception', or the God of a live human being.

And if one lacks that, one has nothing.

So wretched is my plight that serious illness, fear of death, the impact of circumstance and people, have sufficed to capsize and shatter
my entire outlook as I formerly conceived it—everything which once
gave my life its joy and significance. No wonder, then, if I have
blackened my last months with thoughts and feelings worthy of a
slave and savage, no wonder I'm so listless and don't notice the break
of day. Unless a man has something stronger, something superior to all
outside influences, he only needs to catch a bad cold to lose his balance
entirely, to take every bird for a fowl of ill omen, and to hear the baying
of hounds in every noise, while his pessimism or his optimism, together with all his thoughts, great and small, are significant solely as
symptoms and in no other way.

I am beaten. And if so, there's no point in going on thinking and talking. I shall sit and await the future in silence.

In the morning the corridor waiter brings tea and the local paper. I mechanically read the announcements on the front page, the leading article, extracts from newspapers and magazines, and the Diary of the Day.

Amongst other things I find the following item in the Diary:

'Yesterday that well-known scholar and distinguished Professor, Nicholas Stepanovich So-and-so, arrived in Kharkov by express train, and is staying at the Such-and-such Hotel.'

Famous names are obviously created to live their own lives independently of those who bear them. My name is now quietly drifting round Kharkov. In another three months it will be painted on my tombstone in gold letters brilliant as the very sun, by which time I myself shall already be under the sod.

A light tap on the door. Someone wants me.

'Who's there? Come in.'

The door opens and I step back in surprise, hurriedly wrapping the folds of my dressing-gown about me. Before me stands Katya.

'Good morning,' she says, panting after her walk upstairs. 'Didn't expect me, did you? I, er, I've arrived too.'

She sits down.

'But why don't you say hallo?' she goes on in a halting voice, avoiding my eyes. 'I'm here too—came today. I heard you were at this hotel, and I called round.'

'Delighted to see you,' I say, shrugging my shoulders. 'But I'm amazed—dropping in out of the blue like this. What have you come for?'

'Me? Oh, nothing—I just came.'

Silence. Suddenly she gets up impulsively and comes to me.

'Nicholas Stepanovich,' she says, blenching and clasping her hands on her bosom. 'I can't go on living like this, really, Nicholas Stepanovich! Tell me quickly, for God's sake, this very instant—what am I to do? Tell me what to do?'

'But what can I say?' I ask in bewilderment. 'There's nothing I can say.'

'Tell me, I beg you,' she goes on, gasping, and shaking in every limb. 'I swear I can't live like this any longer, I can't stand it!'

She collapses on a chair and starts sobbing. Her head thrown back, she wrings her hands and stamps her feet. Her hat has fallen off her head and dangles by a piece of elastic, her hair is ruffled.

'Help me, help me!' she begs. 'I can't stand any more.'

She takes a handkerchief from her travelling bag, pulling out with it several letters which fall from her lap. I pick them off the floor, and on one I notice Michael Fyodorovich's handwriting and happen to read part of a word: 'passionat—'.

'There's nothing I can say, Katya,' I tell her.

'Help me!' she sobs, clutching my hand and kissing it. 'You're my father, aren't you? My only friend? You're clever, well educated, you've had a long life. You've been a teacher. Tell me what to do.'

'Honestly, Katya, I don't know——'

I am at a loss, embarrassed, moved by her sobbing, and I can hardly stand.

'Let's have lunch, Katya,' I say with a forced smile. 'And stop that crying.'

'I shall soon be dead, Katya,' I at once add in a low voice.

'Just say one word, just one word!' she cries, holding out her hands. 'What can I do?'

'Now, don't be so silly, really,' I mutter. 'I can't make you out. Such a sensible little girl, and suddenly all these tears—whatever next!'

Silence follows. Katya straightens her hair, dons her hat, bundles up her letters and thrusts them in her bag—all without speaking or hurrying. Her face, bosom and gloves are wet with tears, but her expression is now cold and forbidding.

I look at her, ashamed to be happier than she. Only on the brink of death, in the sunset of my life, have I noticed that I lack what my philosopher colleagues call a general idea. But this poor girl has never known—and never will know—any refuge in all her days on earth.

'Let's have lunch, Katya,' I say.

'No thanks,' she answers coldly.

Another minute passes in silence.

'I don't like Kharkov,' I say. 'It's so grey—a grey sort of town.'

'Yes, I suppose so. It's ugly. I shan't stay long—I'm just passing through. I'll leave today.'

'Where are you going?'

'To the Crimea—the Caucasus, I mean.'

'Oh. Will you be away long?'

'I don't know.'

Katya stands up and holds out her hand—smiling coldly, not meeting my eyes.

'So you won't be at my funeral?' I want to ask.

But she doesn't look at me. Her hand is cold and seems alien. I accompany her to the door in silence.

Now she has left me and is walking down the long corridor without looking back. She knows I'm watching her, and will probably turn round when she reaches the corner.

No, she hasn't turned. Her black dress has flashed before my eyes for the last time, her steps have died away.

Farewell, my treasure!

NEIGHBOURS

PETER IVASHIN was in very bad humour. His unmarried sister had gone to live with Vlasich, a married man. Somehow hoping to shake off the irksome, depressed mood which obsessed him indoors and out of doors, he would summon up his sense of fair play and all his high-minded, worthy principles. (Hadn't he always stood out for free love?) But it was no use and he could never help reaching the same conclusion as stupid Nanny: his sister had behaved badly, Vlasich had stolen his sister. It was all most distressing.

His mother stayed closeted in her room all day, Nanny spoke in whispers and kept sighing, his aunt was on the point of leaving every day, so they kept bringing her suitcases into the hall and then taking them back to her room. In house, courtyard and garden it was as quiet as if they had a corpse laid out. Aunt, servants, even the peasants . . . all seemed to give Ivashin enigmatic, baffled looks as if to say that his sister had been seduced and what was he going to do about it? And he blamed himself for doing nothing, though what he should actually *be* doing he had no idea.

Thus six days passed. On the afternoon of the seventh, a Sunday, a messenger rode over with a letter. The address was in a familiar feminine hand: 'Her Excell. Mrs. Anna Ivashin.' Ivashin rather felt that there was something provocative, defiant and liberal about the envelope, the handwriting and that unfinished word 'Excell.'. And female liberalism is intolerant, pitiless and harsh.

'She'd rather die than give in to her unhappy mother and ask forgiveness,' thought Ivashin, taking the letter to his mother.

Mother was lying on her bed fully clothed. Seeing her son, she abruptly sat up and patted the grey hairs which had strayed from under her cap.

'What is it, what is it?' she asked impatiently.

'This came,' said her son, handing over the letter.

The name Zina, even the word 'she', were not spoken in that house. They talked of Zina impersonally: 'this was sent,' 'a departure took place.' The mother recognized her daughter's writing, her face grew ugly and disagreeable, and the grey hairs once more escaped from her cap.

'Never!' she said, gesticulating as if the letter had scorched her fingers. 'No, no, never! Nothing would induce me.'

The mother sobbed hysterically in her grief and shame. She obviously wanted to read the letter, but pride would not permit her. Ivashin realized that he ought to open it himself and read it out, but he suddenly felt angrier than he had ever felt in his life and he rushed out into the yard.

'Say there will be no answer!' he shouted to the messenger. 'No answer, I say! Tell her that, you swine!'

He tore up the letter. Then tears came into his eyes and he went out into the fields, feeling cruel, guilty and wretched.

He was only twenty-seven years old, but he was already fat, he dressed like an old man in loose, roomy clothes and was short of breath. He had all the qualities of an old bachelor landowner. He never fell in love, never thought of marriage, and the only people he was fond of were his mother, his sister, Nanny and Vasilyich the gardener. He liked a good meal, his afternoon nap and conversation about politics or lofty abstractions. He had taken a university degree in his time, but had come to think of that as a sort of conscription incumbent on young men between eighteen and twenty-five years of age. Anyway, the thoughts which now daily haunted his mind . . . they had nothing to do with the university and his course of studies.

In the fields it was hot and still, as if rain was in the offing. The wood was steaming, and there was an oppressive, fragrant smell of pines and rotting leaves. Ivashin kept stopping to wipe his wet brow. He inspected his winter corn and his spring corn, went round his clover field, and twice chased off a partridge and her chicks at the edge of the wood. And all the time he was conscious that this insufferable situation could not go on for ever, that he must end it one way or the other. He might end it stupidly and brutally somehow, but end it he must.

How, though? What could he do, he wondered, casting supplicatory glances at sky and trees as if begging their help.

But sky and trees were mute, nor were high-minded principles of any avail. Common sense suggested that the agonizing problem admitted only a stupid solution and that today's scene with the messenger was not the last of its kind. He was afraid to think what might happen next.

The sun was setting as he made his way home, now feeling the problem to be utterly insoluble. To accept what had happened was impossible, but it was equally impossible not to accept it and there was no middle way. Removing his hat, he fanned himself with his handkerchief and was walking down the road with over a mile to go when he heard a ringing behind him. It was an ingenious, highly successful combination of bells and chimes which sounded like tinkling glass. Only one person went abroad with this tintinnabulation: Inspector Medovsky of the police, a former hussar officer who had wasted his substance and had a pretty rough time, an invalid and a distant relative of Ivashin's. He was an old friend of the family and had a fatherly affection for Zina, whom he much admired.

'I was just coming to see you,' he said as he caught Ivashin up. 'Get in and I'll give you a lift.'

He was smiling and looked cheerful, clearly not yet aware that Zina had gone to live with Vlasich. He might have been informed, but if so he hadn't believed it. Ivashin found himself in an awkward situation.

'You're most welcome,' he muttered, blushing until tears came into his eyes and uncertain what lie to tell or how to tell it.

'Delighted,' he went on, trying to smile, 'but, er, Zina's away and Mother's ill.'

'What a pity,' said the Inspector, looking at Ivashin thoughtfully. 'And I was hoping to spend an evening with you. Where has Zina gone?'

'To the Sinitskys', and then she wanted to go on to a convent, I think. I don't know definitely.'

The Inspector talked a little longer, then turned back, and Ivashin walked home, horrified to think what the other would feel when he learnt the truth. Ivashin imagined his feelings and savoured them as he entered the house.

'Lord help us,' he thought.

Only his aunt was taking afternoon tea in the dining-room. Her face held its usual expression suggestive of a weak, defenceless woman, but one who would not permit herself to be insulted. Ivashin sat at the far end of the table (he disliked his aunt) and began drinking his tea in silence.

'Your mother missed lunch again today,' said his aunt. 'You might bear it in mind, Peter. Starving herself to death won't cure her troubles.'

Ivashin found it absurd for his aunt to meddle in other people's business and make her own departure depend on Zina's having left home. He felt like saying something rude, but restrained himself— realizing even as he did so that the time had come for action and that he could let things slide no longer. It was a matter of either doing something straight away or of falling down, screaming and banging his head on the floor. He pictured Vlasich and Zina, both free-thinking, both well pleased with themselves, kissing under some maple-tree, and then his seven days' accumulated depression and anger all seemed to topple over on Vlasich.

'One man seduces and abducts my sister,' he thought. 'A second will come and cut my mother's throat, a third will set fire to the house or burgle us: and all this under the mask of friendship, lofty principles and sufferings.'

'I won't have it!' Ivashin suddenly shouted, thumping the table.

He jumped up and ran out of the dining-room. His estate-manager's horse was saddled up in the stables, so he mounted it and galloped off to see Vlasich.

Stormy emotions raged within him. He felt the urge to do something striking and impetuous even if it meant regretting it for the rest of his life. Should he call Vlasich a blackguard, slap his face, challenge him to a duel? But Vlasich wasn't the sort who fights duels. As for calling him a blackguard and slapping his face, that would only increase his wretchedness and make him retreat further inside himself. These miserable, meek specimens are the limit, they are more trouble than anyone. They get away with murder. When a miserable man counters a well-deserved reproach with his look of profound guilt and sickly smile, when he submissively bows his head before you . . . then, it seems, Justice herself has not the heart to strike.

'Never mind,' decided Ivashin. 'I'll horsewhip him in Zina's presence and I'll give him a piece of my mind.'

He rode through his woodland and scrub, and imagined Zina trying to justify what she had done by talking of women's rights, of the freedom of the individual, and by saying that there is no difference between being married in church and being a common-law wife. Just like a woman, she would argue about things she didn't understand, and she would probably end up by asking what this had to do with him and what right he had to interfere.

'True, I haven't any right,' muttered Ivashin. 'But so much the better. The ruder, the more in the wrong I am the better.'

The air was sultry, clouds of gnats hung low above the ground and peewits wept piteously in the scrub. There was every sign of rain, yet not a cloud in the sky. Crossing the boundary of his estate, Ivashin galloped over a level, smooth field—he often took this way, and he knew every bush and hollow. That object looming far ahead of him in the twilight like a dark cliff . . . it was a red church. He could picture it all in the smallest detail, even the plaster on the gate and the calves which were always browsing on the hedge. Nearly a mile from the church, on the right, was the dark copse belonging to Count Koltovich and beyond that copse Vlasich's land began.

From behind church and Count's copse a huge black cloud advanced with white lightnings flashing on it.

'Well, here we are, Lord help us,' thought Ivashin.

The horse soon tired of the pace and Ivashin tired too. The thunder-head glared at him, apparently advising him to turn back, and he felt a little scared.

'I'll prove they're in the wrong,' he tried to reassure himself. 'They'll talk of free love and freedom of the individual, yet freedom means self-control, surely, not giving way to passions. It's sheer licentiousness, their freedom is.'

Here was the Count's large pond, dark blue and glowering under the cloud, breathing damp and slime. Near the log-path two willows— one old, one young—were leaning tenderly into each other. Ivashin and Vlasich had walked past this very spot a fortnight ago, softly singing the students' song about it being love that makes the world go round. Wretched song!

Thunder rumbled as Ivashin rode through the wood, and the trees roared and bent in the wind. He must hurry. From the copse to Vlasich's estate he had less than a mile of meadow to cover along a path flanked on both sides by old birch-trees. Like Vlasich they were a wretched, dismal sight, being every bit as spindly and lanky as their owner. Heavy rain rustled in birches and grass. The wind suddenly dropped, there was a whiff of wet earth and poplars. Then Vlasich's yellow acacia hedge, also lanky and spindly, came into view. At the point where some lattice-work had collapsed his neglected orchard appeared.

No longer thinking about slapping Vlasich's face or horsewhipping him, Ivashin did not know what he was going to do at the man's house. He felt nervous. He was afraid on his own behalf and on his sister's— scared at the thought of seeing her any moment. How would she behave towards her brother? What would the two of them talk about? And should he not turn back while there was yet time? Thus brooding, he galloped down the avenue of lime-trees to the house, rounded the broad lilac bushes—and suddenly saw Vlasich.

Bare-headed, in cotton shirt and top-boots, stooping under the rain, Vlasich was going from a corner of the house towards the front door followed by a workman with a hammer and a box of nails. They must have been mending a shutter which had been banging in the wind. Vlasich saw Ivashin and stopped.

'Is it you Peter?' he smiled. 'What a very nice surprise.'

'Yes, it's me, as you see,' said Ivashin quietly, brushing off rain-drops with both hands.

'Well, what a good idea. Delighted,' said Vlasich, but did not hold out his hand, obviously hesitating and waiting for the other to make the first move.

'Good for the oats, this,' he said with a glance at the sky.

'Quite so.'

They went silently into the house. A door on the right led from the hall into another hall and then into a reception room, and there was a door on the left into the small room occupied by Vlasich's manager in winter. Ivashin and Vlasich went into that room.

'Where did the rain catch you?' Vlasich asked.

'Not far from here, quite close to the house.'

Ivashin sat on the bed, glad of the rain's noise, glad that the room was dark. It was better that way—not so unnerving, and he need not look his companion in the eye. His rage had passed, but he felt afraid and vexed with himself. He had got off to a bad start, he felt, and his trip boded ill.

For some time neither man spoke and they pretended to be listening to the rain.

'Thanks, Peter,' began Vlasich, clearing his throat. 'Most obliged to you for coming. It's generous of you, very decent. I appreciate it, I value it greatly, believe you me.'

He looked out of the window and continued, standing in the middle of the room.

'Somehow everything happened secretly as if we were keeping you in the dark. Knowing that we might have hurt you, made you angry . . . it has cast a cloud over our happiness all this time. But let me defend myself. It was not that we didn't trust you, that wasn't why we were so secretive. In the first place, it all happened on the spur of the moment and there was no time to discuss things. Secondly, this is such an intimate, sensitive business and it was awkward to bring in a third party, even one as close to us as you. But the real point is, we were banking heavily on your generosity all along. You're the most generous of men, you're such a frightfully decent chap. I'm infinitely obliged to you. If you should ever need my life, then come and take it.'

Vlasich spoke in a low, hollow, deep voice, all on one note like a fog-horn. He was obviously upset. Ivashin felt that it was his turn to speak now, and that for him to listen in silence really would be to pose as the most generous and frightfully decent of nit-wits—which was not what he had come for.

He got quickly to his feet.

'Look here, Gregory,' he panted in a low voice, 'you know I liked you—couldn't want a better husband for my sister. But what's happened is frightful, it doesn't bear thinking of.'

'What's so horrible, though?' asked Vlasich in quaking tones. 'It would be horrible if we had done wrong, but we haven't, have we?'

'Look here, Gregory, you know I'm not the least bit stuffy, but— well, I'm sorry to be so blunt, but you have both been very selfish, to my way of thinking. I shan't say anything to Zina about this, of course, it would only upset her, but you ought to know that Mother's sufferings are practically indescribable.'

'Yes, very lamentable,' sighed Vlasich. 'We foresaw that, Peter, but what on earth could we do about it? Just because your actions upset someone it doesn't mean they're wrong. It can't be helped. Any serious step you take . . . it's bound to upset somebody. If you went to fight for freedom that would hurt your mother too, it can't be helped. If you make your family's peace of mind your main priority it means good-bye to any idealism in life.'

Lightning flared beyond the window and the flash seemed to switch Vlasich's thoughts into a different channel. He sat down by Ivashin's side and started saying things which would have been far better left unsaid.

'I worship your sister, Peter,' he said. 'Visiting your place, I always felt I was on pilgrimage. I absolutely idolized Zina and now I worship her more each day. She is more than a wife to me! More sacred, I tell you!'

Vlasich waved his arms.

'I adore her. Since she has been living here I have entered my house as if it were a shrine. She is a rare, an outstanding, a most frightfully decent woman.'

What a ghastly rigmarole, thought Ivashin, irked by the word 'woman'.

'Why don't you get married properly?' he asked. 'How much does your wife want for a divorce?'

'Seventy-five thousand.'

'That's a bit much, but why not beat her down?'

'She won't give an inch. She's an awful woman, old man.'

Vlasich sighed. 'I never told you about her before, it has been such a hideous memory, but as the subject has come up I'll go on. I married her on a decent, chivalrous impulse. In our regiment, if you want the details, a certain battalion commander took up with her as a girl of eighteen—simply seduced her, in other words, lived with her a couple of months and then dropped her.

'She was in a most ghastly plight, old man. She was ashamed to go home to her parents, who wouldn't have her anyway, and her lover had deserted her. What could she do—set up as barrack-room whore? My fellow-officers were horrified. Not that they were little plaster saints themselves, but this was such a rotten show, even they found it a bit thick! Besides, no one in the regiment could stand that colonel. All the second lieutenants and ensigns were furious and they decided to do him in the eye by getting up a subscription for the wretched girl, see? So we junior officers met in conclave and each started putting down his five or ten roubles, when I had a rush of blood to the head. The situation seemed to cry out for some heroic gesture, so I dashed off to the girl and said how sorry I was—I spoke with tremendous feeling. On my way to see her, and then as I was speaking, I loved her passionately as a woman insulted and injured. Yes, quite so.

'Well—the upshot was, I proposed a week later. My superiors and comrades found my marriage unbecoming to an officer's dignity. That only added fuel to the flames, though. So I wrote a great epistle, see? I argued that what I had done should be inscribed in regimental history in letters of gold, and all that. I sent the letter to my colonel with copies to my brother-officers. Now, I was a bit upset, of course, and I did rather overstep the mark. I was asked to leave the regiment. I have a rough copy hidden somewhere, I'll let you read it some time. It's written with real feeling—I enjoyed some sublime moments of sheer decency, as you'll see. I resigned my commission and came here with my wife. My father had left a debt or two and I had no money, but my wife embarked on a social whirl from the start, dressing up and playing cards, so I had to mortgage my estate. She was no better than she should be if you see what I mean, and you are the only one of my neighbours who hasn't been her lover. About two years later I gave her some money—all I had at the time—to go away, and away she went to town. Yes, quite so.

'Now I'm paying the ghastly creature twelve hundred a year. There is a certain fly, old man, that puts its larva on a spider's back and the spider can't get rid of it. The grub attaches itself and drinks the spider's heart's blood. That's just how this woman fixed on me. She's a regular vampire. She loaths and scorns me for my folly: for marrying someone like her, that is. She despises my chivalry. A wise man dropped her, says she, and a fool picked her up. Only a wretched half-wit could do what I did, she reckons. It really is a bit hard to take, old man. And by the way, old man, I've had a pretty raw deal, one way and another, it really has got me down.'

Ivashin became quite mystified as he listened to Vlasich. What ever could Zina see in the man? He was not young (he was forty-one), he was lean, lanky, narrow-chested, long-nosed and his beard was turning grey. He spoke like a fog-horn, he had a sickly smile and an ungainly trick of flapping his arms about when he was talking. Instead of being healthy, handsome, manly, urbane and good-humoured, he was just vaguely dim so far as looks went. He dressed so badly, everything about him was so dismal, he rejected poetry and painting as 'irrelevant to modern needs'—didn't appreciate them, in other words. Music left him cold. He was a poor farmer. His estate was in utter chaos, and was mortgaged too. He was paying twelve per cent on a second mortgage and on top of that he owed another ten thousand in personal loans. When his interest or alimony fell due he went round cadging money with the air of a man whose house is on fire. At these times he'd say oh, to hell with it, and he would sell up his whole winter store of firewood for five roubles or a straw rick for three, and then have his garden fence or some old seed-bed frames used to heat his stores. Pigs had ruined his pastures, the villagers' cattle trampled his saplings, and each winter there were fewer and fewer of his old trees left. Beehives and rusty pails bestrewed his vegetable plot and garden. He lacked all talents and gifts, even the humble knack of leading an average life. In practical matters he was an innocent, a weakling easily cheated and done down. No wonder the peasants said he was 'a bit touched'.

He was a liberal and was thought quite a firebrand in the county, but in this too he wore a humdrum air. There was no panache or verve about his free-thinking. Whether indignant, irate or enthusiastic, he was all on one note, so to speak—it all lacked flair, it fell so very flat. Even at times of extreme agitation he never raised his head or stood up straight. But the main snag was his trick of trotting out even his finest and loftiest ideas in a way that made them seem hackneyed and dated. Whenever he embarked on a sluggish, portentous-sounding exegesis, all about impulses of sublime integrity and the best years of his life, whenever he raved about young folk always being, and always having been, in the van of social progress, whenever he condemned Russians for donning their dressing-gowns at thirty and forgetting their *alma mater*'s traditions, it all sounded like something you had read in a book long, long ago. When you stayed in his house he would put a Pisarev or Darwin on your bedside table, and if you said you had already read them he'd go and fetch a Dobrolyubov!

In the county this rated as free-thinking and many thought it an innocent, harmless quirk. Yet it made him profoundly unhappy. For him it was that maggot to which he had just alluded and which had fastened on him to batten on his life's blood. There was his past with that weird marriage *à la* Dostoyevsky, those long letters and the copies written in a poor, illegible hand but with great emotion, there were the interminable misunderstandings, explanations, disillusionments. Then there were his debts, his second mortgage, his wife's alimony and his monthly loans, none of which was any good to anybody, either him or anyone else. Now, in the present, he was still as restless as he always had been, he still sought some great mission in life and he still couldn't mind his own business. There were still these long letters and copies of them in season and out of season, there were still those exhausting, hackneyed tirades about the village community, reviving local handicrafts, starting up cheese-dairies—each speech exactly like the one before as if they were machine-made rather than hatched by a live brain. Finally, there was this scandal over Zina which might end heaven knew how.

And the thing was, Zina was so young, she was only twenty-two. She was pretty, elegant, high-spirited, she liked laughing, chattering, arguing, she was crazy about music. She was good with clothes and books, she knew how to create a civilized environment: at home she would never have put up with a room like this with its smell of boots and cheap vodka. She was a liberal too, but her free-thinking seemed to brim over with energy, with the pride of a young girl, vigorous, bold, eagerly yearning to excel and show more originality than others.

How *could* she love a Vlasich?

'The man's so quixotic, so pig-headed, so fanatical, so lunatic,' thought Ivashin. 'But she's as wishy-washy, characterless and pliable as me. She and I both give in quickly, we don't stand up for ourselves. She fell in love with him—but then I like him too, don't I, in spite of everything?'

Ivashin thought Vlasich a good, decent man, but narrow and one-sided. In Vlasich's emotions and sufferings, in his whole life, Ivashin saw no lofty aims, either near or distant, he saw only boredom and lack

of *savoir-vivre*. Vlasich's self-martyrdom, what he called his achievements and decent impulses . . . they struck Ivashin as so much wasted
effort like firing off purposeless blank shots and using up a lot of
powder. As for Vlasich's obsession with the outstanding integrity and
rectitude of his own mental processes, that struck Ivashin as naïve—
morbid, even. Then there was the man's lifelong knack of confusing the
trivial and the sublime, his making a stupid marriage and regarding
that as a stupendous feat—and then having affairs with women and
calling them the triumph of ideals or something. None of it made any
kind of sense.

Still, Ivashin did like him and felt that there was a certain power
about him. He somehow never had the heart to contradict the man.

Vlasich sat down very near Ivashin in the dark, wanting to talk to
the sound of the rain. He had already cleared his throat to tell some
other long story like the history of his marriage, but Ivashin couldn't
bear to hear it, tormented as he was by the thought of seeing his sister
any moment.

'Yes, you have had a raw deal,' he said gently. 'But I'm sorry, we're
digressing, you and I. This is beside the point.'

'Yes, yes, quite,' said Vlasich, rising to his feet. 'So let's get back to
the subject. Our conscience is clear, Peter, I can tell you. We aren't
married, but that we're man and wife in every real sense is neither for
me to argue nor for you to hear. You're as free from prejudice as I am,
so there can be no disagreement between us on that score, thank God.
As for our future, you have no cause for apprehension. I shall work
my fingers to the bone, I'll work day and night—I'll do all in my
power to make Zina happy, in other words. Her life will be a beautiful
thing. Shall I pull it off, you ask? I shall, old boy. When a man's
obsessed with one idea every minute of the day it isn't hard for him to
get his way. But let's go and see Zina, we must give her a nice surprise.'

Ivashin's heart pounded. He stood up and followed Vlasich into the
hall, and then into the drawing-room. The huge, grim room contained
only an upright piano and a long row of antique bronzed chairs on
which no one ever sat. A single candle burnt on the piano. From the
drawing-room they went silently into the dining-room. This too was
spacious and uncomfortable. In the centre of the room was a round,
two-leaved table with six legs. There was only one candle. A clock in a
large red case like an icon-holder showed half past two.

Vlasich opened the door into the next room.

'Peter's here, Zina,' he said.

At once rapid footsteps were heard and Zina came into the dining-room—a tall, buxom, very pale girl, looking exactly as Ivashin had last seen her at home in her black skirt and red blouse with a large buckle on the belt. She put one arm round her brother and kissed him on the temple.

'What a storm!' she said. 'Gregory went off somewhere and I was left alone in the house.'

She betrayed no embarrassment, and she looked at her brother as frankly and openly as at home. Looking at her, Ivashin too ceased to feel embarrassed.

'But you aren't afraid of thunder, are you?' he said, sitting down at the table.

'No, but the rooms are so vast here. It's an old house, and the thunder makes it all rattle like a cupboardful of crockery.

'Altogether it's a nice little house,' she went on, sitting opposite her brother. 'Every room has some delightful association—Gregory's grandfather shot himself in my room, believe it or not.'

'We'll have some money in August and I'll do up the cottage in the garden,' said Vlasich.

'Somehow one always thinks of that grandfather when it thunders,' Zina went on. 'And in this dining-room a man was flogged to death.'

'It's a fact,' Vlasich confirmed, gazing wide-eyed at Ivashin. 'Some time in the Forties this place was leased to a certain Olivier, a French-man. His daughter's portrait is lying about in our attic now: a very pretty girl. This Olivier, my father told me, despised Russians as dunces and mocked them cruelly. For instance, he insisted that when the priest walked past the manor he should remove his cap a quarter of a mile away, and whenever the Olivier family drove through the village the church bells had to be rung. Serfs and small fry got even shorter shrift, of course. Now, one day one of the cheeriest members of the Russian tramping fraternity chanced to roll along—the lad had a bit of Gogol's theological student Khoma Brut about him. He asked for a night's lodging, the managers liked him and they let him stay in the office.

'There are a lot of versions of the story. Some say the boy incited the peasants, while others have it that Olivier's daughter fell in love with the boy. What really happened I don't know, except that Olivier called him in here one fine evening, cross-examined him and then gave orders to flog him. The master sits at this table drinking claret, see, while the grooms are beating the student. Olivier must have been trying to

wring something out of him. By morning the lad was dead of torture
and they hid the body somewhere. They are said to have thrown it in
Koltovich's pond. An official inquiry was started, but the Frenchman
paid several thousand in the right quarter and went off to Alsace. His
lease ran out just then and that was the end of the matter.'

'What scoundrels,' shuddered Zina.

'My father remembered Olivier and his daughter well. He said she
was a remarkably beautiful girl, and eccentric to boot. Myself, I think
the young fellow did both: incited the peasants *and* took the daughter's
fancy. Perhaps, even, he wasn't a theological student at all, but someone travelling incognito.'

Zina grew pensive. The story of the student and the beautiful French
girl had obviously run away with her imagination. Her appearance
hadn't changed at all in the last week, Ivashin thought, she had only
grown a little paler. She looked calm and normal as if she and her
brother were now visiting Vlasich together. But some change had taken
place in himself, Ivashin felt. The fact was that he had been able to
discuss absolutely anything with her when she was still living at home,
but now he couldn't even bring himself to ask her quite simply how
she was getting on. The question seemed clumsy, superfluous. And
a similar change must have affected her, for she was in no hurry to
mention their mother, their home, her affair with Vlasich. She didn't
try to justify herself, nor did she say that free unions are better than
being married in church, but she remained calm, quietly pondering the
story of Olivier.

Why, though, had they suddenly spoken about Olivier?

'You both got your shoulders wet in the rain,' Zina said with a happy
smile, touched by this small resemblance between her brother and Vlasich.

Ivashin felt the full bitterness and horror of his situation. He remembered his deserted home, the closed piano and Zina's bright little room
where no one went any more. He remembered that her small footprints had vanished from their garden paths and that now no one went
bathing with a noisy laugh before afternoon tea. The things that had
increasingly claimed his affections since earliest childhood, that he used
to like contemplating sometimes when sitting in a stuffy classroom or
lecture-hall—serenity, integrity, joy, everything that filled a home with
life and light . . . those things had gone without trace, they had vanished
and merged with the crude, clumsy story of some battalion commander,
chivalrous subaltern, loose woman and grandfather who had shot
himself.

To start talking about his mother, to think that there could be any return to the past . . . that would mean misunderstanding what was perfectly clear.

Ivashin's eyes brimmed with tears and his hand trembled where it lay on the table. Zina guessed what he was thinking about, and her eyes also reddened and glistened.

'Come here, Gregory,' she said to Vlasich.

Both went over to the window and started whispering. From Vlasich's way of bending down towards her and from her way of looking at him Ivashin again realized that the matter was settled, that it couldn't be mended and that there was nothing more to be said. Zina went out.

'Well, old boy,' said Vlasich, after a short pause, rubbing his hands and smiling. 'Just now I said we were happy, but that was a bit of poetic licence, so to speak. We haven't yet experienced happiness, in fact. Zina has been thinking of you and her mother all the time and she has been suffering, while I've suffered too, watching her. Hers is a free, undaunted nature, but it's hard to go against the grain, you know—besides which she's young. The servants call her Miss. It seems a trifle, but it upsets her. That's the way of it, old man.'

Zina brought in a dish of strawberries. She was followed by a little maidservant, seemingly meek and downtrodden, who put a jug of milk on the table and gave a very low bow. She had something in common with the antique furniture which was comparably torpid and dreary.

The sound of rain had ceased. Ivashin ate strawberries while Vlasich and Zina looked at him in silence. The time had come for a conversation pointless but unavoidable, and all three were depressed by the prospect. Ivashin's eyes again brimmed with tears. He pushed the bowl away, saying that it was time to go home, or else he would be late and it might rain again. The moment had arrived when it behoved Zina to speak of her family and her new life.

'How are things at home?' she asked rapidly, her pale face trembling. 'How's Mother?'

'Well, you know Mother—' answered Ivashin, not looking at her.

'You have thought a lot about what's happened, Peter,' she said, taking her brother by the sleeve, and he realized how hard it was for her to speak. 'You have given it a lot of thought, so tell me: is there any chance Mother will ever accept Gregory . . . and the situation in general?'

She stood close to her brother, facing him, and he marvelled at her beauty, and at his own apparent failure to notice it before. His sister, this sensitive, elegant girl who looked so much like their mother, now lived with Vlasich and shared Vlasich's home with a torpid maid and six-legged table in a house where a man had been flogged to death. And now she wouldn't be going home with her brother, but would stay the night here. All of this struck Ivashin as incredibly absurd.

'You know Mother,' he said, not answering her question. 'In my view you should conform with . . . you should, er, do something, sort of ask her forgiveness or——'

'But asking forgiveness would mean pretending we had done wrong. I don't mind telling lies to comfort Mother, but it won't work, will it? I know Mother.

'Well, we shall just have to see,' said Zina, cheering up now that the most unpleasant bit was over. 'We shall just have to put up with it for five or ten years and see what happens then.'

She took her brother's arm and pressed against his shoulder as they went through the dark hall.

They went on to the steps. Ivashin said good-bye, mounted his horse and started off at a walk. Zina and Vlasich walked a little way with him. It was quiet and warm, there was a delicious smell of hay. Between the clouds stars blazed vividly in the sky. Vlasich's old garden, witness of so many distressing episodes in its time, slumbered in the enveloping darkness and riding through it was saddening, somehow.

'This afternoon Zina and I experienced a number of truly sublime moments,' said Vlasich. 'I read her a first-rate article on the agricultural resettlement problem. You really must read it, old man, it has outstanding integrity. I couldn't resist writing to the author, care of the editor. I wrote only a single line: "I thank you and firmly shake your honest hand."'

Ivashin wanted to tell him not to meddle in other people's business for heaven's sake, but remained silent.

Vlasich walked by his right stirrup, Zina by the left. Both seemed to have forgotten that they had to go back home, that it was damp, that they had nearly reached Koltovich's copse. They were expecting something from him, Ivashin felt, but what it was they expected they didn't know themselves and he felt desperately sorry for them. Now, as they walked by his horse so meekly and pensively, he felt absolutely convinced that they were unhappy—that they never could be happy— and their love seemed a deplorable and irrevocable mistake. Pitying them and aware that he could do nothing to help them, he fell prey to weakmindedness which made him ready for any sacrifice, could he but rid himself of this onerous feeling of compassion.

'I'll come and stay the night with you sometimes,' he said.

But that looked like giving in to them and didn't satisfy him. When they stopped to say good-bye near Koltovich's copse he leant towards Zina and touched her shoulder.

'You're quite right, Zina,' he said. 'You have done the right thing.'

To stop himself saying more and bursting into tears, he lashed his horse and galloped into the wood. Riding into darkness, he looked back, and saw Vlasich and Zina walking home along the path—he with long strides, she at his side with quick, jerky steps. They were conducting an animated conversation.

'I'm like a silly old woman,' thought Ivashin. 'I went there to solve a problem, but only complicated it. Ah well, never mind.'

He felt depressed. When the wood ended he rode at a walk, then stopped his horse near the pond. He wanted to sit and think. On the far side of the pond the rising moon was reflected as a red streak and there were hollow rumbles of thunder somewhere. Ivashin gazed steadily at the water, picturing his sister's despair, her anguished pallor and the dry eyes with which she would hide her degradation from the world. He imagined her pregnancy, their mother's death and funeral, Zina's horror. Nothing but death could break that proud, superstitious old woman. Appalling visions of the future appeared before him on the dark, smooth water, and amid pale feminine figures he saw himself— cowardly, weak, hunted-looking.

On the pond's right bank about a hundred yards away stood some dark, unmoving object—was it a man or a tall tree-stump? Ivashin remembered the murdered student who had been thrown into this pond.

'Olivier behaved cruelly,' he thought, gazing at the dark, ghostly figure. 'But at least he did solve his problem one way or the other, while I have solved nothing, I've only made a worse mess. He did and said what he thought, whereas I do and say what I don't think. Besides, I don't really know what I do think——'

He rode up to the dark figure. It was an old, rotting post, the relic of some building.

From Koltovich's copse and garden came a strong whiff of lily-of-the-valley and honey-laden herbs. Ivashin rode along the edge of the pond, gazed mournfully at the water and remembered his past life.

So far he had not done or said what he thought, he concluded, and others had repaid him in like coin, which was why all life now seemed as dark as this pond with its reflections of the night sky and its tangled water-weed. There was no mending matters either, he thought.

AN ANONYMOUS STORY

I

FOR reasons which I cannot at present specify I was compelled to take a job as footman to a St. Petersburg civil servant called George Orlov, a man of about thirty-five.

I entered Orlov's service because of his father, the well-known politician, whom I considered a serious enemy to my cause. I reckoned to study the father's plans and intentions in detail while living with the son: by overhearing conversations, and by finding papers and jottings on his desk.

The electric bell usually trilled in my footman's quarters at about eleven o'clock in the morning to inform me that my master was awake. When I went into his bedroom with his clean clothes and boots, Orlov would be sitting immobile in his bed, looking not so much sleepy as exhausted by sleeping, and staring fixedly without any sign of pleasure at his awakening. I would help him to dress while he submitted to me reluctantly and silently, ignoring my existence. Then, his head wet after washing, smelling of fresh scent, he would go into the dining-room for coffee. He sat at table, drank his coffee and leafed through newspapers, while Polya the maid and I stood by the door, respectfully watching him. Two adults were compelled to pay the gravest attention to a third drinking his coffee and munching his rusks: all very absurd and barbarous, no doubt, but I found nothing degrading in having to stand by that door though I was Orlov's equal in social standing and education.

I had incipient tuberculosis and there were a few other things wrong with me: a sight worse, perhaps, than tuberculosis. Whether it was the effect of illness, or of some new change of outlook which eluded my notice at the time, I was obsessed day in day out by a passionate, hypersensitive craving for ordinary everyday life. I yearned for peace of mind, health, fresh air, plenty to eat. I was becoming a day-dreamer, and as such I did not know exactly what I wanted. I might feel an urge to go to a monastery and to sit day after day by the window, gazing at trees and fields. Or I would imagine myself buying a dozen acres and settling down as a country squire. Or else I would swear to take up academic work and make a point of becoming a professor at a provincial university. As a retired naval lieutenant I had visions of the sea, of our squadron, of the corvette on which I had sailed round the world. I wanted to experience once again the indescribable sensation of walking in a tropical forest, or of gazing at the sunset in the Bay of Bengal, when you swoon with ecstasy and feel homesick: both at the same time. I dreamt of mountains, women, music. With childlike curiosity I scrutinized people's faces and hung on their voices. As I stood by the door watching Orlov drink his coffee, I felt less like a servant than a man for whom everything on earth, even an Orlov, held some interest.

Orlov was a typical St. Petersburger in appearance, with narrow shoulders, elongated waist, sunken temples, eyes of indeterminate hue and sparse, faintly tinted vegetation on head, chin and upper lip. His face was well-groomed, worn, disagreeable: particularly disagreeable when he was thinking or sleeping. It is hardly necessary to describe a commonplace appearance, though. Besides, St. Petersburg is not Spain, a man's looks don't mean anything there even in affairs of the heart, being of value only to imposing servants and coachmen. If I have mentioned Orlov's face and hair, it is only because there was one notable feature about his looks, to wit: when he picked up a newspaper or book, whatever it might be, or when he met people, whoever *they* might be, his eyes began to smile ironically and his whole face took on an air of gentle mockery free from malice. Before reading or hearing anything he always held this irony at the ready, as a savage holds his shield. It was an irony of habit, an irony of the old school, and it had recently been coming into his face without any effort of will, probably, but as if by reflex. More of that later, though.

At about half past twelve he would take up a brief-case stuffed with papers and drive off, with an ironical air, to work. He would have his meal out and return after eight. I would light the lamp and candles in his study, and he would sit in a low chair, stretching his legs out on to another chair, and start reading in this sprawling position. He brought new books almost every day, or had them sent from the shops, and a mass of books in three languages (not counting Russian), already read and abandoned, lay in the corners and under the bed in my quarters. He read unusually fast. 'Tell me what you read,' it is said, 'and I shall tell you who you are.' That may be true, but it is absolutely impossible to judge an Orlov by the books which he reads. It was all such a hotchpotch, what with philosophy, French novels, political economy, finance, new poets and *Intermediary* editions. He read it all with equal speed, and always with that same ironical look in his eyes.

After ten o'clock he would dress carefully—often in evening clothes, very rarely in his official uniform—and leave the house. He would return towards morning.

I lived there peaceably and quietly, and there were no clashes between us. As a rule he ignored my existence, and he spoke to me without that ironical look on his face—not considering me human, obviously.

Only once did I see him angry. One evening, a week after I had entered his service, he came back from some dinner at about nine o'clock. His expression was bad-tempered and tired.

'There's a nasty smell in the flat,' he said as I followed him into the study to light the candles.

'But it's quite fresh in here, sir.'

'It stinks, I tell you,' he repeated irritably.

'I open the casement windows every day.'

'Don't you answer me back, you oaf!' he shouted.

I took umbrage, and was about to object. God knows how it would have ended but for the intervention of Polya, who knew her master better than I did.

'Yes, really, what a nasty smell,' she said, raising her eyebrows. 'Where can it come from? Stephen, open the casements in the drawing-room and light the fire.'

She clucked and fussed, and went through all the rooms, rustling her skirts and swishing her sprayer. But Orlov's bad mood remained. Keeping his temper with obvious effort, he sat at his desk and quickly wrote a letter. He wrote several lines, then gave an angry snort, tore up the letter and began writing again.

'To hell with them!' he muttered. 'Do they credit me with a super-human memory?'

The letter was written at last. He got up from the desk and addressed me.

'You are to go to Znamensky Square and deliver this letter to Mrs. Zinaida Krasnovsky in person. But first ask the porter whether her husband—Mr. Krasnovsky, that is—has returned. If he has, keep the letter and come back. Hey, wait a moment! If she should ask whether I have anyone with me, tell her two gentlemen have been here since eight o'clock writing something.'

I went to Znamensky Square. The porter told me that Mr. Krasnovsky was not yet back, and I went up to the second floor. The door was opened by a tall, fat, dark-complexioned servant with black side-whiskers. Sleepily, apathetically, churlishly, as flunkey to flunkey, he asked what I wanted. Before I had time to answer a woman in a black dress came quickly into the hall from the drawing-room. She screwed up her eyes at me.

'Is Mrs. Krasnovsky in?' I asked.

'I am she.'

'A letter from Mr. Orlov.'

She unsealed the letter impatiently, held it in both hands, displaying her diamond rings, and began reading. I saw a white face with soft lines, a jutting chin, and long, dark lashes. She looked no more than twenty-five years old.

'Give him my regards and thank him,' she said when she had finished reading.

'Is anyone with Mr. Orlov?' she asked gently, happily, and as if ashamed to be mistrustful.

'Two gentlemen,' I answered. 'They are writing something.'

'Give him my regards and thank him,' she repeated, and went back silently, leaning her head on one side and reading the letter as she went.

I was meeting few women at the time, and this one, of whom I had only had a passing glimpse, made an impression on me. Walking home, remembering her face and delicate fragrance, I fell into a reverie. When I returned Orlov had left the house.

II

Well, I lived quietly and peaceably enough with my employer, and yet the pollution, the degrading element which I had so dreaded on becoming a footman . . . it was present and made itself felt every day. I was on bad terms with Polya. She was a sleek, spoilt little trollop who adored Orlov because he was the master and scorned me because I was the footman. To a real servant or a cook she was probably quite devastating, with her red cheeks, *retroussé* nose, screwed-up eyes and buxom build already verging on the plump. She powdered her face, she tinted her eyebrows and lips, she wore a corset, a bustle and a bangle made of coins. She walked with little tripping steps. When she walked she twisted or 'waggled' her shoulders and behind. Her rustling skirts, her creaking stays, her jingling bangle, this plebeian smell of lipstick, toilet-vinegar and scent stolen from the master . . . when I tidied the rooms with her of a morning, these things made me feel like her accomplice in some foul crime.

Whether because I did not help her to steal, or because I evinced no desire whatever to become her lover—which she probably took as an insult—or else, perhaps, because she sensed in me an alien being, she loathed me from the first day. My clumsiness, my unflunkeylike exterior, my illness . . . she found these things pitiful, and they disgusted her. I was coughing very badly at the time, and I occasionally kept her awake at night because her room was separated from mine by only a wooden screen.

'You kept me awake again,' she told me every morning. 'You ought to be in hospital, not in a gentleman's service.'

So sincerely did she think me not human, but a thing immeasurably beneath her, that she sometimes appeared before me wearing only her chemise like those Roman matrons who had no scruples about bathing in the presence of their slaves.

One lunch-time (we ordered soup and a roast from the restaurant every day) I was in a marvellous contemplative mood.

'Polya,' I asked her, 'do you believe in God?'

'Yes, of course I do.'

'Then you believe there will be a Day of Judgement?' I went on. 'And that we shall answer to God for all our misdeeds?'

She made no reply, only giving a scornful grimace. Now, as I looked at her smug, cold eyes, I saw that this well-integrated, perfectly rounded being was godless, conscienceless and lawless, and that I could never find a better paid accomplice should I ever require to commit murder, arson or burglary.

In this novel setting, unaccustomed as I was to being addressed curtly, and to the constant lying (saying 'the master's out' when he was in), I found my first week at Orlov's rather an ordeal. My valet's tail-coat made me feel as if I had donned a suit of armour. Later on I settled down. I performed my little services like any regular footman, I cleaned the rooms, I ran or drove around on errands. When Orlov did not wish to keep a rendezvous with Zinaida Krasnovsky, or when he forgot that he had promised to visit her, I would drive to Znamensky Square, deliver a note to her personally and tell lies. It all added up to something quite different from what I had envisaged on becoming a servant. Every day of my new life turned out a waste of time both for me and my cause, since Orlov never spoke of his father, nor did his guests either, and all I could learn about that well-known politician's activities was what I contrived, as I had previously contrived, to glean from newspapers and correspondence with my associates. The hundreds of notes and papers which I found in the study and read . . . they lacked even the remotest connection with what I was seeking. Orlov was absolutely indifferent to his father's much-bruited activity, and looked as if he had never even heard of it, or as if his father had died long ago.

III

We had guests every Thursday.

I would order a joint of beef from the restaurant and telephone Yeliseyev's for caviare, cheese, oysters and the like. I bought playing cards. Polya was busy all day preparing the tea things and the supper service. This little bout of activity did rather vary our idle lives, to be honest, and Thursdays were our most interesting days.

There would be three guests only. The most substantial of them—and the most interesting, perhaps—was called Pekarsky: a tall, gaunt person of about forty-five, with a long, hooked nose, a large, black beard and a bald pate. His eyes were big and bulging, and his facial expression was as grave and pensive as a Greek philosopher's. He worked on a railway board and at a bank, he was legal consultant to an important government institution, he was on business terms with a mass of private persons as trustee, chairman of official receivers and so on. His civil service rank was quite low, and he modestly termed himself a 'barrister', but his influence was enormous. A note or card from him was enough to have you received out of turn by a celebrated doctor, a railway director or an important official. One could obtain a pretty senior post through his patronage, it was said, or hush up any unpleasantness whatever. He rated as highly intelligent, but his was a most peculiar and odd sort of brain. He could multiply 213 by 373 in his head in a flash, or convert pounds sterling to German marks without a pencil and tables. He was well up in railway matters and finance, and the entire world of administration was an open book to him. In civil cases he was reckoned a pretty artful advocate, and he was an awkward customer to tangle with at law. Yet this rare intellect was utterly baffled by many things known even to the most limited intelligence. Why do people feel bored? Why do they weep, shoot themselves—and murder others, even? Why do they fret about things and events which don't concern them personally, and why do they laugh when they read Gogol or Shchedrin? All that was utterly beyond his ken. Everything abstract, everything evanescent in the sphere of thought and feeling . . . it was as mysterious and boring to him as music to one who has no ear. He took only the business view of people, dividing them into competent and incompetent. He had no other criterion. Honesty and integrity were merely signs of competence. Drinking, gambling and whoring were all right so long as they didn't interfere with business. Believing in God was rather stupid, but religion must be preserved, since the common people needed some restraining principle or else they wouldn't work. Punishments were only needed as a deterrent. There was no point in going away for one's holidays because life was quite all right in town. And so on. He was a widower without children, but he lived on as ample a scale as a family man, paying three thousand a year for his flat.

The second guest, Kukushkin, was young for the fairly senior rank which he held. He was a short man distinguished by the lack of proportion between his stout, podgy trunk and small, thin face: a highly disagreeable combination. His lips were puckered up, his little trimmed moustache looked as if it had been glued on with varnish. The creature had the manners of a lizard. He didn't enter a room, but rather slithered into it with mincing little steps, squirming and tittering, and he bared his teeth when he laughed. He was a clerk of special commissions to someone or other, and did nothing at all though he was paid a large salary: especially in summer when various assignments were invented for him. He was not so much a careerist to the marrow of his bones as, deeper still, to his last drop of blood, and a petty careerist to boot: one lacking in confidence, who had built his whole career on favours received. For the sake of some wretched foreign decoration, or of being mentioned in the newspapers as present with other august personages at some funeral or other service, he would stoop to any conceivable humiliation, beg, fawn and promise. He flattered Orlov and Pekarsky out of cowardice, considering them powerful, while he flattered Polya and me because we were in the service of an influential man. Whenever I helped him off with his coat he would titter and ask: 'Are you married, Stephen?' This was followed by scurrilous vulgarities by way of showing me special attention. Kukushkin flattered Orlov's weaknesses, his perversity and his complacency. To please Orlov he posed as an arrant cynic and atheist, and joined him in criticizing those to whom he elsewhere grovelled slavishly. When, at supper, the talk turned to women and love, he posed as a refined and sophisticated libertine. It is remarkable, by and large, how the gay dogs of St. Petersburg like talking about their unusual tastes. Some youthful officials of high rank make do very well with the embraces of their cook or a wretched street-walker on the Nevsky Prospekt, but from the way they speak they are contaminated with all the vices of east and west, being honorary members of a round dozen iniquitous secret societies and already having a police record. Kukushkin told the most barefaced lies about himself, and people didn't so much disbelieve him as let his fantasies go in one ear and out of the other.

The third guest, Gruzin, was the son of a worthy and erudite senior official. He was the same age as Orlov, his colouring was fair, he had long hair, he was short-sighted and he wore gold-rimmed spectacles. I remember his long, pale fingers like a pianist's, and there was something of the musician and virtuoso about his whole figure, actually. Orchestral first violins have that same look. He coughed, he was subject to migraine, he seemed generally sickly and frail. At home they probably dressed and undressed him like a baby. He had been to law school, and had first worked in the legal department, had then been transferred to the Senate, and had left that, after which he had received a post in the Ministry of Works through his connections, but had soon left that too. In my time he had a job as section head in Orlov's division, but he used to say that he would soon be back in the legal department. His attitude to his work, and to this skipping from job to job, was extraordinarily flippant, and when people started talking seriously about ranks, decorations and salaries in his presence he would smile complacently and repeat Prutkov's aphorism about government service being 'the only place where you can learn the truth'. He had a little wife with a lined face who was very jealous, and five weedy little children. He was unfaithful to his wife, he loved his children only when he could see them. His general attitude to his family was one of indifference, rather, and he would make fun of it. He and his family lived on credit, and he borrowed here there and everywhere on every possible occasion, not exempting even office superiors and house-porters. His was a flabby nature so lazy that he didn't care what happened to him, but floated with the tide he knew not where and why. He went wherever he was taken. If he was taken to some low dive, he went. If wine was set before him he drank it, and if it wasn't he didn't. If people abused their wives in his presence he abused his, asserting that she had wrecked his life, and when wives were praised he would praise his too.

'I'm very fond of the poor thing,' he would say quite sincerely.

He had no fur coat, and always went round wrapped in a rug smelling of the nursery. When he became absorbed in thought at supper, rolling bread balls and drinking a lot of red wine, I was practically certain, oddly enough, that there was something to him: something which he himself dimly sensed, very likely, but could not really fathom and appreciate, what with having so much fuss and vulgarity around him. He played the piano a little. He would sit down at the instrument, strike a couple of chords and quietly sing:

'What does the morrow hold for me?'

But then he would jump up at once as if scared, and retreat some distance from the piano.

The guests had usually forgathered by ten o'clock. They played cards in Orlov's study, while Polya and I served tea. Only now did I relish the full savour of a flunkey's life. To stand by that door, four or five hours on end, to keep the glasses filled, to change the ash-trays, to dash to the table and pick up a dropped piece of chalk or card—above all to stand, wait, be attentive without venturing to speak, cough or smile . . . all that is harder than the hardest physical labour, I can tell you. I once used to take four-hour watch at sea on stormy winter nights, and watch-keeping is incomparably easier, I find.

They would play cards until two or sometimes three o'clock, then stretch themselves and go into the dining-room for supper: 'a bit of a bite', as Orlov called it. At supper there was conversation. It usually began when Orlov, smiling with his eyes, mentioned a common acquaintance, or a book which he had just read, or some new appointment or project. The fawning Kukushkin chimed in, and there began what to me, in my mood of the time, was a most hideous exhibition. Orlov's and his friends' irony knew no bounds, it spared no one and nothing. They spoke of religion: with irony. They spoke of philosophy, of the meaning and purpose of life: with irony. If the peasant question cropped up there was still more irony. St. Petersburg has a peculiar breed of specialists in deriding every manifestation of life. They can't even pass a starving man or a suicide without some banal remark. But Orlov and his friends did not joke or jeer, they just ironized. They said there was no God, that individuality disappeared completely at death . . . and that there were no immortals outside the French Academy. There was no such thing as true goodness, and never could be since its existence presupposed human perfectibility: a contradiction in terms, that. Russia was just as tedious and poverty-stricken as Persia. Our intellectuals were hopeless, on Pekarsky's reckoning, consisting very largely of futile incompetents. As for our peasants, they were sunk in drink, sloth, thieving and degeneracy. We had no science, our literature was primitive, our commerce was based on fraud and on the idea that 'you can't sell without cheating'. Everything else was the same, it was all absurd.

The wine would cheer them up by the end of supper, and the conversation became brighter. They made fun of Gruzin's family life, of Kukushkin's conquests, and of Pekarsky, who reputedly headed one page in his cash book *To Charity* and another *To Demands of Nature*. There were no faithful wives, they said, there was no wife with whom, given the knack, one couldn't have one's bit of fun without leaving her drawing-room at the very time when her husband was in his study next door. Adolescent girls were corrupt and no better than they should be. Orlov kept a letter written by some fourteen-year-old schoolgirl. On her way home from school she had 'picked up such a nice officer' on the Nevsky, said she, and he had taken her home and kept her there till late at night, and then she had rushed off to write to her girl-friend and share her ecstasies. Chastity had never existed, according to them, there was no such thing, nor was there any need for it, obviously: humanity had managed pretty well without it so far. And the harm done by 'loose living' was much exaggerated. A certain perversion specified in our penal code . . . it hadn't stopped Diogenes being a philosopher and teacher. Caesar and Cicero were lechers, but also great men. Cato married a young girl in his old age, yet continued to rank as an austere, ascetic custodian of morals.

At three or four in the morning the party would break up, or they would drive out of town together—or else to one Barbara Osipovna's on Officer Street—while I would retire to my room where my headache and coughing kept me awake for some time.

IV

I remember a ring on the door-bell one Sunday morning about three weeks after I had entered Orlov's service. It was about half past ten and he was still asleep. I opened the door, and you can picture my astonishment when I saw a veiled lady on the landing.

'Has Mr. Orlov got up yet?' she asked. I recognized the voice of the Zinaida Krasnovsky to whom I had taken letters in Znamensky Square. Whether I had time or wit to answer her, I do not recollect, for I was so taken aback by her arrival. Not that she needed an answer, anyway. She had darted past me in a flash, filling the hall with the fragrance of her scent, which I still remember vividly. Then she disappeared into the flat and her footsteps died away. Not a sound was heard for at least half an hour. Then there was another ring at the door-bell. This time some dolled-up girl (evidently a maid from a wealthy household) and our porter, both puffing, brought in two suitcases and a dress-basket.

'These are for Mrs. Krasnovsky,' said the girl.

She went down without another word. All this was most mysterious and provoked a sly grin from Polya, who doted on her master's capers. 'He isn't half a one,' she seemed to say, and she walked round on tiptoe the whole time. Then, at last, steps were heard, and Zinaida came quickly into the hall.

'Stephen,' she said, seeing me at the door of my room, 'help Mr. Orlov to get dressed.'

When I went into Orlov's room with his clothes and boots he was sitting on his bed with his feet dangling on the bearskin rug, his whole being expressive of discomfiture. He ignored me, having no interest in my menial opinion. It was in his own eyes, in the eyes of his inner self, that he felt disconcerted and embarrassed, that was obvious. He dressed, washed and spent some time fussing with his brushes and combs: silently, unhurriedly, as if taking time to ponder and work out where he stood, and his very back betrayed his dismay and annoyance with himself.

They had coffee together. Zinaida poured out for both of them, then put her elbows on the table and laughed.

'I still can't believe it,' she said. 'When you've been travelling for ages, and at last reach your hotel, you still can't believe you are at journey's end. It's so nice to breathe freely.'

Looking like a mischievous little girl, she sighed with relief and laughed again.

'You will excuse me,' said Orlov with a nod at the newspapers. 'Reading at breakfast is an addiction of mine. But I can do two things at once, I can both read and listen.'

'No, read away, do. You shall keep all your old habits and your freedom. Why are you so glum, though? Are you always like this in the mornings, or is it only today? Aren't you pleased?'

'Oh, very much so. But I must confess to being somewhat non-plussed.'

'Now, why? You've had plenty of time to prepare for my invasion, I've been threatening you with it every day.'

'True, but I had not expected you to execute that threat on this particular morning.'

'Well, I hadn't expected to either, but it's better this way—far better, darling. It's best to take the plunge and get it over with.'

'Yes, of course.'

'Darling!' she said, screwing up her eyes. 'All's well that ends well, but how much trouble there was before we reached this happy ending! Don't mind my laughing. I'm so glad and happy, but I feel more like crying than laughing.

'Yesterday I won a pitched battle,' she went on in French. 'God alone knows how I suffered. But I'm laughing because I just can't believe it. Sitting drinking coffee with you . . . I feel I must be dreaming it, it can't be real.'

Continuing in French, she told how she had broken with her husband on the previous day, her eyes brimming with tears and laughing by turns as she gazed at Orlov enraptured. Her husband had long suspected her, she said, but had avoided the subject. They had quarrelled very frequently, but he had a way of retreating into silence when things reached boiling point—he would retire to his study to avoid blurting out his suspicions in the heat of the moment, and also to cut short any admissions on her part. Now, Zinaida had felt guilty, despicable and incapable of taking any bold, serious step, for which reason she had hated herself and her husband more and more every day, and had suffered the torments of the damned. But when, during their quarrel of the previous day, he had shouted tearfully 'My God, when *will* all this end?' and had retired to his study, she had pounced after him like a cat after a mouse, she had stopped him closing the door behind him, and she had shouted that she hated him from the bottom of her heart. Then he had admitted her to the study and she had told him everything, confessing that she loved another man, that this other man was her true and most lawful husband, and that she considered it her moral duty to go away and join him that very day, come what might, and even under artillery bombardment if necessary.

'You have a marked romantic streak,' Orlov put in, his eyes glued to his newspaper.

She laughed and went on talking, leaving her coffee untouched. Her cheeks were burning, which rather disconcerted her, and she looked at me and Polya in embarrassment. From the rest of her tale I learnt that her husband had replied with reproaches and threats, and finally with tears—it would have been truer to say that it was he, not she, who had won their pitched battle.

'Yes, darling, as long as I was worked up it all went off marvellously,' she said. 'But with nightfall I lost heart. You don't believe in God, George, but I do believe a little and I'm afraid of retribution. God requires us to be patient, generous and unselfish, but here am I refusing to be patient and wanting to build my life my own way. But is that right? What if it's wrong in God's eyes? My husband came in at two o'clock in the morning.

'"You'll never dare leave me," he said. "I'll have you brought back by the police and make a scene."

'Then, a little later, I saw him in the doorway again, looking like a ghost. "Have pity on me, you might damage my career by running away."

'These words shocked me, they made me feel rotten. The retribution's started, thought I, and I began trembling with fear and crying. I felt as though the ceiling would fall in on me, as if I should be dragged off to the police station then and there, as if you'd get tired of me. God knows what I didn't feel, in other words! I shall enter a convent, thought I, I'll become a nurse, I'll renounce happiness, but then I remembered that you loved me, that I had no right to dispose of myself without your knowledge—oh, my head was in such a whirl and I didn't know what to do or think, I was so frantic. Then the sun rose and I cheered up again. As soon as morning came I dashed off here. Oh, what I've been through, darling! I haven't slept the last two nights.'

She was tired and excited. She wanted to sleep, to go on talking for ever, to laugh, cry, and drive off for lunch in a restaurant and savour her new freedom: all these things at one and the same time.

'Your flat is comfortable, but it's a bit small for two, I'm afraid,' she said, quickly touring all the rooms after breakfast. 'Which is my room? I like this one because it's next to your study.'

At about half past one she changed her dress in the room next to the study, which she thereafter termed hers, and went out to lunch with Orlov. They also dined in a restaurant, and they spent the long gap between lunch and dinner shopping. I was opening the door and accepting sundry purchases from shop-assistants and errand-boys till late that night. Amongst other things they brought a magnificent pier-glass, a dressing-table, a bedstead and a sumptuous tea service which we didn't need. They brought a whole tribe of copper saucepans which we arranged in a row on the shelf in our cold, empty kitchen. When we unpacked the tea service Polya's eyes gleamed and she looked at me two or three times with hatred, and with fear that I, not she, might be first to steal one of those elegant cups. They brought a very expensive but inconvenient lady's writing desk. Zinaida obviously intended to settle in permanently and set up house with us.

At about half past nine she and Orlov returned. Proudly conscious of having achieved something bold and original, passionately in love, and (as she supposed) passionately loved, deliciously tired and anticipating deep, sweet sleep, Zinaida was revelling in her new life. She kept clasping her hands tightly together from sheer high spirits, she declared that everything was marvellous, she swore to love for ever. These vows and the innocent, almost infantile, conviction that she was deeply loved in return and would be loved for ever . . . it all made her look five years younger. She talked charming nonsense, laughing at herself.

'There is no greater blessing than freedom,' she announced, forcing herself to say something earnest and significant. 'Why, it's all so silly, isn't it? We attach no value to our own views, however wise, and yet we are terrified of what various half-wits think. Up to the last minute I was afraid of what people might say, but as soon as I followed my own inclinations and decided to live my own way, my eyes were opened, I got over my stupid fears, and now I'm happy, and I wish everyone else could be as happy.'

But then her chain of thought broke and she spoke of taking a new flat, of wallpaper, of horses, of a trip to Switzerland and Italy. But Orlov was tired by his voyage round restaurants and shops, and still felt the self-conscious discomfiture which I had noticed in him that morning. He smiled, but more from politeness than pleasure, and when she said anything serious he agreed ironically.

'Yes, yes, of course.'

'You must hurry up and find us a good cook, Stephen,' she told me.

'There's no need for any hurry on the kitchen front,' said Orlov with a cold look at me. 'We must move into our new flat first.'

He had never had his cooking done at home or kept horses, 'not liking dirty things about the place', as he said, and he only put up with me and Polya in his flat from sheer necessity. So-called domesticity with its mundane joys and squabbles . . . it jarred on him as a form of vulgarity. To be pregnant, or have children and speak of them, that was bad form and suburban. I was now extremely curious to see how these two creatures would manage together in the same dwelling: she domesticated, very much the housewife with her copper saucepans and her dreams of a good cook and horses, and he who so often told his friends that a decent, clean-living man's apartment should be like a warship. There should be nothing superfluous in it: no women, no children, no bits and pieces, no kitchen utensils.

V

Now I shall tell you what happened on the following Thursday. Orlov and Zinaida ate at Contant's or Donon's that day. Orlov came home alone and Zinaida drove off—as I later learnt, to the Old Town to see her former governess and wait till our guests had gone. Orlov was not keen on showing her to his friends: I realized that at breakfast when he began assuring her that he must cancel his Thursdays for the sake of her peace of mind.

As usual the guests arrived almost simultaneously.

'Is the mistress at home?' Kukushkin asked me in a whisper.

'No, sir,' I answered.

He came in with sly, glinting eyes, smiling enigmatically, rubbing his cold hands.

'Congratulations, my good sir,' he told Orlov, vibrating all over with an obsequious, ingratiating laugh. 'Be ye fruitful, and multiply ye, like unto the cedars of Lebanon.'

Making for the bedroom, the guests uttered some witticisms about a pair of lady's slippers, a rug which had been placed between the two beds and a grey blouse hanging on the back of a bed. They were amused by the idea of one so obstinate, one who despised all the mundane details of love, suddenly being caught in female toils in so simple and commonplace a manner.

'That which we mocked, to that have we bowed the knee,' Kukushkin repeated several times. He had, I may say, the disagreeable affectation of parading what sounded like biblical texts.

'Hush!' he whispered, raising a finger to his lips when they came out of the bedroom into the room next to the study. 'Quiet! Here it is that Gretchen dreams of her Faust!'

He roared with laughter as if he had said something terribly funny. I observed Gruzin, expecting this laugh to jar on his musical ear, but I was wrong. His lean, good-natured face beamed with pleasure. When they sat down to cards he said—pronouncing the letter r in his throat, and choking with laughter—that dear Georgie only needed a cherry-wood pipe and guitar for his cup of domestic felicity to run over. Pekarsky laughed sedately, but his tense expression showed that he found Orlov's new love affair distasteful. He could not understand exactly what had happened.

'But what about the husband?' he asked in perplexity after they had played three rubbers.

'I don't know,' answered Orlov.

Pekarsky combed his great beard with his fingers, plunged deep in thought, and did not speak again until supper-time.

'I'm sorry, but I don't understand you two, I must say,' said he, slowly drawling out each word, when they had sat down to supper. 'You could love each other and break the seventh commandment to your hearts' content—that I could understand, I could see the point of that. But why make the husband a party to your secrets? Was there really any need?'

'Oh, does it really matter?'

'H'm,' Pekarsky brooded.

'Well, I'll tell you one thing, old chap,' he went on, obviously racking his brains. 'Should I ever marry again, and should you conceive the notion of presenting me with a pair of horns, please do it so that I don't notice. It is far more honest to deceive a man than to wreck his daily routine and reputation. Oh, I can see what you're after. You both think that by living together openly you are behaving in an exceptionally decent and liberal manner, but I don't hold with this, er—what's it called?—this romanticism.'

Orlov did not answer. He was in a bad mood and disinclined to speak. Still baffled, Pekarsky drummed his fingers on the table and thought for a moment.

'I still don't understand you two,' he said. 'You're not a student, she's not a little seamstress. You both have means. You could set her up in a separate establishment, I take it.'

'No, I couldn't. Read your Turgenev.'

'Oh? Why? I already have read him.'

'In his works Turgenev preaches that every superior, right-minded young woman should follow her beloved to the ends of the earth and serve his ideals,' said Orlov, screwing up his eyes ironically. 'The ends of the earth . . . that's poetic licence, since the whole globe with all its regions is subsumed in the dwelling of the man she loves. Not sharing your dwelling with the woman who loves you, that means denying her high destiny and failing to share her ideals. Yes, old boy, the prescription is Turgenev's, but it's me who has to take the flaming medicine!'

'I can't see where Turgenev comes in,' said Gruzin softly, shrugging his shoulders. 'Do you remember *Three Meetings*, George, and how he's walking somewhere in Italy late one evening, and suddenly hears "*Vieni, pensando a me segretamente*"?'

Gruzin started humming it. 'Good stuff, that.'

'But she didn't force herself on you, did she?' Pekarsky asked. 'It's what you yourself wanted.'

'Oh, do have a heart! Far from wanting it, I couldn't even conceive of such a possibility. When she mentioned coming to live with me I thought she was just having her little joke.'

Everyone laughed.

'How *could* I want such a thing?' continued Orlov in the tone of one put on the defensive. 'I am not a Turgenev hero, and should I ever require to liberate Bulgaria I could dispense with any female escort. I regard love principally as an element essential to my physical nature: one primitive and inimical to my whole ethos. I must satisfy it with discretion or give it up altogether, otherwise it will introduce elements as impure as itself into my life. To make it a pleasure instead of a torment I try to beautify it and surround it with a multitude of illusions. I won't go to a woman unless I am assured beforehand that she will be beautiful and attractive. Nor will I visit her unless I'm on the top of my form. Only under such conditions do we manage to deceive each other, and feel that we love and are happy. But what do I want with copper saucepans and untidy hair? Or with being seen when I haven't washed? And am in a bad mood? In her naïve way Zinaida wants to make me like something I've been dodging all my life. She wants my flat to smell of cooking and washing up. She wants to move into a new establishment with tremendous éclat and drive about with her own horses, she needs must count my underwear, she must worry about my health, she must be constantly meddling in my private life, and she must dog my every step, while all the time sincerely assuring me that I can retain my old habits and my freedom. She is convinced that we're soon going off on our honeymoon, as if we had just got married —she wishes to be constantly at my side in trains and hotels, in other words, whereas I like reading when I travel and can't stand conversation.'

'Then try and talk some sense into her,' said Pekarsky.

'Eh? Do you think she would understand me? Why, we think so differently! Leaving Daddy and Mummy, or one's husband, going off with the man one loves . . . that's civic courage at its highest in her view, whereas to me it's sheer childishness. To fall in love and have an affair . . . to her it means beginning a new life, while to me it means nothing. Love, man . . . they're her be-all and end-all, and perhaps the theory of the subconscious is affecting her here. You just try persuading her that love is only a simple need like food and clothing, that it really isn't the end of the world if husbands and wives misbehave, that one may be a lecher and seducer yet also a man of genius and integrity— and that, conversely, someone who renounces the pleasures of love may be a stupid, nasty animal all the same. Modern civilized man, even on a low level—your French worker, say—spends ten *sous* a day on his dinner, five *sous* on the wine with his dinner, and five to ten *sous* on his woman, and he gives all his mind and nerves to his work. Now, Zinaida doesn't pay for love in *sous*, she gives her whole soul. I might well try to talk some sense into her, but she would answer by crying out in all sincerity that I've ruined her and that she has nothing left to live for.'

'Then don't talk to her,' said Pekarsky. 'Just take a separate flat for her, and that will be that.'

'It's easy enough to say——'

There was a short pause.

'But she is so charming,' said Kukushkin. 'She's delightful. Such women think they'll love for ever, they surrender themselves with such feeling.'

'One must keep one's wits about one,' said Orlov. 'One must use one's brain. Experiences culled from everyday life, and enshrined in countless novels and plays . . . they all confirm that the adulteries and cohabitations of decent people never last more than two or three years at the outside, however much they may have loved each other at the start. That she must know. So all these changes of residence, these saucepans, these hopes for eternal love and harmony simply add up to a wish to bamboozle herself and me. She *is* charming and delightful, no doubt about it. But she has turned my life upside down. All that I have hitherto considered trivial nonsense . . . she makes me elevate it to the status of a serious problem, so I'm serving an idol which I have never worshipped. She *is* charming, she *is* delightful, but when I drive home from work nowadays I'm somehow in a bad mood, as if I expect to find some inconvenience at home like workmen having dismantled all our stoves and left great piles of bricks everywhere. I'm not paying for my love in *sous* now, in other words, but with part of my peace of mind and my nerves. And that's pretty bad.'

'Oh, if only she could hear this wicked man!' sighed Kukushkin.

'My dear sir,' he added theatrically, 'I will liberate you from the onerous obligation of loving this charming creature: I'll cut you out with Zinaida.'

'Go ahead,' said Orlov nonchalantly.

Kukushkin laughed a shrill little laugh for half a minute, shaking all over, and then spoke. 'Now see here, I'm not joking. And don't let's have any of the Othello business afterwards!'

Everyone started talking about Kukushkin's unflagging love life, about how irresistible he was to women, how dangerous to husbands, and how devils would barbecue him in the next world because he was so dissolute. He said nothing, he just screwed up his eyes, and when people named ladies of his acquaintance he would wag his little finger as if warning that other people's secrets must not be divulged.

Orlov suddenly looked at his watch.

The guests understood and prepared to leave. On this occasion I remember Gruzin, who had drunk too much wine, taking an unconscionable time getting ready. He donned an overcoat resembling the coats made for children in poor families, put his collar up and began telling some long-winded story. Then, noticing that no one was listening to him, he shouldered that rug smelling of the nursery, assumed a hunted, wheedling air and begged me to find his cap.

'My dear old George,' he said tenderly. 'Now, listen: how about a trip out of town, old boy?'

'You go, I can't. I now have married status.'

'She's a marvellous woman, she won't be angry. Come on, my good lord and master. It's wonderful weather, there's a bit of a snow-storm and a spot of frost. You need a thorough shake-up, believe me. You're out of sorts, damn it——'

Orlov stretched, yawned and looked at Pekarsky.

'You going?' he asked hesitantly.

'I don't know, I might.'

'A drinking expedition, eh? Oh, all right, I'll come,' Orlov decided after some hesitation. 'Wait a moment, I'll get some money.'

He went into the study and Gruzin waddled after him, trailing his rug. A minute later both returned to the hall. Tipsy and very pleased with himself, Gruzin was crumpling a ten-rouble note in his hand.

'We'll settle up tomorrow,' he said. 'And she's so good-natured, she won't be angry. She's godmother to my little Liza, I'm fond of the poor girl. Oh, my dear chap!'—he gave a sudden happy laugh and pressed his forehead on Pekarsky's back—'Oh, my dear old Pekarsky! You legal eagle, you crusty old fogy, you. . . . But you're fond of women, that I'll wager.'

'Fat ones, incidentally,' said Orlov, putting his coat on. 'But let's be off, or we shall meet her on the way out.'

'*Vieni, pensando a me segretamente,*' hummed Gruzin.

They left at last. Orlov was away all night, and returned for lunch next day.

VI

Zinaida had lost a little gold watch, a present from her father. Its disappearance surprised and alarmed her. She spent half the day going round the flat, looking frantically at tables and window-sills, but that watch seemed to have vanished into thin air.

A day or two later she left her purse in the hall on returning from some expedition. Luckily for me it was Polya, not I, who had helped her off with her coat on that occasion. When the purse was missed it was no longer in the hall.

Zinaida was puzzled. 'This is most odd. I distinctly remember taking it out of my pocket to pay the cabman, and then I put it down here near the looking-glass. Highly peculiar!'

I had not stolen it, yet I felt as if I had and had been caught in the act. Tears even came to my eyes.

'We must be haunted,' Zinaida told Orlov in French as they sat down to their meal. 'I lost my purse in the hall today—and now, lo and behold, it has turned up on my table! But it was in no disinterested spirit that our ghost performed this trick. He took a gold coin and twenty roubles in notes for his pains.'

'First your watch is missing, then it's money,' said Orlov. 'Why does that sort of thing never happen to me?'

A minute later Zinaida had forgotten the ghost's trick, and was laughing as she told how she had ordered some writing-paper last week, but had forgotten to give her new address, so the shop had sent the paper to her husband at her old home and he had had to pay a bill of twelve roubles. Then she suddenly fixed her eyes on Polya and stared at her, while blushing and feeling such embarrassment that she changed the subject.

When I took their coffee into the study Orlov was standing with his back to the fire, and she was sitting in an arm-chair facing him.

'No, I am *not* in a bad mood,' she was saying in French. 'But I've started putting two and two together now, and I understand the whole thing. I can name the day, and even the hour, when she stole my watch. And what about that purse? There's no room for doubt.'

She laughed and accepted some coffee from me. 'Oh, now I understand why I'm always losing my handkerchiefs and gloves. Say what you like, I'm going to dismiss that thieving magpie tomorrow and send Stephen for my Sophia. Sophia doesn't steal and she hasn't such an, er, repulsive appearance.'

'You're in a bad mood. Tomorrow you'll feel differently, and you'll realize that one can't just dismiss a person simply on suspicion.'

'It's not suspicion, I'm absolutely certain,' said Zinaida. 'While I suspected this plebeian with the sorrowful countenance, this valet of yours, I said not a word. I am hurt that you don't trust me, George.'

'If we disagree about something it doesn't follow that I mistrust you.'

'Let us suppose you're right,' said Orlov, turning to the fire and throwing his cigarette-end in it. 'Even so, there is still no need to get excited. Actually, to be perfectly frank, I had never expected my humble establishment to cause you so much serious worry and upset. If you have lost a gold coin, never mind, I'll give you a hundred gold coins. But to alter my routine, to pick a new maid off the streets and wait for her to learn the ropes . . . it all takes time, it's boring, and it's not my line. Our present maid is fat, admittedly, and she may have a weakness for gloves and handkerchiefs, but she is also well-behaved and well-trained, and she doesn't squeak when Kukushkin pinches her.'

'In other words you can't bear to part with her. Then why not say so?'

'Are you jealous?'

'Yes, I am,' Zinaida said decisively.

'Most grateful, I'm sure.'

'Yes, I am jealous,' she repeated, and tears gleamed in her eyes. 'No, this isn't jealousy, it's something worse. I don't know what to call it.'

She clutched her temples. 'Men are so foul,' she continued impetuously. 'It's awful.'

'I don't know what you find so awful.'

'I've never seen it and I know nothing about it, but you men are said to start off with housemaids when you are quite small, after which you get used to it and no longer feel any repugnance. I know nothing whatever about it, but I've even read that——'

Then she adopted a fondly wheedling tone and went up to Orlov. 'You're so right, of course, George, I really am in a bad mood today. I can't help it, though, you must see that. She disgusts me, and I'm afraid of her. I can't bear the sight of her.'

'Surely you can rise above such trivialities,' said Orlov, shrugging his shoulders in perplexity and moving away from the fire. 'It's simple enough, isn't it? Just take no notice of her, then she won't disgust you—and you won't need to dramatize these pin-pricks either.'

I left the study, and what answer Orlov received I do not know. Whatever it was, Polya stayed on. After this Zinaida never asked her to do anything, obviously trying to dispense with her services. When Polya handed her anything—or merely passed by, even, her bangle jingling, her skirts crackling—Zinaida shuddered.

Had Gruzin or Pekarsky asked Orlov to discharge Polya he would have done so without turning a hair, I think, nor would he have troubled to give any explanation whatever, being complaisant, like all apathetic people. But with Zinaida he was stubborn even over trifles for some reason: to the point of sheer pig-headedness on occasion. So if Zinaida took a liking to anything he was sure to dislike it, I knew that by now. When she came back from shopping eager to show off her new purchases he would give them a passing glance, remarking icily that the more the flat was cluttered up with rubbish the less air there was to breathe. Sometimes he would put on evening dress to go out and would say good-bye to Zinaida, but would then suddenly decide to stay at home out of sheer perversity. At such times he only stayed in so that he could be miserable, I felt.

'But why stay in?' Zinaida would ask with pretended annoyance, yet radiant with pleasure. 'Now, why? You are not used to staying in of an evening, and I don't want you to change your habits on my account. So do go out, please, or else I shall feel guilty.'

'No one's blaming you for anything, are they?' Orlov would ask.

He would sprawl in his study arm-chair with a martyred look and take up a book, shielding his eyes with his hand. But soon the book would fall from his grasp, he would turn heavily in his chair and put his hand up again as if to keep the sun out of his eyes. Now he was annoyed with himself for not having gone out.

'May I come in?' Zinaida would ask, hesitantly entering the study. 'Are you reading? I was a bit bored, so I've looked in for a moment just for a peep.'

I remember her coming in one evening in this same hesitant fashion and at some ill-chosen moment. She sank on the rug at Orlov's feet, and her gentle, timorous movements showed that his mood puzzled and scared her.

'You are always reading,' she began artfully, with an obvious wish to flatter. 'Do you know the secret of your success, George? You're an intelligent, educated man. What book have you there?'

Orlov answered. Some minutes passed in silence: minutes which seemed hours to me. I was standing in the drawing-room where I could watch them both, and I was afraid of coughing.

'There is something I wanted to tell you,' Zinaida softly announced, and laughed. 'Shall I? You may laugh at me, you may say I'm flattering myself, but you know, I do so terribly much want to think you stayed in tonight on my behalf, so that we could spend the evening together. Did you? May I think that?'

'Pray do,' said Orlov, screening his eyes. 'True happiness lies in the capacity to conceive things not only as they are, but also as they are not.'

'That was a very long sentence, I didn't quite understand it. Do you mean that happy people live in their imaginations? That is certainly true. I like sitting in your study in the evenings and letting my thoughts carry me far, far away. It's nice to day-dream a little. Shall we dream aloud together, George?'

'Never having attended a girls' boarding school, I am unacquainted with the technique.'

'You're in a bad mood, are you?' Zinaida asked, taking Orlov's hand. 'Tell me, why? I am afraid of you when you're like this. I don't know whether you have a headache or are angry with me——'

More long minutes passed in silence.

'Why have you changed?' she asked softly. 'Why aren't you so tender and cheerful any more, as you were in Znamensky Square? I have lived with you for a month, nearly, but I feel we haven't begun living yet, we haven't had a proper talk. You always fob me off with jokes or with long, bleak answers like a teacher's. There's something bleak about your jokes too. Why have you stopped speaking to me seriously?'

'I always speak seriously.'

'Well, let's have a talk. For God's sake, George.'

'Carry on then. What shall we talk about.'

'About our life, our future,' said Zinaida dreamily. 'I keep making plans for the future, I always enjoy that. I'll start by asking when you mean to give up your job, George.'

'But why ever should I?' Orlov asked, removing his hand from his forehead.

'No one with your views can work for the government, you're out of place there.'

'My *views*?' Orlov asked. 'What views? By conviction and temperament I am an ordinary civil servant: a typical red-tape merchant. You are mistaking me for someone else, I venture to assure you.'

'You're joking again, George.'

'Not a bit of it. The Civil Service may not satisfy me, but still it does suit me better than anything else. I am used to it, and I'm with people of my own sort there. There at least I'm not an odd-man-out, and I feel reasonably all right.'

'You hate the Civil Service, it sickens you.'

'Oh, it does, does it? If I resign, if I start dreaming aloud and letting myself float off into some other world, you don't suppose I'll find that world any less hateful than my job, do you?'

'You're so keen on contradicting me you even disparage yourself.' Zinaida was hurt and stood up. 'I'm sorry I ever started this conversation.'

'But why so angry? I'm not angry because you're *not* in the Civil Service, am I? Everyone lives his own life.'

'But *do* you live your own life? *Are* you free?' Zinaida went on, throwing up her arms in despair. 'Spending all your time writing papers repugnant to your convictions, doing what you are told, visiting your superiors to wish them a Happy New Year, all that incessant card-playing—and then, to cap it all, serving a system which you *must* find uncongenial . . . no, George, no! Don't make such clumsy jokes. Oh, you are awful. As a man of high ideals you should serve only your ideals.'

'You really are mistaking me for someone else,' sighed Orlov.

'Why don't you just tell me you don't want to talk to me?' Zinaida brought out through tears. 'You're fed up with me, that's all.'

'Now, look here, my dear,' Orlov admonished her, sitting up in his arm-chair. 'As you yourself so kindly remarked, I am an intelligent, educated man. Now, one can't teach an old dog new tricks. Those ideas, small and great, which you have in mind when calling me an idealist . . . I know all about all of them. So if I prefer my job and my cards to those ideals I presumably have grounds for doing so. That is the first point. And, secondly, you have never been a civil servant so far as I am aware, and you can only cull your views on government work from anecdotes and trashy novels. It might therefore be a good idea if we agreed once and for all to talk neither about things which we have known all about all along nor about things outside our sphere of competence.'

'Why, why speak to me like that?' Zinaida asked, stepping back in horror. 'Think what you are saying, George, for God's sake.'

Her voice quivered and broke. Though obviously trying to hold back her tears, she suddenly burst out sobbing.

'George, darling, this is killing me,' she said in French, quickly falling to her knees before Orlov and laying her head on his lap. 'I'm so worn out and exhausted I just can't cope any more, I really can't. As a little girl I had that horrible depraved stepmother, then there was my husband, and now there's you . . . you. . . . I'm absolutely crazy about you, and you give me this callous irony in return!

'And then there's that awful, impudent maid,' she went on, sobbing. 'Yes, yes, I see. I'm not your wife or helpmate, I'm just a woman you don't respect because she is your mistress. I shall commit suicide.'

I had not expected these words and tears to produce so strong an impression on Orlov. He flushed, stirring uneasily in his chair, and the irony on his face gave way to a sort of mindless dread. He looked exactly like a schoolboy.

'Darling, I swear you've misunderstood me,' he muttered frantically, touching her hair and shoulders. 'Do forgive me, I implore you. I was in the wrong and I, er, hate myself.'

'I offend you by my complaints and whining. You have such integrity, you're so generous. You are an exceptional man, I'm conscious of that every minute of the day, but I've been so utterly depressed all this time——'

Zinaida embraced Orlov impulsively and kissed his cheek.

'Just stop crying, please,' he said.

'Yes, yes. I have already cried my eyes out, and I feel better.'

'As for the maid, she'll be gone tomorrow,' he said, still squirming in his chair.

'No, let her stay, George, do you hear? I'm not afraid of her any more. One must rise above such trivialities and not imagine silly things. You're so right. You're a rare, exceptional person.'

She soon stopped crying. With the tear-drops still wet on her lashes, she sat on Orlov's lap and recounted in hushed tones some pathetic tale: a reminiscence of her childhood and youth, or something like that. She stroked his face and kissed him, scrutinizing his beringed hands and the seals on his watch-chain. She was carried away by what she was saying, by having her lover near her, and her voice sounded unusually pure and candid: because her recent tears had cleansed and freshened her spirits, very likely. Orlov played with her auburn hair and kissed her hands, touching them soundlessly with his lips.

Then they had tea in the study and Zinaida read some letters aloud. They went to bed at about half past twelve.

That night my side ached mightily, and dawn broke before I was able to get warm or doze off. I heard Orlov go out of the bedroom into his study. After sitting there for about an hour he rang. My pain and fatigue made me forget all etiquette and conventions on this earth, and I went into the study barefoot, wearing only my underclothes. Orlov stood awaiting me in the doorway in dressing-gown and cap.

'Report properly dressed when you're called,' he said sternly. 'Fetch fresh candles, will you?'

I tried to apologize, but suddenly had a terrible coughing fit and clutched the door-post with one hand to stop myself falling.

'Are you ill?' Orlov asked.

I think this was the first occasion on which he had addressed me politely during the whole time we had known each other. Why he did it God alone knows. Wearing underclothes, my face distorted by coughing, I was probably playing my part very badly and little resembled a servant.

'Why do you work then if you're so ill?' he asked.

'Because I don't want to die of starvation.'

'Oh, what a filthy business it all is, really!' he said quietly, going to his desk.

Throwing on a frock-coat, I fitted and lit fresh candles, while he sat near the desk with his legs on the arm-chair and cut the pages of a book.

I left him engrossed in his reading, and his book no longer tended to fall from his grasp as it had in the evening.

VII

As I now write these lines my hand is restrained by a fear drilled into me since childhood, of seeming sentimental and ridiculous. I am incapable of being natural when I want to show affection and speak tenderly. And it is this very fear, combined with lack of experience, which now makes it quite impossible for me to convey with full precision my emotions of the time.

I was not in love with Zinaida, but my ordinary human liking for her contained far more youth, spontaneity and joy than was to be found in Orlov's love.

Plying my boot-brush or broom of a morning, I would wait with bated breath to hear her voice and steps. To stand and watch her drinking coffee and eating breakfast, to hold her fur coat for her in the hall, to put galoshes on her little feet while she placed a hand on my shoulders, and later to wait for the hall-porter's ring from downstairs and meet her at the door—rosy-checked, cold, powdered with snow—hearing her impulsive exclamations about the cold or the sledge-driver . . . ah, if you did but know how much it all meant to me! I wanted to fall in love and have a family, and I wanted my future wife to have a face and voice just like hers. I dreamt of it at mealtimes, on errands in the street and when I lay awake at night. The finicky Orlov spurned women's frippery, children, cooking and copper saucepans, but I garnered all these things together and watchfully cherished them in my dreams. I doted on them, I begged fate to grant me them, and I had visions of a wife, a nursery, garden paths and a little cottage.

Had I fallen in love with Zinaida I should never have dared to hope for the miracle of being loved in return, I knew, but that consideration did not trouble me. In my discreet, gentle feeling, akin to ordinary affection, there was neither jealousy nor even envy of Orlov, since I realized that, for someone as incapacitated as I was, personal happiness was possible only in dreams.

When Zinaida waited up night after night for her George, look-ing at her book without moving or turning the pages, or when she shuddered and blenched because Polya was crossing the room, I suffered with her and I was tempted to lance this painful abscess at once by letting her know what was said in the place at supper-time on Thursdays. But how was I to do it? More and more often I saw her in tears. During the first weeks she had laughed and sung to herself even when Orlov was out, but by the second month our flat was plunged in dismal silence broken only on Thursdays.

She flattered Orlov. Just to win a spurious smile or kiss from him she would go down on her knees and cuddle up like a little dog. Even when she was most depressed she could not pass a looking-glass without glancing at herself and straightening her hair. I was puzzled by her continued interest in clothes and delight in making purchases—some-how it didn't quite square with her deep-felt grief. She followed fashion and ordered expensive dresses. But what use was that to anyone?

I particularly remember one new dress costing four hundred roubles. Fancy paying that much money for one more useless frock when char-women slave away for only twenty copecks a day *and* provide their own food, besides which the girls who make Venice and Brussels lace receive only half a franc a day, being expected to earn the balance by immorality! Why couldn't Zinaida see the point? It puzzled me, grieved me. But she only had to leave the house and I was finding excuses and explanations for all that, and looking forward to the hall-porter's ring from downstairs.

She treated me like a servant, a lower form of life, as one may pat a dog while ignoring its existence. I received orders, I was asked ques-tions, but my presence passed unremarked. The master and mistress thought it unseemly to talk to me more than was accepted. Had I interrupted their conversation or burst out laughing while serving their meals, they would surely have deemed me insane and given me my notice. And yet Zinaida did wish me well. When she sent me on errands—when she explained the workings of a new lamp or anything like that—her expression was unusually serene, kindly and cordial, and she looked me straight in the eye. At such times I always felt that she gratefully remembered my bringing her letters to Znamensky Square. Polya thought me her favourite and hated me for that.

'Go on then, *that mistress of yours* wants you,' she would say with a sarcastic grin when Zinaida rang.

Zinaida treated me as a lower form of life, not suspecting that if anyone was humiliated in that house it was she herself! She failed to realize that I, a servant, suffered on her behalf, wondering twenty times a day what the future held for her and how it would all end. Matters deteriorated noticeably each day. Disliking tears as he did, Orlov began to show obvious fear of conversations and to shy off them after that evening's discussion about his job. When Zinaida began arguing or appealing, when she seemed on the verge of tears, he would make some plausible excuse and go to his study, or else leave the house altogether. He took to spending more and more nights away from home, and he ate out more frequently still. It was now he who asked his friends to take him off somewhere on Thursdays. Zinaida still longed to have the cooking done at home, to move into a new flat, to travel abroad—but day-dreams these day-dreams remained. Meals were brought in from the restaurant, and Orlov asked her not to broach the question of moving house until they had returned from abroad, observing with regard to the said expedition that they could not set off until he had grown his hair long since trailing from hotel to hotel in pursuit of ideals was impermissible without flowing locks.

It was the last straw when Kukushkin began showing up of an evening during Orlov's absence. There was nothing exceptionable about his behaviour, but I just could not forget his once mentioning his intention of cutting Orlov out with Zinaida. Regaled on tea and claret, he sniggered and tried to curry favour by assuring Zinaida that a free union was superior to holy wedlock in every way, and that every respectable person should really come and do her homage now.

VIII

Christmas passed tediously in vague anticipation of some mishap. At breakfast on New Year's Eve Orlov suddenly announced that his office was sending him on some special mission to a Senator who was conducting a certain inspection in the provinces.

'One doesn't feel like going, but one can't think of any excuse,' he said with a vexed air. 'One must go, there's nothing for it.'

At this news Zinaida's eyes reddened instantly.

'Is it for long?' she asked.

'About five days.'

'I'm glad you are going, quite honestly,' she said after a little thought. 'It will make a change. You will fall in love on the way and tell me all about it later.'

Whenever possible she tried to let Orlov see that she was no burden to him, and that he could do as he pleased, but this naïve, blatantly transparent stratagem deceived no one, only reminding him once again that he was not free.

'I am leaving this evening,' he said, and started reading the newspapers.

Zinaida was all for seeing him off at the station, but he dissuaded her, saying that he was not going to America and wouldn't be away five years, but only five days at the most.

They said good-bye at about half past seven. He put one arm round her, kissing her on forehead and lips.

'Now, you be a good little girl and don't fret while I'm away,' he said with a warmth and sincerity which touched even me. 'God preserve you.'

She gazed avidly into his face to imprint those precious features on her memory the more firmly, then twined her arms gracefully round his neck and laid her head on his chest.

'Forgive our misunderstandings,' she said in French. 'Husband and wife can't help quarrelling if they love one another, and I'm absolutely crazy about you. Don't forget me. Send lots of telegrams giving me all the details.'

Orlov kissed her again and left, looking awkward, not uttering a word. When he heard the door-lock click behind him he paused half way downstairs, deep in thought, and glanced upwards. Had but a sound reached him from above just then he would have turned back, I felt. But all was quiet. He adjusted his cloak and began walking downstairs hesitantly.

Hired sledges had long been awaiting him at the door. Orlov climbed into one and I took his two suitcases into the other. There was a hard frost and fires smoked at the crossroads. As we hurtled along, the cold wind nipped my face and hands, taking my breath away. I shut my eyes and thought what a marvellous woman she was, and how much she loved him. People actually collect rubbish in back yards nowadays, and sell it to obtain money for charity, while even broken glass is thought a useful commodity. And yet so rare a treasure as the love of an elegant, intelligent, decent young woman was going completely begging. One of the early sociologists regarded every evil passion as a potential force for good, given the skill to apply it, yet with us a fine, noble passion is born only to fade away: paralysed, aimless, uncomprehended or vulgarized. Why?

The sledges suddenly halted. I opened my eyes and saw that we had stopped in Sergiyevsky Street near the large apartment house where Pekarsky lived. Orlov got out of his sledge and vanished into the entry. Five minutes later Pekarsky's man appeared in the doorway bareheaded.

'You deaf or something?' he shouted at me, furious with the piercing cold. 'Send those drivers off and come upstairs, you're wanted.'

Mystified, I made my way to the first floor. I had been in Pekarsky's flat before—had stood in the hall and looked into the drawing-room, that is—and after the damp, gloomy street it had impressed me each time with the glitter of its picture-frames, bronzes and expensive furniture. Now, amid all this glory, I saw Gruzin, Kukushkin and, a little later, Orlov.

'Look here, Stephen,' said he, coming up to me. 'I shall be staying here till Friday or Saturday. If any letters or telegrams come, bring them here every day. At home, of course, you will say I've left town and sent my regards. You may go.'

When I returned Zinaida was lying on the sofa in the drawing-room eating a pear. Only one candle was burning in the holder.

'You caught the train all right then?' Zinaida asked.

'Yes, ma'am. The master sends his regards.'

I went to my room and lay down too. There was nothing to do, and I did not feel like reading. I was neither surprised nor indignant, I was merely racking my brains to understand the need for such deception. Why, only a boy in his teens would trick his mistress like that! And he, so well-read, so very rational a being . . . surely he could have concocted something a little cleverer! I rated his intelligence pretty high, quite frankly. Had he needed to deceive his Minister or some other powerful man, he would have applied plenty of energy and skill to that, I thought, but now that deceiving a woman was involved any old idea would do—obviously. If the trick came off, so much the better, and if it didn't come off, no matter, for one could tell another lie equally glib and equally hasty without any mental effort whatever.

At midnight there was a shifting of chairs and a cheering on the floor above ours as people greeted the New Year. Zinaida rang for me from the room next to the study. Her energy sapped from lying down so long, she was sitting at her table writing on a piece of paper.

'I must send a telegram,' she said with a smile. 'Drive to the station as quick as you can and ask them to send this after him.'

Coming out into the street, I read her jotting.

'Best New Year wishes. Telegraph quickly. Miss you terribly. Seems like eternity. Sorry I cannot wire a thousand kisses and my very heart. Enjoy yourself, darling,

'ZINAIDA'

I sent the telegram and gave her the receipt next morning.

IX

The worst thing was that Orlov had thoughtlessly let Polya into the secret of his deception by asking her to bring his shirts to Sergiyevsky Street. After that she looked at Zinaida with a gloating hatred beyond my comprehension. She kept snorting with pleasure in her room and in the hall.

'She has outstayed her welcome and it's time she took herself off,' she said triumphantly. 'You would think she could see that for herself——'

She already sensed that Zinaida would not be with us much longer, so she pilfered everything she could lay her hands on while the going was good: scent bottles, tortoiseshell hairpins, handkerchiefs and shoes. On the second of January, Zinaida called me to her room and informed me in hushed tones that her black dress was missing. Then she went round the whole flat, pale-faced, looking frightened and indignant, talking to herself.

'Really! No, I must say! Did you ever hear of such impudence?'

At lunch she tried to help herself to soup, but could not do so because her hands were shaking. So were her lips. She kept glancing helplessly at the soup and pies, waiting for the trembling to pass off. Then she suddenly lost her self-control and looked at Polya.

'You may leave today, Polya,' she said. 'Stephen can manage on his own.'

'No, madam,' said Polya, 'I shall be staying, madam.'

'There is no need for that, you can clear out once and for all!' Zinaida went on, standing up in a great pother. 'You can look for another job. You leave here this instant!'

'I can't go without the master's orders. It was him took me on and what he says goes.'

'I can give you orders too!' said Zinaida, flushing crimson. 'I'm the mistress in this house.'

'Mistress you may be, madam, but only the master can dismiss me. It was him took me on.'

'How dare you stay here one minute longer!' shouted Zinaida and hit her plate with her knife. 'You are a thief, do you hear me?'

Zinaida threw her napkin on the table and rushed out of the dining-room with a pathetic, martyred look. Polya went out too, sobbing aloud and reciting some incantation. The soup and grouse grew cold, and all these restaurant delicacies on the table now wore a meagre, felonious, Polya-like air. Two pies on a little plate had a most pathetic, criminal look.

'We shall be taken back to our restaurant this afternoon,' they seemed to say. 'And tomorrow we shall be served up for lunch again to some civil servant or well-known singer.'

Polya's voice carried from her room. 'Some mistress, I must say! I could have been that kind of a mistress long ago, but I wouldn't demean meself. We shall see who'll leave here first, that we shall!'

Zinaida rang. She was sitting in a corner of her room with the air of having been put there as a punishment.

'There isn't a telegram, is there?' she asked.

'No, ma'am.'

'Ask the porter, there might be one.

'And don't go out of the house,' she called after me. 'I'm afraid to be here on my own.'

I had to run down to the porter every hour after that and ask if there was a telegram. What an unnerving time, though, honestly! Zinaida ate and had tea in her room to avoid seeing Polya, she slept there on a short crescent-shaped divan and she made her own bed. For the first few days it was I who took the telegrams, but when no answer came she ceased to trust me and went to the post office herself. Looking at her, I too anxiously awaited a wire. I hoped he might have contrived some deception: arranging for her to receive a telegram from some railway station, for instance. If he was too engrossed with his cards, or had taken up with another woman, Gruzin and Kukushkin would surely remind him of us, I thought. But we waited in vain. I went into Zinaida's room half a dozen times a day to tell her the truth, but there she would be with shoulders drooping and lips moving, looking rather like a goat. I went away again without a word. Pity and compassion had quite unmanned me. Apparently unaffected by all this, Polya was cheerful and jolly, tidying the master's study and bedroom, ferreting in cupboards, clattering dishes. When she passed Zinaida's door she would hum something and cough. She was glad that Zinaida was hiding from her. In the evening she would go off somewhere and ring the doorbell at about two or three in the morning, when I had to open up to her and listen to her remarks about my cough. At once another ring would be heard and I would run to the room next to the study. Zinaida would stick her head through the doorway.

'Who was that ringing?' she would ask, looking at my hands to see if I was holding a telegram.

When, on Saturday, there was a ring downstairs at last, and a well-known voice was heard on the staircase, she was so happy that she burst into tears. She rushed to greet him, embraced him, kissed his chest and sleeves, and said something unintelligible. The porter carried the suit-cases up, and Polya's jolly voice was heard. It was as if he was just starting his holidays.

'Why didn't you telegraph?' asked Zinaida, panting with joy. 'Why? I've suffered such torments, I've hardly survived. Oh, my God!'

'It's all perfectly simple,' Orlov said. 'The Senator and I left for Moscow on the very first day, so I didn't get your wires. I'll give you a detailed account this afternoon, dearest, but now I must sleep, sleep, sleep. The train was so tiring.'

He had obviously been up all night: playing cards, probably, and drinking a lot. Zinaida tucked him up in bed, and after that we all went round on tiptoe until evening. Lunch passed off quite successfully, but when they went to have coffee in the study the argument began. Zinaida said something rapidly in a low voice. She was speaking French, her words gurgling like a stream, after which a loud sigh came from Orlov, followed by his voice.

'My God!' he said in French. 'Have you really no more interesting news than this eternal lament about the wicked maidservant?'

'But, darling, she did rob me, and she was most impudent.'

'Then why doesn't she rob me? Why isn't she impudent to me? Why do *I* never notice maids or porters or footmen? You are behaving like a spoilt child, my dear, you don't know your own mind. I suspect you may be pregnant, actually. When I offered to dismiss her it was you who insisted on her staying. And now you want me to get rid of her. Well, in a case like this I can be stubborn too, I answer fad with fad. You want her to go away. Very well then, I want her to stay. It's the only way to cure you of your nerves.'

'Oh, all right, all right,' said Zinaida in panic. 'Let us change the subject. Let's leave it till tomorrow. Now tell me about Moscow. How was Moscow?'

X

The following day was the seventh of January (St. John the Baptist's Day) and after lunch Orlov put on his black dress-coat and decoration to go and wish his father many happy returns of his name-day. He had to leave at two o'clock, and it was only half past one when he had finished dressing. How should he spend the thirty minutes? He paced the drawing-room declaiming congratulatory verses which he had once recited to his father and mother as a child. Zinaida was sitting there too, being about to visit her dressmaker or go shopping, and she listened with a smile. How their conversation began I do not know, but when I took Orlov his gloves he was standing in front of Zinaida and peevishly pleading with her.

'In the name of God, in the name of all that is sacred, don't keep churning out the same old truisms. What an unfortunate faculty some clever, intellectually active ladies have for talking with an air of profundity and enthusiasm about things that have been boring even schoolboys to distraction for years! Oh, if you would but eliminate all these serious problems from our connubial programme, how grateful I should be!'

'Women may not dare hold views of their own, it seems.'

'I concede you total freedom. Be as liberal as you like, quote what authors you will, but do grant *me* a concession. Just don't discuss either of two subjects in my presence: the evils of upper-class society and the defects of marriage as an institution. Now, get this into your head once and for all. The upper class is always abused in contrast with the world of tradesfolk, priests, workmen, peasants and every other sort of vulgar lout. Both classes are repugnant to me, but were I asked to make an honest choice between the two I should opt for the upper class without hesitation, and there would be nothing spurious or affected about it because my tastes are all on that side. Our world may be trivial, it may be empty, but you and I do at any rate speak decent French, we do read the occasional book, and we don't go around bashing each other in the ribs even when we are having a serious quarrel. Now, as for the *hoi polloi*, the riff-raff, the beard-and-caftan brigade, with them it's all "we aims to give satisfaction, 'alf a mo', gorblimey," not to mention their unbridled licentiousness, their pot-house manners and their idolatrous superstitions.'

'The peasant and tradesman do feed us.'

'So what? That reflects as much discredit on them as it does on me. If they feed me, if they doff their caps to me, it only means they lack the wit and honesty to do otherwise. I am not blaming anyone, I am not praising anyone, all I'm saying is that where upper and lower class are concerned it's six of one to half a dozen of the other. My heart and mind are against both, but my tastes are with the former.

'Now then, with regard to marriage being an unnatural institution,' Orlov went on with a glance at his watch. 'It is high time you realized that it's not a matter of natural or unnatural, but of people not knowing what they want out of marriage. What *do* you expect from it? Cohabitation, licit or illicit, and all manner of unions and liaisons, good and bad . . . they all boil down to the same basic element. You ladies live exclusively for that element, it's the very stuff of life to you, and without it you'd find existence meaningless. Outside it you have no other needs and so you grab hold of it. But ever since you started reading serious fiction you have been ashamed of grabbing hold of it—you dash from pillar to post, you rush headlong from man to man, and then try to justify the whole imbroglio by saying how unnatural a thing is marriage. But if you can't or won't renounce that essence, your greatest enemy and bugbear, if you mean to go on truckling to it so obsequiously, then what serious discussion can there be? Whatever you say will only be pretentious nonsense and I shan't believe it.'

I went to ask the hall-porter whether the hired sledge had come, and on my return I found them quarrelling. There was a squall in the offing, as sailors say.

'Today you wish to shock me with your cynicism, I see,' said Zinaida, pacing the drawing-room in great agitation. 'I find your words quite disgusting. I am innocent in the eyes of God and man, and I have nothing to reproach myself with, either. I left my husband for you, and I am proud of it. Yes, I swear: proud, on my word of honour.'

'Well, that's all right then.'

'If you have a shred of decency and honesty in you, then you too must be proud of what I have done. It lifts us both above thousands of people who would like to do the same as I, but don't dare through cowardice or meanness. But you aren't a decent person. You fear freedom, you deride an honest impulse because you are afraid of some ignoramus suspecting *you* of being honest. You're afraid to show me to your friends, and there's nothing you hate more than driving down the street with me—that's true, isn't it? Why have you never introduced me to your father and cousin, that's what I want to know?'

'Oh, I am sick of this, I must say,' shouted Zinaida, stamping. 'I insist on having my rights, so kindly introduce me to your father.'

'Go and introduce yourself if you want, he interviews petitioners each morning from ten to ten thirty.'

'Oh, you really *are* foul,' said Zinaida, frantically wringing her hands. 'Even if you don't mean it, even if you're not saying what you think, that cruel joke alone makes you detestable. Oh, you are *foul*, I must say.'

'We're barking up the wrong tree, you and I, this way we'll never get anywhere. What it comes to is this: you made a mistake and you won't admit it. You took me for a hero, you credited me with certain unusual notions and ideals, but then I turned out to be just a common-or-garden bureaucrat who plays cards and isn't the least bit keen on ideals. I am a worthy representative of that same tainted society which you have fled, outraged by its emptiness and vulgarity. Well, why not be fair and admit as much? Lavish your indignation on yourself, not me, for the mistake's yours, not mine.'

'All right, I admit it: I made a mistake.'

'Well, that's all right then. We have reached the point at last, thank God. Now, bear with me a little longer if you will be so kind. I cannot rise to your heights, being too depraved, nor can you demean yourself to my level, since you are too superior. So there's only one way out——'

'What's that?' asked Zinaida quickly, holding her breath and suddenly turning white as a sheet.

'We must have recourse to logic, and——'

'Why, oh why, do you torture me like this, George?' Zinaida suddenly asked in Russian, her voice breaking. 'Try to understand how much I suffer——'

Dreading her tears, Orlov darted into his study and then for some reason—whether to hurt her more, or remembering that it was usual practice in such cases—locked the door behind him. She screamed and rushed after him, her dress swishing.

'What is the meaning of this?' she asked, banging the door.

'What, what *does* it mean?' she repeated in a shrill voice breaking with indignation. 'So that's the kind of man you are, is it? I hate and despise you, so there! It's all over between us: all over, I tell you!'

Hysterical tears followed, mingled with laughter. Some small object fell off the drawing-room table and broke. Orlov made his way from study to hall through the other door, looked around him in panic, swiftly donned his cloak and top hat, and fled.

Half an hour passed, then an hour, and she was still crying. She had no father, no mother, no relatives, I remembered, and she was living here between a man who hated her and Polya who robbed her. How wretched her life indeed was, thought I. Not knowing why I did so, I went into the drawing-room to see her. Weak, helpless, with her lovely hair—a very paragon of tenderness and elegance in my eyes—she was suffering as if she was ill. She lay on the sofa hiding her face and shuddering all over.

'Would you like me to fetch the doctor, ma'am?' I asked softly.

'No, there's no need, it's nothing,' she said, looking at me with tearful eyes. 'It's only a bit of a headache, thank you very much.'

I went out. In the evening she wrote one letter after another. She sent me to Pekarsky, Kukushkin and Gruzin by turns, and finally anywhere I liked if I would but find Orlov quickly and give him her letter. Every time I returned with that letter she feverishly scolded me, pleaded with me, thrust money into my hand. She did not sleep that night, but sat in the drawing-room talking to herself.

Orlov came back to lunch next day and they were reconciled.

On the following Thursday Orlov complained to his friends that he had reached the end of his tether and that life was not worth living. He smoked a lot.

'It's no life, this isn't, it's sheer torture,' he said irritably. 'Tears, shrieks, intellectual conversation and pleas for forgiveness followed by more tears and shrieks, and the result is I can't call the place my own. I suffer agonies and I make her suffer too. Must I really put up with another couple of months of this? Surely not? But I may have to.'

'Then why not speak to her?' Pekarsky asked.

'I have tried, but I can't. With a rational, self-sufficient person you can say anything you like with complete confidence, but here you are dealing with a creature devoid of will-power, character and reason, aren't you? I can't stand tears, they unnerve me. Whenever she cries I'm ready to swear eternal love, and I want to cry as well.'

Not understanding, Pekarsky scratched his broad forehead thoughtfully.

'You really should take a separate flat for her,' he said. 'It's easy enough, surely.'

'It's me she needs, not a flat,' Orlov sighed. 'But what's the use of talking? All I hear is chatter, chatter, chatter, I see no way out. Talk about innocent victims! *I* didn't make this bed, yet it's me who's got to lie on it! A hero's the last thing I ever wanted to be! I could never stand Turgenev's novels, but now (and this is sheer farce) I suddenly find myself a sort of quintessential Turgenev hero. I swear blind I'm no such thing, I adduce the most irrefutable proofs to that effect, but she won't believe me. Now, why not? There must be something heroic about my countenance.'

'Then you had better go and inspect the provinces,' laughed Kukushkin.

'Yes, that's all I *can* do.'

A week after this conversation Orlov declared that he was being assigned to the Senator again, and he took his suitcases to Pekarsky's that same evening.

XI

On the threshold stood a man of about sixty in a beaver cap. His long fur coat reached the ground.

'Is Mr. Orlov in?' he asked.

I thought it was a money-lender at first, one of Gruzin's creditors who occasionally called on Orlov to collect small sums on account. But when the visitor came into the hall and flung open his coat, I saw the thick eyebrows and characteristic pursing of the lips which I had so thoroughly studied on photographs, and two rows of stars on the coat of a dress uniform. I recognized Orlov's father, the well-known statesman.

Mr. Orlov was out, I told him. The old man pursed his lips firmly and looked thoughtfully to one side, showing me a wasted, toothless profile.

'I'll leave a note,' he said. 'Will you show me in?'

Leaving his galoshes in the hall, he went into the study without taking off his long, heavy fur coat. He sat down in a low chair in front of the desk and pondered for several minutes before picking up a pen, shielding his eyes with his hand as if to keep the sun off: just like his son in a bad mood. He had a sad, thoughtful look, with an air of resignation such as I have only seen on the faces of elderly religious people. I stood behind him, contemplating the bald pate and the hollow at the back of his neck, and it was crystal clear to me that this weak, ailing, elderly man was now at my mercy. Why, there was no one in the flat apart from myself and my enemy. I only needed to employ a little force, then snatch his watch to disguise my motive and leave by the tradesmen's exit—and I should have gained incomparably more than I could ever have banked on when I became a servant. I was never likely to get a better chance than this, I thought. But instead of doing anything about it I looked with complete detachment from his bald pate to his furs and back, quietly brooding on the relations between this man and his only son, and on the probability that persons spoilt by riches and power don't want to die.

'You there—how long have you been working for my son?' he asked, forming large letters on the paper.

'Between two and three months, sir.'

He finished writing and stood up. There was still time. I spurred myself on, clenching my fists, searching my heart for some particle at least of my former loathing. How impassioned, how stubborn, how assiduous an enemy I had so recently been, I remembered. But it is hard to strike a match on crumbling stone. The sad old face, the cold glitter of his medal stars . . . they evoked in me only trivial, cheap, futile thoughts about the transiency of all things terrestrial and the proximity of death.

'Good-bye, my good fellow,' said the old man.

He put on his cap and left.

I had changed, I had become a new man: there could be no more doubt on that score. To test myself I began thinking of the past, but at once felt aghast as if I had chanced to peep into some dark, dank corner. Recalling my comrades and friends, I first thought how I should blush, how put out I should be, when I met any of them. But what kind of man was I now? What should I think about? What should I do? What was my goal in life?

None of it made sense to me, and I realized only one thing clearly: I must pack my things and leave with all speed. Before the old man's visit there had still been some point in my job, but now it was just ludicrous. My tears dropped into my open suitcase. I felt unbearably sad, and yet so tremendously vital. I was ready to span all human potentialities within the compass of my brief existence. I wanted to speak, to read, to wield a mallet in some big factory, to keep watch at sea, to plough the fields. I wanted to go to the Nevsky Prospekt, to the country, out to sea: wherever my imagination reached. When Zinaida returned I rushed to open the door and took off her coat with especial tenderness, for this was the last time.

We had two other visitors that day besides the old man. In the evening, when it was quite dark, Gruzin unexpectedly arrived to fetch some papers for Orlov. He opened the desk, took the papers he wanted, rolled them up and told me to put them by his cap in the hall while he went to see Zinaida. She lay on the drawing-room sofa, hands behind her head. Five or six days had passed since Orlov had left on his 'tour of inspection', and no one knew when he would be back, but she no longer sent telegrams or expected them. She ignored Polya, who was still living with us. She just didn't care . . . that was written all over her impassive, dead pale face. Now it was she who wanted to be miserable out of obstinacy, like Orlov. To spite herself and everything else on earth she lay quite still on the sofa for days on end, wishing herself only harm, expecting only the worst. She was probably picturing how Orlov would return, how they were bound to quarrel, how he would cool towards her and be unfaithful to her, after which they would separate, and these agonizing thoughts may have given her satisfaction. But what would she say if she suddenly discovered the real truth?

'I'm fond of you, my dear,' said Gruzin, greeting her and kissing her hand. 'You're so kind.

'Good old George has gone away,' he lied. 'He's gone away, the wicked man.'

He sat down with a sigh and fondly stroked her hand.

'Let me spend an hour with you, my dear,' he said. 'I don't like going home, and it's too early to go to the Birshovs'. Today's Katya Birshov's birthday. She's a very nice little girl.'

I brought him a glass of tea and a carafe of vodka. He drank the tea slowly, with evident reluctance.

'Have you a bite to, er, eat, my friend?' he asked timidly as he gave me back the glass. 'I haven't had a meal.'

There was nothing in the flat, so I fetched him the ordinary one-rouble dinner from the restaurant.

'Your health, dear!' he said to Zinaida and tossed down a glass of vodka. 'My little girl, your god-daughter, sends her love. She has a touch of scrofula, poor child.

'Ah, children, children!' he sighed. 'But you can say what you like, my dear, it's nice being a father. Good old George can't understand that feeling.'

He downed another glass. Gaunt, pale, wearing a napkin on his chest like an apron, he ate greedily, raising his eyebrows and looking from Zinaida to me like a small boy in disgrace. He looked ready to have burst into tears if I had not given him his grouse or jelly. Having satisfied his hunger, he cheered up and laughed as he started telling a story about the Birshov family, but then grew silent, when he noticed that this was uninteresting, and that Zinaida was not laughing. Then a sort of boredom suddenly descended. After the meal they both sat in the dining-room by the light of a single lamp and said nothing. He was tired of lying, while she wanted to ask him something, but didn't dare. Half an hour passed in this way. Then Gruzin looked at his watch.

'Well, perhaps it's time I went.'

'No, please stay. We must talk.'

There was a further silence. He sat at the piano, touched a key, then played and quietly sang: 'What does the morrow hold in store?' Then, as usual, he suddenly rose to his feet and shook his head.

'Play something, my dear,' Zinaida said.

'But what?' he asked with a shrug. 'I've forgotten it all, I gave it up ages ago.'

Looking at the ceiling as if trying to remember, he played two of Tchaikovsky's pieces with wonderful expression, warmly and intelligently. He looked just as he always did—neither intelligent nor stupid—and I found it utterly miraculous that a man whom I was used to seeing in this mean and squalid environment should be capable of flights of emotion so pure, so far beyond my ken. Zinaida flushed and paced the drawing-room excitedly.

'Just a moment, my dear, I'll play you something else if I can remember it,' he said. 'It's something I heard on the 'cello.'

Starting timidly, then picking up, and finally with complete confidence, he played Saint-Saëns's *The Swan*. Then he played it again.

'Not bad, eh?' he said.

Greatly moved, Zinaida went and stood beside him.

'My friend,' she said, 'tell me truly as a friend: what do you think of me?'

'What can I say?' he answered, raising his eyebrows. 'I like you, and I think only good of you.

'But if you want my general views on the problem which concerns you,' he went on, rubbing his sleeve near the elbow and frowning, 'then, my dear, you know. . . . Following one's heart's impulses freely . . . it doesn't always bring happiness to decent people. If one wants to be free and happy at the same time, I think one must face the fact that life is cruel, harsh and pitiless in its conservatism, and that one must pay it back in its own currency: be equally harsh, equally pitiless in one's own drive for freedom, in other words. That's my view.'

'But how can I?' Zinaida smiled sadly. 'I'm so tired, my friend. I can't lift a finger to save myself, I'm so tired.'

'Go into a convent, my dear.'

He said it in jest, but after he had spoken tears glistened in Zinaida's eyes, and then in his.

'Ah well,' he said, 'I have sat here long enough, it's time I was off. Good-bye, dear friend. God give you health.'

He kissed both her hands and stroked them affectionately, saying that he would certainly come to see her again in a day or two. As he put on his overcoat—the one that was so like a child's—in the hall, he spent a long time fumbling in his pockets for a tip for me, but found nothing.

'Good-bye, old chap,' he said sadly, and went out.

I shall never forget the atmosphere which the man left behind him. Zinaida continued pacing the drawing-room excitedly. She was walking about instead of lying down, and that in itself was a good sign. I wanted to take advantage of this mood to speak to her frankly and then leave at once, but hardly had I seen Gruzin out when the door-bell rang. It was Kukushkin.

'Is Mr. Orlov in?' he asked. 'Is he back? No, you say? What a pity. In that case I'll go and kiss your mistress's hand and then run along.

'May I come in, Zinaida?' he shouted. 'I want to kiss your hand. I'm sorry I'm so late.'

He was not long in the drawing-room—ten minutes, no more—but I felt as if he had been there for some time and would never leave. I bit my lips in indignation and annoyance, and I already hated Zinaida. I wondered why she didn't throw him out and I felt outraged, though it was obvious that he bored her.

When I held his coat for him he bestowed a special sign of favour by asking how I managed without a wife.

'But you don't let the grass grow under your feet, I'm sure,' he laughed. 'No doubt you have your bit of slap and tickle with Polya, you rascal.'

Despite my experience of life I had little knowledge of people at that time, and I frequently exaggerated trifles, very possibly, and entirely missed things of importance. Kukushkin's sniggers and flattery had a certain point, it struck me. Perhaps he hoped that, being a servant, I should gossip in kitchens and servants' halls all over the place about his visiting us in the evenings when Orlov was out, and sitting with Zinaida until late at night? Then, when my gossip reached his friends' ears he would drop his eyes in confusion, and wag his little finger. At cards that very evening he would pretend, or perhaps accidentally blurt out, that he had won Zinaida away from Orlov—or so I thought, looking at that unctuous little face.

I was now gripped by the very hatred which had failed me during the old man's visit at midday. Kukushkin left at last. Listening to the shuffle of his leather galoshes, I felt a strong urge to pursue him with some coarse parting oath, but restrained myself. Then, when his steps had died away on the stairs, I went back into the hall and, not knowing what I was doing, seized the roll of papers which he had left behind and rushed headlong downstairs. I ran into the street without my coat or cap. It was not cold, but big snow flakes were falling, and there was a wind.

'Sir!' I shouted, catching up Kukushkin. 'I say, sir!'

He stopped by a lamp-post and looked round in bewilderment.

'I say, sir,' I panted. 'Sir!'

Having no idea what to say, I hit him twice on the face with the roll of paper. Quite at a loss, not even surprised—so unawares had I taken him—he leant back against the lamp-post and shielded his face with his hands. At that moment some army medical officer passed by and saw me hitting the man, but only looked at us in amazement and walked on.

I felt ashamed and rushed back to the house.

XII

My head wet with snow, out of breath, I ran to my room, immediately threw off my tail-coat, put on my jacket and top-coat, and brought my suitcase into the hall. Oh, to escape! But before leaving I quickly sat down and began writing to Orlov.

'I leave you my false passport,' I began. 'Please keep it in memory of me, you humbug, you metropolitan stuffed shirt.

'To insinuate oneself into a household under an alias, to observe domestic intimacies behind a servant's mask, to see all, hear all, and then volunteer denunciations of your mendacity . . . it's all rather underhand, you will say. Very well, but I am not concerned with cultivating integrity at the moment. I have suffered dozens of your suppers and lunches, when you spoke and did as you pleased while I had to listen, watch and hold my peace, and I don't see why you should get away with it. Besides, if there's no one else near you who dares tell you the truth without flattery, let Stephen the footman be the one to knock you off your elevated perch.'

I disliked this beginning, but I was not inclined to change it. What did it matter, anyway?

The large windows with their dark curtains, the bed, the crumpled dress-coat on the floor, my wet footprints . . . they all looked forbidding and gloomy. There was something peculiar about the silence too.

Perhaps because I had dashed into the street without my cap or galoshes, I was running a high fever. My face burnt, my legs ached, my heavy head sagged over the table, and I appeared to be suffering from split personality, each thought in my brain being seemingly haunted by its own shadow.

'Ill, weak and demoralized as I am, I cannot write to you as I should like,' I continued. 'My first wish was to insult and humiliate you, but I no longer feel I have any right to do that. We are both failures, you and I, and neither of us is going to rise again, so however eloquent, forceful and awesome my letter might be, it would still be like beating on a coffin lid: I could bang away for all I was worth without waking anyone up. No exertions can ever warm that damnable cold blood of yours, as you know better than I do. Is there any point in writing to you, then? But my head and heart are burning and I continue writing, somehow excited, as if this letter could still rescue the two of us. My thoughts are incoherent because I am running a temperature, and my pen somehow scratches meaninglessly on the paper, but the question I want to ask you is plain before my eyes as though written in letters of fire.

'It is not hard to explain why *I* have flagged and fallen prematurely. Like Samson in the Bible, I hoisted the gates of Gaza on my back to carry them to the top of the mountain, but only when I was already exhausted, when my youth and health had faded once and for all, did I realize that those gates were too heavy for me and that I had deceived myself. Moreover, I was in constant, agonizing pain. I have suffered hunger, cold, sickness and loss of liberty. I never knew personal happiness, and I still don't. I have no refuge, my memories weigh me down, and my conscience is often afraid of them. But you, now, you... why have *you* fallen? What fatal, hellish causes prevented your life from blossoming forth in full vernal splendour? Before you had even begun to live you hastened to renounce the image and likeness of God, you turned into a cowardly animal which barks to scare others because it is scared itself. Why, though? You fear life, you fear it like the Oriental who sits on a cushion all day smoking his hookah. Oh yes, you read a lot, and your European coat fits you well. Yet with what fond, purely Oriental solicitude, worthy of some eastern potentate, do you shield yourself from hunger, cold, physical effort, pain and worry! How early you began to rest on your oars! What a cowardly attitude you have shown to real life and the natural forces with which every normal, healthy man has to contend! How soft, snug, warm, comfortable you are... and oh, how bored! Yes, you experience the shattering, abysmal boredom of a man in solitary confinement, but you try to hide even from that enemy by playing cards for eight hours out of the twenty-four.

'And your irony? Oh, how well I understand it! Vital, free-ranging, confident speculation ... it's a pretty keen and potent process, that, but not one that a sluggish, idle brain can cope with. So, to stop it encroaching on your peace of mind, you hastened while yet young to confine it within bounds, as did thousands of your contemporaries, by arming yourself with an ironical approach to life or whatever you want to call it. Your inhibited, cowed thoughts do not dare to leap the fence which you have set round them, and when you mock ideals which you claim to know "all about", you're just like the deserter fleeing disgracefully from the battlefield, and stifling his own shame by deriding war and valour. Cynicism dulls the pain. In some novel of Dostoyevsky's an old man tramples his favourite daughter's portrait underfoot because he has treated her unfairly, just as you mock the ideals of goodness and justice in your nasty, cheap way because you can't live up to them any longer. You dread every honest, direct reference to your own decline, and you deliberately surround yourself with people capable only of flattering your weaknesses. So no wonder you're so scared of tears, no wonder at all.

'And incidentally, there's your attitude to women. We are all shameless—that's something we inherited with our flesh and blood, it's part of our upbringing. But what is one a man for, if not to subdue the beast within one? When you grew up, when you got to know "all about" ideas, the truth was staring you in the face. You knew it, but you didn't pursue it, you took fright at it, and you tried to deceive your conscience by loudly assuring yourself that the fault was not yours, it was women's, and that women were as debased as your relations with them. Those bleak dirty stories, that neighing snigger, all your innumerable theories about the so-called "basic element", about the vagueness of the demands made on marriage, about the ten *sous* which the French labourer pays his woman, your never-ending references to female illogicality, mendaciousness, feebleness and the like . . . doesn't it all rather look as if you want to push woman down in the mud at all costs so as to put her on the same level as your own relations with her? You're a wretched, weak, disagreeable person.'

Zinaida started playing the piano in the drawing-room, trying to remember the Saint-Saëns piece which Gruzin had played. I went and lay on my bed, but then remembered that it was time to go. Forcing myself to stand up, I went back to the desk with a heavy, hot head.

'But why are we so tired? That's the question,' I went on. 'We who start out so passionate, bold, high-minded and confident . . . why are we so totally bankrupt by the age of thirty or thirty-five? Why is it that one person pines away with consumption, another puts a bullet in his brains, and a third seeks oblivion in vodka or cards, while a fourth tries to stifle his anguished terrors by cynically trampling on the image of his fine, unsullied youth? Why do we never try to stand up once we have fallen down? If we lose one thing why don't we look for another? Well may one ask.

'The thief on the Cross managed to recover his zest for living and a bold, realistic hope for his future, though he may have had less than an hour to live. You have long years ahead of you, and I'm not going to die as soon as you think, probably. What if, by some miracle, the present should turn out to be a dream, a hideous nightmare, what if we awoke renewed, cleansed, strong, proud in our sense of rectitude? Joyous visions fire me, I am breathless with excitement. I have a terrific appetite for life, I want our lives to be sacred, sublime and solemn as the vault of the heavens. And live we shall! The sun rises only once a day, and life isn't given twice, so hold tight to what is left of it and preserve that.'

I wrote not a word more. My head was seething with ideas, but they were all so blurred that I could not get them down on paper. Leaving the letter unfinished, I signed my rank, Christian name and surname, and went into the study. It was dark there. I groped for the desk and put the letter on it. I must have stumbled into the furniture in the dark and made a noise.

'Who's there?' asked a worried voice in the drawing-room.

At that moment the clock on the desk gently struck one o'clock.

XIII

I spent at least half a minute scratching at the door and fumbling with it in the darkness, then slowly opened it and went into the drawing-room. Zinaida was lying on a sofa and raised herself on an elbow to watch me come in. Not daring to speak, I walked slowly past her while she followed me with her eyes. I stood in the hall for a moment, then went past again while she watched me carefully and with amazement—with fear, even. At last I halted.

'He won't be coming back,' I brought out with an effort.

She quickly rose to her feet and looked at me uncomprehendingly.

'He won't be coming back,' I repeated, my heart pounding violently. 'He can't come back because he hasn't left St. Petersburg. He is staying at Pekarsky's.'

She understood and believed me, as I could tell from her sudden pallor, and from the way in which she suddenly crossed her hands over her breast in fear and entreaty. Her recent history flashed through her mind, she put two and two together, she saw the whole truth with pitiless clarity. But she also remembered that I was a servant, a lower form of life. Some bounder, his hair awry and face flushed with fever, very possibly drunk, wearing a vulgar overcoat, had crudely barged in on her private life, and that offended her.

'Nobody asked your opinion,' she told me sternly. 'You may leave the room.'

'But you must believe me,' I said impetuously, stretching out my arms to her. 'I am not a servant, I'm an independent person just as you are.'

I mentioned my name and quickly—very quickly indeed, to stop her interrupting me or going to her room—explained who I was and why I was living there. This new revelation shocked her more than the first. Hitherto she had still hoped that her servant was lying, or was mistaken and had spoken foolishly, but now after my confession there was no longer room for doubt. The expression in her unhappy eyes and face, which suddenly seemed ugly because it looked older and lost its gentleness . . . it told me that she had reached the limit of her endurance, and how ill it boded, this conversation which I had started. But I continued, quite carried away.

'The Senator and his inspection were invented to deceive you. He did the same in January: he didn't go away, he just stayed at Pekarsky's. I saw him every day and helped to deceive you. They were fed up with you, they hated having you around, they mocked you. If you could have heard how he and his friends jeered at you and your love you wouldn't have stayed here a minute longer. So run away, escape!'

'Oh, all right,' she said in quavering tones, passing her hand over her hair. 'All right then. Who cares?'

Her eyes were full of tears, her lips trembled, her whole face was strikingly pale and breathed anger. Orlov's crude, petty lies outraged her, she found them contemptible and ridiculous. She smiled, but I disliked the look of that smile.

'All right then,' she repeated, passing her hand over her hair again. 'Who cares? He thinks I shall die of humiliation, but I just . . . think it's funny.

'There's no point in him hiding, no point at all,' she said, moving away from the piano and shrugging her shoulders. 'It would have been simpler to discuss things openly than to go into hiding and skulk about in other people's flats. I do have eyes in my head, I'd noticed all this myself ages ago, and I was only waiting for him to come back to have things out once and for all.'

Then she sat in the arm-chair near the table, leant her head on the sofa arm and wept bitterly. There was only one candle burning in the drawing-room candle-holder and the chair she sat in was in darkness, but I could see her head and shoulders quivering, while her hair fell loose and covered her neck, face and hands. In her quiet, even, un-hysterical, normal, womanly weeping could be heard wounded pride, humiliation, resentment and the absolute hopelessness of a situation utterly irreparable and unacceptable. Her weeping found its echo in my agitated, suffering heart. I had forgotten my illness and everything else on earth as I paced the drawing-room, muttering distractedly.

'Oh, what a life! One really can't go on like this, indeed one can't. It's sheer criminal lunacy, this life is.'

'How humiliating!' she said through her tears. 'To live with me and smile at me when he found me such a drag, so ridiculous. What terrible humiliation!'

Raising her head, she gazed at me with tearful eyes through hair wet with tears as she tidied this hair which blocked her view of me.

'Did they laugh at me?' she asked.

'You, your love, Turgenev in whom you were allegedly too well versed . . . these men found it all funny. And should we both die of despair this instant they would find that funny too. They would make up a comic story and tell it at your funeral service.

'But why talk about them?' I asked impatiently. 'We must escape. I can't stay here a minute longer.'

She began crying again, and I went over to the piano and sat down.

'Well, what are we waiting for?' I asked despondently. 'It's past two o'clock already.'

'I'm not waiting for anything,' she said. 'My life is ruined.'

'Don't say such things. Come on, let us pool forces and decide what to do. Neither of us can stay here. Where do you intend going?'

Suddenly the bell rang in the hall and my heart missed a beat. Could Orlov have come back after receiving a complaint about me from Kukushkin? How should we greet him? I went to open the door, and there was Polya. She came in, shook the snow from her cloak in the hall and went to her room without a word to me. When I returned to the drawing-room Zinaida was pale as death and stood in the middle of the room, fixing huge eyes on me.

'Who was that?' she asked softly.

'Polya,' I told her.

She ran her hand over her hair and closed her eyes wearily.

'I'll leave this instant,' she said. 'Would you be very kind and take me to the Old Town? What time is it?'

'A quarter to three.'

XIV

The street was dark and deserted when we left the house a little later. Sleet was falling and a damp wind lashed us in the face. It was the beginning of March, I remember, there was a thaw, and it was some days since the cabmen had started driving on wheels in place of sledges. The back stairs, the cold, the darkness of night, the porter in his sheep-skin questioning us before he let us out of the gate . . . these things utterly fatigued and depressed Zinaida. When we had got into a fly and put the hood up, she shook all over and quickly said how grateful she was.

'I don't doubt your good will,' she muttered, 'but I am ashamed to put you to this trouble. Oh, I understand, I understand. When Gruzin was here this evening I could tell he was lying and hiding something. Very well then, I don't care. Still, I'm ashamed to have you go to so much trouble.'

She still had some doubts. To dispel them once and for all I told our cabman to drive down Sergiyevsky Street. Halting him at Pekarsky's door, I got out of the cab and rang. When the porter came I asked if Mr. Orlov was at home, speaking in a loud voice so that Zinaida could hear.

'Yes, he came back about half an hour ago,' was the answer. 'He must be in bed now. What do you want?'

Zinaida could not resist leaning out of the carriage.

'Has Mr. Orlov been staying here long?' she asked.

'Going on three weeks.'

'And he hasn't been away?'

'No,' answered the porter, looking at me with surprise.

'Tell him tomorrow morning that his sister is here from Warsaw,' I said. 'Good night.'

Then we drove on. The cab had no apron, and snowflakes fell on us, while the wind pierced us to the bone, especially when we were crossing the Neva. I began to feel as if we had been travelling like this for some time, as if we had long been suffering, and as if I had been listening to Zinaida's shuddering breath for ages. In a state bordering on hallucination, as if I was dozing off, I cast a casual backward glance at my strange, feckless life. Somehow a melodrama, *Parisian Beggars*, which I had seen once or twice as a child, came to mind. Then I tried to shake off this semi-trance by looking out from the hood of my cab to see the dawn, and somehow all the images of the past, all my blurred thoughts, suddenly fused into a single clear and cogent idea: both Zinaida and I were now utterly lost. The idea carried conviction, deriving apparently from an air of impending doom in the cold, blue sky, but a second later my thoughts and beliefs were elsewhere engaged.

'Oh, what *can* I do now?' Zinaida asked, her voice rough in the cold, damp air. 'Where am I to go, what can I do? Gruzin said I should enter a convent, and I would, oh, I would! I would change my dress, my face, my name, my thoughts, everything about me, and I'd hide away for ever. But they won't have me as a nun, I'm pregnant.'

'We'll go abroad together tomorrow,' I told her.

'We can't, my husband won't give me a passport.'

'Then I'll take you without one.'

The cab stopped near a two-storey wooden house painted a dark colour. I rang. Taking from me her light little basket—the only luggage we had brought—Zinaida smiled a wry smile.

'My jewels,' she said.

But so weak was she that she could not hold those jewels.

It was a long time before the door opened. After the third or fourth ring a light glinted in the windows. Footsteps, coughing and whispering were heard. Then the key turned in the lock at last and a stout peasant woman with a scared red face appeared at the door. Some way behind her stood a thin little old woman with bobbed grey hair, in a white blouse carrying a candle. Zinaida ran into the lobby and flung herself on the old woman's neck.

'I've been so badly let down, Nina,' she sobbed loudly. 'Oh, Nina, it's such a dirty, rotten business.'

I gave the peasant woman the basket. They locked the door, but sobs and shouts of 'Nina' were still audible. I got in the fly and told the man to drive slowly towards the Nevsky Prospekt. I had to think where I could find my night's lodging.

I called on Zinaida late in the following afternoon. She was greatly changed. There were no traces of tears on her pale, very thin face, and her expression was altered. Whether it was because I now saw her in different and far from luxurious surroundings, or because our relations had changed, or perhaps because great sorrow had left its mark on her, she no longer seemed as elegant and well-dressed as formerly. Her figure had shrunk, rather. In her movements, her walk and her expression I noticed a jerkiness, an excess of nervousness and a quality of urgency, while even her smile lacked its former sweetness. I was now wearing an expensive suit which I had bought during the day. She first cast an eye over this suit and the hat in my hand, then fixed an impatient, quizzical glance on my face as if studying it.

'Your transformation still seems pretty miraculous to me,' she said. 'Forgive me looking at you so inquisitively. You're a most unusual man, aren't you?'

I told her again who I was and why I had lived at Orlov's, speaking at greater length and in more detail than on the previous day. She listened with great attention.

'I am finished with all that,' she interrupted me. 'Do you know, I couldn't resist writing him a note? Here is the answer.'

On the sheet which she gave me I saw Orlov's handwriting.

'I'm not looking for excuses, but you must admit it was your mistake, not mine.

'Wishing you happiness and begging you to forget with all speed

'Your faithful servant

'G. O.

'PS. Am sending on your things.'

There in the drawing-room stood the trunks and baskets sent on by Orlov, among them being my own pathetic suitcase.

'So he must . . .' said Zinaida, but did not finish her sentence.

We were silent for a time. She took the note and held it before her eyes for a couple of minutes while her face assumed the haughty, contemptuous, proud, harsh expression which she had worn at the beginning of our discussion on the previous evening. Tears came to her eyes: proud, angry tears, with nothing timid or bitter about them.

'Listen,' she said, standing up abruptly and going over to the window to prevent my seeing her face. 'I have decided to go abroad with you tomorrow.'

'Very well. We can start today so far as I'm concerned.'

'Recruit me into your organization,' she said, then suddenly turned round and asked if I had read Balzac. 'Have you read him? *Père Goriot* ends with the hero looking down at Paris from a hill-top and threatening the city. "I shall be even with you yet," says he, after which he begins a new life. And when I look at St. Petersburg from the train window for the last time, I'll say the same: "I shall be even with you yet."'

Having spoken, she smiled at her own joke and for some reason shuddered all over.

XV

In Venice I began to suffer attacks of pleurisy, having probably caught cold on the evening when we took the boat from the station to the Hotel Bauer. I had to go to bed on the first day and stay there for a fortnight. During my illness Zinaida came from her room to drink coffee with me every morning, and then read me aloud the French and Russian books of which we had bought a great many in Vienna. These were books which I had known for years, or which did not interest me, but with her delightful, amiable voice sounding so near to me the contents of the whole lot of them boiled down, so far as I was concerned, to the single fact that I was not alone. She would go out for a stroll and come back in her light grey dress and dainty straw hat, cheerful and warmed by the spring sunshine. Sitting by my bed, stooping over my face, she would tell me something about Venice or read these books, and I felt splendid.

At night I was cold, I had pains, I was bored, but during the day I exulted in life: there is no better way of putting it. The hot, brilliant sunshine beating through open windows and balcony door, the shouts below, the plash of oars, the tolling of bells, the thunder-peals of the noon-tide cannon, the sensation of complete and utter freedom . . . these things did wonders for me. I felt as if I were growing mighty, broad wings to bear me off God knows where. And how enchanting it was, what pleasure there was sometimes in the thought that another life was now marching step by step with mine, that I was the servant, protector, friend and indispensable travelling companion of a young woman who besides being beautiful and rich was also weak, insulted and lonely. Even illness can be pleasant when you know that others are eagerly looking forward to your recovery. I once heard her whispering with my doctor behind the door, and when she came into my room afterwards her eyes were filled with tears. It was a bad sign, but I was greatly moved, and it gave me a wonderful feeling of relief.

Then I was allowed out on the balcony. The sunshine and sea breeze lulled and caressed my sick body. I looked down at the familiar gondolas gliding along with feminine grace, smoothly and majestically, like living creatures attuned to the voluptuousness of a civilization so exotic and bewitching. There was a smell of the sea. Somewhere people were playing stringed instruments and singing a two-part song. It was so marvellous, so unlike that night in St. Petersburg with sleet falling and lashing me roughly in the face. Looking straight across the canal now, I could see the open sea, while the sunlight on the far skyline's expanse dazzled till it hurt your eyes. It made me long to go down to the dear old sea to which I had given my youth. I wanted a bit of excitement: a bit of life, that was all.

A fortnight later I was up and about, and could go where I pleased. I liked sitting in the sun, listening to a gondolier whom I could not understand and spending hours on end gazing at the villa where Desdemona was said to have lived: an unsophisticated, sad, demure little place as light as lace, it looked as if you could pick it up in one hand. I stood for some time by the Canova monument, my eyes fixed on the sad lion. In the Palace of the Doges I was attracted by the corner where the wretched Marino Faliero had been daubed with black paint. I should like to be an artist, poet or playwright, I thought, but if that is beyond me a dose of mysticism might not come amiss. Oh, if only I had some scrap of faith to add to the unruffled calm and serenity which filled my heart!

In the evenings we ate oysters, drank wine and went boating. I remember our black gondola quietly bobbing about in one place while the water gurgled beneath it, scarcely audible. The reflections of stars and shore lights quivered and trembled in places. Not far away people were singing in a gondola festooned with coloured lamps which were reflected in the water. Guitars, violins, mandolins, men's and women's voices rang out in the darkness, while Zinaida, looking pale and serious—stern, almost—sat by my side, pursing her lips and clasping her hands. Musing on something, she did not so much as move an eyebrow, and did not hear me. Her face, her pose, her fixed, expressionless glance, those incredibly bleak, unnerving ice-cold memories . . . and around us the gondolas, the lights, the music, the song with its dynamic, ardent cry of "*Jam-mo! Jam-mo!*" . . . what a fantastic contrast! When she sat like this, her hands tightly clasped, petrified, disconsolate, I felt as if we were both characters in an old-fashioned novel with some title like *A Maid Forlorn* or *The Forsaken Damozel*. Yes, both of us fitted: she forlorn and forsaken, and I, the loyal, faithful friend, the introvert, the odd-man-out if you like, the failure no longer capable of anything but coughing and brooding, and perhaps also of sacrificing himself. But what use were my sacrifices to anyone? And what had I to sacrifice, one might ask?

After our evening's outing we always had tea in her room and talked. We were not afraid of touching old wounds which were still unhealed: far from it, for it actually gave me pleasure, somehow, to tell her of my life with Orlov, or make frank allusions to those relations of which I was aware and which could not have been hidden from me.

'There were times when I hated you,' I said. 'When Orlov was behaving like a spoilt child, when he was condescending or lying to you, I was struck by your failure to see and grasp what was going on under your nose. You kissed his hands, you went down on your knees, you flattered him——'

She blushed. 'When I kissed his hands and knelt down I loved him.'

'Was he so very hard to see through? Was he really such a sphinx? A sphinx-cum-bureaucrat—oh really!

'God forbid that I should reproach you with anything,' I went on, feeling a little clumsy and lacking in the urbanity and finesse so essential when dealing with another's inner life, though I had never been aware of suffering from that defect before meeting her.

'But why couldn't you see through him?' I repeated, now more quietly and diffidently.

'You despise my past, you mean, and you are quite right,' she said, greatly upset. 'You are one of those special people who can't be judged conventionally, your moral imperatives are extremely stringent and you are incapable of forgiveness, I can see that. I understand you, and if I sometimes contradict you it doesn't mean I don't see eye to eye with you. I am only talking this antiquated rubbish because I haven't yet had time to wear out my old dresses and prejudices. Myself, I hate and despise my past, I despise Orlov and my love. A fine sort of love that was!

'It all seems so comic now, actually,' she said, going to the window and looking down at the canal. 'These love affairs only dull one's conscience and confuse one. Our struggle is the only thing with any meaning in life. Bring down your heel on the vile serpent's head and crush it. That is where you'll find your purpose, it's either there or there isn't any such thing.'

I told her long stories from my past, describing my exploits—and astounding they had indeed been. But not one syllable did I breathe about the change which had occurred inside me. She always listened with close attention, rubbing her hands at the interesting parts as if irked that such adventures, fears and delights had not yet come her way, but then she would suddenly grow pensive, retreating into herself, and I could tell from her expression that she was heeding me no longer.

I would close the windows on to the canal and ask whether we should have the fire lit.

'Oh, never mind that, I'm not cold,' she would say with a wan smile. 'I just feel weak all over. I think my wits have grown sharper of late, you know. I now have most unusual and original ideas. When I think about my past, say, about my old life—yes, and about people in general —the whole thing merges into a single picture and I see my stepmother. That rude, impudent, heartless, false slut of a woman! And she was a drug addict too! My father was a weak, spineless character who married my mother for her money and drove her into a decline, but his second wife, my stepmother . . . he loved her passionately, he was crazy about her. I had a lot to put up with, I can tell you. Anyway, why go on about it? So, as I say, everything somehow merges into this one image. And I feel annoyed that my stepmother's dead, I would dearly love to meet her now!'

'Why?'

'Oh, I don't know,' she answered with a laugh and a pretty toss of her head. 'Good night. Hurry up and get better. As soon as you do we shall start working for the cause, it's high time we did.'

I had said good night and had my hand on the door handle when she asked: 'What do you think? Does Polya still live there?'

'Probably.'

I went to my room. We lived like this for a whole month. Then, one dull day we were both standing by my window at noon, silently watching the storm-clouds rolling in from the sea and the canal which had turned dark blue. We were expecting a downpour at any moment, and when a narrow, dense belt of rain shrouded the open sea like a muslin veil we both suddenly felt bored. We left for Florence the same day.

XVI

It was autumn, we were in Nice. One morning when I went into her room she was sitting in an arm-chair: legs crossed, hunched, gaunt, face in hands, weeping torrents of bitter tears, with her long, unkempt hair trailing over her knees. The impression of the superb, magnificent sea which I had just been looking at and wanted to tell her about . . . it suddenly vanished and my heart ached.

'What's the matter?' I asked.

She took one hand from her face and motioned for me to go out.

'Now, what *is* the matter?' I repeated, and for the first time since we had first met I kissed her hand.

'It's nothing really,' she said quickly. 'Oh, it's nothing, nothing. Go away. Can't you see I'm not dressed?'

I went out in appalling distress. The serenity and peace of mind which I had so long enjoyed . . . now they were poisoned by compassion. I desperately longed to fall at her feet, to beg her not to bottle up her tears, but to share her grief with me, while the sea's steady rumble growled in my ears like the voice of doom and I foresaw new tears, new griefs, new losses. What, oh what was she crying about, I wondered, remembering her face and martyred look. She was pregnant, I remembered. She tried to hide her condition both from others and from herself. At home she wore a loose blouse or a bodice with voluminous folds in front, and when she went out she laced herself in so tightly that she twice fainted during our outings. She never mentioned her pregnancy to me, and when I once intimated that she might see a doctor she blushed deeply and said not a word.

When I went to her room later she was already dressed and had done her hair.

'Now, that's enough of that,' I said, seeing her once more on the brink of tears. 'Let's go down on the beach and have a talk.'

'I can't talk. I'm sorry, but I'm in the mood to be alone. And when you want to come into my room again, Vladimir, you might be good enough to knock first.'

That 'be good enough' sounded rather peculiar and unfeminine. I went out. My damned St. Petersburg mood came back, and my dreams all curled up and shrivelled like leaves in a heatwave. I felt that I was alone again, that there was no intimacy between us. I meant no more to her than yonder cobweb meant to the palm-tree on which it had chanced to cling until the wind should whip it off and whisk it away. I strolled about the square where the band was playing and went into the Casino. Here I looked at the overdressed, heavily perfumed women, and each of them glanced at me.

'You're an unattached male,' they seemed to say. 'Good!'

Then I went on the terrace and spent a long time looking at the sea. There was not one sail on the horizon. On the coast to my left were hills, gardens, towers and houses with sunlight playing on them in the mauve haze, but it was all so alien, so impassive—it was all such a clutter, somehow.

XVII

She still came and drank her coffee with me in the mornings, but we no longer had our meals together. She didn't feel hungry, she said, and she lived entirely on coffee, tea and oddments like oranges and caramels.

We no longer had our evening chats either, I don't know why. Ever since the day when I had found her in tears she had adopted a rather casual manner towards me, sometimes off-hand—or ironical, even. For some reason she was calling me 'my dear sir'. Whatever had once impressed her as awesome, admirable and heroic, arousing her envy and enthusiasm . . . it left her quite cold now. After hearing me out she would usually stretch herself slightly.

'Yes, yes, yes, but I seem to have heard all that before, my dear sir.'

There were even times when I did not see her for days on end. Sometimes I would knock timidly and quietly on her door, and there would be no answer. Then I would knock again: still silence. I would stand by the door listening, but then the chambermaid would walk past and bleakly declare that '*Madame est partie.*' Then I would pace up and down the hotel corridor. I would see English people, full-bosomed ladies, waiters in evening dress. Then, after I have been gazing for some time at the long, striped carpet which runs down the whole corridor, it occurs to me that I am playing a strange and probably false part in this woman's life, and that I am no longer able to change that role. I run to my room, I fall on the bed, I rack my brains, but no ideas come to me. All I can see is that I have a great zest for life, and that the uglier, the more wasted, the rougher her face looks, the closer does she seem to me, and the more intensely and painfully do I sense our kinship. Call me 'my dear sir', adopt that casual, contemptuous tone, do what you like, my darling, only don't leave me. I am afraid of being alone.

Then I go into the corridor again and listen anxiously. I miss my dinner, I don't notice evening coming on. At last, at about half past ten, familiar footsteps are heard and Zinaida appears at the bend near the staircase.

'Are you taking a stroll?' she asks as she passes by. 'Then you'd better go outside. Good night.'

'Shan't we meet today then?'

'I think it's too late. Oh, all right, have it your own way.'

'Tell me where you've been?' I say, following her into her room.

'Oh, to Monte Carlo.' She takes a dozen gold coins from her pocket. 'There, my dear sir,' says she. 'My roulette winnings.'

'Oh, I can't see you gambling.'

'Why ever not? I'm going back tomorrow.'

I could picture her with that ugly, ill expression on her face, pregnant, tightly laced, as she stood near the gaming table in a crowd of demimondaines and old women in their dotage swarming round the gold like flies round honey, and I remembered that for some reason she had gone to Monte Carlo without telling me.

'I don't believe you,' I said once. 'You wouldn't go there.'

'Don't worry, I can't lose much.'

'It's not a question of what you lose,' I said irritably. 'When you were gambling there, did it never occur to you that the glint of gold, all these women, old and young, the croupiers, the whole complex . . . it's all a filthy rotten mockery of the worker's toil, blood and sweat?'

'But what else is there to do here except gamble?' she asked. 'The worker's toil, blood and sweat . . . you keep those fine phrases till some other time. But now, since you started it, permit me to go on. Let me ask you outright: what is there for me to do here? What am I to do?'

'What indeed?' I shrugged. 'One can't answer that question straight out.'

'I want an honest answer, Vladimir,' she said, her expression growing angry. 'I didn't venture to pose the question in order to be fobbed off with commonplaces.

'I repeat,' she went on, banging her palm on the table as if marking time. 'What am I supposed to do here? And not only here in Nice, but anywhere else.'

I said nothing and looked through the window at the sea. My heart was pounding fearfully.

'Vladimir,' she said, breathing quietly and unevenly, and finding it hard to speak. 'If you don't believe in the cause yourself, Vladimir, if you no longer mean to go back to it, then why, oh why, did you drag me out of St. Petersburg? Why make promises, why raise mad hopes? Your convictions have altered, you have changed, and no blame attaches to you because we can't always control what we believe, but——

'Vladimir, why are you so insincere, in heaven's name?' she continued quietly, coming close to me 'While I was dreaming aloud all these months—raving, exulting in my plans, remodelling my life— why didn't you tell me the truth? Why did you say nothing? Or why did you encourage me with your stories and behave as though you were in complete sympathy with me? Why? What was the point of it?'

'It is hard to confess one's own bankruptcy,' I brought out, turning round but not looking at her. 'All right, I have lost my faith, I'm worn out, I'm feeling pretty low. It is hard to be truthful, terribly hard, so I said nothing. God forbid that anyone else should suffer as I have.'

I felt like bursting into tears and said no more.

'Vladimir,' she said, taking me by both hands. 'You have suffered and experienced so much, you know more than I do. Think seriously and tell me what I am to do. Teach me. If you yourself are unable to take the lead any longer, then at least show me the way. Look here, I am a living, feeling, reasoning creature, aren't I? To get into a false position, play some fatuous role . . . that I can't stand. I am not reproaching you, I am not blaming you, I'm only asking you.'

Tea was served.

'Well?' asked Zinaida, handing me a glass. 'What's your answer?'

'There is more light in the world than shines through yonder window,' I replied. 'And there are other people about besides me, Zinaida.'

'Then show me where they are,' she said briskly. 'That is all I ask of you.'

'And another thing,' I went on. 'One can serve an idea in more than one field. If you have gone wrong and lost your faith in one cause, then find yourself another. The world of ideas is broad and inexhaustible.'

'The world of ideas!' she said, looking me in the face sardonically. 'Oh, we had really better stop. Why go on?'

She blushed.

'The world of ideas!' she repeated, hurling her napkin to one side, and her face took on an indignant, contemptuous expression. 'All your fine ideas, I note, boil down to one single essential, vital step: I am to become your mistress. That is what you're after. To run round with a load of ideals while not being the mistress of the most upright and idealistic of men . . . that means failing to comprehend ideas. The mistress business is the starting point, the rest follows automatically!'

'You're in an irritable mood,' I told her.

'No, I mean it!' she shouted, breathing hard. 'I'm perfectly sincere.'

'Sincere you may be, but you're mistaken and I'm wounded by what you say.'

'Mistaken, am I?' she laughed. 'You are the last person in the world to say that, my dear sir. Now, I shall sound tactless and cruel, perhaps, but never mind. Do you love me? You do love me, don't you?'

I shrugged my shoulders.

'Oh yes, you can shrug your shoulders,' she continued sarcastically. 'When you were ill I heard your delirious ravings, and then we had all these adoring eyes and sighs, these well-meant discussions on intimacy and spiritual kinship. But the main thing is, why have you never been sincere with me? Why have you hidden the truth and told lies? Had you told me at the start just what ideas obliged you to drag me away from St. Petersburg I should have known where I stood. I should have poisoned myself then, as I meant to, and we should have been spared this dismal farce. Oh, what's the point of going on?'

She waved a hand and sat down.

'You speak as if you suspected me of dishonourable intentions,' I said, hurt.

'All right, have it your own way. Why go on? It isn't your intentions I suspect, it's your lack of intentions. If you had had any I should know what they were. All you had was your ideas and your love. And now it's ideas and love with me as your prospective mistress. Such is the way of life and novels.

'You used to blame Orlov,' she said, and struck her palm on the table. 'But you can't help agreeing with him. No wonder he despises all those ideas.'

'He doesn't despise ideas, he fears them,' I shouted. 'He's a coward and a liar.'

'All right, have it your own way. He's a coward, he's a liar, he betrayed me. But what about you? Excuse me being so frank, but what about you? He betrayed me and abandoned me to my fate in St. Petersburg, while you have betrayed and abandoned me here. But he at least didn't tag any ideas to his betrayal, while you——'

'Why say all this, for heaven's sake?' I asked in horror, wringing my hands and going quickly up to her. 'Look here, Zinaida, this is sheer cynicism, it's not right to give way to despair like this.

'Now, you listen to me,' I went on, clutching at a vague thought which had suddenly flashed through my mind and which, it seemed, might still save both of us. 'Listen to me. I have been through a lot in my time—so much that my head spins at the thought of it all—and I have now really grasped, both with my mind and in my tortured heart, that man either hasn't got a destiny, or else it lies exclusively in self-sacrificing love for his neighbour. That's the way we should be going, that's our purpose in life. And that is my faith.'

I wanted to go on talking about mercy and forgiveness, but my voice suddenly rang false and I felt confused.

'I feel such zest for life!' I said sincerely. 'Oh, to live, to live! I want peace and quiet, I want warmth, I want this sea, I want you near me. Oh, if only I could instil this passionate craving for life in you! You spoke of love just now, but I would be content just to have you near me, to hear your voice and see the look on your face——'

She blushed.

'You love life and I hate it,' she said quickly, to stop me going on. 'So our ways lie apart.'

She poured herself some tea, but left it untouched, went into her bedroom and lay down.

'I think we had better end this conversation,' she told me from there. 'Everything is finished so far as I'm concerned, and I don't need anything. So why go on talking?'

'No, everything is not finished.'

'Oh, have it your own way. I know all about that and I'm bored, so give over.'

I stood for a moment, walked up and down the room, and then went into the corridor. Approaching her door late that night and listening, I distinctly heard her crying.

When the servant brought me my clothes next morning he informed me with a smile that the lady in Number Thirteen was in labour. I pulled my clothes on somehow and rushed to Zinaida, terrified out of my wits. In her suite were the doctor, a midwife and an elderly Russian lady from Kharkov called Darya Mikhaylovna. There was a smell of ether drops. Barely had I crossed the threshold when a quiet, piteous groan came from the room where she lay, as if borne on the winds from Russia. I remembered Orlov and his irony, Polya, the Neva, the snow-flakes, then the cab without an apron, the portents which I had read in the bleak morning sky and the desperate shout of 'Nina, Nina!'

'Go into her room,' the lady said.

I went into Zinaida's room feeling as if I was the child's father. She was lying with her eyes closed: thin, pale, in a white lace nightcap. There were two expressions on her face, I remember. One was impassive, cold and listless, while the other, childlike and helpless, was imparted by the white cap. She did not hear me come in, or perhaps she did hear, but paid me no attention. I stood, looked at her, waited.

Then her face twisted with pain. She opened her eyes and gazed at the ceiling as though puzzling out what was happening to her. Revulsion was written on her face.

'How sickening,' she whispered.

'Zinaida,' I called weakly.

She looked at me impassively and wanly, and closed her eyes. I stood there for a while, then went out.

That night Darya Mikhaylovna told me that the baby was a little girl, but that the mother's condition was serious. Then there was noise and bustle in the corridor. Darya Mikhaylovna came to see me again.

'This is absolutely awful,' she said, looking frantic and wringing her hands. 'The doctor suspects her of taking poison. Russians do behave so badly here, I must say!'

Zinaida died at noon next day.

XVIII

Two years passed. Conditions changed, I returned to St. Petersburg and could now live there openly. I no longer feared being or seeming sentimental, and I surrendered entirely to the fatherly—or rather idolatrous —feelings aroused in me by Zinaida's daughter Sonya. I fed her myself, I bathed her, I put her to bed, I did not take my eyes off her for nights on end, I shrieked when I thought the nanny was about to drop her. My craving for ordinary commonplace life became more and more powerful and insistent in course of time, but my sweeping fantasies stopped short at Sonya as if in her they had at last found just what I needed. I loved this little girl insanely. In her I saw the continuation of my own life. This was more than just an impression, it was something I felt, something I had faith in, almost: that when I should at last cast off this long, bony, bearded body, I should live on in those little light blue eyes, those fair, silky little hairs, those chubby little pink hands which so lovingly stroked my face and clasped my neck.

I feared for Sonya's future. Orlov was her father, she was a Krasnovsky on her birth certificate and the only person who knew of her existence or took any interest in it—myself, that is—was now at death's door. I must think about her seriously.

On the day after my arrival in St. Petersburg I went to see Orlov A fat old man with ginger side-whiskers and no moustache—a German, obviously—opened the door. Polya was tidying the drawing-room and failed to recognize me, but Orlov knew me at once.

'Aha, our seditious friend,' he said, looking me over with curiosity and laughing. 'And how are you faring?'

He had not changed at all. There was still that same well-groomed, disagreeable face, that same irony. On the table, as of old, lay a new book with an ivory paper-knife stuck in it. He had obviously been reading before I arrived. He sat me down, offered me a cigar. With the tact peculiar to the well-bred he concealed the distaste which my face and wasted figure aroused in him, and remarked in passing that I hadn't changed a bit—that he would have known me anywhere in spite of my having grown a beard. We spoke of the weather and Paris.

'Zinaida Krasnovsky died, didn't she?' he asked, hastening to dispose of the tiresome and unavoidable problem which weighed on both of us.

'Yes, she did,' I answered.

'In childbirth?'

'That is so. The doctor suspected another cause of death, but it's more comforting for both of us to take it that she died in childbirth.'

He sighed for reasons of propriety and said nothing. There was a short silence.

'Quite so. Well, things are just the same as ever here, there haven't been any real changes,' he said briskly, noticing me looking round the study. 'My father has retired, as you know, he's taking it easy now, and I'm still where I was. Remember Pekarsky? He hasn't changed either. Gruzin died of diphtheria last year. Well now, Kukushkin's alive, and he mentions you quite often.

'By the way,' Orlov went on, lowering his eyes diffidently, 'when Kukushkin learnt who you were, he told everyone you had attacked him and tried to assassinate him, and that he had barely escaped with his life.'

I said nothing.

'Old servants don't forget their masters. This is very decent of you,' Orlov joked. 'Now, would you care for wine—or coffee? I'll have some made.'

'No, thank you. I came to see you on a most important matter, Orlov.'

'I'm not all that keen on important matters, but I am happy to be of service. What can I do for you?'

'Well, you see,' I began excitedly, 'I have poor Zinaida's daughter with me at the moment. I have been looking after her so far, but I'm not long for this world, as you see. I should like to die knowing that she was provided for.'

Orlov coloured slightly, frowned and flashed a stern glance at me. It wasn't so much the 'important matter' which had riled him as what I had said about my not being long for this world—my reference to death.

'Yes, I must think about that,' he said, shielding his eyes as if from the sun. 'Most grateful to you. A little girl, you say?'

'Yes, a girl. A splendid child.'

'Quite so. Not a pet dog, of course, a human being—I must give it serious thought, I can see that. I am prepared to do my bit and, er, I'm most grateful to you.'

He stood up, paced about biting his nails, and stopped before a picture.

'This requires some thought,' he said in a hollow voice, standing with his back to me. 'I shall be at Pekarsky's today and I'll ask him to call on Krasnovsky. I doubt if Krasnovsky will make any great difficulties, he'll consent to take the girl.'

'I'm sorry, but I can't see what this has to do with Krasnovsky,' I said, also standing up and going over to a picture at the other end of the study.

'Well, she does bear his name I should hope.'

'Yes, he may be legally obliged to take the child, I don't know, but I didn't come here for a legal consultation, Orlov.'

'Yes, yes, you're right,' he agreed briskly. 'I seem to be talking nonsense. But don't excite yourself. We shall settle all this to our mutual satisfaction. If one solution doesn't fit we'll try a second. If that won't do then something else will, and this ticklish problem will be solved one way or another. Pekarsky will fix it all up. Now, will you be good enough to leave me your address, and I shall let you know at once what we decide. Where are you staying?'

Orlov noted my address and sighed.

> ' "My fate, ye gods, is just too bad:
>   To be a tiny daughter's dad!" '

he said with a smile. 'But Pekarsky will fix everything, he has his head screwed on. Did you stay long in Paris?'

'Two months.'

We were silent. Orlov was obviously afraid of my mentioning the little girl again.

'You have probably forgotten your letter,' he said, trying to divert my attention elsewhere. 'But I have kept it. I understand your mood of the time and, frankly, I respect that letter.

'The damnable cold blood, the Oriental, the neighing snigger . . . that is charming and much to the point,' he went on with an ironical smile. 'And the basic idea may be close to the truth, though one might go on disputing for ever. That is,'—he fumbled for words—'not dispute the idea itself, but your attitude to the question: your temperament, so to speak. Yes, my life is abnormal, corrupt and useless, and what prevents me from starting a new one is cowardice, there you are quite right. But your taking it so much to heart, and getting so excited and frantic about it . . . now, that isn't rational, there you are quite wrong.'

'A live man can't help being excited and frantic when he sees himself and other people near him heading for disaster.'

'No one disputes that. I am not in the least preaching callousness, all I'm asking for is an objective attitude. The more objective one is the less the risk of error. One must look at the roots, one must seek the ultimate cause of every phenomenon. We have weakened, we've let ourselves go, we've fallen by the wayside in fact, and our generation consists entirely of whimpering neurotics. All we do is talk about fatigue and exhaustion, but that's not our fault, yours and mine. We are too insignificant for a whole generation's fate to hang on our idiosyncrasies. There must be substantial general causes behind all this, causes with a solid biological basis. Snivelling neurotics and backsliders we are, but perhaps that's necessary and useful for future generations. Not one hair falls from a man's head without the will of the Heavenly Father. Nothing in nature or human society happens in isolation, in other words. Everything is based on something, it's all determined. Now, if so, why should we worry so particularly? Why write frantic letters?'

'Yes, yes, all right,' I said after a little thought. 'I believe that future generations will find things easier and see their way more clearly. They will have our experience to help them. But we do want to be independent of future generations, don't we, we don't want to live just for them? We only have one life, and we should like to live it confidently, rationally and elegantly. We should like to play a prominent, independent, honourable role, we should like to make history so that these same future generations won't have the right to call each one of us a nonentity or worse. I believe that what is going on around us is functional and inevitable. But why should that inevitability involve me? Why should my ego come to grief?'

'Well, it can't be helped,' sighed Orlov, standing up as if to let me see that our conversation was over.

I picked up my hat.

'We have only sat here half an hour, and just think how many problems we've solved,' said Orlov, seeing me into the hall. 'All right, I shall think about that matter. I'll see Pekarsky today, my word upon it.'

He stood waiting for me to put my coat on, obviously glad that I was leaving. I asked whether he would mind giving me back my letter.

'Very well.'

He went into his study and came back with the letter a minute later. I thanked him and left.

On the following day I received a note from him congratulating me on a satisfactory solution to the problem. He wrote that Pekarsky knew a lady who kept a boarding home: a kind of kindergarten where she took quite small children. The woman was completely reliable, but before settling things with her it might be as well to talk to Krasnovsky, as the formalities required. He advised me to see Pekarsky at once, taking the birth certificate if there was such a thing,

'With assurances of my sincere respect and devotion,
                                        'Your humble servant——'

While I read the letter Sonya sat on the table looking at me most attentively, without blinking, as if she knew that her fate was being decided.

DOCTOR STARTSEV

I

To visitors' complaints that the county town of S—— was boring and humdrum local people would answer defensively that life there was, on the contrary, very good indeed. The town had its library, its theatre, its club. There was the occasional ball. And, in conclusion, it contained intelligent, interesting and charming families with whom one might make friends. Among these families the Turkins were pointed out as the most cultivated and accomplished.

These Turkins lived in their own house on the main street near the Governor's. Mr. Turkin—a stout, handsome, dark man with dundreary whiskers—used to stage amateur dramatic performances for charity, himself playing elderly generals and coughing most amusingly while doing so. He knew endless funny stories, riddles, proverbs. He rather liked his fun—he was a bit of a wag—and you could never tell from his face whether he was joking or not. His wife Vera—a slim, pretty woman in a *pince-nez*—wrote short stories and novels which she liked reading to her guests. Their young daughter Catherine played the piano. Each Turkin had, in short, some accomplishment. They liked entertaining, and gladly displayed their talents to their guests in a jolly, hearty sort of a way. Their large, stone-built house was roomy and cool in hot weather, with half its windows opening on to a shady old garden where nightingales sang in springtime. When they were entertaining there would be a clatter of knives in the kitchen and a smell of fried onions in the yard—the sign that an ample, appetizing supper was on the way.

No sooner had Dr. Dmitry Startsev been appointed to a local medical post and moved in at Dyalizh, six miles away, than he too was told that he simply must meet the Turkins, seeing that he was an intellectual. One winter's day, then, he was introduced to Mr. Turkin in the street. They chatted about the weather, the theatre, the cholera. He was invited to call. On a public holiday in spring—Ascension Day, to be precise—Startsev set out for town after surgery in search of recreation, meaning to do some shopping while he was about it. He made the journey unhurriedly on foot—he had not yet set up his carriage—humming 'Ere from the Cup of Life I yet had Drunk the Tears'.

He had dinner in town, he strolled in the park. Then Mr. Turkin's invitation suddenly crossed his mind, and he decided to call and see what the family was like.

Mr. Turkin welcomed him in the porch. 'Pleased to meet you, I'm sure. Delighted indeed to see so charming a guest. Come along, I'll introduce you to the wife.

'I was telling him, Vera dear—' he went on, presenting the doctor to his wife. 'He ain't got no statutory right, I was telling him, to coop himself up in that hospital. He should devote his leisure to society, snouldn't he, love?'

'Do sit here,' said Mrs. Turkin, placing the guest next to her. 'You can be my new boy-friend. My husband is jealous—oh, he's quite the Othello!—but we'll try to behave so he won't notice anything.'

'Now, now, ducky!' Mr. Turkin muttered tenderly, kissing her forehead. 'Oh, you are naughty!'

'You're in luck,' he added, turning to the doctor again. 'Mrs. T. has written a whacking great Novel, and today she's going to read it to us.'

Mrs. Turkin turned to her husband. '*Dites que l'on nous donne du thé*, dear.'

Startsev was introduced to Catherine: a girl of eighteen, very much like her mother. Also slim and pretty, she still had a rather childlike expression. Her waist was soft and slender. So beautiful, healthy and well-developed were her youthful breasts that she seemed like the very breath of springtime.

They had tea with jam and honey, sweets and delicious cakes which melted in the mouth. As evening drew on other guests gradually arrived. Mr. Turkin fixed each of them with his grin.

'Pleased to meet you, I'm sure.'

Then they all sat in the drawing-room, looking very earnest, while Mrs. Turkin read her Novel, which began: 'The frost had set in.' The windows were wide open, a clatter of knives was heard from the kitchen, there was a smell of fried onions. It was relaxing to sit in the deep, soft arm-chairs. The lights had such a friendly twinkle in the twilight of the drawing-room that, on this late spring evening— with voices and laughter borne from the street, with the scent of lilac wafting from outside—it was hard to grasp this stuff about the frost setting in and the dying sun illuminating with its chill rays a traveller on his lonely journey over some snow-covered plain. Mrs. Turkin was reading about a beautiful young countess who ran schools, hospitals and libraries in her village, and who fell in love with a wandering artist. These were not things which happen in real life, but they made you feel nice and cosy, they evoked peaceful, serene thoughts—and so no one wanted to get up.

'Not so dusty,' said Mr. Turkin softly.

One of the audience had been carried away by a long, long train of thought.

'No indeed,' he said in a voice barely audible.

An hour passed, then another. In the municipal park near by a band was playing, a choir sang. No one spoke for five minutes or so after Mrs. Turkin had closed her manuscript. They were listening to the choir singing 'Rushlight': a song which conveyed the real-life atmosphere which the Novel lacked.

'Do you publish your stories in the magazines?' Startsev asked Mrs. Turkin.

'No, never,' she answered. 'I keep my writings in a cupboard. Why publish!' she explained. 'It's not as though we were badly off.'

For some reason everyone sighed.

'Now, Pussy, you play us something,' Mr. Turkin told his daughter.

They put the lid of the grand piano up, they opened some music which was lying ready. Catherine sat down. She struck the keys with both hands. Then she immediately struck them again as hard as she could, and then again and again. Her shoulders and bosom quivered, and she kept hitting the same place as if she did not mean to stop until she had driven those keys right inside the instrument. The drawing-room resounded with the din as everything—floor, ceiling, furniture—reverberated.

Catherine was playing a difficult passage—its interest lay in its very difficulty. It was long and tedious. Startsev, as he listened, pictured a fall of rocks down a high mountain: on, on they tumbled while he very much wished they wouldn't. Yet Catherine—pink from her exertions, strong and vigorous, with a lock of hair falling over her forehead—greatly attracted him.

What a pleasant new sensation it was, after a winter in Dyalizh among patients and peasants: to sit in a drawing-room watching this young, exquisite and probably innocent creature, and hearing this noisy, tiresome—yet cultured—racket.

'Well, Pussy, you played better than ever today,' said Mr. Turkin with tears in his eyes after his daughter had finished and stood up. 'A thing of beauty is a joy for ever.'

They all crowded round with their congratulations and admiration, declaring that they hadn't heard such a performance for ages. She listened in silence with a faint smile, her whole figure radiating triumph.

'Marvellous! Splendid!'

Infected by the general enthusiasm, Startsev too said how marvellous it had been. 'Where did you study?' he asked Catherine. 'At the Conservatory?'

'No, I'm still at the pre-Conservatory stage. Meanwhile I've been taking lessons here, with Madame Zavlovsky.'

'Did you go to the local high school?'

'No indeed, we engaged private tutors,' Mrs. Turkin answered for her. 'There might be bad influences in a high school or a boarding school, you know. A growing girl should be under no influence but that of her mother.'

'All the same, I *am* going to the Conservatory,' Catherine said.

'No. Pussy loves Mummy, Pussy won't upset Mummy and Daddy.'

'I *will* go there, I *will*,' joked Catherine, playing up like a naughty child and stamping her foot.

At supper it was Mr. Turkin's turn to display his talents. Laughing with his eyes alone, he told funny stories, he joked, he propounded absurd riddles, he answered them himself—talking all the time in an extraordinary lingo evolved by long practice in the exercise of wit . . . by now it was obviously second nature to him.

'Whacking great,' 'Not so dusty,' 'Thanking you most unkindly——'

Nor was this all. When the guests, contented and replete, were jammed in the hall looking for coats and sticks, the footman Paul—nicknamed Peacock, a boy of about fourteen with cropped hair and full cheeks—bustled around them.

'Come on then, Peacock, perform!' Mr. Turkin said.

Peacock struck an attitude, threw up an arm.

'Unhappy woman, die!' he uttered in a tragic voice. And everyone roared with laughter.

'Great fun,' thought Startsev, going out in the street.

He called at a restaurant and had a beer before setting off home for Dyalizh. During the walk he hummed 'Your Voice to me both Languorous and Tender.'

Going to bed, he did not feel at all tired after his six-mile walk—far from it, he felt he could have walked another fifteen with pleasure.

'Not so dusty,' he remembered as he was falling asleep. And laughed.

II

Startsev kept meaning to visit the Turkins again, but just couldn't find a free hour, being so very busy at his hospital. Then, after more than a year of such solitary toil, a letter in a light blue envelope arrived from town.

Mrs. Turkin had had migraine for years, but recently—what with Pussy now scaring her daily with talk of going to the Conservatory—these attacks had increased. The town doctors had all attended the Turkins, now it was the country doctor's turn. Mrs. Turkin wrote him a touching letter, asking him to come and relieve her sufferings. Startsev went, and then became a frequent—a *very* frequent—visitor at the Turkins'.

He really did help Mrs. Turkin a bit, and she was now telling all her guests what an extraordinary, what an admirable doctor he was. But it was no migraine that brought him to the Turkins' now!

On one of his free days, after Catherine had completed her lengthy, exhausting piano exercises, they had sat for a long time over tea in the dining-room while Mr. Turkin told a funny story. Suddenly the door-bell rang. He had to go into the hall to greet a visitor, and Startsev took advantage of the brief confusion.

'For God's sake, I beg you, don't torment me,' he whispered, much agitated, to Catherine. 'Let's go in the garden.'

She shrugged her shoulders as if puzzled to know what he wanted of her, but she did get up and go.

'You play the piano for three or four hours on end,' he said as he followed her. 'Then you sit with your mother, and one can never have a word with you. Give me a quarter of an hour, I beg you.'

Autumn was approaching. The old garden was quiet and sad, dark leaves lay on the paths and the evenings were drawing in.

'I haven't seen you for a week,' Startsev went on. 'If only you knew how I suffer. Come and sit down, and hear what I have to say.'

They had their favourite place in the garden: a bench under a broad old maple, which was where they now sat.

'What do you require?' asked Catherine in a dry, matter-of-fact voice.

'I haven't seen you for a week, or heard your voice all that time. I long, I yearn to hear you speak. Say something.'

He was fascinated by her freshness, by the innocent expression of her eyes and cheeks. Even in the cut of her dress he saw something unusually lovely, touching in its simplicity and naïve gracefulness. And yet, despite this innocence, he found her very intelligent, very mature for her age. He could talk to her about literature, art or anything else. He could complain about life or people to her, though she was liable to laugh suddenly in the wrong place during a serious conversation. Qr she would run off into the house. Like almost all the local girls, she was a great reader. (Few people in the town read much. 'If it wasn't for the girls and the young Jews we might just as well shut up shop,' they used to say in the town library.) Her reading pleased Startsev no end. He always made a great fuss of asking what she had read in the last few days, and he would listen, fascinated, as she told him.

'What,' he asked her, 'have you read since we met last week? Please tell me.'

'Pisemsky.'

'Which book?'

'*A Thousand Souls*,' answered Pussy. 'What a funny name Pisemsky had: Alexis Feofilaktovich.'

'Hey, where are you off to?' Startsev was aghast when she suddenly stood up and made for the house. 'I must talk to you, I've some explaining to do. Stay with me just five minutes, I implore you.'

She stopped as if meaning to say something, then awkwardly thrust a note into his hand and ran to the house, where she sat down at the piano again.

'Be in the cemetery near Demetti's tomb at eleven o'clock tonight,' Startsev read.

'This is really rather silly,' he thought, collecting his wits. 'Why the cemetery? What's the point?'

It was one of Pussy's little games, obviously. But really, who would seriously think of an assignation in a cemetery far outside town at night-time, when it could so easily be arranged in the street or municipal park? And was it not beneath him—a country doctor, an intelligent, respectable man—to be sighing, receiving *billets-doux*, hanging round cemeteries and doing things so silly that even schoolboys laugh at them these days? Where would this affair end? What would his colleagues say when they found out? Such were Startsev's thoughts as he wandered among the tables at his club. But at half-past ten he suddenly got up and drove off to the cemetery.

By now he had his own pair of horses and a coachman, Panteleymon, complete with velvet waistcoat. The moon was shining. It was quiet and warm, but with a touch of autumn in the air. Dogs were howling near a suburban slaughterhouse. Leaving his carriage in a lane on the edge of town, Startsev walked on to the cemetery alone.

'We all have our quirks, Pussy included,' thought he. 'Perhaps— who knows—perhaps she wasn't joking. Perhaps she will come.' Yielding to this feeble, insubstantial hope, he felt intoxicated by it.

He walked through fields for a quarter of a mile. The cemetery showed up: a dark strip in the distance resembling a wood or large garden. The white stone wall came into view and the gate. The words on the gate were legible in the moonlight: 'The hour cometh when——' Startsev went through the side-gate and the first things to catch his eye were white crosses and tombstones on both sides of a broad avenue, and black shadows cast by them and by the poplars. There was an extensive panorama in black and white, with sleepy trees drooping their branches over the whiteness below. It seemed lighter here than in the fields. Maple leaves like paws stood out sharply against the yellow sand of paths and against gravestones, and the inscriptions on the monuments were clearly visible. Startsev was struck at once by what he was now seeing for the first time in his life and would probably never see again: a world unlike any other . . . where moonlight was as lovely and soft as if this were its cradle, where there was no living thing, but where each dark poplar and tomb seemed to hold the secret promise of a life tranquil, splendid, everlasting. Mingled with the autumnal smell of leaves, the gravestones and faded flowers breathed forgiveness, melancholy and peace.

It was silent all around. The stars looked down from the sky in utter quiescence, while Startsev's footsteps sounded harsh and out of place. Only when the church clock began to strike, and he fancied himself dead and buried here for ever, did he feel as if someone was watching him. This was not peace and quiet, it seemed for a moment, but the dull misery of nothingness: a kind of choked despair.

Demetti's tomb was in the form of a shrine with an angel on top. An Italian opera company had once passed through town, one of the singers had died, they had buried her here, and they had put up this monument. She was no longer remembered in town, but the lamp over the entrance reflected the moon and seemed alight.

There was no one about—as if anyone would come here at midnight! Yet Startsev waited, waited passionately, as if the moonlight were inflaming his desires. He imagined kisses and embraces. He sat near the tomb for about half an hour, then strolled up and down the side-paths with his hat in his hand, waiting. He reflected that in these graves lay buried many women and girls who had been beautiful and entrancing, who had loved and burned with passion in the night, yielding to caresses. Really, what a rotten joke Nature does play on man! And how painful to be conscious of it! So Startsev thought, while wishing to shout aloud that he wanted love, that he expected it—at whatever cost. The white shapes before his eyes were no longer slabs of marble, but beautiful bodies. He saw shapely forms modestly hiding in the shadows of the trees, and he sensed their warmth until desire grew hard to bear.

Then, like the drop of a curtain, the moon vanished behind clouds and everything was suddenly dark. Startsev had trouble finding the gate, for the darkness was now truly autumnal. Then he wandered about for an hour and a half looking for the lane where he had left his horses.

'I'm dead on my feet,' he told Panteleymon.

'Dear me, one really should watch one's weight,' he reflected as he settled down luxuriously in his carriage.

III

Next evening he set off for the Turkins' to propose to Catherine. But it turned out inconveniently because she was in her room with her hairdresser in attendance, and was going to a dance at the club.

He found himself let in for another of those long tea-drinking sessions in the dining-room. Seeing his guest bored and preoccupied, Mr. Turkin took some jottings from his waistcoat pocket and read out a funny letter from a German estate-manager about how all the 'racks' on the property had 'gone to lock and ruin', and how the old place had been so knocked about that it had become 'thoroughly bashful'.

'They're bound to put up a decent dowry', thought Startsev, listening absent-mindedly.

After his sleepless night he felt stupefied, felt as if he had been drugged with some sweet sleeping potion. His sensations were confused, but warm and happy. And yet——

'Stop before it is too late!' a stolid, cold part of his brain argued. 'Is she the wife for you? She's spoilt and capricious, she sleeps till two in the afternoon, while you're a sexton's son, a country doctor——'

'Never mind, I don't care,' he answered himself.

'What's more,' went on the voice, 'if you do get married, her family will stop you working in the country and make you move to town.'

'What of it? Then town it shall be,' he thought. 'They'll give a dowry, we'll set up house——'

Catherine came in at last, wearing a *décolleté* evening dress. She looked so pretty and fresh that Startsev goggled at her, and was so transported that he could not get a word out, but just stared at her and laughed.

She began to say good-bye. Having no reason to stay on, he stood up and remarked that it was time to go home as some patients were expecting him.

'You go, then,' said Mr. Turkin. 'It can't be helped. And you might give Puss a lift to the club.'

It was very dark outside and drizzling, with only Panteleymon's raucous cough to guide them to the carriage. They put the hood up.

'Why did the cowslip?' Mr. Turkin said, helping his daughter into the carriage. 'Because she saw the bullrush, of course. Off with you! Cheerio, chin chin!'

And off they went.

'I went to the cemetery yesterday,' Startsev began. 'How mean and heartless of you to——'

'You actually *went*?'

'Yes. *And* waited till nearly two o'clock. I suffered——'

'Serves you right if you can't take a joke.'

Delighted to have played such a mean trick on a man who loved her—delighted, too, to be the object of such a passion—Catherine laughed, then suddenly screamed with fright because the horses were turning sharply in through the club gates at that moment, and the carriage lurched to one side. Startsev put his arm round her waist while she clung to him in terror. He could not resist kissing her passionately on lips and chin, gripping her more tightly.

'That will do,' she said curtly.

A second later she was out of the carriage. A policeman stood near the lighted entrance of the club.

'Don't hang around here, you oaf!' he yelled at Panteleymon in a nasty voice. 'Move on!'

Startsev drove home, but was soon back again. Wearing borrowed tails and a stiff white cravat, which somehow kept slipping up and trying to ride off his collar, he sat in the club lounge at midnight ardently haranguing Catherine.

'Those who've never been in love . . . how little they know! I don't think anyone has ever described love properly. Does it, indeed, lend itself to description: this tender, joyous, tormented feeling? No one who has ever experienced it would try to put it into words. But what's the use of preambles and explanations? Or of superfluous eloquence? I love you infinitely. I ask you, I implore you——'

Startsev got it out at last. 'Be my wife.'

'Dmitry Startsev—' said Catherine with a very earnest expression, after some thought. 'I am most grateful to you for the honour, Dmitry, and I respect you, but——'

She stood up and continued, standing. 'I'm sorry, though, I can't be your wife. Let us talk seriously. As you know, Dmitry, I love Art more than anything in the world—I'm mad about music, I adore it, I have dedicated my whole life to it. I want to be a concert pianist. I want fame, success, freedom—whereas you want me to go on living in this town, pursuing an empty, futile existence which I can't stand. To be a wife . . . no, no, I'm sorry. One must aim at some lofty, brilliant goal, and family life would tie me down for ever. Dmitry Startsev—.' She gave a slight smile because, while saying his name, she remembered 'Alexis Feofilaktovich'. 'You're a kind, honourable, intelligent man, Dmitry, you're the nicest one of all——'

Tears came into her eyes. 'I feel for you with all my heart, but, er, you must understand——'

To avoid bursting into tears she turned away and left the lounge.

Startsev's heart ceased to throb. Going out of the club into the street, he first tore off the stiff cravat and heaved a deep sigh. He felt a little ashamed and his pride was hurt—for he had not expected a refusal. Nor could he believe that his dreams, his yearnings, his hopes had led to so foolish a conclusion, like something in a little play acted by amateurs. And he was sorry for his own feelings, for that love of his— so sorry that he felt ready to break into sobs, or to land a really good clout on Panteleymon's broad back with his umbrella.

For a couple of days he let things slide—couldn't eat or sleep. But when rumour reached him that Catherine had gone to Moscow to enrol at the Conservatory, he calmed down and resumed his former routine.

Recalling, later, how he had wandered round the cemetery and driven all over town in search of a tail-coat, he would stretch himself lazily, saying that it had all been 'oh, such a lot of fuss'.

IV

Four years passed, and Startsev now had a large practice in town. He hastily took surgery at his home in Dyalizh each morning, after which he left to visit his town patients. From a two-horse outfit he had graduated to a troika with bells. He would return home late at night. He had grown broad and stout, and he disliked walking because he was always short of breath. Panteleymon had filled out too, and the broader he grew the more dolefully he would sigh and lament his bitter fate. 'The driving's got me down!'

Startsev was received in various houses and met many people, but was intimate with none. The conversations, the attitudes—the appearance, even—of the townsfolk irritated him. Experience had gradually taught him that your average provincial is a peaceable, easy-going and even quite intelligent human being when you play cards or have a meal with him, but that you only have to talk about something which can't be eaten—politics, say, or learning—for him to be put right off his stroke . . . or else to launch on generalizations so trite and malicious that there's nothing for it but to write him off and leave. Take the typical local liberal, even—just suppose Startsev should try to tell him that humanity was progressing, thank God, and would manage without passports and capital punishment in time. 'You mean it will be possible to murder people in the street?' the man would ask with a mistrustful sidelong glance. Whenever Startsev spoke in company, at tea or supper, of the need to work—of the impossibility of living without work—everyone took it as a reproach, becoming angry and tiresomely argumentative. What's more, your average provincial never did a single blessed thing. He had no interests—indeed, you just couldn't think what to talk to him about. So Startsev avoided conversation, and just ate or played bridge. When he chanced on some family celebration and was asked in for a bite, he would sit and eat silently, staring at his plate. Their talk was all dull, prejudiced and stupid, which irritated and upset him. But he would still say nothing.

This austere silence and habit of staring at his plate earned him a nickname—'the pompous Pole'—in town, though he was not of Polish origin.

He avoided such entertainments as concerts and the theatre, but enjoyed three hours of bridge every evening. He had another recreation too, which he had slipped into by stages. This was to take from his pockets at night the bank-notes earned on his medical rounds. There were sometimes seventy roubles' worth stuffed in his pockets—yellow and green notes smelling of scent, vinegar, incense and fish oil. When they added up to a few hundreds he would take them to the Mutual Credit Bank and put them in his current account.

In the four years since Catherine's departure he had visited the Turkins only twice—at the behest of Mrs. Turkin, who was still under treatment for migraine. Catherine came and stayed with her parents each summer, but he had not seen her once. It somehow never happened.

But now four years had passed, and on a quiet, warm morning a letter was delivered at the hospital. Mrs. Turkin informed Dr. Startsev that she greatly missed his company, and asked him to visit her without fail to relieve her sufferings. And by the way today was her birthday.

Below was a postscript:

'I join in Mummy's request.
    'C.'

After some thought Startsev drove off to the Turkins' that evening.

'Ah! Pleased to meet you, I'm sure,' Mr. Turkin greeted him, smiling only with his eyes. 'And a very *bon jour* to you.'

White-haired, looking much older, Mrs. Turkin shook hands with Startsev and sighed affectedly.

'You refuse to be my boy-friend, Doctor,' she said. 'And you never come and see us. I'm too old for you, but there's someone younger here. Perhaps she'll have better luck.'

And what of Pussy? She was slimmer, paler, more handsome, more graceful. Now she was Pussy no longer, but Miss Catherine Turkin—her former freshness and childlike innocent look were gone. In her glance and manner, too, there was a new quality of hesitation or guilt, as if she no longer felt at home here in the family house.

'It seems ages since we met,' she said, giving Startsev her hand, and one could tell that her heart was beating apprehensively. 'How you *have* filled out,' she went on, staring inquisitively at his face. 'You're sunburnt, you're more mature, but you haven't changed much on the whole.'

She still attracted him, very much so, but now there was something missing . . . or added. Just what it was he couldn't have said, but something prevented him from feeling as before. He disliked her pallor, her new expression, her faint smile and voice. Before long he was disliking her dress and the arm-chair in which she sat—disliking, too, something about the past when he had come near to marrying her. He remembered his love, remembered the dreams and hopes which had disturbed him four years ago. And felt uncomfortable.

They had tea and cake. Then Mrs. Turkin read them a Novel, all about things which never happen in real life—while Startsev listened, looked at her handsome, white head, and waited for her to finish.

'A mediocrity is not someone who can't write novels,' he reflected. 'It's someone who writes them and can't keep quiet about it.'

'Not so dusty,' said Mr. Turkin.

Then Catherine played long and noisily on the piano, and when she stopped there were lengthy expressions of delighted appreciation.

'Lucky I didn't marry her,' thought Startsev.

She looked at him, evidently expecting him to suggest going into the garden, but he did not speak.

'Well, let's talk,' she said, going up to him. 'How are you? What's your news, eh?'

'I've been thinking about you a lot lately,' she went on nervously. 'I wanted to write to you, wanted to go to Dyalizh myself and see you. I did decide to go, actually, then changed my mind—heaven knows how you feel about me now. I was so excited today, waiting for you to come. For God's sake let's go into the garden.'

They went into the garden and sat down on the bench under the old maple, as they had four years earlier. It was dark.

'How are you then?' Catherine said.

'Not so bad,' Startsev answered. 'I manage.'

That was all he could think of saying. There was a pause.

'I'm so excited,' Catherine said, covering her face with her hands. 'But don't let that worry you. I'm happy to be home, so glad to see everyone. I just can't get used to it. What a lot of memories! I thought we should go on talking and talking till morning.'

Now he could see her face, her shining eyes near by. Out here in the darkness she looked younger than indoors, and even her old childlike expression seemed to have returned. She was, indeed, gazing at him with naïve curiosity, as if seeking a closer view and understanding of a man who had once loved her so ardently, so tenderly, so unhappily. Her eyes thanked him for that love. He remembered what had happened, all the little details—how he had strolled round the cemetery and then gone home exhausted in the small hours. Suddenly he felt sadness and regret for the past, and a spark seemed to come alight inside him.

'Remember how I took you to the club dance?' he said. 'It was dark and rainy——'

The spark inside him was flaring up, and now he felt the urge to speak, to complain about life.

'Ah me,' he sighed. 'Here are you asking about my life. But how *do* we live here? The answer is, we don't. We grow old and stout, we run to seed. One day follows another, and life passes drearily without impressions or ideas. There's earning your living by day, there's the club of an evening in the company of card-players, alcoholics and loud-mouthed fellows I can't stand. What's good about that?'

'But you have your work, an honourable ambition. You used to like talking about your hospital so much. I was an odd girl in those days, thinking myself a great pianist. Young ladies all play the piano nowadays, and I was just one more of them—nothing remarkable about me. I'm about as much of a pianist as Mother is a writer. I didn't understand you at the time, of course. But in Moscow, later, I often thought of you—in fact I thought of nothing *but* you. What happiness to be a country doctor, to help the suffering, to serve ordinary people.

'What happiness!' Catherine repeated eagerly. 'When I thought of you in Moscow you seemed so admirable, so superior.'

Startsev remembered the bank-notes which he so much enjoyed taking out of his pockets in the evenings, and the spark died inside him.

He got up to go into the house, and she took him by the arm.

'You're the best person I've ever known,' she went on. 'We *shall* meet and talk, shan't we? Do promise. I'm no pianist. I've no illusions left, and I won't play music or talk about it when you're there.'

When they were in the house and Startsev saw her face in the lamp-light and her sad, grateful, inquiring eyes fixed on him, he felt uneasy.

'Lucky I never married her,' he thought again.

He began to take his leave.

'You ain't got no statutory right to leave without supper,' Mr. Turkin said as he saw him off. 'Highly perpendicular of you in fact. Well, go on—perform!' he added, addressing Peacock in the hall.

Peacock—now no longer a boy, but a young man with a moustache
—struck an attitude, threw up an arm.

'Unhappy woman, die!' he declaimed tragically.

All this irritated Startsev. Climbing into his carriage, he looked at
the dark house and garden once so dear and precious to him. It all
came back to him at once: Mrs. Turkin's 'novels', Pussy's noisy piano-
playing, Mr. Turkin's wit, Peacock's tragic posturings. What, he asked
himself, could be said of a town in which the most brilliant people were
so dim?

Three days later Peacock brought a letter from Catherine.

'Why don't you come and see us?' she wrote. 'I'm afraid your
feelings for us have changed. I'm afraid—the very idea terrifies me.
Do set my mind at rest. Do come and tell me that all is well.

'I simply must talk to you.

'Your

'C. T.'

He read the letter.

'Tell them I can't manage it today, my good fellow, I'm very busy,'
he told Peacock after some thought. 'Tell them I'll come over—oh, in a
couple of days.'

But three days passed, and then a week—and still he did not go.
Once, when driving past the Turkins' house, he remembered that he
should at least pay a brief call. But then he thought again. And did not.

Never again did he visit the Turkins.

V

A few more years have passed. Startsev has put on yet more weight
—grown really fat. He breathes heavily and goes about with his head
thrown back. Plump, red-faced, he drives in his troika with the bells,
while Panteleymon—also plump, also red-faced, with a thick, fleshy
neck—sits on the box holding his arms straight ahead as if they were
wooden.

'Keep to the r-i-ight!' he bellows at oncoming traffic.

It is an impressive scene, suggesting that the passenger is not a man,
but a pagan god.

He has a vast practice in the town and scarcely time to draw breath.
Already he owns an estate and two town houses, and he is looking for
a third—a better bargain. When, in the Mutual Credit Bank, he hears
of a house for sale, he marches straight in without ceremony, goes

through all the rooms—paying no attention to the half-dressed women and children who stare at him in fascinated horror—prods all the doors with his stick.

'This the study?' he asks. 'That a bedroom? What have we here?' He breathes heavily all the time, wiping sweat from his brow.

He has a lot to do, but still does not give up his council post, being too greedy and wanting a finger in every pie. At Dyalizh and in town he is now known simply as 'the Doc'.

'Where's the Doc off to?' people ask. Or 'Shouldn't we call in the Doc?'

His voice has changed, probably because his throat is so congested with fat, and has become thin and harsh. His character has changed too —he has grown ill-humoured and irritable. When taking surgery he usually loses his temper and bangs his stick impatiently on the floor.

'Pray confine yourself to answering my questions!' he shouts unpleasantly. 'Less talk!'

He lives alone. It is a dreary life, he has no interests.

During his entire time at Dyalizh his love for Pussy has been his only joy, and will probably be his last. He plays bridge in the club of an evening, then dines alone at a large table. He is waited on by Ivan, the oldest and most venerable of the club servants, is served with Château-Lafite No. 17, and everyone—the club officials, the cook, the waiter—knows his likes and dislikes, they all humour him in every way. Otherwise he's liable to fly into a rage and bang his stick on the floor.

While dining he occasionally turns round and breaks into a conversation.

'What are you on about? Eh? Who?'

When, occasionally, talk at a near-by table turns to the Turkins, he asks what Turkins. 'You mean those people whose daughter plays the piannyforty?'.

There is no more to be said about him.

What of the Turkins? Mr. Turkin looks no older—hasn't changed a bit, but still keeps joking and telling his funny stories. Mrs. Turkin still enjoys reading those Novels to guests in a jolly, hearty sort of a way. And Pussy plays the piano for four hours a day. She looks much older, she is often unwell, and she goes to the Crimea with her mother every autumn. Mr. Turkin sees them off at the station, and when the train starts he wipes away his tears.

'Cheerio, chin chin!' he shouts.

And waves a handkerchief.

EXPLANATORY NOTES

THE BUTTERFLY

1 *was a rather junior doctor*: literally, 'was a doctor and held the grade of titular councillor'—class nine in the Table of Ranks introduced by Peter the Great in 1722.

9 *Kineshma*: town on the Volga about 200 miles north-east of Moscow.

11 *Masini*: Angelo Masini (1844–1926), Italian operatic tenor.

14 *Do you know any place in all Russia . . .*: the couplet is a paraphrase of a quatrain from the poem *Razmyshleniya u paradnogo podyezda* (*Reflections by a Main Entrance*; 1858) by N. A. Nekrasov (1821–78).
Polenov: V. D. Polenov (1844–1927), Russian painter.

17 *Barnay*: Ludwig Barnay (1842–1924), German actor.

18 *Gogol's Osip*: the comic servant of Khlestakov, hero of the farce *The Inspector General* (1836) by N. V. Gogol (1809–52).
old fellow called Osip, who 'grew hoarse from a surfeit of gossip': the original tongue-twister reads *Osip okhrip, a Arkhip osip*, literally: 'Osip grew hoarse and Arkhip grew husky.'

WARD NUMBER SIX

24 *official of the twelfth grade*: literally 'a provincial secretary' (*gubernsky sekretar*), twelfth grade in the Table of Ranks.

28 *gendarmes*: founded under Nicholas I in 1826, the Corps of Gendarmes constituted the uniformed branch of the Imperial political police force from then until 1917.

30 *the Order of St. Stanislaus*: one of the numerous orders, or decorations for distinction in peace and war, instituted by Peter the Great and added to as the years went by.

31 *the paralytic*: this refers to the 'tall, lean working-class fellow' mentioned first among the five inmates of the Ward (see p. 24, above).

34 *Pushkin*: Russia's greatest poet Alexander Pushkin (1799–1837) was fatally wounded in the stomach in the course of his duel with a Frenchman, Georges d'Anthès, and suffered for two days before dying.

Heine: Heinrich Heine (1797–1856), the German poet, suffered from spinal disease during the last eight years of his life.

35 *a senator*: founded in 1711 by Peter the Great, the Senate functioned as a supreme court of appeal from 1864 onwards and was also empowered to interpret the laws. The Emperor appointed Senators from among holders of the first three grades in the Table of Ranks.

white tie: a white tie was customary wear for Russian doctors in this period.

Svyatogorsk Monastery: founded in 1566 and situated in Pskov Province, the Monastery was the site of Pushkin's tomb.

35–6 *The Physician*: *Vrach*; a weekly medical newspaper published in St. Petersburg from 1880 onwards.

38 *the ideas of the Sixties*: during the 1860s, the age of Russian Nihilism, an obsession with utilitarianism, materialism and scientific progress was very much in vogue.

40 *Pirogov*: N. I. Pirogov (1810–81), the Russian surgeon and educationist.

Pasteur: Louis Pasteur (1822–95), the French chemist and bacteriologist.

Koch: Robert Koch (1843–1910), the German bacteriologist.

44 *Dostoyevsky*: F. M. Dostoyevsky, the Russian novelist.

Voltaire: Jean François Marie Arouet de Voltaire (1694–1778), the French dramatist and historian, and author of the remark '*si Dieu n'existait pas, il faudrait l'inventer*,' See Voltaire, *Epîtres*, 96, *A l'Auteur du Livre des Trois Imposteurs*.

46 *as an exile—or as a convict*: reference is to the two headings under which a condemned person might be sent to Siberia, the milder status being that of 'exile' (*poselenets*), the more severe that of 'convict' (*katorzhnik*).

47 *Marcus Aurelius*: Marcus Aurelius (A.D. 121–80), the Roman Emperor and Stoic philosopher, author of the celebrated *Meditations*.

49 *Garden of Gethsemane*: reference is to the New Testament, Matthew 26: 36–42; Mark 14: 32–6.

55 *Pripet Marshes*: the Pripet is a tributary of the River Dnieper and flows through marshlands in southern Belorussia.

56 *the Iverian Madonna*: situated near the Red Square in Moscow, the Iverian chapel (*Iverskaya chasovnya*) housed the most celebrated icon in the city, that of the 'Iverian Madonna'. This was an exact copy of an early eighth-century icon preserved in the Iverian Monastery on Mount Athos. The copy was brought to Russia in 1648 and became famous as a 'miracle-working

icon', in which capacity it could be hired out by private individuals.

'*Tsar Cannon' and . . . 'Tsar Bell'*: two well-known sights in the Moscow Kremlin. The Bell was cast in 1733–5, the Cannon in the sixteenth century.

St. Saviour's Temple: this church (in Russian, *Khram Khrista Spasitelya*) was built between 1837 and 1883 on the left bank of the Moscow River, south-west of the Kremlin, as a memorial to the Napoleonic wars of 1812–14.

Rumyantsev Museum: situated in Mokhovoy Street in the centre of Moscow, the Museum was built in 1787, and the core of the exhibits consisted of collections given to the State by Count Nicholas Rumyantsev (died 1826).

Testov's: a well-known Moscow restaurant.

ARIADNE

70 *Volochisk*: name of the actual Russian frontier station in Volhynia Province.

Max Nordau: Max Simon Nordau (1848–1923), Hungarian author of the philosophical work *Entartung* (*Degeneration*; English translation, 1895) and other works.

71 *Weltmann*: A. F. Weltmann [Veltman] (1800–70), minor Russian novelist and poet.

75 *Devichy*: part of south Moscow, the area of the Novodevichy Convent.

the Slav Fair Hotel: a large hotel in central Moscow at which Chekhov sometimes stayed.

the Hermitage Restaurant: in Moscow in Trubny Square, not to be confused with the Hermitage Variety Theatre in Moscow or the Hermitage Museum in St. Petersburg.

79 *Abbazia*: [Opatija]: a seaside resort on the west shore of the Bay of Fiume. It was Austrian before 1914 and is now part of Yugoslavia.

80 *Fiume*: [Rijeka]: North Adriatic port, now part of Yugoslavia. It belonged to Hungary before 1914.

81 *Merano*: health resort in the southern Tyrol in the Italian province of Bolzano.

88 *Boleslav Markevich*: B. M. Markevich (1822–84), a minor novelist who held ultra-conservative political views.

Turgenev: I. S. Turgenev (1818–83), the well-known Russian novelist.

A DREARY STORY

92 *Kavelin*: K. D. Kavelin (1815–85), the Russian philosopher.
Nekrasov: N. A. Nekrasov (1821–78), the Russian poet.

98 *Gruber*: V. L. Gruber (1814–90), anatomist and professor at the St. Petersburg Medico-Surgical Academy from 1858.
Babukhin: A. I. Babukhin (1835–91), Russian histologist and physiologist, founder of the Moscow school of histology.
Skobelev: M. D. Skobelev (1843–82), the famous Russian general who led a punitive expedition against Kokand in central Asia (1875–6) and distinguished himself in the Russo–Turkish War of 1877–8.

99 *Perov*: V. G. Perov (1833–82), the Russian painter.
Patti: Adelina Patti (1843–1919), the operatic singer.

107 *Chatsky . . . Woe from Wit*: Chatsky is the hero of the verse play *Woe from Wit* (1822–4) by A. S. Griboyedov (1795–1829).

108 *Ufa*: city near the Urals, now capital of the Bashkir Autonomous Republic.

110 *Yalta*: town and health-resort on the southern coast of the Crimea.

113 *kasha*: the word describes various forms of gruel and porridge.

115 *Kharkov*: large city in the Ukraine.

122 *How sadly I regard . . .*: the first line of the lyric *Thought* (1838) by the Russian poet M. Yu. Lermontov (1814–41).

123 *Dobrolyubov*: N. A. Dobrolyubov (1836–61), leading Russian radical literary and social critic.

125 *Arakcheyev*: General Count A. A. Arakcheyev (1769–1834), favourite of Alexander I of Russia, who became a symbol of extreme tyranny.

128 *Go, up, thou bald head*: a biblical quotation, 2 Kings 2: 23.

129 *Nikita Krylov*: N. I. Krylov (1807–79), Professor of Roman Law at the University of Moscow.
Revel: German name of present Tallinn, capital of the Estonian Republic.
An eagle on occasion . . .: the lines come from the fable *The Eagle and the Hens* (1808) by the Russian fabulist I. A. Krylov (*c.* 1769–1844).

137 *Berdichev*: Ukrainian town about a hundred miles south-west of Kiev.

138 *World Illustrated*: *Vsemirnaya illyustratsiya*, a St. Petersburg weekly, founded 1869.

The Meadow: *Niva*, a weekly illustrated magazine for family reading, St. Petersburg (1870–1918).

passport system: a Russian citizen was required to possess a passport for purposes of internal as well as external travel.

NEIGHBOURS

143 *Her Excell.*: the honorific 'Your Excellency' (*vashe prevoskhoditelstvo*) was reserved to holders of ranks three, four and five in the official Table of Ranks (see note to p. 1), and to the wives and widows of these high officials.

148 *If you should ever need my life, then come and take it*: Chekhov later used this sentence in his play *The Seagull* (1896). See further *The Oxford Chekhov*, vol. ii, pp. 264, 338 and 356.

152 *Pisarev . . .*: D. I. Pisarev (1840–68), the Russian politico-literary thinker and critic.

Darwin: Charles Darwin (1809–82), the English naturalist.

. . . that weird marriage à la Dostoyevsky: Chekhov must have had in mind such episodes as the marriage of the satanic hero Stavrogin to the idiot girl Mary Lebyadkin in the novel *Devils* (1871–2) by F. M. Dostoyevsky (1822–81).

154 *Khoma Brut*: a character in the story *Vy* in the collection *Mirgorod* (1835) by N. V. Gogol.

AN ANONYMOUS STORY

161 *Intermediary editions*: *The Intermediary* (*Posrednik*) was a publishing house founded in St. Petersburg in 1885 for the dissemination of popular works, including the folk tales of Leo Tolstoy.

162 *Znamensky Square*: the large square at the eastern end of the Nevsky Prospekt, the main thoroughfare in St. Petersburg.

165 *Yeliseyev's*: the most luxurious food store on the Nevsky Prospekt in St. Petersburg.

Gogol or Shchedrin: N. V. Gogol (1809–52) and M. Ye. Saltykov (1826–89, who wrote under the pseudonym 'Shchedrin' and is often known as 'Saltykov-Shchedrin') were the two leading Russian satirists, and—with Chekhov himself—humorous writers of the nineteenth century.

166 *the fairly senior rank which he held*: literally: the 'rank of actual

state councillor' (*deystvitelny statsky sovetnik*): grade four in the Table of Ranks.

167 *Nevsky Prospekt*: the main thoroughfare of St. Petersburg.

the *Senate*: see note to p. 35.

Prutkov: 'Kozma Prutkov' was the collective pseudonym used by the poet and playwright A. K. Tolstoy in conjunction with the brothers Zhemchuzhnikov between 1851 and 1884 for the publication of satire directed against Russian officialdom.

168 *What does the morrow hold for me?*: Lensky's words in Canto VI, verse xxi of *Eugene Onegin* by A. S. Pushkin. The song to which reference is made here is Lensky's aria from Tchaikovsky's opera *Eugene Onegin*, based on Pushkin's novel.

169 *Officer Street*: a street in the west of central St. Petersburg.

174 *Contant's or Donon's*: the restaurants of Contant and Donon, both on the Moyka Canal, are listed in the 1912 Baedeker, the latter carrying one star.

the *Old Town*: literally: 'The Petersburg Side' (*Peterburgskaya storona*). Lying to the north of the River Neva, this was the oldest part of the city now called Leningrad, containing the Peter and Paul Fortress and Peter the Great's house.

176 *Three meetings . . . Vieni, pensando . . .*: reference is to Turgenev's story *Three Meetings* (1852). The line *Vieni, pensando a me segretamente* ('Come, thinking of me in secret') forms part of a quatrain from an Italian song, which Turgenev used as the epigraph to the story.

liberate Bulgaria: reference is to Turgenev's novel *On the Eve* (1860), the hero of which, Insarov, is a Bulgarian struggling for his country's freedom. His inamorata, a Russian girl called Helen, offers (literally) to follow him 'to the ends of the earth'.

183 *a typical red-tape merchant*: literally, 'a hero from Shchedrin': that is, one of those comic civil servants (*chinovniki*) who form the main butts of the satirist Shchedrin (see also note to p. 165 above).

visiting your superiors to wish them a Happy New Year: the practice of paying a formal visit to one's superior officer on this occasion was generally incumbent on subordinate civil servants.

190 *Sergiyevsky Street*: in the eastern part of central St. Petersburg, running east from the Summer Garden.

194 *the beard-and-caftan brigade*: literally 'their worthinesses' (*ikh stepenstva*), an honorific sometimes bestowed on Russian merchants, here used sardonically.

201 *Saint-Saëns*: Camille Saint-Saëns (1835–1921), the French composer.

204   *the gates of Gaza*: reference is to Samson's exploit in carrying the gates of Gaza 'to the top of the hill that is before Hebron'. Judges 16: 3.

205   *In some novel of Dostoyevsky's*: reference is to *Insulted and Injured* (1861) by F. M. Dostoyevsky, which includes an episode where an elderly father, Ikhmenev, tramples on a medallion containing the portrait of his daughter Natasha, cursing her as he does so.

209   *the Neva*: the river on which St. Petersburg (Leningrad) was built.

211   *Père Goriot*: reference is to the novel *Le Père Goriot* (1834) by the French novelist Honoré de Balzac (1799–1850).

213   *Canova*: Antonio Canova (1757–1822), the Italian sculptor, who died in Venice.
      Faliero: Marino Faliero (*c.* 1274–1355), a Doge of Venice who sided with the mob against the nobility. He was beheaded after leading an unsuccessful *coup d'état*, and his portrait in the Palace of Doges was defaced.

224   *My fate, ye gods . . .*: a parody of Famusov's celebrated exit lines from the end of Act I of *Woe from Wit* (written 1822–4) by A. S. Griboyedov (1795–1829). In Griboyedov's original the 'tiny' daughter mentioned by Orlov was 'grown-up'. The couplet is correctly quoted in Chekhov's short play *The Proposal* (1888–9); see *The Oxford Chekhov*, vol. i, p. 77.

DOCTOR STARTSEV

227   *'Ere from the Cup of Life I yet had Drunk the Tears'*: from the poem *An Elegy* by A. A. Delvig (1798–1831).

229   *'Rushlight'*: a well-known folk-song.
      'A thing of beauty is a joy for ever': literally: 'Die, Denis, you'll not write better!' This remark was made to the eighteenth-century Russian playwright D. I. Fonvizin by Catherine the Great's favourite Potemkin after a performance of Fonvizin's play *The Brigadier*.

230   *'Your Voice, to me both Languorous and Tender'*: the first lines of Pushkin's lyric *Night* (1823) read: 'My voice, to you both languorous and tender.'

232   *Pisemsky . . . A Thousand Souls*: reference is to the novel *A Thousand Souls* (1858) by Alexis Feofilaktovich Pisemsky (1820–81).

233   *The hour cometh when—*: John 4: 23.

THE WORLD'S CLASSICS

A Select List

BEN JONSON: Five Plays
Edited by G. A. Wilkes

LEONARDO DA VINCI: Notebooks
Edited by Irma A. Richter

HERMAN MELVILLE: The Confidence-Man
Edited by Tony Tanner

PROSPER MÉRIMÉE: Carmen and Other Stories
Translated by Nicholas Jotcham

EDGAR ALLAN POE: Selected Tales
Edited by Julian Symons

MARY SHELLEY: Frankenstein
Edited by M. K. Joseph

BRAM STOKER: Dracula
Edited by A. N. Wilson

ANTHONY TROLLOPE: The American Senator
Edited by John Halperin

OSCAR WILDE: Complete Shorter Fiction
Edited by Isobel Murray

VIRGINIA WOOLF: Mrs Dalloway
Edited by Claire Tomalin

A complete list of Oxford Paperbacks, including The World's Classics, OPUS, Past Masters, Oxford Authors, Oxford Shakespeare, and Oxford Paperback Reference, is available in the UK from the Arts and Reference Publicity Department (BH), Oxford University Press, Walton Street, Oxford OX2 6DP.

In the USA, complete lists are available from the Paperbacks Marketing Manager, Oxford University Press, 200 Madison Avenue, New York, NY 10016.

Oxford Paperbacks are available from all good bookshops. In case of difficulty, customers in the UK can order direct from Oxford University Press Bookshop, Freepost, 116 High Street, Oxford, OX1 4BR, enclosing full payment. Please add 10 per cent of published price for postage and packing.

OUTSTANDING PRAISE FOR
a piece of the world

"Brings to vivid life a little-known corner of history."
—*USA Today*

"Haunting."—*Christian Science Monitor*

"Transporting." —*New York* magazine

"A pure, powerful story." —*O, The Oprah Magazine*

"Beautiful and stunning." —Daily Beast

"Gorgeous." —*Real Simple*

"Brilliantly imagined." —Erik Larson

"Heartbreaking and life-affirming."—Nathan Hill

"Memorable and unforgettable."
—*Portland Tribune* (Oregon)

"A masterpiece." —Historical Novel Society

"Superb." —*BookPage*

Praise for
A Piece of the World

"The novel evokes the somber grace of [Wyeth's] paintings. . . . Christina's yearning, her determination, her will to dream, occupy the emotional center in both the novel and the painting. . . . *A Piece of the World* is a story for those who want the mysterious made real."
                                                   —*New York Times Book Review*

"Another winner from the author of *Orphan Train*. . . . In this beautifully observed fictional memoir, Kline uses Andrew Wyeth's iconic painting *Christina's World* as the taking-off point for a moving portrait of the artist's real-life muse."
                                                   —*People* (Book of the Week)

"Fans of Kline's phenomenal 2013 best seller *Orphan Train* will recognize the way the new novel moves back and forth between timelines and brings to vivid life a little-known corner of history. The hardships endured by rural women, as well as their triumphs, are a preoccupation of both books. . . . Avoiding sentimental uplift, *A Piece of the World* offers unsparing insight into the real woman behind the painting."
                                                   —*USA Today*

"Kline herself is an artist, drawing on the real history of Christina Olson and Andrew Wyeth to conjure up her own haunting portrait. As in her bestselling novel, *Orphan Train*, Kline's deep research into characters, place, and time period provides the outlines of a compelling story, which she then expertly brings into three dimensions."
                                                   —*Christian Science Monitor*

"Transporting."
                                                   —*New York* magazine

"*A Piece of the World* is . . . the decoding of a mystery. Who has not gazed on Wyeth's picture and wondered, *why does that girl have so very far to go?* . . . Kline's gift is to dispense with the fustiness and fact-clogged drama of some historical novels to tell a pure, powerful story of suffering met with a fight."
                                                   —*O, The Oprah Magazine*

"With beautiful and stunning prose, the novel explores the sensitive and complex bond between artist and muse against the beauty of the rural American landscape." —Daily Beast

"In her absorbing new novel . . . Kline uses the historical record to lay the groundwork, then reimagines life as Christina Olson might have lived it. The result is a portrait of Maine farm life, of an iron-willed spinster with polio and the accidental friendship that changes everything. . . . In the hands of a lesser writer, Christina's plight might seem unwieldy or mawkish. Yet Kline . . . has a graceful, arresting style that lifts the narrative, and her portrayal of Andy leavens the entire story." —*Press Herald* (Portland)

"Like Wyeth's paintings, this is a vivid novel about hardscrabble lives and prairie grit and the seemingly small but significant beauties found there." —*Star Tribune* (Minneapolis)

"A gorgeous read." —*Real Simple*

"*A Piece of the World* is a graceful, moving, and powerful demonstration of what can happen when a fearless literary imagination combines with an inexhaustible curiosity about the past and the human heart: a feat of time travel, a bravura improvisation on the theme of art history, a wonderful story that seems to have been waiting, all this time, for Christina Baker Kline to come along and tell it." —Michael Chabon

"With *A Piece of the World*, Christina Baker Kline gives us a brilliantly imagined fictional memoir of the woman in the famed Wyeth painting *Christina's World*, so detailed, moving, and utterly transportive that I'll never be able to look at the painting again without thinking of this book and the characters who populate its pages." —Erik Larson

"Christina Baker Kline's remarkable novel *A Piece of the World* is the perfect book club pick. An evocative, beautifully written, exquisitely researched historical novel that will both teach and enthrall the reader. A must-read for anyone who loves history and art." —Kristin Hannah

"The inscrutable figure in the foreground of Wyeth's *Christina's World* is our American Mona Lisa, and Christina Baker Kline has pulled back the veil to imagine her rich story. Tender and tragic, *A Piece of the World* is a fascinating exploration of the life lived inside that house at the top of the hill." —Lily King

"With remarkable precision and compassion, *A Piece of the World* transports us to a midcentury farmhouse on the coast of Maine. But just like the painting that inspired it, this novel is about so much more. It's about the terrors and injustices of childhood, the aches of adulthood, the regrets of middle age. It's a story about a woman trapped by family and duty and her own ailing body. It's a book about the façades we erect despite our desire to be seen. This is a novel that does what Andrew Wyeth's famous painting does: it renders a whole universe of love and longing inside a seemingly simple scene. By focusing on this one particular piece of the world, Christina Baker Kline has accomplished something grand. A gorgeous novel, both heartbreaking and life-affirming." —Nathan Hill

"The figure at the center of Andrew Wyeth's celebrated painting *Christina's World* has her back to the viewer, but Kline turns her to face the reader, simultaneously equipping her with a back story and a lyrical voice. . . . Kline lovingly evokes the restricted life of a sensitive woman forced to renounce the norms of intimacy and self-advancement while using her as a lens to capture the simple beauty of the American farming landscape. . . . A character portrait that is painterly, sensuous, and sympathetic." —*Kirkus Reviews*

"The novel provides gorgeous, complicated answers to all the questions the painting stirs, beginning with the day a young painter appears on her porch. Kline has created a memorable and unforgettable voice for Anna Christina Olson, the girl in the field." —*Portland Tribune* (Oregon)

"With delicate palette, stark images, subtle tones, nuanced brushstrokes, and consummate craftsmanship, Christina Baker Kline has written this novel the way Andrew Wyeth painted the canvas. It is a masterpiece." —Historical Novel Society

"Superb. . . . The beauty of Kline's writing and her grasp of her characters is such that at first you want to sink into this book like a warm bath. But she doesn't allow her reader to get too comfortable. Christina is not a woman who accepts her disappointments with saintly forbearance. She is bitter, disappointed and occasionally spiteful. But the good-natured and talented young painter does not pity her—he sees her humanity. Gentle and profound, *A Piece of the World* shows the healing power of simple, unexpected friendship." —*BookPage*

"Epic." —*Cosmopolitan*

"Kline expertly captures the essence of Wyeth's iconic masterpiece and its real-life subject, crafting a moving work of historical fiction." —*Library Journal* (starred review)

"[Kline's] insightful, evocative prose brings Christina's singular perspective and indomitable spirit to life." —*Publishers Weekly*

"Artfully (pun intended) inspired by the Andrew Wyeth painting *Christina's World*." —*Marie Claire*

"Kline's portrait of her main character is moving in an unsentimental way as she evokes the New England landscape, the torment of crippling disease, and the piece of history embodied in Olson's story." —*Sydney Morning Herald*

"A novel about not just art, but family and home—things that last, and what it takes for them to do so." —*San Diego Union-Tribune*

"Readers will savor the quotidian details that compose Christina's 'quiet country life.' *Orphan Train* was a best-seller and popular book-discussion choice, so expect demand." —*Booklist*

"Fantastic and touching." —*Library Reads*

"[A] beautifully rendered portrait of a woman's interior life." —BBC.com

A PIECE *of the* WORLD

Novels by Christina Baker Kline

Orphan Train

Bird in Hand

The Way Life Should Be

Desire Lines

Sweet Water

A PIECE *of the* WORLD

(A NOVEL)

Christina Baker Kline

WM

WILLIAM MORROW
An Imprint of HarperCollins*Publishers*

FIRST WILLIAM MORROW PAPERBACK EDITION PUBLISHED 2018.

Designed by Bonni Leon-Berman

Library of Congress Cataloging-in-Publication Data has been applied for.

ISBN 978-0-06-235627-7

18 19 20 21 22   RS/LSC   10 9 8 7 6 5 4 3 2

For my father,
who showed me the world

"There was a very strange connection. One of those odd collisions that happen. We were a little alike; I was an unhealthy child that was kept at home. So there was an unsaid feeling between us that was wonderful, an utter naturalness. We'd sit for hours and not say a word, and then she'd say something, and I'd answer her. A reporter once asked her what we talked about. She said, 'Nothing foolish.'"

—Andrew Wyeth

PROLOGUE

LATER HE TOLD ME HE'D BEEN AFRAID TO SHOW ME THE
PAINTING. He thought I wouldn't like the way he portrayed
me: dragging myself across the field, fingers clutching dirt, my
legs twisted behind. The arid moonscape of wheatgrass and
timothy. That dilapidated house in the distance, looming up like
a secret that won't stay hidden. Faraway windows, opaque and
unreadable. Ruts in the spiky grass made by an invisible vehicle,
leading nowhere. Dishwater sky.

People think the painting is a portrait, but it isn't. Not really.
He wasn't even in the field; he conjured it from a room in the
house, an entirely different angle. He removed rocks and trees
and outbuildings. The scale of the barn is wrong. And I am not
that frail young thing, but a middle-aged spinster. It's not my
body, really, and maybe not even my head.

He did get one thing right: Sometimes a sanctuary, sometimes a prison, that house on the hill has always been my home.
I've spent my life yearning toward it, wanting to escape it, par-
alyzed by its hold on me. (There are many ways to be crippled,
I've learned over the years, many forms of paralysis.) My ancestors fled to Maine from Salem, but like anyone who tries to

run away from the past, they brought it with them. Something inexorable seeds itself in the place of your origin. You can never escape the bonds of family history, no matter how far you travel. And the skeleton of a house can carry in its bones the marrow of all that came before.

Who are you, Christina Olson? he asked me once.

Nobody had ever asked me that. I had to think about it for a while.

If you really want to know me, I said, we'll have to start with the witches. And then the drowned boys. The shells from distant lands, a whole room full of them. The Swedish sailor marooned in ice. I'll need to tell you about the false smiles of the Harvard man and the hand-wringing of those brilliant Boston doctors, the dory in the haymow and the wheelchair in the sea.

And eventually—though neither of us knew it yet—we'd end up here, in this place, within and without the world of the painting.

THE STRANGER AT THE DOOR

I'm working on a quilt patch in the kitchen on a brilliant July afternoon, small squares of fabric and a pincushion and scissors on the table beside me, when I hear the hum of a car engine. Looking out the window toward the cove, I see a station wagon turn into the field about a hundred yards away. The engine cuts off and the passenger door swings open and Betsy James gets out, laughing and exclaiming. I haven't seen her since last summer. She's wearing a white halter top and denim shorts, a red bandanna tied around her neck. As I watch her coming toward the house, I am struck by how different she looks. Her sweet round face has thinned and lengthened; her chestnut hair is long and thick around her shoulders, her eyes dark and shining. A red slash of lipstick. I think of her at nine years old, when she first came to visit, her small, nimble fingers braiding my hair as she sat behind me on the stoop. And here she is, seventeen and suddenly a woman.

"Hey there, Christina," she says at the screen door, out of breath. "It's been such a long time!"

"Come in," I say from my chair. "You won't mind if I don't get up?"

"Of course not." When she steps inside, the room smells of

roses. (When did Betsy start wearing perfume?) She sweeps over to my chair and hugs my shoulders. "We arrived a few days ago. I surely am happy to be back."

"You surely look it."

She smiles, spots of color on her cheeks. "How are you and Al?"

"Oh, you know. Fine. The same."

"The same is good, yes?"

I smile. Sure. The same is good.

"What are you making here?"

"Just a little thing. A baby quilt. Lora's pregnant again."

"Such a generous auntie." She reaches down and picks up a quilt square, a piece of calico, pink flowers with green leaves on a brown background. "I recognize this fabric."

"I tore up an old dress."

"I remember it. Small white buttons and a full skirt, right?"

I think of my mother bringing home the Butterick pattern and the iridescent buttons and the calico. I think of Walton seeing me in the dress for the first time. *I am awed by you.* "That was a long time ago."

"Well, it's nice that old dress is getting a new life." Gently she places the square back on the table and sifts through the others: white muslin, navy cotton, chambray faintly marked with ink. "All these bits and pieces. You're making a family heirloom."

"I don't know about that," I say. "It's just a pile of scraps."

"One man's trash . . ." She laughs and glances out the window. "I completely forgot! I came up here for a cup of water, if you don't mind."

"Sit down, I'll get you a glass."

"Oh, it's not for me." She points at the station wagon in the field. "My friend wants to paint a picture of your house, but he needs water to do it."

I squint at the car. A boy is sitting on the roof, looking at the sky. He's got a large white pad of paper in one hand and what looks like a pencil in the other.

"He's N. C. Wyeth's son," Betsy says in a stage whisper, as if someone might hear.

"Who?"

"You know N. C. Wyeth. The famous illustrator? *Treasure Island?*"

Ah, *Treasure Island.* "Al loved that book. I think we still have it somewhere."

"I think every boy in America has it somewhere. Well, his son's an artist too. I just met him today."

"You met him today, and you're riding around in a car with him?"

"Yes, he's—I don't know. He seems trustworthy."

"Your parents don't mind?"

"They don't know." She smiles sheepishly. "He showed up at the house this morning looking for my father, but my parents had gone off for a sail. I answered the door. And here we are."

"That happens sometimes," I say. "Where's he from?"

"Pennsylvania. His family has a summer place up here, in Port Clyde."

"You seem to know an awful lot about him," I say, arching an eyebrow.

She arches an eyebrow back. "I plan to learn more."

Betsy leaves with her cup of water and makes her way back to the station wagon. By the way she's walking, shoulders back and chin forward, I can tell she knows he's watching her. And she likes it. She hands the boy the cup and climbs onto the roof next to him.

"Who was that?" My brother Al is at the back door, wiping his hands on a rag. I can never tell when he's coming; he's as quiet as a fox.

"Betsy. And a boy. He's painting a picture of the house, she said."

"Why would he want to do that?"

I shrug. "People are funny."

"Sure are." Al settles into his rocker, pulling out his pipe and tobacco. He starts tamping and lighting, both of us spying on Betsy and the boy out the window and trying to act like we aren't.

After a while the boy climbs down and sets his pad of paper on the hood of the car. He offers his hand to Betsy, who slides down into his embrace. Even from this distance I can feel the heat between them. They stand there talking for a minute, and then Betsy tugs on his hand, pulling him toward—oh Lord, she's bringing him up to the house. I feel a momentary panic: the floor is dusty, my dress soiled, my hair unkempt. Al's overalls are splashed with mud. It's been a long time since I've worried about being seen through the eyes of a stranger. As they walk toward the house, though, I see the boy gazing at Betsy and realize I don't need to worry. She is all he sees.

He's at the screen, now, on the threshold. Lanky, smiling, quivering with energy, he fills the entire doorway. "What a marvelous house," he murmurs as he opens the screen, craning his neck to look up and around the room. "The light in here is extraordinary."

"Christina, Alvaro, this is Andrew," Betsy says, coming in behind him.

He inclines his head. "Hope you don't mind my crashing in uninvited. Betsy swore it was okay."

"We don't stand on ceremony," my brother says. "I'm Al."

"People after my own heart. And call me Andy, please."

"Well, I'm Christina," I say.

"I call her Christie, but no one else does," Al adds.

"Christina, then," Andy says, settling his gaze on me. I detect no judgment in it, only a kind of anthropological curiosity. Still, his keen attention makes me blush.

Turning to Al, I say quickly, "Remember that book *Treasure Island*? His father did the paintings for it, Betsy said."

"Did he now?" Al's face lights up. "You can't forget those pictures. I probably read that book a dozen times. Might be the only book I ever actually finished, now that I think about it. I wanted to be a pirate."

Andy breaks into a grin. His teeth are large and white, like a movie star's. "So did I. Still do, in fact."

Betsy's holding the oversized drawing pad. As proud as a new mother, she brings it over to show me. "Look what Andy did, Christina, in that short amount of time."

The paper is still damp. In bold strokes Andy reduced the

house to a white box with two gables facing the sea. The fields are green and yellow, with bristly blades of grass poking up here and there. Near-black firs, a purple swipe of mountains, watery clouds. Though the watercolor has been done quickly—there's movement in the brushstrokes, as if the wind is blowing through—it's clear this boy knows what he's doing. The windows are mere suggestions, but you have the peculiar sense that you can see inside. The house seems rooted in the earth.

"It's just a sketch," Andy says, coming up beside me. "I'll keep working at it."

"Looks like a nice place to live," I say. The house is snug and cozy, a fairy-tale version of the one Al and I actually live in, the only hint of its decay in smudges of blue and brown.

Andy laughs. "You tell me." Running two fingers over the paper, he says, "Such stark lines. There's something about this place . . . You've lived here a long time?"

I nod.

"I sense that. That it's a place filled with stories. I'll bet I could paint it for a hundred years and never get tired of it."

"Oh, you'd get tired of it," Al says.

We all laugh.

Andy claps his hands together. "Hey, guess what? Today is my birthday."

"Is it really?" Betsy asks. "You didn't tell me."

He puts his arm around her and tugs her toward him. "Didn't I? I feel like you know everything about me already."

"Not yet," she says.

"What's your age?" I ask him.

"Twenty-two."

"Twenty-two! Betsy's only seventeen."

"A *mature* seventeen," Betsy blurts, color rising to her cheeks.

Andy seems amused. "Well, I've never cared much about age. Or maturity."

"How are you going to celebrate?" I ask.

He raises an eyebrow at Betsy. "I'd say I'm celebrating right now."

BETSY DOESN'T SHOW up again until several weeks later, when she bursts into the kitchen and practically dances across the floor. "Christina, we are engaged," she says breathlessly, clasping my hand.

"Engaged?!"

She nods. "Can you believe it?"

You're so young, I start to say; it's too quick, you hardly know each other . . .

Then I think of my own life. All the years, all the waiting that led to nothing. I saw how the two of them were together. The spark between them. *I feel like you know everything about me already.* "Of course I can," I say.

Ten months later, a postcard arrives. Betsy and Andy are married. When they return to Maine for the summer, I hand Betsy a wedding gift: two pillowcases I made and embroidered with flowers. It took me four days to make the French knots for the daisies and the tiny buttonhole-stitch leaves; my hands, stiff and gnarled, don't work the way they used to.

Betsy looks closely at the embroidery and holds the pillow-cases to her chest. "I will treasure these. They're perfect."

I give her a smile. They're not perfect. The lines are uneven, the flower petals spiky and overlarge; the cotton is marked faintly with the residue of ripped stitches.

Betsy has always been kind.

She shows me photographs from their upstate New York wedding ceremony: Andy in a tuxedo, Betsy in white with gardenias in her hair, both beaming with joy. After their five-day honeymoon, she tells me, she'd assumed they would drive to Canada for the wedding of a close friend, but Andy said he had to get back to work. "He'd told me before we were married that was how it would be," she says. "But I didn't quite believe it until that moment."

"So did you go by yourself?"

She shakes her head. "I stayed with him. This is what I signed up for. The work is everything."

OUT THE KITCHEN window I see Andy trudging up the field toward the house, hitching one leg forward, dragging the other, his gait uneven. Strange that I didn't notice that before. Here he is at the door in paint-flecked boots, a white cotton shirt rolled to the elbow, a sketch pad under his arm. He knocks, two firm raps, and pulls open the screen. "Betsy has some errands to do. Is it okay if I hang around?"

I try to act nonchalant, but my heart is racing. I can't remember the last time I was alone with a man other than Al. "Suit yourself."

He steps inside.

He's taller and handsomer than I remember, with sandy brown hair and piercing blue eyes. There's something equine about the way he tosses his head and shifts his feet. A pulsating thrum.

In the Shell Room he runs his hand along the mantelpiece, brushing off the dust. Picks up Mother's cracked white teapot and turns it around. Cups my grandmother's chambered nautilus in his hand and leafs through the filmy pages of her old black bible. No one has opened my poor drowned uncle Alvaro's sea chest in decades; it screeches when he lifts the lid. Andy picks up a shell-framed portrait of Abraham Lincoln, looks at it closely, sets it down. "You can feel the past in this house," he says. "The layers of generations. It reminds me of *The House of the Seven Gables*. 'So much of mankind's varied experience had passed there that the very timbers were oozy, as with the moisture of a heart.'"

The lines are familiar. I remember reading that novel in school, a long time ago. "We're actually related to Nathaniel Hawthorne," I tell him.

"Interesting. Ah yes—Hathorn." Going to the window, he gestures toward the field. "I saw the tombstones in the grave-yard down there. Hawthorne lived in Maine for a while, I believe?"

"I don't know about that," I admit. "Our ancestors came from Massachusetts. Nearly two hundred years ago. Three men, in the middle of winter."

"Where in Massachusetts?"

"Salem."

"Why'd they come up?"

"My grandmother said they were trying to escape the taint of association with their relative John Hathorne. He was chief justice of the witch trials. When they got to Maine they dropped the 'e' at the end of the name."

"To obscure the connection?"

I shrug. "Presumably."

"I'm remembering this now," he says. "Nathaniel Hawthorne left Salem too, and also changed the spelling of the name. But a lot of his stories are reworkings of his own family history. *Your* family history, I suppose. Moral allegories about people determined to root out wickedness in others while denying it in themselves."

"Actually," I tell him, "there's a legend that as one of the condemned witches stood at the scaffold, waiting for the noose, she uttered a curse: 'May God take revenge on the family of John Hathorne.'"

"So your family is cursed!" he says with delight.

"Maybe. Who knows? My grandmother used to say that those Hathorn men brought the witches with them from Salem. She kept the door open between the kitchen and the shed for the witches to come and go."

Looking around the Shell Room, he says, "What do you think? Is it true?"

"I've never seen any," I tell him. "But I keep the door open too."

OVER THE YEARS, certain stories in the history of a family take hold. They're passed from generation to generation, gaining substance and meaning along the way. You have to learn to sift through them, separating fact from conjecture, the likely from the implausible.

Here is what I know: Sometimes the least believable stories are the true ones.

1896–1900

My mother drapes a wrung-out cloth across my forehead. Cold water trickles down my temple onto the pillow, and I turn my head to smear it off. I gaze up into her gray eyes, narrowed in concern, a vertical line between them. Small lines around her puckered lips. I look over at my brother Alvaro standing beside her, two years old, eyes wide and solemn.

She pours water from a white teapot into a glass. "Drink, Christina."

"Smile at her, Katie," my grandmother Tryphena tells her. "Fear is a contagion." She leads Alvaro out of the room, and my mother reaches for my hand, smiling with only her mouth.

I am three years old.

My bones ache. When I close my eyes, I feel like I'm falling. It's not an altogether unpleasant sensation, like sinking into water. Colors behind my eyelids, purple and rust. My face so hot that my mother's hand on my cheek feels icy. I take a deep breath, inhaling the smells of wood smoke and baking bread, and I drift. The house creaks and shifts. Snoring in another room. The ache in my bones drives me back to the surface. When I open my eyes, I can't see anything, but I can tell my mother is gone. I'm so cold it feels like I've never been warm,

my teeth chattering loudly in the quiet. I hear myself whimpering, and it's as if the sound is coming from someone else. I don't
know how long I've been making this noise, but it soothes me, a
distraction from the pain.

The covers lift. My grandmother says, "There, Christina,
hush. I'm here." She slides into bed beside me in her thick flannel nightgown and pulls me toward her. I settle into the curve
of her legs, her bosom pillowy behind my head, her soft fleshy
arm under my neck. She rubs my cold arms, and I fall asleep in
a warm cocoon smelling of talcum powder and linseed oil and
baking soda.

SINCE I CAN remember I've called my grandmother Mamey.
It's the name of a tree that grows in the West Indies, where she
went with my grandfather, Captain Sam Hathorn, on one of
their many excursions. The mamey tree has a short, thick trunk
and only a few large limbs and pointy green leaves, with white
flowers at the ends of the branches, like hands. It blooms all year
long, and its fruit ripens at different times. When my grandparents spent several months on the island of St. Lucia, my grandmother made jam out of the fruit, which tastes like an overripe
raspberry. "The riper it gets, the sweeter it gets. Like me," she
said. "Don't call me Granny. Mamey suits me just fine."

Sometimes I find her sitting alone, gazing out the window
in the Shell Room, our front parlor, where we display the treasures that six generations of sailors brought home in sea chests
from their voyages around the world. I know she's pining for

my grandfather, who died in this house a year before I was born. "It is a terrible thing to find the love of your life, Christina," she says. "You know too well what you're missing when it's gone."

"You have us," I say.

"I loved your grandfather more than all the shells in the Shell Room," she says. "More than all the blades of grass in the field."

MY GRANDFATHER, LIKE his father and grandfather before him, began his life on the sea as a cabin boy and became a ship captain. After marrying my grandmother, he took her with him on his travels, transporting ice from Maine to the Philippines, Australia, Panama, the Virgin Islands, and filling the ship for the return trip with brandy, sugar, spices, and rum. Her stories of their exotic travels have become family legend. She traveled with him for decades, even bringing along their children, three boys and a girl, until, at the height of the Civil War, he insisted they stay home. Confederate privateers were prowling up and down the East Coast like marauding pirates, and no ship was immune.

But my grandfather's caution could not keep his family safe: all three of his boys died young. One succumbed to scarlet fever; his four-year-old namesake, Sammy, drowned one October when Captain Sam was at sea. My grandmother could not bring herself to break the news until March. "Our beloved little boy is no more on earth," she wrote. "While I write, I'm almost blind with tears. No one saw him fall but the little boy who ran to tell his mother. The vital spark has fled. Dear husband, you can better imagine my grief than I can describe to you." Fourteen years later, their teenaged son, Alvaro, working as a seaman on a schooner off the coast of Cape Cod, was swept overboard in a storm. News of his death came by telegram, blunt and impersonal. His body was never found. Alvaro's sea chest arrived on Hathorn Point weeks later, its top intricately carved by his hand. My grandmother, disconsolate, spent hours tracing the outlines with her fingertips, damsels in hoopskirts with revealing décolletage.

MY BEDROOM IS still and bright. Light filters through the lace curtains Mamey crocheted, making intricate shapes on the floor. Dust mites float in slow motion. Stretching out in the bed, I lift my arms from under the sheet. No pain. I'm afraid to move my legs. Afraid to hope that I'm better.

My brother Alvaro swings into the room, hanging on to the doorknob. He stares at me blankly, then shouts, to no one in particular, "Christie's awake!" He gives me a long steady look as he closes the door. I hear him clomping deliberately down the stairs, and then my mother's voice and my grandmother's, the clash of pots far away in the kitchen, and I drift back to sleep. Next thing I know, Al is shaking my shoulder with his spider-monkey hand, saying, "Wake up, lazy," and Mother, trundling through the door with her big pregnant belly, is setting a tray on the round oak table beside the bed. Oatmeal mush and toast and milk. My father a shadow behind her. For the first time in I don't know how long, I feel a pang that must be hunger.

Mother smiles a real smile as she props two pillows behind my head and helps me sit up. Spoons oatmeal into my mouth, waits for me to swallow between slurps. Al says, "Why're you feeding her, she's not a baby," and Mother tells him to hush, but she is laughing and crying at the same time, tears rolling down her cheeks, and has to stop for a moment to wipe her face with her apron.

"Why you crying, Mama?" Al asks.

"Because your sister is going to get well."

I remember her saying this, but it will be years before I understand what it means. It means my mother was afraid I might not get well. They were all afraid—all except Alvaro and me and the unborn baby, each of us busy growing, unaware of how bad things could get. But they knew. My grandmother, with her three dead children. My mother, the only one who survived, her childhood threaded with melancholy, who named her firstborn son after her brother who drowned in the sea.

A DAY PASSES, another, a week. I am going to live, but something isn't right. Lying in the bed, I feel like a rag wrung out and draped to dry. I can't sit up, can barely turn my head. I can't move my legs. My grandmother settles into a chair beside me with her crocheting, looking at me now and then over the top of her rimless spectacles. "There, child. Rest is good. Baby steps."

"Christie's not a baby," Al says. He's lying on the floor pushing his green train engine. "She's bigger than me."

"Yes, she's a big girl. But she needs rest so she can get better."

"Rest is stupid," Al says. He wants me back to normal so we can run to the barn, play hide-and-seek among the hay bales, poke at the gopher holes with a long stick.

I agree. Rest is stupid. I am tired of this narrow bed, the slice of window above it. I want to be outside, running through the grass, climbing up and down the stairs. When I fall asleep, I am careering down the hill, my arms outstretched and my strong legs pumping, grasses whipping against my calves, steady on toward the sea, closing my eyes and tilting my chin toward the sun, moving with ease, without pain, without falling. I wake in my bed to find the sheet damp with sweat.

"What's wrong with me?" I ask my mother as she tucks a fresh sheet around me.

"You are as God made you."

"Why would he make me like this?"

Her eyelids flicker—not quite a flutter, but a startled blink and long shut eye that I've come to recognize: It's the expression she makes when she doesn't know what to say. "We have to trust in his plan."

My grandmother, crocheting in her chair, doesn't say anything. But when Mother goes downstairs with the dirty sheets, she says, "Life is one trial after another. You're just learning that earlier than most."

"But why am I the only one?"

She laughs. "Oh, child, you're not the only one." She tells me about a sailor in their crew with one leg who thumped around deck on a wooden dowel, another with a hunchback that made him scuttle like a crab, one born with six fingers on each hand.

(How quickly that boy could tie knots!) One with a foot like a cabbage, one with scaly skin like a reptile, conjoined twins she once saw on the street . . . People have maladies of all kinds, she says, and if they have any sense, they don't waste time whining about them. "We all have our burdens to bear," she says. "You know what yours is, now. That's good. You'll never be surprised by it."

Mamey tells me a story about when she and Captain Sam were shipwrecked in a storm, cast adrift on a precarious raft in the middle of the ocean, shivering and alone, with scant provisions. The sun set and rose, set and rose; their food and water dwindled. They despaired that they would never be rescued. She tore strips of clothing, tied them to an oar, and managed to prop this wretched flag upright. For weeks, they saw no one. They licked their salt-cracked lips and closed their sunburned lids, resigning themselves to their all-but-certain fates, blessed unconsciousness and death. And then, one evening near sundown, a speck on the horizon materialized into a ship heading directly toward them, drawn by the fluttering rags.

"The most important qualities a human can possess are an iron will and a persevering spirit," Mamey says. She says I inherited those qualities from her, and that in the same way she survived the shipwreck, when all hope was lost, and the deaths of her three boys, when she thought her heart might pulverize like a shell into sand, I will find a way to keep going, no matter what happens. Most people aren't as lucky as I am, she says, to come from such hardy stock.

❧

"SHE WAS FINE until the fever," Mother tells Dr. Heald as I sit on the examining table in his Cushing office. "Now she can barely walk."

He pokes and prods, draws blood, takes my temperature. "Let's see here," he says, grasping my legs. He probes my skin with his fingers, feeling his way down my legs to the bones in my feet. "Yes," he murmurs, "irregularities. Interesting." Grasping my ankles, he tells my mother, "It's hard to say. The feet are deformed. I suspect it's viral. I recommend braces. No guarantee they'll work, but probably worth a try."

My mother presses her lips together. "What's the alternative?"

Dr. Heald winces in an exaggerated way, as if this is as hard for him to say as it is for us to hear. "Well, that's the thing. I don't think there is one."

The braces Dr. Heald puts me in clamp my legs like a medieval torture device, tearing my skin into bloody strips and making me howl in pain. After a week of this, Mother takes me back to Dr. Heald and he removes them. She gasps when she sees my legs, covered with red festering wounds. To this day I bear the scars.

For the rest of my life, I will be wary of doctors. When Dr. Heald comes to the house to check on Mamey or Mother's pregnancy or Papa's cough, I make myself scarce, hiding in the attic, the barn, the four-hole privy in the shed.

❧

ON THE PINE boards of the kitchen floor I practice walking in a straight line.

"One foot in front of the next, like a tightrope walker," my mother instructs, "along the seam."

It's hard to keep my balance; I can only walk on the outsides of my feet. If this really were a tightrope in the circus, Al points out, I would have fallen to my death a dozen times already.

"Steady, now," Mother says. "It's not a race."

"It is a race," Al says. On a parallel seam he steps lightly in a precise choreography of small stockinged feet, and within moments is at the end. He throws up his arms. "I win!"

I pretend to stumble, and as I fall I kick his legs out from under him and he lands hard on his tailbone. "Get out of her way, Alvaro," Mother scolds. Sprawling on the floor, he glowers at me. I glower back. Al is thin and strong, like a strip of steel or the trunk of a sapling. He is naughtier than I am, stealing eggs from the hens and attempting to ride the cows. I feel a pit of something hard and spiky in my stomach. Jealousy. Resentment. And something else: the unexpected pleasure of revenge.

I fall so often that Mother sews cotton pads for my elbows and knees. No matter how much I practice, I can't get my legs to move the way they should. But eventually they're strong enough that I can play hide-and-seek in the barn and chase chickens in the yard. Al doesn't care about my limp. He tugs at me to come with him, climb trees, ride Dandy the old brown mule, scrounge for firewood for a clambake. Mother's always scolding and shushing him to go away, give me peace, but Mamey is silent. She thinks it's good for me, I can tell.

I WAKE IN the dark to the sound of rain drumming the roof and a commotion in my parents' bedroom. Mother groaning, Mamey murmuring. My father's voice and two others I don't recognize in the foyer downstairs. I slip out of bed and into my woolen skirt and thick socks and cling to the rail as I half fall, half slide down the stairs. At the bottom my father is standing with a stout red-faced woman wearing a kerchief over her frizzy hair.

"Go back to bed, Christina," Papa says. "It's the middle of the night."

"Babies pay no attention to the clock," the woman singsongs. She shrugs off her coat and hands it to my father. I cling to the banister while she lumbers like a badger up the narrow stairs.

I creep up after her and push open the door to Mother's bedroom. Mamey is there, leaning over the bed. I can't see much on the high mahogany four-poster, but I hear Mother moaning.

Mamey turns. "Oh, child," she says with dismay. "This is no place for you."

"It's all right. A girl needs to learn the ways of the world sooner or later," the badger says. She jerks her head at me.

"Why don't you make yourself useful? Tell your father to heat water on the stove."

I look at Mother, thrashing and writhing. "Is she going to be all right?"

The badger scowls. "Your mother is fine and dandy. Did you hear what I said? Boiling water. Baby is on the way."

I make my way down to the kitchen and tell Papa, who puts a pot of water on the black iron Glenwood range. As we wait in the kitchen he teaches me card games, Blackjack and Crazy Eights, to pass the time. The sound of the wind driving rain against the house is like dry beans in a hollow stick. Before morning is over, we hear the high-pitched cry of a healthy baby.

"His name is Samuel," Mother says when I climb onto the bed beside her. "Isn't he perfect?"

"Um-hmm," I say, though I think the baby looks as crab apple–faced as the badger.

"Maybe he'll be an explorer like his grandfather Samuel," Mamey says. "Like all of the seafaring Samuels."

"God forbid," Mother says.

"WHO ARE THE seafaring Samuels?" I ask Mamey later, when Mother and the baby are napping and we're alone in the Shell Room.

"They're your ancestors. The reason you're here," she says.

She tells me the story of how, in 1743, three men from Massachusetts—two brothers, Samuel and William Hathorn, and William's son Alexander—packed their belongings into three carriages for the long journey to the province of Maine in the middle of winter. They arrived at a remote peninsula that for two thousand years had been a meeting ground for Indian tribes and built a tent made of animal skins, sturdy enough to withstand the coming months of snow and ice and muddy thaw. Within a year they felled a swath of forest and built three log cabins. And they gave this spit of land in Cushing, Maine, a name: Hathorn Point.

Fifty years later, Alexander's son Samuel, a sea captain, built a two-story wood-frame house on the foundation of the family's cabin. Samuel married twice, raised six children in the house, and died in his seventies. His son Aaron, also a sea captain, married twice and raised eight children here. When Aaron died and his widow decided to sell the house (opting for a simpler life in town, closer to the bakery and the dry goods store), the seafaring Hathorns were dismayed. Five years later Aaron's son Samuel IV bought the house back, reestablishing the family's hold on the land.

Samuel IV was my grandfather.

All of those sea captains, coming and going for months at a time. Their many wives and children, up and down the narrow stairs. To this day, Mamey says, this old house on Hathorn Point is filled with their ghosts.

WHEN YOUR WORLD is small, you learn every inch of it. You can trace it in the dark; you navigate it in your sleep. Fields of rough grass sloping toward the rocky shore and the sea beyond, nooks and crannies to hide and play in. The soot-black range, always warm, in the kitchen. Geraniums on the windowsill, splayed red like a magician's handkerchief. Feral cats in the barn. Air that smells of pine and seaweed, of chicken roasting in the oven and freshly plowed soil.

One summer afternoon Mother looks at the tide chart in the kitchen and says, "Put on your shoes, Christina, I've got something to show you."

I lace up my brown brogues and follow her down through the field, past the humming cicadas and the swooping crows, and into the family cemetery, my legs steady enough that I can almost keep up. I trail my fingers across the moss-mottled, half-crumbled headstones, their etchings hard to read. The oldest one belongs to Joanne Smalley Hathorn. She died in 1834, when she was thirty-three, the mother of seven young children. When she was dying, Mother tells me, she begged her husband to bury her on the property instead of in the town cemetery several miles away so their children could visit her grave.

Her children were buried here too. All the Hathorns after her are buried here.

We continue to the shore on the southern side of Hathorn Point, above Kissing Cove and Maple Juice Cove, where the estuary of the St. George River flows into Muscongus Bay and the Atlantic Ocean beyond. There's an ancient heap of shells here that Mother says was left by Abenaki Indians who spent long-ago summers on the point. I try to envision what it would've been like here before this house was built, before the three log cabins, before any settlers discovered it. I imagine an Abenaki girl, like me, scouring the rocky shore for shells. From the point you can see way out to sea. Did she keep one eye on the horizon, scanning it for intruders? Did she have any idea how much her life would change when they arrived?

The tide is low. I stumble on the rocks, but Mother doesn't say anything, just stops and waits. Across the muddy flats is Little Island, an acre-wide wilderness of birches and dry grass. She points to it. "We're going there. But we can't stay long, or the tide will strand us." Our path is an obstacle course of seaweed-slick stones. I pick my way along slowly, and even so I trip and fall, scraping my hand on a cluster of barnacles. My feet are damp inside my shoes. Mother glances back at me. "Get up. We're nearly there." When we reach the island, she spreads a wool blanket on the beach where it's dry. Out of her rucksack she takes an egg sandwich on thick-sliced bread, a cucumber, two pieces of fried apple cake. She hands me half the sandwich. "Close your eyes and feel the sun," she says, and I do, leaning back on my elbows, chin toward sky. Eyelids warm and yellow. Trees rustling behind us like starch-stiff skirts. Briny air. "Why would you want to be anywhere else?"

After we eat, we collect shells—pale green anemone puffs and iridescent purple mussels. "Look," Mother says, pointing at a crab emerging from a tide pool, picking its way across the rocks. "All of life is here, in this place." In her own way, she is always trying to teach me something.

TO LIVE ON a farm is to wage an ongoing war with the elements, Mother says. We have to push back against the unruly outdoors to keep chaos at bay. Farmers work in the soil with mules and cows and pigs, and the house must be a sanctuary. If it isn't, we are no better than the animals.

Mother is in constant motion—sweeping, mopping, scouring, baking, wiping, washing, hanging out sheets. She makes bread in the morning using yeast from the hop vine behind the shed. There's always a pot of porridge on the back of the range by the time I come downstairs, with a filmy skin on top that I poke through and feed to the cat when she isn't looking. Sometimes dry oatcakes and boiled eggs. Baby Sam sleeps in a cradle in the corner. When the breakfast dishes are cleared, she starts on the large midday meal: chicken pie or pot roast or fish stew; mashed or boiled potatoes; peas or carrots, fresh or canned, depending on the season. What's left over reappears at supper, transformed into a casserole or a stew.

Mother sings while she works. Her favorite song, "Red Wing," is about an Indian maiden pining for a brave who's gone to battle, growing more despondent as time passes. Tragically, her true love is killed:

Now, the moon shines tonight on pretty Red Wing
The breeze is sighing, the night bird's crying,
For afar 'neath his star her brave is sleeping,
While Red Wing's weeping her heart away.

It's hard for me to understand why Mother likes such a sad song. Mrs. Crowley, my teacher at the Wing School Number 4 in Cushing, says that the Greeks believed witnessing pain in art makes you feel better about your own life. But when I mention this to Mother, she shrugs. "I just like the melody. It makes the housework go faster."

As soon as I'm tall enough to reach the dining room table, my job is to set it. Mother teaches me how with the heavy silver-plate cutlery:

"Fork on the left. L-E-F-T. Four letters, same as 'fork.' F-O-R-K," she says as she shows me, setting the fork beside the plate in its proper place. "Knife and spoon on the right. Five letters. R-I-G-H-T, same as 'knife' and 'spoon.' K-N-I-F-E."

"S-P-O-O-N," I say.

"Yes."

"And glass. G-L-A-S-S. Right?"

"What a clever one!" Mamey calls from the kitchen.

By the time I'm seven I can strip thin ribbons of skin from potatoes with a knife, scrub the pine floors with bleach on my hands and knees, tend the hop vine behind the shed, culling yeast to make bread. Mother shows me how to sew and mend, and though my unruly fingers make it hard to thread a needle, I'm determined. I try again and again, pricking my forefinger, fraying the tip of the thread. "I've never seen such determination," Mamey exclaims, but Mother doesn't say a word until I've succeeded in threading it. Then she says, "Christina, you are nothing if not tenacious."

MAMEY DOESN'T SHARE Mother's fear of dirt. What's the worst that can happen if dust collects in the corners or we leave dishes in the sink? Her favorite things are timeworn: the old Glenwood range, the rocking chair by the window with the fraying cane seat, the handsaw with a broken handle in a corner of the kitchen. Each one of them, she says, with its own story to tell.

Mamey runs her fingers along the shells on the mantelpiece in the Shell Room like an archaeologist uncovering a ruin that springs to life with all the knowledge she holds about it. The shells she discovered in her son Alvaro's sea chest have pride of place here, alongside her black travel-battered bible. Pastel-colored shells of all shapes and sizes line the edges of the floor and the window ledges. Shell-encrusted vases, statues, tintypes, valentines, book covers; miniature views of the family homestead on scallop shells, painted by a long-ago relative; even a shell-framed engraving of President Lincoln.

She hands me her prized shell, the one she found near a coral reef on a beach in Madagascar. It's surprisingly heavy, about eight inches long, silky smooth, with a rust-and-white zebra stripe on top that melts into a creamy white bottom. "It's called a chambered nautilus," she says. "'Nautilus' is Greek for 'sailor.'" She tells me about a poem in which a man finds a broken shell like this one on the shore. Noticing the spiral chambers enlarging in size, he imagines the mollusk inside getting larger and larger, outgrowing one space and moving on to the next.

"'Build thee more stately mansions, O my soul / As the swift seasons roll!'" Mamey recites, spreading her hands in the air. "'Till thou at length art free, / Leaving thine outgrown shell by life's unresting sea.' It's about human nature, you see. You can live for a long time inside the shell you were born in. But one day it'll become too small."

"Then what?" I ask.

"Well, then you'll have to find a larger shell to live in."

I consider this for a moment. "What if it's too small but you still want to live there?"

She sighs. "Gracious, child, what a question. I suppose you'll either have to be brave and find a new home or you'll have to live inside a broken shell."

Mamey shows me how to decorate book covers and vases with tiny shells, overlapping them so they cascade down in a precise flat line. As we glue the shells she reminisces about my grandfather's bravery and adventurousness, how he outsmarted pirates and survived tidal waves and shipwrecks. She tells me again about the flag she made out of strips of cloth when all hope was lost, and the miraculous sight of that faraway freighter that came to their rescue.

"Don't fill the girl's head with those tall tales," Mother scolds, overhearing us from the pantry.

"They're not tall tales, they're real life. You know, you were there."

Mother comes to the door. "You make it all sound grand, when you know it was miserable most of the time."

"It *was* grand," Mamey says. "This girl may never go anywhere. She should at least know that adventure is in her bones."

When Mother leaves the room, shutting the door behind her, Mamey sighs. She says she can't believe she raised a child who traveled all over the world but has been content ever since to let the world come to her. She says Mother would've been a spinster if Papa hadn't walked up the hill and given her an alternative.

I know some of the story. That my mother was the only surviving child and that she clung close to home. After my grandfather retired from the sea, he and Mamey decided to turn their house into a summertime inn for the income, the distraction from grief. They added a third floor with dormers, creating four more bedrooms in the now sixteen-room house, and placed ads in newspapers all along the eastern seaboard. Drawn by word of mouth about the charming inn and its postcard view, visitors streamed north. In the 1880s a whole family could lodge at Hathorn House for $12 a week, including meals.

The inn was a lot of work, more than any of them anticipated, and my mother was needed to help run it. As the years passed, the few eligible bachelors in Cushing married or moved away. By the time she was in her mid-thirties she was well past the point, she thought—everyone thought—of meeting a man and falling in love. She would live in this house and take care of her parents until they were buried in the family plot between the house and the sea.

"There's an old expression," Mamey tells me. "'Daughtering out.' Do you know what it means?"

I shake my head.

"It means no male heirs survived to carry on the family name. Your mother is the last of the Cushing Hathorns. When she dies, the Hathorn name will die with her."

"There's still Hathorn Point."

"Yes, that's true. But this is no longer Hathorn House, is it? Now it's the Olson House. Named for a Swedish sailor six years younger than your mother."

My mind is reeling. "Wait—Papa is younger than Mother?"

"You didn't know that?" When I shake my head again, Mamey laughs. "There's a lot you don't know, child. Johan Olauson was his name then." I mouth the strange words: *Yohan Oh-laow-sun.* "Barely spoke a word of English. He was a deckhand on a schooner captained by John Maloney, who lives in that little house down yonder with his wife," she says, gesturing toward the window. "You know who I'm talking about?"

I nod. The captain is a friendly man with a bushy gray mustache and yellow-corn teeth and his wife is a ruddy, broad-faced woman with a bosom that seems of a piece with her middle. I've seen his boat in the cove: *The Silver Spray.*

"Well, it was February. Eighteen ninety—a bad winter. Endless. They were on their way to Thomaston from New York, delivering fuel wood and coal to lime kilns up there. But when they reached Muscongus Bay and dropped anchor, a storm swept in. It was so cold that ice grew around the ship in the night. There was nothing they could do; they were stranded. After a few days, when the ice was thick enough, they got out and walked across it to shore. This shore. Your father had nowhere to go, so he stayed with Maloney and his wife until the thaw."

"How long was that?"

"Oh, months."

"And the boat was just out there in the ice the whole time?"

"All winter long," she says. "You could see it from this window." She lifts her chin toward the pantry. I can faintly hear the clatter of dishes on the other side of the door. "Well, there he was, in that little cottage all winter, down near the cove, with a clear view of this house up the hill. He must've been bored to death. But he'd learned how to knit in Sweden. He made that blue wool blanket in the parlor while he was staying with them, did you know that?"

"No."

"He did, sitting around the hearth with the Maloneys every night. Anyway, you know how people are: they talk, they tell stories—and oh, those Maloneys like to gossip. They would've told him, no doubt, about how this house was on the verge of daughtering out, and that if Katie married, her husband would inherit the whole thing. I don't know for sure, of course; I can only guess what was said. But he'd been here just a week when he decided he was going to learn English. He walked into town and asked Mrs. Crowley at the Wing School to teach him."

"*My* teacher, Mrs. Crowley?"

"Yes, she was the teacher even then. He went to the schoolhouse every day for lessons. And before the ice thawed, he'd changed his name to John Olson. Then, one day, he made his way up through the field to this house and knocked on the front door, and your mother answered. And that was it. Within a year Captain Sam died and your parents were married. Hathorn House became the Olson House. All of this"—she raises her arms in the air like a music conductor—"was his."

I picture my father sitting with the Maloneys in their cozy cottage, knitting that blanket while they regale him with stories about the white house in the distance: how three Hathorns bestowed their new name on this spit of land, and one built this very house . . . the spinster daughter who lives there now with her parents, their three sons dead, no heir to carry on the family name . . .

"Do you think Papa was . . . in love with Mother?" I ask.

Mamey pats my hand. "I don't know. I really don't. But here's the truth, Christina. There are many ways to love and be loved. Whatever led your father here, this is his life now."

I WANT MORE than anything for Papa to be proud of me, but he has little reason. For one thing, I am a girl. Even worse—I know this already, though no one's ever actually said it to me—I am not beautiful. When no one is around, I sometimes inspect my features in a small cloudy fragment of mirror that's propped against the windowsill in the pantry. Small gray eyes, one bigger than the other; a long pointy nose; thin lips. "It was your mother's beauty that drew me," Papa always says, and though I know now that's only part of the story, there's no question that she is beautiful. High cheekbones, elegant neck, narrow hands and fingers. In her presence I feel ungainly, a waddling duck to her swan.

On top of that, there's my infirmity. When we're around other people, Papa is tense and irritable, afraid that I'll stumble, knock into someone, embarrass him. My lack of grace annoys him. He is always muttering about a cure. He thinks I should've kept the leg braces on; the pain, he says, would've been worth it. But he has no idea what it was like. I would rather suffer for the rest of my life with twisted legs than endure such agony again.

His shame makes me defiant. I don't care that I make him uncomfortable. Mother says it would be better if I weren't so willful and proud. But my pride is all I have.

One afternoon when I am in the kitchen, shelling peas, I hear my parents talking in the foyer. "Will she have to stay there alone?" Mother asks, her voice threaded with worry. "She's only seven years old, John."

"I don't know."

"What will they do to her?"

"We won't know until she's looked at," Papa says.

A finger of fear runs down my back.

"How will we afford it?"

"I'll sell a cow, if I must."

I hobble toward them from the pantry. "I don't want to go."

"You don't even know what—" Papa starts.

"Dr. Heald already tried. There's nothing they can do."

He sighs. "I know you're afraid, Christina, but you have to be brave."

"I'm not going."

"That's enough. It's not up to you," Mother snaps. "You'll do as you're told."

The next morning, as dawn is beginning to seep through the windows, I feel a rough push on my shoulder, a shake. It takes a moment to focus, and then I am staring into my father's eyes.

"Get dressed," he says. "It's time."

I feel the soft shifting weight and dull warmth of the hot water bottle against my feet, like the belly of a puppy. "I don't want to, Papa."

"It's arranged. You know that. You're coming with me," he says in a firm quiet voice.

It's cold and still mostly dark when Papa lifts me into the buggy. He wraps the blue wool blanket he knitted around me and then two more, adjusts a cushion behind my head. The buggy smells of old leather and damp horse. Papa's favorite stallion, Blackie, stamps and whinnies, tossing his long mane, as Papa adjusts his harness.

Papa climbs into the driver's seat, lights his pipe and flicks the reins, and we set off down the hard-packed dirt road, the buggy squeaking as we go. The jostling hurts my joints, but soon enough I adjust to the rhythm, drifting to sleep to the lulling sound, *clomp clomp clomp,* opening my eyes some time later to the cold yellow light of a spring morning. The road is muddy; melting snow has created streams and tributaries. Hardy clusters of crocuses, purple and pink and white, sprout here and there in slush-stained fields. In three hours on the road, we pass only a few people. A stray dog emerges from the woods to trot alongside us for a while, then falls back. Now and then Papa turns around to check on me. I glare at him from my nest of blankets.

Eventually he says, over his shoulder, "This doctor is an expert. I got his name from Dr. Heald. He says he will do only a few tests."

"How long will we be there?"

"I don't know."

"More than one day?"

"I don't know."

"Will he cut me open?"

He glances back at me. "I don't know. No point worrying about that."

The blankets are scratchy against my skin. My stomach feels hollow. "Will you stay with me?"

Papa takes the pipe out of his mouth, tamps it with a finger. Puts it back in and takes a puff. Blackie clip-clops through the mud and we lurch forward.

"Will you?" I insist.

He doesn't answer and doesn't look back again.

It takes six hours to reach Rockland. We eat hard-boiled eggs and currant bread and stop once to rest the horse and relieve ourselves in the woods. The closer we get, the more panicked I become. By the time we arrive, Blackie's back is foamy with sweat. Though it's cold, I'm sweating too. Papa lifts me out of the buggy and sets me down, ties up the horse and attaches its feed bag. He leads me down the street by one hand, holding the address of the doctor in the other.

I am woozy, trembling with fear. "Please don't make me, Papa."

"This doctor could make you well."

"I'm all right the way I am. I don't mind it."

"Do you not want to run and play, like other children?"

"I do run and play."

"It's getting worse."

"I don't care."

"Stop it, Christina. Your mother and I know what's best for you."

"No, you don't!"

"How dare you speak to me with this disrespect?" he hisses, then quickly glances around to see if anyone noticed. I know how much he dreads making a scene.

But I can't help it; I'm crying now. "I'm sorry, Papa. I'm sorry. Don't make me go. Please."

"We are trying to make you better!" he says in a violent whisper. "What are you so afraid of?"

Like a slight tidal pull that presages the onset of a huge wave, my childish protests and rebellions have been only a hint of the feelings that well inside me now. What am I so afraid of? That I'll be treated like a specimen, poked and prodded again, to no end. That the doctor will torture me with racks and braces and splints. That his medical experiments will leave me worse, not better. That Papa will leave and the doctor will keep me here forever, and I'll never be allowed to go home.

That if it doesn't work, Papa will be even more disappointed in me.

"I won't go! You can't make me!" I wail, wrenching away from him and running down the street.

"You are a mulish, pigheaded girl!" he yells bitterly after me.

I hide in an alley behind a barrel that smells of fish, crouching in the dirty slush. Before long my hands are red and numb, and my cheeks are stinging. Every now and then I see Papa stride by, looking for me. One time he stops on the sidewalk and cranes his neck, peering into the dimness, but then he grunts and moves on. After an hour or so, I can't take the bitter cold any longer. Dragging my feet, I make my way back to the buggy. Papa is sitting in the driver's seat, smoking his pipe, the blue wool blanket around his shoulders.

He looks down at me, a grim expression on his face. "Are you ready to go to the doctor?"

I stare back at him. "No."

My father is stern, but he has little tolerance for public displays. I know this about him, in the way you learn to identify the weak parts of the people you live with. He shakes his head, sucking on his pipe. After a few minutes, he turns abruptly, without a word, and jumps down from the buggy. He lifts me into the back, tightens Blackie's harness, and climbs back into the driver's seat. For the entire six-hour ride home he is silent. I gaze at the stark line of the horizon, as severe as a charcoal slash on white paper, the steely sky, a dark spray of crows rising into the air. Bare blue trees just beginning to bud. Everything is ghostly, scrubbed of color, even my hands, marbled like a statue.

When we arrive home, after dark, Mother meets us in the foyer, baby Sam on her hip. "What did they say?" she asks eagerly. "Can they help?"

Papa removes his hat and unwraps his scarf. Mother looks from him to me. I stare at the floor.

"The girl refused."

"What?"

"She refused. There was nothing I could do."

Mother's back stiffens. "I don't understand. You didn't take her to the doctor?"

"She wouldn't go."

"She wouldn't go?" Her voice rises. "*She wouldn't go?* She is a child."

Papa pushes past her, removing his coat as he walks. Sam starts to whimper. "It's her life, Katie."

"Her life," my mother spits. "You are her parent!"

"She threw a terrible scene. I could not make her."

Suddenly she turns to me. "You foolish girl. You have wasted your father's day and risked your entire future. You are going to be a cripple for the rest of your life. Are you happy about that?"

Sam is starting to cry. Miserably I shake my head.

Mother hands the squalling baby to Papa, who bounces him awkwardly in his arms. Crouching down in front of me, she shakes her finger. "You are your own worst enemy, young lady. And you are a coward. It is senseless to mistake fear for bravery." Her warm breath is yeasty on my face. "I feel sorry for you. But that's it. We are done trying to help you. It's your life, as your poor father said."

AFTER THIS, WHEN I wake in the morning, I spread my fingers, working out the stiffness that creeps in overnight. I point my toes, feeling the crimp in my ankles, my calves, the dull sore ache behind my knees. The pain in my joints is like a needy pet that won't leave me alone. But I can't complain. I've forfeited that right.

MY LETTER TO THE WORLD

It's not long before Andy is at the door again. Awkwardly lugging a tripod, sketchbook under one arm, paintbrush like a bit between his teeth. "Would you mind if I set up my easel somewhere out of the way?" he asks, dumping his supplies in the doorway.

"You mean . . . in the house?"

He nods his chin toward the stairs. "I was thinking upstairs. If you're okay with it."

I'm a little shocked at his nerve. Who shows up unannounced at a virtual stranger's house and practically asks to move in? "Well, I . . ."

"I promise to be quiet. You'll hardly know I'm here."

Nobody's been upstairs in years. There are a lot of empty bedrooms. And the truth is, I wouldn't mind the company.

I nod.

"Well, good," he says with a grin. He gathers his supplies. "I'll try to stay out of the way of the witches."

His footsteps are loud as he thumps up the stairs to the second floor. He sets up his easel in the southeast bedroom, the one that once was mine. From the window he can watch the steamers pull away from Port Clyde, heading to Monhegan and the open sea.

Through the floorboards I hear him muttering, tapping his foot. Humming.

Hours later he comes downstairs with paint-stained fingers, the corner of his mouth purple from sticking a brush in it. "The witches and I are cohabiting just fine," he says.

BETSY COMES AND goes. Like us, she knows better than to interrupt Andy while he's working. But unlike us, she has a hard time sitting still. She gets a towel and a bucket of water and washes the dusty windows; she helps me feed the wet laundry through the wringer and hang it on the line. Donning one of my old aprons, she crouches in the dirt and plants a row of lettuce seeds in the vegetable garden.

On warm evenings, when Andy has finished for the day, Betsy shows up with a basket and we picnic down by the grove, where Papa built a fire pit long ago and wedged boards between tree trunks for seats. Al and I watch Betsy and Andy collect driftwood and twigs to make a fire in the circle of rocks. From the campfire, the fields that separate us from the house in the distance look like sand.

One rainy morning Betsy shows up at the door, car keys in hand, and says, "Now, madam, it's your day. Where to?"

I'm not sure I want a day, especially if it means I have to gussy myself up. Looking down at my old housedress, the socks bunched around my ankles, I say, "How about a cup of tea?"

"That would be lovely. When we get back. I want to take you on an adventure, Christina." She strides over to the range and lifts the blue teakettle, inspecting the bottom. "Aha. I thought as much. This old thing is on the verge of rusting through. Let's get you a new one."

"It doesn't even leak, Bets. It works just fine."

She laughs. "This whole house could fall down around your ears and you'd still say it's just fine." She points at my shoe. "Just look at how worn that heel is. And have you seen the moth holes in Al's cap? Come on, my dear. I'm taking you to the department store in Rockland. Senter Crane. They have everything. And don't worry, I'm buying."

I suppose, in some abstract way, I'd noticed the rust on the teakettle. And the shaved heel of my old shoe, and the holes in Al's cap. These things don't bother me. They make me feel comfortable, like a bird in a nest feathered with scraps. But I know that Betsy means well. And truth be told, she seems to need a project. "All right," I relent. "I'll come."

Betsy and Al help me into the station wagon in the drizzle and get me comfortably situated, and then we set off down the long drive to Rockland, half an hour away. At the first stop sign she reaches over and pats my knee. "See? Isn't this fun?"

"It makes you happy, doesn't it, Bets?"

"I like to be busy," she says. "And useful. I think those are pretty basic human desires—don't you?"

I have to ponder this for a minute. Do I? "Well, I used to think so. Now I'm not so sure."

"Idle hands . . ." she says.

"The devil's playground. Is that what you think?"

She laughs. "My Puritan ancestors certainly did."

"Mine too. But maybe they had it wrong." I gaze out the windshield at the fat raindrops that land on the glass only to be whisked away by the wipers.

Betsy glances at me sideways and purses her lips, as if she wants to say something. But instead, with a slight tilt of her chin, she looks back at the road.

OVER LUNCH ONE day—split pea soup with ham, on a blanket in the grass—Betsy tells Al and me that Andy's father doesn't approve of her. He objected to their engagement, warning Andy that marriage would be a distraction and babies even worse. But she doesn't care, she says. She finds N. C. arrogant, bullying, presumptuous. She thinks his colors are gaudy and his characters cartoonish, calculated for the marketplace. "Billboards for Cream of Wheat and Coca-Cola," she says disdainfully.

While she's talking I watch Andy's face. He's gazing at her with a bemused expression. He doesn't nod, but he doesn't protest either.

Betsy tells us that Andy needs to differentiate himself from his father. Take himself more seriously. Push himself harder. Take risks. She thinks he should limit his palette to starker colors, simplify the composition of his images, sharpen his tone. "You're capable of it," she tells him, putting her hand on his shoulder. "You don't even know your own power yet."

"Oh, please, Betsy. I'm just dabbling. I'm going to be a doctor," Andy says.

She rolls her eyes at Al and me. "He just had a one-man

show in Boston and won a prize. I don't know why he thinks he's going to be anything but a painter."

"I like the study of medicine."

"It's not your passion, Andy."

"You're my passion." He wraps his arms around her waist, and she laughs, shrugging him off.

"Go mix your tempera," she says.

MOST MORNINGS ANDY rows over by himself in a dory from Port Clyde, half a mile away. On the way to the house, swinging a tackle box full of paints and brushes, he ducks into the hen yard and emerges with half a dozen eggs, cradling them in one hand like juggling balls. He comes in the side door and chats with Al and me for a little while before heading upstairs.

Andy's eye is drawn to every cracked or faded implement and receptacle and tool, objects that once were used daily and now exist, like relics, to mark a way of life that has passed. Through his perspective I see familiar things anew. The pale pink wallpaper with tiny flowers. The red geraniums blooming in the window in their blue pots. The mahogany banister, the ship captain's barometer in the foyer, an earthenware crock on a shelf in the pantry, the blue pantry door scratched by a long-ago dog.

Some days Andy takes his sketch pad and tackle box to the shed, the barn, the fields. I watch from the kitchen window as he roams the property, loping unevenly down the grass to peer at the words on the headstones in the cemetery, sit on the pebbled shore, gaze at the sudsy waves. When he comes back to the house, I offer him sourdough bread from the oven, sliced ham, haddock chowder, apple skillet cake. He settles on the stoop in the open doorway, cradling a bowl in one hand, and I sit in my chair, and we talk about our lives.

He's the youngest of five, he tells me, with three doting sisters. A twisted right leg and a faulty hip kept him from walking properly as a child, from taking part in sports; you've probably noticed my limp? He was plagued with chest infections. His father was his only teacher. Kept him out of school, apprenticed in his studio. Taught him all about the history of art, how to mix paints and stretch canvases. "I was never like the other kids. Didn't fit in. I was an oddball. A misfit."

No wonder we get along, I think.

"Betsy's told me a lot about you and Al," Andy continues. "How Al chops firewood for everybody on the road. And you make dresses for ladies in town, and even quilts." He points to the tiny flowers on my sleeve. "Did you embroider these?"

"Yes. Forget-me-nots," I add, because it's a little hard to tell.

"Interesting, isn't it, what the mind is capable of," he muses, stretching out his hand and flexing his fingers. "How the body can adapt if your mind refuses to be bowed. Those intricate stitches on the pillowcases you gave us, and here on this blouse . . . It's hard to believe your fingers can do the work, but they can because you will them to." He takes his empty bowl to the counter, swipes a slice of apple cake from the skillet. "You're like me. You get on with it. I admire that."

IN SKETCH AFTER sketch Andy focuses on the house. Silhou-etted against the sky, a blot of smoke rising from a chimney. Viewed from a drainpipe, the cove, the eye of a seagull over-head. Alone on the hill or surrounded by trees. As large as a castle, as small as a child's playhouse. Outbuildings appear, dis-appear. But there are constants: field, house, horizon, sky.

Field, house, horizon, sky.

"Why do you draw the house so much?" I ask him one day when we're sitting in the kitchen.

"Oh, I don't know," he says, shifting on the stoop. He stares into space for a moment, drumming his fingers on the floor. "I'm trying to capture . . . something. The feel of this place, not the place itself, exactly. D. H. Lawrence—he was a writer, but also a painter—wrote this line: 'Close to the body of things, there can be heard the stir that makes us and de-stroys us.' I want to do that—get close to the body of things. As close as I can. That means going back to the same material again and again, digging deeper every time." He laughs, rub-bing a hand through his hair. "I sound like a crazy person, don't I?"

"I just think it would get boring."

"I know, you'd think it would." He shakes his head. "People say I'm a realist, but truthfully my paintings are never quite . . . real. I take away what I don't like and put myself in its place."

"What do you mean, yourself?"

"That's my little secret, Christina," he says. "I am always painting myself."

THERE'S A SINGLE bed with a rusty creaking frame—my old bed—in the room upstairs where Andy has set up his easel. When Al finishes his chores in the afternoon, he often goes up there and watches Andy paint for a while before drifting off for a nap.

One day, offhandedly, chatting in the doorway with Al and me before heading upstairs, Andy mentions that he doesn't like being observed. He wants to work in private.

"I'll stop coming up, then," Al says.

"Oh, no, that's not what I'm talking about," Andy says. "I like it when you're there."

"But he's watching," I say. "We're both watching."

Andy laughs, shaking his head. "It's different with you two."

"He's himself around you," Betsy says when I relay this conversation to her. "Because you and Al don't need anything from him. You let him do what he wants."

"It's our entertainment," I tell her. "Not much happens around here, you know."

And it's true. For so long this house was filled to the dormers. I used to wake every morning to a cacophony of sounds coming through the walls and the floorboards: Papa's booming voice, the boys pounding up and down the stairs, Mamey scolding them to slow down, the barking dog and crowing rooster. Then it got so quiet. But now I wake in the morning and think: *Andy is coming today*. The day is transformed, and he hasn't even gotten here yet.

On winter afternoons, when the sun goes down by 3:30 and wind howls through the cracks, we huddle near the woodstove wrapped in blankets, drinking warm milk and tea in the dim light of a whale-oil lamp. Papa shows Al and Sam and me how to make the knots he learned as a sailor: an overhand bow, a clove hitch, a sheet-bend double, a lark's head, a lariat loop. He hands us wooden needles and tries to show us how to knit (though the boys scoff, refusing to learn). He teaches us to whittle whistles and small boats out of wood. We line them up on the mantelpiece, and when the weather warms, we take these boats down to the bay to see whose sails best. I watch my tall, large-limbed father, his blond shaggy head bowed over his miniature boat, muttering to himself in Swedish, coaxing the vessel along in the choppy water. Mamey told me that several months before I was born, Papa's brother Berndt sailed over from Gothenburg to spend the winter here, and the two of them built a crib for me and painted it white. Berndt is the only Olauson who has ever visited us.

On a low shelf in the Shell Room, behind a giant conch, I discover a wooden box filled with a motley collection of objects: a whalebone comb, a horsehair toothbrush, a painted tin soldier from a long-ago children's set, a few rocks and minerals. "Whose is this?" I ask Mamey.

"Your father's."

"What are all these things?"

"You'll have to ask him."

So later that afternoon, when Papa comes in from the milking, I bring him the box. "Mamey said this is yours."

Papa shrugs. "That's nothing. I don't know why I kept it. Just bits and pieces I brought with me from Sweden."

Weighing a black lump of coal in my hand, I ask, "Why did you save this?"

He reaches for it. Rubs his fingers over its metallic ebony planes. "Anthracite," he says. "It's almost pure carbon. Made from decomposed plant and animal life from millions of years ago. I had a teacher once who taught me about rocks and minerals."

"In your village in Sweden?"

He nods. "Gällinge."

"Gällinge," I repeat. The word is strange. *Yah-lee-nyeh*. "So you kept it to remind you of home?"

He blows out a noisy breath. "Perhaps."

"Do you miss it?"

"Not really. I miss some things, I suppose."

"Like . . ."

"Oh, I don't know. A bread called *svartbröd*. With salmon and soured cream. And a fried potato cake called *raggmunk* my sister used to make. Maybe the lingonberries."

"But what about . . . your sister? And your mother?"

And that's when he tells me about the squalid, low-ceilinged two-room hut in the village of Gällinge that his family of ten shared with a cow, their surest hedge against starvation. His father, a drunkard with two moods, brooding and raging, who terrorized him and his seven younger siblings and worked occasionally at a peat farm as a day laborer when he was desperate enough. Papa's own constant stomach-churning hunger. More than once, he says, he avoided jail by eluding police on a long chase through cobbled streets after stealing a rasher of pork, a jug of maple syrup.

From an early age he knew there wasn't much of a future for him in Gällinge; no jobs, none he was qualified for even in the big city of Gothenburg, sixty miles away. Though a quick study, he paid little attention in school, knew how to read only the simplest stories. Never learned a trade. He taught himself to knit so he could help his ma, who earned a few coins making scarves and mittens and hats, but that was no job for a man, he says.

So when he heard about a trading ship bound for New York, he rose in the dark to be the first at the dock at Gothenburg Harbor.

The captain scoffed. *Fifteen years old? Too young to leave your mama.*

But Papa was determined. *She won't miss me,* he told him. *One less mouth to feed, a few more coins for the rest. Sick babies.* The youngest, his brother Sven, not even a year old, had starved to death a month before.

And so he set sail with the captain and his small crew, across and back and around the world. As months turned into years, his past began to recede. He sent money to his mother, and talked, as all the sailors did, about going home, but the more time he spent away from Gällinge, the less he missed it. He didn't miss tripping over his brothers and sisters, not to mention the cow. He didn't miss that dingy hovel with its slop pail in the corner and the rank smell of unwashed bodies. The dank confines of a ship's belly might not have been much of an improvement, but at least you could rise from its depths onto a wide deck and gaze up at a vast sky sprinkled with stars and the yolk of a moon.

IT'S SURPRISING THAT Papa knows as much as he does about farming, given that he grew up in a hovel and spent his twenties at sea. Mother says he's just a quick study at whatever he puts his mind to. He restored the inn to a family home, raises cows and sheep and chickens for milk and meat and wool and eggs. He plants corn and peas and potatoes in the rocky soil, rotating them yearly, and he set up a farm store on the property to sell them. His customers come by boat from Port Clyde and St. George and Pleasant Point, loading their dories with produce and rowing back to where they're from.

Having discovered that seaweed in the fields keeps the ground moist and the weeds down in the summer, Papa corrals Al and Sam and me to collect and distribute it. It takes two of us, our hands encased in thick cotton gloves, to steer a heavy wheelbarrow down to the water's edge at low tide. We rip the kelp from the rocks, pulling up barnacles and crabs and snails, and load the barrow with spongy green strands bubbled at the ends and flat, wide strips fluted like piecrust. The gloves are stiff and unwieldy; it's easier to grab it without them, so we take them off, rinsing our hands in ocean water to wash off the slime. Then we push the wheelbarrow up the hill to the newly furrowed field, where we grab big handfuls of cold kelp, squishing it between our fingers and scattering it down the rows. "Push it back," Papa calls from where he's hoeing. "Don't smother the plants."

Papa is always dreaming up projects to make money. His flock of sheep is growing, and though he sells wool to local people, one season he decides to box up the bulk of it and send it away to be carded and spun and dyed and sold out of state for a higher price. The following summer he constructs a fishing weir with a neighbor in the cove between Bird Point and Hathorn Point. Now that it's winter, he's decided that he will harvest freshwater ice, which can be loaded onto ships and transported easily and cheaply by steamer ship on the nearby sea-lanes to Boston and beyond. He'll store it in an icehouse Captain Sam built that has been standing empty for decades.

Like any crop, ice is delicate and mercurial; bright sun or a sudden storm can ruin it. There's no guarantee, until the ice is received in Boston, that Papa will get paid. He waits until February, when the ice on Vinal's Pond is fourteen to sixteen inches thick, and offers money to other farmers to help him clear the snow with horses and plows. Up before dawn on frigid mornings, they use a workhorse to pull the clearing scraper, a series of boards attached together to create a flat bottom that angles back about eight feet wide, and a three-foot-wide snow scraper to remove heavier, wetter ice. Several men saw through the ice with handsaws fused to long iron T-bar handles, shedding coats and scarves and hats as they warm up. It is hard work, but these men and horses are accustomed to hard work.

When a slab of ice is cut and floating, twelve inches above the syrupy water, the men hold float hooks, long poles with spiky ends, to keep the ice where they want it. After this comes the tedious work of cutting and loading these floats onto flatbed trailers behind horses that will transport them to the icehouse behind the barn. There the blocks will be stacked and stored in sawdust, some set aside to sell to locals and the rest to wait until a carrier bound for Massachusetts is ready in the cove.

The morning of the harvest, after Papa has left the house, I dress in the dark, layering sweaters and trousers over my long underwear and pulling on two pairs of socks. I meet Al in the downstairs hall and we head out into the mist, blowing our breath at each other, and make our way toward Vinal's Pond to watch the horses harnessed to plows trek back and forth on the thick ice, deepening the grooves. Snow falls softly, like flour through a sifter, accumulating in drifts.

We spot Papa in the distance, leading Blackie and the plow. He sees us too. "Stay off the ice!" he shouts. When Al and I reach the edge, we stand silently watching the men do their work. Blackie prances skittishly, tossing his head. He's a nervous horse; I've spent hours in the paddock devising routines to calm him. He's wearing the choke rope I fashioned around his neck several days ago to control him when he gets spooked.

One of the men has broken his float hook in a block of ice, and everyone is distracted, offering suggestions, when I notice that Blackie is sliding in slow motion toward the lip of the ice. All at once there's a high-pitched whinny. His eyes roll in terror as he plunges into the breath-stopping cold, flailing and churning in the water. The plow teeters on the edge. Without thinking, I run toward Papa across the ice.

"Damn it, get back!" Papa yells.

"Grab the choke rope," I call, motioning to my own neck. "Cut off his breath!"

Papa gestures to some of the men, and they join arms, elbow to elbow, Papa in the middle and several holding his belt. He leans far out over the horse's head and grasps the rope, pulling it tight. After a moment, Blackie quiets. Papa manages to pull him up onto the slab by his harness, forelegs first, then belly, and finally his powerful thick haunches. For a moment the horse stands as if frozen, front and back legs apart like a statue. Then he dips his head and shakes his mane, spraying water.

At the supper table that night Papa tells Mamey and Mother that I am the orneriest and most stubborn child he has, and the only reason he didn't wring my neck for running onto the ice is that my quick thinking probably saved Blackie's life. A drowned horse, we all know, would've been a big loss.

"I wonder where she gets that from," Mother says.

IN THE EVENINGS, once or twice a month, local farmers come by the house to drink whiskey and play cards around the dining table. Papa is different from the others, with his quiet ways and his Swedish accent, but the fact that they're all farmers and fishermen is enough of a bond. After Mother and Mamey have gone to bed, Al and I sit on the stairs, just out of sight, and listen to their stories.

The more Richard Wooten drinks, the more he rambles. "There's treasure in that Mystery Tunnel, by God, there is. One of these days, I swear, I'll get my hands on it."

Al and I are fascinated by the legend of Mystery Tunnel. According to local lore a two-hundred-foot tunnel was carved out of rock near Bird Point by early settlers as a place to hide from passing pirates and Abenaki Indians.

"I came this close. *This* close," Richard says. His voice softens, and I have to lean close to the banister to hear. "Pitch black. Not a star in the sky. I sneak down there with a lantern. I'm digging for who knows how long, hours, it's gotta be."

"How many times have you told this story, a hundred?" someone scoffs.

Richard ignores him. "And then I see it: the glint of treasure."

"You do not."

"I do, with my own eyes! And then . . ."

The men grumble and laugh. "Aw, c'mon!" "Now he's just makin' it up."

"Spit it out, Richard," Papa says.

"It disappears. Like—that." I hear the snap of his fingers. "Just as I was reaching for it. It was there and then it was gone."

"Rough luck," one of them shouts. "To treasure!"

"To treasure!"

The next evening Al and I slip out of the house with a candle nub and make our way down to Bird Point. The lip of the tunnel is dark and mysterious; our flickering candle keeps sputtering out. It's eerily silent as we creep along. About fifty feet in, fallen rocks block the path. I feel a strange relief—we probably would've dared ourselves to continue. Would we have found the buried treasure? Or would we have disappeared in the depths of the tunnel, never to be found?

Al and I take our adventures where we can find them. Several weeks later he wakes me up in the middle of the night, a finger to his lips, and whispers, "Follow me." I pull on a housedress over my nightgown and my old leather shoes over my socks and leave the snug cocoon of my bed. As soon as we're outside I see a glowing orange ball several hundred yards out in the harbor, its reflection splashed across the water. Then I realize what it is: a ship on fire.

"Been burning for hours," Al says. "A lime coaster. Headed to Thomaston, no doubt."

"Should we wake Papa?"

"Nah."

"Maybe he could help."

"A dory came ashore with a group of men a while ago. Nothing anybody can do now."

For more than an hour we sit in the grass. The freighter blazes in the dark, its destruction a thing of beauty. I gaze at Al, his face illuminated in the glow. I think about his favorite book, *Treasure Island*, about a boy who runs away to sea in search of buried treasure. Mrs. Crowley, seeing how often Al thumbed through the pages of the copy on her shelf, gave it to him when school let out for the summer. "For our seafaring Alvaro," she wrote on the inside cover in her neat handwriting. "May you embark on many adventures."

Months later, the ribs of that lime coaster are visible when the tide is low. Papa and Al row out to the wreck and strip the hull of its oak planking, and after stacking and weighting them to make them straight, they use them to rebuild the icehouse floor.

EVERY WEEKDAY AL and I walk together to the Wing School Number 4 in Cushing, a mile and a half away. With my unsteady gait it takes a long time to get there. I try to focus on my steps, but I tumble so often that my knees and elbows are constantly bruised and scraped, despite the cotton padding. The sides of my feet are tough and callused.

Al complains the whole way. "Jeez, the cows are faster than you. I could've been there and back by now."

"Go ahead, then," I tell him, but he never does.

It helps if I swing my body forward, using my arms for balance, though even that doesn't always work. When I fall, Al sighs and says, "Come on, now we're really going to be late." But when he pulls me up, he puts all his weight into it.

Sometimes we walk with two neighbor girls, Anne and Mary Connors, but only when their mother insists on it. They cluck their tongues and kick at sticks when I trip and fall behind. "Oh Lord, again?" Mary mutters, and the two of them whisper together so Al and I can't hear.

At school I wait until the cloakroom is empty before taking off my knee pads and armbands and stashing them in my lunch pail. The other kids can be mean. Leslie Brown trips me as I walk up the aisle to get a book, and I crash into Gertrude Gibbons's desk. "Watch it, clumsy," Gertrude says under her breath.

There are things I could say. Few of us at the Wing School Number 4 have picture-perfect lives. Gertrude Gibbons's mother ran off to Portland with a man who worked at the paper mill in Augusta, and never looked back. Leslie's stepfather beats him with a belt. The Connors girls have no father; he didn't go away, he was never here. It's a small town, and we know more about one another than any of us might wish.

One afternoon Al and I are sitting outdoors with our lunch pails under the shade of an elm in the schoolyard when Leslie and another boy begin to circle and taunt. "What's wrong with you? You're not normal, you know that?"

The tips of Al's ears redden, but he stays quiet. He's small and slight, no match for these rough boys with chaw in their cheeks. I don't want him to defend me anyway. I'm more than a year older than he is.

A girl in my grade, Sadie Hamm, strolls over. She's a thin, tough girl, as solid as a sunflower stalk, brown eyed, round faced, with a nimbus of curly sunflower petal hair. Putting her hands on her hips, she juts her chin out at the boys. "That's enough."

"Sadie Bacon," Leslie says with a sneer. "That's your name, right?"

"I don't think you want to play the name game with me, Leslie Brown." Turning to Al and me, Sadie says, "Okay if I join you?"

Al doesn't look too happy about it, but I pat the grass.

Sadie shares her sandwich with me, meatloaf sliced thin on bread with butter. She tells us that she lives with her two older sisters in an apartment above the drugstore, where one sister works behind the counter. She doesn't mention her parents, and I don't ask.

"Mind if I sit with you tomorrow?" she asks.

Al cuts his eyes at me. I ignore him. "Sure you can," I say.

For so long Al has been my only companion. He is as familiar to me as the walls of the kitchen or the path to the barn. It would be nice, I think, to have a friend.

ON LAND AL is shy and awkward. He doesn't talk much. In a crowd of people he acts like he wants to be somewhere, anywhere, else. He doesn't know what to do with his hands, which hang like oversized gloves from his wrists. But out on the ocean, when we pull up to one of Papa's blue-and-white buoys bobbing in the water, he is purposeful and self-assured. With a quick yank on the rope he can tell how many lobsters are in the trap far below.

Al has always wanted to be a lobsterman. The summer he turns eight, Papa decides he's old enough to learn. He takes Al out in an old skiff a few afternoons a week, and sometimes I go along for the ride. We row out so far that our white house looks like a speck on the hill. It makes me nervous to be on the open ocean in the small boat—my balance is precarious enough on land. The water is deep and dark around us; the planks are rough, and saltwater pools between the ribs of the boat, pickling my bare feet and dampening the hem of my dress. I fidget and sigh, impatient to get back. But Al is in his element.

Papa hands each of us a handline. It's a simple rig, cotton line coated with linseed oil and wrapped around a piece of wood he whittled on each end to better hold the line. There's a big hook at the end and a lead weight to make it sink. He teaches us to bait the hook with chum he keeps in an old bucket covered by a board. We let our lines down slowly, and then we wait. I don't catch anything, but Al's line is magic. Is it the way he fastens his bait? The way he jigs his line, making the fish believe it's alive? Or is it something else, a serene confidence that fish will come? Half a dozen times there's an almost imperceptible tug on the line between Al's forefinger and thumb, and he in response pulls hard on the line to set his hook and then, hand over hand, hauls in a flapping haddock or cod from the depths of the sea, over the gunwales into our boat.

With the skill of a surgeon, he removes the hook from the

fish and detangles the line. He insists on rowing all the way back by himself. When we land at the dock, he holds up his palms, red and raw, and grins. He's proud of his blisters.

Within a few years Al has restored Papa's old skiff and learned how to build and rig his own traps, fashioning the bows and sills from scraps of lumber, knitting twine for the heads and using rocks as weights to sink them. The traps he builds are better than Papa's, he boasts, and he's right: they brim with lobster. He constructs a fish house behind the barn to store the lobster traps and bait barrels, boat caulking and buoys, fishing nets and nails. Before long, he has taken over the blue-and-white buoys and is selling lobster to customers in Cushing and as far away as Port Clyde.

Al can't wait to be done with book learning. He's just biding his time, he says, counting the days until he can spend every waking moment in his precious boat.

MRS. CROWLEY TOLD ME once—the nicest thing anybody has ever said to me—that I'm one of the brightest students she's ever taught. Long before the others, I have finished my reading and arithmetic. She's always giving me extra work to do and books to read. I appreciate the compliment, but maybe if I could run and play like the other kids, I would be as impatient and distracted as they are. The truth is, when I'm immersed in a book I'm less aware of the pain in my unpredictable arms and legs.

AT SCHOOL WE'RE learning about the Salem Witch Trials. Between 1692 and 1693, Mrs. Crowley tells us, 250 women were accused of witchcraft, 150 imprisoned, and 19 hanged. They could be convicted by "spectral evidence," an accuser's assertion that they appeared in ghostly form, and "witches' marks," moles or warts. Gossip, hearsay, and rumors were admitted as evidence. The chief magistrate, John Hathorne, was notoriously ruthless. He acted more like a prosecutor than an impartial judge.

"He's related to us, you know," Mamey tells me when I relay this lesson after school. The two of us are sitting by the Glenwood range in the kitchen, darning socks. "Remember those three Hathorn men who left Salem in the middle of winter? It was fifty years after the trials. They were running from the shame."

Pulling another sock out of the pile, Mamey tells me about Bridget Bishop, an innkeeper accused of stealing eggs and transforming herself into a cat. Bridget was an eccentric whose colorful clothing—a red bodice covered with lacework, in particular—was believed to be a sign of the devil. After two confessed witches testified that she was part of their coven, she was arrested, thrown into a dank cell, and fed rotten tubers and broth. It took only a few days in those conditions, Mamey says, for a respectable woman to resemble a trapped and desperate animal.

In the courtroom, in front of a jeering crowd, John Hathorne asked her, "How do you know that you are not a witch?"

She answered: "I know nothing of it."

Justice Hathorne narrowed his eyes. Lifted his index finger. When he jabbed it at her, she stepped back as if struck. "Why look you," he said. "You are taken now in a flat lie." He slammed the flat of his hand on the table in front of him—Mamey slams her hand down, demonstrating—and the accusers and spectators erupted in a frenzy.

Bridget Bishop knew it was over, Mamey says. She'd be condemned to death like the others, left to swing on Gallows Hill until someone took pity and cut down her corpse, probably in the middle of the night. Like many of the condemned she was a middle-aged loner, with a house and property that had already been confiscated. Who was there to show support for her? Who would speak to her character? No one.

Eventually the governor of Massachusetts put a stop to the proceedings. One by one the magistrates of the Superior Court recanted, expressing remorse and sorrow about their rush to judgment. John Hathorne alone was silent. He never expressed the slightest regret. Even after his death twenty-five years later—peacefully, in prosperous comfort—his reputation for cold-blooded cruelty lingered.

Mamey tells me about the curse that Bridget Bishop placed on Hathorne's descendants. Well, not a curse, exactly, but a warning, a reckoning. "You have to admire that woman," she says. "Using the only power she possessed to instill the fear of God into him! Or the fear of something. But I believe it. I think your ancestors brought the witches with them from Salem. Their spirits haunt this place."

"For goodness' sake." My mother sighs loudly in the next room. She thinks her mother fills my head with outlandish ideas. She thinks I should pay less attention to Mamey's stories and more attention to my stitches.

WHEN I ASK Papa about the curse, he says he doesn't know about that, but he does know the Hathorns were a notoriously unruly bunch. A fierce, rugged Scots-Irish clan who emigrated to New England from Northern Ireland in the 1600s, they quickly developed a reputation for sadism against their perceived enemies. "Beating Quakers, double-crossing Indians and selling them into slavery—things like that," he says.

"How do you know all this?" I ask.

"I drank some whiskey with your grandfather once, a long time ago," he says.

THE SPRING OF my tenth year, Mother is heavy with child. Mamey and I are doing most of the cooking, which at the tail end of a long winter consists mostly of old root vegetables from the cellar, dried fish and meat from the smoker, stews and chowders. It's so cold and choppy on the water that Papa and Al can't go out in the dory. Sam has a hacking cough and a runny nose. The earth is soggy; if I fall on my way to school, I end up mud soiled and damp skirted all day. None of us have much to be cheerful about.

On the way home from school one wet afternoon I see Papa's buggy on the road ahead of me, a familiar badger shape with a blue bonnet on the seat beside him, and I know Miss Freeley is coming to deliver Mother's baby. When I get home, my brothers and I sit in the kitchen with Papa. Rain pummels the roof and the windows, heavy, slurry, and we can all feel the dampness in our bones. I peel off my socks and drape them over the range. Even the wood smoke from the Glenwood is damp.

The birth is uneventful. Mother is used to this by now. But after Fred is born, she is different. Slow to rise when he needs her. She hands him to Mamey and goes back to bed in the middle of the day. When Fred cries for her milk, Mother turns the other way and Mamey has to stir together cow's milk and water with a sprinkle of sugar. She puts a soapstone in the oven and wraps it in a cloth to put in his crib when he goes down for a nap, but it's no substitute for his mama, she says.

Al and I hurry home from school to take Fred from his crib and rock him in the chair, give him baths in the tin tub. (Before we bathe him he smells sour and damp, like he's been pulled out of a hole in the field. Afterward he smells like a puppy.) We all try to think of ways to cheer Mother up. Mamey makes pound cake with lemon peel, her favorite kind. Papa builds a four-drawer dresser for her linens. Blue is Mother's favorite color, so I decide I'll surprise her by painting some objects around the house a cheerful blue.

Al shakes his head when I tell him my plan. "Painting a chair is not going to help."

"I know," I say, but I hope maybe it will.

I ask Mamey's permission, knowing Papa might not approve. "Splendid," she says and hands me money for paint.

At the A. S. Fales & Sons General Store after school I pick up a gallon of the most vibrant blue on the chart, two horsehair brushes, a tin tray, and a can of turpentine, stashing it in the woods when I'm too tired to carry it all the way home. The next day, when I check the spot where I left it, it isn't there. I'm afraid someone has stolen it, but when I get to the house, it's sitting in the shed. "I still think it's a silly idea," Al says, "but I can't let you do all the work by yourself."

The wet paint is the color of the bluest feather on a bluebird, as shiny as the surface of a lake. With old rags Al and I wipe down the shed doors, the wagon rims and chassis, the sled and hayrack and geranium pots. Once we start painting, it's hard to stop. We go back to Fales for more supplies and return to paint the front and back doors, all of the wagon beds.

When we persuade Mother to come downstairs and see what we've done, she pulls Al and me into a hug.

Slowly, things improve. As the weather warms, Mother and I resume our walks to Little Island at low tide, but now we bring my brothers too. Al runs ahead through the grass; Sam piles starfish in a tide pool. We roam the pebbled beach, searching for shells and stopping for a picnic under the old spruce tree. Mother takes baby Fred out of his sling and lays him on his back on the beach, where he coos and gurgles. I sit on a rock, watching her. She seems better, I think. But now and then I see her staring off into the distance with a blank expression on her face, and it worries me.

WHEN MRS. CROWLEY COPIES a poem by Emily Dickinson on the chalkboard in her neat cursive, the muttering begins.

"Did a six-year-old write that?"

"What are those dashes? Is that proper grammar?"

"My grandpa told me she was just a strange old lady. A spinster," says Gertrude Gibbons, the class know-it-all.

"Emily Dickinson did have a quiet life," Mrs. Crowley says, tucking a strand of gray behind her ear. "A man broke her heart, and she became something of a recluse. She only wore white. Nobody even knew she was a poet; she was admired for her beautiful garden. She would sit for hours at a little desk, but nobody really knew what she was doing. After she died, a folder of her poems was discovered in a drawer. Page after page in her precise script, with very odd notations, as you can see. Hundreds and hundreds of poems."

As I copy the poem on the chalkboard into my notebook I mouth the words to myself:

> I'm Nobody! Who are you?
> Are you—Nobody—too?
> Then there's a pair of us!
> Don't tell! they'd advertise—you know!

"It doesn't even rhyme," Leslie Brown says.

"So what do you think it means?" Mrs. Crowley asks, holding the chalk in the air.

"I dunno. She feels like her life doesn't matter?"

"That's one interpretation. Christina, what do you think?"

"I think she feels like she's different from most people," I say. "And even if they find her strange, she knows she can't be the only one."

Mrs. Crowley smiles. She seems to be about to say something, then changes her mind. "A kindred spirit," she says.

After class I ask her if I can read more poems by this poet I've never heard of. Picking up a small blue hard-backed volume on her desk, she shows me that Emily Dickinson often used "common meter," alternating lines of eight and six syllables, a form more typical of hymns. That she wrote most of her poems in slant rhyme, in which the rhyming words are similar but not exact. And she employed a figure of speech called synecdoche, wherein the part stands in for the whole—"for example, here, in this poem," Mrs. Crowley says, tapping a page and reciting the words aloud: "'The Eyes around—had wrung them dry.' What do you think this refers to?"

"Um . . ." I scan the first few lines of the poem:

> I heard a Fly buzz—when I died—
> The Stillness in the Room
> Was like the Stillness in the Air—
> Between the Heaves of Storm—

"The people standing around the bed, mourning the one who died?"

Mrs. Crowley nods. She hands me the book. "If you'd like, you may take this home for the weekend."

Sitting on the front stoop of my house after school I thumb through the pages, alighting here and there:

> This is my letter to the world
> That never wrote to me—
> The simple news that Nature told—
> With tender majesty . . .

The poems are peculiar and inside out, and I'm not sure I know what they mean. I imagine Emily Dickinson in a white dress, sitting at her desk, head bent over her quill, scratching out these halting fragments. "It's all right if you don't exactly understand," Mrs. Crowley told the class. "What matters is how a poem resonates for you."

What must it have been like to capture these thoughts on paper? Like trapping fireflies, I think.

Mother, seeing me reading on the stoop, dumps a basket of air-dried sheets in my lap. "No time for lollygagging," she says under her breath.

NEAR THE END of eighth grade—the final year of Wing School Number 4, and the last year of any kind of schooling for most of us—Mrs. Crowley takes me aside during a lunch period. "Christina, I can't do this forever," she says. "Would you be interested in staying on for another few years, to get qualified to take over the school? I think you'd make an excellent teacher."

Her words make me glow with pride. But at supper that evening, when I report the conversation to Mother and Papa, I see a look pass between them. "We'll talk about it," Papa says and sends me outside to sit on the stoop.

When he calls me back in, Mother is looking at her plate. Papa says, "I'm sorry, Christina, but you've had more schooling than either of us ever did. Your mother has too much to do. We need your help around here."

My stomach plummets. I try to keep the hard edge of panic out of my voice. "But, Papa, I could go to school only in the mornings. Or stay home when I'm needed."

"Trust me, you'll learn more on this farm than you'll ever learn from a book."

"But I like going to school. I like what I'm learning."

"Book learning doesn't get the chores done."

The next day I plead my case to Mamey. Later I hear her talking to Papa in a low voice in the parlor. "Let her stay in school a few more years," she says. "What can it hurt? Teaching is a fine profession. And let's face it: There's not much else available to her."

"Katie isn't well, you know that. Christina is needed here. *You* need her here."

"We can manage," Mamey says. "If she doesn't do this now, she might end up on this farm for the rest of her life."

"Is that so intolerable? It's the life I chose."

"But that's it, John. You saw the world and then you chose it. She's never been farther than Rockland."

"And remember what a success that was? She couldn't wait to get home."

"She was young and scared."

"The wider world is no place for her."

"For pity's sake, we're not talking about the wider world. We're talking about a small town a mile and a half from here."

"My decision is made, Tryphena."

Telling Mrs. Crowley at recess the next day that I can't stay in school is one of the hardest things I've ever done. She is silent for a moment. Then she says, "You'll be fine, Christina. There will be other opportunities, no doubt." She seems a little teary. I am teary too. She has never touched me before, but now she puts her delicate hand on mine. "I want to say, Christina, that you are . . . unusual. And somehow . . ." Her voice trails off. "Your mind—your curiosity—will be your comfort."

On the last day of school, I am so full of self-pity that I can hardly speak. On my way out the door I linger in front of Mrs. Crowley's globe, ordered from a Sears, Roebuck catalog, and turn it with a finger. The ocean is robin's egg blue, with bumpy raised green and tan parts representing continents. I run my fingers over Taiwan, Tasmania, Texas. These faraway places are as real to me as the treasure buried in Mystery Tunnel. Which is to say: It's hard for me to believe they actually exist.

AFTER I LEAVE school, time stretches ahead like a long, flat road visible for miles. My routine becomes as regular as the tide. I rise before dawn to collect an armload of firewood from the shed, dump it into the bin beside the Glenwood range in the kitchen, and go back for another. Open the heavy black door of the oven, use the poker to stir the ashes, find the faint embers. Add several logs, coax the fire along with kindling, shut the door and press my cold stiff hands against it to warm them. Then I rouse my brothers from bed to feed the chickens and pigs, the horses and the mule. They grumble all the way down the stairs about who scatters the feed, mucks the stalls, collects the eggs. While the boys are in the barn I fix a pot of boiled oats with currants and raisins for their breakfast and make sandwiches of butter and molasses on thick sourdough bread, wrapped in wax paper, for their lunches; gather vegetables and apples from the cellar, a basket looped over my arm as I make my way down the rickety wooden ladder.

Al forgets a book, Sam his pail, Fred his hat. When they're finally out the door, I wash their dishes in the long cast-iron sink in the pantry. Then I start the process of baking bread, pinching off the sourdough starter I keep in the pantry, sprinkling flour over the wooden board. I make beds, empty night jars, limp to the garden to pick squash for a pie. After school, Sam and Fred help Papa in the barn and the fields and Al goes out in his boat. In the late afternoon, when the boys' other chores are done, they work on the fish weir that stretches between Little Island and Pleasant Point. Before supper they have to be reminded to wash, to take their boots off, to come to the table.

I have plenty to think about, I suppose. Will the bread rise properly if I use a different kind of flour? How many servings will one anemic chicken provide? How much money will the wool of eight sheep bring in, after adjusting for expenses? I know how to get the hens to lay more: give them extra salt, keep the henhouse windows clean to let in light, grind lobster shells into their feed. Our healthy hens produce more than our family can consume, so Al and I start selling the eggs. I spend several hours each month sewing bags out of cheesecloth to store them.

Despite my crooked hands, I am becoming a reasonable seamstress. In the afternoons I darn and patch the boys' hard-worn trousers and shirts and socks and spruce up old dresses with new collars and cuffs. Before long I am sewing all my own skirts and blouses and dresses on Mother's treadle Singer in the dining room, with its pretty red, green, and gold fleur-de-lis pattern, its rounded form like an arm bent at the elbow. From her book of patterns I learn to sew a three-panel skirt, and then one with five panels. Buttonholes are hardest; it takes my clumsy fingers ages to get them right.

Mother believes pockets on skirts are inelegant. She shows me how to sew a secret pouch into the lining so no one can see. "A lady doesn't reach into her pocket in view of others," she says.

I find her formality a little silly. It's only us here, and the boys neither notice nor care.

With no running water, we collect rain and melted snow from gutters and downspouts in the large cistern in the cellar and dredge it up using the hand pump in the pantry. Al figures out how to attach a funnel from the downspout to a hose to collect water for the cistern, making the process more efficient. When we run out of water in the cellar, I harness our mule, Dandy, to a wooden drag loaded with two empty barrels, corral one of the boys to help, and lead her to the pasture spring half a mile away to fill them. Laundry, once a week, takes at least one full day, and sometimes two. I boil water on the range and pour it from the large black pot into a wide steel tub, then scrub the laundry on a ribbed washboard and run it through a handwringer before hanging the dripping sheets and shirts and undergarments to dry. It's not easy, with my uneven balance, to pin clothes on the line outside, but I discover that I can detach the rope from the two poles on either end and pin the laundry on it while it's on the ground, then raise the line, with damp clothes hanging from it like a charm bracelet. When it's too snowy to go outside, I hang clothes in the shed. They stay damp for days; the smell of mildew lingers until spring.

I make soap when we need it by combining water with lye and adding oil, then pouring the mixture into molds and letting it dry for several days before turning the bars onto wax paper and putting them in the pantry to cure for a month. I scrub the floors with bleach and well water until my knees and knuckles are red, splotching my dress with white. With my shaky balance, even these ordinary tasks are fraught with peril. My arms and legs are marred and scarred from run-ins with boiling water, toxic bleach, poisonous lye.

When I mutter about these minor injuries, or that too much is expected of me, Al says, "We have a roof over our heads. Some people don't have that much." It helps to remember this, I guess. But it's hard to shake my sadness at having been taken out of school.

Only Mamey understands. "You inherited my curiosity, child," she says. "More's the pity."

As time goes on I find ways to make it bearable. I save three unwanted kittens and choose a runt from a neighbor's cocker spaniel litter and name him Topsy. I order seed packets and plant a flower garden like the one Emily Dickinson kept, with nasturtiums and pansies and daffodils and marigolds. A butterfly utopia, she called it. When my flowers bloom, they lure yellow-and-black monarchs, cabbage whites, teal blue swallowtails.

I find a poem I copied in my notebook:

> Two butterflies went out at Noon
> And waltzed above a Stream,
> Then stepped straight through the Firmament
> And rested on a Beam . . .
> And then together bore away
> Upon a shining Sea . . .

I imagine these butterflies traveling the world, alighting in my garden for a short time before heading off again. Dream that someday I might grow wings and follow, fluttering behind them down the field and across the water.

I try not to think about what I'd be doing if I weren't tied to the farm. Anne and Mary Connors are both continuing their studies, I hear. Anne wants to be a nurse and Mary a teacher. There's talk about her taking over from Mrs. Crowley. When I'm doing errands in Cushing and see one of them from afar, at the hardware store or the post office, I cross to the other side of the road.

WHEN I WAS a child, Mamey would whisper, "You're like me, Christina. Someday you'll explore distant lands." But she has stopped talking like this. Now she just wants me to get out of the house. Unlike my parents, who don't speak of such things, Mamey is always trying to convince me to "mingle," as she calls it. "Pity's sake, you need to be with people your own age!" she says. "Isn't there a social or a picnic you could go to?"

Al has no interest in the dances that are held on Friday evenings at the Acorn Grange Hall in Cushing, so I go with my friend Sadie Hamm. We walk along the rutted path in the semi-darkness, linking arms with several other girls. Sadie always breaks the chain when I fall behind, as I often do, stumbling in the ruts. She pretends she wants to gossip, but really she's providing ballast.

Sadie wears dresses with lace-trimmed sleeves and pearl buttons, hand-me-downs from her sisters, she says, but fancier than anything I own. I wear navy blue skirts and white muslin shirt-blouses with buttons at the front. A long dark skirt is forgiving; my misshapen legs aren't as obvious behind its folds. On the way to the dance Sadie sings silly songs and makes a fool of herself, turning cartwheels in her dress. She wears pink lip stain and powder that her sisters bring home from the drugstore in little containers. I envy her free and easy laugh, the way she skips along without fear of stumbling. I wish I dared to speak to the boys at the Grange Hall and get out on the dance floor instead of swaying to the music on the sidelines.

Later, when I'm at home in bed, I conjure entire conversations I might've had with a boy named Robert Allan, whose brown eyes and wavy hair I found so appealing that I could hardly bear to look at him directly, even from across the room.

And then, in my imagining, the music starts. "May I have this dance, Christina?" Robert asks.

"Why, yes," I say.

He extends his hand, and when I take it, he pulls me close, his chest warm against mine. Through my blouse I feel his other hand on the small of my back, guiding me gently, firmly, as he moves forward on his left foot and I step backward with my right: two slow steps, three quick ones, hold. Forward, forward, side to side . . .

I drift to sleep, hearing the music in my head, moving my toes to the rhythm. *Two slow steps, three quick ones, hold. Two slow steps, three quick ones, hold.*

AT EIGHTY, MAMEY seems to float more than ever on the aquamarine oceans of her past, where the sand is as pale and fine as sugar and the smell of tropical flowers lingers on the air. Her eyelids flutter as she dips in and out of dreams, sinking deeper into herself. She can't get warm, no matter how many feather ticks and blankets I pile on. I heat a stone in the oven, her old trick, and slide it under the covers to the foot of her bed.

One day I bring her a conch from the Shell Room, its innards as pink and glistening as an inner lip. Gripping the bony conch, she tells me how she found it on a deserted beach on an expedition to Cape Horn with Captain Sam. Sand under their toes and leafy palm fronds overhead, shielding them from the sun. Siesta on a porch and grilled fish and vegetables for supper.

"Next time I'll take you with me," she says softly.

"I would like that," I say.

MAMEY'S HAIR IS thin and yellowed, her skin as freckled and translucent as a meadowlark egg, her eyes searching, unfocused. Her bones are as delicate as a bird's. Mother comes into her room every day and flits around for half an hour or so, fussing over the bedsheets and picking up soiled linens. "It pains me to look at her," she tells me. Perching on the edge of Mamey's

bed, gazing up at the ceiling, Mother sings one of her own favorite songs, an old gospel tune she learned in church as a child:

> Will there be any stars, any stars in my crown
> When at evening the sun goeth down
> When I wake with the blest in those
> Mansions of rest
> Will there be any stars in my crown?

I wonder what those stars are meant to represent. They must
be proof that you are especially worthy, that you shine a little
brighter than everyone else. But if you wake with the blessed
in heaven, isn't that enough? Haven't you achieved the most
you could've hoped for? The words seem at odds with Mother's personality, her negligible ambitions, her lack of interest
in anything beyond the point. Maybe she believes that the way
she lives is the height of righteousness. Or maybe, as she's said
before, she just likes the melody.

My father comes upstairs now and then and lingers in the
doorway. My brothers drift in and out, rendered speechless in
the presence of such profound dissolution. But I can't really
blame them. Mamey always called my brothers "those boys"
and kept a wide berth from them, while pulling me close.
"Mamey, I'm here," I murmur, stroking her arm and holding
it to my cheek. Her breath on my face smells like scum on a
shallow pond.

When she finally dies, it is after days of not eating and barely
drinking, her skin tightening across sunken cheeks, her breath-

ing becoming raspy and labored. I think of that poem: *the Eyes around—had wrung them dry . . .*

The day we bury her is dreary: a colorless sky, gray-boned trees, old sooty snow. Winter, I think, must be tired of itself. Reverend Cohen of the Cushing Baptist Church, in a eulogy at Mamey's grave in the family cemetery, talks about how she will rejoin the ones she loved who are gone. But as I watch her pine casket descend slowly into the dirt, I try to envision the reunion of a frail eighty-year-old woman with her decades-younger husband and their three sons and am left with the lingering feeling that the places we go in our minds to find comfort have little to do with where our bodies go.

WAITING TO BE FOUND

As the war heats up we see transport ships far out at sea. Soldiers sent down from Belfast roam our property in green jeeps, patrolling the coastline, scanning the horizon with binoculars.

Al is amused. "What do they think is going to happen here?"

When one of the soldiers knocks on the door and asks if I'm aware of any "suspicious activity," I ask him what on earth he means.

"Reports of enemy ships in the area," he says darkly. "The Cushing waterfront has been declared unsafe."

I think of the villainous pirates in *Treasure Island* and their telltale black flag with skull and crossbones. Our enemy—if one is lurking around—probably doesn't announce itself so plainly. "Well, I've seen a lot of activity out there lately. More than usual. But I wouldn't know if it's friend or foe."

"Just keep your eyes open, ma'am."

Soon enough Cushing is subjected to intermittent blackouts and rationing. "This is worse than the Depression," Fred's wife, Lora, exclaims. "There's barely enough gasoline to do my errands."

"Cottage cheese is a sorry substitute for ground beef. I can't for the life of me get Sam to eat it," says my other sister-in-law, Mary.

None of it affects Al and me much. A poster on the wall in the post office instructs citizens to "Use it up—wear it out—make it do—or do without!" But that's the way we've always lived. We've never had electricity, so blackouts are nothing new. (They happen every night when we extinguish the oil lamps.) And though we've come to rely on the Fales store for milk and flour and butter, most of what we eat comes from the fields and the orchard and the chicken coops. We still store root vegetables and apples in the cellar and perishables in an icebox under the floorboards in the pantry. Al does his butchering. I boil and crank the laundry as I've always done and hang it in the wind to dry.

It's a cool September day when my nephew John, the oldest son of Sam and Mary, pulls up a chair in my kitchen. A lanky, mild-mannered boy with a lopsided grin, John has been my favorite nephew since he was born in this house twenty years ago.

"I have something to tell you, Aunt Christina." He clasps my hand. "I hitched a ride to Portland yesterday and enlisted in the navy."

"Oh." I feel stricken. "Do you have to? Aren't you needed on the farm?"

"I knew I'd be called up sooner or later. If I'd waited any longer, I'd've been drafted by the army into the infantry. I'd rather do it on my own terms."

"What do your parents have to say about it?"

"They knew it was only a matter of time."

I pause for a moment, absorbing this. "When do you leave?"

"In a week."

"A week!"

He squeezes my hand. "Once you sign on the dotted line, Aunt Christina, you're as good as gone."

For the first time, the war feels starkly real. I put my other hand over his. "Promise you'll write."

"You know I will."

True to his word, every ten days or so a postcard or a pale blue onionskin letter from John arrives at the post office in Cushing. After six long weeks of basic training in Newport, Rhode Island, he is assigned to the USS *Nelson,* a destroyer that escorts aircraft carriers and patrols for enemy ships and submarines. After that the postmarks become larger and more colorful: Hawaii, Casablanca, Trinidad, Dakar, France . . .

Our seafaring ancestors! Mamey would be pleased.

Sam and Mary erect a flagpole in their yard and hang a crisp new American flag for all to see. They are proud of John for serving his country. Mary coordinates scrap-iron drives to collect copper and brass for use in artillery shells and organizes get-togethers with other wives and mothers of servicemen to knit socks and scarves to send to the troops. "Our boy will come back a man," Sam says.

I join Lora's knitting circle and go around the house and barn gathering bits and pieces of metal to send to the war effort. But with John overseas, I sleep fitfully. All I want is for him to come home.

❧

I READ ONCE that the act of observing changes the nature of what is observed. This is certainly true for Al and me. We are more attuned to the beauty of this old house, with its familiar corners, when Andy is here. More appreciative of the view down the yellow fields to the water, constant and yet ever changing, the black crows on the barn roof, the hawk circling overhead. A grain bag, a dented pail, a rope hanging from a rafter: these ordinary objects and implements are transformed by Andy's brush into something timeless and otherworldly.

Sitting at the kitchen window early one morning, I notice that the sweet peas I planted years ago have flourished beyond all reason in their sunny spot beside the back door. Taking a paring knife from the utility drawer and a straw basket from the counter, I make my way to the vine and clip the fragrant blossoms, cream and pink and salmon, letting them tumble into the basket. In the pantry I take Mother's tiny dust-covered crystal vases from a high shelf and wash them in the sink, then fill them with sprigs. I find spots for the vases all over the ground floor: on the kitchen counter, the mantel in the Shell Room, a windowsill in the dining room, even in the four-hole privy in the shed. I set the last vase at the foot of the stairs for Andy to take upstairs.

When he shows up several hours later, I hold my breath as he steps into the hall.

"What's this?" he exclaims. "How glorious!" As he trudges

up the stairs, he calls, "It's going to be a good day, Christina, a very good day indeed."

ONE HOT AFTERNOON I hear Andy pad down the stairs and out the front door. From the window in the kitchen I watch him pacing around barefoot in the grass. Hands on hips, he stares out at the sea. Then he walks slowly back to the house and materializes in the kitchen.

"I just can't see it," he says, rubbing the back of his neck.

"See what?"

He sits heavily on a stool.

"Lemonade?" I offer.

"Sure."

I rise from my chair and grope along the wall to the narrow pantry, using the table, Andy's rocker, and the wall for balance. Normally I'd feel self-conscious, but Andy is so lost in thought he doesn't even notice.

Betsy—seven months pregnant and grumpy in the heat—left a pitcher of fresh-squeezed lemonade on the counter before returning home for a nap. When I lift the glass pitcher with both hands, it wobbles and I splash the liquid all over my arm. Annoyed at myself, I dab at it with a damp dishrag before carefully carrying the glass to Andy.

"Thanks." Absentmindedly he licks the side of his hand where it's sticky from the glass. As I settle back into my chair, he says, "You know, I spend entire days up there just . . .

dreaming. It feels like so much wasted time. But I can't seem to do it any other way." He takes a long swig of lemonade and sets the empty glass on the floor. "Christ, I don't know."

I'm no artist, but I think I understand what he means. "Some things take the time they take. You can't make the hens lay before they're ready." He nods, and I feel emboldened. "Sometimes I want the bread to rise quicker, but if I try to rush it, I ruin it."

Breaking into a grin, he says, "That's true."

I feel a small glow in the pit of my stomach.

"You have an artist's soul, Christina."

"Well, I don't know about that."

"We have more in common than you think," he says.

Later I reflect on the things we have in common and the things we don't. Our stubbornness and our infirmities. Our circumscribed childhoods. His father kept him out of school; we're alike in that way. But N. C. trained him to be a painter and Papa trained me to take care of the house, and there's a world of difference in that.

SOME OF ANDY'S sketches are hurried outlines, a map of the painting to come—a hint of a figure, grasses growing this way and that, geometric slashes of house and barn. Others are precisely shaded and detailed—every strand of hair and fold of fabric, the wood grain on the pantry door. His watercolors are inky greens and browns, the sky merely the white of the paper. Al in his flat-visored cap with his pipe, raking blueberries in the field, sitting on the front doorstep, gathering hay; the fine figure of our dun-colored mare, Tessie, in profile. Andy sketches the scarred wooden table, the white teapot, egg scales, grain bags in the barn, seed corn hanging to dry in a third-floor bedroom. On his canvases these objects look the same, but different. They have a burnished glow.

Andy's father paints in oil, he tells me. But he prefers egg tempera, he says, the method of European masters like Giotto and Botticelli in the late Middle Ages and Early Renaissance. It dries quickly, leaving a muted effect. I watch as he cracks an egg, separates the yolk from the white, and rolls the plump sac gently between his hands to remove the albumen. He pokes the yolk with the tip of a knife, pours the orange liquid into a cup of distilled water, stirs it around with his finger. Adds a chalky powdered pigment to make a paste.

After dipping a small brush into the tempera, he presses out the wetness and color with his fingers and splays the tip to make dry spiky strokes. He layers it over a pale wash of color or pencil and ink on a Masonite fiberboard coated with gesso, a smooth mix of rabbit-skin glue and chalk. Though he works fast, the brushstrokes are painstaking and meticulous, each one distinct. Cross-hatched grass, a dense, dark row of plantings. When wet, the colors are as red as Indian paintbrush, russet as clay, blue as the bay on a summer afternoon, green as a holly leaf. These bright wet colors fade as they dry, leaving a ghostly glow. "Intensity—painting emotions into objects—is the only thing I care about," he says.

Over time Andy's paintings become starker, drained of color, austere. Mostly white and brown and gray and black. "Damn it to hell," Andy murmurs, cocking his head to look at a newly finished watercolor: Al's shadowy figure walking down the rows in his visored cap, the white house and gray barn stark on the horizon. "This is better. Betsy was right."

❧

WHEN HE ISN'T upstairs painting, Andy hovers near me like a bee around honeycomb. He is fascinated with our habits and routines. How are the hens laying, how do you make a perfect loaf of bread without measuring, how do you keep the slugs from the dahlias? What kinds of trees does Al cut for firewood, what type of sail do lobstermen around here use on their boats? How do you collect the water in the cistern? Why are so many things in the house painted the same shade of blue? Why is a dory marooned in the rafters of the shed? Why is that long ladder propped against the house?

"We don't have a telephone," Al explains in his laconic way. "And the closest fire company is nine miles from here. If there's a roof or chimney fire . . ."

"Got it," Andy says.

These questions are easy to answer. But over time his inquiries become more personal. Why do Al and I live here alone, with all these empty rooms? What was it like when it was full of people, before most of the fields went to flower?

At first I'm guarded. "It just turned out that way," I tell him. "Life was busier then."

Andy isn't satisfied with evasions. *Why* did it turn out that way? Did you or Al ever want to live somewhere, anywhere, else?

It's hard to say what's in my head. It's been a long time since anyone cared to ask.

He insists. "I want to know."

So little by little, I open up. I tell him about the trip to Rockland when I refused to see the doctor. The disappearing treasure in Mystery Tunnel. The witches, the sea captains, the ship stranded in ice . . .

What did you miss about going to school?

Why were you so scared of doctors?

He is as gentle as a dog, as curious as a cat.

Who are you, Christina Olson?

In the Shell Room one afternoon Andy finds Papa's wooden box of keepsakes and opens the lid. He strokes the smooth tines of the whalebone comb. Picks up the tiny tin soldier and raises its arms with his forefinger. "Whose is this?"

"My father's. This box is the only thing of his I kept after he died."

"I used to collect toy soldiers," he muses. "When I was a boy, I created a whole battlefield. I still have a row of them lined up on the windowsill in my studio in Pennsylvania." He sets the soldier back in the box and runs a finger over the black lump of anthracite. "Why do you think he held on to this?"

"He liked rocks and minerals, he said."

"This is anthracite, right?"

I nod.

"Coal's glamorous cousin," he says. "In the Civil War—did your father tell you this?—anthracite was used by Confederate blockade runners as fuel for their steamships to avoid giving themselves away. It burns clean. No smoke."

"I've never heard that," I say. But I think: How apt. Papa was never one to give himself away.

"They called them ghost ships. It's a terrifying image, isn't it? These ominous ships materializing out of nowhere." He sets the anthracite back in the box and shuts the lid. "Did he ever go back to Sweden?"

"No. But I'm named after his mother. Anna Christina Olauson."

"Did you know her?"

I shake my head. "It's strange, don't you think—to name your child after a living person you've chosen never to see again?"

"Not so strange," he says. "There's this great line from *The House of the Seven Gables*: 'The world owes all its onward impulses to men ill at ease.' Your father must have felt he had to forge his own path, even if it meant cutting ties to his family. It's brave to resist the pull of the familiar. To be selfish about your own needs. I wrestle with that every day."

SEVERAL MONTHS AFTER Andy and Betsy return to Chadds Ford for the winter, I get a letter from Betsy. In September she gave birth to a sickly child, Nicholas, who needed a lot of special care but seems to be all right. In November Andy was drafted into the army. When he reported for his physical they took one look at his twisted right leg and his flat feet and rejected him on the spot. "He truly feels he's been given a reprieve and is determined to make the most of it," she writes.

A reprieve of one sort, I think. But though I may not have a child of my own, I know all too well how the demands of family life can become consuming. I wonder if, as a father, now, Andy will feel even more torn between the pull of the familiar and the creative impulses that drive him.

I'm in the henhouse early on a warm June morning, gathering eggs, when I hear voices coming closer across the field. We're not expecting visitors. Standing up straight, I lower the warm eggs I'm holding into the pocket of my apron and listen closely.

Ramona Carle—I'd recognize her throaty laugh anywhere.

Ramona, along with her siblings Alvah and Eloise, are summer folk from Massachusetts whose family bought the Seavey homestead down the road several years ago. Alvah is the oldest; Eloise is my age, Ramona a few years younger. They stay in Cushing from Memorial Day to Labor Day. But unlike some other from-aways (with their languid indolence, their impulsive thrill-seeking), the Carles do their best to fit in with the locals. I always look forward to seeing them. They organize egg-in-spoon races at our annual Fourth of July clambake on Hathorn Point, convince everyone to play games like Red Rover and Olly Olly Oxen Free, and bring bags of fireworks to light after dark.

Ramona is my favorite. A friendly, impulsive girl, she is slight and energetic, with hair the color of melted chocolate and eyes as large and shiny as a fawn's. Once, when I was with her in town, an old lady told her she was as cute as a button. (No one has ever said anything remotely like that to me.)

Ducking out of the henhouse with my bounty of eggs and a big smile of anticipation, I nearly run into a man I've never seen before. "Why—hello!" I say.

"Hello!" He's about my age, I think—I've just turned twenty—and about half a foot taller than me, with light-brown hair that flops in front of wide-set blue eyes. He's wearing thin linen pants and a soft white shirt with the sleeves rolled above his elbows.

Self-conscious all of a sudden, I smooth my sleep-matted hair, glancing down at the soiled apron I baked bread in this morning and the wooden clogs I wear to wade through mud.

"Walton Hall," he says, extending his hand.

"Christina Olson." His hand is surprisingly soft. This is a man who has never handled a plow.

"Walton is visiting from Malden," Ramona says. "He and Eloise went to high school together. At the end of the summer he's heading off to Harvard."

"Admit it, you're shocked," Walton says with a small wink. "'Must not be as dull as he looks.'"

"Just because you're going to Harvard doesn't mean you're not dull," I say.

When he smiles, I see that one of his front teeth slightly overlaps the other. He raises an invisible glass in a mock toast. "Good point."

"All right, enough," Ramona says. "Let me remind you, Walton, that an entire household awaits breakfast."

"Ah, yes," he says. "We've come to procure some eggs."

"Right," I say. "How many?"

"Two dozen, yes, Ramona?"

She nods.

"Okay, that'll be fifty cents for the eggs and a penny for the bag," I tell them.

"My word, you drive a hard bargain!"

Ramona rolls her eyes. "You could've asked for fifty cents an egg, Christina. He has no idea what he's talking about."

Once by one I slide the eggs into a bag, counting out twenty-four as he teases: "Not that one! It's not oval enough," and "They must all be exactly the same size." He is standing quite close to me and his breath smells of butterscotch. Ramona's talking about the weather, how dull a winter it was and how she counted the days until June, what a beautiful day it is today, but do you think it might take a turn? Will it be calm enough to go out for a sail later on? She wonders what her mother will do with all these eggs if breakfast is over by the time they get back: a soufflé, perhaps? An omelette? A lemon meringue pie?

"Come with us," he says.

Ramona and I both look up.

"What?" I say, confused.

"Come sailing this afternoon, Christina," he says. "The wind will be perfect."

"You might've said that when I was fretting about the weather," Ramona mutters.

I don't usually take off afternoons, especially to sail with strange boys I've only just met. "Thank you, but—I . . . can't. I have to make bread. And my chores . . ."

"Oh, for heaven's sake, come along," Ramona says. "We have to entertain Walton somehow. And bring your brother Sam. He's such fun. I need someone my own age to flirt with."

"I'm sorry, I don't think so."

"My word, you're a hard sell. Look, I'll sign your hall pass," Walton says.

"Hall pass?"

Seeing my puzzlement, Ramona laughs. "They don't have hall passes in one-room schoolhouses, Walton."

"I can't," I say.

He shakes his head and shrugs. "Ah well. Another day, then."

"Maybe."

"That means yes," Ramona tells him with the confidence of a girl accustomed to getting her way. She flashes me a smile. "We'll try again. Soon."

When I return to the house from the brightness of the yard, I lean against the wall in the dim foyer, breathing heavily. What *was* that?

"Did I hear voices?" Mother calls from the kitchen.

I touch my face. Smooth the front of my blouse. Take a deep breath.

"Was somebody here?" she asks when I come in, untying my apron and taking it off.

"Oh," I say, straining for a casual tone, "only Ramona, to buy eggs."

"I could've sworn I heard a male voice."

"Just a friend of the Carles'."

"Ah. Well, the dough's ready for kneading."

"I'll get to it," I say.

OVER THE NEXT few weeks, Ramona and Walton, sometimes with Eloise and Alvah, stop by every other day or so, seeking eggs or milk or a roasting chicken, staying longer each visit. They bring a picnic basket and an old quilt and we sit on the grass, drinking tea steeped in the sun. I come to expect the sight of them sauntering up the field in the late morning or early afternoon. My brothers, with their gentle ways, tend to shy like deer from the summer folk, but the Carles and Walton gradually win them over. When they're finished with chores, Al and Sam often join us on the grass.

One morning, when it's just Walton and Ramona and me, Ramona says, "We're kidnapping you, Christina. It's a perfect day for a sail."

"But—"

"No buts. The farm will manage without you. Alvah is waiting. Off we go."

As we make our way down the path toward the shore I feel Walton's eyes on me from behind. Aware of my awkward gait, I concentrate carefully on my movements. In front of us Ramona chatters away—"The sun is so bright! Mercy, I did not even think of it, but we do not have enough hats; maybe Mother left one or two on the boat"— seemingly unaware that neither Walton nor I say a word in response. And then the very thing

I fear happens: I trip on a root. My legs buckle; I feel myself pitching forward.

Before I can make a sound, an arm is under mine. In a low voice, so Ramona won't hear, Walton says, "What a long path this is."

Though only moments ago I was flushed with anxiety, now I am oddly calm. "Thank you," I whisper.

I have never been this close to a boy who isn't related to me. My senses sharp, I notice everything in the clean morning light: daffodils pale and bowed; guillemots gliding overhead, black, with bright red legs, squeaking like mice; the trees in the distance, red spruce and firs and juniper and slender scotch pines, that frame the field. I taste the salt on my lips from the sea. But mostly I am aware of the warm mammal scent of this boy whose arm is ballast: sweat, perhaps, and the musky smell of his hair, a whiff of aftershave. Sweet butterscotch on his breath.

"I hope you won't think this impertinent, but did you know that the blue flowers in your dress match your eyes exactly?" he murmurs.

"I did not," I manage to answer.

The Carles' boat is a single-mast sloop, with a jib in the front and a large white mainsail attached to the back of the wooden mast. They keep a wooden dinghy on the shore near Kissing Cove, paddles tucked inside, to row out to the sailboat. When we get to the beach, Alvah is waving from the deck of the sloop, about a hundred yards out in the bay. We drag the dinghy to the water. Walton insists on taking the oars and we meander toward the sailboat, this way and that. I have to bite my lips to keep from laughing: his strokes are choppy and inexpert, nothing like Al's rhythmic motion. When we arrive at the boat, Ramona ties the small craft to the buoy, and Walton, taking Alvah's proffered hand, jumps up first so the two of them can assist us.

"Gallant of you, I suppose, but unnecessary," Ramona says, batting away Walton's hand. I don't protest. I need all the help I can get.

Once aboard, I'm more at ease. It is a mild, warm morning, with a gentle wind, and I know how to sail, having learned with Alvaro on his small skiff. Alvah hoists the mainsail, which flaps dramatically in the wind like a sheet on a clothesline, and I pull down firmly on the halyard until it stops. He turns the boat to starboard, weaving away from the wind, lessening the tilt to bring us to a more comfortable sailing angle as we approach open water. I have to warn Walton to duck so he won't get hit in the head by the boom.

He seems surprised and a little impressed that I seem to know what I'm doing. "So many hidden talents!"

It's a miracle I'm any help to Alvah given how distracted I am by the skin on Walton's neck, slightly sunburned just above his collar. The small flaps of his ears turning pink in the sun. The quick flash of his gray-blue eyes.

Alvah, passionate for sailing in the way that boys who grew up on boats with their fathers and grandfathers can be, is happy to do the brunt of the work, and once we're out on the ocean we fall into an easy rhythm. Ramona opens a basket and cuts chunks of bread, slices of cheese, passes around hard-boiled eggs and salt and a tin canteen of water.

In the course of conversation, I learn bits and pieces about Walton's upbringing. His mother is obsessed with social decorum, his father a banker who stays in Boston in a small apartment several nights a week—"when he has to work late. Or at least that's what he tells us," Walton says. I'm not sure what he's implying and fear it's rude to ask; I don't want to look ignorant but also don't want to pry. It's as hard to picture where Walton grew up as it is to imagine life on the moon. I conjure parlor rooms out of Jane Austen, a redbrick mansion, the walls of the dining room adorned with gilt-framed paintings of Harvard-educated ancestors.

He tells me that he had a curved spine, scoliosis, as a child, and had to wear a plaster body cast for a long, hot summer after an operation when he was twelve. While other boys were climbing trees and kicking balls around, he lay in bed reading adventure stories like *Swiss Family Robinson* and *Captains Courageous*. He doesn't say so, but I know he's trying to explain that he understands what it's like to be me.

As the hours pass, the sky drains of warmth. It's not until I notice goose bumps on my arms that I realize I've forgotten a sweater. Without a word, Walton peels off his jacket and drapes it around my shoulders. "Oh," I say with surprise.

"I hope that wasn't too forward of me. You seemed chilly."

"Yes. Thank you. I just—I didn't expect it." In truth, I can't remember the last time anyone noticed my physical discomfort and did something about it. When you live on a farm, everyone is uncomfortable much of the time. Too cold, too warm, dirty, bone tired, banged up, injured by a tool or hot grate—too preoccupied to worry much about each other.

"You're quite an independent girl, aren't you?"

"I suppose I am."

"You've never met anyone like Christina, Walton," Ramona says. "She's not like those silly girls in Malden who don't know how to light a fire or clean a fish."

"Is she a suffragette, like Miss Pankhurst?" he asks in a teasing voice.

I feel woefully ignorant; I don't know what a suffragette is and I've never heard of Miss Pankhurst. I think of all the years Walton spent in school while I was washing and cooking and cleaning. "A suffragette?"

"You know, those ladies starving themselves for the vote," Ramona says. "The ones who think, God forbid, they can do anything a man can do."

"Is that what you think?" Walton asks me.

"Well, I don't know," I say. "Shall we have a competition and find out? We could split logs for firewood, or fix a drainpipe. Or maybe slaughter a chicken?"

"Careful," he says, laughing. "Miss Pankhurst was just sentenced to three years in jail for her treasonous words."

There is, I am almost certain, a spark between us. A flickering. I glance at Ramona. She raises her eyebrows at me and smiles, and I know she senses it too.

ONE DAY WALTON shows up alone on a bicycle. He's wearing a pin-striped sack coat and a straw boater, not the kind of hat any man around here would wear. (For that matter, they don't wear pin-striped sack coats either.) Around my brothers he looks slightly preposterous, like a peacock in a cluster of turkeys.

Holding his hat between his hands, he kneads the brim with his long fingers. "I'm here to do you the favor of relieving you of some eggs. Can you believe they've entrusted me with this important task?" And then, conspiratorially, "Actually, they have no idea I'm here."

"I'll get my coat," I say.

"Don't think you need one," he says. "It's not actually—"

But I've already shut the door.

I stand in the dark hall, my heart thudding in my ears. I don't know how to act. Maybe I should tell him that I'm needed in the—

A rap on the door. "Are you there? All right if I come inside?"

I reach up to the coat pegs and pull down the first thing I find, Sam's heavy wool jacket.

"Christina?" Mother's voice filters down the stairs.

"Getting eggs at the henhouse, Mother." Opening the door, I smile at Walton. He smiles back. I step onto the stoop, putting on the jacket. "Two dozen, yes? You can come with me if you want."

"Butterscotch?" He holds out a piece of amber candy.

"Uh . . . sure."

He unwraps it before handing it to me. "Sweets to the sweet."

"Thanks," I say, blushing.

He gestures for me to lead the way. "Lovely property," he says as we stroll toward the henhouse. "Used to be a lodging house, Ramona said?"

The butterscotch is melting in my mouth. I turn it over with my tongue. "My grandparents took in summer guests. They called it Umbrella Roof Inn."

He squints at the roof. "Umbrella?"

"You're right," I say, laughing a little. "It looks nothing like an umbrella."

"I suppose it keeps the rain out."

"Aren't all roofs supposed to do that?"

Now he's laughing too. "Well, you find out the answer and let me know."

Walton is right; my brother's scratchy jacket is too hot. After I've gathered the eggs, I peel off the jacket and Walton suggests we sit in the grass.

"So what's your favorite color?" he asks.

"Really?"

"Why not?" The butterscotch clicks between his teeth.

"Okay." I've never been asked this question. I have to think about it. The color of a piglet's ear, a summer sky at dusk, Al's beloved roses . . . "Um. Pink."

"Favorite animal."

"My spaniel, Topsy."

"Favorite food."

"I'm famous for my fried apple cake."

"Will you make it for me?"

I nod.

"I'm going to hold you to that. Favorite poet."

This is an easy one. "Emily Dickinson."

"Ah," he says. "'Not knowing when the dawn will come, I open every door.'"

"'Or has it feathers like a bird—'"

"Very good!" he says, clearly surprised that I know it. "'Or billows like a shore.'"

"My teacher gave me a collection of her poems when I left school. That's one of my favorites."

He shakes his head. "I never understood that last part."

"Well . . ." I'm a little hesitant to offer an interpretation. What if he disagrees? "I think . . . I think it means that you should stay open to possibility. However it comes your way."

He nods. "Ah. That makes sense. So are you?"

"Am I what?"

"Open to possibility?"

"I don't know. I hope so. What about you?"

"Trying. It's a struggle."

He tells me that he is going to Harvard to please his father, though he might've preferred the smaller campus of Bowdoin. "But you don't turn down Harvard, do you?"

"Why not?"

"Why not, indeed," he says.

"HE LIKES YOU," Ramona says, eyes sparkling. "He asks me all these questions: how long I've known you, if you have a boyfriend, if your father is very strict. He wants to know what *you* think."

"What I think?"

"About him, silly. What you think about *him*."

It feels like a trick question, as if I'm being asked to respond in a language I don't understand. "I like him. I like many people," I say warily.

Ramona wrinkles her nose. "You do not. You hardly like anyone."

"I hardly know anyone."

"True," she says. "But don't be coy. Does your heart pitter-patter when you think of him?"

"Ramona, honestly."

"Don't act so scandalized. Just answer the question."

"Oh, I don't know. Maybe a little."

"Maybe a little. That's a yes."

As the summer progresses she goes back and forth between Walton and me like a carrier pigeon, carrying scraps of news, impressions, gossip. She is perfectly suited to the task—one of those girls with boundless energy and intelligence and no place to exercise them, like a terrier with a housebound owner.

❧

AT FIRST MOTHER is formal and a little cool with Walton, but slowly he wins her over. I watch how he calibrates his behavior, deferring to her at every turn, calling her Ma'am, presuming nothing. He coaxes her outside for picnics and afternoon sails. "Well, the boy does have excellent manners," she allows at the end of a long afternoon lunch on the shore. "Must've learned them at an expensive school."

One morning Mother surprises me by returning from town with a bolt of calico cloth, a packet of buttons, and a new Butterick pattern. She hands it to me casually, saying, "I thought you could use a new style." I look at the illustration on the cover: a dress with a seven-panel skirt and fitted bodice with small mother-of-pearl buttons. The calico is pretty, flowers with green leaves on a brown-sugar background. I set to work after my chores are done, cutting out each piece of the pattern, pinning the puzzle pieces of delicate tissue to the fabric, marking it with a nub of chalk, trimming along the solid line. I work in the orange light of an oil lamp and several candles as the sun drops from the sky.

Late into the night I sit hunched over Mother's Singer, feeding the fabric through, my foot pumping the treadle. Mother pauses in the doorway on her way to bed. She comes and stands behind me, then reaches down and traces the hem with her finger, smoothing it flat behind the needle.

When I put on the dress the next morning, it skims closely over my hips. In the pantry I hold the small cloudy mirror in my hand, turning it this way and that to get the full effect, but all I can see are bits and pieces.

"That turned out," is all Mother says when she comes into the kitchen to help with the noonday meal. But I can tell she's pleased.

Later in the morning Walton comes to the door with a bouquet of tulips and daffodils. He takes off his straw boater and bows slightly to Mother, who is sifting flour at the table. "Good day, Mrs. Olson."

She nods. "Good day, Walton."

He hands me the bouquet. "What a dress!"

"Mother bought me the fabric and the pattern." I hold out the skirt and turn so he can see all the panels.

"Lovely taste, Mrs. Olson. It's beautiful. But wait, Christina—you made this?"

"Yes, last night."

He grasps a piece of fabric from the full skirt and rubs it between his fingers, touches a mother-of-pearl button on my sleeve. "I am awed by you."

Behind me, Mother says, "Christina can do just about anything she sets her mind to." This rare praise surprises me—she's usually so restrained. But then I remember that my mother was discovered in this house by a stranger at the door. She knows it's possible.

ONE DAY WHEN Walton is visiting I tell him about the Mystery Tunnel—how I think of it as a mysterious and magic place, holding secrets that may never be revealed. "Some think it's filled with buried treasure," I say.

"Show me," he says.

I know my parents won't approve of our going alone, so we make a secret plan: we'll wait until Mother is resting, Papa is at the fishing weir with the boys, and no one will suspect I'm not where I usually am on a Wednesday morning, wringing clothes behind the house and hanging them on the line. He'll come quietly, on foot; and if anyone is nearby, we won't attempt it.

At breakfast, before heading off to the weir, my brothers help me fill the tubs with water. If anyone cared to notice, they might have seen that my dress is starched, my hair neatly braided with a ribbon, my cheeks pink not from exertion but from being pinched between my fingers, as Ramona taught me to do.

Finding me in the yard behind the house after everyone has left, Walton silently takes the heavy, wet clothes from my hands. He begins to feed them through the wringer, turning the crank with one hand and coaxing them along with the other. At the clothesline he lifts the damp pieces from the basket, shakes out the wrinkles, and hands them to me one by one as I pin them on the line. When the basket is empty, he lifts the rope and secures it to the poles.

How thrilling it is—I am suddenly aware—to be playing house.

Hidden among the damp and flapping clothes, Walton reaches for me, pulling me gently toward him. His eyes on mine, he lifts my hand to his mouth and kisses it, then tugs me closer, tilts his head, and kisses me on the mouth. His lips are cool and smooth; I feel his heart pulsing through his shirt. He smells of butterscotch, of spice. It's such a strange and heady experience that I can barely breathe.

When I take the basket back inside the house, I slip out of my apron and smooth my hair, stealing a glimpse of myself in the fragment of mirror in the pantry. What I see looking back at me is a thin-faced girl with a too-large nose and lively if uneven gray eyes. Her features may be plain, but her skin is clear and her eyes are bright. I think of the man waiting for me outside. His hair, I've noticed, has begun to recede. His chest is lightly concave, like a teaspoon, his spine unnaturally stiff from that summer in a cast. When he's agitated he has a slight lisp. It isn't inconceivable to imagine—is it?—that this imperfect man could grow to love me.

We walk silently, single file, in the shadow of the house and barn to the trees beyond the field. At this time of day, with the shadows as they are, we cannot be seen unless someone is actually looking for us. Walton reaches forward and brushes my fingertips, clasps my hand. Several times, making our way down a steep embankment, through a dense cluster of trees, we drop hands, but he finds my fingertips again like a knitter seeking a dropped stitch. When we are out in the open but hidden by the ridge, I pull on his hand playfully and he pulls back, bringing me to a stumbling stop. He is behind me, his breath on my neck, his arm at his side, holding me against him.

"Heaven could not be better than this," he murmurs.

I don't know whether he's talking about the pelt of water stretching out in front of us, the dancing grasses, the rocks with their mantle of inky seaweed—or me. It doesn't matter. This place, this point, is as much a part of me as my hair and nose and eyes.

We are close to the lip of the tunnel. His hands on my waist, Walton turns me around, his forehead against mine.

"I've already discovered the treasure," he says. "All this time you were here, waiting to be found."

WALTON'S ATTENTION IS like a sun high in the sky, so bright, so blinding, that everything else fades in contrast. The voices of my parents, my brothers, the clucking chickens and barking dog, rain on the roof like rice in a can—these noises simmer like a stew in the back of my brain. I am barely aware of them until my mother or a brother shakes my arm and says sharply, "Did you hear what I said?"

Do other people walk around in this state? Did my parents? What a strange idea—that perfectly ordinary people with mundane lives might have once experienced this quickening, this vertiginous unfolding. Their eyes betray no evidence of it.

Mamey used to tell stories about natives on the islands she visited who'd never seen snow and had no language for it. That's how I feel. I have no language, no context, for this.

My friend Sadie says, "You're a goner. You'll move to Boston and we'll never see you again."

"Maybe I'll convince him to live here."

"And do what? He doesn't seem like the farming type."

"He wants to be a journalist, he says. He can write anywhere."

"What's he going to write about? The price of milk?"

But what does Sadie know? Walton seems smitten with our way of life. "This is so different from how I grew up," he says.

"Your knowledge is real. It's practical. Mine is all in my head. I don't know how to foal a calf or skim cream from milk. I'm hopeless at sailing or harnessing a horse to a buggy. Is there nothing you can't do?"

"You're the one who can do, and be, anything you choose," I remind him.

"What I choose," he says, "is to be with you."

It feels as if my life is moving forward at two separate speeds, one at the usual pace, with its predictable rhythms and familiar inhabitants, and the other rushing ahead, a blur of color and sound and sensation. It's clear to me now that for twenty years I have gone through the motions of each day like a dumb animal, neither daring to hope for a different kind of life nor even knowing enough to desire one.

I am determined to keep up with Walton. I ask my brothers to bring the newspapers from town when they go for supplies. I want to learn enough to discuss politics and current events— the flood in Dayton, Ohio, and Irish Home Rule; the federal income tax and the suffragettes demonstrating in Washington; Woodrow Wilson's views on segregation and the assassination of King George of Greece. At the library in Cushing I check out novels by authors Walton has mentioned, Willa Cather and D. H. Lawrence and Edith Wharton, all of which I read through a filter, thinking of him: "She was afraid lest this boy, who, nevertheless, looked something like a Walter Scott hero," Lawrence writes in *Sons and Lovers*, "who could paint and speak French, and knew what algebra meant, and who went by train to Nottingham every day, might consider her simply as the swine-girl, unable to perceive the princess beneath."

I'm afraid that I am the swine girl. But he treats me like a princess. Papa agrees to let me take Blackie and the buggy one afternoon, and I take Walton on a long tour from Broad Cove, with its views of the outer islands, to the quaint shops in East Friendship, to the pristine Ulmer Church in downtown Rockland. We end up in the grass on the hill overlooking Kissing Cove, eating egg salad sandwiches and home-canned pickles, drinking lemonade from a mason jar. As afternoon fades to evening we watch the sun melt into the liquid horizon, a thin disc of moon emerging faintly above. "The stars are so close," he says, pointing up to the black expanse. "Like you could reach up and take one. Hold it in your hand." He pretends to grab one and hand it to me. "When I am in Cambridge and you're here in Cushing, I'll look up at the stars and think of you. Then you won't seem so far away."

THE FINAL WEEK of August is sodden, cloud heavy, with an unwelcome chill that announces the end of summer as abruptly as a dinner host standing at the table to signal the end of the party.

When Walton comes to say good-bye, I am so choked up I can barely speak. I had not realized how dependent I've become on seeing him. "I promise to write," he says, and I promise, too, but he doesn't yet have an address at Harvard, so I will have to wait for him to write first.

Waiting to hear from him is agony. I plod to the post office once a day at noon.

"I'm taking the buggy into town at three o'clock, as always," Al says. "I can pick up the mail."

"I like the fresh air," I tell him.

The postmistress, thin, fussy, meticulous Bertha Dorset, eyes me with curiosity. I soon learn her routines: she keeps stamps in rolls in a tidy drawer and dusts the coin wrappers with a goose feather. Twice a day, according to a checklist on the wall behind her head, she sweeps the floor. At sunset every evening she lowers the flag outside the post office, takes it off the pole, and folds it neatly into a box.

When I arrive, she hands over the mail in our box, bills and circulars, mostly. "That's it for today," she always says.

I nod and try my best to smile.

I feel like I'm living in a jail cell, waiting for release, the strain of listening for the man with the keys making me tense and jittery. After supper one night, as I'm clearing the dishes, my brothers are debating whether to take up the fish weir; it will be destroyed by ice storms if they wait too long, but on the other hand the sardine catch is good so it would be a shame to dismantle it too soon, and I think I might jump out of my skin. I snap at the boys, surprising myself at my own meanness: "For crying out loud, you clodhoppers, pick up your plates! Were you born in a barn?"

There's thin satisfaction in their wounded surprise.

And then one day, long after I've stopped believing there will be a letter, Bertha slides a pile of mail onto the counter, and here it is: a thick white envelope with a red two-cent George Washington stamp, addressed to me. *Christina Olson.*

"Well, look at that. Hope it's good news," she says.

I can barely wait until I'm out of the post office to open the envelope. I settle on a fallen tree just off the road and unfold the thick paper.

"Dearest Christina . . ."

I read hungrily, skipping forward, shuffling pages (two, three, four) to the end—"Yours"—*mine!*—"Walton." My gaze catches on phrases: "summer I will never forget," "the way you shield your eyes from the sun with your hand, the flat collar of your sailor blouse, the blue-black ribbon in your hair," and finally: "All roads lead back to Cushing for me."

I skip forward and back like a bee trying to escape from a hole in a screen. He can't stop thinking about the summer in Maine. The week he was in Malden was tedious and hot; Harvard is lonely after the sailing and picnics and endless adventures. He misses it all: the sloop moored in Kissing Cove, egg sandwiches on just-baked bread, Ramona's silly jokes, clambakes down by Little Island, pink-orange sunsets. But mostly, he writes, he misses me.

The light is different on the walk home, softer, warm on my face. I tilt my chin up and close my eyes, putting one foot after the other in the left-hand rut of the road. I can only walk like this, with my eyes closed, because I know the way by heart.

EVERY WEEK OR ten days a thick letter in a white envelope with a two-cent stamp arrives in the mail. He writes from the library, from the dining hall, from the narrow wooden desk in his dormitory room, by the light of a gas lamp after his rugby-playing, gin-guzzling roommate has gone to sleep. Each envelope, a package of words to feed my word-hungry soul, provides a portal into a world where students linger in wood-paneled classrooms to talk to professors, where entire days can be spent in a library, where what you write and how you write it are all you need to worry about. I imagine myself in his place: strolling across campus, peering up at thick-paned, glowing windows at dusk, going to expensive dinners with friends in Harvard Square, where the waiters wear tuxedos and look down their noses at the unkempt students, and the students don't care.

As the letters pile up I save them under my bed, tied with a pale pink ribbon. In one he writes: "Every night I look up at the great square in the southeast, nearly overhead, and name the stars in it: Broad Cove, Four Corners, East Friendship, and the Ulmer Church, and wish that I were driving around it with you." After supper I open the shed door and step outside, looking up at the vast expanse of stars, and imagine Walton doing the same in Cambridge. Here I am, there he is, connected by sky.

THE CAMEO SHELL

For years, nobody has seemed particularly interested in the young artist who set up a studio in our house. But this summer is different. In town with my sister-in-law, Mary, doing errands, I'm approached by a woman I don't recognize in the canned-goods section of Fales.

"Excuse me. Are you . . . Christina Olson?"

I nod, puzzled. Why would a stranger know who I am?

"I thought so!" she beams. "I'm renting a cottage near here with my family for the week. I've read about you and your brother. Al, is it?"

Mary, who'd wandered over to the next aisle, comes around the corner. "Hello, I'm with Miss Olson. Can I help you?"

"Oh, I'm sorry! I should've cut to the chase. A famous painter is working at your home, I believe? Andrew Wyeth?"

"How do you—" Mary starts.

"I wonder if I might presume on you to get his autograph for me?" the woman wheedles.

"Oh. Well?" Mary asks, looking at me.

I give the woman a tight smile. "No, that's impossible."

Later, when I mention this to Betsy, she wags her head as if she's not surprised. "Sorry about that, Christina. Andy was on the cover of *American Artist* a while back, and we worried it might change things. Evidently it has."

"Did he say anything about Al and me?"

"A little. Not much. He may have mentioned your names. Of course the article reveals that he summers in Cushing, so it probably isn't hard to figure out. I know he regrets saying anything. He really doesn't like being bothered. I'm sure you don't either."

I shrug. I'm not sure how I feel about it.

Several weeks later, sitting in my chair beside the open kitchen window, I watch a baby blue convertible pull up in front of the house. The driver is wearing a cream fedora, the woman beside him a filmy polka-dotted head scarf.

"Toodle-oo!" she calls, waving pink-tipped fingers. "Hello! We're looking for . . ." She bats the man on the arm. "What's his name, honey?"

"Wyeth."

"That's right. Andrew Wyeth." She gives me a pink-lipped smile through the window.

Andy isn't here yet, but I know I'll see him sauntering up the field from Kissing Cove any minute. "Never heard of him," I tell her.

"He's not painting inside this house?"

"Not last time I checked," I say.

She purses her lips, perplexed. "Frank, isn't this the place?"

"I don't know." He sighs. "You tell me."

"I'm pretty sure. That magazine said so."

"I don't know, Mabel."

"I could swear . . ."

Sure enough, as they're chattering away I see Andy coming toward us through the grass, swinging his tackle box of paints. Following my gaze, Mabel cranes her neck in his direction.

"Look, Frank!" she hoots. "That's probably him!"

"That guy?" I say with a forced chuckle. "He's just a local fisherman." I raise my eyebrows at Andy, who sees me and pivots toward the barn. "We let him store his rods up here."

Mabel sticks her lip out in a pout. "Aw, darn it, we came all this way."

"He might sell you some mackerel. I could ask."

"Ew, no thank you," she sniffs, tightening her scarf around her hair. She doesn't bother saying good-bye.

When they've turned their car around and headed off down the drive, Andy emerges from the barn. "Thanks. That was a close one," he says. "I need to keep my big mouth shut."

"Might be a good idea," I tell him. We've had such a closed-off and intimate existence here that civilization has felt very far away. But slowly it's dawning on me that Andy belongs to the world, and not just to us. It's an unsettling realization.

MANY THINGS ARE disquieting these days. In June of 1944 a torpedo zeroed in on John's ship off the coast of Normandy and killed two dozen men. He almost didn't make it out alive; he clawed his way out of the sinking rubble with only the clothes on his back. "The watch I bought in Brooklyn for $100 was smashed to smithereens," he writes, months after the fact. "A day after we were hit, a seagoing tub towed us back to the English Channel, where we were put on a ship to Plymouth. I slept on a coil of rope and nearly froze to death, but I didn't care. I'm just happy to be alive."

Does he come home after this? He does not. He is sent to England, Scotland, Ireland before a short leave in Boston and forty-five days of training in Newport to become a crew member on an aircraft carrier. Then he heads to the South Pacific to fight the Japanese.

Sadie, whose son, Clyde, also joined the naval reserve, tells me, "I'm always on high alert, listening for the sound of an unfamiliar car up the driveway." I know what she means. I wake in the night with a sense of dread that mostly dissipates by morning but is never entirely absent. At random moments in the day and night I think: this could be the moment Sam and Mary arrive on my doorstep with a telegram. But perhaps not if I knead the dough until it's silky. Not if I pluck the chicken until it's smooth of feathers. Not if I sweep the floor and get rid of the cobwebs in the eaves.

EARLY IN THE winter of 1946, Betsy writes with terrible news: Andy's father and his nephew Newell were killed in October by a train in Pennsylvania. Mr. Wyeth was driving the car, which stalled on the tracks. Andy is bereft, she writes, but hasn't shed a tear.

When they return to Maine for the summer, I can see right away how much his father's death has affected him. He is quieter. More serious.

"You know, I think my father might've actually been in love with her," he says when we're alone in the kitchen. Sitting in Al's rocker, he pushes it back and forth abstractedly with his foot. Heel, toe, *creak, squeak*.

I'm confused. "Sorry, Andy—been in love with who?"

He stops rocking. "Caroline. My brother Nat's wife. The mother of Newell, my nephew, the one who was . . . the one in the car."

"Oh—my." I'm having a hard time grasping what he's saying. "Your father and . . . your brother's wife?" I don't know any of these people by name. Andy has never really talked about them.

"Yeah." He rubs his face with his hand, as if trying to erase his features. "Maybe. Who knows. At the very least he was infatuated. My father was that way, you know. 'A man of great and varied passions,'" he says, as if quoting an obituary. "He never made any bones about that. But I think in the end he was miserable."

"Did something happen just before the accident? Did someone—"

"Nothing happened. As far as I know. But I do know death was on his mind. I mean, it was one of his obsessions; you can see it in his work. It's in my work too. But that's not . . ." His voice trails off. It's as if he's talking to himself, hashing out what he feels, trying to settle on an interpretation. "It was strange," he murmurs. "After the accident, we found his painting gear carefully lined up in his studio. All in a row. He's normally like me, his stuff all over the place, you know?"

I think of the tempera splatters and crusted eggshells and petrified paintbrushes all over the house. I know.

"And maybe it was a coincidence, but the bible in his studio was open to a passage on adultery. Or—not a coincidence; I mean, it's not unreasonable to imagine that he was contemplating the consequences of an affair, whatever actually happened. But it doesn't mean he purposely . . ."

"It seems out of character," I say. "From what you've told me. You always described him as so—present."

Andy gives me a sardonic smile. "Who knows what motivates anyone, right? Humans are mysterious creatures." He lifts his shoulders in a shrug. "Maybe it was a heart attack. Or carelessness. Or—something else. We'll probably never know the truth."

"You know you miss him. That's pretty simple, isn't it?"

"Is it?"

I think of my own parents—how sometimes I miss them and sometimes I don't. "I suppose not."

Rocking slowly back and forth, he says, "Before my father died, I just wanted to paint. It's different now. Deeper. I feel all the—I don't know—gravity of it. Something beyond me. I want to put it all down as sharply as possible."

He looks over at me, and I nod. I understand this, I do. I know what it is to carry mixed feelings in the marrow of your bones. To feel shackled to the past even though it's populated by ghosts.

WHEN HIS FATHER died, Andy was working on a life-sized egg tempera of Al leaning against a closed door with an iron latch, next to our old oil lamp. He started it the summer before, trying, in sketch after charcoal sketch, to render on paper the scratched nickel of the lamp and the solid weight of the latch. Then he pulled out his paints and asked Al to pose next to the door in the kitchen hallway. For hours, days, weeks, Al sat against that door as Andy tried, and failed, to translate the vision in his head onto canvas. "It's like trying to pin a butterfly," he said in exasperation. "If I'm not careful, the wings will crumble to dust in my hand."

When Andy left Port Clyde at the end of the summer, the painting still wasn't finished, so he took it back to his winter studio in Chadds Ford. After the accident, he started working on it again. When he returned to Maine, he brought the painting with him and propped it against the fireplace in the Shell Room.

I'm standing near the fireplace looking at the painting one morning when Andy arrives at the front door and lets himself in. Noticing me in the Shell Room from the hall, he comes to stand beside me. "Al hated sitting still like that, didn't he?" Andy says.

I laugh. "He was so bored and fidgety."

"He'll never pose for me again."

"Probably not," I agree.

Half of the picture is in light and half in darkness. The oil lamp casts shadows across Al's face, on the old wooden door, under the iron latch. A newspaper behind the lamp is stained and wrinkled. Al is staring into the middle distance as if deep in thought. His eyes seem clouded with tears.

"Did it turn out how you wanted?" I ask Andy.

Reaching out a hand, he traces the outline of the lamp in the air. "I got the texture of the nickel right. I'm happy about that."

"What about the figure of Al?"

"I kept changing it," he says. "I couldn't capture his expression. I'm still not sure I did."

"Is he . . . crying?"

"You think he's crying?"

I nod.

"I didn't intend that. But . . ." With a rueful smile, he says, "You can practically hear that wailing train whistle, can't you?"

"It looks like Al is listening to it," I say.

He moves closer, studying the canvas. "Then maybe it did turn out all right."

ANDY HAS NEVER asked me to pose for him, but several weeks after this conversation he comes to me and says he'd like to do a portrait. How can I say no? He sits me down in the pantry doorway, arranges my hands in my lap and the sweep of my skirt, and draws sketch after sketch, pen on white paper. From a distance. Up close. My hair, each minute strand, swept back off my neck. With a necklace and without. My hands, this way and that. The doorway empty, without me in it.

Most of the time the only sounds are the scratch of his pen, the great flap of paper as he turns a large sheet. Squinting, he holds out his thumb. He sticks the pen in his mouth, leaving him inky lipped. Mumbles quietly to himself. "That's it, there. The shadow . . ." I have the odd sensation that he's looking at me and through me at the same time.

"I hadn't quite noticed how frail your arms are," he muses after a while. "And those scars. How did you get them?"

I've become so accustomed to dealing with people's reactions to my infirmity—uncertainty about what to say, distaste, even revulsion—that I tend to clam up when anyone mentions it. But Andy is looking at me frankly, without pity. I glance down at the crisscrossing strips on my forearms, some redder than others. "The oven racks. Sometimes they slip a little. Usually I wear long sleeves."

He winces. "Those scars look painful."

"You get used to it." I shrug.

"Maybe you could use some help with the cooking. Betsy knows a girl—"

"I do all right."

Shaking his head, he says, "You do, don't you, Christina? Good for you."

One day he scoops up all the sketches and heads upstairs. For the next few weeks I barely see him. Every morning he comes toward the house through the fields, his thin body swaying off kilter from that wonky hip, his elbows and knees flailing out, wearing blue dungarees and a paint-splattered sweatshirt and old work boots he doesn't bother to lace. He raps twice on the screen door before letting himself in, carrying a canteen of water and a handful of eggs he's swiped from the hens. Exchanges pleasantries with Al and me in the kitchen. Thumps up the stairs in his work boots, muttering to himself.

I don't ask to see what he's doing, but I'm curious.

It's a warm, sunny day in July when Andy comes downstairs and says he's tired and distracted and maybe he'll take the afternoon off and go for a sail. After he leaves, I realize it's a good time to see what he's working on up there. No one is around; I can hoist myself up each stair as slowly as I want. Resting every other step.

Even before I open the door to the bedroom on the second floor I smell the eggs. Pushing the door wide, I see broken shells and dirty rags and cups of colored water scattered all over the floor. I haven't been up here in ages; the wallpaper, I notice, is peeling off the wall in strips. Despite the breeze from an open window, the room is stuffy. I glance quickly at the painting, propped on a flimsy easel in the far corner, and look away.

Pulling myself up onto the single bed—my childhood bed—I lie on my back, staring at the spiderweb fissures in the ceiling. Out of the corner of my eye I can glimpse the rectangle of canvas, but I'm not ready to look at it directly. Andy told me once that hidden in his seemingly realistic paintings are secrets, mysteries, allegories. That he wants to get at the essence of things, no matter how ugly.

I'm afraid to learn what he might see in me.

Finally I can't put it off any longer. Turning on my side, I look at the painting.

I'm not hideous, exactly. But it's a shock nevertheless to see myself through his eyes. On the canvas I'm in profile, looking soberly out toward the cove, hands awkward in my lap, nose long and pointy, mouth downturned. My hair is a deep auburn, my frame thin and slightly off kilter. The pantry doorway is rimmed in dark, half in shadow. The door is cracked and weathered, the grasses wild beyond. My dress is black, with a slash, a deep V, below my white neck.

In the black dress—not what I was wearing—I look somber. Severe. And utterly alone. Alone in the doorway facing the sea. My skin ghostly, spectral. Darkness all around.

Bridget Bishop, waiting to be sentenced.

Waiting for death.

I roll onto my back again. Shadows of the lace curtains, moving in and out with the wind, make the ceiling a roiling sea.

When Andy comes in the next morning, I don't tell him I went upstairs. He says hello, we chat for a few minutes while I stir up drop biscuits, and he walks into the foyer. Stops. Comes back to the kitchen door with his hands on his hips. "You went up."

I spoon the dough onto a flat metal sheet, dollop after dollop.

"You did," he insists.

"How'd you know?"

He sweeps his hand up with a flourish. "Path through the dust all the way to the top. Like the trail of a giant snail."

I laugh drily.

"So what'd you think?"

I shrug. "I don't know about art."

"It's not art. It's just you."

"No, it's not. It's you," I say. "Didn't you tell me that once? That every painting is a self-portrait?"

He whistles. "Ah, you're too shrewd for me. Come on. I want to know what you think."

I'm afraid to tell him. Afraid it will sound vain or self-important. "It's so . . . dark. The shadows. The black dress."

"I wanted to show the contrast with your skin. To highlight you sitting there."

Now that we're having this conversation, I realize that I'm a little angry. "I look like I'm in a coffin with the lid half shut."

He laughs a little, as if he can't believe I might be upset.

I stare at him evenly.

Running his hand through his hair, he says, "I was trying to show your . . ." He hesitates. "Dignity. Solemnity."

"Well, I guess that's the problem. I don't think of myself as solemn. I didn't think you did, either."

"I don't. Not really. It's just a moment. And it's not really 'you.' Or 'me.' Despite what you think." His voice trails off. Seeing me struggle with the heavy oven door, he comes over and opens it for me, then slides the baking tray of biscuits in. "I think it's about the house. The mood of it." He shuts the oven door. "Do you know what I mean?"

"You make it seem so . . ." I cast about for the right word. "I don't know. Lonely."

He sighs. "Isn't it, sometimes?"

For a moment there's silence between us. I reach for a dishrag and wipe my floury hands.

"So how do you think of yourself?" he asks.

"What?"

"You said you don't think of yourself as solemn. So how do you think of yourself?"

It's a good question. How do I think of myself?

The answer surprises us both.

"I think of myself as a girl," I say.

Everybody in town seems to know about the envelopes postmarked Massachusetts. I can tell that Bertha Dorset has been gossiping by the way she smirks and lifts her eyebrows when she hands me the mail. When I mention it in a letter to Walton, he writes, "I'm sorry that anyone should bother you with their curiosity," and offers to use Ramona as a foil—she can address the envelopes from Boston, he says. "Then they wouldn't know that I was writing. But I'm afraid they would hear of it some other way."

I decide not to let it bother me. People will always talk. At least now they have good reason.

In one of his letters, Walton says that he has tried, and failed, to grow sweet peas, his favorite flower, in his Cambridge apartment. In April, months before he is due to return, I send away for mail-order sweet pea seeds and ask Al to build a trellis. When the packet arrives, I soak the seeds overnight in water, drain them and chip one end with a sharp blade, then plant them in the manure-rich dirt. I feel like Jack anticipating his beanstalk.

Sprigs sprout, grow into skinny stalks, and race up the lattice. By mid-June, when strawberries are ready to harvest, the sweet peas begin to flower. Though Walton has written to let me know the week he'll be back, and though Sam reports an in-town sighting, I am startled to see him coming up the path on a warm morning with a cluster of sweet peas in his hand and a wide grin on his face.

"You're a sight for sore eyes!" he says when he arrives at the kitchen door, pulling me into a quick embrace. Handing me the bouquet, he says, "I know how much you like sweet peas," and I want to say, no, you're the one who likes them; you know how much I like *you*. But I am oddly touched that he has conflated his feelings with mine.

"I have a surprise," I tell him and make him close his eyes before leading him to the trellis. "Open."

He gives me a rueful look. "I'm sorry. Owls to Athens."

"Great minds," I say. "I grew these for you."

"For me?"

I nod.

He moves closer, grasps my hand. "There's enough beauty here to lure me without sweet peas."

Welcome back, I think.

I'VE NEVER PAID much attention to how I look, but all of a sudden I'm acutely aware of it. I notice the soiled patch on my blue chambray dress, the frayed sleeves of my muslin blouse, the dirty hem of my skirt. I run my fingers through my hair, separating it into oily strands. The entire family bathes on the third Monday of each month in the same water in the kitchen, oldest to youngest (though in the summer the boys, never much for baths to begin with, get by with a swim in the lake or the ocean). Every few days I wash my face and under my arms with a wet cloth dunked in a pot of water warmed on the range. But that, I decide, isn't enough. I drag the old galvanized tin tub from the woodshed, with Al's help, and we fill pots with water from the pump in the pantry and carry them to the range to heat. When the water's close to boiling, we dump it in the tub and add buckets of cold water. Then I send him out of the room.

In the tub I rub castile soap across my arms, my legs, my pale stomach, the downy fur under my arms and between my legs. Dipping my head, I wet my hair and run my soapy hands through it, my fingers strange on my scalp, like someone else's. After rinsing my hair, I pour apple cider vinegar into a cupped hand, as Mother taught me, and run it through the strands until they squeak. The water is soothing on my knotted muscles and floating arms, free of gravity's pull. My legs are floating too. When I was younger, I would bathe in the pond with my brothers sometimes, reveling in the weightlessness, the momentary release from pain. Now the bath is the only place I can find this relief. I shut my eyes, savoring it.

Leaning back against the cold tub, I fantasize about what it would be like to leave this place. I envision the moment as if I'm a character in a story: A young woman rises while the rest of the house is asleep, gathers some items into a bundle, makes her way down the stairs as quietly as she can (as she is accustomed to do, waking before the others to stoke the fire and prepare breakfast). She laces her shoes in the shadows of the front hall and opens the door to the outside. Light on her feet as a ballerina, weightless as a butterfly, she slips down the steps and around the corner, beyond the house and the barn to the automobile that waits out of sight, a young man behind the wheel. (Walton, of course. Who else would it be?) He takes her bag, tosses it over the seat. In her bag: a chambered nautilus, an empty picture frame decorated with shells that awaits a moment worth remembering. Almost everything else she leaves behind, bits and pieces of a life outgrown. Whatever she'll need in the future can be found where she's going.

AS THE SUMMER progresses we fall into our routines from the year before: boating with the Carles, clambakes on the rocks by Kissing Cove, picnics in the meadow. One day, as we're meandering down to Bird Point, he says, "It would be terrific if you could come to Boston this fall."

I feel a surge of pleasure. "I would like to."

"You could stay with the Carles, I'm sure. And . . ." He hesitates, and I hold my breath, hoping he'll make the invitation more personal—"perhaps you might see a doctor for your affliction while you're there."

I stop walking in surprise. We haven't ever explicitly talked about my condition, though I've come to rely on his arm under mine. "You want me to see a doctor?"

"These country physicians are well meaning, no doubt, but I doubt they're conversant in the latest advances. Wouldn't you like to find out what's wrong with you?"

"Wrong with me?" I stammer. My skin feels cold.

He taps his forehead with two fingers. "Forgive me, Christina. 'What ails you,' I should have said. You don't complain, but I can imagine how much you suffer. As one who cares about you . . ." His voice trails off again, and he grasps my hand. "I'd like to see if something can be done."

These concerns are reasonable, even logical. So why do his gentle entreaties make me want to put my hands over my ears and beg him to stop? "You are kind to want to improve my welfare," I tell him, striving for a neutral tone.

"Not at all. I only want for you to be well. So will you consider it?"

"I would prefer not to."

"Said Bartleby." He flashes a smile, breaking the tension.

Bartleby. From the recesses of my school brain I dredge the reference: the obstinate scrivener. I smile back.

"I only want what's best for you, you know."

"You're what's best for me," I say.

AUGUST IS EXQUISITE agony. I want each day to last forever. I am fretful, fevered, perpetually irritated by everyone but Walton, to whom I'm determined to show my best self. It's a peculiar kind of dissatisfaction, a bittersweet nostalgia for a moment not yet past. Even in the midst of a pleasurable outing I'm aware of how ephemeral it is. The water is warm but will cool. The ocean is a sheet of glass, but wind is picking up, far across the horizon. The bonfire is roaring but will dwindle. Walton is beside me, his arm around my shoulder, but all too soon he will be gone.

On our final evening as a group, sitting on the beach, making conversation, Walton mentions the almanac's prediction of a hard winter ahead, and Ramona says, "Will Christina ever know anything except a hard winter?" She doesn't look at him when she says it, but we all know what she's asking: if, and when, Walton is going to offer a way out.

He seems oblivious. "Christina's not like us, Ramona. She likes the cold Maine winters. Isn't that so?" he asks me, squeezing my shoulders.

I look at Ramona, who shakes her head slightly and rolls her eyes. But neither of us says anything more.

FLOWERS FADE, FREEZE in an early frost, wither on the vine. Trees burst into flame and burn themselves out. Leaves crumble to ash. All the things about life on the farm that once contented me now fill me with impatience. It has become harder to tolerate the months after summer ends, the plodding regularity of my daily chores, the inevitable descent into darkness and cold. I feel as if I'm on a narrow path through familiar woods, a path that goes around and around with no end in sight.

I spend the early fall canning and preserving and pickling: tomatoes, cucumbers, strawberries, blueberries. Shelving the jars in the shed. Alvaro slaughters a pig, and we carve and cure and smoke every last bit of it, from hoof to curly tail. We trowel up and store unlovely root vegetables, rutabagas and turnips and parsnips and beets. Pluck apples and lay them out on a long table in the cellar for the long winter ahead.

I have too much time to think. I torment myself. All I do is work and think. I feel like the mollusk in Mamey's nautilus, grown too big for its shell. A woman my age, I think, should be laboring for her own husband and children. All around me, friends and classmates are becoming engaged and getting married. The boys I went to school with are settling into lives as farmers and fishermen and shopkeepers. The girls, Sadie and Gertrude among them, are setting up house and having babies.

When I trudge through my tasks, Mother chides me—"Pick up your feet, my girl; life is not as tragic as all that"—and Al looks at me sideways, and I know what they're thinking, that it might have been better if Walton had never come along.

But Walton's letters are hot-air balloons, lifting me out of melancholy. He writes about his classes, his teachers, his thoughts about his future career. Though he's been training as a journalist, news about the war raging in Europe dominates the papers, making it a hard time to break into domestic reporting, he says. He has decided to shift his sights to teaching. Teachers are always needed, whether a war is raging or the stock market is falling. It's not lost on me that he could be a teacher anywhere—even in Cushing, Maine.

WINTER PASSES AS slowly as a glacier melts. Christmas and New Year's provide momentary distraction before we settle into months of ice and snow. Walking back from the post office in the late-afternoon gloom of a February day, I am tucking Walton's letter inside my coat when my shoe catches on a protruding chip of ice and I crash to the ground. I prop myself on an elbow, noting with strange detachment my torn stockings, the thin coating of blood on my shin, a throbbing pain in my right hand, the one I used to break my fall. Tentatively I extend my left arm and begin to hoist myself up. I pat my jacket. The letter must have flown from my pocket when I fell. I feel around on the ground, muddying my skirt even further, my blood pinking the ice. Several yards away I spy the envelope and limp over to

it. Empty. The sky is darkening, the air is cold, my shin is throbbing, and still I continue, as desperate as an opium addict; I can't
leave until I find it. And then I see the folded pages, fluttering
in the ditch.

When I reach them, I find that the ink has run; the letter—
mud spattered, water soaked—appears to have been written in a
diabolical code designed to drive the recipient insane. I can only
identify every fourth or fifth word or phrase (*entertaining . . . I
am glad to say . . . beginning to enjoy*), and after straining to make
out the letters with increasing exasperation, I hold the pages flat
against my dress, inside my coat, hoping they'll be legible when
dry. The walk home is slow and painful. When I step into the
house, I open my coat to find the bodice of my chambray dress
tattooed with ink. A permanent reminder of how important his
words have become to me.

SUMMER AGAIN. WHEN I answer the door one June morning in 1915 to find Walton standing there, he gives me a huge smile and presents me with a package of butterscotch candies. "Sweets to the sweet," he says.

"That's an old line," I tell him. "You've said it before."

He laughs. "I obviously have a limited repertoire."

Soon we fall back into our familiar routines, seeing each other nearly every day. We stroll the property, sail in the afternoon, picnic in early evening with the Carles and my brothers Al and Sam down by the grove. I see Ramona watching as Walton and I go off together to collect driftwood and twigs to make a fire in the circle of rocks, as he pulls me behind a tree and kisses me. At the end of the evening we sit on the rough benches Papa made and watch the cinders crumble and settle. The sky changes from blue to purple to rose to red as the sun sinks like an ember into the sea.

When Walton gets up to talk to Alvah on the other side of the fire pit, Ramona comes to sit beside me. "I need to ask," she says quietly. "Has Walton discussed the nature of his commitment to you?"

I knew this question was coming. I've been dreading it.

"Not exactly," I tell her. "I think our commitment is— understood."

"Understood by whom?"

"By both of us."

"Does he say *anything*?"

"Well, he needs to establish himself before—"

"I am prying, forgive me. I've tried to keep my mouth shut. But my goodness, this is the third year."

It's not like she's articulating anything I haven't thought myself, but her words feel like a punch in the gut. Walton is a scholar, I want to say, studying the classics and philosophy; he cannot make any decisions until he is done with school. Nobody seems to understand this.

I'm not sure I understand it myself.

"It's really not your business, Ramona," I say stiffly.

"It's not, you're right."

We sit in silence, the air between us bristling with words unsaid.

After a few moments, she sighs. "Look, Christina. Be careful. That's all I'm saying."

I know Ramona means well. But this is like telling a person who has leapt off a cliff to be careful. I am already in midair.

IN LATE AUGUST, Walton and I make a plan to sail alone to Thomaston. Since my conversation with Ramona I've been acutely aware of how deftly he evades any talk of commitment. Maybe she's right; I need to raise the issue directly.

I resolve to do it on our sail.

It's early evening, and the air is laced with cool. He stands behind me, unfurling a big wool blanket and wrapping it around our shoulders as I steer.

"Walton——" I begin nervously.

"Christina."

"I don't want you to leave."

"I don't want to leave," he says, wrapping his hand over mine.

I slide my hand out from under his. "But you have things to look forward to. All I have is months of winter. And waiting."

"Ah, my poor Persephone," he murmurs, kissing my hair, my shoulder.

This irritates me further. I pull away a bit. For a few moments we are quiet. I listen to the mournful yawp of seagulls overhead, as large as geese.

"I want to ask you something," I say finally.

"Ask."

"Or—well—tell you."

"Go ahead."

"I love . . ." I start, but my courage fades. "Being with you."

He pulls the blanket tighter around me, enveloping us in a cocoon. "I love being with you."

"But . . . what are we—what are you—"

His hands move up my sides, resting on my ribs. I arch my back, leaning into him, and his hands move to the front, cupping my breasts gently through the fabric. "Oh, Christina," he breathes. "Some things don't need explanation. Do they?"

I decide I will not ask him, press him, insist. I tell myself it's not the time. But the fact is, I am afraid. Afraid that I will push him away, and that this—whatever it is—will end.

AL AND I are clearing the dishes from supper one evening when he says, "So what do you think is going to happen?"

"What?"

He's bent over the plates, scraping leftover potatoes and yams and applesauce into a bucket for the pigs. "You think Walton Hall is going to marry you?"

"I don't know. I haven't thought about it." But Al must know this is a lie.

"All I'm saying is . . ." He is strained and awkward, unaccustomed to the intimacy of speaking his mind.

"'All I'm saying is,'" I mock him impatiently. "Stop hemming and hawing. Spit it out."

"I've never seen you like this."

"Like what."

"As if reason has left you."

"Honestly." Feeling a flare of annoyance, I handle the pots recklessly, clanging them into each other.

"I'm concerned for you," he says.

"Well, don't be."

For a few minutes we work silently, clearing the table, scooping the cutlery into a bowl, pouring warm water from the kettle into a pan for the dishes. As I go through the familiar motions I get even angrier. How dare he—this cautious man-child who has never been in love—pass judgment on Walton's motives and my own good sense? Al knows as much about the nature of our relationship as he does about sewing a dress.

"What do you think?" I blurt finally. "That I am an imbecile? That I have not a thought in my head?"

"It's not you I worry about."

"Well, you needn't worry. I can take care of myself. And besides—as if it's any of your business—Walton has been honorable in every way."

Al lowers a stack of plates into the washing pan. "Of course he has. He likes the diversion. He doesn't want to give it up."

Clutching a fistful of forks, I turn to him. For a brief moment I contemplate striking him with them, but instead I take a deep breath and say, "How dare you."

"Come on, Christie, I don't mean to . . ." Again his voice falters, and I can see, given how unnatural it must feel for him to confront me, how important he considers this. And yet I find him irritatingly simplistic. All the things I ordinarily admire about Al now strike me as deficits: his loyalty no more than fear of the unknown; his decency, merely naïveté; his sense of morality, prim judgment. (How quickly, with a slight twist in perception, do people's strengths become flaws!)

"What I'm saying is that . . ." He swallows. "His options are many."

It's no use trying to explain to Alvaro what love is. So I say, "You might say the same about Papa, when he courted Mother."

An ironic look flits across his face. "How's that?"

"He could've worked on any ship. Traveled all over the world. But he settled here, with her."

"Mother had a big house and hundreds of acres." He flings

his hand toward the window. "You know what this house, the *Olson* House, used to be called."

I splash the cutlery in the dishwater impatiently. "Did you ever consider that maybe Papa fell in love?"

"Sure. Maybe. Just remember—you have three brothers. This house isn't yours to inherit."

"Walton isn't after this house."

"Okay." He dries his hands on a dish towel and hangs it on a hook. "I'm just saying you should be careful. It's not right for him to keep you on a tether."

"I'm not on a tether," I tell him sharply. "Anyway, I'd rather be with Walton for three months in the summer than any of these local boys all year-round."

One morning after gathering eggs, a few weeks later, I step across the threshold into the house and hear my parents' voices in the Shell Room, a place they rarely enter. I stand very still in the foyer, cupping the eggs, still warm from the hens, in my hands.

"She's no beauty, but she works hard. I think she'd make a fine companion," Papa is saying.

"She would," Mother says. "But I'm beginning to wonder if he's toying with her."

My face tingles as I realize they're talking about me. I lean against the wall, straining to hear.

"Who knows? Perhaps he wants to run a farm."

Mother laughs, a dry bark. "That one? No."

"What does he want with her, then?"

"Who knows? To fill his idle time, I suspect."

"Maybe he really does love her, Katie."

"I fear . . ." Mother's voice trails off. "That he will not marry her."

Papa says, "I fear it too."

My cheeks are aflame, my heart beating in my ears. In my trembling hands, the eggs jostle and shift, and though I try to contain them they slip between my fingers and drop to the floor, one after the other, splattering smears of yellow and viscous white across the entryway.

Mother appears in the doorway, looking stricken. "I'll get a rag." She ducks away and comes back; crouching, she mops the floor around my feet. Both of us are silent. I'm aware of nothing but my own humiliation, the shock of hearing my silent fears put into words. The screen door slams and I watch Papa go past the window, ducking his head on his way to the barn.

IN SEPTEMBER, WHEN Walton is back at school, he writes, "I think that night we made the trip to Thomaston was the happiest I ever spent. How could you steer, under the circumstances? I believe I was to blame." He is homesick for Cushing. Homesick for me. "This was the best summer of my life. A large part of that I owe to you," he writes, signing his letter, "With love, Walton."

I feel as if a wall of the house has detached from the rest and fallen gently to the ground. I can see a way out, a clear path to the open sea.

WITH WALTON AND the Carles around all summer I don't need anyone else; my brothers and I buzz around them, moths to their vivid flame. But after they leave, I am lonely. When Gertrude Gibbons, a girl I never particularly liked at school who has grown into a mildly tolerable adult, invites me to a Wednesday night sewing circle run by a professional seamstress, Catherine Bailey, I reluctantly agree. Gertrude, too, makes her own dresses, and between sessions of the group we start sewing together in the evenings sometimes, when the chores are done. It's a way to pass the time.

On a cool November evening, I take my sewing to Gertrude's house in a sack slung over my shoulder, a two-mile walk. All day it's been raining; the road is damp, and I have to walk slowly and carefully to avoid muddy puddles.

"Finally!" Gertrude exclaims when she answers my knock. Round faced and ruddy, with an ample bosom that strains the buttons on her dress, she's chewing a molasses cookie. Her large black dog barks and leaps. "Down, Oscar, down!" she scolds. "Come in, for mercy's sake."

A cat is curled on an upholstered chair. "Shoo, Tom," Gertrude says, flapping her hands, and the cat reluctantly obliges. "Sit here," she tells me. "Cookie? Fresh baked."

"I'm fine for now, thanks."

"That's how you stay so thin!" she says. "You're abstemious

like my sister. I try, honestly I do, but I don't know how anyone can resist a warm molasses cookie."

The house is snug; embers glow in the fireplace. Gertrude tosses on another log while I get settled. Her parents are away, visiting relatives in Thomaston, she says; her brother is out with friends. Oscar sprawls in front of the hearth, his eggplant stomach soon rising up and down in contented sleep.

We chat about the large yield this season of potatoes and turnips; I tell her about the fox that stole three hens out of our coop, and how Al trapped and killed it. She wants to know my famous fried apple cake recipe and I explain it step-by-step: how you peel and thinly slice the apples, fry the slices over a low flame in a heavy black skillet, adding a stream of molasses until the apples are soft in the middle and crispy on the edges, then turn the skillet over onto a platter. (I don't tell her that I can no longer turn the skillet on my own and have to ask one of my brothers to do it.)

The skirt I'm working on is beige cotton, with pleats and pockets. Before I came to Gertrude's I pressed the fabric with a hot iron, one inch all the way around, and now I'm using a slip stitch to hem it. My stitches are small and neat, partly because I have to concentrate so hard to get them right. Gertrude's are sloppy. She is easily distracted, full of gossip she's been waiting to share. Emily Jones had a stillborn baby early in the summer and she still hasn't left the house, poor girl. Earl Standin has a drinking problem. His pregnant wife showed up at Fales with a shiner last week, claiming she walked into a pole. Sarah Stewart married a blacksmith from Rockland she met at a social, but rumor has it she's in love with his brother.

"So what do you hear?" she asks.

I hold up the fabric and frown, pretending to be vexed by a missed stitch. The more she natters on, the less I want to say. I know she is eager for details about Walton, but I hold them close, not trusting that she won't chew them into cud. She waits patiently, her sewing in her lap.

"You are a sphinx, Christina Olson," she says finally.

"I'm just a bore," I say. "Nobody tells me anything."

"What about that Ramona Carle and that Harland Woodbury? I hear he's sweet on her."

A man named Harland Woodbury did, in fact, travel up from Boston to visit Ramona this summer in Cushing. But after he left, Ramona made fun of his chubby cheeks and porkpie hat. "Don't know a thing about it," I tell Gertrude.

She gives me a sly look. "Well, I heard something you might be able to shed light on." She licks her index finger and rubs the frayed edge of her thread into a point. "I heard," she says, threading her needle, "that a certain young man from Harvard can't make up his mind."

A flush moves through me, starting at the top of my head, like heatstroke. My fingers tremble. I put down the cloth so Gertrude won't see.

"Surely you're aware that a man like that . . ." she says gently, as if to a child. She sighs.

"Like what?" I ask sharply, and immediately regret engaging her at all.

"You know. Educated, from away." She reaches over and pats my leg. "So just—what's the saying—don't put all your goods on one ship."

"Okay, Gertrude."

"I know you're private, Christina. And you don't want to talk about this. But I could not, in good conscience, let the moment pass without telling you what I think."

I nod and keep my mouth shut. If I don't speak, she can't answer.

MAKING MY WAY home from Gertrude's house I am distracted, lost in thought, when my foot sinks into a rut in the road and I tumble forward. As I fall I try to pivot sideways to protect the parcel I'm carrying containing my half-finished dress, landing with a thud on my right side. I feel a searing jolt of pain in my right leg. Both of my forearms are skinned. As soon as I brush the gravelly dirt off, blood springs to the surface. My leg is twisted under me, my foot splayed in an unnatural direction. The parcel is torn and muddied.

It's no use calling for help; no one will hear. If my leg is broken, if I can't get up, it will probably be morning before anyone finds me. How stupid was I to venture out like this on a cold night by myself—and for what?

I moan, feeling sorry for myself. People make dumb mistakes all the time, and that's the end of them. A man in Thomaston was found frozen to death last winter in the woods, either because he was disoriented or had a heart attack. People go out in skiffs in cloudy weather, swim in the ocean when there's an undertow, fall asleep with candles burning. Go out alone and break a leg in the middle of nowhere on a frigid November night.

I reach down to touch my right thigh. The kneecap. I bend my leg and feel a sharp jab. Ah, there. The ankle.

Papa urged me to take his walking stick when I left the house, but I refused.

I'm so tired of this mutinous body that doesn't move the way it should. Or the low thrumming ache that's never entirely absent. Of having to concentrate on my steps so I don't fall, of my ever-present scabs and bruises. I'm tired of pretending that I'm the same as everyone else. But to admit what it's really like to live in this skin would mean giving up, and I'm not ready to do that.

"Your pride will be the end of you," Mother often says. Perhaps she's right.

I tuck the parcel into my waistband and struggle to my knees. Bunching my skirt beneath me to buffer my skin from the ground, I drag myself toward the side of the road, moving gingerly to avoid putting pressure on my ankle. I squint toward a clump of birches about a dozen feet away, looking for a stick to use as a cane. After pulling myself to my feet, I stagger to the cluster of trees, picking my way over rocks and ruts, and feel around with my hands. Here. Too short, but it'll do. Limping back to the road, I lean heavily on the stick, grimacing through the pain.

An hour ago I couldn't wait to leave Gertrude's house, but now going back there is my only option. I hobble slowly down the road. When I see her front porch, I breathe a sigh of relief. I pull myself up the three front steps, leaving a sludgy trail, and pause in front of the door. The lights are off. I pound on the door with the side of my closed fist. No answer. I rap hard on the window beside the door with my knuckles.

From deep inside the house I hear footsteps. Through the window I see the glow of a lamp. Then Gertrude's frightened voice on the other side of the door: "Who's there?"

"It's me. Christina."

The door opens and I lurch inside.

"Mercy!" Gertrude flaps her arms like a bird trying to land on a rock. "What happened?"

"I fell on the road. I think my ankle may be broken."

"Oh dear. You are covered in mud," she says with dismay.

"I'm sorry. I'm sorry to bother you." Hot tears spring to my eyes, tears of relief and exhaustion and bitterness—that I can't walk right, that I am back at this house, that, damn her, Gertrude may be right: Walton will never marry me, I will be stuck in this place for the rest of my life, sewing with this wretched woman. I turn my face so she doesn't see the tears streaking through the grime.

Gertrude sighs and shakes her head. "Stay right there. Let me find a cloth so you don't ruin the rug."

"I BROKE MY ankle coming back from Gertrude Gibbons's house," I write to Walton. "It was foolish. I never should have been alone on that road in the dark."

"I am glad to hear you're on the mend, and dearly hope you'll be more prudent in the future," he writes back. "Yours faithfully—."

I scan the letter several times, trying to hear his voice between the lines. But the words are stiff and formal. No matter how often I read them, they sound like an admonition.

I'M APPREHENSIVE ABOUT seeing Walton for the first time after the long winter apart, but he gives me a warm hug and a kiss on the cheek. "I have a present for you," he says, drawing a large shell from the inside pocket of his seersucker jacket and placing it on the table in front of us. "I thought you might add it to your collection."

The shell is shiny and garishly colored—orange red, with bulky knobs on top that get smaller toward the edges.

I pick it up. It's as smooth and heavy as a glass paperweight. "Oh. Where did you find this?"

"I bought it. In a specialty shop in Cambridge." He smiles. "From Hawaii, I believe. It's called a cameo shell. At least that's what the card on the shelf said. It'll look nice in the Shell Room, don't you think?"

I nod. "Sure."

He touches my arm. "You don't like it."

"No, it's—interesting." But I'm disappointed that he doesn't know me well enough to understand that this gaudy bauble from a specialty shop doesn't belong in the Shell Room, filled with discoveries from expeditions. I wish he'd lied and told me he found it on a beach.

I set the cameo shell on the mantelpiece in the Shell Room, but it looks out of place, like an artificial flower in a garden. After a few weeks, I put it in a drawer.

❧

AS THE SUMMER of 1916 progresses, Walton acts exactly as he always has: solicitous, courtly, quick with a smile and an ironic aside. But I am acutely aware that like a slip of paper in the wind, something in his nature eludes my grasp. Even when I ask direct questions, he is evasive, offering only vague generalities about his life in Boston, his family, his plans for the future.

One early July morning Walton and I are making our way through the high grass to Hathorn Point to harvest mussels for dinner when I notice that he's not saying much. He seems uncomfortable, fiddling with his sleeve as he walks.

"What is it? Walton, tell me."

"It's just . . ." He shakes his head as if dislodging a thought. "My parents. Thinking they know what's best for me."

I know his parents live in Malden, near the Carles. As far as I'm aware they've never come up for a visit. "Did you get a letter?"

He bends down, swipes an errant stick from the grass, and snaps it in half with a small, sharp movement. "Yes. A long, tedious letter. Saying it's time for me to grow up, to take a job in Boston in the summers and stop frittering away my time up here with the Carles." He snaps the stick halves in half again before flinging all the tiny pieces onto the ground.

"Is this about . . . me?"

He shoves his hands in his pockets. His grievance has taken on a theatrical air, as if exaggerated for my benefit. "It's not personal," he says brusquely. "They claim to be concerned about my future. They don't want me to limit myself."

My heart skitters ahead of my words. "What—what do they mean by that?"

"It's absurd," he says. "Keeping up appearances. Harvard, all that. The right job. The right wife."

"Meaning . . ." I ask in as neutral a tone as I can muster.

He shrugs. "Oh, who knows. They want me to marry someone"—he lifts forked fingers to convey that he's quoting— "'educated' and 'from a good family.' Which means, naturally, a family they've heard of. A Boston family, preferably. A family that will bolster their social standing. Because that's the important thing."

I find myself shrinking into silence. Of course Walton's parents don't want their Harvard-educated son marrying a girl who didn't even go to secondary school.

"You're upset," Walton says, patting my arm. "But you shouldn't be. This isn't about you. They don't really know about you."

This shocks me into words. "You've never mentioned me?"

"Of course I've mentioned you," he says quickly. "I just don't think they realize quite what . . . quite how much you mean to me."

"Do they know that we are . . ." The word *sweethearts* springs to mind, but I'm afraid it will sound cloying, presumptuous.

He shrugs. "I try not to talk to my parents about much of anything."

"So they don't know that we've been . . . seeing each other for four years?"

"I'm not sure what they know, and I don't care," he says dismissively. "Let's put this aside and enjoy the morning, shall we? I'm sorry I brought it up."

I nod, but the conversation has dampened my mood. It's only later, going over it in my head, that I realize he didn't answer my question.

THE DAY BEFORE Walton and the Carles are to return to Massachusetts, we make a plan to go to the Acorn Grange Hall in Cushing for a dance. Walton shows up earlier than expected with Eloise and Ramona and finds me in the yard behind the house, struggling with a load of laundry. It's wash day, and I can't leave until all the clothes are on the line.

"Go ahead, I'll be along soon," I tell them. I'm hot and perspiring, still wearing my old frock and apron.

"I'll help her finish," he says to the others. "We'll catch up with you."

Eloise and Ramona leave the house with Al and Sam in a clamorous gaggle. I watch them as they make their way down the road—Al and Sam tall and awkward, bending like reeds toward the pretty sisters.

Walton helps me wring the damp pieces, his strong hands far more efficient than mine. He hoists the straw basket to his hip and we make our way to the clothesline; then, crouching, he takes each piece of damp clothing from the basket, shakes it, and hands it to me, and I pin it to the rope. The intimacy of this ordinary task feels bittersweet.

Walton waits on the back stoop while I go inside to change into a clean white blouse and navy skirt. "You look nice," he says when I appear. As we stroll toward the Grange Hall, he rummages in his pocket. I hear the familiar crinkle of wax paper. He pops a butterscotch candy into his mouth.

"Do you have one for me?" I ask.

"Of course." He stops and takes out another, unwraps it, and puts it on my tongue. He rubs my arms. "Autumn in the air already," he muses. "Are you cold? Do you need my jacket?"

"I'm perfect," I say a little stiffly.

"I know you're perfect. I was asking if you're chilly." He smiles, and I can tell he's trying to lighten my mood.

I suck on the candy for a moment. "You're leaving."

"Not for a few days."

"Soon."

"Too soon," he concedes, lacing his fingers through mine.

For a few minutes we walk along in silence. Then I venture, "Teachers are needed all over. Even in Maine."

He squeezes my hand gently but says nothing. Above our heads a riot of birdsong erupts, piercing the quiet. We both look up. The dense tree cover, leaf lush, gives nothing away. Then, suddenly swooping across the road, a dark flurry.

"I've never seen so many crows," he remarks.

"Actually, they're blackbirds."

"Ah. What would I do without you to correct me?" He pulls on my hand playfully, and then, realizing he's yanking me off balance, tucks his arm around my waist. "Such a clever girl," he murmurs in my ear. Then he slows and stops in the road.

I'm not sure what he's doing. "What is it?"

He puts a finger to his lips and tugs me gently down the embankment into a copse of blue-black spruce. In the shadows he cups my warm face in his cool hands. "You are truly something, Christina."

I look into his pale eyes, trying to decipher what he's saying. He gazes back implacably. "I can't tell if you're sad to be leaving," I say, a petulant tone creeping into my voice.

"Of course I am. But admit it—you'll be a bit relieved. 'Finally summer's over, I have my life back.'"

I shake my head.

He shakes his head, mimicking me. "No?"

"No. I—"

He kisses me on the mouth, gathers me closer, kisses my bony shoulder, the hollow of my neck. He runs his hand down my bodice, hesitates for a moment, then continues all the way to the folds of my skirt. I am dizzy with surprise. He pushes me back against the bark of a tree. I feel its knots pressing into my back as he leans into me, running a hand down my side, another under my blouse, up the slight curve of my breast. His mouth on mine jams my head awkwardly against the trunk, an uncomfortable and yet not altogether unpleasant experience.

The butterscotch clicks in my mouth. "I'd better spit this out, or I might choke," I say.

He laughs. "Me too."

I don't care that it's unladylike; I spit it on the grass.

Now his hand is between my legs, lost in the fabric. I feel him cup me there in a proprietary way, and I push my hips toward him, feeling his hardness between us. My skin is alive, every nerve ending pulsing. His breathing ragged, insistent. This is what I want. This passion. This certainty. This clear sign of his desire. Right now I would do anything, anything he asks.

And then—a sound on the road. Walton jerks his head up, alert as a bird dog. "What is that?" he breathes.

I cock my head. Feel a low rumbling in my soles. "An automobile, I think."

The sky is dark now. I can barely see his face.

He pulls back, then sways into me, clutching my shoulders. "Oh, Christina," he murmurs. "You make me want you."

The darkness emboldens me. "I'm yours."

Still holding my shoulders, he rests his head on my breast-bone like a nudging sheep. When he sighs, I feel his warm breath on my chest. "I know." Then he looks up into my eyes with a startling intensity. "We must be together. Beyond"—he waves an arm, indicating the trees, the road, the sky—"all this."

My heart leaps. "Oh, Walton. Do you mean it?"

"I do. I promise."

Though everything in my nature fights against it, I'm determined to find out what he means. Swallowing hard, I ask, "What do you promise?"

"That we will be together. There are things I need to—resolve. You must come to Boston, and meet my parents. But I promise you, Christina, yes."

Blue-black spruce shushing overhead, gravelly dirt under my thin-soled shoes, the smell of pine, a Necco wafer of moon in the sky. Some sense memories fade as soon as they're past. Others are etched in your mind for the rest of your life. This, I already know, is one of those.

When we get to the Grange Hall, Ramona and Eloise are chatting and dancing with whatever stray boys they can round up, gaily pulling them out of chairs. The makeshift band, fiddle and piano and standing bass, is composed of some of the boys I grew up with, Billy Grover and Michael Verzaleno and Walter Brown. They play raucous, sloppy versions of "The Maple Leaf Rag" and "It's a Long Way to Tipperary." Walton croons in my ear: "Leave the Strand and Piccadilly, or you'll be to blame, for love has fairly drove me silly—hoping you're the same!"

When they start to play "Danny Boy," I listen to the words as if I've never heard them before, as if they were written just for me.

> The summer's gone, and all the roses dying,
> It's you, it's you must go and I must bide . . .
> It's I'll be here in sunshine or in shadow—
> Oh, Danny boy, oh Danny boy, I love you so

We dance nose to nose, Walton's hand low on my waist, a tacit reminder of our moment in the woods. "I'll miss this," he says. "I'll miss you."

My voice chokes in my throat. I don't trust myself to speak.

After the last song, we make our way home on the dark road with the others. My legs are tired, but melancholy makes me even slower, like a dog on a leash being pulled where it doesn't want to go. Walton puts his arm around me and we fall back, away from the others. At the turnoff for the Carles' we linger by the gate. I lean my head on his shoulder.

"I wish I could reach up and grab a faraway star and put it on your finger," Walton says. Running a finger over my lips, he bends down to kiss me. I feel in his kiss the weight of his promise.

TEN DAYS LATER I receive a letter postmarked Massachusetts. "Remember a week ago tonight? I shall remember it until I see you again," he writes. "What promises I make, I keep."

DECEMBER IS AS gray as my mood. I haven't received a letter from Walton since September.

Though it's cold, there's little snow. A cat has been hiding under the house, a butterscotch tiger-striped Maine coon with enormous ginger eyes. I tempt it out with a bowl of milk. Shivering, it laps the milk hungrily, and when the bowl is empty, I lift it onto my lap. A female. Her skin is loose around her bones; it's like cradling a bag of hollow pipes. She licks my chin with a sea-urchin tongue and settles on my lap with a purr. I name her Lolly. She's the only bright spot of my entire month.

For Christmas I give my brothers plaid shirts I've sewn out of flannel while they were working outside. Mother knits socks and hats. Papa makes no pretense of giving presents; he says the roof over our heads is present enough. Sam gives me a baking tray, Fred puts a ribbon on a new straw broom, Al carves a set of wooden spoons. Walton sends a thick cream-colored card foil-stamped with a green wreath and a red bow, addressed to The Olson Family. "Sending you warm wishes in this cold season. Happy Christmas and God Bless!" He signs it "Walton Hall."

Instead of displaying his card, as I've done in past years, I take it upstairs to my room. I take the stack of his letters from the shelf where I keep them, untie the pale pink ribbon, and sit on my bed, opening the letters and reading each one. *All roads lead back to Cushing for me. What promises I make, I keep. With love.* I hold the Christmas card between my hands so tightly that it rips a little. Slowly, I tear it down the middle, then rip the pieces again and again until they're as small as butterscotch candies, as two-cent stamps, as faraway stars in the sky.

I WRITE TO Walton after the holidays, wishing him a happy 1917, telling him about the presents I received from my brothers and the flannel shirts I sewed. I describe the suckling pig we roasted in a pit Al built in the yard, the blueberry compote and fried apple cake, the chicken stew with squash dumplings and the drink Sam concocts on New Year's Eve: rum, molasses, and cloves in a mug with boiling water, blended with a cinnamon stick. Whaler's Toddy, it's called. I strive to convey the flavor of our humble rituals, the camaraderie and clamor of a house filled with boys, a feeling of well-being and holiday cheer that isn't so much exaggerated in the telling as enhanced. I do my best to avoid a plaintive undertow.

I don't understand. Why haven't you written?

Days pass, weeks. Months. I thought I was used to waiting. This is a new kind of hell. My soul feels coated with tar.

I berate myself for the letter I sent, filled with mindless chatter about our simple rituals. What I have to share is paltry, insignificant, domestic. And yet it's all I have to give.

As winter turns to spring I slog to the post office, zigzagging through the snow and slush. Bills, flyers, the *Saturday Evening Post*. "Nothing for you today, Christina," Bertha Dorset says, her prim voice threaded with pity. I want to lunge across the counter and throttle her until her face purples and she gasps for breath. But I take the mail and smile.

Even when the snow melts and the crocuses bloom I am cold, always cold, no matter how many blankets I pile on my bed. In the middle of the night, I listen to the wind screaming through gaps in the wall. I remember a story I read once about a woman who goes mad trapped inside her house and comes to believe that she lives behind the wallpaper. I am beginning to wonder if I will stay in this house forever, creeping up and down the stairs like the woman in that story.

IT IS A warm morning in May when I see Ramona out the kitchen window, striding toward the house across the grass, head down, shoulders squared. I've thought about this day all winter. I sink into my old chair beside the red geraniums. Lolly springs onto my lap and I stroke her back. Ordinarily I would get up, put a kettle on for tea, stand in the doorway to welcome her, but I can't rally the energy to cover the conversation that I know is coming with the rituals of a friendly visit.

Ramona isn't surprised to find me in the kitchen. "Hello, Christina. Mind if I come in?" Her smile is wobbly. Stepping across the threshold into the gloom, she squints. "So good to see you."

I muster a smile in response. "You too."

"Did I catch you in the middle of something?"

"Just the usual."

"You look well."

I know I don't. I'm wearing an old apron over a plain checked dress. "I wasn't expecting company." I start to untie the back of the apron.

"Oh, please don't change," she says, adding quickly, "It's just me."

"I'm done with the lunch dishes. About to take it off anyway."

She watches me wrestle with the tie in the back. I can tell she wants to help but knows I wouldn't like it.

For a moment she hesitates in the middle of the floor. She's clutching a paper bag and wearing a style of dress I haven't seen before, yellow and white checkerboard patterned with full white sleeves and three tortoiseshell buttons, a drapey white collar, and a wide waistband. Pale stockings and white leather shoes. Her hair is pulled back in a bun with a yellow ribbon.

"That's a nice dress," I say, though her outfit makes me think she must be stopping through on her way to somewhere more exciting.

"Oh, thank you. It's summery, don't you think?"

"I guess."

As if suddenly remembering, she says, "I brought you something! Mama had a crate sent from Florida." She takes three large oranges out of her bag and sets them on the table. "I'd love to get down to Florida one of these days. I can just see myself lying on a beach on a towel with a big straw hat. Wouldn't that be nice?"

"Maybe so."

"How about we go together? In the winter sometime, when it's so dang cold."

I shrug. "I'm not keen on burning in the sun."

"I forget about your Swedish skin," she says. "Why don't I peel us an orange and I can dream about Florida and you enjoy a healthy treat?"

"Well, I just ate lunch . . ." I begin, then relent. "All right."

She digs into an orange with her thumbs and peels back the thick cratered crust, carefully picks off the white veins. Pulling it apart, she hands me a slice. "Cheers!"

The orange is so sweet, so juicy, that I almost forget how nervous I am.

When we've polished it off, Ramona pulls Al's rocker toward the table and sits down. "I love this old rocker," she says. "So lived in." She rubs the arms where the black paint has worn through to wood.

It's only now, with her hands draped over the arms of the rocker, that I notice a sparkle on her finger—a ring. "My goodness, is that—?"

She blushes deeply, then leans forward and thrusts her splayed fingers toward me. "Yes! Can you believe it? Engaged. I wondered when you'd notice." The false cheer in her voice is evidence of how awkward this is for both of us. "I would've written to let you know, but it happened only a few weeks ago."

The ring, with a sizable central diamond encircled by a pattern of tiny diamond chips, is more ornate than any I've ever seen. I tell her honestly, "It's beautiful. From Harland, I assume?"

She laughs. "Of course Harland. It got quite serious quite suddenly. We plan to marry in the fall, just a small family wedding. There's lots to do, goodness! But I'm so glad to be back here now. And to see you."

"Well." I think of portly Harland in his funny short-brimmed hat. "Congratulations."

"Thank you. It means the world to have your blessing." Spying Lolly sidling through the doorway, she cries, "Oh, what a pretty cat! So big."

"She's a Maine coon. They're little tigers."

"Here, kitty." She clucks her tongue and snaps her fingers.

Lolly freezes, looks back and forth between us.

"She won't come," I say. "She's stubborn and shy. Like me." As if to demonstrate, the cat streaks across the floor and leaps onto my lap.

Ramona smiles. "You're not shy. You just like who you like. That cat's the same way."

Lolly arches into my hand, insisting that I stroke her, and for a few moments her steady purring is the only sound in the room.

A faint citrus scent lingers in the air.

Finally Ramona sighs. "I have been fretting about how to bring this up. Walton . . . I don't . . ." She shakes her head, twists one of the large buttons on her dress. "He's a dear, I adore him, but he can be so *exasperating*."

I can't follow what she's saying. Walton is a dear? She adores him? "He stopped writing," I say.

"I know, he told me."

I grip Lolly's back so hard that she meows and sinks a claw into my palm, then squirms out of my lap. A bead of blood springs to the surface of my hand. I wipe it on my skirt, leaving a pink smear.

"It was abominable of him. I kept telling him so. And— well—cruel."

Though I knew this moment was coming, not a single fiber of my being wants to be having this conversation. "Ramona—"

"Let me bumble through this, horrible as it is—I have to. Walton loves you—loved you, I suppose. Oh, Christina." She sighs. "Every word out of my mouth is as painful for me to say

as it must be for you to hear, and I don't want to do this, but . . ."
She stops. Then blurts: "Walton is engaged to be married."

Walton is. Engaged. To be. Married. Am I missing something? Engaged to be married to me? I look at her blankly.

Walton is engaged to be married.

To someone else.

In all the ways I've thought about his silence, considered its sources, this possibility never occurred to me. But why not? It makes the most logical sense. He stopped writing abruptly. Of course—of course—he met someone else.

I feel as if I am emptied out, filled with thick, heavy air. I can't think or see; it fills me to my eyes. I try to remember what Walton looks like. A straw boater with a black grosgrain ribbon. A linen jacket. Soft girlish hands. But I can't envision his face.

"Christina? Are you all right?" Ramona's face is stretched into a ghastly expression. I look into her eyes. It's as if I'm watching her through a scrim.

"Why." A tiny word, one syllable, not even a question.

She sighs. "I've asked myself a million times, and Walton too; I've begged him for an answer that makes sense. I don't even know if *he* knows, except . . ." Her voice trails off.

"Except . . ."

"Except." She twists in her chair. "The distance. And his parents."

"His parents."

"He told you, he said. That they—disapproved."

"He didn't say that."

"He didn't?"

Leaning back in the chair, I close my eyes. Maybe he did.

"His mother is an awful woman. A striver. She wanted—wants—a certain kind of life for her golden boy. And she kept bringing around the daughter of a friend, a girl at Smith, and I just think after a while he thought, what's the use, I can't fight it anymore; the easiest thing is to give in."

"The easiest thing," I echo.

"I suppose she's not a bad sort, really. She's all right." Ramona shrugs. "Though of course I never said that to him; I only told him how vexed I was, how disappointed. On your behalf."

By the way she's telling me this I can see that she has spent time with this woman, that they have all been out together. "What is her name."

"Marilyn. Marilyn Wales."

I contemplate this for a moment. A real person, with a name. "He never even . . . wrote to explain."

"I know. It makes me so angry. We argued about it. I told him it was unconscionably rude. He said he couldn't do it; he begged me to write to you myself, to tell you, and honestly I refused."

I feel as if I'm being whipped, every word a lash. "You knew I was waiting," I say slowly, my voice rising, "and you wouldn't put me out of my misery?"

"Christina?" Mother calls from upstairs. "Everything all right?"

I look steadily at Ramona and she looks back, her eyes filling with tears. "I am so sorry," she says.

"Everything is fine, Mother," I call back.

"Who's there?"

"Ramona Carle."

My mother is silent.

"He didn't deserve you," Ramona whispers.

I shake my head.

"Yes, he's smart, and he can be charming, but quite honestly he is a weak man. I see that now."

"Stop," I say. "Just stop."

Leaning forward in the rocker, Ramona says, "Christina, listen to me. There will be other fish in the sea."

"No, there won't."

"There will. We'll find you a great catch."

"I have hung up my rod," I say.

This seems to break the tension. Ramona smiles. (It was hard for her to be this serious! She isn't constitutionally cut out for it.) "For now. There'll be more expeditions."

"Not in this leaky boat."

She laughs a little. "You are as stubborn as a Maine coon, Christina Olson."

"Maybe so," I tell her. "Maybe I am."

WHEN I GO to bed, I never want to get up. There's an ache deep in my bones that won't go away; I jolt awake in the night sobbing in pain. Nothing will ever get better. It will only get worse. I pull the blue wool blanket Papa made tighter around me and finally drift to sleep. When I wake several hours later in the astringent light of morning, I bury my face in my pillow.

Al comes into my room. I can hear him, see him, though my eyes are shut and I pretend to be asleep. "Christina," he says softly.

I don't answer.

"I found some bread and jam for breakfast. Sam and Fred are in the barn. I'll bring eggs to Mother and Papa when chores are finished."

I sigh, tacit acknowledgment that I hear him.

Behind my eyelashes I see him look down, hands on hips. "Are you sick?"

"Yes."

"Do you need a doctor?"

"No." I open my eyes, but I can't rouse myself to an expression. He looks back at me steadily. I don't remember ever holding his gaze like this.

"I would like to kill him," he says. "I really would."

My bed feels like a shallow grave.

ॐ

I TAKE THE stack of letters from Walton, tied with their pale pink ribbon, and place them in a box. Part of me wants to set them on fire and watch them burn. But I can't bring myself to do it.

At the top of the first flight of stairs is a small closet door on the side wall. When no one is around, I slide the box into a dark corner of the closet. I don't want to see his letters. I just want proof that they exist.

IN TOWN NOBODY says a word about it, at least not to me. But I see the pity in their eyes. I hear the whispers: *She was abandoned, you know.* Their sympathy fills me with a shame so deep that I can understand why someone might sail off to a distant land, never to return to where he's from.

GETTING READY FOR a late afternoon sail with my brothers on a warm June day, I tuck the shell Walton gave me into my pocket. On the sloop I stroke it with my fingers, probing its rough crevices and silky exterior. It's the perfect weight and shape to nestle in my palm. Toward the end of the trip, as the sun dips in the sky, I move to the back of the small sailboat and sit alone, peering down at the scalloped water. How easy it would be to slip over the side and sink to the bottom of the ocean. Blackness, only blackness, and merciful unconsciousness. I taste the tears running down my face, salty sweet in my mouth. Before long, no doubt, my brothers will marry, my parents will weaken and die, and I will be alone in the house on the hill, with nothing to look forward to but the slow change of seasons, my own aging and infirmity, the house turning to dust.

Walton and I sat together at the back of the boat just like this. *I adore you,* he whispered in my ear. How devoted he was; he couldn't get enough of me, loved only me. Only me. His solid shoulder against mine, his long finger pointing toward the sky, the constellations, all the names I learned so eagerly: Orion the Hunter, Cassiopeia, Hercules, Pegasus. I look up now at the darkening sky, as solid as slate. The stars are washed away, present only in memory.

Closing my eyes, I lean over the side, the salt spray on my face mingling with tears. I weigh the shell in my palm—this cameo shell that has no place with the others. A store-bought trinket with no history, no story. I knew, deep down, when he gave it to me that he didn't understand anything about me. Why didn't I recognize it as a warning?

I feel a hand on my arm and open my eyes. "Nice night, isn't it," Al says mildly. "Careful back here. It's slippery."

"I'm all right."

He tightens his grip on my arm. "Come sit with me."

"In a minute."

"Did anyone ever tell you you're as stubborn as a mule?"

I laugh a little. "Once or twice."

We gaze out into the dusk. On the shore, faint lights glow in the windows of a faraway house. Our house. "I'll stay here with you, then," he says.

"You don't need to do that, Al."

"Wouldn't want anything to happen. Couldn't forgive myself if it did."

The weight of sorrow presses on my chest. I grip the shell, feeling its blunt knobs. Then I let it slip from my fingers. It makes a small splash.

"What was that?"

"Nothing important."

The shell sinks quickly. I'll never have to look at it again, or hold it in my hand.

WHAT PROMISES I MAKE

Hel-loo? Chris-tina?" A woman's artificially high voice comes through the screen.

"In here," I say. "Who is it?"

The woman pulls open the door and steps into the kitchen like she's stepping onto a sinking ship. She's of indeterminate middle age, wearing a worsted wool suit and stockings and pumps and carrying a casserole. "I'm Violet Evans. From the Cushing Baptist Church? We have a hospitality club, and—well—we've put you on our list for a stop-in visit once a week."

My back stiffens. "I don't know about any list."

She smiles with aggrieved patience. "Well, there is one."

"What for?"

"Shut-ins, mostly."

"I'm not a shut-in."

"Umm-hmm," she says, glancing around. She holds up the dish. "Well. I brought you chipped beef and noodles." She squints into the gloom. It's late afternoon, and I haven't lit a lamp yet. Until she came inside, I hadn't really noticed how dark it is in here. "Maybe we could switch on a light?"

"No electricity. I'll find a lamp if you'll wait a moment."

"Oh—don't go to any bother for me. I won't stay long." She

steps gingerly across the floor and sets the casserole on top of the range. "I spilled a little on my skirt, I'm afraid. Can you point me toward your sink?"

Reluctantly I direct her to the pantry. I know what's coming.

"Why, this is—a pump!" she says with a little surprised laugh, just as I knew she would. "My heavens, you don't have indoor plumbing?"

Obviously we don't. "We've always managed fine without it."

"Well," she says again. She stands in the middle of the floor like a deer poised to bolt. "I hope you and your brother like chipped beef."

"I'm sure he'll eat it."

I know she expects me to act more appreciative. But I didn't ask for this casserole, and I don't particularly care for chipped beef. I don't like her haughty manner, as if she's afraid she'll catch a disease by sitting in a chair. And something in my nature bridles at the expectation that I must be grateful for charity I didn't ask for. Perhaps because it tends to be accompanied by a kind of condescending judgment, a sense that the giver believes I've brought my condition—a condition I'm not complaining about, mind you—on myself.

Even Betsy, who understands me, is always wanting to improve my lot. She washes the dishes with her delicate hands and puts the crockery back in the wrong places. I find the broom behind the door and the dishrag drying on the back stoop. One day she showed up with a pile of blankets and sheets and plunked them on the table in the dining room. "Let me take those old rags you sleep on," she said. "I think it's time you had some fresh linens, don't you?" (Everyone knows I'm proud. Betsy's the only one I'll tolerate speaking to me like this.) She gathered up my bedcovers—which, it's true, had seen better days, especially the threadbare blue blanket Papa knitted—and hauled them outside, tossing them in the back of the station wagon to take to the dump.

"Don't worry about the Pyrex," the woman from the Baptist church assures me. "I'll collect it next week."

"You don't need to keep doing this. Really. We get along just fine."

She leans over and pats my hand. "We're glad to help, Christina. It's part of our mission."

I know this woman from the Baptist church means well, and I also know she'll sleep well tonight, believing she's done her Christian duty. But eating her chipped beef and noodles will leave a bitter taste in my mouth.

MOST SUMMER DAYS, around midmorning, when heat thickens over the fields like a gelatin, Andy is at the door. There's a new intensity to his demeanor; his son Nicky is almost three years old and Betsy is pregnant again, due in a month. Andy needs, he says, to produce some work that will support his growing family.

Sketch pad, paint-smeared fingers, eggs in his pocket. He kicks his boots off and roams around the house and fields in his bare feet. Makes his way to the second floor and moves from one bedroom to another, trudges up another flight to a long-closed room. I can hear him opening windows on the third floor that haven't been cracked in years, grunting at the effort.

I think of his presence up there as a paperweight holding down this wispy old house, pinning it to the field so it doesn't blow away.

Andy doesn't usually bring anything, or offer to help. He doesn't register alarm at the way we live. He doesn't see us as a project that needs fixing. He doesn't perch on a chair, or linger in a doorway, with the air of someone who wants to leave, who's already halfway out the door. He just settles in and observes.

All the things that most people fret about, Andy likes. The scratches made by the dog on the blue shed door. The cracks in the white teapot. The frayed lace curtains and the cobwebbed glass in the windows. He understands why I'm content to spend my days sitting in the chair in the kitchen, feet up on the blue-painted stool, looking out at the sea, getting up to stir the soup now and then or water the plants, and letting this old house settle into the earth. There's more grandeur in the bleached bones of a storm-rubbed house, he declares, than in drab tidiness.

Andy sketches Al doing his chores, picking vegetables and raking blueberries, tending the horse and cow, feeding the pig. Me sitting in the kitchen beside the red geraniums. Through his eyes I am newly aware of all the parts of this place, seen and unseen: late-afternoon shadows in the kitchen, fields returned to flower, the flat nails that secure the weathered clapboards, the drip of water from the rusty cistern, cold blue light through a cracked window.

The lace curtains Mamey crocheted, now torn and tattered,

blow in an eternal wind. She is here, I'm sure of it, watching her life and stories transform, as stories will, into something else on Andy's canvas.

ONE CLOUDY DAY Andy blows through the door with a grim expression and stomps up the stairs without stopping to chat as he usually does. I hear him banging around up there, slamming doors, swearing to himself.

After an hour or so of this, he plods back down to the kitchen and sinks into a chair. Mashing his palms over his eyes, he says, "Betsy is going to be the ruin of me."

Andy can be dramatic, but I've never heard him complain about Betsy. I don't know what to say.

"She's decided she wants to restore an old cottage on Bradford Point for us to live in. Without even consulting me, I might add. Damn it all to hell."

This doesn't strike me as entirely unreasonable. Betsy told me they're living in a horse barn on her parents' property. "Do you like the cottage?"

"It's all right."

"Can you afford to fix it up?"

He shrugs. Yes.

"Does she want you to help?"

"Not really."

"Then . . . . ?"

He gives his shaggy head a violent shake. "I don't want to be shackled to a house. The way we're living is perfectly adequate."

"You live in a barn, Andy. In two horse stalls, Betsy said."

"They're fixed up. It's not like we're sleeping on hay bales."

"With one child and another on the way."

"Nicky likes it!" he says.

"Hmm. Well . . . I think I can understand why Betsy might not want to live in a barn."

Picking at a patch of dried paint on his arm, Andy mutters, "This is what happened to my father. Houses and boats and cars and a dock that needed constant repairs. . . . You get in too deep, start hemorrhaging money, and then you're making decisions based on what will sell, what the market wants, and you're ruined. Goddamn *ruined*. This is how it starts."

"Fixing up a cottage isn't quite the same as all that."

Andy narrows his eyes and gives me a curious smile. Except for my unhappiness with his portrait, I've never really disagreed with him. I can tell it startles him.

"I've known Betsy since she was a girl," I say. "She doesn't care about material things."

"Sure she does. Not as much as some women, maybe. But I would never have married those women. You bet she cares. She wants a nice house and a new car . . ." He sighs heavily.

"She's not like that."

"You don't know, Christina."

"I've known her a lot longer than you have."

"Well, that's true," he concedes.

"Did she tell you how we met?"

"Sure, she was bored one summer and started coming to visit."

"Not just to visit. She knocked on the door one day—she was only nine or ten—and came in, and looked around, and set to work washing dishes. Then she started showing up every day or so to help out around the house. She didn't want anything for it. She was just being . . . herself. She used to braid my hair . . ." I think about Betsy pulling the clips from my long hair and working through it with a wide comb, patiently teasing out tangles. My eyes closed, head tilted back, the sky orange inside my lids. The strands of hair caught in her brush threaded with silver. Her small hands strong and firm as she separated my hair into three strands and wove them together.

Andy sighs. "Look, I'm not saying she isn't a lovely person. Of course she is. But girls grow into women, and women want certain things. And I don't want to think about any of that. I just want to paint."

"You do paint," I say with rising impatience. "All the time."

"It's the pressure I'm talking about. It's hard not to be— influenced."

"But you aren't. You wouldn't be. It's all about the work, you always say that. *She* always says that."

He sits there for a minute, drumming his fingers on his knee. I can tell there's more he wants to say that he isn't sure how to articulate. "My father loved all that stuff, you know. The trappings of fame. It just makes me angry."

"What makes you angry? That he valued that stuff, you mean?"

"Yeah. No. I don't know." He stands abruptly and goes to the window. "I was almost hit by the same train that killed him, did you know that? At the same intersection, several years ago. I was driving along, thinking about something else, and I looked up and jammed the brakes at the last second and the train went firing past. So I know what it was like for him to see that train bearing down. The horror of it. The futility of realizing there's nothing you can do." He hesitates, then adds, "And I'm filled with rage. At—at losing him. Losing him too soon."

Ah, all right, I think.

"I'm angry at losing him, but I'm also angry at the waste," he says. "The time wasted, the energy squandered on meaningless possessions, the compromises . . . I don't want to make the same mistakes."

I think of the mistakes my own father made toward the end of his life. I know how the death of a parent can be both a release and a reckoning.

"You won't."

"I'm about to."

"Let me make you a cup of tea," I say.

He shakes his head. "No. I'm going back up. Rage is good for the work. I'll pour it in. And sorrow, and love, all mixed together." Standing in the doorway, gripping the frame, he says, "Poor Betsy, it's not her fault. She wanted a normal life and she got me instead."

"I think she knew what she was in for."

"Well, if she didn't, she does now," he says.

For the first time in years, the summer days hold more hours than I know what to do with. I order wallpaper from a catalog in the Fales store and enlist Mother's help in transforming the rooms downstairs. (If this is to be my home, let it at least be papered with small pink flowers on a field of white.) Mother persuades me to join groups I've previously disdained—the Friendly Club, the Helpful Women's Club, the South Cushing Baptist Church sewing circle, with their ice cream socials and apron sales and weekly meetings. I borrow books from the library that Walton didn't recommend. (*Ethan Frome* in particular, with its bleak New England winters, its agonizing compromises and tragic mistakes, keeps me up at night.) I take sewing orders for dresses and nightgowns and slips from ladies in town. I even agree to go to the Grange Hall on a Friday night with Ramona and Eloise and my brothers, though when I hear the cheerful piano and fiddle music wafting through the trees as we get closer—"Tiger Rag" and "Lady of the Lake"—I want to vanish into the woods.

As soon as we arrive, everyone disperses. "You poor dear!" Gertrude Gibbons yelps from across the room when she spots me. She rushes over and grabs my hand. "We were all so sorry to hear."

"I'm fine, Gertrude," I say, attempting to fend her off.

"Oh, I know you have to say that," she stage whispers. "You are so *brave*, Christina."

"I'm not."

She squeezes my hand. "You are, you are! After all you've been through. I would crawl into a hole."

"No, you wouldn't."

"I would! I would just collapse. You are so . . ." She sticks her lip out in a pretend pout. "You always make the best of things. I admire that *so much*."

And just like that, I've had enough. I close my eyes, take a breath, open them. "Well, see, now, I admire *you*."

She puts a hand on her chest. "Really?"

"Yes. I think it would be hard to have such a slender sister, when you try so desperately to watch your weight. That doesn't seem fair at all."

She stands erect. Pulls her stomach in. Bites her lip. "I hardly think—"

"It must be very difficult." Reaching out, I pat her shoulder. "Everybody says so."

I know I'm being unkind, but I can't help myself. And I don't regret it when I see the hurt look on her face. My heart is shattered, and all that's left are jagged shards.

MOTHER HAS BEGUN spending entire days in her bedroom with the shades drawn. Dr. Heald comes and goes, trying to figure out what is wrong. I hover in the shadows out of his way. "It appears that she has a progressive kidney disease and possibly a heart condition," he tells us finally. "She needs to rest. When she feels up to it, she can venture out into the sunshine."

She has good days and bad. On bad days, she doesn't come out of her room. (When she calls for tea, I make my way up the stairs slowly, rattling the teacup in its saucer, splashing the hot liquid on my hand.) On good days, she appears after I've finished washing the breakfast dishes and sits with me in the kitchen. Now and then, when she's feeling particularly well, we'll take a picnic to Little Island, timing our walks to the ebb of the tide. We are quite a pair: a sickly woman short of breath and a lame girl lurching alongside.

Mother keeps Mamey's black bible, worn and faded from years of travel, on the table beside her bed, and often thumbs through its gossamer pages. Now and then she murmurs the words aloud she knows by heart: *We rejoice in our sufferings, knowing that suffering produces endurance, and endurance produces character, and character produces hope . . . For this light momentary affliction is preparing us for an eternal weight of glory beyond all comparison . . .*

One morning I come to the barn to bring Papa a jug of water and find him slumped against the mule in its stall, a strange grimace on his face. Startled, I drop the cup and stumble forward.

"Help me, Christina," he gasps, reaching out a hand. "I can't get up." His muscles constrict and spasm; his legs are so painful, he says, that he can barely move them. When I finally get him into the house, he lies on the floor of the kitchen and kneads his calves, trying to dull the pain.

Al goes to fetch Dr. Heald. After examining Papa, he announces that it must be arthritis, and there's not much he can do.

With Mother in and out of bed and Papa increasingly infirm, the duties of the household fall even more heavily on my brothers and me. We have no choice, or the whole farm will slide into entropy—animals unfed, the cows needing milking, tasks doubled for the next day. To get it all done I have to dim my brain, turn it down by notches like the flat-turn knob on a gas lantern, leaving only a nub of flame.

AS SUMMER TURNS to fall, envelopes with two-cent stamps postmarked Boston begin to arrive for me at the post office again. Ramona's "small family wedding," she reports, has grown, predictably, into a more lavish affair. Her dress will be modern, despite her mother's objections—a white satin V-neck with a skirt just below the knee, a wide satin belt, and a bridal cap veil (not, God forbid, her grandmother's, with its crumbling yellowed lace). "If suffragettes can picket the White House, I can express my emancipation from long skirts and old veils," Ramona declares. She will carry a bouquet of irises like the bride on the cover of *Hearst's* magazine.

The invitation—on thick cream card stock, hand-painted with pastel flowers—arrives in an oversized cream envelope. I stand in the road and read the words etched in florid black script:

Mr. and Mrs. Herbert Carle
Respectfully request the honor of your presence
At the marriage ceremony of their daughter
Ramona Jane
And Harland Woodbury . . .

Equally respectfully, on notebook paper, I decline to attend. My brothers are busy with the harvest and I must prepare for the holidays, but we all send our best wishes to the happy couple. (And later a silverplate tea service marked down on sale at a home goods shop in Thomaston.)

After the wedding, held in early November, I receive a honeymoon postcard postmarked Newport—"Such magnificent houses! All the ladies here wear furs"—and, a few weeks later, a note describing the sunny apartment in a new brick building that the newlyweds are renting in Boston. "You must come and visit in early spring. I know Al will be busy with the planting, so bring dear Sam," Ramona writes. "He needs an adventure, and so do you. It's neither haying nor holiday season, so no excuses. A few weeks only! Nothing will be disrupted."

The idea of traveling to Boston under such vastly different circumstances than the one I envisioned sends me to bed with a headache for the afternoon.

"YOU KNOW WE can't possibly go," I tell Sam when he confronts me with the letter, which I foolishly left open on the dining room table.

"Why not?"

"The distance . . . my infirmity—"

"Nonsense," Sam says. "I've never been anywhere. Nor have you. We're going."

Looking at tall, handsome Sam, with his strong jaw and aquiline nose and piercing gray eyes, I think of all those seafaring Samuels he was named after, setting off to explore the world. Sam is twenty years old. Ramona is right—he needs an adventure. "You go," I urge him.

"Not without you."

"But—Al can't manage the farm on his own."

"He's not on his own. Fred is here. And Papa will help."

I give him a skeptical look. Papa hasn't been much help for a while now.

"Al will be fine. I'm not taking no for an answer."

So it is that early on a March morning in 1918, despite my trepidation, Al drives us through the fog to Thomaston, where Sam and I will catch a train bound for North Union Station in Boston. The staircases and ticket lines, narrow hallways and train platforms are a bewildering obstacle course for both of us, made even more difficult by my tight new shoes. Sam carries both suitcases and an overcoat and still manages to keep a firm arm under mine, steadying me as we slowly make our way toward the gate. When we finally get to our railway car, we collapse onto the red leather seats.

A few minutes after we've left the station, Sam asks, "Got anything to eat?"

I had packed a few dry biscuits in my bag, but when I pull

them out, they crumble in my hand. Just as I'm thinking we might have to wait until Boston, the conductor, a red-faced man with a bristly mustache, happens along to collect our tickets. Sam fumbles through his jacket for them. "Let me guess," the conductor says. "First time on a train?"

I nod.

"Thought so." He leans over the seat. "Lavatories are in the next car . . ." He points a meaty finger toward the right. "And the dining room is four cars down. You can get a hot meal or a cup of tea. Or whiskey, if you prefer," he says, chuckling. His breath is briny, like lobster.

"Thank you," I say. But after he moves along, I tell Sam, "I don't think we should. We need to budget." We've brought $80 for the entire visit; the round-trip fare has already eaten up $5.58 each. But I'm also reluctant to make a spectacle of myself, jerking back and forth.

"What we need to do is eat," Sam says.

"You go and bring me something small."

Sam knows what I'm thinking. Four long cars. He stands with a flourish and holds out his arm. I take a deep breath and rise to my feet. But now there's another question: Do we take our things with us so they won't be stolen, or do we leave them here? An elderly woman with a face like a cellar apple leans forward in her seat across the aisle. "Don't worry, dears, I'll watch your bags."

The swaying of the train actually disguises my infirmity. Accustomed to having to work to keep my balance, I adjust to it more quickly than Sam, who weaves from side to side like a drunkard.

In the dining car, we eat ham sandwiches and drink tea with milk and sugar, gazing out at the rushing dark. For years I've dreamed of this moment—or rather, a moment like this. How different it is from my imaginings! My ankles are cold, my feet pinched in these new shoes, the air sour with tobacco smoke and body odor, the bread stale, the tea weak and bitter.

And yet—here I am, going somewhere new. How shockingly easy it was to pick up and go, to buy a ticket and board a train and head off into the unknown.

Portland, Portsmouth, Newburyport. We slow into stations one after another that never have meant more to me than words on a map. When we arrive in Salem, I think about our ancestor who lived here. I imagine Bridget Bishop standing on the scaffold, trying desperately to use the sentence against her to her own advantage. *If you truly believe I'm a witch,* she must have thought, *then you must also believe I have the power to harm you.* I've always assumed that John Hathorne trumped up those charges against rebels and misfits as a way of enforcing social codes. But now I wonder: What if he really did believe those women were capable of ensnaring his soul?

When we pull into South Station, it's dark and cold and we must take three different trains to get to the Carles'—one of them elevated, which requires dragging our bags up and down stairs. With Sam's arm under mine I concentrate on my steps, one foot up, the next one down. When I dreamed of a life with Walton, I hadn't thought about what it would be like to navigate city living. Everything comes back to this body, this faulty carapace. How I wish I could crack it open and leave it behind.

DESPITE MY TREPIDATION about being in Boston, it's exciting to be in a new place and easy enough to pretend that everything is all right—to chat amiably with Ramona as she fries eggs for breakfast, exclaim over her wedding gifts and the charming view of the cobblestoned street from the apartment window, play card games in the evenings at a square folding table in the living room with her and Harland and Sam. (Though I can't help flinching when Harland suggests we play Old Maid.)

But just under the surface, my heart feels raw, painful to the touch. Beneath my smiles and nods and exclamations, I drift through each day like a ghost, silently keening for what might have been. Here, in Harvard Yard, Walton and I might have rested on a park bench. At Jordan Marsh Department Store we would have selected furniture and dishes. On the banks of the Charles we'd spread a quilt for a picnic and I'd lean back against his chest, watching the rowers go by. At night I fall into bed exhausted, overwhelmed by a grief so overwhelming that I can hardly breathe.

In spite of my best efforts, Ramona isn't fooled. One morning she says, apropos of nothing, "It was brave of you to come." The two of us are sitting at the breakfast nook eating soft-boiled eggs in china cups and toast propped in a silver rack. Sam and Harland have gone for a stroll.

"I'm happy to be here."

She takes a sip of coffee. "I'm glad. It couldn't have been an easy decision to make the trip."

"No," I admit. "But Sam insisted."

"I know. He told me. But—you are having a nice time, aren't you?"

I nod, buttering my toast. "Of course, a lovely time."

"I want to tell you, Christina . . ." She sets down her spoon. "You must be wondering. Walton lives in Malden. He rarely comes into the city these days."

I look in her eyes. "I was wondering."

"I hope that sets your mind at ease."

"Does he know I'm here?"

"I told him. I felt I had to. In case . . ."

"It makes sense. You're friends." I can hear the bitter edge in my voice.

She bites her lip. "Family friends. From childhood. It's hard to just cut people off . . . even though . . ." Shaking her head, she says, "I don't know how to explain it. I feel like a traitor. I know how painful it was for you. He behaved abominably."

Ramona seems so sincerely distressed that I feel a trickle of empathy for her. "You don't have to explain. I understand."

"Do you?" she says hopefully.

"The past is past."

I know it's what she wants to hear. She smiles, clearly relieved. "I'm so glad you feel that way. I do too! And by the way, I know you said you aren't interested, but Boston is filled with eligible bachelors."

"Ramona—"

She flaps her hand. "Yes, yes, I know, you've hung up your rod. You can't blame a girl for trying."

A FEW DAYS later, Ramona says, "I can't imagine it's easy for you, Christina dear, all this perambulating around."

She's right. Every inch of Boston has been treacherous for me, from the cobblestoned streets to the crowded sidewalks. She and Sam and even bumbling Harland steer me into the elevator and down the steps, offering steady arms for our afternoon strolls. Even so, I trip and stumble. "I truly appreciate your help," I tell her.

"Oh, well—it's nothing. But it does seem, perhaps, that your situation is more acute than it used to be. I see you wincing sometimes. Are you in pain?"

I shrug. The pain has become part of me, just something I live with, like my pale eyelashes and skimmed-milk skin. But when I wake in the morning now, it takes several minutes of stretching and kneading before I can move my hands. And my feet often feel mired in glue; I can't walk more than four or five steps on my own without losing my balance.

"Christina, Walton told me he had a conversation with you about this some time ago. He said he urged you to come to Boston to see if something could be done."

I feel my face flush. "He didn't have any business—"

She raises a finger. "This is not about Walton. I spoke with a doctor—a very good doctor—at Boston City Hospital, and he thinks they might be able to help. It wouldn't be right away. Not this visit. We'd need to make an appointment. All I'm asking is for you to consider it. Look"—she sighs—"don't you want to have a normal life, with normal opportunities? You refused before, and . . ."

Her unsaid words linger on the air. I know what she's implying: that my unwillingness to consider treatment may have cost me the relationship. I feel a surge of anger. Yes—this was exactly what I feared at the time. That Walton's feelings for me were conditional. That he was telling me to get better, or else.

But the anger subsides as quickly as it arose. It would be nice to have a normal life. I'm tired of pretending to be strong, of hiding the fact that even the smallest chores exhaust me. I'm tired of the bruises and scrapes and the pitying looks of people on the street. Maybe this doctor could actually help me. Who knows? Maybe he can even make me well.

"All right," I tell Ramona. "I'll consider it."

She smiles. "Good! We just might get that leaky boat of yours patched up after all."

NEWSPAPERS ARE FILLED with dispatches from the front. *The Boston Globe* reports that the United States is sending nearly ten thousand soldiers to France every day. In Cushing we heard occasional stories about boys who enlisted, or, after the Selective Service Act was passed last year, were drafted. (My farmer brothers, like many in our area, were exempt.) We listened to radio reports. But here the news is not an abstract event, happening far away. Walking across Harvard Yard, Sam and I come upon several thousand young men in blue regulation sailor suits, new recruits attending Radio School. Boston Common is lined with Red Cross tents, where volunteers collect and pack supplies to ship overseas.

When the suffragettes who've been picketing in front of the White House for more than two years are disparaged in opinion columns, Ramona and Eloise are incensed and talk about it at length. They know the names of some of the ladies, the arguments for why women should be given the vote. They talk about these events as if they have a stake in the outcome. As if they have a right—an obligation, even— to an opinion.

"But this has nothing to do with us," I say.

"It has everything to do with us," Ramona replies indignantly.

None of the tasks that fill my days in Cushing are relevant in Ramona's world. It's as if she's playing house in her four-room apartment overlooking the street, four flights up, with no one to take care of but her well-meaning but slightly ham-fisted husband and plenty of money with which to do it. How different my life would be with electric lights and an indoor toilet, hot water that comes out of a faucet in the kitchen and the lavatory, gas burners on the stovetop that ignite with the flick of a match, cast-iron radiators that heat every room. If I weren't spending all my time stoking the fire, maybe I, too, would know what's going on in the wider world. Ramona attends the opera, the latest plays; she browses in the millinery store and the ladies' shops. She has a girl (Ramona calls her that, though she's older than us) who comes in twice a week to take the laundry, scrub the floors, change the bedding, dust the breakfront, and wash the dishes while Ramona sits at the table in her dressing gown reading the *Boston Herald*.

Ramona refuses to step outside without a hat and a dress in the latest style, freshly starched and ironed. I—who have two plain dresses, two skirts, two blouses, and two slightly crumpled hats to choose from—spend a lot of time waiting for her to get ready. "Oh, Christina, you must be exasperated," she says with a sigh, hurrying out of her bedroom, pinning on one of her many hats in front of the hall mirror while I idle by the door. "All this folderol, primping and pin curls and hatpins—I expend so much energy worrying about how I look! You just are who you are. I envy that."

I don't believe her. She is living the life she wants to lead. But I don't really envy her, either. Even without an infirmity it would be hard to adjust to these narrow streets clotted with buildings and pedestrians and endure incessantly clanging streetcars, blaring horns, squealing brakes, music drifting from doorways, human chatter. The Boston sky, watered down by lamplight, is never completely dark. I miss the thick, star-sprayed blackness of Hathorn Point at night, the soft glow of gaslight, the moments of absolute quiet, the view of our yellow fields and the cove and the sea in the distance, the horizon line beyond.

RAMONA AND EVEN Harland, bless him, are more than generous, but when it's time to leave, I am ready to go. The day of our departure is brilliantly sunny. Snow is melting into puddles in the streets. Yellow and purple crocuses in the park have burst overnight through the slush. I'm in my tiny bedroom, tucking my few belongings into my suitcase, when there's a rap at the door. "It's Sam. May I come in?"

"Sure."

When he opens the door, I look up. His eyes are sparkling and he has a huge grin on his face. "So are you nearly ready?"

"Yes. Are you?"

"Not quite."

"Well, hurry up then." I hold up a long skirt and fold it in half. "We don't want to miss the train."

He wavers in the doorway, half in the room and half out, his hand on the knob. "I'm not ready to go back."

I look up in surprise. "What?"

He presses his forehead against the door and sighs. "I've been thinking. If I'm going to spend my life in a tiny place in the middle of godforsaken nowhere, I want at least to see something of the world."

"Isn't that what we've been doing?"

"I think I'm just getting started," he says.

I'm having trouble wrapping my mind around this. "So— you want to stay on with Ramona and Harland? Have you asked them if they mind?"

"Actually, Herbert Carle has offered me a position as a mail clerk in his company and a room in their house. So I wouldn't need to stay here."

It dawns on me slowly that he's been hatching this idea for a while. "Why haven't you told me about this?"

"I'm telling you now."

"But what will . . . how will . . ."

"You'll be fine," he says, as if reading my mind. "I'm going to escort you to the station. And then I'll turn right around and go to work."

"Well, what about the farm?"

"Al and Fred can manage. Anyway, it'll be good for Fred to step up and help out more—he's been the baby of the family for too long."

I feel stung. "You've thought this through."

"I have."

"Without even consulting me."

He squirms in the doorway like a dog being scolded. "I was afraid you wouldn't approve."

"It's not that I don't approve. It's that I . . . I . . ." What is it, exactly? "I suppose it's that I feel . . ."

"Abandoned," he says. It's as if we both realize it at the same time.

My eyes fill with tears.

"Oh, Christina," he says, coming over and putting a hand on my arm. "I've only been thinking of myself. I wasn't thinking of you at all."

"Of course you weren't," I say, choking on the words. I know I'm being melodramatic, but I can't help myself. "Why should you? Why should anyone?" Turning away from him, I reach for a folded handkerchief in my suitcase and weep into it, my shoulders shaking.

Sam steps back. He's never seen me like this. "I'm being self-ish," he says. "I'll come home with you on the train."

After a few moments, I take a deep breath and dab my eyes with the handkerchief. Outside the window I hear the clatter of a streetcar, a honking car. I think of Mamey's wanderlust. Her desire to see the wider world. Her frustration that no one in the family seemed to share her ambitions. Why shouldn't Sam stay in Boston? He has his entire life ahead of him.

"No," I say.

"No . . . ?"

"You shouldn't come home."

"But you—"

"It's all right," I tell him. "I want you to stay."

"Are you sure?"

I nod. "Mamey would be proud."

"Well, I'm hardly sailing around the world," he says with a smile. "But perhaps Boston is a start."

Sam, as promised, escorts me to the station and puts me on a train. He looks so young and handsome and happy standing on the platform, waving good-bye as the train pulls away.

As Boston recedes into the distance, the domestic concerns that have receded from my thoughts swim back into focus: How is Mother's health? Has she been sleeping well? Did she manage the cooking? I think about the dirt I'll find in the corners of the kitchen, the piles of laundry that no doubt await, the ashes piled up in the range. The mule, the cows, the chickens, the pump behind the house . . . I look out at the horizon—horizontal bands of color, black to blue to russet to orange, a line of gold and then blue again. Heading north is like going back in time. When the train pulls into Thomaston it's cold and muddy and gray, exactly how Boston looked when I arrived there several weeks ago.

A FEW MONTHS after I've returned, Mother sits me down at the dining room table, a letter in her hand. Papa stands behind her in the doorway. "Sam and Ramona would like for you to go back to Boston to be evaluated. The Carles know a very good doctor who—"

"Yes, she mentioned it," I interrupt. Now that I'm home again, back to my familiar routines, Boston seems very far away. The disruption of my chores, the effort of the journey, not to mention the almost certain painfulness of the procedure and the far from certain outcome: It's hard to imagine why I would put myself through such an ordeal. "I said I'd consider it. But honestly, I don't think there's any point."

Mother reaches for my wrist and grasps it before I can pull away. She turns it over, revealing raised red strips on my arm. "Look. Just look at what you've done to yourself."

I've started using my elbows, my wrists, my knees to lift heavy pots, balance the teakettle and fill it with water from the pump, lug it to the range. My forearms are striped with burns. Partly for this reason and partly because over the years my arms have become thinner and more sticklike, I hide them as often as I can in voluminous sleeves. I yank my arm away, slide the sleeve down to cover it. "There's nothing anyone can do about it."

"We don't know that."

"I get along fine, Mother."

"If it continues getting worse, you will not be able to walk. Have you thought about that?"

I busy myself brushing some crumbs on the table into a pile. Of course I've thought about it. I think about it every day when I navigate the fourteen-foot-long pantry by using my elbows along the walls.

"Do you think you'll get along fine when your legs don't work at all?" she persists.

"It's decided," Papa says abruptly. We both turn to look at him. "She's going to Boston, and that's the end of it."

Mother nods, clearly surprised. Papa rarely asserts his opinion with such force. "You heard your father," she says.

It seems there's no use arguing. And who knows, maybe they're right—maybe something can be done to reverse or at least slow my decline. I pack two equally weighted bags to help me keep my balance, and Al borrows a neighbor's car to drive me to Portland so I won't have to change trains by myself. When I reach Boston, Sam and Ramona pick me up in Harland's brand-new sky-blue Cadillac sedan and drive me to City Hospital on Harrison Avenue in the South End—a stately brick building with giant columns and a turreted dome—where I'm admitted for a week's "observation."

A hen-breasted nurse pushes me in a wheelchair into an elevator, accompanied by Sam and Ramona, and up to a small private room on the eighth floor with an iron bed and a view of the neighboring rooftops. It smells of paint thinner.

"When are visiting hours?" Ramona asks.

The nurse consults my chart. "No visitors."

"No visitors? Why on earth not?" Sam asks.

"The prescription is rest. Rest and solitude."

"That hardly seems necessary," Ramona says.

"Doctor's orders," the nurse says. "I'll leave you alone with her for ten minutes. Then you need to let her settle in. You can come back to collect her in a week." Looking over at me, she lifts her beak. "There's a hospital gown on the bed for you to wear. The doctors will do their rounds later in the afternoon. Any questions?"

I shake my head. No questions. Except—"What is that smell?"

"Ether," Ramona says. "Horrid. I remember it from when I had my tonsils out."

"And overcooked peas," Sam adds.

When the nurse leaves, Ramona pulls a book out of the bag she's carrying and places it on the nightstand. *My Ántonia.* "I haven't read it, but apparently it's all the rage. Country life in Nebraska." She shrugs. "Not my cup of tea, but if you get bored . . ."

Looking at the book jacket, gold with bronze lettering, I realize that this must be the third in Cather's prairie trilogy. I read the other two at Walton's suggestion. A line from *O Pioneers!* pops into my mind: "People have to snatch at happiness when they can, in this world. It is always easier to lose than to find . . ."

"We'll ask the nurse exactly when you're being discharged so I can be here to pick you up," Sam says.

"I'll be counting the minutes," I say.

"If you finish that book, I can bring more," Ramona says. "Sherwood Anderson has a collection of stories everybody's talking about."

Once a day a gaggle of doctors, gooselike in their white coats, march into the room and gather around my bed, led by a specialist I come to think of as "Big Bug" because of his eyes, enormous behind oversized spectacles. The doctors instruct me to stand up, wave my arms, and stomp my legs, and then, muttering among themselves, troop back out again. They act as if I don't have ears, but I hear everything they say. The first few days they speculate that perhaps electricity will help. By day four they decide that electricity would be disastrous. Nobody seems to have the slightest idea what's wrong with me. On the seventh day, Big Bug releases me into the care of Sam and Ramona with a sanctimonious smile and a prescription.

"You should go on living as you've always done," he declares, steepling his fingers at me while the other doctors scribble notes on their pads. "Eat nourishing food. Live out of doors as much as you can. A quiet country life will do you more good than any medicine or treatment."

"I don't suppose she needed to travel all the way to Boston to learn that," Ramona mutters under her breath.

On the train home I squint out the window at a silver-dollar moon framed in a blue-velvet sky. I've done what my parents wanted me to do. They don't have to fret about a cure we didn't seek. This disease—whatever it is—will advance as it will. I think about the destructiveness of desire: of wanting something unrealistic, of believing in the possibility of rescue. This stint in

Boston only confirms my belief that there is no cure for what ails me. No matter how long I hold a stick with fluttering rags above my head, no trawler in the distance will be coming to my rescue.

Though I am only twenty-five, I know in my bones that my one chance for a different life has come and gone.

I pull the now-dog-eared copy of *My Ántonia* out of my satchel—I've read it twice—and leaf through the pages, looking for a line that comes near the end. Ah—here it is: "Some memories are realities and are better than anything that can ever happen to one again." Maybe so, I think. Maybe my memories of sweeter times are vivid enough, and present enough, to overcome the disappointments that followed. And to sustain me through the rest.

IF ALVARO HAD been born in a previous generation, he would have been a ship captain like our ancestors. His stoic temperament is ideal for sailing. His passion for the sea—up before dawn in all kinds of weather, out on the ocean as light seeps into the sky—is in his blood. But when Papa's hands stiffen and gnarl, when Sam shows no sign of returning from Boston and Fred gets a job at a dry goods store in Cushing and moves to an apartment in town, Al is the only one left to run the farm.

"This farm is in fine shape," I overhear Papa telling him one spring morning. "I've managed to save more than two thousand dollars. The horse team and the equipment are paid off. Now it's up to you to keep it going."

Later that morning Al clips our mare, Tessie, to the runner, guides her down to the shore, and loads up his dory—the boat he goes out in every day. He brings it up to the house, hauls it into the shed attached to the kitchen, and stores it upside down, high in the haymow, with all his fishing gear. Then he dry-docks his sailboat, the *Oriole*, on the tip of the point of Little Island.

"What are you doing?" I ask him. "Why put the boats away?"

"That time is past, Christie."

"But maybe someday—"

"I'd rather not be reminded," he says.

Over the next few months, thieves pillage the dry-docked

sailboat, stealing the fixtures and lanterns and even pieces of wood, leaving its decimated carcass to rot in the grass. The fish house behind the barn falls into disrepair, the tools inside languishing like relics from a long-ago era: decoys, bait barrels, boat caulking, lobster traps as dry and bare-boned as fossils.

In the late afternoon, when his chores are done, I sometimes find Al in the shed, fast asleep beneath the dory on a pile of horse blankets. I feel badly for him, but I understand. It's painful to hold out hope for the things that once brought you joy. You have to find ways to make yourself forget.

ONE DAY A deliveryman from Rockland shows up with a wheelchair, and from then on Papa is rarely out of it.

"What do you need that thing for?" I ask him.

"We should get you one, too," he says.

"No, thank you."

Papa's bones ache, he says, when he tries to do just about anything. His arms and legs have thinned and weakened; they're contorted in a way that's familiar to me. But he calls his condition arthritis and refuses to believe it has anything to do with mine.

Both of us are proud, but we wear our pride differently. Mine takes the form of defiance, his of shame. To me, using a wheelchair would mean that I've given up, resigned myself to a small existence inside the house. I see it as a cage. Papa sees it as a throne, a way to maintain his fleeting dignity. He finds my behavior—my limping and falling—undignified, shameless, pathetic. He is right: I am shameless. I am willing to risk injury and humiliation to move about as I choose. For better or worse, I think, I am probably more Hathorn than Olauson, carrying in my blood both intractability and a refusal to care what anybody thinks.

I wonder, not for the first time, if shame and pride are merely two sides of the same coin.

In a fit of optimism—or perhaps denial—Papa buys a car, a black Ford Runabout, for $472 from Knox County Motor Sales in Rockland. The car, a Model T, is shiny and powerful, and though Papa is proud of it, he is too infirm to drive it. I am too. So Al becomes the family chauffeur, taking Papa and the rest of us where we need to go. He drives to the post office every day, whatever the weather, and picks up the mail for our neighbors along the road, distributing it on his way back. He does errands for Mother in Thomaston and Rockland. The car provides Al a measure of freedom: he starts going out at night now and then, usually to Fales, where a group of men can be counted on for a card game, old Irving Fales making a dime or two barbering in the middle of it.

During one such evening, Al hears about a treatment in Rockland that supposedly cures arthritis, administered by a Doctor S. J. Pole. The next day he drives Papa into Rockland to find out more. The two of them come back talking animatedly about apples and surgery-free treatments, and at supper we pore over the contract Papa has been given to sign. The gist of it is that he will be required to eat many apples. There's a small orchard behind our house that he planted fifteen years ago; the trees are laden with shiny red and green apples. But these, apparently, are not the right kind. He has to eat a specific variety, one he can only get in Thomaston for five cents apiece.

I flip through the pages of the contract. "It is fully understood by me that while S. J. Pole believes that he can help and perhaps cure me, he in no way guarantees anything," it reads. "It is mutually agreed that no money paid by me for his services shall be refunded. I am of lawful age."

"Fifty-seven. That's lawful age, isn't it?" Papa laughs.

Mother purses her lips. "Has this worked for other people?"

"Dr. Pole showed us page after page of testimonials from people he cured," Al says.

"Katie," Papa says intently, putting his hand on Mother's, "this could be the remedy."

She nods slowly but doesn't say anything more.

"How much money is it, exactly?" I ask.

"It's reasonable," Papa says.

"How much?"

Al looks at me steadily. "Papa hasn't had hope for a long time."

"So what does it cost?"

"Just because nothing worked for you, Christie . . ."

"I can't understand why we have to buy apples when we have a perfectly good orchard full of them."

"This doctor is an expert. Papa could be cured. You don't want that?"

I once read a story about a man named Ivan Ilych who believes he has lived justly and is outraged to discover that he must suffer a horrible fate, an early death of unknown cause.

My father is like this. He is furious that he has become a cripple. He has always believed that industry and cleanliness equal moral rectitude, and that moral rectitude should be rewarded. So I'm not surprised that he is so eager to believe this preposterous story about a cure.

Papa signs the contract and pays for thirty sessions over thirty weeks, the minimum required. Every Tuesday Al helps him into the passenger seat of the Model T and drives to Rockland. At each appointment—which, as far as I can tell, consists merely of paying more money for mysterious tablets and cataloging his intake of those expensive apples—a divot is punched in his contract.

Papa has always run the farm with a firm hand, selling blueberries and vegetables, milk and butter, chickens and eggs, cutting ice and managing the fishing weir for extra money. He's always stressed the importance of saving. But now he seems willing to spend whatever this doctor tells him to in the hopes of getting well.

One Tuesday morning, about four months into the treatment, only an hour after Al and Papa have left for the weekly trip to Rockland, I hear a car door slam and look out the kitchen window. They're back. Al has a grim look on his face as he helps Papa get out of the car. After taking him upstairs to his room, Al comes into the kitchen and sits down heavily. "Oh Lord," he says.

"What happened?"

"It was all a ruse." He rubs his hand through his hair. "When we got to Pole's office, the whole building was shuttered. A few days ago, they told us, he was chased out of town by angry patients. A lot of people lost their shirts."

Over the next few months, the severity of our situation becomes starkly clear. Papa's two thousand dollars in savings are gone. We can't pay our bills. More infirm than ever, Papa is listless and depressed and spends all his time upstairs. I try to be sympathetic, but it's hard. Apples. The fruit that tempted Eve lured my poor gullible father, both seduced by a sweet-talking snake.

IT'S A CHILLY Thursday morning in October when Papa asks Al to carry his wheelchair down to the Shell Room. An hour later, a sleek four-door maroon Chrysler glides up to the house and a woman in a trim gray suit steps out of the back. The driver stays in the car.

Hearing a knock on the front door, I make a move to answer it, but Papa says gruffly, "I'll handle it."

From the back hallway I can hear some of their conversation: . . . *generous offer . . . wealthy man . . . desirable shorefront . . . doesn't come twice* . . .

After the woman leaves—"I'll let myself out," she says and does; I watch out the window as she ducks into the backseat of the Chrysler and taps the driver on the shoulder—Papa sits in the Shell Room for a few minutes by himself. Then he wheels awkwardly into the kitchen. "Where's Alvaro?"

"Milking, I think. What was that all about?"

"Fetch him. And your mother."

When I'm back from the barn, Papa has wheeled himself into the dining room. Mother, who spends most of her time upstairs, sits at the head of the table, a shawl around her shoulders. Al troops in behind me and stands against the wall, grimy in his overalls.

"That lady brought with her an offer from an industrialist by the name of Synex," Papa says abruptly. "Fifty thousand dollars for the house and land. Cash."

I gape at him. "What?!"

Al leans forward. "Did you say fifty?"

"I did. Fifty thousand."

"That's a hell of a lot of money," Al says.

Papa nods. "It's a hell of a lot of money." He pauses for a few moments, letting the news sink in. I look around—all three of us are openmouthed. Then he says, "I hate to say this, but I think it would be wise for us to accept this offer."

"John, you can't be serious," Mother says.

"I am serious."

"What an absurd idea." She sits up straight, pulling the shawl tight around her shoulders.

Papa raises his hand. "Hold on, Katie. My savings have been spent. This could be a way out." He shakes his head. "I hate to say it, but our options at this point are few. If we don't take this now . . ."

"Where would you—we—go?" Al asks. I can tell as he stumbles over the words that he's trying to assess Papa's state of mind, wondering if he and I factor into it at all.

"I'd like a smaller house," Papa says. "And with the money I could help you set up your own homes."

We are all quiet for a moment, contemplating this. Except for the time with Walton—which seems to me now like a fever dream, hallucinatory and indistinct, unrelated to my life before or after—I have lived in this house like a mollusk in its shell, never imagining that I might be separated from it. I've taken for granted my existence here—the worn stairs, the whale-oil lamp in the hall, the view of the grass and the cove beyond from the front stoop.

Mother rises abruptly from her chair. "This house has been in my family since 1743. Generations of Hathorns have lived and died here. You don't walk away from a house simply because someone offers to buy it."

"Fifty thousand." Papa raps his misshapen knuckles on the table. "We will not see an offer like this again, I can tell you."

She tugs at her dress, her jaw clenched, the veins on her neck like rivulets of water. I have never seen the two of them in conflict like this. "This is my house, not yours," she says fiercely. "We will stay on."

Papa's face is grim, but he doesn't speak. Mother is a Hathorn; he is not. The conversation is over.

Papa will spend the next fifteen years confined to a wheelchair in a small room on the ground floor of the house he was so eager to sell, rarely venturing outside. Al and I, with the help of our brothers, will scrape and save, learn to live with even less. We'll manage, just barely, to save the farm from bankruptcy. But sometimes I will wonder—all of us will wonder—whether it would have been better to let it go.

IN JULY OF 1921 Sam, laughing, gathers our family together in the Shell Room. Clasping the hand of his bespectacled choir-leader girlfriend, Mary, he announces that he has asked for her hand in marriage.

"Of course I said yes!" Mary beams, holding out her left hand to show us the modest engagement ring she inherited from her grandmother.

This news isn't a complete surprise: the two of them met in Malden, where Mary grew up, when Sam stayed to work for Herbert Carle, and have been together for several years. I watch as he moves closer and whispers something, as she blushes and he brushes her hair behind her ear. "I'm so happy for you both," I tell them, and though I feel a pang of sadness for myself witnessing their casual intimacy, I mean it. Dear kind Sam deserves to find love.

Sam and Mary's wedding is held on the "lawn," as Mary calls it, though we Olsons have never thought of it as anything but the field. Al and Fred build a pergola and set up two rows of twenty chairs borrowed from the Grange Hall. Over several days I bake rolls, blueberry and strawberry pies, and a wedding cake, Sam's favorite: lemon with buttercream frosting. Mary wears a lacy dress and veil; Sam is dashing in a dark gray suit. A three-piece band from Rockland plays on the bluff above the shore, where Fred has organized a clambake at the water's edge.

After their honeymoon, the newlyweds move into our family homestead to save money for a house of their own. I like having another woman around, particularly one as young and friendly as Mary, who is solid and kind and laughs easily. She is good company in the house, helping me cook and clean.

Sam and Mary settle into a bedroom on the third floor, away from the rest of the family, and soon enough, Mary is with child. Unlike Ramona—as reported in her letters—she has no morning sickness. We sit by the hearth as she knits blankets and I sew frocks for the baby, talking about the weather and the crop yield and the people we know in common, such as Gertrude Gibbons, who was married recently herself. (She sent an invitation to the wedding, but I didn't go.)

"That girl's got some border collie in her blood. Can't help herding and nipping. But she's all right," Mary says.

The image makes me smile, both because it's exactly what Gertrude does and because Mary says it so matter-of-factly, without rancor. I don't mention my waspish comment to Gertrude at the dance. It's hard to feel proud of that.

MONTHS LATER, WOKEN in the middle of the night by a low moan, I lie in the darkness of my bedroom, my breathing the only sound. Sitting up, I strain to listen. Minutes pass. Another moan, louder this time, and then I know: it's time for the baby to be born. I hear Sam's heavy footsteps down two flights of stairs and out the front door. The Ford engine revs; he's on the way to get the midwife.

I bend and unbend my legs, as I do every morning, and carefully swing them over the side, holding onto the spindle frame as I reach for my dress on the peg on the back of the door. In the darkness I pull on stockings and lace my feet into shoes, then make my way downstairs, leaning on the banister. Papa is in the foyer in his wheelchair, bumping around, muttering under his breath in Swedish, trying to navigate the doorways to get to the kitchen. He must've roused himself from bed, a task Al usually helps him with.

I fill the kettle from the urn of water on the floor, fire up the Glenwood, and take out oats for porridge and bread for toast as the sun rises in the sky. After some time, I see the car pull up in front of the house. The midwife steps out, carrying a large tapestry bag. Then the back door opens and Gertrude Gibbons emerges. What is she doing here?

"Look who I found," Sam says, stepping into the kitchen. "Mary thought it might be useful to have another set of hands."

"How are you, Christina?" Gertrude says, just behind him, smiling brightly.

"I'm fine, Gertrude," I say, trying to keep my voice neutral. We haven't seen each other since that long-ago dance, and it feels stiff and awkward between us.

"I know you have difficulty with those stairs, and your mother isn't well," she says. "I'm honored to fill the gap. Where is dear Mary?"

When everyone has trooped upstairs, I step out into the cool air of the backyard, shadowed at this early hour by the house. Al has been plowing the garden plot, and the dirt smells fresh and damp from yesterday's rain. Tessie neighs in a distant field. Lolly winds between my legs, pressing against my calves. Sinking onto the stone step, I pull her into my lap, but she yowls and slinks away. I feel low, heavy, weighted to the earth. Earlier in the spring a birth announcement arrived from Ramona and Harland: a girl named Rose, seven pounds, nine ounces. In June, Eloise married Bill Rivers, and Alvah eloped with Eva Shuman a few weeks later. I'm glad for Sam and Mary, for all of them, but every ritual—weddings, births, christenings— reminds me of how alone I am. My own life so barren in contrast.

Tears well in my eyes.

"Why, there you are!" Glancing over my shoulder, I see Gertrude's face cross-hatched in the screen. "I've been looking for you all over. The midwife doesn't need me at the moment. She says Mary is a natural."

I wipe my face with the back of my hand, hoping she didn't see, but nothing gets past Gertrude. "What on earth is wrong? Are you hurt?"

"No."

She tries to open the screen, but I'm sitting in the way. "Did something happen?"

"No."

"Can I come out there?"

The last thing I want to do is explain my tears to Gertrude Gibbons. She is here out of curiosity, after all, and boredom, and her endless desire to know what's going on. "Please, just give me a minute."

But she will not. "Mercy, Christina, if—"

"I said," I tell her, my voice rising, "leave me alone."

"Well." Affronted, she pauses. Then she says coldly, "I was coming down to help with breakfast. But I see you have let the fire go out."

I stand up unsteadily. Then I yank open the door, startling her, tears clouding my vision. I lurch into the kitchen. My awkwardness irritates me even further; everything is a blur, and Gertrude is looking at me in her usual obtuse, judgmental, pitying way.

I hate her for it. For seeing me clearly, for not seeing me at all.

I careen through the pantry, forcing her to step back against the wall. I want to be upstairs in my bedroom, with the door shut, but how can I navigate the stairs without her watching? And then I realize I don't care. I just need to get there. Leaning against the wall, I pull myself along the hallway until I reach them. I use my forearms and elbows to hoist myself up the narrow stairs, stopping to rest every few steps, knowing that Gertrude is listening to every grunt. When I reach the landing at the top, I look down. There she is, standing in the foyer with her hands on her hips. "Honestly, Christina, I do not under—"

But I won't listen. I can't. Turning away, I wrench myself along the floor to my bedroom, where I kick the door shut behind me.

I lie on the floor of my bedroom, breathing heavily. After a few minutes, I hear footsteps plodding up the stairs.

Then a rap on the door.

"Christina?" Gertrude's voice is laced with affected concern.

Scooting backward I grasp the bedpost, then turn around and

heave myself up onto the mattress, trying to slow my pounding heartbeat. Her presence on the other side of the door radiates a nasty heat; I am flushed with it.

Another rap.

"Go away."

"For mercy's sake, let me in."

There's no lock. After a moment, I watch the white porcelain knob turn. Gertrude steps into the room and shuts the door, her doughy face pinched with pantomimed worry. "What is wrong with you?"

I wish I could dart around her, but my only recourse is words. "I did not invite you here."

"Well, your brother asked me to come. Honestly, with three of you infirm in this household I should think you'd be grateful for it."

"I assure you, I am not."

For a moment we glare at each other. Then she says, "Now listen. You make breakfast for this family every single day of the year. You need to pull yourself together and prepare some food right this minute. Why are you being so hateful?"

I'm not sure I understand it myself. But my flinty anger feels good. Better than sadness. I don't want to let it go. I cross my arms.

She sighs. "We are about to welcome this wonderful new life—this baby! I'm sorry to be blunt, but you are acting like a child. Maybe nobody else is saying this to you, but I assure you they're thinking it." She runs her hands down the bedspread near my leg, smoothing the wrinkles. "Sometimes we all need a good friend to tell us what's what."

I flinch from her hand. "You are not a friend to me. Much less a good friend."

"Why . . . how can you say that? What do you mean?"

"I mean that . . ." What do I mean? "You take pleasure in my misfortune. It makes you feel superior."

Her neck reddens. She puts a hand to her throat. "That is a terrible thing to say."

"It's how I feel."

"I invited you to my *wedding*! Which—let me remind you— you did not attend. Nor send a gift."

I feel a little twinge. I'd forgotten about the gift. But I'm in no mood to apologize. "Let's be honest, Gertrude. You didn't want me at your wedding."

"Do not presume to know what I want or don't want!" she says, her voice rising in a hiss. Then she pokes at the ceiling and puts a finger to her lips. "Shh!"

"You're the one raising your voice," I say evenly.

"Christina, this is foolishness," she says, suddenly imperious. "No doubt it was devastating for you, what happened with that man. Walton Hall." Hearing his name on her lips makes me shudder. "But it's time to move on. You have to stop stewing in your misfortune. Don't you wish the best for your brother and Mary? Now let's forget this ever happened and go make some food for those hungry people."

Bringing up Walton is the final straw. "Get out of my room."

She gives a little disbelieving laugh. "Why, I—"

"If you don't leave my room this minute, I swear I will never speak to you again."

"Now, Christina—"

"I mean it, Gertrude."

"This is outrageous. In all my days . . ." She looks around as if some unseen presence in the room might come to her aid.

I shift on the bed, turning my body away from her.

She stands in the middle of the floor for a moment, breathing heavily. "You have a very cold heart, Christina Olson," she says. Then she wrenches open the door and walks out into the hall, slamming it behind her. I hear her hesitate on the landing. Then heavy footsteps down the stairs.

Muffled voices. She is speaking to Papa in the dining room. The screen door opens with a creak and swings shut.

WHAT PROMISES I *make, I keep,* Walton once said. His words were empty, but mine are not. Despite the fact that we live in a small place and are bound to run into each other, I keep my promise to Gertrude Gibbons. I will never speak to her again.

By the time my nephew—John William, given his grandfather's American name—is born on the third floor a few hours later, I've made my way downstairs to the pantry, where I wash my face with a cool cloth and tame my hair with a horsehair brush. I coax the fire back to life and lay a table with sliced turkey and pickled beans and fried apple cake. When my brother Sam places the small bundle in my arms, as warm and dense as a loaf of bread fresh from the oven, I look down into the face of this child. *John William.* He stares up at me intently with dark eyes, his brow furrowed, as if he's trying to figure out who I am, and my melancholy lifts, lightens, evaporates into the air. It's impossible to feel anything for this baby but love.

THORNBACK

Only traces of white remain on the sun-bleached, snow-battered clapboards and shingles of this old house. Inside, wood smoke, fuel oil, and tobacco have darkened the wallpaper. Sometimes it feels as if Al and I are living in a haunted house with the ghosts of our parents, our grandparents, all those sea captains and their wives and children. I still keep the door between the kitchen and the shed open for the witches.

Ghosts and witches, all around. The thought is oddly comforting.

Much of the time, these days, the house is quiet. I've come to think of silence as another kind of sound. After all, the world is never totally silent, even in the middle of the night. Beds creak, a wolf howls, wind stirs the trees, the sea roars and shushes. And of course there's plenty to see. In springtime I watch the deer, noses to the wind, trailed by speckled fawns; in summer rabbits and raccoons; in autumn a bull moose loping across the field; a red fox vivid against December snow.

Hours accumulate like snow, recede like the tide. Al and I drift through our routines. Get up when we want to, go to bed when light drains from the sky. Nobody's schedules to attend to other than our own. We hunker down in the fall and winter, slow our heartbeats to a hibernating rhythm, struggle to rouse ourselves in March. People from away arrive in cars laden with bags and boxes in June and July and head out in the opposite direction in August and September. One year melts into the next. Each season is like it was the year before, with minor variations. Our conversations often revolve around the weather: Will this summer be hotter than last; can we expect an early frost, how many inches of snow by December?

This life of ours can feel an awful lot like waiting.

In the summer I'm usually up before sunrise, lighting the Glenwood range and making porridge. (I rarely sleep through the night on my pallet; my legs throb, even in my dreams.) I'll scoop a cup for myself and eat it in the dark, listening to the sounds of the house, the gulls cawing outside. When Al comes into the kitchen, I'll hand him a cup of porridge and he'll take it to the counter and sprinkle sugar on it from Mother's cut-glass bowl.

"Well, I suppose it's milking time," he says when he's finished. He carries the cup to the sink in the pantry and dredges water from the pump.

"I can wash that," I sometimes protest. "You've got chores."

But he always rinses his cup, and my cup too. "It's no trouble."

When Al heads out to the barn, I sit in my old chair looking out the window toward the road to town in one direction and the St. George River, and beyond it the sea, in the other. The sun shimmers on the water and the wind carves patterns in the high grass. Around mid-morning Andy usually shows up, disappears upstairs, emerges for lunch, leaves in the late afternoon. With the door propped open, Topsy and the cats come and go as they please. Sometimes a friendly porcupine climbs up the steps, waddles across the kitchen, and disappears into the pantry. I might drift to sleep and wake to purring, which sounds to my sleep-clotted brain like a faraway motor. Lolly, seeing my eyes flicker, stretches toward my face, her paws digging into my shoulder. I reach under her rib cage, feeling through her warm skin the quick thrumming of her heart.

Later in the day I'll weed and prune my flower garden, brilliant with color—poppies and pansies and an assortment of sweet peas, pale blue, peach, magenta. Red geraniums grow fat and healthy in the window in their Spry shortening cans and old blue-painted pots. I fill vases with the white lilacs that have grown beside the shed for a hundred years alongside Al's favorite pink roses. The cats sprawl in the sun, blinking lazily. I can't imagine anywhere I'd rather be.

But in the winter, when it's so cold in the early morning that you can see your breath as you lie in bed, when getting to the barn requires a hoe to cut through the icy crust on top of the snow, when the wind slices branches off the trees and the sky is as dull as a stone, it's hard to see why anyone would live here if they have a choice. Heating this old house is like heating a lobster trap. The three woodstoves must be fed constantly or we will freeze. It takes eleven cords of wood to keep the fires burning until spring. Darkness comes early without electricity. Before turning in, Al banks the stoves high with firewood to keep the embers glowing through the night. I heat bricks in the oven to wrap in towels and slide under the covers. Many nights we are in bed by eight o'clock, staring at the ceiling in separate rooms.

Do our natures dictate the choices we make, I wonder, or do we choose to live a certain way because of circumstances beyond our control? Perhaps these questions are impossible to tease apart because, like a tangle of seaweed on a rock, they are connected at the root. I think of those long-ago Hathorns, determined beyond all reason to leave the past behind—and we, their descendants, inheritors of their contrarian tenacity, sticking it out, one generation after the next, until every last one of us ends up in the graveyard at the bottom of the field.

THE POSTCARD, STAMPED Tokyo, features a scenic view of an arched bridge leading to a mansion with a curved roof. "Nijubashi: The Main Entrance to the Imperial Palace," the caption says, in English, on the front, next to a string of Japanese characters. Though it's not unlike the half-dozen postcards I've received in the past few months of 1945, the scrawled message from John on the other side is a surprise: "Finally, Aunt Christina—I'm coming home!"

My old friend Sadie Hamm also has reason to celebrate: her son Clyde was injured, but he is coming home with only a flesh wound to his upper arm and some shrapnel in his legs. She's teary when she tells me the news. "It could've been so different for us," she says. "When I think about what others have to endure . . ."

The postmistress Bertha Dorset's two sons were drafted into the army, and her youngest died in France. And Gertrude Gibbons's nephew, who grew up in Rockland and was trained as a fighter pilot, was killed over the Pacific. I never would have guessed, seeing the soldiers on Boston Common all those years ago, that another world war would engulf us. I couldn't have imagined how much more there was to lose.

"You could drop Gertrude a note, you know," Sadie says gently. "I'm sure it would mean a lot to her."

"I could," I say.

"A lot of time has passed."

"It has."

But though I feel a pang of sadness for Gertrude, I know I won't reach out. I am too old, too stubborn. Her meddlesome insensitivity was something I could not—cannot, in the end—forgive.

And if I'm honest, there's something else. Gertrude has become a stand-in for anyone who ever pitied me, didn't try to understand me, abandoned me. She gives my bitterness a place to dwell.

IT TAKES SEVERAL weeks for John to travel by boat from Japan to Treasure Island in the South Pacific and, from there, by ferry to San Francisco, and another five days on a train to Boston, where he is officially discharged from the navy on Christmas Eve, 1945. He shows up at our house in uniform on Christmas Day with a chestful of medals, colorful packets of pastel-colored hard sugar candies called Konpeito that I don't care for, and a newly acquired, un-Olson-like propensity to hug.

John is taller, thinner, and flinty featured, but still as mild-mannered as ever. "I can't wait to pull my lobster boat out of the shed and get out on the water," he tells me. "I've missed this place."

He doesn't waste any time getting settled. By spring 1946 he's engaged to a local woman named Marjorie Jordan. "You'll come to the wedding, won't you, Aunt Christina?" he implores, taking my hand.

How will I ever get to a wedding when I can barely walk? "My land, you don't need me at your wedding."

"I most certainly do. You're coming if I have to carry you there myself."

I motion for him to come closer. I don't know what to say, but I want to say something. I'm touched that he wants me there. "I'm glad you survived," I tell him when he crouches down beside me.

Laughing, he kisses me on the cheek. "I'm glad I survived, too. So you'll come?"

"I'll come."

Sadie claps her hands together when I tell her the news. "What fun! All right, then, we need to find you a dress. I'll take you into Rockland."

"Not store-bought. I'm going to make it myself."

She looks at me doubtfully. "How long has it been since you sewed anything?"

"A while, I guess." I hold my gnarled hands out, palms up. "I know they look frightful, but they work just fine."

Sighing, she says, "If you insist, I'll take you to get some fabric."

The next morning Sadie helps me into her cream-colored Packard sedan and drives me to Senter Crane in Rockland. On the ride I begin to worry. How is she going to maneuver me inside? When she parks the car, Sadie leans over and pats my knee. As if reading my mind, she says, "Why don't you let me go in and get you some samples? What would you like?"

I let out a breath I didn't know I was holding. "That's probably best. Maybe a flowered silk?"

"You got it."

I watch her whisk through the revolving door. She spins out ten minutes later with a dress pattern and three squares of fabric. "Thanks to rationing, no silk," she says. "But I found some decent options." She hands me the squares: a sky-blue dotted Swiss, a floral rayon, and light pink cotton broadcloth. I choose the pink, of course.

At home, in the dining room, I spread the fabric across the table and study the picture on the cover of the pattern: a thin, elegant woman who looks nothing like me in a dress with a fitted bodice and a long paneled skirt. I take the flimsy folded pattern out of its envelope and lay it over the cloth, find the pincushion in my sewing basket, and attempt to secure it. I'm startled to find that my fingers are shaking badly. Only with laborious effort do I manage to pin a section of the pattern to the cloth. I slice into it with my heavy silver scissors, but the line is jagged. When I open the sewing machine, I sit at it for a few minutes, running my hand over its curves, touching the still-sharp needle with my finger.

All at once I'm afraid. Afraid I'll ruin the dress.

I sit back in my chair. It's not just the dress, or my wretched hands; it's all of it. I'm afraid for my future—a future of inevitable debilitation. Of increasing reliance on others. Of spending the rest of my years in this broken shell of a house.

When Sadie stops by a few days later, she runs her finger along the erratic line of the pins. Inspects the ragged cut. "You made a start," she says gently. "Shall I take it over to Catherine Bailey in Maple Juice Cove to finish it up?" She doesn't look in my eyes; I can tell she doesn't want to embarrass me. When I nod, she says, "Right, then," and carefully folds the pattern with the fabric, gathers the spools of pink thread and the instructions. Unfurling the yellow measuring tape from my sewing box, she encircles my waist, my hips, my bodice, scratches the numbers on a scrap of paper, and tucks it all into a bag.

SEVERAL WEEKS LATER I'm sitting in the kitchen, wearing my new dress, about to leave for the wedding, when Andy shows up, unannounced as usual, at the door.

Stopping abruptly in the doorway, he says, "My God, Christina." He strides over and runs his hand down my sleeve, whispering to himself, "Magnificent. Like a faded lobster shell."

In the summers, now, I make my way to the Grange Hall in Cushing most Fridays, but instead of swaying with the music and chatting with friends as they jostle on and off the dance floor, joking and laughing and carrying on, the bolder ones smoking cigarettes outside and tippling from a flask, I am consigned to the role of fruit-punch server, pound-cake cutter, molasses-cookie arranger. I pick up soiled napkins and wash dirty glasses in the sink behind a partition. Most of the women who play this role are older than I am and married. Only a few are my age: the unchosen and childless.

I have not gotten used to it. I'm not sure I ever will. For a while I continue to bring my dress shoes in a bag, as I always have, and put them on as soon as I arrive. But one evening when the hall is particularly hot, I excuse myself from the serving table, go outside, roll my stockings down, slip them off my feet, and put my flat-heeled walking shoes back on. What does it matter?

It's a damp Friday in August and I'm walking to the Grange Hall with Fred and his fiancée, Lora, wearing a white dress I finished sewing hours earlier from a new McCall's pattern, when I slip in a rut in the road. I put my hands out to stop my fall, but my arms aren't stable enough to support my weight. I drop heavily into the muck and gravel, tearing my sleeves, scraping my chin.

"Oh!" Fred shouts, leaping toward me, "Are you all right?"

My chin drips blood, my wrists throb, I am facedown in the wet, soiled dress it took me weeks to sew. The skirt is bunched up round my hips, my bloomers and misshapen legs exposed. Lifting myself slowly on my elbows, I survey my torn bodice. All at once I am so tired of this—of the constant threat of humiliation and pain, the fear of exposure, of trying to act like I'm normal when I'm not—that I burst into tears. No, I am not all right, I want to say. I am fouled, degraded, ashamed. A burden and an embarrassment.

"Can you get up?" Lora asks kindly, standing over me. She crouches down. "Let me help you."

I turn my face away.

"Doesn't seem to be a break," Fred murmurs, running his expert farmer's hands over my wrists and ankles. "But you'll have some bruises and swelling, I'm afraid. Poor thing." He tells me to flex my hands, not the easiest maneuver even when I'm not in pain. When I grimace, he says, "Probably a nasty sprain. No fun at all, but it could be worse."

Lora waits with me while Fred jogs back to the house to get the car. At home the two of them carry me through the front door and upstairs to my room, where Lora finds my nightgown on a peg and discreetly helps me undress and Fred gently washes my face and arms. Once they've shut the door behind them, I burrow into my blankets and turn toward the wall.

How did I go from being the maiden in a fairy tale to a wretched old maid so quickly? It happened almost without my realizing it, the transition to spinsterhood. Mamey said that in her day a woman who had not married by the age of thirty was called a thornback, named after a flat, spiny, prehistoric-looking fish. It's what they called Bridget Bishop, she said. *Thornback.* That's what I have become.

WHEN MOTHER'S HEALTH becomes so precarious that she and Papa need separate bedrooms, I offer to give up mine. She's in pain; her kidney issues are worse, her legs puffed with fluid. She has started sleeping upright in a parlor chair. I move downstairs, where my bed is a pallet on the dining room floor that I roll up each morning and tuck in the closet. It's not so bad; I'm closer to the kitchen and the privy, secretly relieved not to have to navigate the stairs.

In the mornings I prepare the noon meal and carry it through the narrow pantry to the round oak table in the dining room for Al and Papa and me, making a separate plate for Al to carry upstairs for Mother. Baked or boiled potatoes, green beans, roast chicken or turkey or ham, a stew of beef and carrots and onions and potatoes. Every few days I make bread with the sourdough starter. Watch the bread rise, punch it down, watch it rise again. In the summer and fall I can the berries Al rakes from their bushes and the strawberries he grows in the garden for jams and jellies, cakes and pies.

We mark the days by the chores that need to be done, the

way farm families have always done. Al feeds the hens and horses and pigs, splits wood in the fall, slaughters a pig when the weather turns cold, cuts ice in the winter. I collect eggs from the laying hens and Al drives me into town to sell them. He times the planting so that by the Fourth of July we'll have new peas and by September there's a whole field of corn. Gulls lunge for a feast, ravaging the crop, so Al kills a few and hangs them from poles as warning. During haying season in midsummer, I see him from the dining room window in his visored cap, scything the hay by hand with six hired men walking abreast, forking the newly mown hay onto the hayrack. They haul the hay to the barn, where a block-and-tackle hoist lifts it into the mow. Swallows, disrupted from their nests, swoop in and out.

In late July and August, blueberry season, Al uses a heavy steel hand rake to harvest the small dark berries from their low bushes. It's grueling work, stooping over those low bushes in the hot sun, dumping the berries into a wooden box to be winnowed and weighed, and all summer the back of his neck is burnt and peeling, his knuckles scraped and scarred, his lower back constantly sore.

Aside from the Grange Hall socials, the sewing circle I go to now and then, and the occasional visit with Sadie, I don't see many people. Most of my old friends and acquaintances are busy with their new husbands and new lives. At any rate, I have little in common with most of the girls I went to school with who are married and having children. I can tell, when we're together, that they are self-conscious talking about their husbands and pregnancies. But this difference only highlights what has always been true. I've never shared either their fluid ease of movement or their quick laughter. My wit—such that it is—has always been more sardonic, stranger, harder to recognize.

Now and then I leaf through the small blue volume of Emily Dickinson poems that my teacher, Mrs. Crowley, pressed into my hand. I remember her words to me when I left school: *Your mind will be your comfort.*

It is, sometimes. And sometimes it isn't.

With no one to talk to about the poems, I have to try to parse the meanings myself. It's frustrating not to be able to discuss them with anybody, but also strangely freeing. The lines can mean anything I want.

> Much Madness is divinest Sense—
> To a discerning Eye—
> Much Sense—the starkest Madness—
> 'Tis the Majority
> In this, as all, prevail—
> Assent—and you are sane—
> Demur—you're straightaway dangerous—
> And handled with a chain—

I imagine Emily sitting at her small desk, her back to the world. She must've seemed very odd to those in her orbit. A little unhinged. Even dangerous, perhaps, asserting, as she does, that it's the people who lead conventional lives who are the mad ones.

I wonder about that chain that held her. I wonder if it's the same as mine.

❦

MY CATS, AS cats will do, have kittens. Al takes boxes of them into town and gives away as many as he can, but before long I'm feeding a dozen. They swarm underfoot, mewling and jumping and sometimes hissing at one another. Al grouses about it, pushes them off the table with an open palm, kicks at them when they wind around his legs, mutters about solving the problem with a rock-heavy sack in the pond. "It's too many, Christie, we've got to get rid of them."

"Oh? And then what, I'll go around talking to an empty house?"

He chews his lip and goes back out to the barn.

LATE ONE EVENING, I'm lying on my pallet in the dark in the dining room when I hear a commotion upstairs, directly above me. Mother's bedroom. I sit up quickly, fumble for a candle and match, and make my way to the foyer. "Mother?" I call. "Are you all right?"

No answer.

Al is out with Sam, playing cards. Papa is sound asleep in his room. (There's not much point in waking him; he's frailer than I am.) I haven't been upstairs in months, but I know I have to get there now. I haul myself up the stairs as quickly as I can on my elbows, sweat dampening my neck from the effort. When I reach the top, I pull myself to my feet and grope my way down the hall to Mother's door, push it open. In the moonlight I see that she is on the floor on her knees, fumbling at the quilt in a kind of panic, trying to claw her way up back onto the bed, her nightgown bunched around her thighs.

She turns and gives me a bewildered look.

"I'm here, Mother." Stumbling forward in the dark, I collapse on the floor beside her. I try to help her up with my hands, my elbows, even my shoulder, but her weight is like a sack of flour, and I can't get any traction.

She begins sobbing. "I just want to go to bed."

"I know," I say miserably. I feel helpless and angry: at myself for being so feeble, at Al for going out. After a few minutes, her sobbing turns to whimpering, and she rests her head on my lap. I pull her nightgown down over her legs and stroke her hair.

Some time later—fifteen minutes? Half an hour?—the front door opens downstairs. "Al!" I shout.

"Christie? Where are you?"

"Up here."

Footsteps pound up the stairs, the door slams open. I see the confusion in Al's eyes as he takes in the sight of Mother collapsed on the floor, me cradling her head in my lap. "What is going on?"

"She fell off the bed, and I couldn't lift her."

"Lord a mercy." Al comes over and gently hoists Mother up onto the mattress, then pulls the quilt over her and kisses her on the forehead.

After he's helped me down the stairs and onto my pallet in the dining room, I say, "That was terrible. You can't leave me alone with her like that."

"Papa's here."

"You know he's no help."

Al is silent for a moment. Then he says, "I need a life of my own, Christie. It's not too much to ask."

"She could've died."

"Well, she didn't."

"It was hard for me."

"I know." He sighs. "I know."

SEVERAL MONTHS LATER, about a week after Thanksgiving, I wake early, as usual, to stoke the fire in the kitchen and begin the process of making bread. The floorboards above my head creak with the ordinary sounds of Al getting up and dressed and going to Papa's room to check on him, the muffled sounds of Papa's deep bass and Al's higher tenor. I scoop flour into the earthenware bowl and add a sprinkle of salt, my hands going through the motions while my head is free to plan the day: pickled beets and sliced ham, warmed in the oven, for the noontime meal; gingerbread cookies if I have time, a pile of mending . . . I add a scoop of yeasty starter, a dollop of molasses, warm water from the saucepan on the range, and start kneading, folding in the flour.

Upstairs, Al knocks on Mother's door—or perhaps I only think I hear it, so accustomed am I to his routine. And then I hear, sharply, "Mother." Furniture scrapes along the floor.

I feel it before I know it. I look up at the ceiling with my hands in the dough.

Al clatters down the stairs. Materializes, panting, in the kitchen.

"She's gone, isn't she?" I whisper.

He nods.

I sink to my knees.

The next day Lora brings a mourning bouquet to hang on the front door. It's round and black, with long streamers and artificial flowers pasted in the middle. Mother would've hated it. She didn't like fake flowers, and neither do I.

"It's to show the community that this is a house of mourning," Lora says when she sees me scowling.

"I suspect they know that," I say.

The wind blew so hard all night it swept most of the snow into the sea. Neighbors swoop toward the house like crows, in groups of two and three, black scarves and coats flapping. They rap on the front door, hang their coats on hooks in the foyer, file past Mother's body in the Shell Room. The women bustle into the kitchen. They know what to do in a situation like this: exactly what they've always done. Here is Lisa Dubnoff, unwrapping a loaf of spice cake. Mary-Violet Verzaleno, slicing turkey. Annabelle Weinstein, washing dishes. The men jam their hands in their pockets, talk about the price of lobster, squint out at the horizon. I watch some of them out the kitchen window smoking cigarettes and pipes in the yard, stamping their feet and hunching their shoulders as they pass around a flask.

These neighbors leach pity the way a canteen of cold water sweats in the heat. The slightest inquiry is freighted with words unsaid. *Worried about you . . . feel sorry for you . . . so glad I'm not you. . . .* The women in the kitchen stop talking as soon as I come in, but I hear their whispers: *Lord help her, what will Christina do without her mother?* I want to tell them, My mother hasn't actually been present for a long time; I'll get along fine. But there's no way to say this without sounding harsh, so I stay quiet.

In the late afternoon of the third day, we huddle around Mother's burial plot in the family graveyard, strafed by the wind, the sky as yellow gray as a caul. Reverend Carter from Cushing Baptist Church opens his bible, clears his throat. When you live on a farm, he says, you are particularly aware that God's creatures are born naked and alone. Given only a short time on this earth. Hungry, cold, persecuted, afflicted, released. Each one of us experiences moments of doubt, of despair, of feeling unduly burdened. But there is solace to be found in giving yourself to the Lord and accepting his blessings. The best we can do is appreciate the wonders of God's green earth, try to avoid calamity, and put our faith in him.

This sermon sums up Mother's life perhaps all too well, though it does little to improve the general mood.

Before we leave the gravesite, Mary sings Mother's favorite gospel hymn:

Oh, what joy it will be when His face I behold,
Living gems at His feet to lay down;
It would sweeten my bliss in the city of gold,
Should there be any stars in my crown.

Mary's lovely voice rises and lingers in the air, and by the end of the song most of us are crying. I am too, though I still don't know what those stars are meant to represent. My mistake, I suppose, is in thinking they should mean something.

ONE MORNING IN July I'm sitting in my chair in the kitchen, as usual, when there's a rap on the window. A slip of a girl with straight brown hair and large brown eyes is staring at me. The side door is open, as it always is in the summer. I nod at the doorway and she comes to the threshold and steps cautiously inside.

"Yes?"

"I'm hoping I might impose on you for a glass of water." The girl is wearing a white shift dress, and her feet are bare. She is watchful but clearly unafraid, as if accustomed to walking into the homes of strangers.

"Help yourself," I tell her, motioning toward the hand pump in the pantry. She sidles across the room and disappears around the corner. From my chair I hear the screech of the heavy iron arm moving up and down, the chortle of water.

"Can I use this cup here?" she calls.

"Sure."

She comes back around the corner, drinking noisily from a chipped white mug. "That's better," she says, setting the cup on the counter. "I'm Betsy. Staying up the road with my cousins for the summer. And you must be Christina."

I can't help smiling at her forthrightness. "How did you know that?"

"They told me there's only one woman living in this house, and she's named Christina, so I figured."

Lolly, who's been winding around my feet, leaps into my lap. The girl strokes her under the chin until she purrs, then glances at the other cats milling around the kitchen. It's time for their breakfast. "You sure have a lot of cats."

"I do."

"Cats only like you because you feed them."

"That's not true." Lolly sinks down, exposing her belly to be rubbed. "I'm guessing you don't have a cat."

"No."

"A dog?"

She nods. "His name is Freckles."

"Mine is Topsy."

"Where is he?"

"Probably out in the field with my brother Al. He doesn't like cats much."

"The dog, or your brother?"

I laugh. "Both, I guess."

"Well, that's no surprise. Boys don't like cats."

"Some do."

"Not many."

"You seem awfully sure of your opinions," I tell her.

"Well, I think about things a lot," she says. "I hope you won't mind my asking: What's wrong with you?"

I have spent my life bristling at this question. But the girl seems so frankly curious that I feel compelled to answer. "The doctors don't know."

"When I was born, my bones were kind of deformed," she says. "I had to do all kinds of exercises to get better. I'm still a little crooked, see? Kids made fun of me." She shrugs. "You know."

I shrug back. I know.

The girl raises her chin at the pile on the sideboard. "Look at that pile of dirty dishes. You could use some help." She goes over to the sideboard, makes a pile of dishes, and carries them over to the long cast-iron sink in the pantry.

And then, to my surprise, she washes them.

WHEN PAPA DIES at the age of seventy-two in 1935, he has been so unwell and so unhappy for so long that his death comes as a relief. For decades I did my best to care for this man who ended my schooling at twelve, who squandered the family fortune, such that it was, on a crackpot scheme, who expected his only daughter— possessed of an infirmity as debilitating as his own—to manage the household, and never once said thank you. I fed him, cleaned up after him, washed his soiled clothes, inhaled his sour breath; and his own discomfort was all he could see.

I have to remind myself that once I saw this man as kind and just and strong.

When my brothers and their wives arrive at the house, we go through the familiar motions of mourning, serving cake and tea and slicing ham, accepting condolences, singing hymns. The body in the Shell Room, the burial in the family plot. As I stand at Papa's grave I think of how he was at the end, miserable in his wheelchair in the front parlor, clutching a chunk of anthracite in his fist and gazing out through the window toward the sea. I don't know what he was longing for, but I can guess. His robust youth. His ability to stand and walk. His family of origin in the land of his birth, to which he never returned. A clear sense of where he belonged, and to whom, and why. Did he regret the calculations and miscalculations he made that opened up the world to him and eventually narrowed it to this point of land?

Though I lived with this man for my entire life, I never really knew him. He was like a frozen bay himself, I think—an icy crust, layers deep, above roiling water.

AFTER ALL THE mourners leave, I am struck by the vast emptiness of this house, stretching up three floors to the dormers. All these unused rooms. Sam and Fred have started their own family farms and gone into business together, manufacturing lumber and hay. Now it's just Al and me—and the wheelchair, taking up space in the middle of the Shell Room.

"It's yours if you want it," Al says. "Still in pretty good shape."

I look at the nasty contraption, with its sagging stained seat and rusted wheels. "I hate that chair. I never want to see it again."

His eyes widen. I guess it's the first time I've said that aloud. He stands there for a moment, sucking on his pipe. Then he goes over to the woodstove, knocks the ashes out of his pipe, and says, "All right. Let's get rid of it, then."

I watch as Al drags the wheelchair out the front door and down the steps, where it teeters to its side and crashes over. He disappears into the barn and comes back a few minutes later with Tessie hitched to the small wagon. Pulling on her harness, he leads her close to the wheelchair and heaves it into the wagon, then doffs his hat to me with a smile and leads the horse and wagon down to the cove.

About half an hour later I see Al through the window, trudging back up the field with Tessie. The wagon is empty.

"What'd you do with it?" I ask when he comes through the kitchen door.

He sits in his chair, takes off his cap, sets it on the bench in front of him. Fiddles inside his jacket, pulls out his old brown pipe and a pouch of tobacco. Finds a matchbook in his trouser pocket. Takes a pinch of tobacco, packs it into the pipe, tamps it down with his finger. Adds more tobacco, tamps it down again. Sticks it in his mouth and lights it, cupping a hand around it to protect the flame. Shakes out the match. Sits there inhaling the smoke and blowing it out.

I know better than to rush him. Anyway, we have all the time in the world.

"You know the boulder by the Mystery Tunnel? That drop-off below?" he says after a while.

I nod.

He sucks on the pipe. Takes it out of his mouth and blows a stream of smoke. "I rolled that wheelchair up to the top of the rock and dumped it over."

"Gone," I say. "Good riddance."

"Good riddance," he says.

For the rest of my life I will think of that wheelchair lying smashed and rusting in the salty water near Mystery Tunnel, a place that once opened me to a world of magic, of possibility, but that over the years has come to mean something else. A place where Walton spun his false promises. A path strewn with anticipation that ends at a pile of rocks. A repository for my broken dreams, the treasure vanishing as soon as I reach for it.

The wheelchair, fool's gold, in the depths below.

SADIE IS STANDING in my kitchen, dropping off a chicken dish, when she says, "Are the rumors true? I hear Al's got his eye on that new teacher at the Wing School."

My skin prickles. "What are you talking about?"

"Angie Treworgy, I think her name is. She's boarding with Gertrude Gibbons."

Boarding with . . . Gertrude Gibbons? "I haven't heard a thing about it."

"He would make some lucky girl a wonderful husband, don't you think?"

"No, I do not think," I say stiffly.

Al has started going out three or four nights a week, usually to join the card game at Fales. He knows I don't like being left alone at night, but still he goes. On Saturdays he often drives to Thomaston, where the stores and bars stay open until nine. Or at least that's what he tells me. Now I wonder if he's going instead to Gertrude Gibbons's.

I don't mention what I've heard about the teacher, but for several days I give Al the silent treatment. He doesn't ask why.

I hear no further news of any woman until a few weeks later, when Al mentions casually that he's going to help out a man who lives with his daughter down near Hathorn Point. "They could use some firewood," he says. "I told him I'd cut some logs for them later in the week."

"How old's the daughter?" I ask.

"What?"

"You heard me."

"Why do you want to know?"

"I just wonder."

He gives me a look and scratches his head. "Old enough that it's rude to ask her age."

"As old as you are?"

He shifts his feet. "Well, no."

"Is she even in her forties?"

"I'd say not."

"Married?"

Sighing heavily, he says, "Divorced, I believe."

"I see." A few days later, I ask Sadie, "So who's that divorcée down on Hathorn Point?"

"You mean Estelle Bartlett?"

I shrug.

"Lives with her father?"

"That's the one."

Sadie leans close. "Word is she's been married three times, each time to someone older and wealthier. Who knows, it could be idle gossip. But she does appear to be well-off. Bought her father a brand-new Pontiac. Why do you ask?"

"Al's doing some odd jobs for her father."

Sadie's eyes shine. "She's a pretty lady. Wavy brown hair. That devil, your brother! Good for him."

Al keeps to his routine. He does his chores in the house, in the barn. But more and more these days he comes and goes as he pleases.

It's a sunny Fourth of July, the day of the annual clambake down at the shore near Little Island. My sister-in-law Mary's in charge—she pickled carrots and made wild rhubarb pies; Lora fried chicken and made yeast rolls. They've gathered blankets and bonnets and cutlery and dishes and piled them into baskets to be transported to the beach. My only task this year is drop biscuits, which I could make in my sleep. I start on them early in the morning. By the time people start showing up, just before noon, five dozen biscuits are cooling on racks in the pantry. I've had time to change my apron, which I can never help soiling (a dousing of flour, a smear of lard), and I'm sitting in the kitchen when they arrive.

"You look well, my dear!" Lora says.

"Doesn't she?" Mary says.

I know they mean to be kind, but their chipper tone makes me feel like I'm a hundred years old.

While Lora packs up the biscuits, Mary helps me into the car. She drives to the grassy area above the water, where they set up a chair for me away from the treacherous rocks. A gaggle of children, my nieces and nephews and some of their friends, are already on the beach, skipping rocks far out into the sound, competing to see whose goes the farthest, whose skips the most, their voices rising and mingling with the cawing of gulls.

My fourteen-year-old nephew, John, the oldest of the bunch, climbs up from the beach to sit with me for a while. We watch the others play games in the grass: Red Rover and Red Light/ Green Light and Giant Steps and hide-and-seek. They climb pine trees and gaze out at the small islands like Al and I used to do, sailors on the mast of a ship, the fields below a yellow ocean. The adults lounge on wool blankets, poke at the fire, pour fruit punch, squint up at us with a wave and a smile. Only Al is absent.

After some time, I hear the familiar clacking of the old Ford engine up near the house. The motor cuts off. I twist around to see Al climb out, go around to the other side, open the passenger door. Out steps a slim smiling woman with light brown pin curls.

Estelle—it must be. My stomach lurches. He did not mention a word to me about bringing her here.

"Well, look at that," John says. "Al's got a girl."

Here they come, now, down the path, Al in front, grinning shyly, wearing a crisp white shirt I've never seen before, the woman behind in a blue dress, sure-footed, laughing, dimple-cheeked, swinging a basket in one hand and a straw bonnet in the other. I want to run away, but I can't. I am caught like a fox in a trap, squirming, panicked, stuck.

"Beautiful day, isn't it?" Al says. As if we were acquaintances running into each other at the hardware store.

"Sure is," John says.

I gaze at Al steadily, saying nothing.

Color creeps up his neck. He clears his throat. "Christina, this is Estelle. I think I told you I've been doing some work for her father."

"There's work that needs to be done at our house," I say.

Estelle's smile fades.

"How about we head down and see the others?" Al says to her.

She looks at him, then inclines her head toward me and John. "Nice to meet you," she says in a tiny voice.

"Likewise," John says.

They turn and pick their way down to the rocks.

John cracks his knuckles. "Well, guess I'll grab another slice of rhubarb pie."

I nod.

"You okay, Aunt Christina?"

"I'm fine."

"Can I bring you anything?"

"No, thank you."

When John goes back to the clambake, I watch Al and Estelle, smiling and chatting and pointing at a sailboat, accepting plates of food. I sit glowering above them like a hot coal.

Lora clambers up to sit beside me, then my brother Fred, bearing offerings from below: an ear of corn, still warm in its charred green husk, a bowl of clams, a slice of blueberry cake. I shake my head. No. I will not eat. Their voices falsely cheerful, they exclaim over the blue sky, the glassy water, those delicious drop biscuits, what a lovely dress.

It was on this very bank that I sat with Walton—how many years ago? I know what everyone is thinking. *Poor Christina. Always left behind.*

I feel myself battening down, fortressing.

Sam climbs up and sits on the grass beside my chair. "What's going on?" he asks, patting my knee.

I look down at his hand on my knee and then at him. He removes his hand.

"Nothing's going on," I say.

He sighs. "This is no good, Christina."

"I don't know what you're talking about."

"You are ruining this picnic."

"I'm doing no such thing."

"You are, and you know you are. And you're making Al very unhappy."

"If he's going to bring that—that gold digger—" I blurt.

Sam puts his hand over mine. "Stop. Before you say something you'll regret."

"He's the one who's going to regret—"

"Come on," he says sharply. "Don't you think Al deserves to be happy?"

"I thought Al was happy."

He sits back on his heels. "Look, Christina, you know that Al has always been here for you. And he always will be. To begrudge him this—this relationship feels a little . . . well . . . mean-spirited."

"I'm not begrudging him anything. I'm just questioning his judgment."

Sam sits with me a minute longer, and I know he wants to say more. The words are sitting on his tongue. I can guess what they are. But he seems to think better of it. He pats my knee again and stands up, goes back to the others.

A few minutes later Al and Estelle climb the bank and up to the Ford, looking away when they pass me. Even the children seem wary, giving me a wide berth as they play their games in the grass. Within the hour Lora and Mary are packing up blankets and putting food into hampers. When they pick me up and help me into the car, they don't say much, but their faces are grim.

Mary and Lora settle me into my chair in the kitchen and go back to the car for some foil-covered leftovers—"to tide you over for a few days," Mary says. After carefully placing the dishes in the icebox under the floorboards, she gives me a small strained smile. "You're all set?"

"I'm fine."

"Well. Happy Fourth."

"Happy Fourth," Lora echoes.

I nod. None of us seem very happy.

After they leave, I scoop Lolly into my lap. I notice that the geraniums have wilted in their blue pot with the crack running up the side. The fire in the range has died out. The air is damp, rain is on the way. And all at once I have the peculiar sensation of watching myself from above, in the same spot where I have sat nearly every day for the past three decades. The geranium, the cracked pot, the cat in my lap, the fire that must be fed, rain on the horizon, the road to town in one direction and the St. George River in the other, stretching all the way to the sea.

I don't know how much time has passed when I hear Al's car crackling up the drive. The door creaking open, slamming shut. Footsteps to the kitchen stoop, the squeak of the screen door.

He flinches when he sees me. "Didn't know you were in here."

"Yep."

"It's dark."

"I don't mind."

"Want me to light the lamp?"

"It doesn't matter."

He sighs. "Well, okay, then. Guess I'll turn in." He hangs his cap on the hook beside the door and turns to leave.

"She's been married three times," I say. My heart is thumping in my chest.

"What?"

"Did you know that?"

He inhales sharply. "I don't think—"

"Did you know that, Al?"

"Yes, of course I know that."

"And I hear she's . . . ambitious."

"What's that supposed to mean?"

"Her motivations are questionable. I'm told."

He winces. "Who told you that?"

"I'm not at liberty to say." I know I'm hurting him, but I don't care. I like the sharpness of the words. Each one of them a dagger. I want to wound him for wounding me.

"What 'motivations' could Estelle possibly have?" he says quietly, hands on his hips. "I have nothing to offer. Except myself."

"She probably wants this house."

"She doesn't want this house!" he spits. "Nobody wants this house. I sure don't."

I feel like I've been slapped. "You can't mean that. We have a responsibility. Our family . . . the Hathorns. Mother—"

"Mother is dead. To hell with the Hathorns. And damn it, we should've sold this house when we had the chance. It's become a prison, can't you see that? We're inmates. Or maybe you're the inmate and I'm the warden. I can't do this anymore, Christie. I want a life. *A life*." He slaps himself on the chest, a dull thwack. "Out there in the world." He sweeps his arm toward the window.

I don't think I've ever heard him string so many words together at a time. I hold my breath. Then I say, "I never knew you felt that way."

"I didn't used to. But now I see . . . I see that maybe things could be different for me. You know what that feels like, don't you?"

Al has never spoken to me so directly. I think I've assumed he didn't feel things as deeply as I do—but obviously I was wrong. "That was a long time ago. This is different."

"Why? Because it's not about you?"

I flinch. "No," I snap. "Because we're older. And this is where we belong."

"No, it isn't. It's just where we ended up."

His voice sounds choked. I think he might be crying. I'm crying too. "So what about me? I've spent my whole life cooking and washing and cleaning for this family. And now you'd just—throw me out with the trash?"

"Come on," he says. "Of course not. You'd be welcome with me wherever I go, you know that."

"I'm not a charity case."

"I never said that."

"This is my home, Alvaro. And yours."

"Christina . . ." His voice is weary, leaden. By the time I realize he isn't going to say anything further, he has already left the room.

IN THE MORNING I wake to silence. My first thought is: Al is gone. But when I look out the window, I see the Ford in the same place where he parked it last night. I go about my morning routine as usual, and as usual Al comes in from the barn for the noonday meal. He doesn't say a word until he clears his plate, and then he says thank you and heads back outside. As I'm setting newly churned butter in its earthenware pot in the shed, my eye is drawn to the dory, high in the rafters.

We should've sold this house when we had the chance. You're the inmate and I'm the warden. The words hang in the air between us. But as long as neither of us mentions them, we can pretend they were never said.

For the next few months, each morning when I wake up, I think he'll be gone.

Al doesn't bring Estelle to the house again. He doesn't speak her name. One day Sadie casually mentions that she heard Estelle met a man with two kids and moved to Rockland.

Over time, Al and I settle back into our old ways. But he is changed. A bird flies into a windowpane on the second floor, breaking the glass, and instead of fixing it he stuffs a rag in the hole. He leaves the old Model T to rot behind the shed. He rarely cleans out the woodstoves anymore, just shoves the ashes back to make room for new logs. Long winters strip the white from the house, exposing gray boards underneath, and he doesn't bother to paint. One after another the fields go fallow, farm equipment abandoned to rust. Within a couple of years, Al is farming only one small patch.

It's as if he has chosen to punish the house and land for needing him. Or maybe he's punishing me.

CHRISTINA'S WORLD

1948

In the middle of the field the earth smells like sourdough. Each sharp blade of grass is separate and distinct. Dainty yellow cowslips hang on their stems like tiny wilting bouquets; a yellow-and-black tiger swallowtail butterfly hovers overhead. It's a mild May afternoon, and I'm on my way to visit Sadie in her cottage around the bend. She offered to come and get me in her car, but I prefer to make my own way. It takes about an hour to get there, pulling myself along on my elbows, hitching my body forward. My cotton knee pads are frayed and grass stained. This close to the ground, the only sound is my own rough panting and the chirp of crickets. Blackflies circle, nipping my ears. The air tastes of salt and lavender and dirt.

I can't walk at all anymore. My chair has worn a deep groove into the kitchen floor between the table and the Glenwood range. I will not use a wheelchair. So I have a choice: I can stay inside, in the security of the kitchen and my pallet on the dining room floor, or I can get where I need to go as best I can. That's what I do. Once a week or so I visit Mother and Papa, crawling through the yellow expanse of grass to the family graveyard where they are buried, overlooking the sound and the sea. On mild afternoons I take a small pail with me and pick blueberries.

I like to rest in the grass and watch the fishing vessels as they pull away from Port Clyde, out past Monhegan Island and into the open ocean.

When I arrive at Sadie's, she's on the front porch waiting for me. "Mercy," she says with a wide smile. "Look at you. I'll bet you could use a glass of iced tea."

"That'd be nice."

Sadie disappears inside the cottage while I drag myself up the steps and lean against the wooden railing, breathless from the effort. She comes back out with a bowl of berries, a pitcher of iced tea with mint, two glasses, and a wet washcloth on a large tray.

"Here you go, my dear." She hands me the cool cloth. "So glad you came for a visit, Christina."

"It's a lovely day, isn't it?" I say, wiping my face and neck.

"It surely is. I hope we have a temperate summer like last year, not like the one two years ago. Remember that? Even nighttime was miserable."

"It was," I agree.

Sadie and I don't talk about much. A lot of our time is spent in companionable silence. Today the water in the cove shimmers like broken glass in the late-afternoon sun. The lilacs beside the porch smell like vanilla. We eat the raspberries and blackberries that she plucked earlier in the day, and drink the iced tea, the cool tingle of mint leaves slipping into our mouths like wafers.

The older I get, the more I believe that the greatest kindness is acceptance.

ANDY HASN'T ASKED me to pose since I complained about the portrait in the doorway. But one mild afternoon in early July, out of nowhere, he comes into the kitchen and says, "Will you sit for me in the grass? Just for twenty minutes. Half an hour at most."

"What for?"

"I have an idea in my head, but I can't envision it."

"Why not?"

"I can't get the damned angle right."

He knows I don't want to. I feel shy, self-conscious. "Ask Al."

He shakes his head. "Al's done posing, you know that."

"Maybe I am too."

"You're always posing, Christina. It's not as hard for you."

"What are you talking about?"

"Al is restless. You know how to be still."

Patting the arms of my chair, I say, "Let's face it, Andy, I don't have much choice."

"That's true, I suppose. But it's more than that." He strokes his chin, thinking. "You know how to be . . . looked at."

I laugh a little. "What an odd thing to say."

"Sorry, that does sound odd. What I mean is I think you're used to being observed but not really . . . seen. People are always concerned about you, worried about you, watching to see how you're getting on. Well-meaning, of course, but—intrusive. And I think you've figured out how to deflect their concern, or pity, or whatever it is, by carrying yourself in this"—he raises his arm as if holding an orb—"dignified, aloof way."

I don't know how to respond. No one has ever spoken to me like this, telling me something about myself that I didn't know but understand instantly to be true.

"Right?" he says.

I don't want to give in too soon. "Maybe."

"Like the queen of Sweden," he says.

"Come on."

He smiles. "Ruling over all of Cushing from your chair in the kitchen."

"You're just teasing me now."

"I swear I'm not." He reaches out his hand. "Pose for me, Christina."

"Are you going to make me look like death warmed over?"

He laughs. "Not this time. I promise."

AFTER ANDY LEAVES the kitchen to get his painting supplies, I slide off my chair, pull myself along the floor to the open door, and winch down the steps to a shaded spot in the grass. It feels cool and springy under my fingers. I rest there, waiting, propping myself on my arms. When Andy comes to the doorway and sees me, he squints. Walks down the steps and circles me slowly, cocking his head. Directs me: "Like this. Tucked under. Leg back." I feel like a heifer at the livestock fair. He has a pencil in one hand and the sketch pad in the other. Then he opens the pad, settles with a grunt on the stoop ten feet away, and starts to draw.

After a while, my back starts to feel sore. I say, "It must've been at least an hour already."

"It's not so bad, is it? Out here in the sunshine?" Andy looks at me and back at the pad, sketching.

"You said twenty minutes."

Holding the piece of charcoal aloft, he gives me a big smile. "Come on, Christina. You know a boy will say anything when he's trying to seduce you."

"That's for sure."

He raises his eyebrows.

I don't say anything more.

A few minutes later he says, "Hey, where is that pink dress? The one you wore to John's wedding?"

"In the hall closet."

"Would you put it on?"

"Right now?"

"Why not?"

I'm tired. My legs are throbbing. "We've already been out here longer than you promised. This is enough for today."

"Tomorrow then."

Though I roll my eyes, we both know I'll agree.

Early the next morning, I ask Al to get the pink cotton dress from the closet. He lays it on the dining room table and I shoo him out of the room before wriggling into it and pulling it down over my hips, then call him back in to fasten the buttons. When he's done he says, "I always did like that color."

Al's not one for compliments. This is as good as it gets. I give him a smile.

When Andy appears in the distance an hour later, I watch from the kitchen window. He makes his way up the hill with his tackle box, hitching one leg forward, pivoting slightly, grunting with the effort, and I find myself oddly moved by his sweet mix of bravado and vulnerability.

Strangely, my hands are clammy. Like a girl waiting for her date.

"Oh, Christina!" He gives a low whistle when he comes through the door. "You are—marvelous."

Despite myself, I blush.

"It's a nice day to be outside. Let's get something for you to sit on so you'll be more comfortable." He sets his tackle box on a chair. "I saw a pile of quilts in one of the front bedrooms." He disappears upstairs, emerging a few minutes later with an old double wedding-ring I made over one arm and his rickety easel and sketch pad under the other. "I'm taking these outside. Shall I come back and get you?"

"Well . . ." Ordinarily I would say no. But dragging myself down the steps and across the grass in this dress might ruin it. "I suppose."

I watch as he sets up his easel in the same patch of grass as the day before. He unfolds the quilt and lays it on the ground, pulling the scalloped edges to smooth it. Then he comes back inside to get me, standing very close, and puts his shoulder under mine as he pulls me up from my chair. I haven't been this close to a man I'm not related to since I was with Walton. I am acutely aware of my body next to Andy's, my fragile bones and papery skin against his warm solid chest, his muscular arm clasping my gaunt one. My senses suddenly sharpen; I possess the eye of an eagle, the ear of a cat, the nose of a dog. His breath on my face is sickly sweet. I hear a faint click between his teeth. My stomach lurches as my brain registers the smell. "Is that . . . butterscotch?"

"Sure is."

He doesn't notice that I turn my head away.

With his arms wrapped around me, under my elbows, to support my weight, he half walks, half carries me outside. My heart is beating so loudly I almost wonder if he can hear it. Gently he sets me on the quilt adjusting my legs, smoothing my dress, tucking my hair behind my ear—before rooting around in his jacket pocket. He pulls out a cellophane bag filled with the wrapped amber candies. "I warn you, they're addictive."

"No, no—I don't want one," I say, putting up my hand. "I can't abide the smell. Much less the taste."

"How can that be? Everybody likes butterscotch."

"Well, not me." The memory is so painful I have to catch my breath: Walton's scratchy cheek against mine, one hand on the small of my back, his breath on my neck as we dance at the Grange Hall . . . "Someone I knew was always . . . sucking on them."

"There's a story," he says, tucking the cellophane bag back into his pocket. "Let me guess. The boy you alluded to yesterday?"

I look away. "I didn't allude to any boy."

He spits the butterscotch into his hand and flicks it into Al's rosebush. Adjusts the easel, props his pad on it, opens the tackle box. "I'm sorry to tell you this," he says, pulling out his pens and brushes, "but I suspect we'll be here for more than an hour today as well. In case, you know, you're concerned you won't have time to tell me about him."

For a while I am silent. I listen to Andy's pen scratching the paper. Then I take a deep breath. "It was . . . a summer visitor."

"One summer?"

"Four. Four summers."

"How old were you?"

"Twenty, the first year."

"Around the age I was when I met Betsy," he says, holding his hand out in an L shape and squinting at me through it. "Was it serious?"

"I don't know." I swallow hard. "He promised me that . . . that we would be together."

"You mean that you'd get married?"

I nod. Is that what he promised? I'm not quite sure.

"Oh, Christina." Andy sighs. "What happened?"

Something in his manner makes me want to confide things to him I've never told anyone. Even painful things, shameful things.

I didn't know how badly I wanted to share them.

"HONESTLY, CHRISTINA," ANDY says, shaking his head, when I finish telling him the story. "That man sounds very dull. Very conventional. What in the world did you see in him?"

"I don't know." I think, again, of my mother opening her

front door to a Swedish sailor, the stuff of fairy tales: Rapunzel letting down her hair, Cinderella sliding her foot into the glass slipper, Sleeping Beauty awaiting a kiss. All were given one chance to step into a happily ever after—or at least it must've seemed that way. But was it the prince who attracted them, or merely the opportunity for escape?

How much of my love for, obsession with, Walton was about my fantasy of rescue—a fantasy I didn't even know I harbored until he came along?

"I suppose I just wanted . . ." To be loved, I almost blurt. But I'm ashamed to say it. "A normal life, I guess."

Andy sighs. "Well, that's the problem, isn't it? Look, I don't mean to be rude, but you could never have a normal life, even if that's what you thought you wanted. You and me, we're not 'normal.' We don't fit into conventional boxes." Shaking his head again, he says, "You dodged a bullet, if you ask me. If that man lives to be a hundred, he'll never know the strength of his convictions."

I swallow the lump in my throat. "He knew he didn't want me."

"Pah. He was weak. Easily swayed. Believe me, you avoided a lifetime of misery. That man would've chipped away at your heart bit by bit until there was nothing left. It may have been bruised, but at least it's whole."

He may be right; my heart might be whole. But I think about the people I've kept at arm's length, even those I love. I think about how I treated Al and Estelle. What I said, and meant, to Gertrude, who had come only to help that morning during my nephew's birth: *I swear I will never speak to you again.* Maybe she was right when she told me I had a cold heart. "I feel as if . . . as if it's been encased in ice."

"Ever since?"

"I don't know. Maybe it always was."

He caps the pen in his hand. "I can see why it might feel that way. But I don't believe it. You're guarded, perhaps, but that's understandable. Jesus, Christina, you've been dealt a rough hand. Taking care of your family your whole life. Your goddamn legs that don't work the way they're supposed to." He looks at me intently, and again I have the uncanny sense that he can see straight through me. "It's obvious to me—it's always been obvious—that you have a big heart. Just watching you with Betsy, for one thing. The affection between you. And your love for your nephew—there's no mistaking that. But most of all, you and Al, in this house. Your kindnesses to each other. This guy—this guy *Walton*," he says, mocking his name, "has no consequence here. You scared the poor bugger off." He laughs drily. "What did Al think of him?"

"Not much."

"Didn't think so." Closing the sketchbook, he says, "Al knows what's what."

My heart—bruised, battered; who knows, possibly thawing—constricts. *Your kindnesses to each other.* Andy doesn't know the whole story.

He's right about one thing, though: Al does know what's what. Has always known. And I rewarded his empathy, his loyalty, by taking him for granted, by ruining his relationship with a woman who probably would have been good for him. Who would've changed his life. I can picture the small, neat cottage that the two of them might've lived in. His pale pink roses on another trellis. Al up before dawn and out on the water in his lobster boat, checking traps, calculating the yield with a tug. Home in mid-afternoon to a cozy kitchen, wingbacks by the fire, a child to play a game with, a wife to ask about his day . . .

In my own grief and panic, I denied him the respect he has always given me. What right did I have to deny him his one chance for love?

"I NEED TO say something, Alvaro," I tell him in the kitchen at dusk, when we are drinking tea by the range. "Not that it will make any difference now. But . . . I had no right to force you to stay."

I can barely make out his features, but I see him flinch.

"I am sorry."

He sighs.

"You could have been happy with her."

"I'm not unhappy." His voice is so quiet I can barely hear it.

"You loved her, didn't you." I choke out the words. "I kept you here."

"Christie—"

"Will you ever forgive me?"

Al rocks back and forth in his creaky chair. Reaches into his pocket and pulls out his pipe, tamps down the tobacco, swipes a match against the oven door and lights it. Mumbles something under his breath.

"What?"

He sucks in the smoke and blows it out. "I said, I let myself be kept."

I think about this for a moment. "You felt sorry for me."

"It wasn't that. I made a choice."

I shake my head. "What choice did you have? I made you feel like you were abandoning me, when you were just trying to live your life."

"Well." He swipes at the air with his hand. "How could I leave all this?"

It isn't until he gives me a wry grin that I realize he's making a joke.

"Nobody else knows how I like my oatmeal," he says. "And anyway. You would've done the same for me."

I wouldn't have, of course. Al is being kind, or maybe it's easier for him to believe this. Either way, it doesn't excuse what I did. Here we are, the two of us, not partners but siblings, destined to live out our lives together in the house we grew up in, surrounded by the phantoms of our ancestors, haunted by the phantom lives we might've lived. A stack of letters hidden in a closet. A dory in the rafters of the shed. No one will ever know, when we're gone to dust, the life we've shared here, our desires and our doubts, our intimacy and our solitude.

Al and I have never hugged, that I can remember. I don't know the last time we've touched, except when he is helping me get around. But here in the murky darkness I put my hand over his, and he lays his other hand over mine. I feel the way I do when I lose something—a spool of thread, say—and search for it everywhere, only to discover it in an obvious place, like on the sideboard under the cloth.

I think of what Mamey told me long ago: there are many ways to love and be loved. Too bad it's taken most of a lifetime for me to understand what that means.

A FEW DAYS after Andy started sketching me in the pink dress in the grass, he takes his drawings upstairs. I work in the kitchen all morning, scraping my chair around the floor. I leave biscuits cooling on the counter, a pot of chicken soup on the range. At noontime he comes downstairs and helps himself, scooping a biscuit through his bowl of soup, gulping water from the pump in the pantry, wiping his mouth with the back of his hand. Heads back upstairs. In the afternoon I bake a blueberry pie, cut a warm slice, push it ahead of me on a plate to the stairs, and call for him to come and get it. It's worth the effort for the grin on his face.

He rows home at dusk. Comes back the next day and troops upstairs, his heavy thudding footsteps the only sound in the quiet house. I hear him pacing around up there, opening doors, shutting doors, walking into different rooms.

This goes on for weeks.

One month, then two.

There are traces of Andy everywhere, even when he's gone. The smell of eggs, splatters of tempera. A dry, splayed paintbrush. A wooden board pocked with color.

The weather cools. He's still working. He doesn't leave for Pennsylvania as usual at the end of August. I don't ask why, half afraid that if I speak the words aloud, they'll remind him that it is past time for him to return home.

While he's upstairs I go through the motions of my routine. Heat water for tea. Knead the bread. Stroke the cat on my lap. Watch the grasses sway out the window. Chat with Al about the weather. Settle in to enjoy the sunset, as vivid as a Technicolor movie. But all the time I'm thinking of Andy, tucked away in a distant room like a character in a fairy tale, spinning straw into gold.

One October morning Andy doesn't show up. I haven't seen Betsy in weeks, but the next day, when I'm darning socks, she pops her head in the kitchen door. "Christina! Will you and Al come to dinner?"

"To your house?" I ask with surprise. They've never invited us before.

She nods. "Andy talked to Al, and they agreed Al can bring you in the car. Please tell me you'll come! Just a simple meal, nothing fancy. We'd adore it. A nice send-off before we head back to Chadds Ford."

"Andy's finished for the season, then?"

"Finally," she says. "It'll be nice to have some peace and quiet, I'll bet."

"We don't mind. We have a lot of peace and quiet."

IT'S LATE IN the afternoon a few days later when Al—wearing a light-blue collared shirt I made for him years ago that I rarely see him in—lifts me out of my chair in the kitchen and carries me down the steps and into the back of the old Ford Runabout. It's been a long time since I've been anywhere in a car—since

I've been anywhere except Sadie's, in fact. I'm dressed in a long navy cotton skirt with forgiving panels and a white blouse—an old uniform, but at least it isn't torn or stained. Hair smoothed back and tied with a ribbon.

The backseat of the car is dark and cool. As we bump down the drive I lean back and close my eyes, feeling the vibrating thrum of the motor against my legs and a flutter of nervousness in my stomach. I've never seen Andy anywhere except in our house, with his paint-spattered boots and pockets bulging with eggs. Will he be a different person in his own home?

Al turns right at a stop sign, then drives mile after mile on a smooth road. I hear the loud blinker; we make a slow right turn. Then the crackle of gravel. "We're here, Christie," he says.

I open my eyes. White clapboard cottage, trellis of white clematis, dark windows, neat green arborvitae. I knew they'd moved out of the horse stalls, but seeing the cottage reminds me anew: Betsy got her house after all.

And here she is, standing on the porch in slim black pants, a mint-green blouse, a red-lipped smile, waving. "Welcome!" Behind her, Andy waves too. It is strange seeing him here, out of context, wearing a crisp white shirt and clean, unsullied trousers and shoes, his hair neatly combed. He looks like a nice, ordinary man in a nice, ordinary house. The only hint of the Andy I know is his hands stained with paint.

Al gets out and opens my door. He and Andy cradle me up the steps and into the house. Betsy holds the door open; two young boys dart back and forth like minnows.

"Nicholas! Jamie!" Betsy scolds. "You two go play upstairs. I'll bring you some cake if you're good."

Al and Andy carry me into a sparsely furnished room with a long red couch, a low oblong wooden table in front of it, and two striped wingback chairs. They settle me onto the couch while Betsy disappears through a swinging door and emerges with a tray of radishes in a small bowl, a platter of deviled eggs, and a little jar of green olives with red tongues. (I've seen olives like this before, but never tried one.) She sits beside me and directs Andy and Al to sit across from us in the wingbacks.

Andy seems a little jittery. He shifts in his chair and gives me a funny smile. Al glances above my head and then looks at Andy. He seems jittery too.

"Toothpick?" Betsy offers.

I take one and spear an olive into my mouth. Briny. Texture like flesh. Where to put the toothpick? I see a small woodpile on Andy's plate and balance the toothpick on my own. Looking around the room, I see Andy's familiar pictures in frames all over the walls: a watercolor of Al raking blueberries, his pipe and cap in profile. A charcoal sketch of Al sitting on the front doorstep. The large egg tempera of Mamey's lace curtains in a third-floor room billowing in the wind.

"They look nice in frames," I tell Andy.

"That's Betsy's domain," he says. "She names them and frames them."

"We divide and conquer," Betsy says. "A glass of sherry, Christina?"

"No, thank you. I only drink at the holidays." I don't want to say it, but I'm afraid I might spill on my blouse.

"All right. Al?" Betsy asks.

"A drink would be nice," he says.

Al and I, not used to being served, are stiff and formal. Betsy's doing her best to put us at ease. "It's supposed to rain tomorrow, I hear," she says as she hands Al a tiny glass of sherry.

"Good thing, we can use it," Al says and takes a sip. He winces. I don't think he's ever tasted sherry before. He sets the glass on the table.

I glance at Betsy, but she doesn't seem to notice. Laughing lightly, she says, "I know rain is good for the farm, but it's no fun to be stuck inside with the children on a rainy day, let me tell you."

Al gives Andy a droll look. "You should get them painting," he says.

Andy shakes his head. "Finger painting is more like it. Actually, Nicholas seems to have no aptitude for it whatsoever, but Jamie—I think he might actually have some talent."

"For heaven's sake, he's two years old," Betsy says. "And Nicky's only five. You can't know that already."

"I think maybe you can. My father said he saw that spark in me when I was eight months old."

"Your father . . ." Betsy rolls her eyes.

Spearing another olive, I ask, "So you're headed back to Pennsylvania in a few days?"

Betsy nods. "Starting to pack up. It's always hard to leave. Though we stayed longer than usual this year."

"It feels like you just got here," I say.

"Goodness, Christina, you can't mean that! With Andy bothering you day in and day out?"

"It wasn't a bother."

"Except when I made her pose." Andy catches my gaze. "Then it was a big bother."

I shrug. "I didn't mind it so much this time."

"Glad he didn't ask me again," Al says.

Andy laughs, shaking his head. "I learned my lesson."

"Well," Betsy says, standing up, "I need to go up and check on the boys. Andy, can you clear these plates?"

I see a look pass between them.

"Yes, ma'am," he says. When Betsy leaves the room, he gathers the bowls and puts them back on the tray. "You two will have to entertain each other. I'm just the hired help." We watch him shuffle backward through the swinging door, holding the tray aloft.

"Nice house, isn't it," Al says when it's just us.

"Very nice." We're artificial with each other, unaccustomed to small talk. "I could get used to those olives."

He grimaces. "I don't care for them. Too—rubbery."

This makes me laugh. "They are kind of rubbery."

As we sit in strained silence I see Al's gaze rise up the wall above my head again. He looks at me for a moment, then back at the wall.

"What?" I ask.

He lifts his chin.

I shift on my seat, craning my neck to see what he's looking at.

It's a painting, a large painting, and it fills almost the entire wall above my head. A girl in a yellow field wearing a light pink dress with a thin black belt. Her dark hair blows in the wind. Her face is hidden. She's leaning toward a shadowy silver house and barn balanced on the horizon line, beneath a pale ribbon of sky.

I look at Al.

"I think it's you," he says.

I look back at the painting. The girl is low to the ground but almost appears to float in space. She is larger than everything around her. Like a centaur, or a mermaid, she is part one thing and part another: my dress, my hair, my frail arms, but the years on my body have been erased. The girl in the painting is lithe and young.

I feel a weight on my shoulder. A hand. Andy's hand. "I finally finished it," he says. "What do you think?"

I look closely at the girl. Her skin is the color of the field, her dress as bleached as bones in the sun, her hair stiff grass. She seems both eternally young and as old as the land itself, a line drawing in a children's book about evolution: the sea creature sprouting limbs and inching up from shore.

"It's called 'Christina's World,'" he says. "Betsy titled it, like she always does."

"Christina's world?" I repeat dumbly.

He laughs. "A vast planet of grass. And you exactly in the middle."

"It's not quite . . . me, though, is it?" I ask.

"You tell me."

I look at the painting again. Despite the obvious differences, this girl is deeply, achingly familiar. In her I see myself at twelve years old, on a rare afternoon away from my chores. In my twenties, seeking refuge from a broken heart. Only a few days ago, visiting my parents' graves in the family cemetery, halfway between the dory in the haymow and the wheelchair in the sea. From the recesses of my brain a word floats up: synecdoche. A part that stands in for the whole.

Christina's World.

The truth is, this place—this house, this field, this sky—may only be a small piece of the world. But Betsy's right: It is the entire world to me.

"You told me once you see yourself as a girl," Andy says.

I nod slowly.

"I wanted to show that," he says, gesturing at the painting. "I wanted to show . . . both the desire and the hesitation."

I reach for his fingers and draw them to my lips. He's startled, I can tell; I've never done this before. It surprises me too.

I think about all the ways I've been perceived by others over the years: as a burden, a dutiful daughter, a girlfriend, a spiteful wretch, an invalid . . .

This is my letter to the World that never wrote to Me.

"You showed what no one else could see," I tell him.

He squeezes my shoulder. Both of us are silent, looking at the painting.

There she is, that girl, on a planet of grass. Her wants are simple: to tilt her face to the sun and feel its warmth. To clutch the earth beneath her fingers. To escape from and return to the house she was born in.

To see her life from a distance, as clear as a photograph, as mysterious as a fairy tale.

This is a girl who has lived through broken dreams and promises. Still lives. Will always live on that hillside, at the center of a world that unfolds all the way to the edges of the canvas. Her people are witches and persecutors, adventurers and homebodies, dreamers and pragmatists. Her world is both circumscribed and boundless, a place where the stranger at the door may hold a key to the rest of her life.

What she wants most—what she truly yearns for—is what any of us want: to be seen.

And look. She is.

AUTHOR'S NOTE

WHEN I WAS EIGHT YEARS OLD, growing up in Bangor, Maine, my father gave me a woodcut by a local artist inspired by Andrew Wyeth's *Christina's World*. It reminded him of me, he said, and I understood why: our shared name, the familiar Maine setting, the wispy flyaway hair. Throughout my childhood I made up stories about this slight girl in a pale pink dress with her back to the viewer, reaching toward a weathered gray house on a bluff in the distance.

Over the years I came to believe that the painting is a Rorschach test, a magic trick, a slight of hand. As David Michaelis writes in *Wondrous Strange: The Wyeth Tradition*, "The down-to-earth naturalism of Wyeth's paintings is deceptive. In his work, all is not as it seems." Andrew Wyeth's paintings always have an undercurrent of wonder and mystery; he was fascinated with the darker aspects of human experience. You get glimpses of this in the arid, dry-as-bones grasses rendered in startlingly precise detail, the wreck of a house on a hill with a mysterious ladder leading to a second-story window, a lone piece of laundry floating like an apparition in the breeze. At first glance the slim woman in the grass appears to be languidly relaxed, but a closer look reveals odd dissonances. Her arms are strangely thin and twisted. Perhaps she is older than she appears. She seems poised, alert, yearning toward the house, and yet hesitant. Is she afraid? Her face is turned from the viewer, but she appears to be gazing at a darkened window on the second floor. What does she see in its shadows?

After I finished writing my novel *Orphan Train*, I began to look for another story that would engage my mind and heart as completely. Having learned a great deal about early-to-mid-twentieth-century America as part of my research, I thought it would be fruitful to linger in that time period. I'd become particularly interested in rural life: how people got by and what emotional tools they needed to survive hard times. As with *Orphan Train*, I liked the idea of taking a real historical moment of some significance and, blending fiction and nonfiction, filling in the details, illuminating a story that has been unnoticed or obscured.

One day, several months after that novel came out, a writer friend remarked that she'd seen the painting at the Museum of Modern Art in New York and thought of me. Instantly, I knew I'd found my subject.

For the past two years I've immersed myself in Christina's world. I sat in front of the actual painting for hours at the Museum of Modern Art in New York, listening to the enthused, perturbed, intrigued, dismissive, passionate comments of passersby from all over the globe. (My favorite, from a Danish woman: "It's just so . . . creepy.") I studied the work of all three famous-artist Wyeths—N.C., his son Andrew, and Andrew's son Jamie—to get a sense of the rich and complex family legacy. In Maine I became intimately familiar with the Farnsworth Museum in Rockland, which has an entire building devoted to Wyeth art, and the Christina's World homestead in Cushing, an old saltwater farm that is now part of the Farnsworth. I interviewed art historians and American historians and was lucky to get to know several tour guides from the Olson house, who sent me articles and letters I never would have discovered on my own. I read biographies, autobiographies, obituaries, magazine and newspaper articles, art histories, art books, and criticisms. I read more than I needed to about the Salem Witch Trials, which play a role in the family's history. (So interesting!) I collected postcards and even bought a print of *Christina's World* to hang on my wall.

Here's what I discovered. Christina Olson, descended on one side from the notorious chief magistrate in the Salem Witch Trials and on the other from a poor Swedish peat-farming clan, was uniquely poised to become an iconic American symbol. In Wyeth's painting she is resolute and yearning, hardy and vulnerable, exposed and enigmatic. Alone in a sea of dry grass, she is the archetypal individual against a backdrop of nature, fully present in the moment and yet a haunting reminder of the immensity of time. As MoMA curator Laura Hoptman writes in *Wyeth: Christina's World*, "The painting is more a psychological landscape than a portrait, a portrayal of a state of mind rather than a place."

Like the silhouetted figure in James Whistler's *Whistler's Mother* (1871) and the plain-featured farm couple in Grant Wood's 1930 painting *American Gothic*, Christina embodies many of the traits we have come to think of as distinctively American: rugged individualism and quiet strength, defiance in the face of obstacles, unremitting perseverance.

As I did with *Orphan Train*, I tried to adhere to the actual historical facts wherever possible in writing *A Piece of the World*. Like the real Christina, my character was born in 1893 and grew up in an austere house on a barren hill in Cushing, Maine, with three brothers. A hundred years earlier, three of her ancestors had fled from Massachusetts in midwinter, changing the spelling of their family name to Hathorn along the way, to escape the taint of association with their relative John Hathorne, the presiding judge in the Salem Witch Trials and the only one who never recanted. On the scaffold, one of the convicted witches put a curse on Hathorne's family, and the specter of the trials clung to the family through generations; it was said among the townspeople of Cushing that those three Hathorns had brought the witches with them when they fled. Another relative, Nathaniel Hawthorne—who also changed the spelling of his name to obscure the family connection— wrote about his great-great grandfather Hathorne's unremitting ruthlessness in *Young Goodman Brown*, a tale about how those who fear the darkness in themselves are the most likely to see it in other people.

Another true story became an equally significant part of my novel. For generations, the house on the hill was known as the Hathorn house. But early in the winter of 1890, in the midst of a raging snowstorm, a fishing vessel bringing lime to make mortar and bricks became stuck in the ice of the nearby St. George River channel, and a young Swedish sailor named Johan Olauson was stranded. The ship captain, a Cushing native, offered to take him in. Olauson walked across the ice to Captain Maloney's cottage, where he hunkered down for the winter, waiting for the thaw to melt the ice so he could put back to sea. Just up the hill from the cottage was a magnificent white house belonging to a respected sea captain, Samuel Hathorn. Johan soon learned the story of the family on Hathorn Hill: they were on the brink of "daughtering out," meaning that no male heirs had survived to carry on the family name. Within several months, the young sailor had taught himself English, changed his name to John Olson, and made his presence known to the "spinster" Hathorn daughter, Kate—at 34, six years his senior. In a one-month span, Samuel Hathorn died and John Olson married Kate, taking over the farm. Their first child, Christina, was born a year later, and the big white homestead became known as the Olson house. The Hathorns had daughtered out.

❧

BY ALL ACCOUNTS, from an early age Christina was an active and vibrant presence. She had a lust for life, a fierce intelligence, and a determination not to be pitied, despite the degenerative disease that stole her mobility. (Though she was never correctly diagnosed in her lifetime, neurologists now believe she had a syndrome called Charcot-Marie-Tooth, a hereditary disorder that damages the nerves to the arms and legs.) Christina refused to use a wheelchair; as she became increasingly immobilized she took to dragging herself around. Several years ago the actress Claire Danes portrayed Christina Olson in an hour-long tour-de-force dance performance that emphasized her ferocious desire to move freely despite her devastating disease.

Quick of wit and sharp of tongue, Christina was a force to be reckoned with. Late in life—with her straw-like hair and hooked nose, her spinsterhood and independent nature—she was rumored among some of the townspeople of Cushing to be a witch herself. Andrew Wyeth variously called her a "witch" and a "queen" and "the face of Maine."

Wyeth first appeared at Christina's front door—along with Betsy James, his future wife, who'd been visiting the Olson farm since she was a girl—in 1939. He was twenty-two, Betsy seventeen, Christina forty-six. He began coming around almost daily, talking with Christina for hours, and sketching and painting landscapes, still lifes, and the house itself, which fascinated him. "The world of New England is in that house," Wyeth said "—spidery, like crackling skeletons rotting in the attic—dry bones. It's like a tombstone to sailors lost at sea, the Olson ancestor who fell from the yardarm of a square-rigger and was never found. It's the doorway of the sea to me, of mussels and clams and sea monsters and whales. There's a haunting feeling there of people coming back to a place."

In time, Wyeth began incorporating Christina into his paintings. "What interested me about her was that she'd come in at odd places, odd times," he said. "The great English painter John Constable used to say that you never have to add life to a scene, for if you sit quietly and wait, life will come—sort of an accident in the right spot. That happened to me all the time—happened lots with Christina."

For the next thirty years, Christina was Andrew Wyeth's muse and his inspiration. In each other, I believe, they came to recognize their own contradictions. Both embraced austerity but craved beauty; both were curious about other people and yet pathologically private. They were perversely independent and yet reliant on others to take care of their basic needs: Wyeth on his wife Betsy and Christina on Alvaro.

"My memory can be more of a reality than the thing itself," Wyeth said. "I kept thinking about the day I would paint Christina in her pink dress, like a faded lobster shell I might find on a beach, crumpled. I kept building her in my mind—a living being there on a hill whose grass was really growing. Someday she was going to be buried under it. Soon her figure was actually going to crawl across the hill in my picture toward that dry tinderbox of a house on top. I felt the loneliness of that figure—perhaps the same that I felt myself as a kid. It was as much my experience as hers."

"In Christina's World," Wyeth said, "I worked on that hill for a couple of months, that grass, building up the ground to make it come toward you, a surge of earth, like the whole planet . . . When it came time to lay Christina's figure against the planet I'd created for her all those weeks, I put this pink tone on her shoulder—and it almost blew me across the room."

In becoming an artist's muse—a seemingly passive role—Christina finally achieved the autonomy and purpose she craved her entire life. Instinctively, I believe, Wyeth managed to get at the core of Christina's self. In the painting she is paradoxically singular and representative, vibrant and vulnerable. She is solitary, but surrounded by the ghosts of her past. Like the house, like the landscape, she perseveres. As an embodiment of the strength of the American character, she is vibrant, pulsating, immortal.

For many reasons, this was the most difficult book I've ever written. Christina Olson was a real person, as were—and are—many of the people in this novel, and I did a tremendous amount of research into her life, her family, and her relationship with Andrew Wyeth. But at a certain point I had to let the research go and allow my characters to move the story forward. Ultimately, *A Piece of the World* is a work of fiction. Biographical facts regarding the characters in this book should not be sought in these pages. I hope readers intrigued by the story I tell here will explore the nonfiction accounts I mention in the acknowledgments. And above all else, I hope I have done this story justice.

ACKNOWLEDGMENTS

I WAS BORN in Cambridge, England, and spent my early years with my parents and younger sister in a small nearby village called Swaffham Bulbeck, in a house built in the thirteenth century. When you stood in the living room and looked up, you could see the circular outline of what had once been the hole in the roof above the space where the original inhabitants had built fires. There was no refrigerator or central heating; we used an icebox and a small gas heater that required coins to operate. Several years later we moved to Tennessee and lived on an abandoned farm, in an unheated house that had only recently been wired for electricity. Eventually we moved to Maine, into a normal house with basic amenities. But we spent weekends, holidays, and summers at a camp my father built on a tiny island on a lake with an outdoor pump for water, gas lanterns and candles for light, a fireplace for warmth, and an outhouse. We snowshoed across the frozen lake in the winter and chipped ice from the front door to get inside. My sisters and I would huddle in our coats around the hearth until the fire my parents built was robust enough to warm us.

So I want to thank my father, William Baker, and my late

mother, Christina Baker, who taught their four daughters that living close to the elements can make you more attuned not only to the world around you, but to the world within. I have no doubt that my unusual childhood shaped me as a writer. And in my last two novels, *Orphan Train* and now this one, I've drawn explicitly from those early experiences to create characters who live simply, without the modern-day amenities that most of us have come to expect.

One sunny afternoon in July 2013 I took a tour of the Christina Olson house in Cushing, Maine, led by a young woman named Erica Dailey. Erica noticed that I was taking notes and asked if I was writing an article; I confessed that I was thinking about writing a novel. As I was leaving the house, another docent, Rainey Davis, pulled me aside, slipped her card into my hand, and told me to reach out if I had more questions. I did—and Rainey and I became fast friends. We met in Rockland, Maine and even Sarasota, Florida, where she has a house and I was giving a lecture. Some months later, another docent, Nancy Jones, sent me an email offering to introduce me to some people close to Christina. Through her, I met Andrew Wyeth's nephew David Rockwell, whose knowledge about the Wyeths and the Olson House is encyclopedic; Jean Olson Brooks, Christina's niece, who knew her intimately for many years; ninety-year-old Joie Willimetz, a distant cousin of Christina's who shared her childhood memories of visiting Christina in the 1930s and '40s; and Ronald J. Anderson, M.D., a Harvard Medical School professor who, in *The Pharos* medical journal, argued persuasively that Christina had a hereditary motor sensory neuropathy called Charcot-Marie-Tooth disease. Nancy and I attended his lecture "Andrew Wyeth and Christina's World: Clues to Christina's Secret Illness" at the National Society of Clinical Rheumatology conference in 2015 that happened to be in Maine.

As I worked on this novel I read everything I could get my hands on about the Wyeths and the Olsons. Two biographies were my touchstones: *Christina Olson: Her World beyond the Canvas* by Jean Olson Brooks and Deborah Dalfonso, and *Andrew Wyeth: A Secret Life* by Richard Meryman. Both books became so tattered that I needed to buy multiple copies. (Special thanks to Elizabeth Meryman and Meredith Landis, Richard's wife and daughter respectively, for their help along the way.) Betsy James Wyeth's beautiful book of paintings, pre-studies, and reminiscences, titled simply *Christina's World*, was also tremendously important to my research. Other relevant sources were *Andrew Wyeth: Autobiography*, with an introduction by Thomas Hoving; *Andrew Wyeth, Christina's World, and the Olson House* by Michael K. Komanecky and Otoyo Nakamura; *Wyeth: Christina's World*, a MOMA publication by Laura Hoptman; *Rethinking Andrew Wyeth*, edited by David Cateforis; *Wondrous Strange: The Wyeth Tradition*, with a foreword by David Michaelis; and *Andrew Wyeth: Memory and Magic* by Anne Clausen Knutson. For details about Christina's life and rural life in general, I turned to *John Olson: My Story*, as told to his daughter, Virginia Olson; *Old Maine Woman* by Glenna Johnson Smith; *We Took to the Woods* by Louise Dickinson Rich; and *Farm Appliances and How to Make Them* by George A. Martin, among others.

A number of videos were useful to me, including *Christina's World*, a Hudson River Film & Video documentary narrated by Julie Harris; *Bernadette*, the story of a contemporary young woman named Bernadette Scarduzio afflicted with Charcot-Marie-Tooth disease; a BBC film titled *Michael Palin in Wyeth's World*; and a Boston Museum of Fine Arts video in which Jamie Wyeth, Andrew's son, talks about his creative process while working on a painting titled *Inferno*.

My trusted friend John Veague, a gifted writer and editor, read the manuscript long before anyone else—and not once, but over and over. (I'd wake up in the morning to emails time-stamped 3 A.M. saying, "I've just thought of one more thing . . .") The manuscript is stronger as a result of his rigor and thoughtfulness.

My three sisters, Cynthia Baker, Clara Baker, and Catherine Baker-Pitts, are my ideal readers; their notes on my manuscript were sharp and intelligent. I'm indebted to Michael Komanecky, Chief Curator at the Farnsworth Art Museum, for patiently answering my many questions and giving the manuscript a shrewd and incisive read. Rainey Davis, Nancy Jones, and David Rockwell fact-checked the novel; Anne Burt, Alice Elliott Dark, Louise DeSalvo, Pamela Redmond Satran, and Matthew Thomas improved it in ways large and small. Marina Budhos gave me the germ of the idea. My husband, David Kline, cheered me on and provided invaluable notes. Laurie McGee did such a brilliant job copyediting my last novel that I requested her again (and once again benefited from her thoroughness and exactitude). My wry, savvy agent, Geri Thoma, has supported me every step of the way; Simon Lipskar and Andrea Morrison at Writers House were also hugely helpful.

I've been working with my editor, Katherine Nintzel, for a long time. With each novel, my admiration for her grows. In her calm and gentle way, she is relentless. This book is infinitely better as a result of Kate's skillful guidance and perceptive editing. I also want to thank my team at William Morrow/HarperCollins for their unstinting support: Michael Morrison, Liate Stehlik, Frank Albanese, Jennifer Hart, Kaitlyn Kennedy, Molly Waxman, Nyamekye Waliyaya, Stephanie Vallejo, and Margaux Weisman.

On a personal note, I am so grateful for my husband David and my sons Hayden, Will, and Eli, without whom my own small piece of the world would be barren indeed.

CREDITS

About the author

About the book

Read on

Insights,
Interviews
& More . . .

Christina Baker Kline
Talks with Kristin Hannah

Karin Diana

KRISTIN HANNAH is an award-winning and bestselling author of more than twenty novels, including the international blockbuster *The Nightingale*. Her latest novel is *The Great Alone*.

Hey, Christina, I am so glad to be talking with you about your latest book, **A Piece of the World.** *I know you have a strong personal connection to Andrew Wyeth's iconic painting* Christina's World. *What is it? How did that connection develop into the idea for this novel?*

My family moved to Maine from North Carolina when I was six. On weekends, my parents, young professors fresh out of graduate school, packed my three sisters and me into our trusty station wagon for family excursions, from coastal islands to museums to notable landmarks. One summer afternoon, when my mother's mother was visiting from the South, we drove to the small town of Cushing to see the Olson house, made famous by Wyeth's painting. My grandmother was born within a decade of Christina Olson and was raised, similarly, in a rural white farmhouse with few amenities. She, my mother, and I share the same name: Christina. Ever since that long-ago visit to the Olson house, I have felt a deep-rooted kinship with Christina Olson.

A few years ago I was brainstorming ideas with a novelist friend for her new book, and she said, out of the blue, "You know, the painting *Christina's World* reminds me of you, for some reason. Have you ever considered writing about that mysterious woman in the field?" (How did she know?) I realized instantly that I'd found my subject.

What sort of research did you do for this book? What surprised you the most? How long did the novel take to write?

I pored over books and articles; interviewed people who knew the Wyeths or the Olsons, or both; went to Wyeth exhibits in museums in Maine, New York, Pennsylvania, and New Jersey; attended a neurological ▶

**Christina Baker Kline Talks
with Kristin Hannah** *(continued)*

convention; watched documentaries
and profiles. The more I learned, the
more determined I became to try to stick
to the facts of the real-life story, which
were more interesting than anything I
might invent. Even more important, I
wanted to understand Andrew Wyeth,
an intensely complicated man. I was
surprised to discover that, unlike many
artists, Wyeth had the ability and the
desire to probe and analyze his own
impulses and methodology—partly
because his biographer, Richard
Meryman, was such a deep thinker
himself, and pushed Wyeth to articulate
so much about his artistic process
and psychological motivations. Their
conversations contributed enormously
to my interpretation of Wyeth's
relationship with Christina Olson.
The book took a little more than two
years to research and write.

*How was writing this book a different
experience from writing* Orphan Train?
*Can you tell us a little bit about your
process? (I am like all readers—I love
to hear how writers do what they do.)*

Unlike *Orphan Train,* the characters in
this novel are mostly real people, some of
whom are still living. I felt an enormous
responsibility to render their lives and
their stories as sensitively and accurately
as I could, while at the same time
creating an inner life for Christina
that is entirely imagined. Furthermore,

Christina Olson lived a quiet, somewhat ordinary life, with few peaks and valleys. Like most, she had her own small personal crises and heartbreaks; I needed to dig deep into them to create moments of internal and external drama. For these reasons this was a much harder book to write than *Orphan Train*. Every sentence was hard-won. The story inhabited my head like nothing I've ever written; I obsessed over it and lived in a kind of feverish dream state for months. Somehow I did manage to function in the world, most of the time. But the story was always lurking just under the surface. I came to think of this novel as a kind of sestina: a complex poetic form with exacting requirements, which only succeeds when the poet is able to transcend the restrictions.

It can be hard to follow a book that so many people adored. How did the success of Orphan Train affect your writing of A Piece of the World?

I should ask you, Kristin. Next time we'll turn the tables!

The reception to *Orphan Train* has been a surprise to me, a lovely surprise, but not something that I can—or even want to—engineer again. My books are quite varied; I never want to feel constrained by writing a novel for a specific audience. *A Piece of the World* is similar to *Orphan Train* in some ways (it takes place in the early- to ▶

5

**Christina Baker Kline Talks
with Kristin Hannah** (*continued*)

mid-twentieth century; it's about
hardscrabble life in rural America),
but it's a very different kind of story:
more internal, more philosophical,
more close to the bone.

The success of *Orphan Train* has
definitely made some things easier.
I think people were more willing to talk
to me when I was researching this book.
I've also gained time and flexibility.
I need to travel quite a bit to talk about
my books, but I'm not attempting to
juggle paying jobs, like editing and
teaching, with parenting and writing
the way I was several years ago. My kids
are older, too. I have a lot of empathy
for women who fit their writing into the
crevices of their too-busy lives, as I once
did. In a larger sense, I think the success
of *Orphan Train* confirmed my desire to
write about things that scare me, topics
I might've rejected when I was younger
because they felt foreign, or too vast.
I discovered how exhilarating it is to
take big risks.

*Other than the central character in
your first novel,* Sweet Water, *who is a
sculptor, you haven't written about the
act of artistic creation—or about being
an artist's muse. Was this difficult to do
in* A Piece of the World? *Were you able
to tap in to anything from your own
experience?*

One of the wonderful things about
being a writer is that you're constantly

dredging up some arcane knowledge or long-forgotten experience, rediscovering old passions and interests. In my teens I fancied myself an artist; I hung out with the eccentric art teacher at my high school, painted still lifes and portraits and landscapes in watercolor and acrylics, took private lessons, won some blue ribbons for my earnest renderings. My lack of talent did little to dampen my enthusiasm. In college I thought I'd continue, but, like Salieri, I quickly realized that while I had the ability to appreciate art, I wasn't actually very good. Instead of painting, I studied art history. As I wrote *A Piece of the World* I drew on my love of painting and my understanding of twentieth-century American art to create Wyeth's character.

Is A Piece of the World *a "New England" novel? How much of your depiction of Christina Olson takes into account her deep New England roots?*

While I was writing this novel I thought of it as not only a New England story but a specifically American one, with its depiction of ruggedly independent people forging a path out of the wilderness and claiming a piece of the world for themselves. Christina Olson's story is linked—IRL, as the kids say— to the Salem Witch Trials, Nathaniel Hawthorne, and many Maine sea captains. But having traveled recently ▶

**Christina Baker Kline Talks
with Kristin Hannah** *(continued)*

to remote islands like Iceland and
Tasmania, and having read accounts
of people's lives in those places, I now
view this novel more broadly as a story
about the human impulse to persevere,
to put down stakes, and to carve a life
out of the flintiest of circumstances.

What are you working on now?

My father, a historian, has written many
nonfiction books and biographies. I've
always written novels. I didn't realize,
until I wrote *Orphan Train* (my fifth),
the extent to which I, like my father,
enjoy immersing myself in a different
time and place. The novel I'm working
on now is about the hidden history of
the destitute women who were sent
from Britain on convict ships in the
nineteenth century to an island off
the coast of Australia, and how they
shaped the society in which they came
to live. ༄

Reading Group Guide

1. Christina Olson's life is limited by her parents, her illness, and the realities of a rural life in the first half of the twentieth century. But she does make decisions that affect the course of her life. What are some of the major consequences of Christina's choices? Which choices did you agree with, and with which did you disagree?

2. Consider Christina's relationship with her parents and her relationship with Mamey. What does Mamey offer Christina that her parents do not? What are the limitations of that relationship? How do Christina's brothers have different relationships with both Mamey and their parents?

3. How do the poems of Emily Dickinson engage with the themes of this novel?

4. How might Christina's life have been different if Walton had actually married her? What do you think their marriage might have been like?

5. What does Christina's behavior toward her brother reveal about her character?

6. What is it about Andy that compels Christina to share her very private world with him? Why does she allow him to paint her, and why does she like being a model more than Al does? ▶

7. What draws Andy toward Christina? How are they similar? How does Betsy's relationship with each influence the relationship with the other?

8. Discuss the ways in which Andrew Wyeth's iconic painting *Christina's World* interacts with this story. Were you familiar with the painting before you read the novel? How did that familiarity (or lack of familiarity) color your reading?

9. Which parts of Christina's life are probably based on biographical fact? What parts do you think the author added? Did your reading of the Author's Note at the end of the novel change the way you thought about any aspect of the book? What about seeing the painting at the end of the novel?

10. Would you characterize Christina as an unlikeable narrator? Why or why not?

11. Is *A Piece of the World* a "New England" novel? To what extent do the characters and the setting take into account their New England roots?

12. The majority of historical fiction revolves around important or influential figures: monarchs, cultural beacons or warmongers. Christina, by contrast, lives a "quiet, ordinary life." How does Kline

extract drama and complexity in
Christina's character?

13. Does Christina's approach to her
    disability evolve? How does this
    reflect her personality, and in what
    ways is it a reaction to the times she
    lived in? How does her disability
    affect her relationship with her
    family? ∾

Stranded in Ice

An early draft of *A Piece of the World* contained an abundance of Olson family background, much of which ultimately was not included in the finished book. Kline repurposed the story of how Johan Olauson, Christina Olson's father, came to America and made a life for himself on the coast of Maine, for the stand-alone story "Stranded in Ice" originally published in LitHub (February 2017).

FEBRUARY 1890. The bleak heart of a Maine winter. On Hathorn Point, above Kissing Cove, where the St. George River flows into the Atlantic Ocean, a storm sweeps in, sending the temperature plummeting. Wind whips up the hill, strafing the white clapboard house at the top. In the kitchen, a retired sea captain and his wife and daughter pull on wool socks and leather boots and hurry to feed the animals in the barn. To be outside for more than a few minutes is to risk freezing to death. Returning to the warm kitchen, they carry firewood from the attached shed and stack it beside the hearth, pull the doors shut tightly behind them, line windowsills and doorframes with blankets.

Far below them, in the St. George River channel, the roiling sea hardens, quickly and almost imperceptibly, into a bumpy sheet of ice.

*

A young Swedish sailor wakes to silence. All the sounds of a ship in the ocean are absent: the slap of water against the hull, the creak of boards shifting and settling in the waves, the giant bird's-wing flap of the sail.

Johan sniffs the air. Exhales. His breath is fog, dense and opaque. He blinks: even in the depths of the ship, he can see bright whiteness through the cracks. It is tempting to turn over in his cocoon of blankets and burrow deeper.

What would he be doing now if he'd stayed in the small village of Gällinge, where he was born? Little imagination is required for this exercise, but it comforts him to picture it. There is Birgid, with her wide blue eyes and straw-colored hair, lingering near the dock at the end of the day, waiting for him when the fishing vessels come in. Pale fingers like taper candles, her breasts small globes—entire worlds—under the cotton ticking of her bodice. For years this memory has lulled him to sleep on his hard narrow cot, distracted him from seasickness (which still plagues him, after all these years), tamped down the fear that swells in his chest on every trip. He is twenty-seven years old and has been working on boats since he was fifteen, and it never gets easier.

In these daydreams Johan chooses not to dwell on other aspects of life in Gällinge. The squalid, low-ceilinged two-room hut his family of ten shared with a cow, their surest hedge against ▶

starvation. His father, a drunkard with two moods, brooding and raging, who terrorized Johan and his seven younger siblings and worked occasionally at a peat farm as a day laborer when he was desperate enough. Constant stomach-churning hunger. More than once he avoided jail by eluding police on a long chase through cobbled streets after stealing a rasher of pork or a jug of maple syrup.

From an early age, Johan knew there wasn't much of a future for him in Gällinge; no jobs, none he was qualified for even in the big city of Göteborg, sixty miles away. Though a quick study, he'd never paid much attention in school, knew how to read only the simplest stories. Never learned a trade. He'd taught himself to knit so he could help his piteous God-fearing Ma, who earned a few coins making scarves and mittens and hats, but that was no job for a man, was it?

So when he heard about a trading ship bound for New York, he rose in the dark to be the first at the dock at Göteborg Harbor.

"Fifteen years old, eh." The captain spit on the cobblestones. "Too young to leave Mama."

Johan didn't understand much English, but *Mama* he knew. "She won't miss me," he said. "One fewer mouth to feed, a few more coins for the rest. Sick babies." The youngest, his brother Sven, dead a month before, not even a year old. Johan would've told the captain this if he'd trusted himself not to cry.

The captain listened to a rough translation, shrugged. "*Det* är *ditt liv, antar jag.*" It's your life, I suppose.

And so Johan set sail with the captain and his small crew across and back and around the world. He stowed his few possessions in a wooden box under his bed: a whalebone comb, bitter cream of tartar and a horsehair brush for his teeth, a painted tin soldier from a long-ago children's set, and a small collection of rocks and minerals. He'd been ten when a kind, eccentric teacher taught him to identify and collect these specimens—to separate isometric minerals like garnet and pyrite from tetragonals like zircon and andalusite. Unlike rocks, he'd learned, which have no specific chemical composition, minerals have an ordered atomic structure. Johan was fascinated by their sharp edges and smooth surfaces, the way their many facets refracted light. His favorite, anthracite, was not actually a mineral but a sedimentary rock, a hard, compact form of coal. He loved the metallic, inky sheen of its planes, the fact that it was derived from decomposed plant and animal life from millions of years ago. He loved that it was almost pure carbon, which meant that it burned hard and bright. Even as an adult, anthracite was what he reached for when he felt anxious or seasick or lonely. Its angles and planes fit perfectly in the palm of his hand.

As months turned into years, Johan's past began to recede. He sent money home and flirted with Birgid when he was back, but she didn't want a husband at sea, did she? Gone half the year, no idea when he'd return. Birgid had never been anywhere and had no desire to travel. She wanted a simple life with a dependable husband who would stoke the fire first thing in the morning and cut and haul the wood in the afternoon. Who'd go to church with her on Sundays and chip the ice from the well when it froze.

In truth, the more time Johan spent away from Gällinge, the less he missed it. He didn't miss tripping over his brothers and sisters, not to mention the cow. He didn't miss that dingy hovel with its slop jar in the corner and the rank smell of unwashed bodies, boiled cabbages and its aftereffects. The dank confines of a ship's belly might not have been much of an improvement, but at least you could rise from its depths onto a wide deck and gaze up at a vast sky sprinkled with stars and the yolk of a moon.

What he did miss was the countryside surrounding Gällinge, jade fir trees and lush dark dirt, lingonberries red against the snow. His sister's fried potato cake called *raggamunk*, the feral smell of pumpernickel with cured salmon and soured cream. His sense memories of Birgid, preserved and sweetened like flies in honey. And though he adapted to the rhythms of life on the ocean, he joked with his mates and came to know every inch of the ship, he never quite grew to love it. (That pervasive queasiness, for one thing, even in anticipation: waking in a sweat the night before an expedition with a mouth full of saliva and a roiling gut.)

A fellow seaman, Karl, joked that Johan was amphibian: longing for land, yet pulled toward water. He did not know whether to tuck his legs under him or retire his gills. Yes, Johan ▶

Stranded in Ice *(continued)*

had to admit, it was true. He took to looking for signs to point him in the right direction: a clear path out of the thicket of his own ambivalence. And like anyone looking for a sign, eventually he found one.

*

They were bored, so bored, on board. Karl took to reading out loud in the bunks at night—he practically held them hostage. Endured howls of abuse: "Shut up, Karl, will ye? Nobody's listening."

"Just a story," he'd insist. "Only one."

Karl was the only Englishman on the ship. He told them that his Swedish mother, who worked in London as a domestic, sent him on a train every summer to visit his grandparents in Trosa, near Stockholm, to teach him manners and give herself a rest. On the schooner Karl spoke a funny patois of English and Swedish, mostly, he said, to amuse himself. He was different in other ways, too: loud, quick-witted, a spark of mischief. Bushy brown mustache and dark shiny eyes, coarse dark hair. Always with a book in his hand. He read to them in halting Swedish from *The House of the Seven Gables*, translating as he went, laughing, "American to English to godforsaken Swedish, this is wrong, all wrong." The rest of them agreed, throwing soiled underclothes in his direction, a wet boot. But Karl persevered. "I'm going to teach you louts about sin and evil before it's too late!" he shouted. "Learn from the master."

What other dungeon is so dark as one's own heart! What jailer so inexorable as one's self! . . . The world owes all its onward impulses to men ill at ease. The happy man inevitably confines himself within its ancient limits. . . .

These words punctured Johan's soul, as if intended for him alone. Here he was, in a dungeon of his own devising, propelled out of Gällinge by his own dissatisfaction, uncertain of the path ahead. Ill at ease was an understatement.

Karl looked up, right into Johan's eyes, his finger holding his place in the book. "You like this, don't you?"

Johan flushed, mortified to be so transparent.

Karl just grinned. "I knew you weren't like the rest of these hooligans," he said, and went back to reading.

In late January, after a month at sea, they docked in New York harbor. On the first night Karl persuaded Johan to venture out to a bar.

New York had always frightened Johan a little. It was never quiet, it seemed, nor truly dark. The streets were full of drunken, marauding sailors. Johan didn't even want to drink—his legs were wobbly, and alcohol only made seasickness worse. Closing his eyes on a street corner, he curled his toes against the cobblestones and felt the water churning beneath him. He listened to the chatter around him on all sides—cacophonous tongues; wasn't this what Ma said Gomorrah was like? So many voices, so many languages. He thought of Gällinge, its streets silent at 8 p.m., not a soul outside, most already asleep.

Like many sailors, Johan sought adventure but craved the familiar. On board the schooner this oxymoronic state was easy enough to maintain: the cast of characters small, the walls unchanging; the outside world, in all its bewildering excess, rolling by at a distance. Up close, now, New York was vast and disorienting and cold, and all he wanted was to return to his nest and go to sleep.

But Karl was having none of it. "Sleep is for babies. You're staying with me." He reached over with both hands and turned up Johan's thick wool collar. "Besides, you'll regret it if you go back. Everybody needs stories to tell."

They trudged through the slush. Walked for blocks and blocks. The falling snow was God spitting at them, Karl said, taunting them to find a drink. Finally—"There." He pointed toward a set of glowing windows in the distance, as welcome as a lighthouse beacon. When Karl opened the heavy door they stepped into a saloon filled with sailors.

Johan shrank back. But Karl nudged him forward, his flat hand guiding him toward the bar. "An ale for my friend here, and one for me," Karl told the bartender, and Johan nodded. "Ale" he knew. "Friend," too. They stamped snow off leather boots, shook damp wool caps, waited for the warmth to penetrate as they settled on two stools. Karl, as was his inclination, struck up a conversation with the man next to him.

"John Maloney. Captain. *The Silver Spray*," the man grunted, holding out a meaty paw.

Karl shook it. "Karl Butler. And Johan Olauson, not so good with the English. From the godforsaken land of lutefisk and lufsa."

John Maloney reached over to shake Johan's hand. It was like grasping a pork loin. "Sweden, eh? Cold over there." He laughed. "I'm not one to talk. I'm from Maine. You know it?"

Johan shook his head uncertainly.

"Beautiful place. Damn cold, though, this time of year."

Karl started talking about all the warm places he'd been: the West Indies, Belize, Portugal, then he and the captain were off and running. Johan understood every fourth or fifth word. Dark-eyed, dark-haired girls in dresses that showed their limbs, brown-sugar sand, brandy and rum and oranges. The words washed over Johan, a warm thrum. The bar was foggy with tobacco smoke and the conversation around him a stew of sound. He looked around for someone, anyone, from the boat he might converse with, but couldn't see beyond the crush of bodies close to the bar.

Warm now, he shrugged off his coat, lifted the glass to his lips. The ale was cold, a welcome change from the piss-warm brew they kept in barrels onboard. It must have been stored in an ice house. *Ice*—this word he knew. "Ice," he mouthed to himself.

"What's that?" the captain said, leaning in.

Johan waved a horizontal hand at the two of them—don't mind me, keep talking, I'm fine here.

But Karl leaned forward. "Captain Maloney is looking for crew," he said in Swedish. "Had to jettison some drunkards. Needs to deliver fuel wood to lime kilns up north." He chugged his beer and set it down. "Nathaniel Hawthorne lived in Maine, did you know that?"

"I'm going to Thomaston," Maloney said.

"Thomaston." Karl rolled his eyes. "*Vart i helvete som* är. Ändå är *han erbjuder en vacker slant.*" Wherever the hell that is. Still, he's offering a pretty penny.

For a moment Johan wasn't sure what Karl was saying. And then he got it. The realization propelled him upright on his stool. Karl switched boats like an acrobat switches ropes, but Johan had always been on the same crew. To abandon his schooner, his bunk and mates, the ease of camaraderie and routine—not to mention a common language—was almost unthinkable.

And yet . . .

"Kom igen, varför inte?" Karl said. Come on, why not? He lifted his arms wide. *"Vad har vi att förlora?"* What do we have to lose?

Usually people with Karl's assemblage of traits—confidence and gregariousness, easy familiarity with strangers, a shrewd gaze and quick smile—made Johan feel invisible, but Karl had the opposite effect on him: Karl made him feel seen.

Varför inte?

Weaving down the dark street with Karl's arm around his shoulder a few hours later, after the bar closed, Johan felt the dizzying stirring of change. Yes, he was going to do it. He was twenty-seven, after all, and unencumbered, accountable to no one. Though the idea terrified him, he knew that this might be his only chance to resist the pull of the familiar. And Karl would be there. Really, what did he have to lose?

The snow falling around them was softer now, a downy blanket, and Johan leaned into his friend for warmth and stability. He was so tired he could lie down right there on the sidewalk and go to sleep. Karl swayed against him, tipping both of them a little, his arm tightening around his shoulder. Johan laughed. *"Enkelt,* fella"—easy—and all of a sudden felt himself pushed around a corner, shoved against a building. It was so dark he couldn't see a thing. He felt Karl's breath on his neck, the bristle of his mustache, Karl's rough hand pulling up his shirt, cold against his abdomen, resting on his belt.

"Du vill ha det också," Karl whispered. You want it too. He pressed against his body, the full twinned length.

Johan—woozy, drunk, confused—froze. What was happening? Karl's mouth found his, open, warm lips and searching tongue, and Johan's mind reeled. He surged forward, not sure whether to push Karl off or succumb to the embrace. In a short minute the hot blood in his head would melt any last shred of . . . ▶

And then, with a sudden surge of clarity, he knew. As clearly as he had seen the choice between safety and adventure, he saw that he didn't have the stomach for this. He wasn't sure what he felt, but he knew that the rickety persona he was attempting to construct would collapse altogether under the weight of . . . of what? Of fear and shame and taboo. He put his hand over Karl's. *"Nej."*

Karl's hand on his stomach trembled. His shoulders tensed. Then his hand moved again. *"Johan—"*

"Nej, nej, säger jag." No, no, I say.

Karl stood back. Wiped his mouth with the back of his hand. *"Du säkert?"* You sure?

Johan nodded. His eyes had grown accustomed to the dark; fat white flakes fell so slowly it was as if time were suspended. With both hands Karl yanked his collar up so it stood in two points around his face. Johan could feel his eyes on his, studying him, dark and shiny as coal. As anthracite. He looked at the ground, at the trail of their intermingled footsteps in the foamy snow. As Karl stepped away, Johan watched his boots pivot and disappear.

Johan leaned back against the wall and shut his eyes, feeling the warmth of his own exhalation on his face. When he got back to the schooner, Karl's bunk was cleared out. There was no note. On Johan's bed was the dog-eared copy of *House of the Seven Gables*. The next day Johan found *The Silver Spray* and signed on. Two days later he was carrying fuel wood and coal to the lime kilns in Thomaston. He would never set eyes on Karl again.

*

Merciless moon. It grew fuller each night, sloshing light across the ice-slippery deck, shiny as a rink. The sky dribbled snow, too chilly for big flakes. Frigid air found any slice of exposed skin: the back of Johan's long neck, his bony wrists, a patch of ankle. Had he ever been this cold? If so he couldn't remember it.

The Silver Spray was fairly small. Only two masts with four-cornered sails. Maloney was a good captain, firm and jovial in just the right amounts, and the two other crewmen were friendly enough. An experienced sailor needs few words; the tasks on board require little language, and Johan got by with pantomime and gesture. He was a quick study. Alone on deck at night, he went through the same checklist he performed on the Swedish schooner. Maloney shadowed him the first few days, observing him closely, and then relaxed. Johan could tell he was pleased.

On the evening of the eighth day, Johan completed the check and they dropped anchor. He crawled into his narrow cot below deck and pulled the wool blankets and furs around him. He'd grown accustomed to the smell of his unwashed body, salt and dirt, perspiration and grime, and now he found it vaguely comforting, like a child inhaling the scent of a beloved threadbare blanket. Drawing his knees to his chest and wrapping his arms around himself, he burrowed in like a hibernating mammal.

*

Even before he fully rouses to consciousness, before he opens his eyes, Johan is aware of a vast stillness. He waits as his eyes adjust to the gloom, then wills himself awake. In one quick movement he flings the covers back and reaches for his trousers, trying not to think, not to absorb the cold. Pulls a salt-stiffened sweater over his heat, yanks off the wool cap he slept in, runs forked fingers through his lank hair, pushes the cap back on, over his ears.

It's barely light. The other two crewmen are still asleep. He hoists himself up the stairs like a chimpanzee, arms on the rails. On the deck a sheen of fog makes it feel like he's walking through a cloud.

Captain Maloney is there already, gazing out at the whiteness. He turns around. "Olauson."

"Captain."

The captain shakes his head. "Stuck in the ice," he says. "Stranded."

Ice.

Johan struggles to find words. "We are where?"

"Well, that's the irony. Only six miles from Thomaston." The captain points into the fog, toward nothing Johan can see. "We're at Hathorn Point. My home is right over that hill." ▶

*

Stranded in Ice *(continued)*

They must abandon ship. There is no option; the ice grew around them in the night. They wait a few days for the ice to thicken before packing their belongings and venturing down a rickety ladder. Take toddler steps toward shore as the new ice bruises under their feet, creating spider web fissures. No fog, now; Johan sees evergreens, spiky and sharp, in the distance.

Johan follows the captain and crew up a rocky beach sugared with snow and across a barren field. The other two sailors are from these parts; they'll be on their way. But he has nowhere to go.

"You'll stay with me until the thaw," the Captain says, matter-of-fact. "That old boat ain't going nowhere. Neither are you."

"And who is this?" the Captain's wife says, greeting her husband at the door as if he'd left on an errand an hour before. She's a ruddy, broad-faced, round-shouldered woman, with a bosom that seems of a piece with her middle. Johan looks back and forth between them. They could be siblings.

"Hullo, Mrs. Maloney," the Captain says.

"Hullo, Captain," she says with obvious fondness, a smile spreading down from her eyes to her mouth, which opens to reveal little yellow-corn teeth.

"Swedish lad," the Captain says. "Olauson. Doesn't speak much English."

"How'm I supposed to communicate with him? Smoke signals?"

"He's learnin'."

"Pleasure to meet," Johan says.

"What'd I tell ya?" the Captain nods at his wife.

She rolls her eyes. "All right, come in the house before you catch your death."

And like that, he's in. Mrs. Maloney leads him up the stairs and opens the first door on the right. "You can stay here," she says. It's a small room, with only a narrow bed and a mirrored dresser, but it's kingly to Johan, who has never slept in a room on his own in his life. When she leaves, shutting the door behind her—saying she'll boil water for his bath in a tub downstairs, have a rest now, it'll be a while—he goes to the window and lifts the lace curtain. A white house on a distant hill is the only other building in sight.

Three full stories with a commanding view of the cove. Who lives in such a dwelling?

Dropping the curtain, Johan turns to inspect the room and catches his own reflection in the large oval mirror above the oak dresser. It's been years since he's seen himself clearly; washrooms on the schooners provided only a convex disk of tin for shaving. He is a good-looking man, or so his mama said—and his sisters, when they were trying to heave him out of the house on a Friday night. He thinks he resembles a horse: large, pale-lashed eyes, a sloping, prominent nose ending in flared nostrils, a mane of coarse, honeyed hair. His body, too, is equine: muscles quivering under skin stretched thin, veins visible on his calves.

Sitting on the bed, he bounces a little, marveling at the coils in the mattress and the vivid colors, blue and pink and green, of the patchwork quilt pulled tight around the frame. He digs his fingers into the soft blue wool of the knitted blanket folded at the bottom. Then he stretches out, the full length of him, careful in his grimy clothes not to move around too much, lest he leave a stain. He leans his head back on the soft lumpy bulk of a down pillow and closes his eyes. *The happy man inevitably confines himself. . . .*

What is happiness, then? Is this it? He doesn't know, but is glad enough to have a chance to find out.

*

With no vessel to attend, Johan finds, the days and nights are long.

Mrs. Maloney, bless her, is impatient. It's not easy having a rough-mannered, awkward, monosyllabic Scandinavian underfoot. "Cup!" she cries, holding it out as if to an idiot or a beggar. "Candle!" Wax dripping on her thumb. "Window!" Rapping hard on the glass. Johan stands around, equally frustrated, long arms hanging at his sides. Her pantomimes become increasingly exaggerated. "Outside, you big lug, *firewood*," she says, miming a sawing action, "See?"

Mrs. Maloney keeps a snug, cozy home, with braided rugs on the kitchen floor and mahogany chairs in the parlor. She is constantly in motion, cleaning, cooking, mending. Johan does ▶

Stranded in Ice *(continued)*

what he can to help out, repairing three cane chairs that have lost
their straw webbing, patching a crumbling wall, rising in the dark
after a snowfall to clear a path to the barn, mucking out the two
old horses. He fixes an old black buggy's busted wheel, then clips a
horse to it and drives into Cushing, a mile and a half away, to pick
up flour and sugar and lard and whatever else the lady of the
household requires.

("More yarn!" Holding up a flap of maroon knitting suspended
between two needles.)

At the general store the boy behind the counter shakes his head
at Johan's pathetic attempts to communicate. "You could learn
English," he says, ringing up the items.

Johan nods, the tips of his ears pinkening. "I am try."

The boy hands him some change. "I mean really learn. With a
teacher. Teacher, you know? My brother is a sailor, like you.
Married an Italian gal a few years ago and brought her over here.
She learned in a winter with the kids at the Wing School here in
town."

Johan only catches a few words, but it's enough to get the point.
"Where?"

The boy leads him to the door, points down the street. "There."
He pulls out a pocket watch. "Almost noon. Lunch time. The
teacher won't mind you stopping by."

The teacher, Mrs. Crowley, wiry and bespectacled, is in her
early fifties and has seen stranger things than this. "All right," she
sighs, "as long as you do the work." Johan begins with a primer
for five-year-olds, but within weeks he progresses enough to read
simple sentences and moves up to seven and eight. It's a little
peculiar having a grown man in the classroom, but Johan proves
useful, chopping firewood and chipping ice from the walkway.
Mrs. Crowley, a recent widow, seems to warm to the idea of
having another adult around, especially one who hangs on her
every word.

This desolate corner of Maine feels both strange and strangely
familiar. So much reminds Johan of Sweden: Dalmatian-skinned
birches, pipe-cleaner trees, dense clouds in a pebble-colored sky,
snow and more snow. More than a few of the people he meets
possess a laconic Swedish diffidence. But the saltbox houses are

nothing like the thatched-roof huts in Gällinge, and the food is bland. He misses the sour tang of horseradish and pickled herring.

Soon enough the odd becomes routine. He is learning English. Finding his way. He walks the mile and a half to Cushing every weekday in all kinds of weather, sleet and fog and snowstorms that swallow the ruts in the road, almost obliterating the path, which has become so familiar he could trace it in his sleep. At the Captain's house Mrs. Maloney packs Johan a lunch every morning, sets a plate of warm gingerbread or molasses cookies for him on the counter in the afternoon. As the language of this place takes root in Johan's head, his shyness diminishes. People stop to talk to him on the street, the Maloneys include him in conversation. Supper at home is lively, even jovial sometimes.

Johan discovers a hole in the knitted blanket on his bed and buys a skein of blue yarn to patch it, and before long he is spending evenings after supper with the Maloneys in the living room, surrounded by baskets of yarn. Three wingback chairs pulled close around the hearth, a plate of currant bread and tumblers of whiskey on the rough bench that serves as a table, two cats purring on the rag rug—both black, Mrs. Maloney says, because a black cat in the home of a Captain's wife protects her husband at sea. Johan and Mrs. Maloney knit sweaters and scarves and throw blankets while the Captain carves small intricate ships out of wood, adding each one to a collection on the mantelpiece above the fireplace as he finishes it.

Johan thinks of Sweden only occasionally now, and mostly with unease. To return to Gällinge would almost certainly mean being pulled back into his desperate family. There are so many of them, and their needs are so dire. What would he do for work if he returned? What is he qualified for, beyond life on the seas? The miserable subsistence of peat farming, that's what.

As the days turn into weeks and months, Johan's mixed and wavering feelings undergo a sedimental settling, gradually layering on top of each other until they are as solid as stone. He will not spend his life on a schooner, with its attendant boredom and queasiness and fear. He will not return to Sweden. He will find a way to stay here, right here, in this place. He will change ▶

Stranded in Ice *(continued)*

his name and become an American citizen. All the serendipitous twists and turns his life has taken have propelled him out of one kind of story and into another—a new narrative filled with possibility. God Bless America!

In the evenings, to the click-click of knitting needles and the scrape of the paring knife, the Captain and his wife regale Johan with village lore about the house on the hill: how three Hathorn men fled north from Salem to outrun an abominable legacy—the disgrace of their connection to John Hathorne, presiding magistrate of the witch trials, and the only justice who never recanted—and bestowed their new name on this spit of land . . . their connection to a famous writer, Nathaniel Hawthorne (have you heard of him? Johan nods in surprise), who wove family legends into his own stories . . . the successive generations who lived in the same spot . . . the retired sea captain, Sam Hathorn, who lives there now with his wife and spinster daughter.

Captain Sam, Mrs. Maloney says, began his life on the sea as a cabin boy. When he married a whip-smart beauty named Tryphena, he took his young bride with him on his trips around the world, transporting ice from Maine to the Philippines, Australia, Panama, the Virgin Islands, and filling the ship for the return trip with brandy, sugar, spices, and rum. Their four children, three boys and a girl, were born at sea, and they traveled the world with him until, at the height of the Civil War, Captain Sam insisted they stay home. Confederate privateers were prowling up and down the East Coast like marauding pirates, and no ship was immune.

But his caution could not keep his family safe: his three boys all died young. One succumbed to scarlet fever. His four-year-old namesake, Sammy, drowned in a river one October when the captain was at sea. Fourteen years later, their teenaged son, Alvaro, working as a seaman on a schooner off the coast of Massachusetts, was swept overboard in a storm. News of his death came by telegram, blunt and impersonal. His body was never found. Weeks later Alvaro's sea chest arrived on Hathorn Point, its top intricately carved by his hand. Tryphena, disconsolate, spent hours tracing the outlines with her fingertips, damsels in hoopskirts with revealing décolletage.

Finely attuned to her mother's
sadness, Katie—the only surviving
child—stayed close to home. A shy and
somewhat awkward girl, she clung to
her parents, and they to her. Years went
by. One by one, the few eligible bachelors
in Cushing married or moved away.
Now Katie is thirty-four years old and
well past the point of meeting a man.
But it's all right; she is resigned to it.
She will live in the house and take care
of her parents until they are buried in
the family plot between the house and
the sea.

There is an expression in Cushing,
Mrs. Maloney tells Johan: daughtering
out. It means that no male heirs have
survived to carry on the family name.
Katie is the last of the Cushing Hathorns.
When she dies, the Hathorn name will
die with her.

*

Like many sailors, Johan is a
superstitious man. He believes in
portents and omens, refrains from
whistling on board a vessel, and refuses
to cut his hair or trim his nails while at
sea. He rubs the heads of Mrs. Maloney's
black cats to ward off danger. The fact
that he is stranded in this place, at this
time, strikes him as a sign he'd be a fool
to ignore. Why did he arrive on this
point, within a stone's throw of a house
belonging to relatives of Nathaniel
Hawthorne? A house containing a
spinster daughter and naming rights
to the man who marries her? Frozen ▶

Stranded in Ice (*continued*)

in place in Kissing Cove! What greater omen could there be than that?

And so it is that before even striding across the field and knocking on the Hathorns' front door, before meeting the slim, dark-haired woman six years his senior who lives there with her parents, before setting foot across the threshold, he has devised a plan. He will change his name to John Olson, and he will marry this woman, heir to the estate. He'll take over the farm, and the big white homestead on the hill will become the Olson House. The Hathorns will daughter out. ❧

BIRD IN HAND
A Novel

"Gripping … A realistic and, at times, heartbreaking look at love and friendship."

—*Real Simple*

THE WAY LIFE SHOULD BE
A Novel

"An unassumingly beautiful story of human relationships and self-discovery...the ideal page-turning light read, with a tremendous payoff."

—*People*

DESIRE LINES
A Novel

"Has the staying power of art. I hesitate to call Kline a 'serious novelist' for fear of obscuring her easy style and fluid metaphor-making, but she's the real deal."

—*Boston Globe*

SWEET WATER
A Novel

"Kline keeps us glued to the page."

—*Newsday*